THE SUN THAT ROSE FROM THE EARTH

THE SUN THAT ROSE FROM THE EARTH

SHAMSUR RAHMAN FARUQI

Translated from the Urdu
Savaar aur Doosre Afsane by the Author

HAMISH HAMILTON
an imprint of
PENGUIN BOOKS

HAMISH HAMILTON
Published by the Penguin Group
Penguin Books India Pvt. Ltd, 7th Floor, Infinity Tower C, DLF Cyber City,
Gurgaon 122 002, Haryana, India
Penguin Group (USA) Inc., 375 Hudson Street, New York, New York 10014, USA
Penguin Group (Canada), 90 Eglinton Avenue East, Suite 700, Toronto, Ontario,
M4P 2Y3, Canada
Penguin Books Ltd, 80 Strand, London WC2R 0RL, England
Penguin Ireland, 25 St Stephen's Green, Dublin 2, Ireland (a division of Penguin Books Ltd)
Penguin Group (Australia), 707 Collins Street, Melbourne, Victoria 3008, Australia
Penguin Group (NZ), 67 Apollo Drive, Rosedale, Auckland 0632, New Zealand
Penguin Books (South Africa) (Pty) Ltd, Block D, Rosebank Office Park,
181 Jan Smuts Avenue, Parktown North, Johannesburg 2193, South Africa

Penguin Books Ltd, Registered Offices: 80 Strand, London WC2R 0RL, England

First published in Urdu as *Savaar aur Doosre Afsane* by Aaj ki Kitaben, Karachi, Pakistan,
2001; and by Shabkhoon Kitab Ghar, Allahabad, India, 2003
First published in English in Hamish Hamilton by Penguin Books India 2014

Copyright © Shamsur Rahman Faruqi 2014

10 9 8 7 6 5 4 3 2 1

ISBN 9780670086917

Typeset in Dante MT by R. Ajith Kumar, New Delhi
Printed at Thomson Press India Ltd, New Delhi

A PENGUIN RANDOM HOUSE COMPANY

To the memory of Muhammad Ozair Farooqui
of Koriapar, Azamgarh, then Koriapar House, Karachi
Loving brother-in-law, almost a father to all of us

What terms would'st give to gain his company?
Any.
But how would'st serve him, with thy best endeavour?
Ever.
What would'st thou do if here thou could'st behold him?
Hold him.

Contents

Bright Star, Lone Splendour

Bright star! Would that I were as steadfast as thou art—
Not in lone splendour hung aloft the night
And watching, with eternal lids apart,
Like nature's patient, sleepless Eremite
The moving waters at their priestlike task
Of pure ablution round earth's human shores

'Bright Star', John Keats

Talking about Ghalib's station isn't something that sensible people do:
I am drunk today, so I'll give some news of him.

From the Persian Divan of Mirza Asadullah Khan Ghalib of
Delhi (1797–1869)

I am of Rajput lineage; the place where I was born and brought up is Nizamabad, in the district of Azamgarh. Formerly in the kingdom of Awadh (or Oudh or Oude, as the English prefer to call it), Azamgarh had been part of John Company Bahadur's dominions from about the end of the eighteenth century. During the times of the Exalted Presence, Mahabali, King Akbar, whose place is now in the Eternal Paradise, some bhumihar zamindars of our nearby city of Ballia and its environs became somewhat fractious; some elements of the Imperial Army were dispatched to put down their rebellion, from Patiala, Jaipur and Jhunjhunu in the far west. These contingents contained some Rajputs, and also Pathans and some Sayyids.

The unrest was put down in short order; some cavalrymen, infantrymen and even middle-level commandants fell so much in love with these eastern territories that many of them decided to stay back and settle here. Sarai Rani, Sarai Mir, Sanjarpur and Khurasan (now called Khurason) were settled during those days. Albeit Nizamabad had been there from much more ancient times. It is said that my ancestors were part of the royal armies which were dispatched to quell the recalcitrant bhumihars, and they settled in Nizamabad. But our House achieved its real prominence when the Emperor of the Deccan and Hindustan, the Exalted Presence, Reviver of the Creed and the Faith, King Aurangzeb Alamgir, in his auspicious reign and puissant governance, awarded to two brothers, over the Royal Hand and Seal, the favour to be Resident Plenipotentiary of these purlieus. The brothers were called Azmat Khan and Azam Khan: Azam Khan settled in the city of Azamgarh, and at a distance of about forty miles in the north-east, Azmat Khan settled the town of Azmatgarh.

There is no doubt that among the cavalrymen and commandants of Azam Khan were my ancestors who had risen from the territory of Panjab and they now settled in Nizamabad near the newly founded city of Azmatgarh.

We are Chandrabanshi Rajputs, claiming descent from the Moon. Our own clan is called the Hay Hay Bansh, and we have always been known for both our prowess in battle and our love of learning. Some property disputes arose among us during the Reign of Auspicious Foundation of the Exalted Presence, Raushan Akhtar Muhammad Shah Padishah, Warrior for the Creed, and who now rests in Paradise. These disputes became so bitter that my great-grandfather removed himself from the traditional pale, and this withdrawal turned so deep that my ancestor adopted the religion of Islam. Even today, those of his progeny who are still in the world of the living, wherever they may be, are Muslim, by Grace of God. My own direct ancestor continued to follow the Hindu Faith, and by Parameshwar's Grace I too remain firm in the old Faith.

With the passage of time we Hindus and our Muslim brethren began to come closer; we began visiting with each other on festive occasions, each participating in the other's rites and ceremonies without any sense of incongruity. Indeed, there were one or two occasions when matters came to marriage between the two branches, leading even to drawn swords and actual warfare. But all this acrimony was swept off in the stream of time. Gradually, the strained strings regained equanimity, and lives regained their even tenor.

My grandfather had a passionate interest in weaponry and even took up weapon-making as a hobby. He would often say that a man must know as much about his weapons, and must have as much confidence in them as he has knowledge of and confidence in his offspring or wife. Another of his favourite sayings was that for a soldier there's no better way of making the best acquaintance with his weapon than to fashion it with his own hands. In the beginning, he devoted his skills to making our traditional weapons like tiger's claw, broadsword and heavy cutlasses. Once a Christian padre sneered at him, and said, 'Well, you natives would find it rather difficult to make our sorts of weapons.' He took the matter to heart and soon acquired exceptional skill in making carbines, double-barrelled shotguns, and long-barrelled single shotguns.

My grandfather soon became known everywhere in the neighbouring areas for his excellence in gun-making, and his work came to be admired so much that the soldiers of the Company Bahadur and even the dacoits from the forested areas to the north-east became his clients and paid his rather high prices without demur. By the time he retired from active work, my father had taken over the business. Our profession thus effectively changed from weapon-wielding to weapon-making.

In the immediate surrounds of our village of Nizamabad, many rain-fed or perennial ponds yielded—and I hope they still do—a special kind of deep-black, rich clay which was very suitable for fine pottery— from simple household pots to ornamental vases, hookah bases, trays and cups. This pottery of ours was exported to even faraway markets and cities. By chance I struck up a friendship with a potter's son and, quite clandestinely from my father, I learnt quite a bit of his craft by way of fun. Little did I know that my skill at that lowly profession would be of some use to me at a dire time.

Both the branches of our House regarded loyalty in the service to the descendants of Azam Khan and Azmat Khan, and thus to the Timurid Prince who ruled from Delhi, as dearly as our own Faith and Dharma. In the fateful battle of Buxar (1764), Buxariya mercenaries, hired ponies with allegiance to no side, fought on both sides—the forces of John Company against the Mughal Emperor Shah Alam II and his supporter, Shuja-ud Daulah, the Navab Vizier of Awadh. But all those from our House, whether Hindu or Muslim, were to be found under the Exalted Presence, the Emperor's benign banner of Power and Law. Twenty-one champions from both the branches of our family quaffed the cup of martyrdom in that fateful battle.

Even after their defeat at Buxar, the Emperor and the Navab Vizier continued to command our loyalties. But a thousand pities, he of the Exalted Portal, who now has his abode in Paradise, Emperor Shah Alam Secundus, soon gave away the authority of Revenue Collection and Administration to the Company Bahadur. The Navab Vizier, a few years later, was summoned into the loving shelter of Allah. He who now has his abode in Paradise, could not, in despite of all his sagacity and excellent qualities of statesmanship, get out of the net that the Englishman had knit to hold him in their thrall. Finally, in 1771, the great Maratha Chieftain Mahada ji Sindhia rescued the Emperor from his Golden Cage in Allahabad, and ably ruled, armed with the Emperor's Power of Attorney, as Absolute Plenipotentiary and Minister in Chief. The death in April 1782 of Zulfaqar-ud Daulah Najaf Khan had practically rendered the Emperor ineffectual on the country's chessboard of power and politics, and more or less extinguished the last hope of Mughal India. The Maratha restored his power, even if in name. Once the Maratha was dead (1794), the Englishman got his chance again and in 1803 he retook the Emperor under his 'protection'.

We were under the safe and auspicious rule and nurture of Navab Asaf-ud Daulah, Greatest in Munificence, Scatterer in alms of hundreds of thousands of rupees in a single day, of whom everyone spoke nothing but good, and who stays in the Paradise of Eden since he died in 1797. Then his son, Wazir Ali Khan, who has God's Forgiveness, became our master, but the Englishman had him removed and placed Mirza Mangali (Sa'adat Ali Khan) on the Seat of Governance. That noble lord also is now in the shade of God's Mercy and rests in Paradise.

The troubles and frustrations borne by one of the chief officers of the Court, Tafazzul Husain Khan, more commonly known as Khan-e Allama, and his colleagues in effecting the removal of Wazir Ali Khan and installing Mirza Mangali were numerous, but the mammoth and climacteric price that was paid was the alienation of nearly half of the territory of Awadh and letting it pass into the claws of the English. Azamgarh was one of the districts so ceded. We were now both literally and metaphorically in the Firangi's shackles.

Khan-e Allama and my grandfather had been friends of old, and the main reason for their first getting acquainted was my grandfather's old hobby of weapon-making. The Khan was extremely fond of my grandfather's long-barrelled single shotguns. He often had them made specially for his own use and also presented them to his English friends on appropriate occasions.

In 1798, when he was on his way to Calcutta to assume the station of the Navab Vizier's Chief Representative at the Court of the Grand Lord Sahib, Khan-e Allama stopped at Azamgarh to visit with some relatives and also my grandfather who presented to him, as usual, a carbine and a long-barrelled musket of his own making. But this time my grandfather regretted that in getting the Navabi to Saadat Ali Khan, he had permitted a whole vast swath of Awadh's territory, from Bareilly to Banaras, to be gobbled up by the Englishman. In extenuation, the Khan-e Allama uttered a dire prophecy, which was my evil destiny to see coming true. He said, 'Bhowani Singh, remember that I saved Awadh by giving away those few districts. It's only a matter of time that not just Awadh, the whole land of Hindustan will be forced to recognize Calcutta as Delhi.'

*

The only child of my parents, I was born in 1840. As was usual in our families, I was taught the martial arts as also the literate arts. At home, I learnt Persian and Arabic, and some mathematics. Then I was enrolled in a boys' school whose headmaster was a pupil of the renowned Maulana Muhammad Faruq of Chirayya Kot. In 1837, some Christian padres had opened an English Education School in the city of Azamgarh. It was called Wesley High School. A friend of my father's who had served under the Company Bahadur, insisted upon my father that I be sent to that school, because, he said, in a few years from now matters of administration and governance would all be conducted in the language of the Firangi. Unable to resist his importunacy every day, and in fact slightly miffed, my father had me enrolled in Wesley High School. I was at that time ten years old.

In the English madrasa, along with some instruction in the Firangi Faith, they taught us Persian, English, mathematics, history and also something quite unfamiliar which was called 'Hindi'. In fact, it was effectually no other than or no different to the language that we spoke at home, but it was written in the Sanskrit script, from left to right. And as for its vocables, the poor thing's back seemed to be crippled under the weight of unfamiliar, hard-to-pronounce Sanskrit vocabulary which had replaced the dulcet and easy-flowing Hindi that I and all our menfolk spoke at home. (Women mostly spoke Bhojpuri.) This new language made me uncomfortable: I used to imagine that when I grew up, I'd write poetry in Rekhtah (or Hindi, the names were completely interchangeable, except that the written language was more often called Rekhtah). But I wasn't able to quite visualize how a poetry like that of the Presence, Mir Taqi Mir of Delhi—may God enhance his station—or Mir sahib, the worshipful Babr Ali Anis, of Lucknow, could be written in this new Hindi. Above all, I most passionately wanted to follow the style of my most revered Mirza Naushah Ghalib sahib—to write even one ghazal in the sonorous, mysterious and intellectually challenging mode much favoured by Mirza Ghalib sahib would have been the apogee of achievement for me.

Here in the mission school, the new Hindi was the rising star; I even heard some of the masters say that Hindi is a separate, independent language; it is the language of the Hindus, whereas the language of the Muslims is known as Rekhtah, or Urdu. We were further informed that Urdu meant 'language of the Court of the Mughal', or 'the language of the *lashkar*', a word that was loosely translated as 'army, cantonment' and so forth.

There were quite a few boys in Wesley School who were viewed and treated with special favour by the masters. They were quite like us in appearance, physical features and general deportment. Though most of them were from rather lower in the caste system, their names were somewhat strange: half Indian and half Firangi. For example, one of the boys with whom I became good friends was called Samuel Singh. Another one was called Laran Das. I came to know much later that actually his name was Lawrence Das which we had corrupted to Laran. Yet another boy, who was older than all the rest of us, was John Masihuddin. Taller and heftier than most of us, he was a typical school bully, never hesitating to deliver a drubbing to whoever offended him. All these boys had had something called 'Baptism' done to them. It entitled them to be called Christian, like the English. I was under the delusion that this Baptism must be something like circumcision, but Laran Das disabused me of this foolish notion and told me that it was a ceremony in which words from the Bible were pronounced and the person being given Baptism was sprinkled with some sort of holy water.

Well, the thing I remember most about those boys was the total unity among them, even to the extent that they all made conscious efforts to look and speak differently from us whom they contemptuously called 'desi'—something lowly, because home-grown. There were a couple of Firangis also among our masters and this was the first time for me to observe an English, or Firangi, person from close quarters. For some obscure reason, they inspired a sort of terror in me, though they were invariably polite with us. This was perhaps because their speech was incomprehensible to me, and partly also because they were inscrutable: soft-spoken and even gentle ordinarily, but unhesitating in giving the severest caning and pandying when they thought the offence deserved it.

Once, it was announced for some reason that school would be out two hours sooner. Overpowered by the joy of it, I ran out from the large assembly hall, shouting my pleasure. Unfortunately, I was loud enough for the headmaster to hear me. Instantly, I was summoned to the august presence and ten of the best was declared condign for me and the punishment was meted by a particularly harsh master, 'Hangman' Mr Emmanuel Lall.

One thing that I most disliked at that school was its excessive emphasis on punctuality. I was a chronic late riser and would be often late for school, even if by minutes. I was always punished for my lack of punctuality. It was quite right, I suppose, but it still stung, even worse than grazing my shins against something very hard and prickly.

Well, you can imagine that I wasn't long for Wesley School. My saintly father was often taunted by his peers for facilitating my conversion to the Firangi religion by sending me to a 'mission school'. On the other hand, the imposition upon me of courses and subjects that I disliked, like 'manual training' (carpentry, bookbinding), science and 'Hindi', and the behaviour of John Masihuddin, that all-time bully, was progressively pushing me towards a state of active alienation. I barely got through the sixth grade when happily my father withdrew me from the school. All that I took away from there was a bit of the English language. I was now back to my madrasa and to my beloved Persian and Arabic, some mathematics and logic and astronomy, with plenty of freedom to learn and practise the myriad arts of armed and unarmed combat at which my people had always excelled. To the traditional arts was added marksmanship with different kinds of guns. I developed some taste for wrestling and joined a nearby club—such clubs were called *akhara* and were run with the support of a patron and many voluntary contributors.

My village Nizamabad is situated eight miles to the east of Azamgarh where my madrasa was located. I always walked to the school and this helped me develop good musculature and endurance with no extra trouble. But the thing I was totally committed to become was a Hindi poet. I composed ghazals in the solitude of summer noons and the frost of winter nights when everyone kept indoors and had little to do. I had the luxury of having a small room of my own. I recorded my immature little verses in a large notebook, and sometimes overwhelmed by my pleasure at versification, I would start singing them. Once I was mortified to have my father overhear me and he had no difficulty in divining that I was singing my own compositions.

12

I don't quite remember if it was the singing, or the versification that annoyed my father the most, or perhaps it was both. Anyway, he boxed my ears and slapped me—albeit gently—and presented me at the court of my grandfather. My grandfather, may Parameshwar save him from rebirth, was the gentlest and most sagacious of men, despite his past fondness for weaponry and the hunt. He loved me perhaps even more than my father. He chided my father gently for disapproving my bent towards poetry, and said, 'Well, Karni Singh, where's the harm in all this? We have just this one child among the two of us. Let him do what he likes best. Poetry was never forbidden among the well born. Don't you please reprimand him for it.'

This was like the grant to me of a freehold on a valuable, tractable parcel of land, with nothing to pay to the revenue collector and to do with it as I pleased. My next two, three years passed in comfort and happiness, with much of my time spent in perfecting my martial prowess and some of it in poetry. My grandfather, may God's Mercy be upon him in plentiful measure, was very old by then, or perhaps he seemed very old to me. My parents didn't expect any more children to be born to them. Contrary to the prevalent practice among most Rajput clans, there was no polygamy in my family. Extramarital liaisons, open or clandestine, were of course always a possibility. Such things were not necessarily approved or encouraged, but were tolerated as nothing below the high standards of Rajput behaviour.

I thus grew up as the sole offspring, the pupil of everyone's eye, the centre of everyone's prayers and good wishes. Once, suddenly, my grandfather said to me: 'Hey, you young stripling, I just heard that Maulavi Khadim Husain Nazim has taken over as Magistrate at Muhammadabad Kohna.' He paused a moment, because I hadn't responded. 'Do you know who he is?'

'No, Presence, I have never heard of him. Is he a relative?'

'No,' he guffawed. 'But he's just like one. He is the grandson of a renowned and learned person, Mullah Sabiq of Banaras. And this Mullah sahib happens to be the father of our Khan-e Allama's ustad,

Mufti Ibrahim. So we have some sort of a connection there, Khan-e Allama being a friend of mine.'

'Yes, Presence,' I replied dutifully.

'You want to be a poet, so you need a proper ustad. One doesn't make one's mark at anything, and poetry especially, without excellent mentoring. I'll take you to Maulavi Khadim Husain Nazim sahib and request him to take you under his wings.'

The next day we rode early to Muhammadabad, twelve miles to the south-west. I rode my beloved Kathiawari pony, a dear friend and companion, aptly named Mitwa. My grandfather chose a magnificent bay, taller than me even who was rather tall for my age. We cantered into Muhammadabad by the time the sun was up, having quite lost the orange-red typical of the dawn in our part of the country. Now in his true colours, the good God Surya was fierily beating down on us poor humans. Having reached the imposing official residence of Maulavi Nazim sahib, we had our names sent in, citing the Khan-e Allama's name by way of introduction, and waited in the front veranda. Maulavi Khadim Husain came out shortly after, welcomed us and escorted us to his divan khana, a spacious, if somewhat dimly lit chamber.

We were treated to the application of a small quantity of the attar of the khas gently between our neck and shoulder, and to betel cones and cool drinks. Maulavi Khadim Husain sahib wore a four-cornered hat in the Mughal mode, and a silk cloak embroidered in the modernist style. Under the cloak he wore a long kurta of fine white muslin. Light-blue cotton trousers, very wide bottomed in the approved Delhi style, and a pair of silk embroidered Salim Shahi shoes, open at the back, adorned his feet. In his hands, he had a heavy rosary of red agates, which he was perhaps telling in his heart, because I could see the beads moving under his fingers.

At first, I was quite overawed by the whole ambience and ensemble, but soon realized that Maulavi sahib's personality exuded a sense of

14

comfortable lightness. My grandfather stated the purpose of our visit. Maulavi Khadim Husain sahib smiled a gentle, brief smile, and asked me, 'Mian, your *takhallus*?'

I submitted in nearly a whisper, 'I have chosen no takhallus yet, Your Honour.'

Maulavi Khadim Husain sahib again smiled his brief smile, uttered an impersonal 'Ah, I see', and was silent for a while; then he spoke: 'So, Mian Beni Madho Singh, I note that you, a relict of the illustrious Rajput Hay Hay clan who were noted for their prowess in battle, are ready to bring disgrace to them by turning to poetry.' He smiled a friendly, somewhat mischievous smile. 'So I determine your takhallus to be Ruswa. Is that acceptable?'

Ruswa does mean 'disgraced', but because social disgrace of a kind is often the portion of true lovers, it was an excellent choice.

'Very well indeed, Your Honour,' both my grandfather and I said in unison.

Maulavi Khadim Husain sahib raised his hands in prayer, in which we joined. He prayed for the takhallus to be auspicious and for wisdom and perfection being vouchsafed to me in my new role as poet. He then passed his hand on my head, as if caressing or praising me, and commanded: 'Right, young fellow. Now let's hear something from your verses.'

I was stunned and almost stopped breathing, and looked at grandfather with the corner of my eyes, hoping for his support, or somehow to get me off the hook. But he pretended to be quite unconcerned; he didn't even give me a glance of encouragement. I cleared my throat and in a low voice said the opening verse of a recent ghazal of mine. My throat was dry and I hated the choked voice in which I croaked out my verse:

Understand existence to be nothing more than a bubble;
Understand each breath to be just water.

Maulavi Khadim Husain sahib said, 'Yes, quite good.' Then he paused a moment, and continued, 'Young sir, you have used the word *samajhiye* to scan as *samjhiye* which is quite correct, but somewhat archaic. Why not substitute *janiye* for it? The scansion is perfect, the meaning the same, and the idiom is more current.'

I was just about to say something to thank him for the excellent correction when he continued: 'And there's no real proof, poetic or logical, to describe "breath" as "water"; also, there's very little connection established between the two lines by using "breath" and "water". How about saying *alam* instead of *sans*?'

I clearly saw that describing *alam*, which means 'world', as being transient like water was much stronger and created a better, self-sustaining statement than created by *sans* which means 'breath'. Also, there was a small twist in the prosody, which I liked.

'Do you know some prosody, young man?'

'I do, sir, and can see that your correction sets up an unusual prosodic situation which I make bold to say is extremely attractive.' I spoke haltingly, but with an inner certainty that my answer was quite correct.

Maulavi sahib again commanded, 'Yes, quite good.'

My grandfather now entered the dialogue, as if he had just arrived: 'Only God is free from all blemish! Presence, how appropriate are the corrections that you have commanded!'

On Maulavi sahib's request, I said another verse of mine from another ghazal:

> *More's the pity; my friends committed an act of enmity*
> > *against me:*
> *Had I stayed on in her alley, I would at least serve as attendant.*

Maulavi sahib paused a beat, then said, 'Yes, good. It's a verse in the manner of Shaikh Nasikh. The Shaikh, as you must know, preferred to speak in hints and suggestions. As he himself said:

The meaning intended by the poet who's given to abstract thought is
                                        contained in the poem itself:
It's quite near, that which people think is distant.

But in your verse the words are not set properly and elegantly. I suggest you rephrase your first line as follows:

Of what use is the kingdom of the world to me?

Now your verse is a very elegant, finished one, even if it's now less oblique than the original:

Of what use is the kingdom of the world to me?
Had I stayed on in her alley, I would at least serve as attendant.'

He finished his instruction: 'Be sure to understand, more than anything else, that a beginner needs clarity of expression and elegance of phrase.'

I didn't quite follow his drift, but grandfather had no comments other than 'very good', 'very appropriate'.

Maulavi Khadim Husain sahib closed the audience in a firm but kindly way. He said, 'Look, little boy, I really don't have the leisure to suggest corrections to your verses regularly. You are a young man, your temperament bubbles with poetry and boils with the heat of your imagination. Do, of course, be sure to visit and show me your verses whenever you pass this way.'

On coming out, we were surprised and abashed to see that in return for the five sers of sweets that we had brought as offering, Maulavi sahib had organized nearly a whole month's worth of foodgrains, fruits and vegetables, loaded on a bullock cart and ready to accompany us. Maulavi Khadim Husain sahib had already returned to his chamber, and there was no opportunity for us even to thank him. We left, admiring his bountifulness and his poetic prowess. He was, after all, a magistrate and not a full-time poet.

*

Becoming a pupil of Maulavi Khadim Husain Nazim was something like a certification of completion of studies for me. I stopped attending the madrasa, devoting all my time to poetry, and refining my skills with the sword and the gun. And soon, an affair of the heart began to burgeon and brighten my daily outings and nightly imaginings. There were, indeed, some hints from the other side as well. The matter didn't grow into the passion that our poets talk about so eloquently, but it certainly was an *affaire d'amour*, light-hearted, giving me more pleasure than pain. I was sixteen years old now. With my hair worn fashionably long so as to come down in a slightly wavy fashion below my ears, my body slim and athletic, I thought I cut quite a dashing figure for the village belles and certainly for my parents and my most loved grandfather. There was no dearth of good food, fresh venison and fowl. Sword, gun, books, the hesitant drafts of a letter or two that I hoped to send her, were my most important possessions in the little room that I had called my own since the age of twelve—a marriageable age, though none in my family looked upon me in that light.

But oh, that year of 1856 passed over me in heavy pain and puzzlement. Where and why did the cool, friendly days and nights full of the potential for fine activity and fun go away? It was a niggle, the point of a sharp needle that I could not wish away from my spirit. We were directly affected by the seizure of the kingdom of Awadh by the English in an unexpected way. A wave of unrest, anger and sorrow rose from all around us and engulfed the space of our daily life, separating it from the pastures and orchards of hope and stability. The resentment was against the Grand Lat Sahib of Calcutta, as much as the Englishman Sleeman whom in some vague way rumour associated with the launching of the whole shocking affair.

Stranger things began to happen: prices of foodgrains and other essential commodities began to rise daily and inexplicably—inexplicable because there had been no floods, no drought of late. Even petty things, but things essential for the life of the poor, began to soar beyond their reach. It seemed that the produce of Awadh had now ceased to come to the markets in the east. Coarse grains or fine, all began to sell at the impossible price of eight, nine rupees to a ser. Rumours were circulating everywhere that the Company was seizing or buying all the merchandise and food products, and sending them off to *vilayat* daily on very large ships, ships that people swore on oath were driven by fire and vapour.

Within a few days of the King of Awadh, the popular Jan-e Alam of Lucknow, being settled in the Company's custody in Calcutta, people began to talk in whispers that the kingdom not just of Awadh, but also of the Throne of Delhi was about to be restored in some mysterious manner. Occasionally, someone would whisper the word 'chapati' and imply that the dispatch of a chapati meant sending some secret message to someone who lived and worked hidden from all eyes. I wondered how the chapati, unleavened thin bread, thinner almost than a cotton kerchief, could be used as a medium of communication.

Suddenly, passing by a busy shop, someone would whisper loudly enough to be heard in the bustling bazaar: The army that the Company Bahadur kept stationed at Mandiahu near Lucknow as an engine of intimidation to the king, had rebelled, or was just about to rise in mutiny. News or word of Danka Shah of Arcot in faraway Madras began to be on everyone's lips. It was reported that everywhere he was preceded by loud drums (hence the word *danka* as part of his name), perhaps to alert the people to his coming, or also perhaps to indicate that the old drums of power are now replaced by the new. The drummer went about crying that the 'Leader of the Mussulmans' is on his way to this place. In his speeches, Maulavi Ahmadullah—which was later revealed to be Danka Shah's real name—openly incited both the Hindus and the Mussulmans to rebellion, battle and jihad. Funnily enough, both Hindus and Muslims used the word 'jihad'. Danka Shah declared that the rule of the English was based on godlessness and falsehood. He insisted that someday soon, the English would forcibly alienate the natives of this country from their ancient faiths and would drag them far away from their God.

These sensational developments made my blood feel hotter and course joyfully through my young body; in fact, I began to dream of some things most unusual and quite illogical for my age and state.

But the event that signalled the greatest unexpected change in my life was my dear grandfather's death towards the very end of 1856. His illness was extremely short and mild and apparently didn't at all presage his death. Certainly, he was eighty-six years old, but he was so well preserved—his muscles hardly slack, nor his sight dim. He could easily beat us youngsters at wrestling, which he practised weekly in our private arena. No one ever imagined that he would take the route to the Land of Nothingness so soon. In later years, it often would occur to me that perhaps his sacred soul had somehow felt the shadow of what was to come—the tyranny and the atrocities visited by the English on our countrymen—and decided that it was better to close one's eyes than to live on to witness those horrors.

Only a couple of months had passed over the new year that the news of Danka Shah's capture and arrest in Fyzabad—about eighty miles to the north-west of Azamgarh—was on every surreptitious tongue, then repeated overnight across the whole countryside. A strange unrest, quiet but palpable to us Hindis, seemed to spread all around. My puzzlement and anxiety weren't diminished when I heard my father tell my mother one day that Beni Madho should be dispatched to the safety of his maternal uncle's farmhouse in Shahjahanpur. It was a district far to the west of us. I heard my father also say words to the effect that things are going to change and life will become extremely uncertain very soon.

Then suddenly, a rumour spread like wildfire: In Meerut, where there was a large English cantonment, the native soldiers had behaved extremely badly, in fact rebelliously, with their English officers. Losing their nerve, the English were running away wherever they could; they were leaving that city, and also the nearby cities of Bulandshahr and Aligarh in the north-western provinces, hot on the road to Panjab which was at that time considered secure.

None could ascertain what exactly happened, and why. All that was heard, in very vague terms, was that the Company Bahadur's sepoys had been issued with cartridges of a new kind, one end of which needed first to be bitten off or cut with the teeth before being loaded into the matlock, or any other similar gun. It was said the cartridge was coated with cow's fat, or pig's fat, thus making it an object of disgust and horror to both Hindu or Muslim sepoys. Whisperings were abroad that a sepoy called Mangal Pandey, a Brahmin by caste, rather than bite the cartridges, shot his English commandant dead. The English had the news suppressed, but word was abroad in spite of strictures, and the sepoys were out everywhere in rebellion. The Exalted Presence, the Shadow of God, Abu Zafar Sirajuddin Bahadur Shah the Second was installed on the Peacock Throne inside the Exalted Fort with the title of Emperor of India.

News arrived the very next day that the native soldiers and the followers of Danka Shah, storming the prison in Fyzabad, had freed Danka Shah and all his imprisoned followers and they were on the road to Lucknow with a multitude of combatants in tow.

A curious thing happened late that night. In the depth of the silence, a tall and strongly built old man knocked softly on the back door of our house—called *garhi*, that is, little fortress—and sought admittance in a most secretive manner. His face and head were wrapped in a thick cotton scarf, revealing just a hint of the eyes. He said that he was a messenger sent by Babu Kunwar Singh of Ballia, a district neighbouring ours, and had something to convey to my father. Babu Kunwar Singh at that time was nearly eighty years old; he ruled a small princely state, but his name inspired fear and respect over areas far and wide. He hated the Englishman and encouraged his people to openly heap abuses on

21

any English that passed through Jagdishpur, his headquarter town.

My father grasped the purpose of the messenger's visit without a word having been exchanged. He had me dispatched that very night to Shahjahanpur, escorted by an assistant of the old messenger. I did my best to persuade him to let me stay with him, but he heard not a word of my or my mother's entreaties. Go I must, for he had so ordained. Quite contrary to grandfather, my father had a short fuse and a terrible temper. I never saw anyone ever withstand him for more than a minute or so. And I was a mere child in his eyes, anyways.

I later found out that my father too, accompanied by a few of his bravest friends and servants, left our garhi for Babu Kunwar Singh's headquarter town. He left my mother and some ancient but trusted servants behind.

*

All that inordinately long-sounding duration of the war against the English I spent in helpless desolation in the hunting lodge of my maternal uncle in a remote place outside the small town of Roza, itself about a dozen miles east of Shahjahanpur. My uncle's people kept a severely vigilant eye on me lest I escape my ignominious prison. News of the battles trickled down to us occasionally, and often very late. My heart would leap up on the news of each victory of the Indian armies, and would sink equally low on the news of every setback suffered by us.

The war seemed to be all but over by about the middle of 1858. And the cup of my patience was now running over. I determined to somehow jump the high wall of the hunting lodge and escape as soon as I could and go join the Indian fighters under Prince Birjis Qadr, King of Awadh, who was then carrying on the fight from the nearby forests of Pilibhit.

I was quietly looking for a suitable mount for myself. The moon was on the wane and I hoped to take advantage of the coming dark nights and quietly slip away when a trusted servant of my uncle told me in secret that Birjis Qadr, Begam Hazrat Mahal and Maulavi Ahmadullah

Shah, having been defeated severally in individual battles, were now planning to gather their remaining smatter of forces in the forests of Pilibhit, and from thence march away in secret to Nepal in order to continue their fight from there. None of the remnants of their armies had surrendered to the English, nor was such a surrender likely at all.

And that very evening information about Maulavi Ahmadullah Shah thrilled me to the core of my heart: Maulavi sahib intended to seek refuge and regroup in the fortress of Jagannath Singh, the Raja of Pawayan, who was a distant kin of my uncle. Now was the time for me to break my shackles and go and join Maulavi sahib at Pawayan, which wasn't quite near, but was within a hot night ride's distance.

I made a makeshift lasso from two horses' reins, and somehow succeeded, after several throws, in getting one end of it snagged to a stone of the perimeter wall which stood a little out of true. I had my most faithful attendant stand in wait for me some distance away with a couple of hardy mounts. We galloped fast and yet faster and hit the outskirts of Pawayan a little after daybreak, only to see a banner-wielding mass of English cavalry and even more of the sepoys of the infantry surround the village of Pawayan from all sides. There was something clearly and badly wrong here. I thought I heard one of the sepoys speak to another in a whisper; he said something to the effect that the Raja's treasonous conduct cost Danka Shah sahib his life. And the matter became quite apparent shortly thereafter when I saw a throng of the women of the village coming out of their homes, weeping the chants of mourning and beating their breasts. They were followed by yet another host of women who were cursing Jagannath Singh, raising their hands towards the heavens. A posse of the Company Bahadur's cavalry and infantry were pushing them back towards the village.

I felt the world darken around me. It was now plain that the Indian armies had tasted defeat everywhere. Nothing was now left to fight for. But I did not want to return to the hunting lodge, for I was anxious to get news and possibly take care of my mother and my people. I dismissed my servant, took both the horses, and left for distant Azamgarh, taking care to travel quietly and only through by-roads and little-frequented areas.

*

The story of that journey I must put off for some other time. I was on the road like a fugitive criminal for two and a half months, hiding myself as best I could from anyone who seemed to represent authority, especially a Company sepoy or policeman. The entire route bore living witness to the cruelty and mindless brutality of the Company Bahadur's dauntless, dreadless soldiers. Dogs, jackals, crows and other carrion eaters were so gorged with gore and flesh that they lay on the roadside or on the trees and minarets in unmoving, uninterested lassitude. Hyenas, even vultures, were sick of, and sick with overstuffed maws and gullets. For miles and miles along the roads, there were makeshift gibbets, most of them still bearing their pitiful burdens of the stinking, soiled bodies of humans with their blackened tongues hanging out, as if begging for a drop of water.

Throughout my painful, slow and appallingly fearful progress, I heard news, the saddest news: Shah Mal Jat of Baraut and Baghpat in the far west near the district of Muzaffarnagar, and Debi Singh of Raya Mahaban from near Brindaban just to the south of Delhi, and their armies, had been cut down, slashed and sliced away like so much vegetable. In Allahabad, the Mughal Banner raised by Maulavi Liaqat Ali on the ramparts of Emperor Akbar's Fort could display its glory for a bare three days. Neill sahib visited the most heinous punishments on all whom he could capture, even on the slightest suspicion: many were hanged in figures of the English numeral eight or six from the branches of a neem tree near the Kotwali. Maulavi sahib too was reported captured, though later I learnt with great relief that he had made good his escape to fight another day.

Having reached Azamgarh, I prudently stayed at a caravanserai in Rani ki Sarai, eight miles west of the city. My idea was to stay, practically incognito, and quietly seek news, information, or even rumours about the fate of my people at Nizamabad, which lay six miles to the north. I roamed far and away, but found no one whom I could call an acquaintance even. And no stranger would ever open his mouth to tell me about what may have transpired. All that I heard was that the Rajputs of Nizamabad had been decimated—man, woman, child, none survived in battle, or was spared after the English victory.

Having waited for many nights, and leaving my inn for another one nearer to Nizamabad, one dark night I gathered my faltering fortitude of mind and visited my deserted village. Our beloved garhi was now razed to the ground, as if kissing the earth in honour of the victorious Englishman. There was no one residing there, not even some homeless hobo, sheltering there against the dark of the night.

I wandered through the night, like a ghost returning to the place where he had departed the world. My nightlong search and inquiry yielded just this much: My father tasted martyrdom with Babu Kunwar Singh in the battle of Jagdishpur. In that last battle, fought in April 1858, Babu sahib's army delivered a decisive defeat to the English, putting the English to the rout. My father lost his life in that battle; Babu sahib was grievously wounded, but he still could return to Jagdishpur, remove the English flag that the Company soldiers had put there in his absence, and breathe his last: a free warrior in his free home. The English army then proceeded westward and in due course destroyed and dismantled our garhi, having first put to death the remnants of the tiny servant force left there by my father. Fearing for her honour, my mother jumped into the well inside the garhi. There is no doubt that she drowned, but her body wasn't recovered; in fact, none at that time had even thought of trying to recover it.

The sepoys and some spies of the English, I heard people say in frightened whispers, were looking for me. No one knew if I lived, or died somewhere in the far west at my uncle's estate. Some of my

Muslim relatives could escape the English sword or musket, but there was now no trace of them.

It seemed that there was no life left for me to live, no land for me to seek. And where could I go, after all? I didn't know what had happened with my uncle and his people in Shahjahanpur. For all I could imagine, they too were dead, or missing. I had no way of transporting myself to any distance anyway, for I had sold off my mounts during my dire journey from Pawayan. I, in fact, walked during the last couple of weeks of my journey to Azamgarh. I wasn't the suicidal type, the Rajput male rarely was—and I had in fact not even the means to do so, having no sword, no capability to procure poison. No doubt I had my gun, but I had no ammunition for it. I'd used the last of it in hunting fowls or similar edible beasts during my long journey. And trying to buy ammunition was worse than walking into the jaws of death. I'd be informed against most promptly and put in a Firangi prison to suffer torture and an ignominious death. Death by drowning was my only option. Quite unconsciously, I began to walk towards the pond that was reputed to be the deepest in the village. Proximity to the pond and its unique black clay called to my mind my old friend, the potter's son. Perhaps there was a possibility there? Perhaps he or his family had escaped the carnage? I could hide with them, at least for some time.

I walked back stealthily towards the village and soon found the mud hut that had been my friend's home. Having reached as close to the door as possible, and risking the crowing of the occasional rooster, for the dawn wasn't too far, I coughed gently and called out his name in the special way that we had developed to signal between us. The door opened instantly, and I found myself in the close embrace of my friend, both of us sobbing and hugging each other hard as if our lives depended on it.

Apparently, he had heard rumours about me and was vaguely hopeful, being at the same time cautious enough not to try inquiring openly. He pulled me inside, and said: 'Dada, this is your house. Live here as long as you like, and live the way you like in as much comfort as we can give you. You have to do nothing but keep silent, not ever saying a word, for your speech will betray you. I'll tell everyone that you are the son of a distant uncle from Banaras who lost his life in the recent upheaval so you've sought shelter here. You are dumb and mentally retarded, so none will try to socialize with you.'

I spent many days, then weeks and months, in peace and without fear, with my potter friend. The little skill at pottery that I had acquired in my past life stood me in great stead now, for I could easily pass off as to the manner of pottery born, always tinkering with the pots or the clay or the wheel.

*

By the year 1860, the fire of revenge and retribution began to burn somewhat slow in the Englishman's breast. Many of my village who had run away were now returning, in trickles, but in no apparent fear. But who did I have among us to return to our garhi? For me it was like the gut-wrenching verse from Mir Taqi sahib, the Lord of Poetry:

We, the people of pain—
Not dry in the summer's fieriness, not wet in
The season of the rains; but the greensward
Of our eyelashes was always wet to saturation.

Living like a potter, I was of necessity separated from reading and writing, the enjoyment of poetry and letters. It seemed to me that paper and pen were no longer destined to adorn my life. But then, suddenly one day, my potter friend, who had been to Azamgarh on some errand, came and gave me the news that the Englishman had set up a gun factory in Kampu. He said, 'Dada, you must send in your application for employment there. You are quite familiar with guns and all, and know the English language too. They're recruiting in large numbers now; so there won't be much investigation or inquiry about who you are. You were not made for making pots and pans, Dada. My heart hurts all the time, seeing you waste your life like a potter. Your ancestral lands are still in the Company Bahadur's hands, they were confiscated when they destroyed your garhi. Perhaps some day they'll release them and I'll let you know at once so that you can return and reclaim them.'

I heard him out in silence. Kampu! The city that the English called 'Cawnpore', a corruption of our Kanhpur, or 'Kanha's city', Kanha being an affectionate name for Sri Krishna whose songs of love sung by Mira Bai were household words everywhere. When the Glorious Sahibs established a big military cantonment or camp there, most people began to call it 'Kampu', which became the city's popular name among the rustics.

Cawnpore! Kampu! The very name struck terror in the heart of every Indian and inspired the most flagrant fury in the heart of every Englishman. The city where the famous 'massacre' of the English took place during the war and where the Company wreaked a brutal vengeance on the Indians! So that was the city now where I was perhaps fated to go and serve the English.

I could see the sense in my potter friend's advice. My chances of gainful employment were good and Cawnpore was far enough away from Azamgarh for anyone to have heard about me or my people. So, soon enough, I found myself standing in a long, straggling queue of applicants at the factory gate in Cawnpore. They must have been in dire need of able-bodied workers, for the recruiting sahib made the most perfunctory of inquiries of the applicants. Their only question for me was if I had taken part in the fighting against the Company Bahadur. To this I gave the truthful reply: 'No, not at all, sahib.' At the end of the day I found my name among those who were selected. I reported for duty the next day. My knowledge of guns, and of English, helped me gain quick promotions. I soon became a foreman, which was something like a supervisor over a group of skilled workers.

Thus far, I had been living in a free public inn and buying my frugal victuals from the market every day. Now a foreman, I could afford a small house near the big bazaar called Parade, at the rent of two and a half rupees a month. I hired a cook—a man of all jobs—and set up house, gradually stocking my little house with books of poetry and trying to compose some poetry of my own. Cawnpore did not have an acknowledged ustad in Urdu or Persian in those days. The city was barren after the departure of Mirza Rajab Ali Beg Surur just before 1857. Shaikh Nasikh used to visit Cawnpore often in the early part of the century, but unlike Mirza Rajab Ali Beg sahib, he never developed a liking for the city and left no important pupil behind him. In fact, I remembered with wry pleasure a verse from him about Cawnpore:

The people of Cawnpore—
They claw and clutch human beings
Just as crows eat the carrion that floats
On the Ganga River.

These days, it was only Agha Hajju Sharaf who visited occasionally from Lucknow. Among the local poets, each regarded himself as the ultimate ustad. Almost every senior poet regularly hosted mushairas, both formal and informal, but I rarely participated in any of them. I spent my time mostly in reading Shaikh Nasikh sahib and Mirza Ghalib sahib. Shaikh Nasikh sahib was lucky to have died much before 1857 and so he didn't share our misfortune of having to live in these times whose days were worse than the darkest nights.

Mirza Ghalib sahib was, of course, alive and well in Delhi, having weathered more or less successfully the stormy days and nights of death and destruction that swept through Delhi after the English retook the city in September 1857. It was Mirza Ghalib sahib who was now the sole pivot and centre of my little poetic universe. It was my strongest desire, my most ardent ambition, in fact my life's ambition, to write like Mirza Ghalib sahib, to go to him and hear his words, learn his ways, and come back after spending some considerable time in his company and learning even to speak and behave like him.

I perfectly remembered my ustad Maulavi Khadim Husain Nazim's instruction to me: The beginner must learn, first and foremost, the art of achieving flowingness, clarity and appropriately idiomatic speech. Rather than wandering about in the uncharted, thorny routes to new and untested themes, a technique commonly called *khiyal bandi* (that is, using abstractions in poetry), of which Ghalib sahib was the greatest exponent of the day, the beginner must be cautious, for too much ambition shackled a poet to whims and fancies. Still, my heart hankered after the status of a khiyal band. I didn't much worry about the 'chastity' of language and 'smoothness' of expression. I wanted to surprise my reader or listener, to make him think, by a fine excess. Frugality in word or thought was not my preferred way.

It was now early June 1862 and the day was Sunday. I was walking along rather aimlessly, intending ultimately to visit the Sunday market on Parade to look for old books. Passing just in front of the Kotwali police station in the Topekhana Bazaar, I noticed Maulavi Abdur Rahman, owner of Nizami Press, walking briskly and purposefully towards me. He stopped in mid-stride and said, 'Here, Mian Ruswa,' he practically collared me as he spoke, 'I give you something to remember! You always talk of Mirza sahib to me, in fact, you take his name so frequently as if you were telling it on some beads in your heart! Well, I have something—will you believe it?—I just printed Mirza Ghalib's entire Urdu divan!'

He practically thrust in my hands a medium-sized and slim book triumphantly, as if delivering a conjuring trick. Thrilled, I immediately looked at the last page, which traditionally bore printing information and other essential details. And indeed, there was Maulavi Abdur Rahman sahib's own seal; the name of the press: Nizami Press, 'situated in the city of Cawnpore'; and the date of its printing: the month of Zil Hijja of the year 1278 of the Hegira. Like everyone in these days, I used the Hegira calendar in my private affairs, and the English calendar for official use. So I knew that the month of Zil Hijja, 1278 hijri, had begun on 30 May in 1862.

There was a formal, beautifully carved ornate seal impressed at the bottom, which read:

Muhammad Abdur Rahman bin Haji
Muhammad Raushan Khan Hanafi, the year 1273

All this text, perfectly legible, with some small floral decorations was in a seal, which was barely an inch high and an inch and a quarter wide. In order to leave absolutely no doubt about the authenticity of the divan, Maulavi Abdur Rahman's rather uncouth signature was also reproduced in facsimile. It was also claimed that the text was fully error-free: 'The Multitudinous in limitless Kindness, Muhammad Husain Khan Sahib of Delhi sent us a copy with corrections in the Honourable Author's Own Hand . . . and I printed it with perfect correctness and total accuracy . . .'

I immediately bought a copy from Maulavi sahib, but could barely suppress a smile when I noticed an error on the very first page: Ghazal 2 of the divan had just one verse, but it was not numbered as a ghazal, so the total number of ghazals (incomplete or complete) had the error of one. Of course, I said nothing about it and praised Abdur Rahman sahib appropriately for the fine printing and excellent calligraphy.

*

From that time on, that new divan became my friend and interlocutor of my days and nights. It often occurred to me that the publication of this new edition of Mirza sahib's divan should somehow provide me the occasion for establishing some contact with Mirza sahib, but how? I was quite unlettered in the protocols of the elites of Delhi and had none here, or in Nizamabad even, to guide me. That copy of the divan must have been seen by thousands of admirers since publication. So what was there special about my possessing a copy, even if I had it from the printer's own hand? The fact that it was printed in Cawnpore, and I too was in Cawnpore at that time, could be a delicious coincidence for me, but could have no significance for Mirza sahib.

I let a whole month pass, cogitating on the matter. The bazaar of the Parade then came to my rescue. Once I noticed a small crowd around a padre; and it seemed that people approached from different directions and obtained his signature—'autograph', as I learnt later— on some book. I went up close and discreetly asked what was going on there. I found that the padre himself was the author of that book; people bought a copy from the bookstore and brought it to him for his autograph. I was a little mystified, but learnt on further inquiry that it was a token of appreciation for the book and the author: to buy his book and then ask him to sign it so that it could become an even more valuable possession for the buyer.

The thought suddenly flashed in my brain: How about my doing it for my friends? I could buy copies of Mirza sahib's new divan, go to Delhi, pay my respects to him, and perhaps get him to sign the copies and bring them back. What better gift could there be from Delhi than those volumes? I would hit two targets with one arrow: fulfil my dearest desire, and also find occasion to do a gratuitous favour to my friends.

The first thing that I did was to go to Nizami Press in Chaman Ganj and buy twenty-five copies of the divan. The price was just half a rupee each, low even for the standards of those days. Then I had each of the volumes bound in fancy, presentation binding. The bindings cost me six annas each, that is, just a little less than a copy of the divan itself. Maulavi sahib had printed the book on thin, unimpressive machine-made paper; fortunately the calligraphy was excellent, the printing even more so, making the volume quite respectable. Now each sumptuously bound volume became truly a presentation item.

Still, I let another month pass; I was quite unable to gather up the energy to make a decision. Should I go or not? It wasn't such a difficult question as was the question of the divan volumes. Mirza Ghalib sahib was clearly a man of sophistication and refinement, and was brought up in the elite Navabi environment where everything was governed by strict protocols. Who knows, Mirza sahib might feel affronted at my newfangled idea of subjecting him to the inconvenience and cumber of signing so many volumes which did not even belong to him? Many of my friends, younger than me, and even more keen than me to own a copy of Mirza Ghalib's autographed divan, pressed me to go, and go with the divans, and then play it by ear, or use my intuition. Also, the weather was still quite hot and humid at present; the rains were going to be worse before they got better, so I should wait for a change of weather, a cooling of the breezes to make my journey less arduous.

*

I kept those bound volumes practically against my bosom for four months. It was nearly the end of Jumad-l Awwal 1279, or November 1862, when I travelled out by Post Coach to Qannauj, Farrukhabad, then Beawar, finally stopping at Kol (now called Allyghur, actually Aligarh) for a few days to rest and recuperate. I recommended my journey two days later and travelled through Bulandshahr, Ghaziabad, Shahdarah and Delhye, the last being just a name now, because the area had been destroyed sometime ago. I stopped at a small caravanserai near Pahargunj, just outside Bara Hindu Rao. I understood that Billimaron (also called Billimaran), where Mirza sahib lived, was not too far from there.

The iron road hadn't passed from anywhere near Cawnpore yet, though there was talk about its coming there shortly. It was in Delhi already, though I didn't expect to have to travel on it ever at all. The halting place on the iron road, called 'station', was somewhat close to my inn at Pahargunj and I could observe at first-hand the noises, the rough and tumble of heavy carts carrying large parcels, the smoke, the steam-and-fire-driven injans (it was, of course, 'engine' in English, but we somehow liked to say 'injan'). I first came to know about the injans in Cawnpore, but never saw one before I came to Delhi. All this looked somewhat forbidding and unnerving. I disliked especially the crowds, the hurry and anxiety that seemed to drip from their bodies. The Firangi railway sahibs naturally lorded it over in comparative ease and comfort.

The wintry evening was fast becoming dark. I had two kebabs made at the inn, ordered a couple of parathas from a nearby shop, and sat down to eat. But I was so tense and so tired that I couldn't eat much and retired early to bed.

I rose early, again because of uneasiness and tension in my body and mind. I inquired from the mistress of the inn about Mirza sahib. She informed me gravely, as if advising on something of import: 'Mian sahib, the daily routine of these types of people—navabs and poets—is that they rise late, attend the courts and offices of the grandees, meet the Quality, and go out to take the air of an evening. Thus the best time to pay them a visit should be just after sundown, when the lamps are lit and the streets are bright. I have heard about Mirza Naushah sahib; well, he's not from Delhi. Possibly his ways of life and spending the time were different then, but now he has become a proper Dilliwallah and he is surely dyed in the same hues as those of the people here. Actually, I saw him once or twice passing through the Rajwaron ki Gali in a carriage. (I later learnt that Rajwaron ki Gali was a street where dwelt many dancing girls, professional women, and so forth.) So, Mian sahib, you take things easy, go out now to see the sights of the city. In the evening, I will have a torchbearer, a horse and syce made ready for you. Go then in comfort, and come back in your own good time.'

So I changed into proper, formal clothes just a little before the fall of the evening. For the base and to make a snug fit, I put on a cap made of fish scales and tied a colourful turban upon it. I wore in each of my ears a large, thin gold ring with pearls. Below my silk dhoti, I wore long socks, on my feet I had a pair of Jodhpuri slippers. Then I hung my powder horn by the pommel of my horse and hung on my shoulder the long single shotgun made by my beloved grandfather. As presents for my venerable and honoured Mirza sahib, I had brought with me silk cloth for two lungis and another two silk pieces for turbans. I had these made specially by a weaver in Mubarakpur, a village near my native one, and known since ancient days for its silk weavers. I also had earthenware pieces for the hookah, with silver work done profusely on them, made with the special black clay from my own village of Nizamabad.

I had all this loaded on to a large, round copper tray, had the books too placed on it and had everything covered with a green silk square sheet called *khvanposh*, especially made for covering such trays. I entrusted the tray to my syce, had the torchbearer proceed a few steps ahead of me, and rode my horse into the city.

Evening had fallen everywhere deep and wide by now. The dark was like a vague curtain on the dilapidated and deserted havelis and bazaars plundered by the victors more than seven years ago. The environs and the wide, tall stairs of the Jama Masjid were thronged with the lovers of spicy food, or of the good life, or with audiences of the *dastan*, as usual. I was sorry to find that my torchbearer and syce were both from Mewat, and strangers to Delhi. They often stumbled or lost their way and blamed the changes in the city for their ineptness. My syce was a particularly gabby type. He proceeded ahead in his bumbling way and also talked away in his bumbling way: 'Mian sahib, who could now find the correct road, and how, indeed could one know it even if one found it? There is nothing here but a huge wilderness from Jama Masjid all the way to Rajghat. And nothing is to be found there but heaps of stone and brick; and in them, homes and sanctuary for snake and scorpion. The nether part of the garden and orchard of Mirza Gauhar Alam sahib was lower than the front part by several bamboo-lengths. Now all that hollow declivity is full of rubble and the lowland has risen to lie level with the *chandni*.'

This word 'chandni' was not familiar to me. A bit of thought let me upon its meaning. A chandni was what we called *chabutra*, that is, a stone or brick and masonry platform set in a garden for people to sit on and enjoy the sights of the garden.

'It was right in the middle of the garden,' my syce was talking away, unaware or uncaring if I was listening or not, while I was trying to solve the riddle of chandni. 'Mian sahib, do you hear? The chandni was right in the middle of the garden, and now the lower end of the garden is level with it!'

I made some vague noise, perhaps cleared my throat, as if I wanted to take part in his reminiscences. But he was floating in the steady stream of his own words.

'And here is more: for the iron road, the land has been levelled to look like a maidaun, from Kashmiri Darwaza to Kabuli Darwaza. Old alleys and lanes are chock-full with people. All routes and roads have become lost, in fact, eradicated. So where should a newcomer or visitor go?'

Suddenly he paused in his flow, looked back towards me to make sure that I was within hearing distance and was attentive. He went on: 'And Mian sahib, did you know? Panjabi Katra, Dhobiwara, Katra Saadat Khan . . . Well, dear sir, these were whole districts, and these and God knows how many others have now ceased to exist. The roads and alleys that remain do not look the same. Mian sahib, this Dilli is definitely not the Dilli that was. It is now a kump (camp), a barak (barracks), a forest of desolate, dweller-less homes.'

He again turned towards me, and raised his eyebrows, as if to give more emphasis to his story. 'In the times of the Presence, Mirza Abu Zafar Sirajuddin Bahadur Shah, all these alleys, by-lanes and road were alive with bright lights . . . alive, dear sir, with myriads of lights and lanterns. And now, one's own hand can't find the other hand.'

I remembered the short *qita* of Mirza sahib that he wrote during the days of the fighting with the English. It hadn't yet been printed for fear of being declared treasonous or seditious, but it had been on the tongues everywhere since those very times:

Going out to the marketplace from one's home,
Is an occasion for the spleen to turn to water;
The Chandni Chowk? It is now a site of massacres,
And the home? It is just like a prison house.

And about the Delhi of today that was before my eyes, I recalled a verse from many such composed by the most Eloquent of his times, the most Superior among the poets, the Lord of Poetry, the Presence, Mir Taqi Mir:

The city now is a maidaun, everywhere;
Did such desolation–destruction prevail here ever before?

I said to myself in my heart: May Ishwar ordain the return of Dilli's fortunes, may the throne of Delhi be adorned by him whose it is by right.

These conversations—mostly monologues—stumblings around, losing and finding the right way, cost me a full two hours. I was sick with anxiety. Mirza sahib was an old man, he might retire for the night before I could present myself at his portal. And it would be worse if he had retired, and was obliged to rise and return to the divan khana just because I had come calling. And here were my torchbearer and the syce, entirely unable to find Kale sahib's compound. One door of Mirza sahib's haveli opened on Katra Alam Khan; the other opened on the mosque of Kale sahib. It was the main entrance, just adjacent to the door of Kale sahib's house.

A Sufi's house was commonly called a *khanqah*—a convent or hospice—though actually it consisted mostly of the Sufi's residence, an always open and free guest house, an open-to-all meeting place, and a mosque. I don't know how such establishments came to be called 'khanqah'. I recalled, with a half smile, one of Ghalib sahib's most delectable jokes. After release from the prison where he was incarcerated for some minor intransigence of the law of the English, he changed his residence to the current address. Someone asked him: 'How are you doing, sir?' Mirza sahib drew a sigh, and said with perfect gravity: 'Oh well, I was until recently in the Gora sahib's penitentiary. Now I am in Kale sahib's jailhouse.'

Anyway, my recalling the joke was a good omen, apparently, for presently we stumbled upon Kale sahib's khanqah and immediately sighted Mirza sahib's haveli. I saw a couple of servants standing at the gate, apparently waiting for their masters, and found almost a new breath of life, for the servants' presence denoted that Mirza sahib was still receiving.

I had my name sent and was immediately summoned to the Presence. There were two others present; Mirza sahib had begun his evening's occupation already, perhaps there was not much concealment between him and his visitors.

Oh, how could I ever describe the form and figure of Mirza Ghalib! He was tall, his body was neither heavy nor emaciated, and his shoulders were wide and strong. He was old, in fact very old in my young eye, but there was no droop or bend to his shoulders. His colour was golden, like the champak flower's, and on his face he had a beard, not too long, and pure white. His head was shaven—I remembered he once said that when he grew a beard in his old age, he had his head shaved. A bright, no, a luminant and smiling visage; his eyes were large, and perhaps because of the onset of a little effect of the wine, they inclined to a little redness, making them even more beautiful; in spite of the effect of the wine, his eyes shone with intelligence, alertness and sharpness of acumen. He looked more like a recently arrived Turk from Turkmenistan or Iran than an Indian. Were his beard not of the Hindi style and his head not shaven, even the brightest of strangers would be convinced that he was in the presence of a Turanian Agha. His cheeks were somewhat sunken, perhaps because he had lost many of his teeth, especially the molars on both sides. But for this deficiency, he could easily win a contest of male handsomeness and personality.

His voice was quite clear, his enunciation perfect. Drink or not, there was no mumbling or loss of word or phrase. The dulcet-streaming and suppleness of the Braj of Akbarabad could still be discerned in his voice, although there was on it now a clear overlay of Delhi's harsh intonations. What would these people think of my 'soft and lowly' eastern tones and voice, which still bore distinct traces of the Bhojpuri of Nizamabad, I thought to myself, somewhat uncomfortably.

And how great was his humility, how kind his behaviour towards an uninvited stranger! He came up to the end of the carpet in my welcome, and seated me to his left. The person who sat to his right was in the dress of the Mughal grandees: his upper dress, or the *jamah*, was very wide towards the bottom, his trousers of some costly fabric; a silk dupatta was tied around his midriff like a sash, from which hung a dagger, bright in its jewel-encrusted sheath. On his head he wore a five-sided cap in brocade, its cut somewhat different from the standard Mughal cloth cap. His whiskers and beard were both very dense, with the moustaches turned up at the ends; the beard, somewhat square, was cut with extreme care; not a single hair was out of true or improperly combed. He wore a large emerald ring on his right index finger, a signet perhaps: in spite of the wrong angle and distance, I could discern some inscription on it, though I couldn't decipher the text. In short, he was an extremely handsome and manly person. I learnt that he was Navab Ziauddin Ahmad Khan. He wrote poetry in Hindi with the pen name of Naiyar; for Persian prose and verse, his ustad Mirza Ghalib sahib had bestowed upon him the pen name Darakhshan. Both had affinities with his name Zia, which means 'light', whereas *naiyar* means 'the sun' and *darakhshan* means 'shining bright'.

The moment I was introduced to him, I rose to my full height and paid obeisance. He smiled, did a simple Mughal salaam in return, and gave beneficence with the words: 'May you be happy and flourish always; may your prosperity and advancement ever increase.'

The gentleman seated in front of Mirza sahib had an extremely dense beard and whiskers, not bounden to a comb, or a barber—just like a bird's nest, though without artifice, I thought somewhat irreverently. He wore a hard velvet cap, taller than the usual, and his body was enclosed almost fully in a heavy English-style coat. Below the coat, one could see a somewhat coarse pair of woollen trousers above which a tunic of the same fabric could be glimpsed. All this was made noticeable because of his smiling, bright eyes. I learnt that the gentleman was Munshi Shiv Narain Aram, a very dear pupil of Mirza sahib's. He lived in Akbarabad, but was in Delhi to visit with Mirza sahib, and also for treatment of some chronic ailment. I again rose to my full height and made a salaam in submission. Munshi sahib's words of beneficence were almost the same as had been uttered by Navab Ziauddin Ahmad Khan sahib.

Mirza sahib commanded: 'Dear boy, this is a house free from the rituals of form, so tell me plain: do you have some inclination for my special activity?'

I replied in low, respectful tones, but quite clearly: 'Presence, I am a Rajput, son of a Rajput. I even break the statutory fast with a sip of the pure and double distilled.'

A tiny smile played on Mirza sahib's face. Shiv Narain Aram sahib looked at me with approval and some admiration. Navab sahib commanded: 'Dear young sir, you answered in practically a verse of our venerated and most respected Mirza sahib!'

I immediately understood what he meant, and recited the following Persian verse of Mirza Ghalib sahib:

*Just look at my shame, among my good deeds they didn't find anything
But a fast, correctly kept and broken with wine!*

I then folded my hands in humility and submitted: 'It is no more than a little miracle of my Guide and Mentor that I could find such an answer. The Guide and Mentor occupies the station of the Tongue of the Unseen.'

I did not need to explain that the 'Tongue of the Unseen' denoted none else but Hafiz Shirazi. Those present then spoke in unison: 'Doubtless, doubtless!'

Mirza sahib then summoned his steward Kallu and ordered him to fetch a glass and some savouries for me. Then he asked me the reason for my visit from such a long distance. I submitted brief details. I then presented the lungi and the turban fabrics. Luckily, they met with approval. He commanded: 'Very nice indeed. It's good that the turbans have no red in them, not even a thread. I really don't like wearing a turban which has red in it.'

I bent low in salaam; I then presented the Nizamabadi earthenware, the clay jet-black and worked over in silver. Those little items from the east were something quite new for the people of the far north-west and were admired by all present.

Navab sahib and Munshi sahib took their leave presently; it was now I and Mirza sahib, enjoying our tipple. It was some English wine, utterly without colour and very, very strong. Perhaps it was shampane (champagne), for I knew that Mirza sahib liked foreign wines. When the night became deep, and damp with dew, and the activity of the bazaar outside quite abated, I begged Mirza sahib's leave. He commanded: 'It's getting quite late, so all right, you must go now. I'll sit up a little longer, trying to compose a verse or two. Hah, I just recalled one from my days of youth:

Racking the brain, trying to compose poems,
It's nothing but dwelling in the prison house of silence
Through and through:
The spiral of smoke rising from the lamp burning
At midnight, is in fact a silent chain.

'Yet, I too am not up very long; I don't have the stamina,' he smiled and concluded.

I submitted in a low voice, not without much trepidation: 'Presence, if that divan had verses of such high excellence, why did you stand drawing the line of cancellation through it?'

It was as if he fell silent, suddenly. I feared that my misgivings had come true; I had annoyed him by asking about things that were far above my station to inquire about. But he answered slowly, in very soft tones. 'Mian, I am ashamed to confess at this stage of my life, when I am so old and experienced,' he paused. 'But the fact of the matter is that I am now sorry for rejecting all those verses and poems. Though I did declare once that I wandered aimlessly in my nonage, and gabbed on without caring for sense, and I went on to say that when some sense was knocked into me, I tore off those pages from end to end, and left only a few verses by way of sample in my current divan . . . but it wasn't a matter of walking the straight and moderate path in search of themes, or composing in the standard register rather than in a language that was practically of my own making . . . ' He paused again, as if somewhat exhausted by the long speech.

He drew on the hookah before going on: 'Actually, it was the high ambition of youth, and also a belief that poetry is meant to be studied in a quiet corner at home in a tranquil mood more than it being heard at assemblies and mushairahs. Also, the words of the great Persian poet Mirza Abdul Qadir Bedil sahib—may Allah Raise his station—resided deep in my heart when I read him saying that Word and Meaning are two alien beings. In fact, the Word cannot sustain the Meaning. Potentially, a word has more meaning than it can convey on its surface. Mirza Bedil sahib commands:

Oh, the thousands of themes, that for all their
Brilliance and bold beauty, discouraged by the
Alien nature of language,
Remained hidden behind the veils of mystery.

'But I found that we are more comfortable with the ancient practice of hearing poetry, rather than reading poetry; and like Mirza Bedil sahib, my thoughts were anyway shy of embodiment in the language. So I made it a habit of expressing my meaning through hints and subtle suggestions. But then once I felt so disgusted with the whole situation, the obtuseness and conventionality of my compatriots that I decided not to write in Rekhtah at all from then on. I should confine myself to Persian where I felt I had people, at least in the past, who spoke the same tongue as me.'

He drew on the hookah, looking at the fragrant smoke and the burning coals that were now darkening a bit. 'I'll let you in on a secret,' he smiled.

'Sir?' I answered in confusion.

'I'll say to you a Rekhtah verse of mine. Everyone believed that it was a poetic conceit, merely. Well, it was that too—all poetry is conceit, do you hear, young man?—but I was dead serious as well. I said:

Only he is able, somewhat, to appreciate my utterances,
Though the Angel Gabriel and I don't speak with the same tongue!

'Wah, wah! Presence, I for one will testify to it!' I spoke impulsively, though I should have held my tongue.

As if he didn't hear my interruption, he said, 'Actually, I did mean what I said. These old-fashioned Dilliwallahs couldn't come up to scratch when it came to comprehending my poetry.'

He paused. 'So, in order to please my so-called friends in the Hindi world, I declared that I'll discard all the hard and obscure verses and will permit only the simpler and more comprehensible verses to go into my divan. But, in fact, the poems that I discarded were not quite bereft of easy, comprehensible verses.'

He laughed briefly, and went on, 'So, I didn't really make a systematic selection. One night, when I was rather much in my cups, I just scratched randomly the lines that I felt like discarding. The fact of the matter is that the ghazals which practically compelled the literary circles here in Delhi to accept my station as ustad, mostly date from those days, the days of my early youth, before I turned twenty-five.'

'Oh, I didn't know that!' I ejaculated. I almost went on to say, 'So you were a born master,' but I didn't know if he would like my speaking almost as his equal, capable of judging his value.

Mirza sahib smiled a wan smile. 'Well, most people have short memories, and most people want to remember only what they want to remember. And I was an outsider here. There was much prejudice those days against outsiders. Even the Presence, Mir Taqi sahib, took some time to establish himself here.'

'Presence,' I said somewhat haltingly, 'is there no hope of recovering that treasure?'

'I don't really have a good retentive memory for my own poetry,' he said with a hint of apology, or perhaps just without any emotion. 'I'll now get to look at those poems only on the Day of Resurrection.'

Somewhat impudently, I said before him a verse of Mir sahib's:

On the Day of Judgement, by way of punishment,
My own divan was hurled upon my head!

He smiled. 'So you too are a Miri like me, not a Saudai.' He was referring to Mir sahib's great rival and contemporary, Mirza Sauda. The point of the joke was that in Hindi *saudai* means 'crazed'. It wasn't hidden from me. I said in admiration, 'Only Allah is free from blemish,' then submitted: 'I beg that the Honourable Portal may grant permission to this slave to take his leave. And . . . and is it possible that the Guide and Mentor summons me tomorrow at some such time when the Presence may be free from other visitors?'

Actually, I wanted badly to request his autographs on his divans, but I was just unable to get up the courage at that time. I was hoping that I'd have gathered myself overnight to make the request.

He paused to consider for a moment, then commanded: 'Mian, then the best thing would be that you should dine with me tomorrow. I eat

44

at about midday, then rest for a while. None are permitted to intrude at that time. I'll save that leisure for you.'

I did not have the courage to say more, although I wanted to submit that it was very hard for me to intrude thus upon his rest and privacy. I salaamed him and returned to my lodging.

*

I was feeling poorly the next day. So I slept late and it was almost twelve by the time I was ready to go out. I rode to Billimaron alone. In many places I could clearly see the signs of the jarnaili bandobast that had just come to an end—broken-up buildings, desolate mosques and temples, empty or ravaged shops, or shops with their doors shut firmly. I could also see preparations for more buildings and places to be pulled down to make things easy for the coming of the iron road. I rode on, my eyes strictly on the path in front. There was no roaming or going astray this time and I reached Mirza sahib's haveli quickly enough. Mirza sahib, extremely kind and hospitable as always, was waiting for me. Dinner was served immediately upon my arrival. There was so little for Mirza sahib to eat—like the teardrops of a bulbul, as they say—and a full panoply of variety, and in plentiful quantity, for me.

Dinner over, the Guide and Mentor had his bed brought out into the inner courtyard, but placed not directly in the sun. A light chair, more like an *aram kursi* than chair, was placed for me in front of Mirza sahib's bed. The hookah was refreshed. Mirza sahib drew on it lightly once or twice, then paused for me to speak. Sometimes he granted me the favour of sharing the hookah with him.

Having enjoyed the hookah, Mirza sahib dismissed the servants, and commanded: 'So, sahib, say what is it that you want to say; we're alone now.'

I unwrapped the bundle of the divan copies and extended my hand towards him with a copy of the book. I was about to say something by way of explanation when he took it from my hand, opened it, and

45

said in a wondering voice: 'This is nothing but my own divan! What shall I do with it?'

I submitted: 'There is some purpose in presenting them before Your Honour. I pray that the Presence may enhance the beauty of these volumes by autographing them. I will present them to my close friends. What better gift of the road could be than these invaluable volumes.'

Mirza sahib frowned. 'But dear young man, why should *I* sign those books? They are not my property.'

I entreated: 'Honourable sir, among the Sahibs of Great Glory there is, among others, a convention to express appreciation and admiration for an author by purchasing a copy of his book and getting it autographed by him. They regard such an autographed book as a thing of great worth for those who value such things.'

Mirza sahib laughed briefly. 'I always thought that the way to express one's appreciation of a poet's work is to have him wear a robe of honour consisting of seven or even fourteen pieces, present to him a necklace of twenty-one gems, especially pearls; bedeck his head by tying round it a *jigha* encrusted with seven gemstones. I didn't know that buying a little book worth half a rupee and getting it autographed by the author for distribution among friends was also a proper way of expressing appreciation for the author. Anyway, now that you have made this request, let me then impress my seal on each of those volumes. By a happy chance, I had a new seal made dated 1278 just a few months ago.'

He summoned his steward and asked for his inkstand. He thought a bit, put his seal on twenty-four of the volumes, and then wrote on the last one:

My young friend Beni Madho Ruswa, of prosperous fortune and long life

This was followed by a famous Persian line of welcome:

Oh you whose coming causes happiness to my heart!

46

Below it he wrote:

Asadullah Khan Ghalib, inscribed 16 Rajab-ul Murajjab 1279

He extended the book towards me, and said: 'Here, young fellow, you should be happy now!'

In a daze, for I never expected him to actually inscribe and sign my copy, I rose and bent low in salaam; then I gingerly took the book in both hands. I kissed it, and touched my eyes with it. I immediately pleaded to be excused so that he could have some moments of rest now.

He commanded, 'No, no. Stay a little longer. I like the way you talk and speak. You never told me about your life in the composition of poetry. Do you have a divan already, and who is your ustad in the art of poetry?'

In a soft voice I submitted some details about my Ustad Maulavi Khadim Husain Nazim of Banaras, and Mullah Sabiq of Banaras, his late grandfather. He listened intently—I then realized that he was a little hard of hearing. I even recalled a famous Hindi verse of his and knew that it was based on reality:

> *I am deaf, so it is proper that I should be given twice*
> *as much regard as others;*
> *For I am unable to hear your words unless they're spoken twice over!*

I was about to say something about the verse, or apologize for my thoughtlessness, but I checked myself, for both the things would have been inappropriate.

Mirza sahib spoke thoughtfully: 'I don't have the honour to know Maulavi Khadim Husain sahib, but during my stay in Banaras I had occasion to go through Mullah Sabiq sahib's *masnavi, Tasir-e Muhabbat*. He was a person of great erudition.'

Led by the irresponsibility of callow youth, I thought I could become a little bold. This was possibly because he said that he liked the way

47

I talked. I submitted: 'Honourable Guide and Mentor, if I am spared my life, I would like to say something.'

'Yes, yes,' he commanded cordially, but looked at me with some interest. 'So, what is it?'

I screwed my courage to the sticking place, and spoke haltingly, as if I had difficulty in enunciation: 'In the opinion of the Presence, the Indian poets of Persian are not worth much, because they have no true command over the language. But that Exalted Portal also belongs to Hind?'

His face crimsoned slightly and I feared that I was going to face the fury of his wrath. But he seemed to check himself, paused a little, and commanded: 'Look, my boy. The subtle points and mysteries of the Persian language are implanted and imprinted in my soul, just like the natural grain or streak in steel, or the moisture of the morning breeze in the delicate veins of a flower. As against me, where are those lowly lexicographers and grammarians like Mullah Ghiasuddin of Rampur or Dilwali Singh Qateel, a Khatri, of Faridabad! Their remotest ancestors even wouldn't have had a glimpse of the Iranian soil!'

He paused for breath. I should have let go at that point. But I wasn't a Rajput only in name. I persisted: 'But, Presence, there are other Hindi poets, aren't there? Amir Khusrau, Mullah Faizi, Mullah Ghani of Kashmir, Abul Barakat Munir of Lahore. They are not all like Ghias and Qateel and others of their ilk.'

His tone now had a little heat. 'Among the Indians, none is canonical in language and idiom except Amir Khusrau. Do you follow me? Even Mian Faizi stumbles sometimes. As for Ghani and Munir . . . well, they are good poets, doubtless. They have a knack of finding new themes. But they have no natural flair for the language. Their usage is non-standard, at best.'

I felt like asking, 'Presence, words and themes go together, don't they? In fact, there can be no theme without words. So how could it be that the elegance of themes may be achieved without the elegance of words?' But such utterances would have been outrageously impertinent. Still, I thought, let's open the discussion with Mirza Bedil. But even that was risky, because, in spite of all his past admiration for him, Mirza Ghalib sahib had changed his mind long ago about Bedil's mastery of idiomatic Persian. He was just not prepared to grant that Bedil, or any other Indian Persian poet for that matter, could possibly be in total command of Persian, an alien language. Still, I said, somewhat mischievously: 'Presence, there was a time when you greatly admired Bedil . . .'

He cut me short, and spoke with something like cold disdain: 'I admire him, but I don't believe that his Persian is idiomatic and can compare with an Iranian master who has Persian as his native tongue. Bedil, Nasir Ali Sarhindi, Ghanimat of Kunjah . . . ugh! Of what account can their Persian be—they were mere Hindustanis.'

He then called to Kalyan, his other manservant, to refresh the hookah. I spoke haltingly, but stubborn as before. 'Honoured sir, I fear that the future may discard you and keep you out of the poets' mansion, just as you are denying a place to your compatriots. Those who come after you might say . . .'

He sat up with almost a jerk. He commanded, his voice full of passion: 'That is not possible! That is just not possible! I hold the reins of the Persian language in my hands. My temperament is secure in its right-minded affability; my taste is impeccable. And most of my themes are such that the world for ever after will read my powerful verse and try to fathom its depth.'

He then recited a Persian verse of his, with a supremeness of confidence and with such mastery of mood that I was stunned:

My station cannot be discerned by any eyes but mine;
For my star is so far up that it doesn't shine bright.

I swear by all that is holy: that voice, that mood, that time and that environment were so kingly in their total confidence and assertiveness

49

that the very air seemed to stop flowing, trying to hear what Mirza sahib was pronouncing. And the theme was so entirely new. I was almost moved to rise up and dance, and try to catch those powerful rhythms through the movement of my limbs.

Dear Reader, please remember that the year was 1862 and a very great deal of the night sky was unexplored at that time. Many decades later, I read in a newspaper somewhere that astronomy had now established that some stars are so far from us that from them, only a dim light reaches us here on this planet. So they look much less bright than they actually are. I recalled that afternoon, and Mirza sahib saying that verse, which now seemed prophetic to me. Did he have some intuitive sense of the future? I thought. How could he know so many years in advance that an extremely bright star may be so far up above all others that it may appear dim rather than bright? For, how else could he have found that metaphor?

Well, to go back to my story. I spoke words of praise as best I could, and said them most enthusiastically. But my devil was still not quieted. I was still not inclined to stop teasing him. (Also, I surely wanted to learn from him by saying provoking things.) So I said, after an appropriate hiatus: 'Sir, you are like my Kabah and I prostrate myself before you, always. But you might recall that the great Mirza Saib was an admirer of Ghani of Kashmir?'

He very nearly snorted. 'Who? Saib? Well, an Iranian he was, but a long sojourn in Shahjahanabad had corrupted his language. He said *intiqam kashidan* which is correct, but also *intiqam giriftan* which is a direct translation of the Hindi "to take revenge".'

Mirza sahib emphasized 'to take' which according to him wasn't correct with intiqam (revenge). He declared, 'Intiqam giriftan is plain, blind, bad Persian. No, it is Hindi.'

'But, Honoured Guide and Mentor,' I continued to prod him and point out the weakness of his argument, 'what would you say about Urfi? Was he not an Iranian too who spent a very large part of his life in Akbarabad?'

'Ha! Why do you bring in Urfi's name? He is the one whom we all obey; we subserve to him in full. *He* can do no wrong.'

Whatever little logic I picked up long ago in the madrasa urged me to contradict him. But I had already gone too far, I realized, and anyway my basic purpose was to hear him talk, and learn from what he commanded. I wasn't there to do a debating match with him. Still, I persisted, gently and tentatively: 'Sir, may I submit something?' Finding him silent and somewhat pensive after his outburst, I blurted: 'Sir, didn't Khan-e Arzu hold that Indian masters of the Iranian idiom had as much right to innovate and make creative changes in it?'

'Yes, but where *are* the masters of that idiom among the Indians? Would you accord the rank of master to Qateel, who pronounces strictly idiomatic phrases like *hama ja, hama alam* to be incorrect?'

He continued passionately without pausing: 'Was it not the asinine Qateel who wrote the Hindi *khak* (dust=nothing) *na bood* instead of the standard Iranian *heech na bood*?'

I persisted, most foolhardily, I realized in retrospect. He was the master. He had the right to his ideas, even if I feared that they might affect him too adversely sometime in the future. Anyway, I submitted, in the gentlest, most cajoling of tones: 'Sir, there are others among the Hindustanis. If the Presence, Amir Khusrau, may Allah Raise his station, could be fully authoritative, why not some others too? And after all, the Iranian ustads didn't all come from the same place. They were Shirazi or Isphahani or Balkhi, Ghaznavi and so on.' I finished somewhat lamely, because Balkh and Ghazni are in Afghanistan, and Mirza sahib might have excluded them from his canon on that ground.

'Look, if you want to be disputatious and contentious, that's another matter; for the straight, God-approved truth is that the Hindustanis do not know Persian as it should be known.' He paused. 'My case is different. First, I have an inborn, very nearly spiritual and eternal affinity with Persian. Second, I had an Iranian ustad who more or less poured all the subtleties and obscure points of the language down my young throat. And I absorbed them and digested them as a part of my blood.'

Saying this, he lay back on the bed and closed his eyes. After waiting a moment or two, I decided that he was exhausted, and had dozed off, and I was about to do a quiet salaam and go away, when he spoke, though his eyes were shut: 'Remember that the mother tongue exerts its pull on the non-native speaker of a language. The mother tongue of the Hindustani, be it Hindi or Bengali or Bhakha, always pulls at him and leads him astray when he tries to write Persian.'

Somehow, and regrettably, I must say, my native pride intervened here and I had to say: 'Sir, Exalted Presence, we who produced past masters in Persian—Khusrau, Faizi, Ghani, Tek Chand Bahar and others—must surely be given some right on the Persian language?'

'You won't understand these things,' he spoke kindly, with a tinge of tired disdain. 'You are a mere child. Just look at Tek Chand Bahar: he has picked hundreds of holes in the pronouncements of Khan-e Arzu and he has always found his mark. Yet, the moment he lets his own inference guide him, he stumbles and falls on his face. Only a native master can truly understand the matters of his language.'

'Please pardon me if I am being impertinent, Honourable Guide and Mentor, sir. But I still believe what I believe in the light of what I have learnt from my elders. People like Tek Chand Bahar, Mirza Bedil and Anand Ram Mukhlis who spoke and wrote Persian throughout their days and nights, and who thought and must have even felt in Persian, should be admitted to the rank of native speakers . . .'

He drew a deep sigh, thought for a few seconds, then observed: 'You are, after all, a Rajput, and a young Rajput at that. I have no cure for your recalcitrance. So go now, it's late. I need to rest.'

I was rocked to the depth of my soul. This kindly, angelic person, this master poet who discommoded himself purely for me—a callow and uncouth young visitor—and I had managed to upset him. Shame on me!

I rose in a most submissive, tentative manner, went down on

my knees, folded my hands close to my chest in the Rajput gesture of utmost humility, and said: 'Exalted sir, I annoyed you by my impertinence and stubbornness. I'd rather die at your hands than have the feeling that I hurt Your Honour's sentiments. This useless slave begs to be forgiven.'

He sat up, and asked Kalyan to give him the support of a couple of heavy pillows. When this was done to his satisfaction, he gestured that Kalyan should go away. He had his eyes half closed; I didn't know if he was still feeling sleepy, or was considering the reprimand with which he should dismiss me. Thank God, he wasn't apparently minded to have me thrown out by his servants. Had I known him well, I would have had no such fears. In fact, a more tolerant, affectionate and forgiving human being never walked the earth, as I came to know much later when I read his disciple Maulavi Hali's biography of him, published in 1897, long after he was dead and gone to his Maker.

He opened his eyes, but didn't look me directly in the face. As if I wasn't there, he spoke in a half whisper a verse of Momin Khan sahib:

My breath may stop due to my feebleness,
But I never am displeased with anyone.

Then he continued: 'There's nothing for me to be upset with you, dear boy. As Momin Khan—Allah Elevate his station—said, "I am angry at no one, angry with no one." I am unhappy with my fate: the true taste for Persian disappears fast from this land, this city. So how can I expect anyone to appreciate my subtleties, the high flights of my mind. I once said, and not without reason:

Of what use is it to bring Ghalib
Into your conversation? His heart is burnt to nothing,
And you are in a place where they don't know
Naziri from Qateel.'

I wished that the earth may open and I disappear down the hole. I had no words even to apologize. Sensing that I was entirely discomfited, he said: 'Right, young man. You may go now. Come tomorrow at this time again, if you feel so inclined.'

He pushed the extra pillows away and lay down, closing his eyes. I salaamed low, and tried to disappear as stealthily as I could. But Kallu the steward was alert to my going; he came up, salaamed, and said as he let me out, 'Mian sahib, do come again tomorrow.'

I hated myself all the while. I had no cause, nor qualification, to enter into a disputation with Mirza Ghalib sahib. Everyone acknowledged that there was none above him in the whole of Hindustan in Persian, and also Hindi poetry. And who was I? A half-educated rustic who didn't even have enough Hindi, not to speak of Persian. Clearly, I was far out of bounds in engaging him. True, I did so more because I foolishly felt that I loved him and he had some regard for me too. But still, I was nothing but a piece of dried grass, and he a towering tree of learning and poetic capability. *Tab'-e vaqqad*, 'brilliant, hot, shining temperament', as someone said about Amir Khusrau.

And there were conflicting signals: Was there a hint of sarcasm or displeasure in Mirza sahib's words that I should come tomorrow if I were so inclined? Did it mean that I should not come, or did it mean even worse: Since I had been so obstreperous all this while, I should apparently not like to revisit, and need not come, in fact? Hey Bhagwan! What had I done to myself?

But then there was Kallu, inviting me so reassuringly that I must come tomorrow. Was I meant to understand that the Presence was not really angry at me?

And Mirza sahib, and the Hindustani Persian poets . . . I was still being obstinate, in fact hatefully cussed and intractable in my heart. I was sure that justice was with me. When a people use an alien language for a very long time, they gradually develop a natural proclivity for it and some of them may well achieve mastery in that tongue. Oh well, who was I to impose my callow beliefs on him? From now on, I shall hear more, much more, than I'll speak.

*

Morning dawned, cool, grey and depressing. Or perhaps it was I who was depressed. I still had fearful thoughts: Did Mirza sahib really mean that I was no longer welcome? No, that could not be. He was a gentleman of the old class. They forgave, they had compassion, especially for well-meaning country louts like me. I decided to go.

I waited until about midday, then rode out as usual. While passing through the fruit market of Fatehpuri, I saw that the whole market was displaying extremely good Kabuli grapes. Quite on impulse, I bought a whole basketful of them as a small present for Mirza sahib.

I found him friendly and kind as before. If he was upset yesterday by my argumentativeness, there was no apparent trace of it today. He was pleased with my basket of grapes, but it wasn't his favourite fruit, the mango—about which it was said that he wanted his mangoes to have just two qualities: they should be sweet, and they should be plentiful. So he said, 'Very nice fruits, these. The children will surely enjoy them. I too will eat a couple of the bigger ones. But, oh dear, how I wish that every season was the season of mangoes! Do you recall my short poem on the mango?'

Before I could answer, he said one of the verses from that poem:

It can do nothing at all before the mango:
The grapevine does no more than pick at its blisters!

Before I could utter a word of praise for the delightful wit and delicate wordplay, he said, 'Hey, Mian Ruswa, you know what? I feed grapes to my pious and mullah friends like Mufti Azurda and the rest. Do you get the point?'

He was clearly testing me. I was nonplussed, but I always had a good memory, and the Goddess Saraswati saved me from error. A Persian verse of Mirza sahib's flashed upon the inward eye, as if the page was open before me. Almost ecstatically, I recited:

Pious man, don't regard my gift of a bunch of grapes
With contumely. Hey, man! Don't you know?
I wasted a whole wine cupful to treat you!

May Allah open the doors of Paradise to him in his grave from all sides. Mirza sahib smiled with delight and observed: 'Young fellow, you seem to have good taste. Should you visit some evening, I'd treat you to liqueur.' He pronounced it 'likore', and I didn't quite understand his meaning. He continued, 'Its taste has the effect of mango. Its colour is very pleasing, its texture thin and sweet like the heated and thickened mixture of sugar and water. I don't like the Indian wine, fermented from molasses and the skin of sugar cane.'

I inquired more about this mysterious 'liqueur' when I returned to Cawnpore. I found out that Mirza sahib most probably meant the French wine, Chartreuse, which was a popular liqueur in those days.

Dinner was served as we spoke. Dinner over, we washed our hands with chickpea powder, and Mirza sahib's bed was placed in the courtyard, a little away from the sun, as before, and a chair placed for me near the bed. His Honoured sir enjoyed the hookah in quiet content. My mental brow was clear of anxiety now. The Presence had forgiven me, exhibiting the magnanimity with which he had treated me so far.

I made bold to ask: 'You quoted Hakim Momin Khan sahib yesterday. I take it that you liked him and his poetry.'

'Yes,' he drew a sigh and fell silent for a moment or two. 'I had many friends in Delhi, but Momin Khan was my friend of fifty years' standing. Young fellow, you won't now find an enemy of half a century's standing; a friend as old as that is now a very far cry. Gone are those days when we had Momin, Zauq and Nizam-ud Din Mamnun, and many, many others. They were lucky to have died before the fearful and cruel tumult. I am now practically alone in this benighted place. Among our men of learning, Fazl-e Haq Khairabadi, Sahbai and Muhammad Baqar suffered the wrath of the Glorious Sahibs, and there were many more like them.'

He seemed to have fallen into a brown study. Who could say what his gloomy meditations were? But I blamed myself, rather unjustly, that I should have triggered them off by bringing up Momin's name. I dared not intrude upon his thoughts now.

Suddenly, there was a brief commotion in the back of the haveli, perhaps at the door that led into the inner quarters. It was quickly hushed, but an extremely handsome, if sickly looking young boy of about ten appeared at the door, followed by Kalyan.

'No, let me go to Dada jan!' The boy was saying in a fierce, confident whisper.

Ghalib sahib opened his eyes and looked up smilingly. 'So, it's that young rascal Husain Ali Khan!' He said. 'Kalyan, let him come in. What does he want?'

'Presence, I tried to restrain him . . . '

'No, no. It's quite all right. So, Husain Ali Khan Bahadur, what is it that the Glorious Sahib desires of this old man?'

The boy went past Kalyan quickly, came close and stood with slightly defiant eyes. 'Dada jan, I need some money, now!'

'Well, what do you want it for, child? Do you need something?'

'Dada jan, I hear that there is some celebration today in the Chowk, to prepare for the Basant. Everybody is flying kites. I too want to fly kites. But Dadi ji says I am too old to fly a kite.' He went on petulantly: 'Too old to fly the kite, but too young to go out alone! This is indeed tyrannous!'

Ghalib sahib laughed indulgently. 'Well, sir, you may be too old to fly the kite, but you are certainly too young to go out alone. Kallu, take some money from my cash box, give it to Bi Vafadar with strict instruction to go to the Billimaron bazaar and buy a couple of the best kites. But she must not let Husain Ali sahib out of her sight for a moment. Is that clear?'

'Sir, Presence. Quite clear. I will summon Vafadar to the outer gate at once.'

The boy laughed in high glee, put his head in Mirza sahib's lap and nuzzled. Mirza sahib ruffled his ample hair, disarranging his cap in the process, and patted him gently on the back.

'So, sahib, are you happy now? And be sure,' he said in a stage whisper, 'not to let Dadi jan know that you went out!'

The boy jumped up before Ghalib sahib finished and followed Kallu into Mirza sahib's chamber.

Mirza sahib looked at me. 'That was Husain Ali Khan, fatherless and motherless. His father was Navab Zainul Abidin Khan Arif, who died young, of phthisis, or as the Persians say, *ranj-e barik* (the subtle and wasting disease).'

I said, 'Exalted Presence, why is the disease also called *tap-e diq*?'

'Well, actually,' he promptly observed, 'they are the same, ranj-e barik and tap-e diq, because in Arabic *diqq* means any fever that lasts and lasts and is subtle, and its patient wastes away.'

'Presence, I heard somewhere that the good lady who was the mother of the two boys also died of the ranj-e barik. As I recall, Navab Arif sahib was particularly dear to you, and in fact the elegy in ghazal form that you wrote on his death is one of the most famous in the language.'

A wan smile appeared on his lips. 'Yes,' he said. 'Nowadays I often recall the concluding verse. It is so appropriate to my old age: bereft of friends, and with Persian, the light of my heart, going out in no uncertain fashion in today's world.' He recited:

Ghalib, they don't know, those who ask, why do you live still?
In fact, it's only a few days for me before I cease to long for death.

In spite of myself, I ejaculated: 'Marvellous, how marvellous! Only a perfect ustad like His Honour could bring off such an effect: equating the fact of life with the fact of longing for death.'

Mirza sahib was pleased. I heaved a huge sigh of relief in my heart; perhaps his mood was now going to change and I was instrumental in bringing it about. I thought of observing that his love for Arif sahib's orphaned sons was exemplary; for, Arif sahib was just a distant relation, and that too by marriage. But I desisted. It would have been intrusive, if not invasive on his private life and emotions.

'Yes, Zainul Abidin Khan's ancestors and mine had been friends from before they came to India more than a century ago.'

Did he somehow sense what was in my heart? Hey Ram, was he some sort of a clairvoyant, and could also descry things that were far into the domain of knowledge in the future, as the example of his star verse proved later? But Mirza sahib was speaking, I realized.

'They were not blood relations, but they were closer than blood relations, in fact. Your ustani ji and Zainul Abidin's mother were sisters. Zainul Abidin's wife died first, leaving two sons. Arif too died soon after remarrying. Over that short period of time your ustani ji had fallen in love with the infants. We are childless, as you know.'

He became pensive. Perhaps he was grieving for his babies, all of whom died one after the other, almost immediately after they were born.

'So, these two are our babies now. When they were small, they spent much of their time in the men's haveli with me. Allah, those naughty goblins! They left nothing untouched, and they left everything grubby.'

He smiled briefly. 'Do you know, Mian Ruswa, someone asked me if it was irksome for me to correct their poems? I wrote in reply: Dear fellow, your poems are like my children in spirit. They don't irk me, any more than my physical children who play havoc in my bedroom and divan khana all the time! They spill water where no water should be, leave imprints on my pristine white bed sheets with their muddy boots, steal my ink and my pens to make drawings on my walls. *They don't irk me, so how could those mute little spiritual children?*'

He laughed in pleasure, as if remembering those pranks.

'The Exalted Portal's magnanimity and lovingness are almost godlike and are known all over the land of Hind.'

'Oh well, maybe. It's your love for me, really. But Allah didn't give me a thousandth part of the means that were needed to satisfy the urges of love and munificence that He endowed me with. If nothing, I wish He'd given me enough to spare me the sight of a hungry or naked soul in at least the city where I live.'

I recalled an absolutely marvellous Persian verse of his and spoke it on impulse:

Whatever the Heaven didn't desire,
None desired from Heaven.
The theologian's cup didn't seek wine
And my wine needed no relish.

'Well, young sir,' he observed, obviously pleased but not without a hidden tinge of regret, 'you know quite a few of my verses. But beware, fingers of malice may point towards you if you go on loving and remembering my poems!'

'Exalted Portal, God made you the envied one,' I ventured, 'and not the envier. You should be prepared to pay the price.'

He looked at me intensely, as if silently reprimanding me for not ceasing to take liberties with him. Then he spoke gruffly, perhaps more to himself than to me: 'There's very little that comes together for me, and there's much that breaks into pieces. And my self-respect,' he smiled a pale, almost colourless smile, 'some would say self-regard, and my pride, and my heedlessness of those who can give, none of it comes without a price.' He recited a line of verse from Bedil:

Life was slung round my neck, Bedil, like a collar; there's no way
of getting rid of it.

He didn't give me time to answer, but changed tack, perhaps because Bedil's name had cropped up. He commanded: 'Dear boy, remember. Writing poetry is not measuring the rhymes and ensuring that the metre is correct. Poetry means creation of new themes, new meanings. You might ask, how could there be new meanings? Well, if you compose a verse where everything is on the surface and nothing is left for the intellect, for the brilliant mind to discern, then you are no poet. Let the poem make you pause, and ponder, then you'll see that it seems to say more than it seemed to, at first flush.'

This was rather hard for me to follow. But I held my tongue. Mirza sahib recited a verse from Saib of Tabriz. There was an unequalled grace and fluency in his recitation which I recall even today with wonder. He said:

Our way of luxury is
To catch hold of a subtle, delicate theme;
We, whose imagination is subtle, and complex,
For us the subtle thought is the crescent moon of the Id.

'I am not much given to saying the obvious,' he observed with some passion. 'I believe in complexity; I walk faithfully the path of the *tazah khiyal* masters, poets who believed in the Freshness of the Imagination, in using the resources of the language to the ultimate limit.'

'Would such a poet compose poems that were apparently simple, but difficult to imitate?' I asked.

'No, perhaps not. But remember, all great poetry is difficult, if not impossible, to imitate. Good poets don't imitate. They go forward to welcome the masters of the past.' He smiled, 'And in going forward in welcome, they go beyond them. That was the point hidden in the term *istiqbal* invented by the poets of a few generations ago in the context of their true begetters, the Poets of the Past.'

I said, with no little hesitation: 'Presence, in spite of the rather obvious complexity of your poetic creations, I sometimes seem to feel that they have a certain fluency which I do not find in most poets of your style. Am I right in believing so?'

Mirza sahib was obviously pleased. 'Yes, others too have felt something of the sort. You know, there's the term *sahl-e mumtane*. It is supposed to mean a poem which is deceptively easy, but whose effect is very nearly impossible to reproduce. It is not a precise term. But I feel that such a state does seem to supervene in most of my prose and verse.'

'In Lucknow, we have a famous poet from your own Delhi,' I submitted. 'He also seems to believe that love is not necessarily the only thing that a poet must write about.'

'Yes, I expect you mean Navab Asghar Ali Khan Nasim,' he returned. 'Pity he had to leave here because of property disputes with his siblings. A proud and honourable man, and a poet after my own heart, though he was a pupil of Momin's.'

'Sir, Nasim sahib has a verse which I seek your permission to say to you.'

'Yes, yes. Let's hear it.'

I recited:

It's quite proper if the poet tries
To find other themes.
It's not necessary to regard the ghazal
As a poem about love alone.

Mirza sahib was pleased. 'Yes, that is exactly what we need to do now. The ghazal has vast potential for all kinds of themes, but,' he said with emphasis, 'the theme should be made to conform to the World of Ghazal.'

'By which Your Honour means . . .'

'What I mean is that the ghazal has its own language, its own rules. The main condition is that a verse of the ghazal should have, at its best, layers of meaning.'

Quite without intending to, I recited a verse from the great Mir Taqi Mir sahib:

Each utterance of mine, oh Mir, has many sides and layers:
How much, and how varied are the utterances of my poem's tongue!

'That was well said,' Mirza sahib observed. He fell silent; perhaps he was lost in the mood evoked by Mir's verse. In the meantime, his hookah was refreshed and presented. Seeing him enjoy the hookah with obvious content, I thought that it was the best time to seek permission. I submitted: 'Presence, may I be permitted to be in attendance at your Portal tomorrow evening? I'll be leaving the day after.'

'Hey, you just came and now you want to leave! But see, you reminded me of a verse from the blessed Mian Zauq sahib.' He recited:

You snatched the lover's burning heart and left;
My dear, did you come to borrow a bit of the burning coal?
You came, and you took your leave!

He continued, 'Is your office leave nearing its end?'
'No real hurry, Presence,' I submitted.
'So does someone watch the road for you at home?' he persisted.
As if someone stabbed me in the heart, my eyes misted over, in spite of myself. 'Exalted Presence, I have no home. Live I do in Cawnpore, but I am a stranger there. There are none in the dwelling I call my home.'

Mirza sahib was immediately moved to compassion. Speaking gently, almost like a loving mother to a young son, he asked what the matter was. I demurred, but he pressed, and pressed more. 'Nay, I do want to share your pain, dear boy. And I assure you, it'll be safe with me.'

Then I had no choice but to tell him my tale. I spoke in a soft voice, almost in whispers. He listened intently, as if he was too absorbed to even move his head.

He sighed deeply when I finished. 'So that's the reason. I understand now. I used to wonder how and where this young lad acquired such a pain-filled heart, so full of empathy. So you too are fated to wander, aimless and homeless like the morning breeze . . . All right, I permit you to go back home . . . no, go back to Kampu where you reside at present. And look, do come here tomorrow evening. We have a dastan recitation session before dinner, but it is in Persian, come hear the dastan reciter too, if you are interested.'

*

As promised, I was at Ghalib sahib's haveli at about four next evening. It was quite cool, but pleasant. I had noticed that the sun goes down much later in Delhi than in my easterly Azamgarh or even Cawnpore. So there was plenty of light, and bustle. The street of Billimaron looked almost narrow because of the multitude. And there were more people at the haveli's gate than usual.

I entered to a warm welcome by Navab Ziauddin Ahmad Khan sahib, Mirza Ghalib sahib and an extremely good-looking and impressive young man who I was delighted to know was Dagh sahib, the famous poet. His bearing was so erect and his manner so self-assured that I would have taken him for a visitor from some northern Arab country like Palestine or Iraq.

The dastan began soon after I arrived. The *dastango*—that is, the dastan narrator—was a tallish, but frail, almost wispy old man called Mir Mujid. He and his uncle Mir Sajid had been employed at the Red Fort before the holocaust of 1857; he now lived on the munificence of Hakim Mahmud Khan sahib, a great friend of Mirza sahib's. Hakim sahib was also present. I learnt later that the dastango was a pupil of the Exalted and Noble Presence, Prince Mirza Rahimuddin Haya, a scion of the royal family who now lived in Rampur.

The dastan was an excerpt, or episode, from the famous dastan of Amir Hamza. Perhaps because of me being among the audience, the excerpt related to the famed Landhaur bin Sa'dan, Emperor of Hindustan. The language was Persian, though the dastan's Hindi versions were also becoming popular. My Persian didn't come quite up to the mark when the narrator spoke fast, though I could, even then, follow the drift. As for the dastan itself, I cannot tell you how and what it was. Nor can anyone else, I am quite certain. Once he began, the narrator no longer seemed human. He was more like a force of nature. He was utterly fluent, capable of changing his rhythm and enunciation and tone as and when he willed. His voice seemed moderately strong, but it seemed to carry easily to every listener. He could speak like a woman— though without distorting his voice or making it sound high—or like a commoner, or like a king, or like anyone, in fact, with an absolute lack of effort. He sat, entirely unmoving, with his feet tucked under his thighs in the rather uncomfortable style called *do zanu*, through the two-hour-long performance. But for his eyes and his tongue, no other part of his body moved. It wasn't a performance: it was a creation.

As I said, the dastan had lasted two hours, and no one so much as sneezed or coughed. The dastan narrator didn't even shift on his seat, not to speak of relaxing his posture or stance. The listeners had quickly become participants. Cries of admiration and appreciation filled the air. 'Wah, Wah!'; '*Subhanallah*'; 'Such narrative artistry is yours, and yours alone, Mir sahib'; 'Do let's hear it again, the episode of Sarsar the female *ayyar!*' These and similar words were spoken in Persian, and sometimes in Hindi. The dastango merely smiled; he didn't do even the customary salaam. It was after he was done that he rose to his full height and made a very low salaam, saying, 'I am nothing but a pale shadow of my master. May God bless this august assembly and may it never be dispersed.'

I didn't notice any money changing hands when the dastan session ended. Perhaps Mirza sahib paid him on a regular, monthly basis. Perhaps the great and extremely rich Hakim Mahmud Khan sahib didn't suffer a protégé of his to accept gratification from others. Anyway, the host and the dastango seemed to be on cordial terms.

The audience left quickly; no one dared linger or tarry for small talk after such a virtuoso performance. Only a handful of the visitors remained. Of them I was one, and a bearded, middle-aged Maulavi sahib was another. His simple dress and plain appearance suggested that he taught at some small madrasa. Mirza sahib turned towards him, and commanded: 'So, Maulavi sahib, do let's hear about your problem again, Mian Ruswa should also benefit from our pondering your question.'

'Presence, it is a verse from the great Khaqani of Sharvan. I wasn't able to make head or tail of it. Mufti Azurdah sahib explicated it to me, but I am still somewhat uncertain.'

I felt shaky and insecure in my heart. Khaqani, I knew, was one of the greatest Persian poets. He was from the twelfth century and widely reputed to be extremely difficult. My small Persian barely reached up to knowing the names of his books. I waited, my breath almost still. The Maulavi sahib said, 'Exalted sir, I present the verse.' He now spoke a verse of which I swear I couldn't comprehend a word.

Without the least pause, Mirza sahib replied, 'Well, how could you get to its sense if you read this verse by itself? The verse that is causing problems to you is from the Noble Hakim Khaqani's long masnavi, *Tuhfatul Iraqain.* You must link it to the preceding verse to get to the poet's meaning.'

After the smallest of pauses to reflect, Mirza sahib quoted the verse that preceded the problematic one and explained its meaning so well, and pointed out its subtleties so clearly as if many commentaries on that admittedly difficult masnavi were open in front of him.

The Maulavi sahib expressed the keenest satisfaction with the explication of the Exalted Presence and we joined him in uttering words of enthusiastic admiration. Only a few close friends remained after the Maulavi sahib took his permission. Dinner was taken somewhat late. I, and some others joined Mirza sahib at drinks after dinner. The night was well past its heart when I begged leave. Mirza sahib granted permission, but I could see that he was truly sorry to see me go away.

His voice somewhat choked, he said: 'I entrust you to the Protection of God and to Imam Zamin, the Guarantor of all Protection. Do visit again, and write when you can.'

I bent to touch his feet, but he embraced me, and said, 'Be careful as you go.'

I salaamed as low as I could and crossing the courtyard, reached the gate of the haveli when Kallu the steward overtook me and put in my hand a silken pouch, saying: 'Navab sahib has bestowed this little something for your way expenses.'

I was taken aback, but there was no way that I could refuse. I gave Kallu a Company rupee by way of thanks and left. Having reached my room, I opened the pouch: it contained fifty-one Company rupees.

*

After that one visit, I could not go to Delhi again. Or perhaps I should say, I did not go to Delhi again. I have tried my best, and again and again, to examine myself in my heart and to understand the reason for it, but I never could arrive at a convincing reason. No, it was not a sense of inadequacy. In fact, my poetry and personality both gained confidence as a result of my visit and the hours that I spent with the greatest poet of the age, or perhaps the greatest poet of all time. I felt ennobled by him and by his tolerance of my youthful, rebellious ideas—remember I was only twenty-two years old at that time. When I went to Delhi I was an enthusiastic, but raw student of poetry, and a petty practitioner of it. When I returned, I was elevated, in fact ennobled in my own eyes, and this elevation gave me a power of confidence, a confidence that I never had since I left my home on that windy, fateful night in May 1857.

So, why didn't I try to gain more from Mirza sahib's munificence? Why should I not have done the obvious thing to gain more elevation, more ennoblement?

I think I did find some sort of answer for my unexplainable conduct, but I cannot be sure. It seems to me that I knew myself well enough when I went to Delhi, but now . . . ? I just don't know. But sometimes in my dreams I see vague shapes of mysterious people visiting somewhere, taking away some valuable things. 'For honour's sake,' they seem to say to me.

Once I left my home, I never did return, because nothing had remained for me to return to. Is it possible that I found my second home, equally warm, equally secure as the first one, in Mirza sahib's heart? And perhaps I had the unreasonable, nearly insane fear that once I return to Mirza sahib's haveli, I'll find it empty just as I found my original home empty when I went back. Or that it will become empty soon enough. I wanted to save in my heart, in my mind, the living, laughing, poem-explicating, benevolent poetic spirit that was Mirza Asadullah Khan Ghalib when I saw him that winter of 1862.

I know this sounds weak, but it will sound strong enough to anyone who found a changed sky, a different earth when he returned home. I know I wasn't the cause, or even the reason, for the new emergences. Perhaps I was like the old women of my village who did not want to take the name of a dead relative for fear that more deaths would occur in the family. Similarly, I did not want to go to Mirza sahib again: I feared that he won't be there when I returned.

I had been hearing about Mirza sahib's illnesses through the *Awadh Akhbar* and other newspapers. His deafness, I understood, was now almost total. He developed some sort of papules on his left calf; suddenly one of them grew large and hard, swollen almost like a carbuncle. It did not burst in spite of poultices and liniments. Finally, it was opened by a *jarrah*, that is, a local Indian surgeon, without being given any *behoshi*—opium or some English preparation of it that was now becoming common. The jarrah made a deep, X-shaped incision, but nothing much would flow out by itself; the carbuncle had to be drained by pressing the poisonous stuff out. Someone told me that my redoubtable Mirza sahib bore the excruciating ordeal without any outward expression of pain or hurt. But the boil still did not heal. The jarrah visited every day and probed the depth and width of it with a blunt knife, cleaned the wound and stuffed it with unguent. Day after day, Mirza sahib wordlessly stood the pain. The wound healed finally, but left a hole the size of a ball in the calf muscle.

Honest to God, I did not want to see my Ghalib sahib after all this had happened. No. That's not true. The truth is that I feared to go back. I did not want to break my dream and face reality. I knew that if I went back, I would find no one there.

*

I made a practice of sending some present to Mirza sahib once or twice a year: Fine mangoes from Malihabad near Lucknow; very deep-fried jalebi-like *imirtis* from Jaunpur which are soft, instead of the usual hard ones, and which stay very long, not going bad in the hottest weather; or turban or jamah fabrics in silk from Mubarakpur. Once or twice I would make bold to send him a ghazal. But he never returned the ghazal, nor suggested any correction. Occasionally, he would send a brief, affectionate acknowledgement, always ending with the inquiry: *Ab tumhara Dilli ka phera kab hoga?* (When will you be coming round to Delhi next?) I dare hope that he considered my ghazals didn't need any correction. Or maybe he saw in me not a pupil but a casual friend or marginal acquaintance. Oh, for me any kind of connection with him was like a heavenly honour. As some Persian Master said:

In all, the smallest connection with you
Should be sufficient for me;
It's more than enough for the bulbul to rhyme with gul.

In 1868, almost exactly ten years after the Englishman's perpetration of death and devastation on us, I heard from my potter friend that my confiscated properties had been released by the government and my clan had been pardoned. My friend joyfully invited me to come and resume the properties. But it was just like Delhi for me: There would

69

be, there could be, nothing there to benefit me from the pardon and the lands. My mother had saved her honour by jumping in the well in our courtyard. She must have drowned a painful drowning; none had dared even to recover her body for cremation.

I recalled that a relative of my mother's was living in penury in a village in Banaras. Everything that he had was lost, one way or another. I asked him to take charge, and then the possession of the properties. In due course, I transferred the entire property to him for no payment.

Cawnpore gave me no hurt, no anguish but aloneness. I never married; in due time I gained some reputation as a poet and as a 'friend' of the great Mirza Ghalib sahib. In terms of the days' standard of prosperity, I lived in comfort, for I drew good pay from the gun factory. I was well regarded by my neighbours because I was a respectable employee of the government, and had no bad habits except the occasional drinking. But I never drank alone.

It was some date in February 1869 that I read in the *Awadh Akhbar* that the Nightingale of India, Star of the Realm, Scribe of the Kingdom, Mirza Asadullah Khan sahib Ghalib was joined with his Maker. I drew a cold, deep sigh, put away the paper, and lay down with my body fully covered as in a shroud. I didn't go to the factory that day.

I read somewhere, or maybe I heard him say, that by the Grace and Kindness of the Creator of Time and Space, I have managed and organized matters in the Kingdom of Prose and Verse in the best way possible. Now, if He so wills, my name will remain inscribed upon the world's page until the Day of Resurrection. My heart said, Amen, and Amen yet again:

> *It remains written for hundreds of years:*
> *That which someone writ—*
> *And he who writ, that crazy man*
> *Decays, and decays, and becomes dust.*

*

The name Mirza Ghalib rode higher and higher in the Firmament of Renown after he went away. His pupil, Khvajah Altaf Husain Hali had already earned a high reputation by a famous preface to his divan. In that book, he held Mirza sahib's compositions in the greatest of regard when judged by the newer standards of literature. He then wrote a whole biography of Mirza sahib. It had some discussion of his poetry too, but the main service he did to his Honoured Master was to establish his personality as a lively, witty, dynamic, erudite and generous individual. Once you read that book, you felt that you had become a personal acquaintance of a great man and a great poet. I am proud to report that it was first published in Cawnpore, in 1897, and I became the owner of its very first copy.

A few years later, Salahuddin Khuda Bakhsh, a scholar in Azimabad, Patna, wrote a paper saying that Mirza sahib's poetry could be compared favourably with some German poet of a very high reputation in Europe.

Many poets wrote elegies on Ghalib sahib; the most famous was again by Maulavi Hali sahib. I made numerous starts with my own elegy, but could never go beyond a line or two. My eyes would well up as I felt that I was writing my own and also my father's and my ancestors' elegy. I didn't know anyone close to Mirza sahib to whom I could send my condolence on his death. I thought for some time. My acquaintance with Navab Ziauddin Ahmad Khan sahib was so slight that it would have almost been an offence against good taste to write him a letter of condolence. I could decide nothing better than having five sers worth of *sheermals* and an equal quantity of sweets distributed among the poor at the Dargah of Dada Mian sahib, the chief Sufi saint of Cawnpore. Quranic verses and prayers were read by many visitors, then a prayer was made to Allah that the merit earned by today's recitation and distribution of food to the poor may accrue to the Sacred Soul of Navab Mirza Asadullah Khan sahib Ghalib, may Allah pardon him and accord him His Pleasure and Favour.

I came back home, wept a few tears, kissed and touched to my eyes

Shamsur Rahman Faruqi

the copy of the Nizami Press divan that bore his kindly words for me. On that day too, I didn't go to the factory.

*

Today is the last day of November 1918. I am seventy-eight years old, according to the English calculation. It's a long, long time to have lived. I hope my summons are on the way now. I had much to say, but as Amir Khusrau's friend Hasan Sijzi said:

You ask: Why do you not tell me the story of your heart?
Well, I can start telling it, but who will bring it to its end?

I have recorded these things so that the reader (should there ever be a reader of these incoherent babblings) should know something about who I was, and more about those whom I have had the honour to be in conversation with. Half a century and more has passed since the events I narrated here. Yet, they seem bright before me like yesterday's writing. Or as if I saw them in a dream just a moment ago. My mother's sweet, ethereal face; the heart-tugging person of my father; the luminant visages of my grandfather and Maulavi Khadim Husain Nazim; the press and crush of English forces on the border of Pawayan, and the array of its women, out in mourning for Danka Shah sahib and cursing the Raja of Pawayan; Mirza sahib's awesome personality, which exuded power, but also had a beauty that nothing could surpass; his witticisms which hid a strange anguish; the handsome, learned Navab Ziauddin Ahmad Khan; the pleasant, simple but dignified Munshi Shiv Narain Aram; Dastango Mir Mujid; and why not, even my hostess at the inn who spoke beautiful Urdu with quiet elegance and who still regarded Mirza Ghalib sahib as an outsider and not a native of Delhi.

And the ravaged, half-burnt, looted or just desolately shut down bazaars of Delhi, they still had a Presence, and the holy sadness of loss pervaded there. They still looked unbent, unbeaten in their pride.

Then my refuge, my potter friend, without whom I could never have survived. And she . . . whom also 1857 gobbled up like a python swallowing a small bird. She, on whom my amorous eye fell so often and so innocently. The great Shah Hatim, Sauda's ustad, wrote with prescience perhaps for us:

> *My heart was ensnared at the very moment*
> *When you touched my hand;*
> *Our souls and bodies were one, with no gaps,*
> *But at that moment, the hearts of us both*
> *Pined to exchange just one word.*

The Englishman won the Great War even when he came perilously close to losing it. Mirza sahib used to quote the Sufi Ghausi Ali Shah sahib who'd said, perhaps half jokingly, that the Englishman's Fortune is in the ascendant—even his women have no visitation from the jinns and evil spirits! I do not now hope to see that star begin to suffer eclipse. Allah is Sufficient; all else is mere wandering in the night.

The Rider

He would not stay for me; and who can wonder?
He would not stay for me to stand and gaze.
I shook his hand and tore my heart asunder
And went with half my life about my ways.

A.E. Housman

The flame of my little lamp was dim; or should I say, it was smoky, tremulous like a worm? Having written these words, I smiled in my heart a little. The reason is that the word that I used, *doodi*, is a medical term to describe a patient's weak pulse. It was just a few days since I learnt this word and its meaning. Ashraf-ul Atibba—Noblest of Physicians—Hakim Sharif Khan sahib, may his shadow lengthen more, and even more, occasionally took time to visit our madrasa, and give us a lesson or two in the science of medicine. During his last visit, he spoke to us most concisely on the art of understanding the significance of the beat of a patient's pulse. Well, it wasn't so much a lecture as a lesson in the ideal way of teaching the subject.

So this is how Hakim Sharif Khan sahib taught: A comparatively senior student would read out a sentence from Avicenna's *Al Qanun fi-Altibb*. Needless to say, the book was universally referred to as *Qanun*, the Canon, and Avicenna as Shaikh Al-Rais, the Presiding Master. If the student made an error in reading, or the manuscript itself contained an error, Hakim sahib would immediately correct the student, or the text. He did not, of course, have the text in front of him. He always taught from memory. After the text had been established, Hakim sahib would translate the original Arabic into Persian, but then while he commented on it, he spoke in Arabic.

Once the text had been explicated and commented upon adequately, Hakim sahib would invite each student to feel the pulse of the student who sat next to him, and comment upon the rhythm of the pulse—actually, give a diagnosis—in light of the points made by the Presiding

Master in the Canon. (The student's own commentary could be in Persian, even in Hindi.) Sometimes a student would hesitate, for fear of misreading the pulse or diagnosing some disease which wasn't there, or say something indiscreet while diagnosing a condition that his 'patient' wanted to keep hidden. The Hakim sahib would then order the diagnosing student to come forward. He would feel his pulse, press it in different ways, such that each time he did so, the rhythm of the pulse would change. Sometimes he would order the student to feel his own pulse, not at the wrist but somewhere else—for example, on his neck just below his Adam's apple.

Now this was a harder task, though not without its delights; for, it was more of an intuitive art than a science to read the pulse anywhere on the body, but especially on the neck. It was during these demonstrations that we were told about the doodi pulse. There were two interpretations for the word: In Persian, *dood* means 'smoke'. So a doodi pulse was an extremely weak pulse, something like the tremulous wisp of the smoke that rises from a lamp when it is about to go out. In Arabic, *doodah* means 'worm'. So the interpretation now was that a pulse that moved extremely sluggishly, with very little volume, like the movement of a worm, was doodi.

A discussion ensued about the comparative merits of the two interpretations. Hakim sahib preferred the Arabic connotation, but most of us students felt that the Persian connotation was more apt.

So that was exactly the state of my lamp: its light was dim and smoky. And the hot weather was something over and above the dimness of the light. Sweating, I held in one hand a small fan made from a date palm leaf, and my notes of a lecture on Rhetoric and Poetics, in the other. I needed to hold the hastily scratched notes as near to the lamp as possible, but if I played the fan over me, the lamp would sputter with a tremor and threaten to die. The heat and the humidity threatened me with death at the same time. So I mopped the perspiration on my face and eyes with a sleeve, and pressed my unhappy, burning eyes on the page. It was a point from Taftazani's *Mutawwal*, the well-known fourteenth-century Arabic treatise on Grammar, Rhetoric, Figures of Speech and much else besides.

I just could not make head or tail of Taftazani's point: The meaning of an utterance depends on the speaker's intent, and also on the hearer's state of mind. He gave some examples by way of illustration. My task today was to provide my own examples to prove the great man's theory, or propose some objections to the theory. It was a Thursday night. Once I finished my task, I was free to go home and spend the Friday with my mother. Unfortunately, I was not able to follow Taftazani's argument clearly. So where was the question of finding illustrations or objections pertinent to it?

I was a student at the Rahimiya Madrasa, situated just behind the Fatehpuri Mosque and established by the Presence, our Master and our Certification, Shah Abdur Rahim sahib Faruqi, may the Mercy and Forgiveness of God be upon him. The Worshipful Senior Shah sahib had long been joined with God in the month of Safar of the year of the Hijra 1131 (January 1719). The madrasa's affairs were in the auspicious hands of his son, most Learned of the Learned of the World, most Knowledgeable of all Men of Knowledge, Leader and Exemplar for those who have given themselves up to God, the Cream of the Cream of those who have attained the True Knowledge of the Almighty, Standard and Prover for those who Walk the Path of Truth, the Presence, Shah Valiullah sahib of Delhi, the undisputed master scholar of the Prophet's Traditions.

This worthless one had the good fortune to sit in on the lessons of the Presence, Valiullah sahib, for about two years. It is a matter of mourning, a hundred times a matter of mourning, that a few months ago, on the 29th of Muharram 1176 (19 August 1762), our Worshipful Presence, Shah Valiullah sahib also became finally joined with Allah, the Truth. All the learned ones, and even the common people of Delhi still remember him with sorrow and mourn for him. The management of the madrasa is now in the hands of the Ghazali of the Times, Master of the Prophet's Traditions throughout the Earth, Aristotle of the Age, the Presence, Shah Abdul Aziz sahib, may his grace be perpetual and may his beneficences to the people extend more and yet more.

I was nudging my fifteenth year at that time—just about the age when young men believe that they are rising in the world and also in manly confidence. The down on my upper lip was quite distinguishable now in spite of my brown visage. Like my late father, may he be forgiven and counted among the good, I was strong of constitution, and tall and powerful for my age. My father, may God grant him Paradise every time he stirs in his grave, was martyred in a small skirmish in Bihar, fighting under the command of the Presence, Shah Alam Secondus. At that time, that Prince had not assumed the Throne in the Red Haveli with the titles of Lord of the Time, Sovereign of Hindustan, Ruler of both the Realms of Knowledge and the Dominion of Hind, Abul Muzaffar Jalaluddin Muhammad Shah Alam Secondus, may God perpetuate his Kingdom and his Law. At the time of the skirmish, which took my father's precious life, that Sahib was a Prince of the Realm and he was spending those auspicious and fortunate days as just Prince Ali Gauhar, with the title of Shah Alam.

I was about three years old, and my dear sister had just been born. Our names, Khairuddin for me, and Sitti Begam for my sister, were in fact bestowed upon us by that Prince of Great Fortune and Influence. The Worshipful Sahib-e Alam, benevolent Prince that he was, showed his munificence and his desire to nurture the poor, by granting my mother a small lifelong pension. That noble lady fed us, clothed us and brought us up in a respectable manner, thanks to that pension. When I was ten years old, my mother sent me to Madrasa Rahimiya, for my ambition in life was to become a man of learning and be remembered by the title of Maulavi. I had been in that madrasa for about five years now.

I had a small room of my own at the madrasa, about three and a half yards by three; low ceilinged, the room had a stone floor covered with a hay or reed mat, depending on the season. I had a long, low table on which were scattered my books and papers. As needed, I also used it as a dining table. We had no chairs and no beds; in fact, such luxury items were prohibited. A rather grubby, thin cotton carpet, of the type made best in Akbarabad, covered the mat. Sometimes I could manage to get a white cotton sheet from the housekeeper of the madrasa, to spread on the carpet. Pillows were not needed; I used anything thick that came to hand—a register, a book, even a brick, for resting my head.

Some rich and friendly neighbour most often sent our food. In case nothing came on any given day, I could buy an excellent meat dish for the sum of one and a quarter *dams* or at the most one and a half dams; chapatis came free with the meat. Occasionally, the baker also put a bit of dry vegetable on a chapati. The sum of one and a quarter rupees per month paid to each student by the madrasa management was enough to suffice for the month and still save a bit. I always presented the saving to my mother, but she never put it to any use for herself; instead, she spent it on new clothes or other necessities for me.

Often, in the winter, some philanthropic patron would send extra thick or woollen clothes to defend against the cold. It could even be an expensive double shawl, or a duvet or quilt filled with fine, carded cotton. Some of these welcome goods fell to my share. The madrasa provided books and writing material to all students at no cost to them. There was also the stipend: enough attractions for a seeker of knowledge.

My life thus floated on, with nothing to worry about, and particularly not about what the morrow would bring. But I was also conscious of the fact that I was in my last year at the madrasa and on passing out I must look for employment and make necessary arrangements for the marriage of Sitti Begam, who was now in her thirteenth year.

Oh, I have reached far in my ramblings and to no purpose at that. I was talking about my given task. I was in a hurry to understand and learn properly the relevant text of the *Mutawwal*, marshal my arguments for or against, invent effective examples to support my views, and be on the road to home. Friday was always a holiday and we were allowed to leave for our parents' or our guardians' home on Thursday evenings. I tried to concentrate on the *Mutawwal* for a second, or perhaps a third time. What is the meaning of the 'hearer's state of mind'? Does this imply that every hearer derives the meaning of every utterance in accordance with his own presumptions?

May God save me from error! That was a dangerous road to take. If meaning depended on the recipient, then how to arrive at an authoritative, authentic meaning of a Quranic verse? Should I understand Taftazani to mean that the hearer's purpose, or at least his understanding, stood higher than the intent of the one who made the utterance? No, I must rethink the matter.

Rather than rethink the issue, I dozed off into a nap. I woke up with a start after a few moments, or maybe almost a half hour. It seemed to me that a spider had woven its thickest cobweb not only around my brain, but also my eyes. Everything seemed dull, deprived of its natural brightness; the cobwebs had not even a chink to permit some light in. I rubbed my eyes hard, trying to restore some light in them. But the call for the late-evening prayer sounded from the Fatehpuri Mosque, the muezzin's voice so near as to be almost next door to me. In some confusion and not a little hurry, I rose to go to the mosque, do my ablutions and join the prayer. I must leave for home after the prayers; let the Great Savant Taftazani take care of his own problem. Maybe he will whisper something in my ear by way of inspiration as I wended my way home. Nothing, I was sure, was going to happen here in my little cell now.

I rolled tight the papers containing the *Mutawwal*, and my class notes, and was about to stow them safely in my box. Suddenly, I heard someone whisper something in my ears from somewhere (for, there was none nearby that I could see or even sense as a presence). I couldn't quite understand what it was: a command, or the inspiration that I was hoping for, or just my fevered brain? I tried to recreate in my mind the rhythms of the phrase again, and felt my flesh creep when I realized that it was a line of Persian poetry:

The rider of everlasting prosperity appeared on the highway

I am no poet and I am not much of a student of Persian poetry either. I have read Persian just enough as necessary for me to understand the Persian texts set for study in the class. And as regards the ghazal, it is certainly not a thing to be read, so much as heard. The breezes that blew so pleasantly through the lanes and bazaars of Delhi resonated anyway with the poetry of Mirza Bedil, his disciple Achal Das, his friend Muhammad Afzal Sarkhush, and younger poets like Anand Ram Mukhlis, Mirza Mazhar Jan-e Janan and scores of others. The winds wafted away the poetry to far-off places. In spite of the ghazal enjoying such popularity, I had never composed a line of verse in Persian. If ever in the future I thought of turning my hand to poetry, I would choose Rekhtah, or Hindi, as that language was often called nowadays. The better poets today were turning to Rekhtah in large numbers. Rekhtah had a brilliancy of wit and a freshness of colour that seemed to be lacking in Persian.

So it wouldn't certainly be I who had composed the line of Persian that I just heard. Heard or imagined? But it certainly was a line to remember, somewhat mysterious, but very well turned, though it seemed incomplete. Was it waiting for me to compose the second line and complete the verse? Nonsense, crass nonsense. But I do wish it were I who had composed it . . . and what does the line mean? Were the holy spirits of Taftazani and Sakkaki sending out to me a message from beyond? Did they mean to hint that it was up to the hearer, that is I, to make sense of an utterance, any utterance? But did I actually *hear* that line, or had I invented it, unknowing that I was composing a line of poetry?

But how, oh how, was that possible? If it is up to the hearer to make sense of the utterance that he hears, then there will be nothing to distinguish truth from falsehood. All right, so be it. But if *I* composed this line, and I don't understand what it means, then what *is* the meaning of an utterance? Is it as if I didn't compose it at all? Or am

I supposed to be, qua Taftazani, both the speaker and the finder of meaning here? So what is my intention, my state of mind, that I must take into account in order to perceive the meaning here?

But who is this rider, and where is the highway on which the information, or the story of his appearance is being narrated? Perhaps the line will make sense when I add another to it, making it a full two-line verse. But how can I compose the second line when I haven't the faintest notion of the meaning of what has been stated in the first one?

All along, I had believed that the poets, when they think of composing poems, ponder and concentrate, adding a word here, deleting a word there, making sure that the verse truly conveys what they want to say. And for creating an excellent, perfect two-line verse, I am sure it was like burning your heart's blood for the oil in your midnight lamp, worrying over each and every word, each and every thought, taking as much care as rolling wafer-thin, brittle papads with a large and heavy rolling pin so as to maintain their smoothness and integrity . . . and God knows what else. Was it not Nemat Khan-e Ali, dead just these last few decades, who had said:

> *The name of those who are given to poetry rises high because of poetry,*
> *There is no offspring better and worthier than a well-turned line of verse.*

But young fellow, how and why would you be counted among those who are 'given to poetry'? All that I long for in this life is to teach at some good, reputed madrasa, to convey to others what I have learnt and gained from my elders and seniors. To be a poet is nowhere in my little scheme of things. But by Allah, what an excellent, moving, mysterious line it is. Quite without intending to do so, I began to hum the line under my breath. Music is not something that I favour, though my schoolmates say that I have a good singing voice. I hummed as I wended my brief way to the mosque.

I don't recall which Quranic verses the Imam sahib recited, and which were those that I recited when after the group prayer, I offered my prayers alone. It was just the line, that abominable line that rang through my brain like a horse whose rider has lost his stirrups.

The prayers finished, I made straight for home. The day's heat was now abated; the wild westerly that had blown through the day was dying down, if not actually cooling off. Lights flared and scintillated on both banks of Sa'adat Khan's Canal and the air was almost visibly pleasant under the flowering shrubs around which the lights had been lit.

We lived just inside Phatak Teliyan. The straight path to my home was easy: I had to walk halfway down Chandni Chowk, then take a turn into Kinari Bazaar, leave the Jama Masjid on my left and enter Chowri Bazaar. Instead of walking the whole length of Chowri Bazaar, I had to take a right turn just halfway down the bazaar into Sui Walan. There was a complex network of lanes and alleys after this, but the best way was to take a right again into Bazaar Sita Ram and get to Phatak Teliyan, passing Bulbuli Khana and Turkman Darwaza on my right. A fast clip would let me traverse the route in about half an hour or a little more.

But there was another, longer route too, and I sometimes favoured it. The advantage in this was that I could enjoy the flower-sellers' market in Mali Wara on my way. I would go down Chandni Chowk a hundred or so yards from the Fatehpuri Mosque, enter Billimaron to my right, then passing the recently named Gali Qasim Jan, take another left and enter Mali Wara. That very road then would bring me back, through Chowri, to my wonted road. I did this often enough so the flower-sellers now knew me by sight, if not name. Sometimes they would ask me to say the proper Quranic verses and prayers on sweets or other delicacies, which they then distributed among the poor. The merit thus earned was then given away through prayer to their revered dead, or some well-known Sufi saint. I accepted no remuneration, but the flower-seller would always present to me, in token of gratitude and appreciation, a big bunch of Iranian jasmine, or a bouquet of red roses from Mangalore in the far south, or a thick garland of absolutely ravishing white double mogra from Jaunpur or Banaras farther in the east. It was a rare day when I got the present of a bunch of champak blossoms. When they bloomed to their full, their scent would, of a hot summer night, disseminate through the whole neighbourhood.

These blooms were always my best presents for my mother. As I perhaps said above, Amma ji was widowed at a comparatively young age. Her face was still youthful and her skin so free of blemish that if we sometimes inveigled her into putting on clothes of bright hue and better quality, she would provoke the envy of much younger and richer begams in an assembly.

Mali Wara was always overcrowded: buyers, sightseers, takers of the evening air, all were shoulder to shoulder. To cap the sounds of their talking to, or at each other, there was the noise and sales calls of the flower-sellers. Flowers of myriad hues, and fragrances that ranged from the outlandish to native, and sometimes the open palanquins of the ladies from Rajwaron ki Gali, which was mostly inhabited by dancing girls and courtesans, brought their own scents and colours.

'Hey, Mian! This Iranian houri awaits your attention!'

'Young gentleman sir, listen to me please; come and exchange a few words with my stylish Telangi belle from Hyderabad!'

'Respected Maulana ji, are there better beads for your rosary than these budding mogras?'

'Come, take them, buy them cheap! Here are roses from Mehrauli, nay, pure wine made from honey and dew.'

'Sir, just look, these are nosegays in the manner of Shahjahan, the Sahibqiran!'

'Please trouble your noble feet, Mian sahib. Come and see, *each flower has its own fragrance, its own colour.*' (This was said in Persian.)

'*Oh dear Rose, I love you because you are fragrant like someone!*' (This was again in Persian.)

There were exceedingly heavy garlands and head ornaments, each more beautiful than the next—it was common for the heavier ones to bend the scale at five or six sers. Clients had to book three, four days in advance for the heavier ones. But those who came to collect their order always stayed for a while to enjoy the sight and the fragrance and the calls of the flower-sellers. The heart of the visitor was always captivated, his feet always secured by the scenes and sounds.

These many-coloured blooms—from distant places and strange climes as they came—how was their youthful bloom and hue preserved? I always wondered. How did their roseate freshness manage not to diminish? Clearly, by the time the earlier stock was cleared, newer stock arrived. Still, for how long could those delicate beauties tarry after they were snapped off from their native branches? I recalled a marvellous Persian verse by Mirza Razi Danish:

In the flower-sellers' hands the rose contracted a sickly hue
The waters of a strange country agreed ill
with the child brought up in the flower garden with love.

One of the flower-sellers' tricks, or an example of their cleverness, was that I never saw a pale visage among their flowers. God knows what happened to those poor little things when they saddened and wilted. The flower shops opened very early in the morning and remained open until very late. Perhaps they waited for the last spectator in the assemblies of Rajwaron ki Gali or Chowri Bazaar, and the last visitor at the nightly meetings of dance, song and poetry at the stately abodes of the Quality before they surreptitiously took the dead beauties home for consigning them to the dustbin or the river? Anyway, the flower shops remained bedecked and their contents artistically arranged until the flower-sellers were sure that there was no one left. I was sure the flower-sellers quietly removed the stale ones in the small hours of the night when they were sure that they had seen the back of the last visitor.

On the day that I am talking about, my present was a bunch of Jaunpuri double jasmines. Very large, almost like wild roses and whiter, their fragrance was so strong that often one felt like swooning away, drenched in their exotic scent. Of a night, they were placed on the bed, but their scent persisted even after three, four days of being crushed and displaced by the sleeper's body. I have never been to places in the east, and there was no possibility of my going to live there anyway. But I greatly loved the flowers from the east; for, my father's last resting place was in the east.

I didn't buy any food from the bazaar that night; for, I was hoping for a treat from my loving Amma ji. I bought a little clay pot full of Bengali rasgullas for my little sister. As I turned into the gateway of Phatak Teliyan, it seemed that the whole neighbourhood was aglow with the scent of the milk, ghee and saffron sheermal breads prepared by Amma ji. Sitti bibi stood behind the door and no sooner had I stepped in than she spoke impulsively: 'Bhai jan, Bhai jan, did you hear the news?'

'What news? My little baby sister might have heard something right behind the closed door here in her home, but there's nothing in the bazaar, not even a cheep of a rumour.'

'Bhai jan, you'll have your joke always, won't you? Actually, I heard that a Mighty Rider will appear in the bazaar tomorrow.'

She stressed particularly the words 'mighty' and 'rider', as if they were written in bold letters before her.

'Hey, you! Come gulp down these rasgullas quickly, or they'll go lose their full freshness. As for your Mighty Rider, he's none of you starving types to roam the bazaar aimlessly.'

'Now look at that! So I roam the bazaars aimlessly! Listen, please for God's sake, listen, Bhai jan! Please, please to get me too a glimpse when he appears.'

'Have you lost your mind, Bibi? Come nigh a little bit and let me feel your pulse! Did you hear, she'll now go out and look at some beefy, obscure rider strutting about in the open bazaar like a bull?' I replied, but my smile robbed the words of any harshness that might have been taken as implied in them.

'Allah's Truth, Bhai jan. He's not a beefy bull, as you say. He is a Sufi of the highest order. He has attained unto God's Own Presence.' She paused for breath, and continued. 'Tomorrow, when it's about an hour for the day to wester, he'll suddenly appear, riding his favourite mount called Siyah Qitas, right here, near Turkman Darwaza. He will ride an easy pace through Bulbuli Khana, Bazaar Sita Ram, Hauz Qazi, Chowri Bazaar and will arrive at the North Gate of the Masjid,' she went on hurriedly, as if apprehending interruption from me. 'Leaving the North Gate, he'll come out to Chandni Chowk through Kinari Bazaar.'

'Then?' said I, pretending to be interested.

'Then? Then nothing. He'll . . . he'll disappear suddenly, the way he appeared. But, Bhai jan . . . '

She tarried a moment. It seemed to me that she was trying to pick up courage; get some strength in her voice to say what she wished to say.

'Come, out with it!' I said in affectionate tones and re-covered her head with her dupatta, which had slipped to her shoulders.

'Yes, well . . . well, they say . . . ' She paused, and then carried on boldly, in a rush. 'Well, Bhai jan, they say that if one blocked his way for a second, and . . . and then asked for something too, some boon . . . everything will be granted. It's just a matter of a moment of courage, stopping him and speaking to him!'

'The girl has the shadow of some evil spirit on her,' Amma ji mumbled in a tired voice. 'She has babbled of nothing else throughout the day. What's the boon that you'll ask him for at all, silly girl?'

'I will ask for a bride for my dear Bhai jan, a bride who should be beautiful as the moon!'

'I beg the forgiveness of God! A feat of such magnitude, needing so much pluck, just to pray for something so tawdry! Oh look, look! What's the matter with my Khairu?' Amma ji cried in consternation.

Entirely oblivious to my mother's words and my sister's eagerness to catch a glimpse of the mythical rider, I stood motionless, in a daze, looking somewhere faraway, repeating to myself a line of verse that someone seemed to have whispered in my soul:

None held his reins to stop him. He rode away.

I muttered to myself, as one demented. It's a whole verse now, really:

The rider of everlasting prosperity appeared on the highway
None held his reins to stop him. He rode away.

So I didn't compose the verse? Rather, I was made to utter it by some Power whom it is beyond me to understand? Will some true saint or Sufi really appear here tomorrow? And if someone were to stop him on the way . . . But the line that just came to me was inspired in me? The line says that none will stop him, really. Though it seems that he does desire that someone should step up and almost block his progress? Oh God, what's that supposed to mean? Should I really go up to him and ask him to give some boon for my Sitti? Well, a poem is a poem, just that, a poem. Even if I—or someone—did say that none held his reins to stop him and he rode away, it is not a prophecy. A poem is something and hard facts are something else again. I remembered the tenth-century Arab critic Qudamah Ibn Jafar's dictum: *The best in a poem is that which is the most false in it.*

I stood rooted to the spot. Amma ji was ransacking our little home for some medication to help bring me out of what she obviously thought was a faint, though I hadn't fallen down. 'Where is the jar of the *khamira* of *gao zaban*, Sitti? Or at least, let me have a small bottle of rose water . . . or something, anything. Ya Allah, what should I do now?'

Poor Sitti Begam was fanning me as she stood on her toes to reach my head. She pronounced the Prophet's Salutation over and over again and blew on me. I collected my senses as best I could and said reassuringly, 'Nothing, it's nothing at all, Amma ji. It is so very hot, you see. Just dizziness. And have no worry, ladies. It is Delhi, the Presence, and city of rumours and dreams of the supernatural and the phantasm. Not a day passes here before rumours come flying in about someone clad in green, or in black, a dromedary rider, a stallion rider, a person flying in the sky. Not for nothing are the people of Delhi known to favour spicy food. Such rumours are also like chutney to their plain fare. Amma ji, all this talk of food redoubles my appetite. So let's have some food now. Amma ji, your sheermal breads have made a fragrant zone of our lane.'

There was no talking as we ate. Contrary to the custom, all three of us ate together, though not at the same tablecloth. No one ever talked much while eating anyway. Both Sitti and I had our own phantoms to contend with. I remembered an incident of more than six hundred years ago at the time of the Presence, Baba Qutbuddin Bakhtiar Kaki, may the Mercy of God be upon him. It was Delhi again, and a holy man appeared here. He rode his mount, wandering apparently without purpose through the streets and alleys of all Delhi. It was said about him that whoever cast even a glance at him would go straight to Paradise after death. A whole multitude poured out into the streets to have his holy glimpse. The only one who did not go was Bakhtiar sahib's chief disciple, Baba Farid-ud Din Ganj-e Shakar, may God's Mercy be upon him. The Presence, Bakhtiar sahib, commanded, 'Mian Farid, you didn't go to get a glimpse of that holy man?'

'No, Mentor and Guide, I didn't.'

'Why ever so? Don't you long for Paradise?'

'Exalted Presence, I do have the longing.'

'So?'

'May I be spared my life,' Baba Farid spoke with some hesitancy.

'Yes, speak out without fear. In my presence you have what the Quran describes as "the contented soul". So go ahead.'

'The Exalted Presence didn't go out to get a glimpse of him. And there is no incontrovertible proof from independent sources that entry into Paradise shall be Your Honour's lot. But that glance would have, according to what is upon the people's lips, guaranteed Paradise for the Exalted Presence. Thus there's no knowing if Paradise will have the privilege of kissing your auspicious feet. So why should I seek a Paradise which could possibly be devoid of the noble presence of my Kabah, my Spiritual Beloved, my Guide and Mentor?'

The Presence, Baba Bakhtiar, was so moved by his favourite pupil's display of love, his faith in his Mentor, and the vehement puissance of attachment to the Shaikh that he was overcome by a storm of passion and prophesy, and commanded, 'Farid-ud Din, they say about that holy man that he who looks at him will go to Paradise. As God, the Lord of Honour, and Power, and Authority, is my Witness, I say that whoever visits your grave will go to Paradise!'

True enough, I mused to myself, as the great Rumi had said:

His speech was God's speech
Though it fell from the mouth of one who was a mere slave of God.

So is it not possible that there be some Sufi, some saint today who could grant whatever was demanded of him, provided someone stopped his progress? Really, that one who asked him would be given what he prayed for? Maybe, maybe not. But my little sister was almost burning with hope. She had absolute faith in the truth of that rumour. Why should I then disappoint her, deny her what she wanted: no more than a look at him and possibly a word with him. It won't cost me anything, not even madrasa time.

I asked, as I was polishing off the last of the sheermal, 'Sitti bibi, is that holy man the Presence, Amir Hamza, the Prophet's uncle?'

'I don't know. But why do you ask?'

'Because in his dastan, one of Amir Hamza's favourite mounts is called Siyah Qitas.'

'I don't know. I have never heard a dastan recitation,' she spoke, her brow knitted in concentration. 'The woman who gave me the news about the Rider told me nothing about the Holy Presence, Amir Hamza sahib.'

'Well, then your informant was playing you for a dolt. But, no matter, I will certainly satisfy your wish. I am friends with the grandson of Ustad Khairullah, the architect. Their haveli is right on the road and is very spacious. Adequate arrangement for the ladies in purdah can be laid on without difficulty. So I'll take you there tomorrow evening.' I smiled with a faint hint of derision. 'And I, too, thanks to your kindness, shall avail the merit of getting a blessed glimpse of your revered saint.'

'Oh, for wisdom's sake,' Amma ji cried, 'son, your wits have been destroyed with too much reading! You would now take a girl of marriageable age out in the open, would you? God knows who that Venerable Person is. I never heard of such a thing. A young girl to lose her good sense for the sight of him, is it not totally ridiculous?'

'Amma ji, there is no Rider. There is nothing really,' I replied soothingly. 'No Venerable Person, no Mentor, no Prophet. But I do wish to fulfil our little sister's wish, so I'll personally escort her to Baqaullah's haveli and be there with her all the time.'

'Well, I don't know. The times are bad. We'll be nowhere should something untoward happen. I leave it in your hands.' Amma ji relented with manifest unwillingness. Apparently, Sitti had tired her out with day-long cajoling.

Sitti Begam blossomed up like a dew-drenched flower of the morning. 'Yes, yes, Amma ji, please,' she pleaded. 'We'll return in no time. You won't even realize that we went away anywhere at all! Do not please be anxious.'

*

I did not sleep well that night. It was very hot, and my thoughts were scattered all over my brain, like tiny shells on a seashore, unfocused, without a pattern or rhythm, not letting me fall into a proper nap. So who could that redoubtable, holy, venerable man be? And if I really dared to stop his progress for a few seconds, what should I ask of him? What *could* I ask of him? Was I worthy? Should I ask him to grant a suitably rich and refined groom for my Sitti? A great quantity of erudition and renown for me? Continued good health, economic ease and comfort for Amma ji? I hear that sometimes when such boons are asked for and granted, something somewhere has to be given up later, or forcibly lost, as a sort of ironical conclusion, proving the vanity of human wishes. So why should I run that risk?

I would occasionally fall into a brief, light doze and would wake up again with a start. This went on for the whole night, or so it seemed to me. Amma ji and my sister slept somewhat better, I think. God is particularly kind to those who labour all day. It is rare that they have the problem of having somehow to entice sleep to come to them anight.

But Sitti Begam had to be married off, and sooner rather than later. His Majesty still graced the eastern territories. So who should take my petition to his Exalted Court, and how? And would he now be inclined especially to add some grant to the small monthly pension that was already being paid to us? Mirza Sulaiman Shikoh Bahadur, may his fortune remain forever, looked after the affairs of state from the Fort. So should I have a plaint submitted at his Elevated Porte? But how? Should I directly make myself a supplicant at Court, or should I choose the embassy of the Presence, Shah Abdul Aziz sahib—may his shadow lengthen over the land of Hind forever?

Yet the fact was, the thought of being separated from my little sister weighed very, very heavy on me. Marry her off and send her away? Her, whom I used to always look after, seat her on my knee and lull her to sleep in my lap? In looks, in deportment, in the arts of house management, in her expertise at needlework, darning and embroidery, she was very nearly the equal of Amma ji, and in temperament, she was even more delicate, almost finicky. She would change her clothes every day, even when they didn't apparently need washing; leftover food, however good tasting and even if a delicacy, was entirely unacceptable. She gladly and promptly gave away all the leftovers the same day, if not immediately after a given meal. Amma ji would protest, sometimes aloud, sometimes under her breath, 'Who is going to cook fresh chapatis and other food for this begam twice a day, day after day!' But Sitti would ever reply confidently, 'Amma ji, I am here. I will cook four times a day, if needed. And I'll never, never fret or pet or even pull a face.'

She was a begam in observance and comportment, and a budding maulavi to boot. She had read the whole of the Quran (though without understanding the Arabic) at least a dozen times before she considered herself proficient in Quranic recitation. Since then, thanks to her reading from the Holy Book every day, she could immediately identify the source of any given verse. She knew all the regular and irregular Persian verbs and was capable of carrying out simple correspondence in that language. She knew enough arithmetic to maintain the household accounts and agree the total without difficulty.

But where to find a suitable husband for her? In our stratum of society, even the better-looking and talented girls had often to be satisfied with a widower, or even have to become a second wife. I hated the thought of such a fate for her. But where was the money or family status to negotiate and execute a suitable marriage for her? So, why not . . . why not ask that Magnanimous Rider for such a boon?

*

Evenfall is always slow in the summer season, but today it seemed that the sun would never take itself towards the west.

It was quite early, in fact just after the asr prayers, that I settled myself in the haveli of Ustad Khairullah, the architect. The haveli was just a little beyond Bulbuli Khana. It was right on the roadside, and the stated route of the Rider of Siyah Qitas passed just in front of it. I found out that special arrangements for purdah were in place. Obviously, I wasn't the only one to have escorted or helped his womenfolk there for a glimpse of the Holy Rider. There was a little desultory chit-chat; mostly, people were quiet, lost in their own thoughts or fears.

It was at least an hour and a quarter to sundown when the entire environment became empty, silent, as if frozen in some alien space. There was no movement, no activity. I couldn't find anyone at all on the road, in the doorways, or inside the shops. It seemed as if the whole city, having chosen a vantage place on the upper windows, balconies, doorsteps and shop counters, had planted itself there like self-propelled stone, and then stayed there, motionless and almost breathless. On the two sides of the road was, of course, a solid phalanx of people: none was willing to give room or move his place for a sick or elderly person even. No beggars called or sang their poems; no shopkeepers' agents could be heard enticing and cajoling a prospective buyer; no hawkers hawking their goods—be it victuals or household objects; there were no bazaar frequenters—those loose-living, loose-talking youths—to be seen or heard.

Imagine an evening of high summer in Delhi, without the water-sellers clashing the drinking cups together to create pleasant music, imitating the flow of water over stone; imagine no one selling ice or sherbet; imagine no itinerant flower-sellers calling out with their ware; imagine no one, far less a throng, at the attar-sellers' kiosks. Do you think Delhi could ever be thus? Well, tonight it was so.

Once, when I was small, I witnessed a full solar eclipse. I won't ever forget the deadly quiet, the silent terror of that afternoon. Gradually, but quite visibly, the sun covered itself somewhere in the sky, or it was driven to go away somewhere else, trying to hide its huge, burning bulk in some sort of a grey, winding sheet. Not a bird's twitter, not a cicada's call, not a dog's bark could be heard. The birds had, in fact, disappeared somewhere, as they do at fall of night. The dogs lay silent, like the dead, not even panting. Their mouths were tightly shut, as if they feared that the evil spirit, or whatever it was, would take possession of them if they kept their mouths open. Leaves, twigs and branches on all nearby trees had darkened, as if their sap was run dry. All human beings were either hiding in corners in their homes, or were silently saying prayers. Some of the more intrepid ones were trying to observe the sun through a piece of black cloth with a hole pricked in it, or through a grubby piece of glass, or even a black dupatta.

It was the same kind of evening today, except that it was like a normal urban evening, in the sense that people were out on the streets, in the alleys, wherever they hoped they could see the Mysterious Rider pass.

Suddenly, a vague noise, or disturbance. Its source seemed to be somewhere around Turkman Darwaza. A subdued sound, somewhat like a buzz, or the murmur of hundreds of people praying under their breaths. Then silence. Many of those who stood near me began to pronounce the Salutation to the Prophet in low tones. That vague, uninterpretable noise rose again. It lasted for a few moments, or a few minutes, this time. Some of those who stood near me tried to crane their neck as far as they could, gazing towards Turkman Darwaza. Some others gestured to them fiercely to desist. Perhaps afraid of disrespecting the Mighty Rider, or apprehending that their own line of sight would be blocked. But what was that noise? Was everyone there pronouncing some prayer, some benediction? Did anyone make an appearance at all at that end?

It was hotter, somehow. Actually, Delhi's weather cools fast as soon as the sun approaches the lower end of the horizon. I felt a drop of perspiration flow down my brow, touch my right eye and drop from the tip of my nose. I needed to scratch, but somehow didn't move, as if the least movement would destroy the apparition that was still to come. It seemed to me that many around me were losing patience, or perhaps having the jitters. 'What is it?' I whispered in my friend's ear. 'What's happening here?' He whispered back, 'I really don't know. My heart is heavy with premonition, as if some calamity is going to befall us.'

I was just about to reply when the sound of weeping and keening began to be heard, out of our sight, where the road turned towards my friend's haveli. The words of the Salutation to the Prophet were joined, or almost dissolved, in the sound of weeping, as if the onrush of tears and of crying wasn't due to pain or terror. It was just that everyone there was overcome by some uncontrollable emotion, an emotion that lay too deep for words. Soon, the voices muted to a murmur, as if the thing—the Presence—that caused the boiling over of emotion was past the onlookers. And my body began to shake and quiver as if struck by a freezing gust of wind. Some of my neighbours pulled their hands to their eyes; some began to weep with the same keening sound that was now muted elsewhere. Some began to pronounce aloud the Salutation to the Prophet, but their voices were heavy, almost choked.

Siyah Qitas. Black horse, absolutely black, jet-black, black as ebony—I have no words to describe the depth and intensity of that colour. Very tall, taller than the best Arab or Iraqi, mammoth, like a densely foliated hillock seen from a distance in the middle of a city square. None could discern at first glance that it was something equine. Stirrup, saddle, mouth ornament, blinkers, tail ornaments, everything encrusted with brilliant gems of many hues. The shoes adorning the stirrup seemed more a cluster of diamonds than shoes. The reins tight, in full control of the rider, and made of some bejewelled leather thongs with which silver thread was intwined and twisted. Very nearly each individual hair of the mane strung with pearls, the massive head adorned with gold- and silver-threaded white, red and azure feathers of some wild bird.

His head covered with a black, fully black, tall turban, his upper body clad in *char qub*, the style of dress associated with Mughal emperors alone. His lower body—I don't recall what he wore on it, but I do recall that when I looked again, his feet didn't seem to be shod in any kind of footwear, the shoes were invisible behind a bright light, and not just the reins, but both bit and bridle were covered with gold, silver and small gem quality stones.

High neck erect and eyes looking at something in front, or not at anything at all. It was as if he wasn't passing through a teeming city, which was always noisy with people, and pigeons, and turtles, and mynahs, and swooping kites, and dogs, and innumerable carriages of every description. As if it was a vacant wilderness that he was passing through. There was nothing of interest there to catch his eye or slow his speed. His face looked radiant, fresh as if he had made his ablutions, and not with ordinary water, but with some life-giving water. The freshness was of youth, but the sense of youth was coupled with a sense of superiority, of disdain and supercilious disregard of the world and its petty business. The face was bright, but there was no lack of hauteur; a face that made one feel safe and well protected in front of it, but also fearful, fearful of unknowingly doing something to offend, even by making a tiny movement—to bring down a cloud of annoyance and darken the brightness of it. An awe-inspiring face, but also devoid of the sense of oppression; yet, the awe that it caused was so great that one didn't dare raise one's eyes and avail oneself of a full look. A very tall lance in one hand, taller than an average human male's, and so lustrous and lambent that one couldn't decide where the hasp ended and the blade began. It was a streak of lightning, frozen along the length of the horse. And the rider's body too was motionless, like his head, but his whole person seemed to overflow with life and movement, like the portraits of princely riders painted at Akbar and Jahangir's courts by Ustad Manohar or Ustad Mansur. With all this profusion of picturesqueness, it wasn't possible to determine the details of the rider's personal appearance or his personality, if personality is the word that I want here.

The stallion was in motion; very slow, deliberate, precise movements, which seemed to be very nearly mechanical, but those who knew the art of riding could observe the rider's gentle manipulation of his bridle. There was also, muffled and remote but distinct enough to me, the tinkle of bells. Did Siyah Qitas have bells around its ankles, I wondered. Nothing was visible. Was a dromedary following him?

No one was weeping now, not even the sound of the Salutation could be heard. Was everybody struck dumb? I stole a glance from the corners of my eyes: Was anyone there bold enough to step into the road and—God have Mercy on me—stop him? I, at least, did not have it in me. But there was no movement from any side at all. I was by now bathed in warm perspiration, my trousers were now very nearly dripping on my shoes. It seemed to me that every one of us was now desirous of the passing of the Mystery Rider. Let him pass from our sight, at least. Though it had been barely two minutes or even less since we set our eyes on him, and he was now about to disappear behind the next bend of the road anyway, it seemed to me that a very long moment had elapsed between his appearance and his turning the bend. I have the strength no more to stand here. None of us has strength any more to remain in his presence, or for his presence to remain among us.

He disappeared. Surprisingly, the sound of weeping arose yet again. As if no one was relieved at his going, though his presence may have hung heavy on all of us. There was a sense, perhaps, of an opportunity lost, a favourable chance not accepted.

The voices died down almost at once, but the city took a long time to return to its normal brash and noisy self. Things began to wake up and look up. As if a paralysis had supervened miraculously, and was now going away equally miraculously. My sister was lost in some unfathomable thoughts on the way home.

Once we entered the familiar comfort and simplicity of our home, I spoke, half in badinage, but in fact in order to make myself able to negotiate with the event in my heart.

'So, did you get to look at your precious Rider?'

'How could I see anything?' She was almost in tears. 'She was a purdah lady, her body fully covered in a black sheet. Just her face was open, but I could see nothing of her face. I could only get a holy glimpse of that Bibi sahib's white horse. I didn't dare go up and speak to her, far less stop her and ask her for some boon.' She dried her tears and looked at me with almost accusing eyes.

'What garbage is it?' I cried almost sharply. 'Or are you telling me some stupid joke? It was a man, young lady, and he rode a black mount. And here are you, silly little girl,' I softened my tone and lowered my register, 'claiming the Rider to be some Rajji Sajji Bibi like the Sultan Razia Begam of centuries ago!'

I laughed a bit, partly to cover my own misgivings. 'Little girl, return to your senses! Hey, I quite wasted my time escorting you there and back. I hope you don't have some problem with your eyes?'

She spoke with some heat: 'Bhai jan, such things are not to be joked about. It's a matter of sacred beings and holy souls. The Rider sahib might take offence, you know. And Allah will be surely displeased! You are describing a lady, a maid, who is among Allah's chosen, as a man, and above that, you say that her snow-white horse was jet-black. Please beg Allah's pardon! What has come over you, Bhai jan, that you say such things?'

'You little foolish darling, nothing is the matter with me. It is you whom a great deception—'

Before I could finish, we had a visitor. She was Hajjin bibi, a neighbour, pretty ancient of days, and a woman whose main function in life was to go from house to house among the genteel families, exchange gossip, and do little jobs in or around the house in return for a little politesse and some compensation, given to her quietly, with the pretence that nothing was happening. Her main need was that she should be treated as genteel, and not as a lowly artisan or manual worker. She entered without rattling the door chain or calling out. Quite breathless, obviously in a hurry, and too excited to stop and exchange salaams, she said, 'Ay hay, Bibi, did you see Sultan Razia Begam? What an impressive horse, absolutely of the best pedigree! She rode with royal dignity, like the Queen of Delhi that she was!'

I pricked up my ears. Was she talking about Sitti's Rider? 'There, Hajjin bibi, you are another victim of the illusion! Here was a properly equipped, powerful male rider passing in front of all of us and you claim that he was a woman!'

'Illusion or mirage, and me?' she returned somewhat hotly, certainly with the emphasis of conviction. 'Young man, my eyes are perfectly sound. I don't even wear spectacles. My eyes are still as good as those of the young people. I will thank you not to question my eyes.'

Surreptitiously, I looked at Sitti. She didn't seem smug, or even satisfied at my being wrong. On the contrary, she looked somewhat confused, even upset. It was clear that I described what I saw, she described what she saw, and Hajjin bibi described what *she* saw, and each of us was quite persuaded of the truth of our sight, and the power of our eyes. My heart suddenly lurched and jumped hard against my ribs. My pulse quickened, my heart rate raced to I don't know how many hundreds, and my breath, shallow and compulsive, made breathing difficult for me. I felt nauseous, as if all my internal organs were pushing to come out from the depth of my throat at the same time. Fortunately, Amma ji had engaged Hajjin bibi in some dispute about where Razia Sultan was buried; Sitti was lost in thought, her delicate brow knitted. I took advantage of their being lost in their own occupations, and quietly went to an inner room, the room which had been mine ever since I was able to sleep alone on my cot. On the way, I drew a cup of cool water from Amma ji's earthen pitcher and gulped it down.

It was suffocatingly hot and airless in that little room, better described as a cell now that I had become tall and even somewhat gangly, quite a grown-up man. Still, I remained quietly lying on my cot, pretending to sleep. Amma ji and the two ladies were still conversing in low tones. The call for the night prayers came, and not too soon. I made the necessary ablutions and went off to the Kali Masjid. Actually, it is Kalan Masjid, that is, Big Masjid, but it had been called Kali Masjid, or Black Mosque, for many centuries, I am sure, because of its massive, fortress-like appearance. Its stone facade had grown somewhat dark with age, giving rise to the misnomer.

Since Amma ji knew my routine, I didn't need to tell her where I was going. At the mosque, I was not a little irritated and surprised that everybody was talking about that phantom rider. An extremely grave, white-bearded, quite neatly dressed old man was saying, 'Actually, I saw him with these very eyes. It was a dromedary Rider.' The word 'actually' suggested that someone had questioned the veracity of his narrative. The old gentleman went on, 'I say again, he rode a golden red dromedary; the rider was also very tall, he wore a turban of the same colour, its plume high and flowing into the breeze.'

I couldn't believe my ears, but it soon became clear to me that each and every one of us had seen the Rider of everlasting prosperity in their own way: no two visions of him seemed to agree. But why am

I describing him as the Rider of everlasting prosperity? Who awarded this title to him? It was certainly not I.

My heart began again to feel heavy and uneasy. It felt like the intimation of cardiac deficiency, though I knew that I had no such ailment. What has been going on here? Was something unusual really going to happen? Countless eyewitnesses, and each telling a different story. Did this portend something? There would certainly be quarrels and disagreements among Delhi's citizens, young or staid or frivolous. I tried to look at the possibly lighter side of the thing. I finished the prayer with only half my heart in it and forced myself to eat some dinner, forgetting all my appetite for Amma ji's sheermals. I quietly retired to bed, though I could not, in all fairness to my mother and sister, pretend to them that I was not out of sorts. I did not want to tell them anything about it. There was no need to add to their burdens.

I was to report to the madrasa very early, after the predawn prayer, but I could sleep little that night. Before I left for work the next morning, Amma ji said the Prophet's Salutation and other beneficent prayers on Sitti and me for many a minute, then blew on our face and head.

*

A new day. All of us back to the grinding routine of studying, disputatious argufying, memorizing, composing. Everyone was driven by the demon of examinations. Granted, there were many months to go yet for the examinations, but students are by nature restless and fussy. But suddenly a very good thing happened.

Perhaps it was the beneficence of the Rider, or just one of those happy accidents of life. The season of rains was not yet under way when a 'message', that is, a marriage proposal, for Sitti Begam came from the House of Ustad Khairullah, the architect. The proposed groom was Baqaullah, the very friend in whose haveli we were guests and spectators for the Rider. The women of his House saw Sitti bibi that afternoon and liked what they saw. After the usual investigations, they sent us the marriage message. I and Amma ji, after our own deliberations and inquiries—though nowhere as thorough as those that must have been mounted by the groom's family—accepted the proposal. It occurred to me that I should tell Sitti bibi too, but I had cold feet every time I thought of introducing the subject to her. I prayed most desperately that she like the proposal. I knew that she would know—girls get to know these matters through some mysterious means of their own. She never made a hint one way or another. And that was what I had to content myself with. I was sure, though there was no reason to be so, that if she disliked the proposal she would have let her disapproval known to Amma ji, though not to me.

Baqaullah was my friend; his family were prosperous, in fact rich beyond most people's comprehension. Baqaullah and his father didn't follow their ancestral calling of architecture and engineering. They weren't poets even. Baqaullah's grandfather, Ustad Khairullah, the renowned architect, was still among us at that time. Aside from engineering, architecture and astronomy, he was an acknowledged master in poetry and lexicography. The famous lexicographer Tek Chand Bahar, in *Bahar-e Ajam,* his massive dictionary of the Persian language, often quotes Ustad Khairullah and always with the appellative *khair-ul mudaqqiqin,* 'the best among those who know all the subtle points'. For his own ustad, the renowned Sirajuddin Ali Khan-e Arzu, Tek Chand sahib uses the title *siraj-ul muhaqqiqin,* 'the guiding lamp of all those who seek the truth'.

Ustad Khairullah was the chief designer and architect of the extremely large observatory constructed a few miles outside the city of Delhi at the behest of Sawai Raja Jai Singh of Jaipur. Highly popular among the specialists and common people alike, the observatory is still an important destination for visitors. Astronomers from as far as Transoxiana, Turkey and Egypt frequently go there to consult the state of the celestial formations and derive benefit from its extensive library.

Baqaullah's father, Maulana Safiullah, was much given to thought and meditation on the Divine Being, and Sufism. So he, instead of earning and acquiring the goods of the world, chose to build a small cell for himself at the luminant mausoleum of his father's older brother. The uncrowned king of Delhi, the Shaikh of the age, the Qutb of the times, our Master and our Protection, the Presence, Shah Kalimullah sahib Jahanabadi's tomb is in the busy maidaun and bazaar below the Jama Masjid, on the eastern side. Baqaullah's temperament inclined towards the esoteric arts of geomancy and *jafar*, which is the art of divining with secret characters. His aptitude and achievement in these nearly secret and very difficult disciplines were so great that even though a young man, he was counted the equal of the city's most eminent practitioners of those arts. I was thus confident that my little sister would have more than enough of both mundane wealth and spiritual wealth.

It was decided that the marriage would be performed after my graduation from the madrasa. The weather would have softened its rigour by that time, and I too might gain some employment somewhere. Fortunately, it happened just as planned. By Allah's Grace and Munificence, the air in Delhi at that time was much favourable for teaching and learning. It so happened that some years ago, Maulana Nizam-ud Din, an individual from among the most honoured descendants of the Presence, Sayyid Bandah Nawaz Gesu Daraz, arrived in Delhi from Aurangabad in the Deccan. He gave his hands in the Truth-worshipping hands of Shah Kalimullah sahib Jahanabadi, the Presence, the Shaikh of the times, and in due course became his eminent disciple and pupil. At that time Nizam-ud Din sahib's son, the worshipful Presence, Shah Fakhruddin sahib, was in his nonage. The Shaikh of the age soon left this transient place for the Space filled with the Higher Ones. Soon after, Shaikh Nizam-ud Din sahib also was joined with God. He was at Aurangabad at the time of his departure from this world. Now Shah Fakhruddin sahib decided to make Delhi his place of residence.

Having arrived here about thirty years ago, Shah Fakhruddin sahib began to teach at the madrasa of Ghaziuddin Firoz Jang. Within a few years, by dint of the quality of his discourses and the beneficence contained in them, the madrasa was teeming with students, resulting in frequent need for more teachers. Some of the graduates from that school obtained employment there, and sometimes, lucky ones from other schools were also inducted. Thus it came to pass that I, freshly minted Maulavi Khairuddin, was appointed fourth assistant master at that august institution. The date was 5 October 1764. My pay was fixed at eleven rupees a month. Above the wonted salary, students from well-to-do homes frequently presented fruits of the season, or clothing like shawls for the winter. Thus, my average intake often reached fourteen or fifteen rupees a month. My pay itself was sufficient for living the life of a respectable young man who had no vices. In fact, I would occasionally save enough to contribute some money to my mother's household expenses.

My sister, beloved of her mother, and her mother's son, left for her new home after a simple but dignified marriage ceremony. The Presence, the worshipful Shah Abdul Aziz sahib, may Allah extend his benefits far and wide, and the Prince, Sahib-e Alam Mirza Sulaiman Shikoh Bahadur, may his fortune remain forever ascendant and may his dominions remain forever, sent special sets of trousseau for the bride, and the Prince also vouchsafed a bag of one hundred Shah Alami gold mohurs as present for the bridegroom. Our Mentor, the Presence, Shah Abdul Aziz sahib, himself adorned the glory of the occasion for a short while.

*

All that was very well and I hoped that my sister was also happy. I certainly had no reason to believe to the contrary. But my heart often felt heavy, always under the shadow of a nameless anxiety. As if I had some important thing to do and I had forgotten to do it and now for the life of me couldn't recall what duty it was. What carked me even more was the feeling, or the fear that I would soon be called to account for my omission.

News of Raja Ram Narain Mauzun's utterance in the last moments of his life had been the subject of common talk in Delhi for some time. Raja sahib was the chief treasurer and confidant of the Martyr Navab, Siraj-ud Daulah of Murshidabad. One of the talking points was that he was falsely accused by the English and they caused him to be awarded the appalling and macabre punishment of death by drowning in the river Ganga. The Presence, the Raja, was a proficient poet in Persian and sometimes composed in Rekhtah too. It was said that while being thrown into the river's roiling waters, the Raja had the following Persian verse on his lips:

The thirsty lips of Husain went to their end, deprived of you,
Waters of the river, turn to dust, for no honour, no lustre is left for you.

The beauty of the verse, and the self-restraint, the dignity, even the pride of the Raja sahib in the moment of death were talked about in every coffee house, every roadside meeting place. But the verse, and the incident both seemed to have some personal meaning for me, and me alone. Was there a sign there? Was I expected to understand here that it was not the pomp of riches, the train of lackeys and servants, the throng of well-wishers and mourners that made a man's death worthy of him? Man's essence seemed to consist in the dignity of his end, and the dignity of the end consisted in not giving up one's essential self.

So what was my essential self? Did it consist in making me compose the verse about the Rider of everlasting prosperity, and then in having me prove that *he* was real? Not to speak of holding him by the bridle and stopping his progress, I didn't, or couldn't even make a gesture to move towards him. But was he necessarily a Chosen One of God? Apparently, instead of being a man of God, he was (Allah pardon me) a magician or master of illusions and appearances. A spirit of the air or even of the earth, maybe? Were that not the case, why should different people see him as a different person, and that too at the same time?

But why did that verse fall from my lips, and without any volition on my part? Was it not as if someone, some Power perhaps, motivated me or composed that verse and put it in my mouth? No, that's bad logic. It is not necessary that I was the conscious or unconscious author of that verse. Perhaps I read it long ago, somewhere, or heard someone recite it somewhere, and it remained locked in my brain, only to suddenly get unlocked and make its escape from the dark labyrinth of memory? Such instances were rare, but not unknown. What else was *tawarud* then, if not such coincidence in composition? I recalled the subtle discussion of tawarud and *saraqa* in Taftazani. If I wrote a verse, which accidentally resembled another one composed by someone else, it was tawarud. Actually, it meant 'coming together at a watering place', thus, a chance occurrence. But if I wrote it knowing that there was another like it already in existence, then it was saraqa, that is, stealing. There were many convolutions and subtleties in the whole thesis, and I felt that even then, Taftazani or his predecessors like the great Abd-ul Qahir Jurjani weren't being entirely logical.

Hey, what did it matter to me that Taftazani or his mentors were subtle and/or illogical? Am I already on the way to irrationality? The question was just this: Was it possible to retain someone else's verse in your head and not know it, and then was it possible for that verse to get released from under the surface of the brain and make a sudden appearance much later? Well, put that way, it didn't seem possible. So I am back at the lowest rung of the ladder.

I had heard poets say that such and such a person composed a whole ghazal by his own self, that is, he believed that he composed it, but in actuality the ghazal turned out to be someone else's creation, composed in some distant or recent past. But wasn't that just hearsay and couldn't constitute proof in formal disputation? But then, was there anyone here whom I could consult about the authorship of the verse? There was Tek Chand Bahar sahib, but I didn't know him. Mir Shamsuddin Faqir sahib was a person who would know. I didn't know him either, and it was perhaps improper for a minor, insignificant person like me to approach such luminaries of the world of learning without a suitable introduction. Our own worshipful Shah Abdul Aziz sahib or his younger brother Shah Abdul Ghani sahib, may Allah preserve them, had very good knowledge of Persian poetry. Yet, I hesitated to trouble them for such a trite matter. Both brothers, may Allah save them from harm, were the very picture of kindness and considerateness to the seekers of knowledge. But to make such an inquiry of them was appropriate for one, I felt, who had the privilege of at least occasional presence in their assemblies. Surely they would know me as a past student of Rahimiya, once I went there, but frankly, I would feel like a fool, asking such a silly question, and that too in the presence of many others.

No, the authorship of the verse was not what mattered. What affected me, and in fact drove me almost to the brink of melancholia, were the meaning and the occasion. I apparently conceived the verse by myself, in two parts, and on two separate occasions. And on both the occasions, a special meaning could be attributed to the two lines: one was something like a prophecy; the other something like the ending of a story. So if there was a prophecy here, what did it portend for me? And was the prophecy also applicable to the end of the story?

So all right, let's look at it this way. Could not this whole construct be anything but an imaginary play, its truth being nothing more than what the philosophers call 'appearance', that is, an allegorical exemplification? Siyah Qitas, the reported name of the Rider's mount, seemed to be suggesting some such thing. Qitas, as far as I know, means nothing at all. There is a constellation called *qaitis* or *qitus*, which is supposed to look like a huge fish. But in the *Dastan of Amir Hamza*, Siyah Qitas is the name of a favourite horse of the Amir. Could that be a corruption of 'qitus'? So does it suggest that he was some heavenly being?

Now that's too much. The whole world knows that the *Dastan of Amir Hamza* is pure invention; it has no basis in fact. So is it not probable that some extremely clever but impudent professional impersonator decided to play a joke on all of us, and in order to suggest that it was a joke, had it bruited about that he rode one of Amir Hamza's favourite horses mentioned in the dastan? Well, quite likely, but to what purpose? I know there are professional male impersonators who can impersonate women, and female impersonators who can assume the men's disguise, and no one is the wiser. These people can impersonate even the King, the Shadow of God on Earth. These people are called by different names; *saangi* is the commonest of them.

Enough of this wild surmising. I should presume that such a person as the Rider of everlasting prosperity did appear in the city. And that there was some sign in it for me, because the Persian verse had occurred to me and me alone.

Was there a test in it for me? If so, it was clear that I had failed that test. This feeling of something undone often pricked and pinched my heart. But please, let someone tell me what the test was. Testing someone and not telling him that he was being tested, or revealing the subject of the test was cruelty; I almost felt like weeping in frustration. Or perhaps it was more the sense of loss that I suffered because of my sister's departure to her new (and, in fact, real) home. I hadn't reconciled myself to our being separated. Granted that she lived not half an hour's distance from my mother's house where I lived. Granted that I could freely visit her. But the real distance between our homes was much greater. If I went there more frequently than propriety permitted, her in-laws could suspect that she was not happy there and needed her brother to console her or give mental support to her. Or they might suspect that it was I who somehow believed that my sister wasn't happy in her marriage, so I came to see her often, to reduce her sense of (what in my imagination was) loneliness. Either way, it was a losing game, and a foolish game. Perhaps it was I who felt guilty, first for letting her go away in marriage, and second for not going to visit her as frequently as I wished. Sitti bibi might think: Bhai jan has quite given me up to strangers.

I think the truth was that I was still not reconciled to the fact that my little sister was now a grown-up, and had become quite capable of managing a household and a husband. She was now the mistress of her own home and no longer manager of her mother's home. More important, an outsider possessed her; she was now something worth possessing. And all girls, whether willingly or against their will, have to pay the price of ownership; to own her house, she had to accept ownership of someone else over her. I was hoping that for my sister, the bargain had her approval, and she was happy in it, or at least, she was content with her lot.

But I perhaps unconsciously missed the Sitti bibi who had me tell her stories every night and quarrelled with me by day in her prattling tongue. Amma ji occasionally hinted at the need for me to get married, but I always managed to change the subject without seeming to do so.

*

Another six months passed. I lived on, like a lost sheep, that wanders the jungle desperately for food, and hopes that she'll find her way home before the marauding wolf overtakes her.

The year was 1765, the Islamic month of Safar was about to end. News was abroad that our King Emperor, who had the majesty of Jamshed, Abul Muzaffar Jalal-ud Din Shah Alam the Second, had transferred the revenue administration of the provinces of Bengal, Bihar and Orissa to the Company Bahadur. We hadn't mourned the defeat at Buxar the previous year as much as this apparently uncoerced transfer of effective power to an entity known for treachery and chicanery. Defeat or victory, these were the original writs for kings and peoples. Was it not right here in Delhi, just about fifteen years ago, that the Durrani Chieftain Ahmad Shah delivered a crushing defeat to the forces of the Maratha? Did not Delhi recover? Did it not become again the heart of empire within a few years? So Buxar could be avenged, its losses recouped. But transfer of power by treaty was something final, like death.

I realized the quiet irony of Destiny or of God Himself: Our

Emperor had the title of Abul Muzaffar, which means, 'Owner of the Victorious', and the month was Safar which in Arabic is another form of *sifr* (cypher, cifer, cipher) which means 'empty' and signifies the zero. The month was called Safar because it was, by convention, empty of fighting: the tribes were expected to be at peace during this month.

True, the Maratha is apparently on the ascendant again; Delhi is not entirely safe. But someone, something, can deal with internal threats, these are transient in their nature. It seemed to me that our King with the majesty of Jamshed would have to spend his days in Allahabad, under the shade of English canopies, in durance if not ignominy. The Red Fort will never wear red again.

Who really would incline to study, and to teach, under these disheartening conditions? Certainly not I. But duty was duty. And by some mischance caused by fate or by the Writer of People's Destinies, I was assigned to teach an advanced course in logic. The text was Mir Zahid Hiravi's famous commentary on Mulla Jalal's opus on logic. Mir sahib was also the teacher, in the seventeenth century, of the All Respected and Admired Mulla Abdur Rahim sahib—may God's Mercy be upon him—the founder of my original school, the Rahimiyya. Known among learned circles as *Mir Zahid Mulla Jalal*, a copy of the book was in the madrasa library. Unfortunately, it was defective, motheaten in many places, and was also full of scribal errors. I decided to go to the Antique Books and Maps Bazaar, which convened every Friday at Jama Masjid and look for a sound copy.

I arrived just after break of day and found the bazaar quite crowded. I found out that a bookseller from Qandahar was offering excellent copies of the divans of, among others, Abu Talib Kalim, Mulla Ghani Kashmiri, Abul Barakat Munir Lahori and some others of the previous century. The book that I sought wasn't at the booksellers' on the stairs of the Masjid. So, braving the throng, I proceeded into Urdu Bazaar, but I almost stopped in my tracks to look at a powerful roan, richly caparisoned, guarded over by a tall and burly syce from the mountains.

A mount with muscles so taut, the coat so shiny, the neck so proud, I never saw, except perhaps under the thighs of the Phantom Rider.

God save me! The thought of the Rider was almost always like the Persian saying, 'to remind the inebrious of their favourite tune'. My mind always then went off at a tangent, imagining or trying to imagine the situations where the Rider of everlasting prosperity could be relevant to my fate.

Suddenly, my eye fell on the rider. What a handsome youth, what a noble visage. His person tugged and pulled at the viewer's heart in spite of the fact that we were total strangers. Of their own accord, my feet took me towards him.

I am more or less two yards tall, thus I stood out among my peers or in any average assembly of men. But that young man was a couple of finger-width taller. Aged twenty-two or twenty-four, his complexion fair, his black beard not very dense, but pointed and cut stylishly in the Turkish or Mughal fashion of the day. His forehead high, his bluish-green eyes glinting like pieces of topaz set in gold. His headgear was a piece of twisted silk, bright green and yellow. He wore a long necklace of lapis lazuli on his slim, high neck, his ears adorned with short earrings with pearls strung in them.

He wore on his upper body a light-green silk caftan, or *nima*, densely embroidered like the *jamahvar* from Kashmir. Following the fashion of the Mirzas of the day, the caftan was open on the left-hand side of the chest; his full-sleeved tunic under the nima was of so fine a muslin that the powerful leonine muscles of his chest could be seen clearly. The sleeves of the nima were very delicately picked to give the effect of wavelets. His arms practically filled the sleeves, which ended just a little before his broad wrists.

He stood before a shop counter, perusing a slim volume. I stole a look: it was the divan of Ghani Kashmiri, its margins beautifully painted in blue and gold. The main title page must be even more richly splendid. Fortunately, the bookseller and I were slightly acquainted. He was attending another customer, but he beckoned me to come nearer.

When I approached close, he picked up a book from the lot in front of him and handed it to me. It was a fine copy of the *Mir Zahid Mulla Jalal* that I had come searching for. Indeed, my coming here seemed to have been guided and approved by some Power above! The moment my friendly bookseller was done attending the earlier customer, he turned towards me and I asked the price of my book. I clinched the deal at one and a quarter rupees after the usual bargaining. Now I had no reason to stay there. The young beau also bought the Divan of Ghani at the asking price of eight and a half rupees, and turned to leave.

I stole a furtive glance at him. I wanted so much that we should get acquainted, but speaking first without introduction would be speaking out of turn. The young man was about to put his foot in the stirrup when my friend the bookseller again came to my aid. He gestured towards the nearly departing rider, and said, 'Maulavi sahib, perhaps you haven't met this gentleman before. He is a person of the most sterling qualities . . .'

Perhaps that stylish rider too was looking somewhat keenly for an introduction. Quickly, he alighted, turned towards me, and said, 'Maulavi sahib, I submit my services. This dweller in the dust is called Budh Singh Qalandar.'

Quite without my knowing, my face blossomed like a flower. I extended my hands for a warm handshake, and said, 'And I, the lowest of creation, am Khairuddin. Sorry, I am not a poet like you.'

'Well, I am not truly a poet. I occasionally do a little rant in Rekhtah, not quite seriously.'

'So whom did you take as ustad?'

'I am nobody's pupil in the regular sense. Occasionally, though, our worshipful Mirza Mazhar Jan-e Janan sahib puts a dot or two on a ghazal or half a ghazal, by way of a sacred gift of correction.'

'Only God is free from all blemish! Mirza sahib is a holy man and a Sufi of high station. A whole world is his disciple in Sufism. And in poetry, be it Persian or be it Rekhtah, he is the Shaikh Sadi of the Age.'

'You are right, sir, but unfortunately that August Portal is no longer much given to poetry. He didn't collect whatever he commanded in Rekhtah. What irony from the heavens, he who created numerous ustads in Rekhtah, and his own divan was never put together! And in Persian too his divan is worth barely thirty or forty pages.'

We walked side by side, engrossed in our exchanges, while Qalandar sahib's mount remained in the syce's charge. I knew a bit of Persian poetry and used it effectively in our conversation. This helped warm his heart quickly towards me. We asked about each other's life and circumstances. It transpired that Qalandar was the only offspring: born in a prosperous and well-educated Khatri family of Lahore, he obtained his education there, and is now resident here, managing the extensive Delhi properties of his parents. In addition to poetry, his temperament inclined towards Sufism and Jog Bidya. He obtained training and experience in both his avocations in the Exalted Mirza sahib's court. And he was not yet married.

We talked on, absorbed in getting to know each other. By and by, we arrived very close to Kali Masjid. The Rajji Sajji Mausoleum was hard by; situated adjacent to it was Mirza sahib's monastery, and his zenana just behind it.

'Oh, we are now almost at the monastery!' I spoke in anxious tones. 'And here I am, entirely empty-handed. I should present myself before him for the first time and not make an offering! That's an unthinkable and horrid breach of manners. So let me take my leave from you,' I continued in my best possible politeness. 'I must beg leave of you now. My humble home—no more than a shoebox for you—is right here, a minute away. So I'll go home now, inshallah, we shall meet again, and soon.'

'No, no. That's not how it should be!' he cried. 'To turn away from the stream of the water of life without quenching your thirst, that's not what wise men do, my dear sir. Believe me, there is no such protocol at the Presence, the Mirza sahib's threshold. Let him who wishes to present something, do so, and let him who has no such wish, not do so.'

'Presence, it is not a question of wishing or not wishing. I would most gladly present something suited to my station. But at this time, I have no preparation at all.'

'Just take the plunge. Come and see. I will warrant for the worshipful Mirza sahib not to mind at all.'

'But my mother will mind, will she not?' I returned somewhat testily. 'My conscience will be unhappy.'

'I beg pardon; I was a trifle slow in seeing your point. So then, here is the newly bought divan of Ghani Kashmiri. I wanted it for me, but let's make it a present for the Exalted Presence.'

'I seek refuge in God! Such a valuable present, and I? Really, I could board for a whole month with the price of this single volume. No, sahib, no. I can't do such a thing, ever!'

'All right, please consider it a loan from me, with no limit of time for repayment. Or better still, in return thereof, teach me a little advance-level Arabic. I am rather backward in Arabic.'

I didn't want to seem churlish by arguing further. Further refusals would indeed sound meretricious as well.

'So be it decreed,' I attempted a little levity. 'Come and read Arabic with me every Friday.'

*

The monastery's door was open. There was no doorkeeper or guard either. We entered without let. A very small hall, then on both sides of it, two small rooms, cells more than rooms. A large courtyard in front, open to the sky and enclosed by double verandas. A tiny stream flowed down the middle of the courtyard. Flowering shrubs on both the dainty banks of the canal. Some birds twittered on a few of the shrubs. I couldn't determine if they were wild or tame. The inner of the double veranda in front of us was wider than the other. It was there, on a slightly elevated platform, that Mirza Mazhar Jan-e Janan sahib's radiant presence enhanced the holy aura of the house. There were people in both verandas: the entire assembly seemed so civilized, so soberly golden and sophisticated that I couldn't pluck up courage to advance and look for a place, as if my presence would nullify the chastity of the assembly, like a patch of soot on a milk-white bedspread.

We stood, hesitant, at the front of the outer veranda, when someone, one of the inner assembly, spoke with quiet authority, of his own volition or maybe at the flicker of the eye from Mirza sahib, 'Here, please come over to this side. There is room here for both of you.'

We advanced, our eyes firmly on the floor, stepping gingerly as if we were walking on eggs. Budh Singh sahib placed his right hand on the left side of his chest, bent a little, made obeisance, and spoke in very low, respectful tones, 'Worshipful and Noble Kabah, I submit salutations. How does the Master feel today?'

Mirza sahib smiled, and then spoke in an extremely mellifluous, heart-warming voice, 'May you live long. May your prosperity and good fortune increase.'

I just salaamed quietly, my eyes on my feet, and stood in quiet apprehension. He then flicked his eyes towards me, almost imperceptibly, perhaps to know my identity and purpose. I again salaamed, bending low, with my eyes strictly on the ground. Then I folded my hands on my chest, as in doing the namaz, and submitted: 'This servant goes by the name Khairuddin. Qalandar sahib gave me a little fortitude, so I presented myself just to look at his Honour and kiss his shoes.'

He spoke a famous Persian line of verse with the same winning half smile:

The qalandar reports what he sees.

As of then, I was unable to comprehend the true meaning of Mirza sahib's commandment. Back home, and arranging the events in their proper sequence, reviewing all that transpired, I divined Mirza sahib's real meaning—at work here was his power of reading people's minds and seeing with his mind's eye things which most people didn't see. I was hesitant, in fact unwilling, to present myself at his monastery, and Budh Singh Qalandar had sought to alleviate my misgivings by assuring me that there was no convention of bringing presents when presenting oneself at Mirza sahib's portal. So the Presence was reinforcing that assurance or was putting his seal of confirmation on it.

I placed the divan of Ghani on my palms, creating a makeshift tray, and presented it to Mirza sahib. He cast a casual glance at the volume, and commanded, 'Maulavi sahib, that's a good present that you brought. As Allah Wills.' This was yet again an instance of his mind reading, or should I say thought reading? The book was bound in plain vellum, with no inscription or sign to indicate its character, but he knew that it was the divan of Ghani. Then there was some imperceptible hint from him, because the same person who had suggested to us the place where we should be seated, came forward. In the meantime, Mirza sahib accepted the volume from me, turned over a leaf or two, and spoke, half to himself, 'This was a poet after my own heart and purpose.' Mirza sahib handed the volume over to the person who had come forward, and recited a verse from Ghani in an absolutely marvellous manner. I have no words to describe the way he recited, except that I never heard such affective reading before, or since:

> *Love spreads its snare over the high land and the low*
> *Farhad was captured and confined in his Besutun,[1] Majnun in his desert.*

I noticed that his eyes were misting over, but he kept a hold on himself. We stood as before, not knowing whether to withdraw. In his gentle voice, he said, 'Please seat your noble selves.' The command was like a new life for me, I'd felt so inadequate, standing before that august assembly. We sat down after giving a brief salaam, our feet tucked under our thighs.

Now that I was settled a bit, I looked around cautiously, to get

---

[1] Literally, 'without columns, free standing'; the name of the mountain which Farhad was required to cut through in order to let a milk stream flow through it.

a better feel of the assembly. At the back of Mirza sahib stood a tallish, rather lean but not feeble individual. Of an extremely refined deportment and visage, he wore a cloak in light pistachio colour, green, but not quite so, and under it a white tunic in muslin, closely buttoned up to his throat. His cap was made of plain, embroidered cloth called chikan, much favoured by the people of Lucknow and other eastern climes. His face, though somewhat wrinkled, had a strangely attractive softness, as if the owner of that face never saw or did anything the least unpleasant. He was fanning Mirza sahib with a fan made of peacock feathers. I later found out that his name was Ghulam Ali, and he was one of the chief disciples of the Presence, but he ran around like a humble menial, doing even the smallest chores for him.

The person who was a sort of aide to Mirza sahib, and who had welcomed us, was Maulavi Naimullah Bharaichi, as I found out later. He was a sort of nominated successor to the Presence for the eastern areas, but spent the best part of the year at the feet of his Mentor and Guide.

I gathered courage to raise my eyes and take a look at the Presence's face. His complexion was very fair, though somewhat wan; he was quite tall but thin, in fact thinner than Ghulam Ali sahib. His beard was white, slightly pointed and short, clearly trimmed with extreme care. His moustache was much less dense than the beard, but not excessively so. He wore a very light-green nima in muslin; extremely fine, it must have been obtained from Dacca. Under the nima was a tunic in milk-white *shabnam*, so white that the muslin's green hue was almost not noticeable. He wore no cloak over his nima, but I could see near him on the flat wooden seat a neatly folded Sufi's cloak in very lightly embroidered jamahvar from Kashmir. On his lower body he wore wide-bottomed trousers in green with light, burnt-orange stripes. Very large eyes, with folded eyelids, revealing a little of the redness of the eyes, red perhaps because of his nightlong prayers and meditations. He wore a four-cornered cap in embroidered velvet; one could see a few snow-white locks of longish hair peeping down the slim neck. One of the locks seemed to have escaped and hung around his right ear, as if he was not mindful enough to push it back under the cap.

In spite of his almost phenomenal thinness, he was more handsome, and his personality more impressive, than anyone I ever saw or knew. I had often seen our revered and loved Shah Abdul Aziz sahib, may God lengthen his shadow over the world, and may God grant him a long life. He is an impressive person, and the radiant power of learning and piety exudes from him like a visible emanation. But Mirza sahib? By Allah, Mirza sahib was something else again. If by virtue of the awe and near terror and trembling that he inspired, he was like the Presence, Muhiyuddin Aurangzeb Alamgir, may God keep his grave cool, then by virtue of his attractiveness and physical beauty, and the dazzling aura of spiritual refinement, he was like the Presence, the Qutb of his age, Khvajah Baqi Bi-Allah sahib, may Allah sanctify his grave and fill it with radiant light.

Now, I also noticed a middle-aged person, clearly a Maulavi, who stood in the middle of the first veranda. His head bowed, his hands just below his chest as in prayer, perspiration flowed copiously from his face, practically drenching his face and his rather thick foliage of a beard, though I noticed that the beard and the whiskers were trimmed somewhat neatly, almost like a designer's work. No, it wasn't sweat, it was tears, I realized with a sense of grotesque horror. The poor visitor was blubbering, not perspiring. I looked, not a little in terror about his unknown crime and the punishment, which should surely follow. The Maulavi sahib was submitting in the most abject tones, his voice hoarse with emotion, or for lack of courage: 'I appeal to His Honour in the name of his Royal Pleasure and Pity. The offence committed by this worthless, sinful and unfortunate person may be pardoned, and this mean and despicable slave pronounced fit to take his seat at the good fortune-ensuring feet of the slaves of this portal.'

I didn't understand anything at all. Surely, this Maulavi sahib couldn't be a criminal like a thief or a cony catcher? If not, what was his crime? How did he come to offend such an angelic, kind soul as our Mirza sahib? The self-styled offender must have stood there from before we entered. Maybe Qalandar sahib saw him even. But I—like the Arabic saying, 'Whoever is a newcomer is full of terror'—didn't have the good courage to look at anything other than Mirza sahib. Now, I dared at least look at Naimullah sahib with mild inquiry. He spoke in conversational tones, 'This respected Maulavi sahib brought his noble presence from Karnal, seeking to be admitted to the circle of the disciples of the Presence of Exalted Value.'

The lachrymose Maulavi, perhaps gaining, or imagining some support from Naimullah sahib, checked his tears as he spoke, looking at Naimullah sahib, but in fact addressing Mirza sahib, 'I have carried out the commandments of His Honour of Exalted Station.'

'Yes,' I heard Ghulam Ali sahib's voice, somewhat mocking, somewhat compassionate. So far, Ghulam Ali sahib had been so intent and unmoving at his task that he reminded me of the Quranic verse, *As if they had birds perching on their heads.* He said, 'But somewhat tardy, if not quite retarded.'

There was reprimand in his tone of voice, but very little, just like a dash of pepper in a sweet drink. His mien remained grave, his words, measured. 'His Honour of Exalted Station commanded you twice, not once, to have trimmed the spiky, dense bird's nest that you had on your face in the name of beard and whiskers. It was desired by His Honour that you should stop looking like a bear, and adopt a human visage. No? But you stuck to your Noble Theological tracts.'

'B . . . but His Honour m . . . must now observe that I have re . . . repented.' He was almost in tears again.

'Yes, but when? When you had repeated instruction in your dreams that if you truly desired spiritual progress and betterment, you must tie yourself to the Sacred Hem of our Presence's garment, nowhere else and nothing else would do.'

He smiled an enigmatic smile, maybe slightly humorous too. 'So, will Mian Qalandar now present and plead your case before the Exalted Presence?'

'Qalandar? Who and where?' the Maulavi sahib inquired in desperate confusion.

Before the Maulavi sahib had finished speaking, the Presence, Mirza sahib, raised his holy head, and commanded, 'He has had enough chastisement now. Let him come tomorrow, it's a Friday, I will then admit him among my pupils.'

It seemed to me that Mirza sahib, who was reputed for his sense of humour as much as for his sophisticated comportment, which was more like that of a true 'Mirza', that is, a person of noble birth and ample means, had somewhat enjoyed the foregoing exchange.

The Maulavi sahib now made bold to advance to centre stage, touch Mirza sahib's knee, and kiss the hem of his nima. As he tried to dry his tears with his sleeve, he said in a choked voice, 'It is Your Honour's benevolence, truly your benevolence.'

But before he could say anything further, a loud, rough and harsh female voice was heard from the door in the narrow lane leading to the zenana. The words were pronounced in the manner of a Jat though literate woman of Mewat, but the intonation was as hard as a piece of seasoned rosewood, even the sharpest saw wouldn't cut it easily. We all heard, utterly consternated: 'Where is that pimp of a Mirza? Is he gone and expired somewhere? He gives airs to himself, fancying himself as a mentor and guide, heh? I should butcher him and put little pieces of him on small copper coins and feed them to kites and crows! Tell him to display his flirtatious coquetry elsewhere. I have no patience for those things. Look, oh you people, the third watch of the day is about to commence and the out-runners with my palanquin haven't shown their swine-faces yet! I stand here at my doorstep, parching in the harsh sun, and there are none of my out-runners to go with me. Tell me, people, how can I, a woman and all alone, go all the way to the Exalted Threshold of Hare Bhare sahib at the Jama Masjid? And if I didn't do this favour to him, shall he dispatch his mothers and sisters for it? Who will pray for his good health and longevity? Who will organize the gatherings of his disciples who would stand his strict demands, his so-called severe canons?'

I don't know about others, but I was stricken dumb and motionless. As if I was caught stealing from the charity box in some sacred place. This pearl-scattering, almost kingly court, this throng of admirers and askers for favours, and such lese-majesty? Undoubtedly, I had heard vaguely about this lady and her treatment of Mirza sahib, but the waters of shame here exceeded the height of a man; indeed, deep enough to sink several elephants. I begged protection and forgiveness from God; does this venerable person have no fear of Hell's fire?

I had no strength to raise my head, far less rise, make my obeisance and beg permission to leave. But I felt, and then confirmed this feeling by looking from the corner of my eyes: there was no surprise, no chagrin among those present, and the Presence himself betrayed not the least sign of being affected by the demonstration of irreverence, and a temper even more flagrant than the demonstration of irreverence. The Presence sat through it quiet and motionless, and there was no question at all of any kind of emotional response. He sat still, as always; his head somewhat bent, as if giving serious thought to some disciple's problems or presentation.

Even that Maulavi sahib from Karnal remained where he was, hugging a leg of Mirza sahib's rather low chair—a wooden platform that he favoured during pubic assemblies. Before any of us could move, Ghulam Ali sahib made some slight gesture, and a couple of the visitors, who sat on the outer side of the assembly near the shoes, rose unobtrusively, salaamed and, walking backwards, proceeded towards the lane where the zenana's door was situated. Another servant almost immediately came out from the zenana and respectfully whispered something to Ghulam Ali sahib. Apparently, the Presence was expecting some such message, because as Ghulam Ali sahib bent towards him, he smiled his usual half smile, sweeter and more refreshing than a thousand roses.

I later learnt that the two hapless out-runners had presented themselves well before time at the zenana and had been directed, with a bit of abuse and slaps to their head from the Pirani sahib, to await summons and not importune and upset her repose before the appointed time.

Finding that the Presence was now something like his normal, equanimous self, a gentleman, whose dress and appearance suggested that he was from Bokhara, or Samarqand, stood up, folded his hands just above his stomach, and submitted, speaking chaste and fluent Persian, 'His Honour's discourse on the *Tafsir-e Mazhari* was fixed to take place today. Should His Honour be pleased to so command, the relevant pages may be taken out from the box, Bismillah pronounced, and reading from the text commenced.'

I recalled that Qazi Sanaullah sahib, of Panipat, was one of the most distinguished disciples and deputies to the Presence and was then writing a large commentary on the Quran, which he named *Tafsir-e Mazhari*.

Before replying, the Presence cast a most kindly glance at us, as if indicating that we could now go if we wanted to. Both of us rose and, after seeking permission to visit again, I took a step backward towards the courtyard, where we had left our shoes near the steps of the outer veranda. But when Budh Singh Qalandar sahib raised his head after kissing Mirza sahib's hand, he commanded, 'Mian Qalandar, Maulavi sahib, always keep in the front of your mind the holy commandment of the Sovereign of the Universe.' He then recited, in the original Arabic and in marvellously pure accents, the Prophet's saying which can be translated as: *So should I not be a slave who is grateful?*

I remembered instantly that the chain of attribution of the tradition that he recited originates with Ayesha, the Prophet's favourite wife. And it occurred to me that the Presence was suggesting to us that having such a wife as his was, in his eyes, a divine boon. For, the constant presence of a termagant in the house kept him from pride and vanity, reaffirming his status as just another human being. All the time, she trampled to non-existence his sense of self and his pride of achievement.

*

Budh Singh sahib's syce waited for us right beside the main door. But he didn't ride at once, thus making me walk some more with him. I was quite delighted. He was quiet; perhaps he was trying to find words suitable to his purport. And in fact, I was also not sure what I should say in the context of what we saw. But I was apparently wrong, for he stopped hard by Rajji Sajji's tomb, and began to say, 'A student arrived at the Presence, Bayazid Bustami's august door; having travelled a far distance and passed through hill and river, his one desire was to cast his eyes at the Presence's sacred visage, seek his blessing, and perhaps learn from him, should he deign to teach him at all. During those days the Shaikh kept his estate hidden, not letting many people know of the high station that he had arrived at in his journey towards God. There were no seekers, no students, not to speak of any servitors or attendant at that auspicious door.'

He paused, looked at me briefly, perhaps wanting to ascertain if he wasn't wearying me. But I was quite attentive. He went on, 'He knocked, and a woman replied in harsh, strident tones, "Go! Get! You stupid lout who knocks at the door of that feckless, jobless lazybones! That pretender to hard labour, he would be asleep somewhere under the shade of a tree. Go; look for him in the jungle. There's none called Shaikh Bayazid here!"

'Obviously, the tired and exhausted student hadn't ever heard such dulcet syllables or such a honeyed voice. He lost his nerve and ran to the jungle at the outskirts of the city. Directly as he entered a coppice, he was vouchsafed a vision, or the sight of the Shaikh, riding a powerful lion. The young man flinched at this out-of-the-world vision, and was about to turn tail when the Shaikh commanded: "Have no fear. I lend my ears to her, he lends himself to me."'

I said, 'Kind sir, you tell a telling anecdote, and so well suited to the occasion. I too knew that because of the extreme delicateness of his temperament, and his love for beauteous persons and things, the Presence, Mirza sahib, was commanded from somewhere that he should marry such and such a lady. But I keep before me always the True Utterance of the Almighty, and always repeat it to myself in my heart. The worshipful Presence has been apportioned so heavy a load, but he also has been bestowed with the strength to stand it. My prayer is the same as the Quranic prayer that the Lord not place a burden on me such that I am unable to sustain it. The kind of burden that is the Presence's fortune would certainly crush me into the dust.'

Qalandar smiled. 'But don't you remember the Almighty's sacred words to the effect that Allah does not burden a soul above that soul's capacity? Were it not so, weaker ones like me would have long ago been riding on the shoulders of four of our fellow human beings!'

Well, this certainly is a brilliant and witty individual, I said in my heart. May God preserve him. Mir Muhammad Taqi says in his *tazkirah* about Tek Chand Bahar sahib that God may guide him and bestow Islam upon him. But really, who knows who is fated to receive guidance, and at whose hands?

I brought myself back to the world and, extending my hands for a warm handshake, I said, 'I hope to see you one week from today at the appointed time in the madrasa. You remember it's Friday today?'

'How could I forget, Maulavi sahib? I will see you then, as Allah Wills,' he said, and turned to ride away on his truly magnificent mount. I walked on, but I was so immersed in my thoughts that I found myself very near Sitti Begam's house. Perhaps the little, though extremely sour, glimpse of Mirza sahib's married life put my mind, by some strange power of association, to the married life of my dear sister. How was she doing? Was she well looked after? Properly valued by her in-laws? May God save her, my sister was so even-tempered, so equable in her dealings, and she spoke and talked so engagingly, there was no doubt at all of her being not happy there. I congratulated Mian Baqaullah in my heart over his good fortune to be married to her. One among many contrary examples was the Presence, Mirza sahib—may God preserve him and save him—whose wife was nothing more than a continual test of his self-respect, fortitude and forbearance. Being husband to such a one, I thought, had surely placed him among the ranks of living martyrs.

I didn't actually enter my sister's house. Visiting her without notifying her and her people in advance was not in the best taste. I said a prayer for her safety and continued happiness, and retraced my steps towards Phatak Teliyan.

*

Teaching *Mir Zahid Mulla Jalal* to young (and perhaps not very interested) students absorbed a little too much of my energy and kept my attention focused on just that abstruse text, that it was many months before I thought of anything personally significant to me. Except, that is, the image of the mysterious Rider, which seemed to have been stamped on my brain. It was more like, really, a face, or a scene, which I had dreamed once, long ago. But whenever the stamp, however dim, rose up in my thinking and feeling mind, I experienced the same sense of some unfinished task, some duty not done. That fiery question mark which had seared my soul in the early days was no longer there, but the image remained.

And then, one day, I actually saw the Rider in my dream. Or perhaps I was wide awake. I didn't really understand the way it happened. But I must have been awake—no, I must have been sleeping over my book.

I beheld him clearly and saw that he left no shadow behind him— so I must have been dreaming. I saw him at the principal gate of the school. I saw him turning towards the gate, making over the bridle of his mount to a syce. My little seat in the school's common room was actually in a corner, and the common room could not be descried from it, anyway. The wide gate seemed like a mirror, reflecting everything, or was it actually the gate? I rose in confusion. The book that I had been studying fell to one side; my formal chador, the *tailsan*, worn by all faculty when they were in school, somehow impeded my rising properly and I stumbled. By the time I disengaged myself from the chador, the scene, or the dream, the Rider, if it was he, had disappeared.

I didn't mention the incident (or the dream?) to anyone, not even to Budh Singh sahib, who visited every Friday. Yet, in fact, there wasn't much learning or teaching for me or him. Most often, something in the Arabic lesson reminded him of something else, especially a verse in Persian, and he would be off at a tangent, joyously reciting verse upon Persian verse. It was a very rare occasion, though, that he said any of his own verses to me. But one day, he closed the Arabic lesson abruptly and without my asking him, began to recite his verses:

My heart has no inclination towards living
What use is living then, when I have no heart?

His recitation was so passionate, so emotion arousing, that it seemed to me that the poem must be about his own self. I felt rather anxious, and in fact seriously troubled. Poets rarely used themselves as the subject of their poems. A recent Persian verse of our Mirza sahib, though, did seem to be somewhat personal. It was on everyone's tongue in Delhi ever since it was first heard on some occasion, though Mirza sahib was, as usual, not present there:

It's a whole lifetime
since he has been composing lamentations before his beloved in poetry's
form
And yet, it seems that Mazhar is still not counted among the poets.

So it was the case, I mused, that sometimes the poets spoke of themselves and didn't just compose a theme to express their virtuosity. But Qalandar sahib was now on his next verse:

Dear my counsel giver, the tears shall stop very gradually
It is no laughing matter: it is weeping.

By Allah, the second line was so utterly eloquent, so stunningly moving, it burst into my consciousness like an explosive. One would have liked nothing better but to say the line over and over again, enjoying its emotional affect, its verbal dexterity. Praise the verse as much as I could, Qalandar sahib was oblivious. His eyes closed, his body swaying like a slender branch in gentle breeze, he seemed not to have heard me at all.

I suddenly noticed that his voice was becoming hoarse, as if something was choking him, or God forbid, as if he was breaking into tears. I rose in a hurry, thinking to fetch him a cup of water, but he opened his eyes, looked at me gravely, as if he was to impart some important secret, and began to recite his *rubai*:

When, sometime, Qalandar will incline to do so
He will snatch his heart back from you, and go away
And your looking at him every day with knotted brow
Will avail nothing to anyone, unnoticed in the coign of neglect.

Before he finished speaking the rubai, he rose and, quite contrary to his style, embraced me, and spoke in tones of sad finality, 'All right, Maulavi sahib, I am now going away. Do you hear me, Maulavi sahib? I am dead.'

Then he recited the following Hindi verse almost in the same tone:

I am dead, but just in order that I may have a sight of you
A little breath of life remains in my eyes, like air in a bubble.

He recited the verse, threw down the paper on which he had written the poem as well as his Arabic textbook, and disappeared at a trice. By the time I sprang up and ran out of the gate, he was lost in the swarm of busy shoppers and sightseers around Fatehpuri. It occurred to me that today he was perhaps quite by himself, without his horse, its appurtenances and even his syce. Why was he alone today?

I didn't know what to do. There was none within my immediate reach or in my family whom I could consult and seek advice. And what was there to seek advice or instruction about? Was my Qalandar stricken in his brain, had he gone out of his mind? Is he in love with someone? But most young gentlemen who loved took the travails and joys of love in their stride; they passed through every stage in laughter or in tears, yet it was rare for someone to leave hearth and home, or pretend to be in love with death. Or perhaps there was no pretence there? But why did he wish to die, then? What affliction pained his spirit, his heart? Should I present myself before the Exalted Presence, Mirza sahib, and seek succour from him? But what should I tell him, and what inquiry should I make of him? He might even get suspicious? I was nobody to push my nose into the affairs of others. And I don't know if it was at all proper to bruit such matters before the Presence, privately or in open assembly.

Qalandar sahib was my friend, though older in years and from a different stratum of society. Or perhaps he was more than a friend. Still, the distance between us was too great to be ignored. They were a business family; he was rich beyond my imagining. Or at least his family were rich beyond my imagining. I didn't know anything more about them. Should I dispatch a fast messenger to Lahore and inform his parents? Again, that would seem like unforgivable meddling. Surely, there were others in Qalandar sahib's business establishment who would keep his parents informed of what seemed to be happening here?

Budh Singh Qalandar: In that one being were gathered, for me at least, father, brother, friend. Riches of which I had ever remained deprived. True, my relationship had not yet progressed to open friendliness, such as that exists among peers or siblings. But I remained confident that Qalandar was the person to turn to, if I ever had a difficult problem or had a difficult decision to make. I knew he would pay his best mind to untangle my sleave of care, if it ever came to that. But now it was he who apparently stood in need of succour and rescue. Rescue from . . . ? From himself, maybe. Or had he some secret, some disease of the heart or body? Oh, how I wished that I could be of some assistance, lend him my helping hand in whatever hazardous enterprise he was about to embark upon!

A whole day passed in these cogitations, then the night, and the next day. I wasn't able to eat or sleep well despite Amma ji's loving ministrations. She applied the balm to my forehead, pressed my back and legs, said prayers and blew upon me. I pretended overwork at the madrasa, and a problem about teaching a new and abstruse text.

It was the evening of the third day since Qalandar sahib's last visit, so fraught with incomprehensible premonitions. I was stowing my workbooks and lecture notes at the end of the day when it occurred to me that I should consult, or perhaps plainly inquire from Baqaullah about what was wrong with Qalandar sahib. Was he not reputed to be an expert geomancer and master of the art of divination? Let him be of some real use to me as well.

*

The next day, I proceeded to Baqaullah's haveli immediately after doing my late morning prayers. He was in his meeting room already, with a couple of inquirers who sat respectfully at some distance from him. The moment Baqaullah saw me, he rose and, spreading his arms wide, he spoke a line of Persian verse:

Come close, and closer, that I may hug thee hard.

'My worshipful Bhai jan, welcome,' he continued. 'How may I serve you? Would you like me to let you on to some news of Budh Singh sahib?'

I was shaken. I had never told Baqaullah about my friendship with

Qalandar sahib; perhaps my sister had mentioned something to him in passing. But how did he know of my purpose, that I came to inquire about Qalandar sahib? I prevaricated. 'Well, can I not visit my own sister and brother-in-law in love and friendship?'

He saw that I was being evasive and needed privacy before I would card out and unknot my skein of anxieties and questions before him.

'Let's to the zenana,' he said to me and, turning towards his visitors, he spoke politely, almost humbly: 'Please to wait for a short while, dear sirs. I'll be back soon.'

He then took me to his private chamber, a small sanctum sanctorum where he studied and meditated and where none could enter without prior and explicit permission. I hadn't yet properly seated myself, reclining against a bolster, that he began to say, 'Bhai jan, he is now a traveller of other paths, other destinations. He rides a mount which flies with the speed of the wind. You cannot reach him now.'

I was somewhat piqued. I was hoping for some good tidings, and tidings *en clair*, not those metaphoric conceits. 'Hey, come on. Say what you wish to say in plain words, don't expect me to solve your riddles.'

I realized that I had spoken rather more sharply than I intended. But Baqaullah's humour remained unruffled. He answered, 'You will see for yourself in a day or two. His body and soul are now feverish with another kind of fire, and it is but a matter of time that it becomes a conflagration. He is not among us for long.'

'What do you mean, God forbid, is he sick with some mortal disease?'

'Don't talk like an immature youth, Bhai jan.' He laughed lightly. 'There are sicknesses and sicknesses. His eye was entangled with another's, but his purpose was not achieved, or perhaps he himself didn't want to bring the business to the wished-for consummation. I haven't examined this matter in any detail, but I can do that, if you so desire. But . . .'

He paused. It was unusual for him to pause when making predictions. Some doubt, or maybe fear, seemed to grip him for a moment.

'But what? Can we not do something to help him?'

He smiled a wan smile. 'We certainly can, but he doesn't want to be helped. I told you, he is now a traveller of paths untrodden by most men. Previously, the matter wasn't much more than what Hafiz said.'

He recited a famous verse from Hafiz:

A proud beauty-idol took my heart and went away
She came into my house, snatched the burning coal, and went away.

He went on: 'Dear Bhai jan, sorry, but that fire has now burnt down the harvest of his sense to ashes. You are an Arabic scholar, you must be aware of the proverb 'Love is a fire that destroys all but the desired one', but the difference here is that his desired one is no longer what he desires. So in just one jump, he vaulted across the barrier between Appearance and Reality.'

'So what should I do now? Should I send word to his parents?'

'It's not necessary. The parents can't do a thing, and they'll soon get to know anyway.'

'But how did you get to know all this?'

'Actually, last night during meditation and later when I drew up the map of all your stars, I got a suggestion that I find out about Budh Singh Qalandar for the benefit of Khairuddin. You know, we normally don't get to know specific things unless some interested party wants them to be revealed to them. In other words, we can answer questions, but not raise questions ourselves. But sometimes, especially when the subject is important to us and we are in good earnest, we can do some investigations on our own asking.' He paused. 'Well, actually, that is my modus. I can't say about others.' He fell into a grave silence. I had no further notions and didn't know what to ask.

He raised his head, 'Bhai jan, his fortunes are looking quite the other way now.'

'I'll go to him directly from here,' I said urgently.

'It won't solve anything. Do as you please. You may go there or not, but he is gone.'

'What do you mean? Is he dead, God forbid?'

'No, but he is dead for you and me and all of us.'

My interview with Baqaullah terminated on this enigmatic note. Since it was school time by then, I went off to the madrasa.

I passed the hours, somehow. Teaching, contemplating, explaining, asking and answering questions, but I was like an automatical doll, such as the Chinese make. I went through the motions, as those dolls do, without the sense of those motions.

After the asr prayers of early evening, before going home, I took the left turn from Billimaron towards Tiraha Bairam Khan, just a little beyond Jogi Wara where stood the sky-kissing haveli of Qalandar sahib's parents. I wasn't quite arrived there when I noticed an unusual medley: people coming and going with some serious purpose or urgency writ on their faces; people talking, gesticulating among themselves; a profusion of pack animals and carts. I noticed that everybody had some luggage, in hand or on the head, or loaded on a cart or animal. Allah, what's going on here? I heard someone say that Budh Singh Qalandar has declared open day for all comers: Let anyone come and take away whatever they fancied in his haveli. What does that mean? I was nearly at my wits' end. I wanted to stop and reprimand those idle wastrels who were enjoying the frenzied plunder.

'He let go all the cash early in the morning. His coffers were open to all. And now it is the household effects,' I heard someone say in a matter-of-fact voice, and hurried on to find out for myself.

Heavy carpets from Bokhara on someone's head; someone sporting a blue Chinese flower vase; another lugging on his head a huge man-sized Aleppo mirror that had a wide and exquisitely painted border. Obviously, he couldn't afford a labourer or draught animal to carry it and it was all he could do to balance it on his bent head, supported by his hands. Another had on his shoulders a bolt of Kashani velvet. A lout, certainly not a fancier, had a pair of huge Shirazi pigeons, tall, erect of head, apparently enjoying the sights and sounds of the bazaar. They were grey-eyed, a beautiful white and ash-grey in colour. I hoped he wasn't going to slaughter them for food. Someone had a dog handler and trainer with him, holding on the leash a pair of absolutely magnificent Arabian hounds, tall, of narrow waist and deep chest, their coat tawny and silken, eyes a strange reddish brown. I then noticed a whole gang of seven or eight, supporting a master bed on their shoulders, not supporting so much as just letting their shoulders and bodies manage its weight and let them carry on, out of breath. The legs of the bedstead were solid silver, its frame and head made of ebony, the counterpane of thin, yellow, silken Mirzapuri carpet. Upon the bed were two large pillows in light-blue satin with Kashmiri embroidery, two small pillows for placing under the cheeks, and very light but large quilts from Jaipur, soft as flower petals. Yet another fellow had a silver washbasin, so heavy that he managed to hold it with difficulty. A whole cartload of books, apparently lifted indiscriminately by a bookseller from the library, glinted with gold decorations on their spines. A pair of glittering brass candlesticks, as tall almost as a man, loaded on a mule mercilessly, along with a bundle of cords for burning. A copper and silver betel box, nearly twenty pounds in weight, thrown together with a pair of large copper and bronze trays.

The procession, or the pillage, seemed endless. Was it a repeat of Nadir Shah's depredation or were they Ahmad Shah Durrani's soldiers, carrying off whatever booty they could find? God, did so much remain in the haveli even after Nadir Shah and Ahmad Shah? The day was about to end, but not the rape of the haveli. And where was Budh Singh Qalandar himself?

I crept along, or in fact was pushed along by the marauding multitude. The crush was so great at the main gate of the haveli that I could hardly stay on my legs. I turned to go back, most unwillingly, but unable to understand what I should do there if I stayed. In the throng, I glimpsed the syce, but no horse. What a magnificent beast it was. I hoped and prayed that Qalandar sahib kept it, or it fell to the lot of someone who would know its value and not destroy it by yoking it as a packhorse. I tried to elbow my way towards the syce, but I couldn't. Cursing the multitude in my heart, I arrived at the main road and found further progress blocked. Perhaps the crowd was assembled to look at Qalandar sahib? I could no longer behave in a civilized manner, and jostled and elbowed to the centre.

It was he. By Allah, it was he. He had on a plain dress, ochre-saffron in colour, and he was barefooted. I was glad to see him riding the horse. A short dagger hung by his waist, neck held high, a large turquoise worn round the neck like an amulet. A very brief smile on his lips, as if regarding the world as the playground of fools, or as if he were in a marriage party and he the bridegroom. The people surrounded him like a vulgar mob, stretching their necks, extending their arms and hands like beggars: someone entreating for a son; someone asking for the boon of employment; someone asking for his son to come back safe from a far journey; a widow was praying for death being granted to her, she wept and cried that she could not bear poverty and loneliness any longer. But he seemed to hear nothing, unaffected by the cries and tears. The road was not open for him to pass; nor did he seem to ask the horde to let him pass. Perhaps he awaited someone?

Our eyes met for a fleeting moment. I sensed a slight smile in his eyes even, as if he were saying to me: So what do you think of all this? Don't you find it fun? Then it seemed to me that he nodded at me, as if asking me to come up to him, or rather, approving of such a step if I did take it.

I took a step forward, trying to wade through the host that separated me from him. But I immediately felt discouraged. I don't know if it was because of the solid phalanx before me, or because my heart was not in it. I said to myself, so what will you do there? Budh Singh Qalandar had countless ancestral wealth to open it up for the world to pillage. He had riches more than sufficient for a hundred generations. Above all, he had a heart; it's the heart that makes people go the way they do. And what do you have? You are a petty schoolteacher; you don't own a horse even. He who has the heart of a man, of a lion, let him do what he will. Let him love and give away his heart to his desired one. Let him cherish his heart, and worship the heart of whom he desires. Let him give away his life, his soul, to the object, the purpose, that he craves.

In fact, it is the poet types who talk about such things. Poets and their flights of fancy. They don't do what they say; is that not the Quranic pronouncement? But don't the Sufis also talk of *ahl-e dil*, 'he who has the heart', and of *sahib dil*, 'he who is the owner of a heart'? Maybe, I was as much a stranger to Sufism as to the world of writing poems. The Sufis say that it is the heart which knows Truth; it is the heart that absorbs Truth. Those who have no heart cannot perceive the Radiant Glory of Truth. That's what the Persian poet meant when he said that without the heart, everything is devoid of meaning:

Without the heart, none of the colour and design of the world has
meaning
The object of life was there, on the page that is darkened now.

Aren't we back in the realm of poetry? I must remember the Quran again: 'Poets are those who have lost their way.' It seems to me that much of Sufism is to be understood in terms of poetry. So? So, nothing. Let the poets fly on their imagined wings. I don't care.

I could see that he was about to depart, and I didn't know where. I pushed and jostled to get near him. I took a small step towards him. But my spirit was hot in its bitter harangue to me: Who are you, the Great Maulavi of the Rahimiya? Where is your heart? You have only trained and polished your mind a bit, it's not enough to let you fly in the open skies of knowledge. Are you prepared to let your learning crash into your heart, as the great poet Rumi said one should do if one wants to do well before the eyes of God? But your heart, it's less than a blank page. The page that burns to ashes in the invisible fire of non-existence is not to be found in the learned treatises of Mulla Abdul Hakim Sialkoti and Mir Zahid.

Qalandar's parents? They aren't a poor, supportless widow, like your mother. Who will take care of her? Qalandar's parents are immeasurably rich; their money will be the surrogate for their son. They will weather the storm. But your poor mother? Her life has been the target of one storm after the other. Do you want to leave her alone?

I hesitated, then stopped struggling against the throng. Our eyes met again. Budh Singh Qalandar bent his head a little, and placed his right hand on his heart. His face bore no smile now, but a strange gravity, as if he were telling me, I accept your decision with all my heart and soul.

Was that some kind of a signal for the people who blocked my progress towards him? Suddenly, the swarm opened a path for him and he went away at a fast trot, proud and self-composed, not looking to right or left, ignoring the supplicants, ignoring me. I heard someone clearly, saying to me:

None held his reins to stop him. He rode away.

My hair stood on end; for a moment it seemed to me that the speaker was right by my side. But there was no one there, naturally. It was my superstition, or my heated mind at best, that was making me hear things that were not. Not even as much as the breath that one emits as one speaks. I tried to reason with myself. You must have heard or read that line of poetry somewhere. It just rose up, like a phantom, from your memory and you thought you composed another line to make it a whole verse. In fact, you must have read a story where that second line occurred, as a part of the narrative, and the propulsive power of the narrative took you far away, misleading you down the road of memory. You think destinies are made and unmade like this? Be assured, that Rider was a phantom, a phantom of your mind, the function of the power of suggestion. If that wasn't the case, why did different persons see a different Rider, even to the extent of seeing a dromedary as against a stallion, a woman as against a man? Do you need more proof of the fact that it was all a play of the mind? If there *was* a Rider, he must have been a master juggler, or conjurer, a warlock, a king of magicians, like Afrasiab in the *Dastan of Amir Hamza*. Hasan bin Sabbah, Hakim Ibn-ul Muqanna, Hakim Qistas-ul Hikmat, numerous conjurers, sorcerers, appeared upon the world, and went away, obliviated forever. Were everyone to believe them to be authoritative and sacred, the world today would not be the workshop of God that it is, but the stamping ground of devils, and ghouls, and Satan himself.

I beg God's protection! So should I understand that Rider to be the devil, or the work of Satan? No. Not at all. You don't need to understand anything at all. There are many things happening, and have happened in this world of creation and mischief, which cannot even be dreamed of in your philosophy. Things happen the cause of which, or even the name of which, remains hidden from the eye or understanding of man. Why should you worry about things that don't concern you? Look to yourself, look to your life and welfare. You are not here to solve riddles or probe depths.

But tell me, someone again whispered to my heart, why did that line of poetry occur to you alone? Or should I rather say, why were you alone inspired to compose that line, and then the second line? God knows, I am no poet, and certainly never wrote anything in Persian.

Well, do you think that you are someone special? I ask, are you the vehicle of destiny? And are destinies fashioned or unfashioned through insignificant persons like you? Are lines of poetry repositories of fate and fortune?

Worried by my thoughts, or worrying my thoughts like a puppy worrying an old slipper, I reached home. There was no question of passing through the flower-sellers' market that evening. I barely ate my food, though Amma ji had again prepared a special dish for me. Amma ji asked, and asked again, what was the matter with me, but I told her some fib about having a bad headache. And if I was minded to tell her, what could I tell her, after all? She had heard about Budh

Singh Qalandar, and was sorry, but she had no idea of the depth of my feelings for him. And even if she knew, how could she understand my suspicion that Qalandar sahib was also a kind of . . . A kind of what? Let me say the word: A kind of Rider. Is that not folly, a supreme kind of folly? I reprimanded myself.

Folly? All right, it was a folly, my great folly. But still, there was a thistle somewhere in the thickets of my heart, and it went on pricking, sometimes to the quick, sometimes gently. And occasionally, I would encounter him, though from far. And when I saw him, the thorn seemed to reach yet deeper into my soul. He had very soon become known everywhere as a saintly person, a true man of God, and one who had reached the closest to the Divine Gates. Thus wherever he appeared, seekers of favour surrounded him. But no one ever saw him speak a word. If he needed to convey something to a favour seeker, he would beckon with his fingers, his gestures so vague, or mysterious, that nobody could dare interpret them with any degree of certainty. Still, this did not deter the needy, the favour seeker, and the hungry for his blessings.

He had not left his haveli, but he rarely went inside. He made the small gatehouse his abode. His parents came from Lahore to look after him, if not to actually persuade him to live in the haveli as befitted his status in society. But he would never let them come near him; he always gestured to them, as if to say, I am all right without you or your attentions. Utterly frustrated, his father returned to Lahore, but his mother stayed back to serve him and look to his needs as best she could. She would have his favourite dishes cooked under her supervision, but he never ate even a morsel and had the entire food distributed among the poor.

Another strange thing happened after some months, or weeks, had passed. It was talked about among his neighbours that Qalandar sahib ate very sparsely, and in fact not more often than once in a week or ten days. His mother still had the food prepared as before, hoping to attract his appetite. A perhaps stranger thing was that though he was practically starving himself, his face showed no sign of frailness, like the sinking of the cheeks, black shadows around the eyes, or inability or unwillingness to move about. There was no emaciation, no wasting away.

As for me, after that day, I hadn't even looked him in the eyes, far less spoken to him. Still, perhaps both of us were acutely conscious of each other's existence in our lives. Every week or ten days, I made it a point to pass in front of his haveli. I am unable to explain now, as I was then, why I did this. All that I can say is that perhaps this was our way of telling each other of having a place in each other's life. My feet touched those paths and that threshold which Budh Singh Qalandar's feet had also touched. Because his mother stayed on, the haveli was full of the usual drove of servitors: doorkeeper, palanquin bearer, cook, male servants for outdoor duties, and housemaids for the interior. In spite of this, except when Qalandar sahib made an appearance, that huge house felt silent and desolate. Or perhaps it was the desolation of my heart. Once, as I passed that way, I heard someone say that Qalandar sahib used occasionally to answer his mother in monosyllables, but had now completely stopped talking.

Then, one day, I heard people say that Qalandar sahib has left Delhi and has gone to live in Bareilly, a hundred and fifty miles away in the north-east. Why did he go away, or did he really go to Bareilly, none could say for certain. He had, indeed, a large number of followers and admirers in those areas, especially Saharanpur, Moradabad, even Agra in the south, but no special disciple or follower was reported to be in Bareilly. I didn't stop passing by his haveli occasionally, though it was now quite silent. Even his mother had left Delhi; I didn't know where she went. Perhaps crazed by the fire of motherly love, she went to Bareilly to look for her son. Or perhaps she went back to Lahore to be with her ageing husband. All that I knew was that an ancient water carrier would be seen going into the haveli, or coming out of it. His duty was to give water and food to a rosy-headed parakeet, much loved by Qalandar sahib's mother; to water and give minimum care to the *maulsari*, the pomegranate and other trees in the inner garden;

to water the sacred tulsi plant in front of the small temple she and her husband had constructed at one end of the inner veranda. He spoke to none and none spoke to him. A professional lamp-lighter from Tiraha Bairam Khan would appear every evening, light a small chandelier in the gateway, and leave.

*

Days became months, and the months soon became years. My melancholia was with me, as ever. Sometimes I was deep in it and sometimes it was just below the surface of my heart. However, it did not interfere with my teacherly duties. In fact, my reputation as a teacher grew with my temporal age. I commanded a small reputation in the circles of good teachers and scholars. In the eyes of the world, I was a fortunate young man: Fatherless, I had still made good in life. I had a small family, a family that doted on me. What else could one pray for before Allah's Exalted Throne? True, I wasn't married yet, while most males of my age would have long been married and would have fathered a baby or two. But some of us Dilliwallahs married late, and some never. So I wasn't something queer in my peers' eyes. Amma ji certainly tried often to cajole me into marriage, but she had given up, of late. It seemed clear to her that I would take my time before I married, if ever I did.

I was now in my twenty-third year. I was clearly taller and stronger. I was fond of physical exercises, which I did twice a week at a local akhara where actual or aspiring wrestlers, weightlifters and others who wanted to improve their bodies, practised at a nominal fee. My body was quite supple and muscular; my beard had grown to a really manly size, but I did not wear it long, or very thick. Unlike other men of religion, I did not trim or shave the hair on my upper lip. I wore it more like a pair of moustaches, not long or heavy, but prominent, and slightly twirled on both sides. In fact, I looked more like a soldier than a teacher at a madrasa.

The year was 1769, the season of Basant was on us. The sun was just arrived in the station of Aquarius. The weather was changing, with winter on its way out and the arrival of summer on the horizon. There were holidays at the madrasa, ostensibly in honour of various days of holy visitation to the tombs of Delhi's great Sufi saints, but actually to celebrate the Basant. The whole city was drenched in yellows, saffrons, ochres—the colours of the Basant. Hindu, Muslim, Sikh, Jain or Nanak Panthi, all had a taste for the Basant, a desire to be among the yellow flowers of the mustard, the last of the bright yellows of the numerous varieties of marigolds, the last of the yellow Firangi flowers whose name I could never pronounce.

The Exalted Pavilion of the Presence, Sultan ji Nizam-ud Din sahib, was almost drowning or choking under the crush and conflux of yellow- or saffron-clad devotees of all persuasions.

It is said that in the beginning, the Muslims had no taste for the Basant or its fairs and its songs and dances. But from the day the Presence, Sultan ji sahib, and Amir Khusrau reportedly became connected with the Basant, the Muslims, giving way to their natural desire for gaiety and for intermixing, began to celebrate it in their own way. Muslim celebrations began in the middle of the month of Pus, or Pausha—almost the time of the apogee and then the decline of the winter sun. Specific celebrations by the Muslims to 'offer the Basant' began from the night the Basant moon was sighted. The first Basant, offered on the night of the moon, was for Allah, at the foot of the Bhojla Hill, just below the last stair of the Jama Masjid, on the eastern side. Then, as the sun was rising, the second Basant was offered at the Holy Footprint of the Prophet. This was followed the next day by the offering of the Basant at the Holy Sepulchre of the Pole of Poles, the Exalted Presence, Khvajah Bakhtiar sahib Kaki, may God have Mercy upon his soul, at Mehrauli (or the Khvajah Sahib, as the village was called by king and commoner alike). The next Basant to be offered was by the qawwals, who presented it at the Sacred Mausoleum of the Sultan of all the Friends of God, the Presence, Nizam-ud Din sahib Auliya Sultan ji.

And so on, the Basant was offered at the Exalted Courts of the remaining of the twenty-two Sufi masters, or Khvajahs, of Delhi. Accompanying each Basant was a horde of visitors, seekers of blessings, singers, dancers, courtesans, the beautiful ones of Delhi, that City of Beauty. Present at each Basant were acrobats, conjurers, flower-sellers, curio-sellers and numerous other professionals. I always wondered if the same professionals thronged every Basant, or there were professionals specific to each Basant. Whatever, but the beautiful people were always there, and almost always the same.

It was the twelfth day of Magha, I too was out to enjoy the sights and sounds and the music of the Basant and thus beguile my melancholy at bit. It was the day of the Basant to be offered to the Presence, the patron Sufi saint of the city, Shah Kalimullah sahib of Jahanabad. A posse of qawwals was on its way to the Sacred Presence, singing a Hindi ghazal from Shah Mubarak Abru sahib, may God shower His Kindness upon him:

The yellow-clad people, celebrating the Basant
with pomp and radiance,
From all four sides of the world, will arise today
the Basant.
The colours of autumn have crowded over, bubbling
with the colours of spring;
Beauty and love have been brought together
by the Basant.
Why are all those, afflicted by love, yellow all over?
Whose beauty is the heart's desire of the Basant?
These are live coals, not the flowers of the dhak:
It's the season of madness in love, and the fire of
disunion is lit by the Basant.

I wasn't clad in yellow—I had to keep some dignity as a teacher, after all. But it really seemed that the whole environment was burning, blazing with the fire of the beauty of the yellow-clad ones. And Shah Mubarak sahib's ghazal, it was so moving, so powerful, that even my heart craved for someone whose remembrance might make my face look pale.

Almost quite opposite the Exalted Portal of the Presence, Kalimullah sahib, was a mendicant, a fakir—his looks and his dress both comely—singing some verses of the eleventh-century Persian poet, Sanai Ghaznavi. Oh, those verses, and the voice, they were so thrilling, and the mendicant's total obliviousness to the celebrant crowd, his absorption in the poem so enchanting—his whole self seemed to be the embodiment of raptness and assimilation. There was a slight crease on his brow, but not of pain, but of masterly concentration, as he sang:

Don't make bare your life-enhancing beauty
And if you do so, go burn yourself like
a grain of bitter rue crackling on live coals.
And what is that beauty of yours?
Your intoxication,
And what that grain of bitter rue?
Your whole being.

I said to myself in my sceptical heart: Well, let there *be* someone before whom one could reveal the intoxication of one's life-enhancing, intoxicating beauty. And then destroy one's self, one's being, in the fire of unity, saying in silent words: There's no one now. You and only you are everywhere.

Suddenly, it seemed to me that there was someone, someone looking at me.

I raised my eyes in surprise; maybe it's an old schoolmate. Who else could be here who would know me? I saw a *havadar*—that is, an open palanquin—borne by four bearers. And someone clad in the colour of the Basant, looking at me. I didn't want to look for one second more, but my eye somehow quite forgot for a moment to look down, as I had been taught to, in front of women or strangers.

Very light-brown complexion, almost the colour of newly harvested wheat. Large, dark-black, radiant eyes, under the arch of dense eyebrows, looking at me. *Me?* Very long black hair, two braids, braided one over the other, falling on the left breast; though unadorned, the braid was heavy, as if it was depressing the prominent breasts somewhat. Wide upper garment, or jamah, in yellow muslin, which was light, but the sulphur-coloured gold embroidery gave it sufficient body. The jamah was very narrow at the waist, or perhaps the waist itself was narrow—I thought of the mythical single hair which grew from the waist, or which *was* the waist of the beautiful beloved. A very short, but not unduly tight tunic on the upper body, short enough to let a glimpse of the velvet stomach. A gold-embroidered tight bodice under the tunic, the embroidery heavy on the sleeves, light on the actual breast-hills. Tall, proud neck, adorned by a long necklace of grey pearls. Just in the centre of the barely suggested cleavage, a breast-and-neck ornament called *dhukdhuki*, for it was supposed to rise and fall with the wearer's breath. The dhukdhuki in pale gold, with the jewel itself being a deep blue, encrusted with yellow sapphires all around. A single-stone emerald earring in each ear, pendant with long gold threads and chain. The emerald itself was set in Jaipur's blue enamel work. A nose pin of light-red ruby, affixed in gold, and the ruby the size of a pea. She wore green and yellow, thin, delicate glass bangles whose lightness was ameliorated by heavy, solid gold bangles whose circles were closed with gold clasps shaped like the lion's jaws. On her feet, very light, very small shoes, their toes very small and their wall so low that the arabesque artistry of the henna work on the feet could be seen. The shoes had betel-shaped toes, fully encrusted with gemstones, white sapphires, I supposed. A ring on one finger of each hand, a diamond on the ring finger of the right hand, and a large, yellow sapphire on the index finger of the left hand. The nails of the fingers and the toes were polished in a natural colour polish, somewhat roseate but not obvious. The fingers and the palms of each hand were again bursting into red with arabesque henna work. She wore a wide, red leather band on her left hand; on the band, a young falcon, looking at the world with cold eyes. The skirt of the jamah was raised a little, so that the delicate ankles and a hint of the rise of the delicately made calves could be glimpsed. Heavy ankle ornaments in silver from somewhere in the eastern part of the land, their design complex and full of little silver bells. Her trousers were in the heavy flowery silk called *gulbadan*, so tight all over as if it was pasted, not worn on the body. But there must needs have been some fold, some wrinkle, if it was a true fabric. Here, what I could see was just a slope of body, cylindrical, smooth and easy, like silk. I recalled Navab Dargah Quli Khan's book *Muraqqa-e Dihli* (A Delhi Album) of a generation ago. In it, he had told of a courtesan called Ad Begam, who didn't wear trousers, but had her lower body painted so cleverly and with such finesse, that though naked below the waist, she created the illusion of being properly clothed. So was this begam too . . . ? I almost took a step backward, in shock, and promptly lowered my gaze.

Actually, at that time, I dared take just a brief look at that lovely rose of the garden of grace and loveliness. The details were somehow printed on my brain, just as a master printer prints flowery designs on a piece of cloth in myriad colours. Needless to say, I recalled every detail, every grace, when I was back at home, comparatively free from her enchantment.

And then, the moment I recalled Ad Begam, and I had that vile suspicion about . . . about her clothed or unclothed body, it was as if no blood would flow if one were to cut me. I no longer had the power, or the pluck, to raise my eyes again. I kept my eyes glued to my shoes. Who knew when a breeze would arise, or she changed her stance, and the loose jamah would be raised higher, or be rucked up, to reveal . . . ? God help me, I had no power in my will to walk away, no strength in me to raise my eyes.

At last, at long last, I raised my eyes, slowly, timidly, like a criminal raising his eye to the judge's face before pronouncement of sentence.

Those eyes were still on me, not intensely, or with any degree of deliberate absorption, but just as the eye alights upon an interesting sight, and stays there.

I didn't know what to do. Should I salaam her, and thus acknowledge that I knew she was looking at me, and she knew that I knew? But how, or why, should I greet her? I didn't know her at all. And it was clear even to me that although she had the dignity, the self-confidence and the assurance of a princess, a woman who let herself be carried through a rolling, roiling multitude in an open bazaar, couldn't be anything else but a courtesan. I had been taught to run even from the shadow of the likes of such, far less have any kind of connection, or even acquaintance with them. But how long should I stand here, rooted to the earth like a clown who had lost the role that he was playing? And I didn't at all have the courage, or the heart, to turn away. Involuntarily, or in spite of myself, my right hand rose up in salaam, my head bent low, and then my hand moved of its own accord to the left side of my breast.

The moment my hand rose, the faint light of the smile, which had so far been confined to her eyes, moved down to her lips and face. I noticed now that the lips were utterly shorn of any kind of artificial support to their rosy redness. Not even the most popular redness, of betel nuts chewed occasionally, was evident: the redness was native to the lips. I don't now remember if it was only her head that was bent in acknowledgement, or if the hand was also raised. I knew that I was totally, utterly destroyed:

It's not easy to take away your head safe from that sword,
Oh Mazhar, someone bent before me in salaam!

I was now in a different kind of trouble: Should I go forward and open some kind of conversation, and if I do, what should I say? Do I introduce myself? Hah, even a rustic blockhead won't be so rustic!

My difficulty was partly solved by the lady herself, or her attendant. I noticed a young, good-looking girl, about thirteen or fourteen years of age, return from the Exalted Portal of Shaikh sahib, with something enclosed in a packet made from large, fresh leaves, in her hand. Obviously, she was returning from the Pavilion with some sweets, something like a portion of the sweets presented for benediction at the Exalted Threshold. She wore yellow, as the whole of the city did on this day: a long cotton tunic, quite clean and well cut, a pair of trousers called *ara* made of a plain cotton fabric called *sangi*, in the style of her mistress, but nothing so tight. Her ears adorned with plain earrings of apparently genuine pearls, part of her thick tresses in short braids falling on her forehead, a colourful dupatta covering her upper body quite effectively. She cast a casual, careless glance at me and took her seat in the open palanquin opposite her mistress.

The bearers effortlessly lifted the palanquin the moment she took her seat and went off briskly towards Matia Mahal. I had a vague hope that her departing mistress would look at me briefly before the palanquin turned away. But she was talking to her maid, and didn't even notice apparently, that they had moved away. I took an impulsive step forward, to walk, or even run after the palanquin, but my self-respect—whatever was left of it—pulled me back. I, and running after such a rider? Impossible. I quite suddenly recalled a Hindi verse of Mir Taqi sahib:

Loving is bad business, Mir ji yesterday
Ran after reed-riding young boys like a lowly servant.

Reed-riding young boys, heh, these poets, always these poets come to tease and harass me. But how will I find her then? And again I shrank back. What is all this drivel about finding her, or not finding her? My world is different, my afterworld is different. My truths are not her truths. My fables are not her fables. What connection could there be, or could be possible, between a person from the community of the people of enjoyment and carnal pleasure, and me, a Maulavi? Mian Khairuddin, do drive some sense into your thick head! Open your mouth after due thought; talk about sensible things. But what is the problem here? I just want to know who she is. I know she cannot have any fancy for me, and God forbid, nor do have I any such craving, or even the lightest interest. But this is Delhi, city of lovers, fanciers of the courtesans, hankerers after the boys. These matters are just purely spectatorly, purely of day-to-day watching, like sightseeing, casual coming and going. But I am not a spectator even, I am just a wayfarer. An uninterested passer-by.

My eyes were on nothing else but that open palanquin, which was now about to disappear in the crowd.

'*As-salam alaikum*, Maulavi sahib!' A strange, sudden voice assailed my ears. I felt like a thief, caught red-handed. I had no choice but to turn and face my accuser. It was the water carrier of my neighbourhood.

'*Wa-alaikum-as salam*, Mian Lal Muhammad. How do you happen to be here today?'

'Nothing much, Maulavi ji, but Ismat Jahan, whose havadar just passed this way, I and she are from the same part of the country. She commanded that I should present myself at the Portal of Shah Kalimullah today and offer free water to all visitors. I have been at this task for much of the day.'

'Ismat Jahan, who is Ismat Jahan?' I feigned ignorance. I did so by design, perhaps.

'The lady whose havadar just passed by close to Your Honour. Her tall, many-storeyed building is known to all in the Rajwaron ki Gali. Navab Ashraf-ud Daulah Afrasiab Khan Bahadur, the adoptive son of Zulfiqar-ud Daulah Najaf Khan Bahadur, he's a frequent visitor there.'

I mumbled some suitable reply, tipped him something and bade him goodbye. My heart was a battlefield of anxieties and desires. Where should I go? What should I do? I couldn't obviously go to her palatial haveli without introduction. Introduction or no, I must not go there.

The madrasa was closed due to the Basant, and I wasn't at all inclined to go home. I could certainly visit Sitti bibi and stay there awhile. But most probably she too would be at some Basant fair.

The bald truth was that I didn't want to go anywhere but to the one place and I was trying to find a reason for going there and not anywhere else.

I walked on, an aimless wanderer, until I found myself on the busy bank of the Jamna. But it was like vitriol in my ears, the noise and bustle, and the sight of so many attractive faces was poison ivy to me. As I approached the river, I had a faint hope that maybe Ismat Jahan would go there at sundown to watch the display of fireworks and the sight of the decorated, well-lighted budgerows frolicking upon the river. But why should I long for her sight? Is that not folly, callow, laughable folly? It's nothing but idle thought, it's impossible, it's madness!

My good birth, my closeness to the elders in the realm of learning and religion, my frequent presence at the assemblies of Men of God, the honour of being a teacher at a noble madrasa, was all this given for being blown away into the wind of lust? But did not Hafiz, the Tongue of the Unseen, advise:

Free living, and the life of desires, these are preferable when one is young.

Indeed, my learned Maulavi, you frown at them and berate them when the poets don't talk to your purpose, and you quote them gladly when their discourse suits you. I beg refuge with the One and only One Who has the Capability and Power. And it is He, none but Allah. Should I live the life of desires, the life of the rake and the roué, and give up all pretence to good birth, good breeding, good learning? Does an innocent desire, to look at Ismat Jahan again, and perhaps exchange a few words with her, have the same evil force of living a roué's life? I asked my heart, and someone answered. But that road leads to that destination, as Rumi said:

I fear, oh pious man, that you'll never reach Mecca
For the road that you walk, goes to Turkestan.

153

Marry her? But I haven't spoken a word to her. I don't know who she is, where she comes from . . . She is obviously a lady of high status; man, you wish to fly so much above your station! It is for dimwits like you that the women have the proverb, 'Let him piss into a Chinese pot and look himself in the face!' Who are you and what do you propose to bring to her? She is the favourite, if not whole-time mistress of Ashraf-ud Daulah; she plays with white and red bullion in the hundreds of thousands, and you, an insignificant Maulavi, and almost a pauper. Come to your senses, man! Think at least of the next few steps before trying to walk on water. It's not the first day even, and who knows what transactions, what dealings, what steep and narrow steps would have to be negotiated before you touch her door curtain even? And then, what next? Even after she admits you to her presence, even if she then lets you come closer, there could be a thousand twists and turns before you can touch her. You don't have even an inkling of what she intends to do with you. You are obviously besotted, but you must still be aware that women of her ilk are experts at playing with the hearts and lives of those who desire them. Those who are the likes of you, and who go to them, gamble with their lives, their honour, and they come back, their Faith, their peace of mind, their respectability, their social status, all destroyed forever. My business is with Mir Zahid and Taftazani, not with Chapter V of Saadi's *Gulistan,* which is about 'Love, and the Prime of Youth'.

The host on the Jamna's banks increased minutely, and so did my anxiety, and the crush and confusion of my thoughts. The drivers of the budgerows were now quite ready to float their boats; the women of the Hindus were already floating lamps in the river with prayers and pious vows. But who knows, there might be some Muslim women too among them? False beliefs and silly superstition were on the rise among the Muslims too. So what? Will you also float a lamp of prayer? God protect me from satanic evil inspirations and practices! It's too late now. I must go home.

*

But somehow it took me very long to reach home. Amma ji was frantic with worry, almost in tears. I made some weak, meaningless excuse, picked at my food, and went to bed silently, after doing my late-night prayer. The next morning, Amma ji unwontedly raised the question of my marriage. She hardly, if at all, broached the topic ever since I had made clear to her that I did not intend to, far less want to marry, at least for quite some time. This time, she didn't speak in any firm or questioning tone, she entreated: 'Dear son, it's becoming unbearable now, living in this empty house. Were a moon to shine here in my courtyard, my heart would be diverted.'

I felt unable to stay silent, and equally unable to say 'no'. A strange thing that happened then was that I didn't feel irritated or put upon at the mention of marriage. I sat there, not speaking, my head bent. This was encouragement enough for Amma ji. She said in almost eager tones, 'I know of an extremely good family, acquaintances of your blessed father, and like him, of soldierly background. In fact, I felt like sending my proposal immediately, and telling you later. But may Allah preserve you, for some reason you do take offence the moment your marriage is mentioned. So I thought I should ask you first.'

'Amma ji, I am not a tongueless girl child whom you can tie to anyone, anywhere at will.'

'Just see now, you are peeved to hear of marriage, as expected.' She spoke in conciliatory, almost imploring tones. 'Did I ever say that I even began to discuss the matter with them, not to speak of settling the issue? I was merely submitting a proposal. And the truth is, I don't have the stamina any longer to do all the housework. I have pain in the chest frequently. I don't know if I am long for—'

'Pain in the chest?' I cut her short, urgently. 'What kind of pain? Is it inside the chest? You never told me before, Amma ji.'

'Go on with you, young man. Am I going to tell you about my petty illnesses? I am no longer young. Old age brings all kinds of ailments with it. Pain in my joints, pain in my back, pain in my chest . . .'

'No, no. A pain inside the chest is something different. I will to Hakim sahib just right now. Please to tell me your symptoms, Amma ji. Does the pain radiate to your shoulders, and is it the left shoulder or the right? Does it go down to your arms?'

Seeing that I was so upset, she was obviously remorseful. 'There, there. What pain, and where was the pain? The cold weather is at its end, and old people always have some kind of pain when one season gives way to another. I'll have it rubbed with Hakim Rukn-ud Din sahib's medicinal oil. Just a couple of days ago your old maid-to-play was here, she said, Bibi ji, please remember me if there's some service that I can do for you.'

'Please, I want you to swear on my head. The next time such a pain happens, let me know at once. At once, do you hear?'

'All right, boy. Have your way. But won't you say anything about . . . about the proposal?'

I was silent for a few moments. I didn't want to lie to her, but I had no truth to reveal to her. 'Amma ji, please let me have two, three days' time. I will think seriously and answer you the day after tomorrow.' I smiled a tiny smile. 'I think I must marry now.'

She blossomed up, like a tender leaf parched for want of rain sighing with joy at the first drop of the nectar. It was the first time that I gave her some cause for hope.

'Sure, quite sure,' she said, wiping her eyes. 'Think as much as you wish, dear boy. I am in no hurry. Should my little child incline to marriage, there is no dearth of brides for him.'

*

I should have made inquiry with some physician about her complaint of pain in the chest. The little medicine that I had been taught was enough for me to be suspicious of such pain. She was slim, and very light of weight; in despite of what she said about her age all the time, she wasn't really old. I was born many years after my parents'

156

marriage. Even so, her age would not exceed forty or forty-five. She was neither of the age nor had a body normally conducive for her to develop the disease of the heart. Frequent pains in the chest? I should have been alerted immediately. But I was running blindly after my lusts, my laughable ambitions. My brain bloated and inflated my own problems. It insisted on looking at her problem through the wrong end of a telescope.

When I came out of my home that morning, I was firmly decided that I would visit Rajwaron ki Gali after school and identify her haveli. But my resolve evaporated when the moment came. Like the dust devil, I went round and round and arrived nowhere. Finally, I decided to go to Chowk Sadullah Khan and divert myself, if possible.

The bazaar in front of the Lahori Darwaza was absolutely enchanting in its colourfulness, if one had a heart willing to be enchanted. As it is, the bazaar was always colourful with the host of buyers, sellers, performers, the envy of Isfahan and Rum, but the season of the Basant was something else again. Everything and everyone was right there in front of your eyes. Dastan reciters, preachers, men of learning of all persuasions, dancer boys, nautch girls, astrologers, palmists and geomancers, conjurers, hakims and vaids, especially those who claimed to be expert in curing 'hidden' diseases, or who sell aphrodisiacs, cheaters all. Then, there were the daily droves of birders, dealers in wild animals, sellers and trainers of dogs and cheetahs, dealers in arms and ammunition of all kinds, cage-builders, mirror-makers, and God knows who else. Acrobats and snake charmers, certainly. During the days of the Basant, the horde of attar-sellers, flower-sellers, clothiers, and male or female dancers became bigger and noisier.

I left the bazaar to its attractions and stopped for a short while at a coffee house in Chandni Chowk, just before one turned into Katra Neel on the right, and next to a large coffee and spice merchants' establishment. All coffee houses, and especially this one, were the haunts of poets and singers of *dhrupad*s or khiyals, or the occasional player of music from Bokhara or Samarqand. The day I visited, a young follower of our well-known poet and Sufi, Khvajah Mir Dard sahib, was singing a Persian rubai of his with a three-stringed instrument, but with no percussion:

> *For a lifetime, I heard of her from a distance,*
> *In my imagination, I hugged her hard to me.*
> *Now, when I reached in front of her,*
> *Like the mirror, she saw herself. I didn't see her.*

True, the poem was actually about divine love, but the ambiguity of the grammar permitted a profane interpretation as well. That was my interpretation. My eyes bedimmed of their own accord. I left quietly, before anyone could notice my estate.

Ordinarily, were I going home, I should now have walked down almost the whole length of the Chowk, enjoyed the sight of the flowering shrubs on both sides of the canal, looked at the glittering shops, at the perfumed young men who thronged at every corner; then just before I reached Fatehpuri Mosque, I should have turned left into Billimaron. But my feet, of some mysterious volition apparently, turned to the left well before Fatehpuri, into the alley that took me to Chowri Bazaar and on to Rajwaron ki Gali. The scented air and the many betel-sellers' shops, bright with mirrors and coloured lights, alerted me that I was elsewhere. I was, in fact, in Rajwaron ki Gali.

So, fate was playing a hand in my favour. I smiled in my heart, but also quaked inwardly. What if someone saw me here? Well, Maulavi sahib, if there was an acquaintance of yours around, he would have the same apprehension. And how to find her haveli, and whom to ask? I was sure that no one would know me here at all, but I was the guilty sneaker. It seemed to me that everyone in that street was looking at me meaningfully. But I must find her, now that I am here.

According to Lal Muhammad, her house of many storeys was famous, and prominent; but that wasn't enough for an address. Now, fate played another hand in my favour: I saw that very young girl coming from somewhere towards me, the one who had disdained to look at me at the shrine. More welcome than her sight was her coming towards me. She knew me immediately, came near and did a salaam, throwing me into confusion again. What should I say to her? But she didn't let me grope for a reply, she said in a most cordial tone, 'Maulavi sahib, you came just in time. Bibi ji is about to go out somewhere in a minute or two. In fact, I had been to Ustad Amin-ud Din Khan sahib to inform him that there would be no *talim* today.'

Talim, I again fumbled in my mind. Did she receive some education still? Then realization dawned soon; 'talim', or 'education', was the technical word among these people for musical training.

Just about to go somewhere? My heart seemed to shrink and hurt. But the next moment, I drew a sigh of relief inwardly: so I don't have go *there*, and I know where she lives. The maid walked fast with me and stopped in front of a huge gate, which pierced a high wall. Beyond the gate, I could see buildings and a garden. A sumptuous Firangi-style carriage, something like a small, modified rath drawn by two sturdy Kathiawari ponies, stood just inside the gate. The doors and wheels of the carriage were decorated with inlay work in brass and ivory, the ponies skittish but well in control of the syce who stood alongside two tall spear wielders, apparently to accompany the carriage. Two burly, cold, almost sneering Afghan doorkeepers stood on both sides of the gate, each carrying a musket. At the same time as I arrived at the gate, Ismat Jahan had walked up to the carriage from inside the haveli.

She hadn't noticed me, obviously, or if she did, she didn't know me. She looked at the maid, and spoke sharply, 'Saghir-un Nisa, where have you been? Why did you take so long?' She now noticed me, and oh, wonders of wonders, she knew me instantly, and cried, 'Please. Maulavi sahib?' Her voice had some surprise, and a bit of pleasure, perhaps? Then she continued in a more composed, even somewhat inviting tone: 'I swear on your head, Maulavi sahib, I would have stayed, but I already am very, very late. I fold my hands in submission and excuse.'

By all that is holy, did anyone ever speak in a voice so refined, so caressing, so sweet, so well formed, as if cast in a mould of light? Did the houris of Paradise ever speak thus? I was unable to utter a word. I was unable to look her in the face. Somehow, in some way I gathered my wits, plucked up courage, and spoke a line from the great Persian poet Urfi:

The power of hearing fell into the Heavenly streams of Kausar, and Tasnim.

'Go on with you, don't make fun of me! I am not learned like you so as to say a verse from Urfi every now and then.' She paused. 'All right, please grant me permission. And please, see that you return tomorrow, at this very time.'

She stepped daintily into the carriage, and left a storm of jealousy and pain raging in my heart. She had to go somewhere? Why did she have to go somewhere? Does someone employ her? If so, what kind of connection would she make with me? My mind intervened bitterly: You fool; you talk of a connection when you haven't even touched the dust of that portal?

Seeing me lost in thought, Saghir-un Nisa spoke, 'Maulavi sahib, is your temper out of sorts somewhat? Please to come inside, have a cool, refreshing drink. Take a few minutes' rest.'

But who had the fortitude of mind to stay in that place? I made her a perfunctory salaam and took my leave. My heart heaved and ached all the way back. Did anyone ever command such beauty, such quality of being lovely and being desired with a madness of desire? But who is her lover? And if that despicable fellow is not her lover, then who is he with whom she is connected? What should I do with a beloved (the word came to my lips for the first time, but how appropriately) whom I cannot make mine?

I recalled the verses of Sanai, those I had heard at the Shrine of the Protector of the City, the Presence, Shah Kalimullah sahib:

Don't make bare your life-enhancing beauty
And if you do so, go burn yourself like
a grain of bitter rue crackling on live coals.
And what is that beauty of yours?
Your intoxication,
And what that grain of bitter rue?
Your whole being.

So, according to Sanai, one should not exhibit oneself as a lover, and if one does so, one must also burn one's whole being like the merest kindling, or even less. I remembered a Hindi line of Mir Taqi Mir sahib:

Love's serpent swallowed up those
who suffered the agony of your love.

You do not need the agony of love to encounter the serpent of love. Ismat Jahan is a serpent in herself, beautiful but deadly. And there's no antidote, no magic panacea, no mantra against her sting. I recalled the story of Navab Abdullah Khan, son of the Rohila Navab, Ali Muhammad Khan. Abdullah Khan kept numerous snakes. His boast was that he knew the mantra against every kind of snake's venom. There was no snake but would be like a limp rope in his hands. Yet, it was a snake whose bite delivered death to him. Someone brought a particularly venomous snake to him, he pronounced the appropriate mantra and took the snake, an exceptionally vicious kind of viper, in his hands. The viper turned and struck, biting him in the face. Abdullah Khan died within hours, in spite of the application or imbibition of every kind of antidote. God knows, I am no snake expert; I know no mantras, no antidote against a snake, except the power of prayer . . . So, you want to invoke God for your selfish, immoral purposes? You are sure to meet a more perditious end than Navab Abdullah Khan.

Repent, and go home. Go and serve your mother.

But does man live only for gain? Is there no other, higher objective to strive for, no more superior view to enjoy? House and household, a so-called respectable, even honourable life, teaching and learning, assemblies of the learned and of the people of good taste—all these are meaningful when a man has nothing better to do, nothing more noble to aim for. To live like the deer in the Sanctuary of the Kabah, is that some kind of life? For the first time I had been granted the taste of something like a new life. Before it, all that I had imbibed so far seemed insipid, food for the invalid, the valetudinarian. I am young, healthy, and now I know what appetite means. Why should I swallow food that tastes like paper, if not dried hay? What are these false pretences, of home, of earning a safe, valueless living? Wasn't there, after all, a man like Budh Singh Qalandar, a person who lacked for nothing? But he gave up everything for nothing. He even gave up eating. He was a true practitioner of what Sanai taught in that same poem:

Take to forest and hill, like the beasts of the wild—
Surrender your home to the cat, the mouse.
If there be any who make use of the house for living
They are none but the ant, the wasp, the spider.

Tell me, who is luckier today than Budh Singh Qalandar? He gave up his house to public plunder, but is in no wise the loser. I am not even giving up my house to a plundering mob, an ignorant host driven by greed. I am doing nothing but throwing my so-called respectability to the winds. And so long as Amma ji lives I am not going to leave my home either. I will make Ismat Jahan my bride; I'll bring her to my humble home, which I know she will cheerfully accept. If I can't do that, I will spend my life roaming, wandering, and going round her alley. I will certainly, surely go visit Ismat Jahan at this time tomorrow. I will tell Amma ji all.

*

But far from visiting there the next day, I didn't ever visit Ismat Jahan's house. By the time that night passed, innumerable nights, each of them longer than the Wilderness of the Dark, had passed over my head. I breathed a sigh of relief when I heard the muezzin's call for the predawn prayer. The sigh of relief wasn't so much at the passing of the night as for the passing of the last such night over me—a night of resolution of difficulties, a night of self-knowledge, or apocalypse even. I had reached the conclusion that there was no game for me to play with Ismat Jahan. When I was small, I and Sitti Begam and other children of a similar age used to play the game of 'Home'. We created a make-believe of relationships and acquaintances, children, parents, people living in different houses, visiting each other, socializing, sometimes quarrelling even. We knew that it was all play-acting, but it did not diminish our absorption in the game, our care about getting all the details right, all the narratives properly set out. But I couldn't play even such a play with Ismat Jahan. It was not my station to become the dust in her path, or anyone's path, for that matter.

A lack of interest in things, a desire to distance myself from everything, a feeling of being a stranger even in the company of Amma ji or Sitti bibi, supervened over my psyche, though I intensified my devotion to Amma ji, to ensure her pleasure in everything, and also my attention to my duties as teacher. I lived two lives, in two selves, it seemed to me. But the true moments of unwillingness to face the truth and reality, of the desire to go away from it all, were those moments when I was alone, on my bed and sleepless. On occasion I did encounter Ismat Jahan in different places, riding her open palanquin, and on each such occasion it seemed to me that there was a question in her eyes, and also some kind of glad tiding. But I never looked her full in the eye, though I once did raise my hand in greeting. Her lips moved in reply, but I didn't hear what she said.

I had given my consent for the marriage proposal that Amma ji had talked about to me. But only a few days passed before Amma ji was herself no more. I rose one morning for the predawn prayer and found her lying motionless on the prayer mat. Apparently, she rose for the late post-midnight prayer as usual, but her heart didn't support her and she fainted. She was unmoving, but her face was grey with lines of pain on it. I shouted for the ladies in my neighbour's house, and ran to Sitti's house, called out to her with the terrible news and ran again to the haveli of Ashraf-ul Atibba Hakim Sharif Ahmad sahib. That noble, angelic person rode with me at once to our home where the women of my neighbour's house and Sitti Begam waited in fear and anxiety, though all could see that there was nothing that anyone could do for her. By the time we arrived, she had been summoned to God.

Sitti bibi wept and wailed so much that she fainted. She would do the same again when she was brought round. Spending all the time in weeping, she took no part in preparing her mother for the grave.

That afternoon, our mother was buried in the holy precincts of the Mehndiyon graveyard near the Dilli Darwaza, just outside the limits of Shahjahanabad, a place where people foregathered at all times because of the numerous holy or learned men buried there. Sitti bibi remained with me until the fortieth-day ceremonies. She read through the Quran numerous times, and prayed for the merit of those readings to be bestowed on our mother. She gave to the poor most lavishly. Save one pair of clothes, all our mother's outfits she gave away to the needy. At last, she left for her home on the forty-first day, her eyes wet and red, and one hand always busy trying to dab her tears.

My temperament became even more bilious after Amma ji's death. Ultimately, I couldn't stand the humdrum life at the madrasa, so I left my job and stayed at home, doing nothing. Sitti Begam insisted, again and again, for me to marry. I was always stubborn in my refusal and she always importunate, more and yet more. One day, I scolded her so harshly and cold-heartedly that she broke down, and went away to her home.

*

No Rider appeared in the city ever again. I adopted Ismat as my pen name and began to write poetry. In due course, I also collected a few pupils. The meagre offerings, money or goods, that they brought from time to time was sufficient for my even more meagre needs. Night or day, I sleep very little. I hope and resolve every day that tonight I will sleep well, and dream. But I never do sleep well. And it has been ages since I dreamt.

In Such Meetings and Partings, Ultimately

In such meetings and partings, ultimately
Lives are lost. There is no end to Love
And Beauty never relents.

From the First Divan (1752) of Mir Muhammad Taqi Mir

It was now the beginning of the fifth week since Labiba Khanam had been out of her home. But this was not the first occasion for her people to leave their hearth and door. Her grandfather Ephraim Çaudat Begovic had left the Balkans at the turn of the last century, making his new home in the Armenistani city of Nakhjavan. Much before that, towards the end of the fifteenth century, when Philip V forced the choice on the Jews and Moors of Granada, and in fact on the Jews and Moors of the whole of Andalus, to convert to Christianity, or else lose their lives, or leave the country, Labiba's ancestor, Zeyeb bin Saleh, Grand Rabbi, theologian and poet, embraced exile, setting fire to the four-hundred-year-old house and library, that his people had owned for generations, took refuge in the Serbian city of Beoghrad (present-day Belgrade), which was then governed by the Ottomans. In that city at that time, Muslims, fire worshippers, Christians, Jews, a few even from the distant lands of Iran and Hind, all lived in harmony under the benign, bright and long-lasting shade of Sultan Bayezid Secondus.

Like almost all other Jews of Andalus of that time, Zeyeb spoke Arabic, and his way of life and religious and social beliefs were much influenced by the teachings of the Cordovan Jewish philosopher Musa ibn Maimun. Known now in the modern world as Moses Maimonides (1135–1204), the philosopher had been himself driven out of Cordova by a fanatical Muslim sect and finally found refuge with Sultan Salah-ud Din Ayyubi (Saladin). Nevertheless, Maimonides always taught that while Jewish law, religious and social practices, and rules of daily existence were superior to all others, all revealed religions were equal

171

as far as the matter of leading human beings to the Path of Truth was concerned.

Life under the Umayyad of Andalus and the Balkans of the Ottoman was equally salubrious for Zeyeb. The only difference was that while he had been using Arabic for general and worldly purposes all his life, his descendants adopted the local languages because Arabic was not spoken anywhere outside their home. In due course, Zeyeb's progeny acquired, in addition to the local Serbian or Bosnian tongue, proficiency in Turkish, Circassian and Persian languages. These last named two had in fact come to the House of Zeyeb as dower, in a manner of speaking, because large numbers of Jews, speaking one or both languages, thronged to Beoghrad from Tabriz and Yarvan for the purpose of trade, commerce or in the service of the Sultan. The Circassians of the south of the Caucasus were almost all of them Sunni Muslim, but there was an occasional Jewish family among them, especially those who were professional clerks and secretaries; they had been settled in Beoghrad for many centuries. These people were prominent in society for their physical beauty, and also their secretarial skills were greatly valued among the Sultan's administrative circles.

A couple of centuries, or a bit more, passed in peace and prosperity. The facial structure and distinctive family looks of the descendants of Zeyeb bin Saleh had begun to dim and alter somewhat on account of their mixing with the local Jewish, Turkish or Christian families. None from his direct, biological progeny were now extant, but Zeyeb's name lived on as their distant but distinguished fountainhead. The teachings of Musa ibn Maimun were still remembered, if not always practised. Many families claimed descent from Zeyeb, one way or another. Among them was the initial ancestor of Labiba Khanam.

Her people were descended from those Iranian Jews who had begun settling in Beoghrad after the year 1400, that is, after the Balkans had come under total Ottoman control and the Jews no longer went in fear of the local Christian population or petty officials. These people, who settled in the Levant during and shortly after the times of Prophet

Moses, had—because of the vagaries of the times, then the tyranny of Rome, to be replaced later by persecution at the hands of the Christian governments—fallen so far away from their roots and original physical and racial provenience, that they believed themselves to be Arab, or Iranian.

Among the Arabs, though, especially those from the central areas of Najd, it was not a rarity to encounter persons or families the azure or blue of whose eyes and fairness of whose complexion deceived people into the belief that they were Caucasian. The most attractive feature of the looks of the original Levanter was a darkness of complexion, very light and delicate, produced by the admixture of the genes of the Arabs of Arabian Iraq in their people. The ancestors of Labiba Khanam had introduced among the local Jewish people a little bit of the arch fairness of the Iranians. Their long, dark and heavy tresses, however, gave a hint of Greece as well.

The families of Labiba Khanam's great-grandfather and great-grandmother were closely connected. By the time the great-grandparents arrived on the scene, the churnings of the blood, bone structure and general looks among the progeny of Zeyeb—the Iranian Jews of the Levant, the Iranians of Armenistan, and the Jews and Christians of the Balkans—had bestowed a radiant, almost angelic light of beauty on the human features of Labiba's people that everyone swore by their burnished gracefulness, and some were even prepared to state on oath that in their view, the women of Labiba's family were created for being worshipped, not for being taken to bed and have babies made out of them.

The power of the Ottomans began to pale and decline in Eastern Europe by the end of the seventeenth century. They reigned, but did not actually rule, the real power having passed into the hands of local potentates and warlords. Muslims, Arabs and Turks, who had settled as far as England and even farther in the North, now tended to return one by one, or in clans and groups, to the security of the territories still firmly under Ottoman rule. The failure of the famous siege of Vienna in 1683 had diminished respect for the military prowess and logistical expertise of the Turk. The crescent-shaped bun, or the croissant, invented by the people of Vienna to commemorate the defeat of the Turk at the siege, reminded the Europeans every morning at breakfast of the near-humiliation of the all-powerful Turkish generals, and the gradual retreat of Ottoman presence in Europe.

Far-sighted people, particularly the Jews among them, trembled at the thought of the day when the European countries would revert to Christian rule and the space of life would again become tight and straitened for all non-Christians. Memories of the massacre of the Jews and Muslims, including women and children, at the hands of the victorious Christian armies in 1099, the destruction and rapine of their property, the dismantlement and demolition of their dwellings, and their ultimate exile from the Holy City after the Christian conquest of Jerusalem, were dim in the collective Jewish mind, but not quite lost. The older and more worldly-wise among the Jews and Muslims said that if we now became slaves of the Firang, no other Saladin would come to liberate us.

In the year 1699, Ephraim Çaudat Begovic, paternal grandfather to the yet-unborn Labiba Khanam, was given a rare opportunity to quit Beoghrad and return to the Levant. This is how it came to pass: A most dreadful and totally destructive earthquake visited the Armenistani city of Nakhjavan. Large parts of the city, including its main market, were razed to the ground. The quaking, splitting, growling earth swallowed much of the human population. An equal number lost their lives under the roofs and walls of collapsed and collapsing dwellings. Palace, hovel, fortress, all suffered the fury of the earthquake. Shahram Yafe, a maternal uncle of Çaudat Begovic, also became a victim to the earthquake. He was killed inside his vast warehouse of imported merchandise. Shahram was unmarried, and Çaudat, though not his extremely close relative, was his only extant relative. So Shahram had willed away all his property, trade and wealth to Çaudat. Since Shahram was barely forty, it was believed that he had made the far-living Ephraim

Çaudat Begovic his heir pro forma, with no real expectation for Çaudat to inherit. It was believed that Shahram might still marry, set up a married quarters, and live the life of a man with a family. He would, in due time, produce biological heir or heirs to his immense wealth.

All that was buried under the rubble left by the earthquake. Now, not to mention an heir for Shahram Yafe, there was none in Nakhjavan to search for his body in the ruins and give it a decent burial. Ephraim Çaudat Begovic was obliged to leave his job under the Sultan's administration, his friends, his settled household and economy, to make for Nakhjavan, accompanied by his wife and daughter, an only child. There was no problem of adjusting to new social mores or language, because the Armenistanis and the Jews and Muslims of Beoghrad had much in common as far as social culture was concerned. And the Armenistani language was so much coloured by Persian that though the two languages were not mutually comprehensible, it was easy for the speaker of one to learn the other within a short time. Ephraim was quite comfortable with Persian because it was the second most popular language in Armenistan at that time.

It was expected, or it was practically everyone's conviction that the inheritor of Shahram's wealth and commerce would recuperate the finances and economic power of the Business House of Shahram Yafe. The opinion was quite widely held that Shahram's heir, already known for his acumen in worldly matters, industry and integrity, would prove a worthy successor to his uncle. But all this was fated not to be.

It had been barely five months since the arrival of Ephraim and his small family in Nakhjavan that the ravaged city became the victim of another earthquake. Richter's scale was not existent at that time, but the older citizens—that is, those who survived—held that there had been no such earthquake in living memory.

The new earthquake inflicted full and fearful upheaval everywhere. In addition to the city of Nakhjavan, the entire western shore of the Caspian Sea suffered grievously. One of the direst effects of the earthquake thus was that the coastal waters of the Caspian Sea, with waves as tall as twenty or twenty-five feet, snarling and roaring in at speeds exceeding forty miles an hour, occupied the hinterland up to thirty and more miles. All the ships in the harbour and all the ships approaching the harbour within five miles were battered, thrown up and down by the force of the water, shaking loose all the humanity clinging to the ropes or below deck, and sunk in the water, or buried in the muck before being drowned.

Godowns, warehouses, havelis and houses big or small, on the shore or near the shore, ceased to exist within a horrifyingly short time. But it was much harder on the unfortunate ones who battled the raging, imperious sea for as long as they could. Nothing was saved, not even those items which were bolted down to the floor, or which were believed to be safe behind practically waterproof and windproof walls. Officials and offices of the government, customs records, goods held in bond, employees' pay lists, most of them functioning from makeshift or temporary structures since the last earthquake, weren't given time to prepare for evacuation. They just disappeared with everything else. Harbour police and coastguard were swept away before they could realize that there was nothing left to guard or to police.

When the water wearied a little of its apparently entertaining climb up the steep hilly shore and the mountainous land beyond, its fury abated somewhat. And it decided to stay on. Wherever the land had cracked into big fissures or split open like a dead crocodile whose stomach bursts under the pressure of the gases accumulated in it, lakes and watery valleys came into existence, some of them deeper than three elephants' height. The water that these lakes and valleys could not accommodate began to search for its return path to the sea. The small, shallow rivers of the hinterland did not have the capacity or the temperament to handle millions of cubic feet of water, and that too, within the short time that would be available to them before they sank under the flood that resulted.

Water and land having become one, the water decided to go back home, regardless of the cost to itself or to the land.

During the oceanic invasion, hundreds of thousands of dead or half-dead sea animals, birds, shells, tortoises and snakes were washed up at the shore. These were followed by the heavier sea life: sharks, squids, octopuses, again half dead by the shock resulting from loss of habitat and being struck forcibly by the water against the rock-hard shores. Then came half-rotten dead bodies of drowned humans or beasts, and skeletons of long-dead life. The last to arrive were the wooden boards and beams of ships that had sunk and disappeared in the distant past. The flood dredged them up at almost the same speed as the rushing waves. The boards and planks inflicted murder and mayhem upon the buildings and the people trapped in them, beheading them, breaking their legs or spines, flattening their faces, and pushing their splintered fragments and the accompanying mud down the throats and gullets of whatever came in the way.

This uncontrolled horde of destructive elements, during its frightful progress, created large or small, high or less high hillocks of debris—some of the hillocks large enough, or close enough to each other, to prevent rescuers or escapers from making effective progress or taking effective action at escape or removal. Half-starving humanity, worn out with fear and fatigue, tried its best to find meliority, scratching and digging for their missing or dead, or for whatever valuables they could retrieve. The swarm of people, busy in their efforts at meliorative action, was impeded. The impediments were, naturally enough, the bodies of their own dead, and the mass of debris created by the oceanic and seismic activity. They did their best to dig holes or trenches through the debris. They created the impression of a swarm of ants, making small, infinitesimal holes in the hard ground with infinite labour over a long time. And in fact, in the background of the cataclysm, human efforts and the status of humans in that world seemed more insignificant than ants.

Now, when the water returned to the sea, gathering the speed of a flood in many places, it took away with it much of the baggage that it had brought; it also took away a little more from what was left of human life and property at that time. It took away much of the debris, garbage, rotting wood from the houses which had fallen down, and many dead and some living humans and cattle. It also left many things as its terrible souvenirs and remembrancers, the most revolting, nauseating and fearsome of them an immense, almost immeasurable quantity of viscous, thick, dense, foul-smelling, sticky, gummy, slimy black mud, which clung to everything, as if for dear life. More than gummy mud, it felt like the froth and spittle from the mouth of some satanic serpents, one of those primordial beasts whom men feared to face even in their dreams. This mud was everywhere, somewhere as thick as the span between thumb and little finger, somewhere it was less, but even so it was of the thickness of a thumb.

There weren't enough crows, kites, vultures and hyenas to account for all the dead of the land within a week, or even two. The Sublime Porte at Constantinople did undertake relief works, especially by granting cash subsidy, organizing the burial of the dead, and the removal of the injured to safer sites. But there was no concerted effort to clean the land, rural or urban, and to reconstruct private buildings. Reconstruction of official buildings was not a priority, so the officials, on relief duty or routine duty, sometimes ended up occupying vacant houses regardless of their ownership. Epidemics spread because of the contamination caused by the rotting matter, and also by the beetles, worms and insects that grew in large numbers in the organic debris and in the land made fertile by the dead organisms being absorbed in the soil.

Fortunately, the Haj caravans, numerically heavy and causers of pollution themselves, had been sent off to Damascus and Baghdad shortly before the earthquake and the invasion of the natural forces that followed it. Otherwise, all the gold and silver granted by the Sublime Porte to defray the Haj expenses would have had to be diverted to disaster relief.

The earthquake, and the calamities and misfortunes that followed shortly, destroyed not only the goods and properties of Ephraim Çaudat

Begovic: they also made him bankrupt because he was unable to pay for the merchandise ordered before the earthquake, nor could he realize any price for the merchandise already sold and invoiced. In other words, his treasure became buried treasure, entirely unrecoverable. The few outlying houses that could be saved were just enough to sustain his small family.

By the time normal life was restored in Nakhjavan, people noted that the young Ephraim was an old man, his hair white and thin, his beard straggly, his cheeks sunken, his waist bent. Like a newly fledged bird snapped up by the falcon at his first flight, Ephraim's life in trade and commerce ended when it began. By the time the lights of the old year were extinguished to give place to the new, the weak and smoky taper of Ephraim's life sputtered and died.

It was the month of Urdibihisht 1080, corresponding to April 1701. Nakhjavan, after two destructions in one year, each to rival the Doomsday, and two winter–autumn upheavals again in that one year, was regenerating into the spring. For Shahram and Ephraim, the gong had finally sounded. No hopes of regeneration could revive them now. Among their surviving relatives, there were only Emmanuel bin Ephraim, Labiba's father and a woman, Naomiah, who was a distant poor relation. Labiba was four years old, but none knew Naomiah's true or even approximate age. She had been looking the same since countless years, as if her personal appearance and her body were fossilized at some distant time. Deaf at birth, she was unable to talk, and was legally and practically dumb. She attended to minor household duties in Ephraim's house, and managed to subsist on leftovers or whatever crusts she could cadge from the kitchen. She slept, uncomplaining even in winter, in the sparsely furnished attic. Now, of course, even crumb or crust had become scarce.

Repeated shocks, one shortly after the other, turned Emmanuel into a mentally defeated and practically inutile individual, utterly valueless as an effectual human being. A secret opium addict, he now became an open opium wreck. But if there was no restraining presence of the father, there was no money either, to give full rein to his foolish and vicious enslavement. He began to steal Labiba's few silver anklets and toe ornaments, going on to the heavy silver amulet that she wore around her neck to ward off the forces of evil. He pretended that Labiba had lost it somewhere as she played among the debris. Thence he proceeded to pawn or sell outright the rustic, ancient, almost valueless silver trinkets that Naomiah possessed and had cherished for as long as one could remember. That done, he began to put in hock, one by one, the few habitable rooms of the last of their houses, the others already destroyed by the flood and earthquake, or sold off to keep the wolf from the door. When they were reduced to one room and one kitchen and no toilet, Naomiah began to often starve herself to feed the tiny life and the worthless, emaciated, lice-ridden, matted-haired body of Emmanuel. Naomiah was reduced to a bundle of dried sticks, entirely devoid of the juice or power of life. There was nothing more left in her body to melt, to be burnt for energy.

Armenistan's murderous cold weather took Naomiah's life finally. She had been a long-time patient of phthisis of the backbone, which they called 'fever of the bone'. One morning, she was found dead in her attic, shrivelled by fever and hunger, her body still in rigor due to extreme cold. She lay on the bare floor, foetus fashion, clinging to one of Labiba's woollen dolls. A few weeks later, Emmanuel died of exposure to the cold. His body, already wasted to brittle bones and sunken cheeks and eyes, was unable to withstand the cold on the roof of the opium house where his fellow addicts had left him when they were unable to wake him from his opium-laden stupor.

The persons who held the several rooms of the house in pawn foreclosed on them. They were kind enough not to insist on recovery of interest. But there was one who was owed money. He took possession of five-year-old Labiba and sold her to Zohra the Egyptian, a local madam. It wasn't anything to shock the morals or offend the custom. Those times were not kind, or even soft, to displaced or parentless children, and especially the girl child, and to the children bought from someone privately or in the slave market. The only difference between a purchased animal and a bought human child was that while the former was often sent out in halters to graze on whatever fodder it could find, the human child was rarely allowed to peep at the outside world from an upper-storey window from behind a curtain. To stand at an open door or window was absolutely forbidden.

The tyranny, the hardship, the cruel deprivations suffered by Labiba Khanam when she was a growing child are better left to the mind to imagine, or not imagine. From the scrubbing of dirty plates and pots and pans to doing the laundry, sweeping and dusting the house, her duties took a substantial part of the day. At night, her duty was to press and knead Zohra the Egyptian to sleep. But that came only after both Labiba and Zohra the Egyptian had spent a couple of gruelling hours over Labiba's musical training. She ate only when all else had eaten and gone to bed. She was the first to rise, almost always before sunup, and the last to go to bed. Her bed was in an attic no better than that of Naomiah's, but she shared it with two other girls, bigger and older than her.

As she grew up to a more sensible age, she was often deputed to the nearby stores to buy groceries. Sometimes she was forced to help fetch water from a well at some distance from the house. This happened when the water level went down in the small, open masonry-built rain-fed tank in the inner courtyard. When the rains hadn't been sufficient of a season to keep its water accessible, it became a sore burden for the householder to maintain water supply in the home. Called *birka* in Turkish and Armenistani, the tank was the lifeline of many a household. Its water was used for everything, from ablutions to cooking.

As she grew older, Labiba's trips outside became less frequent. Her body was filling up and coming in fruit, and likewise, the gaze of the local riff-raff, the flâneur, the lounger, the ne'r-do-well, fell on her more frequently, their eyes bright with lewd hunger, their mouths polluted with lewd remarks. She didn't dare protest or complain to

Zohra the Egyptian, but the Egyptian was quite aware of the value of her property. She would never permit it to be molested by eye, gesture, word or hand. The more pristine the property, the better its future value. So she forbade Labiba's outdoor duties as soon as her sharp eyes saw, or felt, the coming changes in Labiba.

Beauty, Zohra the Egyptian knew to her own cost sometime in the faraway past, will always come into its own when it will, regardless of circumstance, regardless of restraint, regardless of hunger and poverty. Violet or wild rose, tulip or lily of the valley, when they are driven by the organic force of youth, no autumn, no sere can approach them. Its legs paralysed, its eyes wide in wonder, winter can't challenge them.

By the time she stepped into her thirteenth year, Labiba was no longer the orphan, the homeless, the tyrannized Labiba of yesterday. Now it was she whose beauty ruled the whole city of Nakhjavan like a queen. She listened to no entreaty, she looked at no one, she cared for no one. Avid visitors would arrive of an evening in droves, entreating admittance to her presence. One of them, half in jest and half in exasperation-charged anger, called out a Persian verse, loud enough for all the inmates of the house to hear:

To rule the territory of the heart is a major undertaking,
You are a new-rich in beauty, you can't do this job properly.

Zohra the Egyptian heard, and was happy. Labiba heard, and flounced into her own room—yes, she had a small room to herself now—without waiting to observe Zohra the Egyptian's reaction.

And was there ever a beloved, a desired one, a sought-after one like Labiba? She was unique in her belovedness as she was in her beauty. Earnest lovers, desirers—perfervid with inflamed passion—casual visitors to Beauty's Bazaar, there was none whom she didn't somehow lead into the error that she favoured him, and there was none whose expectation was fulfilled in the most infinitesimal degree. Labiba had intuitively acquired or adopted all the wayward ways of coquetry—

cruelty, cold look, disdainful glance—which other and older girls had to attain through practice and education, as the Persian poet said, perhaps with a girl like her in mind:

> *The meaning is one, even if the words are numerous*
> *The beauty of Joseph is one, even if there are a thousand dresses.*

What avails the dress, what the tone of voice, what the little lightning of the sidelong glance; what avails the gait and the deportment, what the manners of conducting oneself among an assembly—there was nothing about Labiba Khanam that didn't sing with the murmur of the brook of beauty, there was nothing in a single hair of her head, nothing in the soft and gentle curves of her body, nothing in every virtue, every grace of her body, which didn't cry out to be adored, to be possessed.

She had an intuitive grasp of her role as the desired one, and of her power to deceive, almost without meaning to. Whoever saw her just once, and that too for a mere moment, immediately persuaded himself that it was just a matter of time, of a little effort, and this Bird of Paradise would fall into the snare of his love. I swear, he told himself, her eyes clearly suggest that we wait for you—there is the scent of a rose, which can persuaded by the special breeze of a loverly heart to open negotiations, to create a chain of connections, so that every wave of the breeze carries off a minute particle of the scent from the rose to the lover. It's not a rose garden which is open to all; but I, I am the privileged one for whom its door will open, and very soon.

Every one of Labiba's desirers arrived at the Egyptian's door with the hope that this time, the eye will fall on me. Yesterday, or the last week, she couldn't really notice me because of the press of visitors. It is just a matter of her looking at me once, just once. There'll then be none else but I. There was never even a hint of privacy there, the faintest suggestion of an inner door waiting to be opened for someone. But everyone believed with the fiercest of beliefs that Labiba Khanam desired him, and him alone.

She avenged herself on her madam to her heart's content, if the heart could be content ever in such matters. She took count of every humiliation, every cruelty, every deprivation, and took her revenge for each. The tyrant Zohra the Egyptian, the slave-driving Zohra the Egyptian, the merciless mistress Zohra the Egyptian, was now the suppliant, the beggar. She would plead with Labiba, would practically shed tears of rectitude and repentance and ask Labiba to be just a little kind, vouchsafe just a few words' worth of softness, a little inclining of the head, a little half smile, shy but consciously alluring, and such and such Prince of Merchants, such and such nobleman from Turkey would be her slave; but it seemed as if Labiba didn't know *those* arts, and knew everything else.

One day, an Azeri, young scion of a noble family, arrived suddenly, on foot and with a dagger in hand. He stood mute, his eyes pleading, for a few minutes. Then he stabbed himself in the throat, saying this Persian verse:

I banish myself from your street.
Tell me, oh you who practised tyranny on me all the time, tell me
Who will you now torture to pass the time?

Zohra the Egyptian stood silent, her head bowed in shame, or perhaps in terror. Labiba didn't even deign to appear on her balcony. And what could Zohra do, after all? Her wildest wishes were fulfilled, more than fulfilled. A horde of admirers, lovers, lust-filled old men, fiery young men hot with the urge to possess and expend, and—above all—spectators, enjoyers of the scene, was always to be found in her street. They brought money, and gifts, and entreaties. Labiba came out of her room only twice, and at fixed times: In the early afternoon, to sing, and very late in the evening, to dance. That was all.

She never left the house, not because she was used to imprisonment, but because she didn't consider anyone, any place, fit to be visited by her.

Occasionally, a haughty or stubborn mayor, or commander of the city garrison, or local governor felt insulted and tried to use his power over Zohra the Egyptian and her establishment. She always capitulated and sent word that Labiba Khanam was no longer in her control; her admirer was free to come and take her away. She was secure in her knowledge that no one would dare appear in her street with adverse intent. Once, though, a chief of police commanded her presence in his haveli at a given time, and added that if his demand was not carried out, armed policemen would be dispatched to bring Labiba to him forcibly, and from then on, Zohra the Egyptian couldn't expect any favour, any protection from him.

Well before the appointed time, the people of Nakhjavan were consternated with a strange sight: a whole caravan of camels, mules, ponies and horses, bearing household goods and personal effects, was coming forth from Zohra the Egyptian's spacious house; closed palanquins, which were reportedly conveying Labiba, Zohra and all the women of the establishment to some unknown destination, were conspicuous in the middle of the train. The caravan wended its way through the city's twisting streets and arrived at the city gates. None had the courage to challenge them about their destination or ask for their laissez-passer.

The report reached the chief of police with the additional information that there was a likelihood of rioting in the city, and picketing at all the roads leading out of the city unless Zohra the Egyptian's caravan was stopped from leaving the city. The police chief had to eat the humble pie on this occasion. On another occasion, it was the governor of the city who had to be respectfully warned by the police chief that should his desire be carried out to remove Labiba from her dwelling and present her before the governor under durance, there would be no guaranteeing the peace in the city.

*

185

Although a Coptic Christian herself, Zohra the Egyptian made no effort to indoctrinate Labiba in matters of her religion, nor did she have her educated in the Talmud and the Law of Moses. Thanks to some of her Jewish admirers, Labiba did pick up a smattering about her religion. For instance, at the beginning of the Jewish New Year, she made sure to keep the fast on Yom Kippur. She revered Moses as her true Lord and Master, but hadn't thought to learn more about his teachings than what she had casually imbibed. The one thing that she was convinced about religion was that it required her always to play the game of 'keep bent, do not drop' with the seekers of her favour. This Persian phrase involved a person with a full bottle in his hand. He was required to keep the bottle bent at an acute angle, but not let fall a single drop from it. That's how she dallied with her suitors: Keep everyone dangling; keep everyone strongly convinced that he would be the first past the post. But even the most deluded suitor knew that he would not necessarily become the owner of her charms.

Did she stop to consider if her treatment of her admirers was based on some natural, intuitive wisdom and far-sightedness, or if it was what every woman did to anyone whom she did not love? Was her decision based on some blood-and-gut feeling: to cling to her greatest wealth, her body? She wouldn't oblige anyone to come away from her doorstep permanently frustrated, never to return, nor would she permit anyone to cross the Rubicon. The obvious result would be for her true wealth, her incomparable jewel, her physical beauty—not to be lent or given away to anybody at all—to increase in value by the minute, and her purse, never empty, keep getting heavier.

Did she ever analyse her decision? Was it a revenge strategy, rather than a defence strategy? Was a great river of hate and avengement rolling in her heart like a wave from a primordial ocean whose nature she didn't understand? Revenge against the world, against the masters and managers of Fate and Destiny? Was she settling scores, and this was the best way open to her to do so? The world had kept her deprived, with a gut-wrenching longing for a safe corner, a coign of peace, not of comfort, far less luxury, but just the little warmth of parental love, the care of an attentive and loving—even if largely ineffectual—maid, like the deaf and dumb Naomiah. She wanted to psychologically maltreat, physically disrespect, materially ignore her suitors, her peers, her madam. She wanted power over them, as they once believed they had power over her.

The full truth is perhaps not in this or in any other explanation. Some unerring instinct, in spite of a life of total mental seclusion, had made her regard, in some mysterious and self-evaluating way, as her life's axis and centre, the open and secret changes that were taking place in her body undiscernibly yet somehow obviously. True, the usual transition of the seasons, from childhood to girlhood and then to youth, did happen with her, but she was so utterly absorbed in her work, swallowed up by the daily swarm of tasks and chores—scrubbing the pots and pans, washing the laundry, carrying out odd jobs for madam, learning and honing up her music—that she hadn't had sufficient time to evaluate the things that were happening to her body, happening in her psyche, maybe. Whether they were bad or good, she couldn't decide, until, finally, she became aware that she was different from other girls.

She certainly appreciated the fact that people's eyes, which in the initial years used to stop at her face, were now slipping down to her neck, and below the neck, to her waist, and below the waist, and sometimes even lower down, apparently searching or eager for things that were there. As this realization grew, she began to see, sometimes fearfully, sometimes with a nameless pleasure, changes in the way she walked, the morning-like brightness of her brow which seemed apparently to cloud over or shine of its own accord, her bending to pick up something from the floor or a low table, lifting her head in a certain way before tossing something over to one of her peers, her turning away shyly from something (was this what people called coquetry?), the maturing music of her voice. As these fraught changes slowly became palpable to her, she experienced a frightening desire for more.

For, she could see that many of those things were not to be found, and certainly not in the same measure, in other girls of madam's house.

She began to enjoy looking and contemplating her body when she was alone. There was a pleasure, a delight surpassing all delights, in regarding the subtle changes heralding the blossoming of her body and then using her imagination—of which she had plenty—to delineate them further in the eye of her thoughts, anticipating their coming, and their effect on her and others.

Another pleasant change was the cessation of corporal punishment. Zohra the Egyptian rarely hit her now, and if she did, it was never on her face or chest or hips. No stroke of the slap or the birch was delivered which could leave a mark anywhere on her body.

Now she was granted certain toiletries every month: a cake of fragrant soap, a length of coarse cloth for towelling herself dry after washing. Previously, she had no time or permission to take a bath; all she was allowed was an occasional washing of the body. She was allowed to use her own clothes to dry herself, and even in the wetter seasons, she had to wear the same wet clothes again, denying to herself the feel of dryness when everything around her was damp. The day she was granted, in addition to a towel, a small leathern bottle of jasmine oil and an old, hard wooden comb, was the day she felt herself human for the first time in her life.

Zohra the Egyptian had been looking forward to the day when Labiba would need those special toiletry things: clean rags for the time of the month, rouge for the face, softening unguent or lotion for the body to prevent her dry skin from cracking, and mechanical or chemical depilatives. But here too, Labiba deprived her of the triumph of being the provider. As she realized the value of her body, she also developed haughtiness, aloofness, a sense of being above the ailments and pains that other girls seemed to suffer. Zohra, in fact, was a little afraid of her. When she experienced flowers for the first time, Labiba didn't panic. She didn't cry, or go tripping to madam for advice and instruction. Perhaps other girls had warned her, perhaps she solved her problem on her own, realizing that what was happening to her, though somehow revolting, was nothing special, not a disease that had overtaken her. The thirteen-year-old, having suffered nearly every mental and physical hardship, having closely observed the present and the past of other girls in the house, found a suitable solution to her problem. She also vaguely understood that it too was a step towards empowerment for her.

*

Nine years passed over Labiba with her newfound haughtinesses and felicities of body and mind. On both sides—her suitors and her endowments—there was nothing but excess, a fine excess. Each and every crevice of her boat was laden with ore; ore that each and every one of her seekers was willing to buy with his life.

It is said that true youth arrives upon a girl when she is twenty-one or twenty-two. Those who said so should have consulted the hearts of the suitors of a thirteen-year-old Labiba, and who had never given thought to the nearly impossible event of a decline in her magic. And it's not as if she had the same suitors, the same importunate desirers from year to year. The Hindi poet Mir's line seemed more relevant:

Were one to escape with his life, there appeared two more, intent upon dying.

Labiba's moods and ways were as before. Still, when one took an account of her lovers, one found one or two unusual individuals. Among them was a half-Iranian, half-Circassian young man, apparently slightly crazed; he had no occupation, no fixed address. He roamed from place to place, a hanger-on to a roaming Samarqandi troupe, doing nothing but singing the ghazals of Hafiz or Rumi. His singing voice was liquid, and sharp and sweet, like the juice of an orange. It was difficult to believe that even such a feckless one could have the courage or gumption to desire *her*—that Paradigm of the Land of Beauty, that seductive Rose of the Garden of Loveliness.

Tall, slim of body, his eyes blue, his hair a mass of brown curls, the features of his face were soft, so soft that if he put on female apparel—which some members of the troupe sometimes did—he deceived everyone into taking him for a young woman. Yet, none knew how old he was, where he originally belonged, and so forth. One day, he arrived in Nakhjavan along with the troupe. The voice of this young man, called Bayazid Shauqi, took the city by storm. Some young men even began to imitate his voice, put on clothes in his style, wore their hair ruffled and rumpled in his manner; some even walked like him, a willowy, almost feminine gait, though firm and unerring.

It was on the second or third day of his advent in Nakhjavan that he appeared, none could say why, in the square opposite Zohra the Egyptian's house. Perhaps he didn't even know where he was, and what kind of people lived on that street. It was very early in the morning; the faces of even the dozing, or early rising dogs of the alley weren't clearly discernible. A dim lamp or two could be descried in the nearby mosque, in its last tremors. Pale light from yellow, white and red candles still escaped but ineffectually from behind the slatted screens on Zohra the Egyptian's balcony. The square had just begun to be peopled by an occasional labourer, some going on duty for Allah and some for the humans. Suddenly, Bayazid Shauqi came into song on a *sih tar*, with the famous ghazal by Hafiz Shirazi whose opening verse is:

Oh, heavenly and angelic beloved
Who unties the strings of your veil?
And oh, bird of Paradise
Who gives you grain, and water?

The air became still. It seemed as if even the birds in Labiba's garden, themselves travellers from some far land, and singing in the memory of the freshly blown, fragrant wild roses which they had left behind, intently listened to the new voice. Who is it whose tune is one, quite uniform, from city to jungle? It pierces the heart and goes down into the soul and stays there.

By this time, more of the pious were about, going for the predawn prayers. They stayed, rooted to the spot. Some imagined that this stranger wanted to attract the attention of Labiba Khanam by showing his beguiling visage and displaying his captivating voice before her. Some felt sad: such a sweet young man, himself almost angelic, was destined to be roiled in the dust at this spot. Little does he know that this place is surrounded by the graves of countless unfulfilled longings, myriads of desires that went unanswered. But Bayazid was lost in an ecstasy of his own, an ecstasy high as the sky, restless like the sea. He poured forth his soul abroad, unaware of his surroundings, perhaps of his own voice even. Sometimes he would repeat a single line for several minutes, delivering the words in all the possible ways permitted by the music of his voice. Sometime he would stay silent, as if recharging his spirit before going on:

> *You went away from me, destroying my wounded self,*
> *Say now, whose place is your destination, and in whose home your*
> *bedchamber?*
>
> *Sleep went away from my eyes because of a liver-searing anxiety:*
> *Whose embrace is your destination where you will go to bed?*
>
> *The inebrious eye waylaid the hearts of the lovers.*
> *This makes clear that your wine intoxicates strongly.*
>
> *Oh heart-luminating mansion, where love*
> *Comes to stay, may the Time's bane not do you harm.*

He sang, rapturous, lost in song. By the time he arrived at the concluding verse, it seemed to the listeners that his soul would leave his body and fly away with the sound as his voice rose and was lost in the surrounding air:

Hafiz is not a slave that would run away
From his master.
Please be kind and take back your wrath
For, I am totally shattered
By your displeasure.

Those who could, now saw that the doors of Zohra the Egyptian's haveli opened, an old doorkeeper came out, and escorted Bayazid Shauqi inside. No one knows what he saw or heard there, but a few days later when the Samarqandi troupe struck camp and left Nakhjavan, Bayazid was not there to depart with them.

None could know where Bayazid lived. With some strange, intuition-driven strength, he seemed to draw sustenance from his song. Every morning, he was seen at the square opposite the Egyptian's haveli where he sang. Sometimes Hafiz, sometimes Rumi, occasionally Khvaju-e Kirmani, these were his entire repertoire. He sang on, uninterrupted, until he was summoned inside.

Two, then three years passed. Ever since his original group left, Bayazid hadn't done anything remunerative. Not accepting any invitations to sing, not joining any other band of singers, local or itinerant, he became a fixture of Nakhjavan. All assumed that Bayazid would now live and die there.

Then suddenly, the news was on every man, woman and child's lips: that Labiba Khanam and Bayazid Shauqi are tied in wedlock, with Labiba quitting the Egyptian's haveli at night by stealth and the city itself by the morning.

There was no door that Zohra the Egyptian didn't knock at to gain redress from the 'wrong' done to her. There was no clamour that she didn't raise, from breast-beating and wailing to howling in rage and shouting piteously for succour. She had informers sent out to unearth the facts: Where is Labiba gone? Who aided and abetted her? She must have secretly arranged with some foreign guides and a caravan manager. There was no caravan, no group of people that was newly arrived in the city and was scheduled to leave that day, or a day or two later. In order to persuade the city's governor and chief of police to her cause, she claimed that Bayazid must have seized and stolen Labiba against her will, because Labiba actually disliked Bayazid and tolerated him merely because of his singing. No one was convinced. Everybody knew Labiba's history, briefly or in greater detail: they knew that Labiba, if not exactly a prisoner in Zohra the Egyptian's establishment, lived there under durance.

The equation of power had changed in the haveli a long time ago. The scale now dipped in Labiba's favour. If Zohra the Egyptian didn't quite subserve to Labiba, she had no actual power over her.

It is true that according to the Ottoman law, Zohra the Egyptian was Labiba's rightful owner, because she'd bought Labiba from another who had jurisdiction over her. But there was no provision in Ottoman law to penalize an escapee slave if she or he was recovered and if at all such recovery was effected. There were no administrative arrangements in place to launch a search for such escapees. It was a matter between the owner and the slave: the State didn't come into it. In fact, in the matter of Labiba and her 'owner', all sympathies lay with Labiba. None, except perhaps a Qazi, held that Labiba was really a slave, owned by Zohra the Egyptian.

A whole age had passed over Labiba since she was sold into the custody of Zohra the Egyptian. A lifetime of manual labour, tyranny and physical deprivation, forcibly being taught music and dance, then, just by her strength of will, avoiding being raped by Zohra's patrons, the duration of Labiba's enforced stay there was twenty-five years. She was now a mature woman, above the age of thirty. In fact, she was at that stage of her life from where old age was just round the first turn. Women of thirty-five became grandmothers; they were treated as venerable ladies, or dried up hags, depending on their circumstances.

None, even the most unsympathetic Qazi, could give credence to the story that Labiba, a mature, almost grandmotherly woman, had been abducted—if she was worth abducting, that is.

No one knew how old Bayazid was. None also knew that his light golden complexion, the colour of the champak flower, a complexion which the Ottoman and Iranian appreciators of male beauty termed 'the colour of the moon', was actually due to the disease called ranj-e barik (the subtle and wasting disease). It was also known as tap-e diqq; western physicians of the nineteenth century termed it phthisis, or consumption. He rarely coughed, or complained of heaviness in the chest, which often happens in pulmonary consumption when the lungs are unable to clear the phlegm generated by the bacilli. Phthisis was the commonest of all conditions of the tap-e diqq, and most people were familiar with it, or had at least heard of it. Thus Labiba, or anyone else, had no idea that Bayazid was ill, and that he had fever in the bones, which was a rare kind of tuberculosis and which had little to do with his lungs.

Bayazid would occasionally, almost to himself, say a verse from Khusrau, that great poet from Hind:

The fire of thought burns each and every joint
In my body, my bones burn from inside:
Should someone have the fever in his bones,
May God forgive him all his sins.

Since 'the fever of the bones' is also a well-known trope, Labiba didn't at all imagine that Bayazid was talking of a real such condition, his own. He was feverish even on the morning they departed Nakhjavan, but he never let on. On top of it, his guide, on his instruction, took a route that passed over a difficult terrain and didn't go direct to their destination. Labiba knew and agreed with the decision.

It was September 1727; cold and easterly winds from the Caspian Sea, and similar westerly winds from the Black Sea, blew fast and cruel. The rain began to fall soon enough, the thinly travelled road was potholed and muddy and narrow, making progress still more difficult. Their true destination was Tabriz, in the northern part of Iran, where Turkish and even Armenistani were widely understood. In order to deceive and evade possible pursuers, they had decided to go north-west, rather than due south. The magnificent Abbasid Highway, which started at Isfahan and, touching Hamadan and Kirmanshah, went up north-west, and ran side by the side the shores of Lake Arumiah for a considerable distance before passing through Yerevan, finally went on to Tblisi in the far north. Their planned route was expected to join with the highway at some point somewhere near Yerevan. Obviously, this almost doubled their travel distance, but more important, they were obliged to travel through many minor, unimportant towns, which offered little comfort or convenience by way of resting or staying places. In fact, Tabriz was barely sixty miles straight to their south.

Another point in favour of the otherwise hazardous and long route was that almost the entire country to the north-east and north-west of Nakhjavan was Ottoman territory, whereas the Iranian frontier was just a few stages to the south. Relations between the Ottoman and Iranian, almost never cordial, were particularly skittish in those days. The current de facto ruler of Iran, Nadir Quli Khan, was looked down upon by the Ottomans as a man of lowly origins, no refinement and unworthy of holding any kind of negotiation with the sophisticated Ottoman Sultan. Thus, it was hoped that even if the fugitives were declared runaway thieves or criminals by the Ottoman administration of Nakhjavan, no Iranian official would take any interest in apprehending them and returning them to their place of origin.

The three-day journey to Tabriz thus took them something like three weeks, but they were happy. Safe in Iran, with plenty of gold and silver, and their art to commend them to all, Labiba and Bayazid quickly settled into a comfortable routine, anxiety-free and as happy as they could be. No one knew anything about the disease that was slowly burning away Bayazid's bones. Labiba was once again confined to the four walls of a house, but this was confinement of the bird which had finally found its perch and its nest, infinitely better than being a bird in a cage, obliged to sing at every beck of Zohra the Egyptian.

*

The date was 10 January 1731 when a girl was born to Labiba. She was named Nurus Saadat. On the third day of her birth, Bayazid caught a cold and began to cough a heavy, growling sort of cough, which made him breathless. He took to bed, but lay in it for barely a week. He didn't allow a physician to see him during his short illness.

'I will now let only death look at me, Labiba Khanam,' he spoke between gasps, in a hoarse voice. 'I am culpable before you. I should have refused to come when you summoned me for the first time. If, out of my crass selfishness, I didn't do that, I should have revealed my secret to you at the first opportunity. My light, florid complexion is only on the surface. Death has been seeking me for a long time, and now very soon death will have to seek no more.'

'Why, why should you be considered culpable?' Labiba spoke sharply. 'What kind of justice is this? What have you done? You lose your life and you are also culpable! The true crime is of the power which some call Fate and some . . .'

'Shush! Don't say things for which you may have to repent later. Labiba, listen. The purpose of our creation was that each of us should strive to achieve the limit of our potential, the perfect bliss and sole felicity of the fruition of the seed of Eternity that is in us. What else could be the perfection of bliss and felicity for me, indeed for anyone other, than arrive at the Mansion where you reside, where Love resides, as Hafiz said? In fact, my potential was not worthy of you. This sickly, polluted, sinful bosom was not fit to be crushed under your feet, far less receive a reflection of your radiant, peerless beauty.'

196

He paused, his breath shallow and noisy. 'I didn't need to live after I reached you. It was just your love that sustained my dead self by the power of your life.'

He sat up on the bed and, suddenly, with full of power and strength, spoke in a strong voice:

When you arrive at the beloved's alley,
Surrender your restless life to her.
For, lest you never again get a chance
To attain your heart's desire.

He lay back on the bed, against the bolster, said the same verse again in an undertone, and closed his eyes.

*

That first winter was very severe on Nurus Saadat. And why Nurus Saadat, it was severe on everyone in Tabriz. Older citizens narrated that they never encountered a colder, more callous weather in fifty winters. Nurus Saadat caught a cold every five or seven weeks; if the cold didn't clear quickly enough, phlegm would congest in her chest; if untreated or not properly treated, incipient pulmonary oedema would then affect her breathing. Insufficient oxygen in her blood soon caused cyanosis: her tender skin, already translucent like a rose petal, would start turning bluish dark. The physicians diagnosed primary, congenital asthma, or perhaps the native warmth of her body was poor, like her father's. Modern-day physicians would have perhaps declared her allergic to cold, damp weather, but some physicians at that time did suggest that a drier climate might suit her better. If she survived another few months, she should be taken to a more suitable place, say Isfahan, where the air was drier and the winter less severe.

But Labiba, widowed at the young-old age of thirty-six, still beautiful, alone in the world, where would she find support or base in

Isfahan? Going back to Nakhjavan was out of all reckoning, and anyway the climate there was as cold and hard as Tabriz, if not worse. Let alone Isfahan, there was nowhere she could go in the whole of Greater Iran. In Tabriz, shortly after widowhood, there had begun to arrive hints and overtures, or clear suggestions, from some of the richer, older and debauchery-laden men for her to marry or live as a concubine with any whom she favoured. Some young men, more interested in short liaisons, were also occasionally seen hovering about her house.

These hints and offers, whether clothed in sophisticated language or made with the leering brashness of youth, were extremely hateful to Labiba. Still, she could descry, though quite dimly, a tremulous ray of hope for the future in Tabriz: Possibly, she won't be a rank outsider in Tabriz. She won't be like the sward in the garden, which is not a native there and is always weeded out or mowed down. Here, if she could not live like a rose in the garden, she won't be the wild grass that grows on the riverside, to be invariably trodden underfoot by unheeding sightseers.

Labiba no longer commanded that self-confidence, that imperturbable aplomb, that haughty remoteness, which had characterized her adult life so far. She no longer had that assurance that the certainty of her own beauty generates in a young woman, the certainty that the world's eyes, lit by desire, fall on her whenever she reveals her face, the knowledge that she has no enemies, only lovers, however lustful and deceiving. Bayazid, who treated her every word as law, had left not only an emotional vacuum in her life; it was also a psychic vacuum, which could not be filled—rather stuffed—with anything, and certainly not a physical presence. Though she had lost all that she had, yet she still had enough pride, self-confidence and consciousness of her self-worth, that there was nothing to choose between the Labiba who had, in her lonesomeness, seen the opening of a door when Bayazid appeared on her horizon, and the Labiba who now dispatched messages to her new suitors to the effect that in her life, the high, bright terrace from which could be viewed, far or near, new prospects of love or friendly concord had turned black forever.

Nurus Saadat very nearly died two or three times before she reached the age of seven months. Winter was gone, but the air in Tabriz was still humid, leaving no security of health for the little baby. She was thin, almost emaciated; her arms and legs were just a little better than brittle spindles, and because of their delicate form and her naturally pink hue, she looked more like a large-sized doll than a tiny baby. Just the eyes were prominent on her face: deep, green, burning with fever, but also bright with the light of awareness, awareness with which she seemed constantly to judge the world and its people. Golden, curly hair formed something like a halo around her pale face, reducing somewhat the sickly hue of disease and consumption. The green scintillation of the eyes, though dim due to her fragility of body, was still able to reflect a little gleam on her profuse tresses.

The world became somewhat easeful on Nurus Saadat when the season changed to true summer. Still, her physical being was like that of the captive bird whose wings are free but whose legs are tied together. It can fly, but not too far and not for too long. Her sickness was the thread that binds the legs of the bird. At age a year and a half, Nurus Saadat fell seriously ill with congestion of the trachea, severe laryngitis, persistent cough and constant catarrh, necessitating not only medication round the clock, but also lying always away from the windward side of the house. The physicians' brutal prognosis was that even if she survived this episode, she wouldn't stand the next winter. Now Labiba Khanam was obliged, once again, to leave home for hopefully better climes.

She hired two reliable guides who organized an experienced caravaneer, sturdy pack animals and comfortable rides for the delicate travellers. She departed for Isfahan in September 1732, well before the advent of winter. The graveyard, which housed Bayazid's grave, was just a little outside the city, not far from the highway. She made the short diversion to the grave, stopped to say a prayer from the Mishnah, taught to her by Bayazid. She said the whole prayer, dry-eyed and determined, bid Bayazid goodbye in her heart, and promised to return, if she lived. She vowed, 'I will die only after I have visited your grave.'

As she left the graveyard, she turned for a last look, saying to herself in her heart the famous poem by the twelfth-century Persian poet, Ibn Yamin:

If I live, I'll repair some day
My garment torn by your disunion.
And if I die, do accept my apology—
Oh for the myriads of longings that turned to dust.

In those days, the better road to Isfahan passed through Mianah, Zinjan, Qazvin, Qum, Tehran and, having skirted the carpet city of Kashan, finally arrived at its end at the famed city at the foothills of Demavand. The route was somewhat longer, but safe, its main merit being that no major river needed to be crossed. It was not free from danger to cross by boat a river flowing fast with the power of the rains. Bridges on this road, and in fact on most roads in that part of the country, were few and far between. Doubtless, the road was steep and mountainous some part of the way. Between Qazvin and Tehran they had to go up the heights and then go down the rather treacherous slopes of Mount Elburz. Traversing the damp, forested foothills and lowlands, they came into the open before they encountered the heights of the Kargas range, just before Isfahan. But in the event, their road took them through the lower ranges and they suffered no hardship, except having to slow down.

They rode Iraqi dromedaries. Extremely fast, and smooth in their gait, large-eyed like the gazelles, they were almost human in understanding what was required of them at a particular point. Quite contrary to your average camel, bull or dromedary, they were famous for their equable temper. Their silky coat was long, reddish and slightly wavy. In fact, to a casual observer they gave the impression not of pelage, but silk sheets.

It was the first time in the brief existence of Nurus Saadat that she encountered such an open, free-flowing environment where the air was sweet and moisture-free. The birds above seemed to twitter and sing in tune with her cackles and gurgles. Riding a fast but smooth-running mount was another rare experience for the little girl. On Labiba Khanam's brow, for the first time since Bayazid's death, there was a light ray of hope blossoming in its true colour of rosy pink. She now dared to imagine that the ardent desire for her daughter's well-being in pursuit of which she had left her lover alone in the alien graveyard would surely see the face of success, and soon.

The journey took two uneventful weeks. She put down in the Royal Inn, and said farewell to all members of her caravan with sumptuous gifts and rewards. She hired a largish room to store her effects, and a smaller one for herself. Two days later, she went into the city, looking for a suitable home.

Very soon, she found out that whereas Isfahan may have been 'half the world' *(nisf-e jahan)*, for her it was worse than the darkest of dark forests. Apparently, there was no corner of safety and peace in that city for her to take refuge from the world. Without a male guardian, or at least a female chaperone, she couldn't gain admittance to any respectable house or dwelling. In some places, prospective landlords looked at her with concealed or open looks laden with carnal desire. They implied that mother and daughter could get accommodation, even rent-free quarters, if there was a quid pro quo from her, and the implication of the quid pro quo was obvious enough. And in the rare case where it was a landlady whom she encountered, it was made equally clear to her through unmistakable hints that she was no widow, and had in fact never been married, and couldn't thus qualify to live in 'respectable' neighbourhoods.

Most women seemed to believe that Labiba Khanam was a 'fallen' woman, if not an honourless harlot, deserted by her lover-customers. As for the tale that she was in Isfahan for the sake of her daughter's health, well, did anyone hear of health being won by change of place?

And did anyone travel so far as from Tabriz to Isfahan for health reasons? Granted that the girl was rather sickly, but what did that prove? The lady's deportment, her obviously haughty speech, her self-confidence—weren't these proof positive that she had been the woman of many a lover, and not one? She didn't at all carry herself as a married woman, in fact.

So, if the women rejected Labiba out of petty jealousy, or groundless suspicion, the men evaluated her not too differently. To them, it was as obvious as day was from night that she must have been active somewhere in the oldest profession, or was at best a nautch girl, employed by some rich grandee. There was some falling out between them, for reasons which were not hard to guess, so she left her original habitat to spread her net and seek a new fortune in Isfahan.

Finally, Labiba Khanam found suitable quarters in a neighbourhood famous all over Isfahan and nearby cities as Baghat (The Gardens). The locality was home to all the 'ladies of the profession'—dancers, singers, nautch girls and sellers of their bodies.

Labiba Khanam, in six years of marriage, hadn't forgotten the ways and manners of the house where she was brought up. She was also quite capable of comporting herself as of old—the remote beloved, the haughty, self-willed beauty, desired by all but available to none. She hated the idea of tying herself to the purse strings of some rich nobleman, to be hated by the ladies of the household, to be talked ill about in her absence, to be fawned upon by those very men and women in her presence. She was well aware that women, especially good-looking women, were bought, used and discarded like carrots and radishes, meat from the butcher to be enjoyed and then the leftovers given away for the use of the menials and the inferior classes, or thrown away on the dunghill.

Better than all this, she thought, to live as a woman of the profession, be her own mistress, give herself all the airs of the sought-after beauty. However revolting to her, that role was better than being in bond:

What would be the state of a warbler
After the rose had been, and gone?
She had to bind that unopened blossom, her heart
To the thorn and dry weeds of the garden.

Whatever little life of honour was possible for her was in the role of a woman of charms, apparently accessible to some, if not all, but tied to none. She was confident that she wouldn't let herself be preyed upon by the lusting, rutting males of her new environment.

What then, of the years of beauty and charm left to her? Surely, she was nearing the evening of her life as a sexually desirable woman? The fact, however, was that it was only now that Labiba had attained the full force of mature youth. Her unconscious gestures, her walk, her manner even of just entering or leaving a room, her manner of speech, all had acquired a new glow, a new power, a new quality of allurement, since she became pregnant and then a mother, a mother as *ravissante* as the baby that she gave birth to. And she could turn this quality on and off at will and move effortlessly from cold hauteur to warm givingness. The living redness of the blood now spoke from each and every pore of her body. Her 'pure and eloquent blood' seemed now to speak through her whole body, from the lips and eyes to the toenails. So it seemed as if the blood didn't just course through her body, it also spoke to her interlocutor. As another poet, more than a century before her in a faraway clime infinitely colder and damper than Tabriz even, wrote:

Her pure and eloquent blood
Spoke in her cheeks and so distinctly wrought
That one might almost say, her body thought.

Her body, always slim and inclining to delicate, almost brittle slenderness, had now filled up a little. The curves of her breasts and hips, and just below the stomach, were now tantalizingly prominent without being openly seductive. She was of middle height, or perhaps just a little on the elfin side. When she stood up to greet and salaam someone or when she stood to acknowledge someone's greetings, even the most unctuous and seasoned men of society couldn't withstand her charismatic power and involuntarily looked down at her sandals, or bare feet, as if looking for a suitable moment to lay their heads there in compelled submission.

No sooner had she set up home and house in Baghat than queues of pleasure seekers, lovers of the good life, aficionados looking for an evening of music and interesting conversation, began to form at her gate. Not all could gain permission to enter, and even those who did, could come only by appointment. Such a regime of discipline always had the potential to engender unpleasantness. Isfahan was obviously not Nakhjavan where every man and child knew how to behave and to do what was necessary to enter the sanctorum where Labiba performed.

Labiba had heard much about the loyalty, hardiness and stout-heartedness of certain Kurdish tribes. They worked on the principle that guarding, or bodyguarding someone meant dying before the person or persons whom they were guarding came to any harm. Accordingly, she hired a team of powerfully built Kurds, experts in martial arts and fearless of man or beast, to guard her entrance gate and parameter wall in eight hourly relays round the clock. They carefully screened all visitors; even those who were regular visitors needed to be cleared by a command from the Khanam. But she couldn't impose any restriction on onlookers when she went out to take the air, or took Nurus Saadat out to a public park. At a little distance from her entrance gate, enthusiasts would sometimes line up as a welcoming party, just to obtain a glimpse. As the Persian poet said:

Those who have gained admittance to your assembly
Have their hearts turning to blood
With anxiety: Lest you go away.

In Such Meetings and Partings, Ultimately

A host is outside on road, waiting
For the moment when you will come out.

In Nakhjavan, as we saw, she had two assemblies. In Isfahan, she had just one, not exceeding two hours, which included formal welcome to the guests and their entertainment with coffee, nuts and condiments. Alcohol was not served, except very occasionally, red Portuguese wine, sometimes mixed with hot water and sugar to cut its astringency. There was no dance. Most often, she sang the ghazals of Rumi or Hafiz. This, in her mind, confirmed and strengthened more and more her spiritual and physical affinity with Bayazid. Sometimes, in deference to Tabriz, she presented a ghazal of the seventeenth-century poet Saib, of Tabriz. Rarely, but without any hesitation when asked, she sang a ghazal of Kamal Ismail or Mohsin Tasir, both of Isfahan. Kamal Ismail belonged to the ancients; Mohsin was of the previous century and had served as Vizier to the Ruler of Isfahan. One of his verses, which was quite apposite to Labiba Khanam's assemblies, went as below:

On no occasion, from any view, the lover's purpose
Wasn't fulfilled. Every part of her body was
More delectable than the other. He didn't know
Where to look.

It so happened she once began her session with a rubai from Kamal Ismail. Her starting pitch was from the *Ushshaq* (The Lovers), a famous manner of the Iranian way of singing. The emotional affect was so strong that choked sobs and muffled screams could be heard not only among those who were in her immediate presence, but also from even those who were outside, intent upon listening to whatever sound of singing could reach their eager ears:

She went away, and my tears were flowing still,
And some life was left in my body still,

205

She said a few words, and I hung upon her words still,
She said: Poor thing, he was quite young still.

*

Months, then years passed. Labiba Khanam was ageing, though slowly. Her self-confidence, the highly regulated culture of her assemblies, the throngs at her house, all were as before. Her beauty's perfection, as also the perfect beauty of her art, both gained a reputation in many places beyond Isfahan. To her admirers, she embodied all that womanhood could imply: beauty, charm, polish, self-confidence, discipline. She was a model mother and an accomplished host. Curiosity about her origins faded as time passed. Her story, that she was widow to an artistic young man who died much before his time, was gradually accepted as rumours of her past life in Tabriz travelled down to Isfahan.

The major change that occurred in her style of life was the growing up of Nurus Saadat as a girl of surpassing beauty and almost bewitching charm. Labiba Khanam, as we know, had had no formal education; she knew nothing of the learned disciplines. Yet, by dint of her industry and native intelligence, and thanks to some teaching by Bayazid Shauqi, she had acquired a smattering of theology, a little bit of astronomy, logic and mathematics. Except for the languages, of which she had only Armenian and Persian, she could be considered an exceptionally well-educated woman for her times. But what she didn't have of formal education in literature, she compensated by her phenomenal memory. She knew by heart thousands of verses of the master poets of the past. She was familiar with the methods of argument and deduction, and could hold her own in most such situations. (Be it noted that in Isfahan, her salon was not avoided by the pious and the learned, who came for the poetry and the sophisticated company.)

Isfahan's temperate climate had the hoped-for salubriousness for Nurus Saadat. She was breathing better, and her bouts of breathlessness or coughing were but rare now. Nothing now stood in the way of her education and training as a lady of refinement, capable of realizing her potential in whichever discipline she chose to do so. Extremely intelligent and talented, she was much like her mother, except that she was haughtier, more given to withdrawing into herself. She was strong-willed, even to the extent of being contumacious, if her wish was thwarted. While her mother was not averse to making her mind clear, Nurus Saadat rarely explained herself, leaving it for the other to grasp her meaning. She could be vocal when aroused. But the occasion for her to be openly angry was an infrequent occurrence.

She seemed to have acquired music and poetry from her mother's womb. Very early in life she could distinguish metrical from non-metrical utterances and had begun to compose poetry by the age of ten or eleven. Ladylike deportment, the proper way of dealing with different people, rhythms of polished speech, where one should put one's hands, the way to sit among people in an assembly, and how to behave with her tutors, all this she learnt by intuition as much as by training.

Not content with the educated women's standard syllabus, Labiba organized teaching for her daughter in other, non-female, subjects: astrology, mathematics, calligraphy, history, archery, horsemanship and even a bit of statecraft. By the time Nurus Saadat entered her thirteenth year, she resembled her mother so much that those who had seen her mother in Nakhjavan were prepared to declare on oath that it was Labiba and she had, by the power of necromancy, made herself look like a young girl.

Very soon she, and her mother too, would have to face a crisis of decision. The matter, which was of the most momentous import for mother and daughter now was the question of Nurus Saadat's future. Given her education and home environment, what was Nurus Saadat to do, or become? No discussion had taken place between them on this, nor did the daughter know by any other means, for example, hearsay, about what Labiba thought of her and about her. There was, possibly, a feeling of guilt, or fundamental inadequacy, in both the women's hearts—a feeling, or fear, of being found out as phony, as having based the girl's life on premises which were untenable. This fear was something that carked their hearts all the time, but both were unwilling to let it out in the open.

Nurus Saadat was educated as a princess, or the daughter of a leading aristocrat-poet of the land, someone like Mohsin Tasir and his children. But God knows she was no aristocrat. Yet, it seemed to all that the palm of Nurus Saadat's hands lacked the marriage line. She was not born to make some average man's wife in some average household. And was it possible for Nurus Saadat to provide the means for entertainment, maybe even the pleasures of the bed, to the loose-living grandees of Isfahan and still behave with the same hauteur, the same disdain as her mother did? The daughter had pride and stubbornness and, when aroused, a scorn bordering on insolence—she could also, perhaps, not imagine a life after her mother, in the manner of her mother, or in the manner of a married, 'respectable' woman. The mother knew the art of making compromises so long as her self-respect and her dignity were not placed at risk. The daughter apparently didn't have the charisma, which enabled her mother to carry off the tightrope walk that she had practised most of her life. But the daughter's charisma in day-to-day dealings with people could only show itself over time. She had been given no opportunity yet to have independent dealings with others.

There was another aspect to Labiba's life and character: she had been lucky, in her own way. She gave birth to a beautiful daughter, she successfully discharged, even if for a few brief years, the functions attaching to the status of a beloved, and also of a woman. Before that, she had behaved pretty much as she pleased after growing up into a woman admired for her beauty and her *ravissement,* her unerring power to suggest an infinity of intimacy and yet maintain a palpable though invisible firewall between her and her favoured suitor, even her hauteur seemed to exude an organic, almost pheromonal attraction.

Good luck was not a quality that could be inherited. Or was it? Wasn't it said by the wise men that everybody made their own destiny?

Did it apply also to a woman like Labiba's daughter, of unknown parentage and provenance? Or would Nurus Saadat be a living example of the irony of fate, to have grown up like a princess and then having to embark upon the boat of life in choppy seas, the boat soon to be battered and sunk against the rock and shale of real life? Or was a Fairy Prince from the realm of Qaf destined to appear and take her away to the land of djinns and fairies?

Mother and daughter both were familiar with the life story of Khadijah Sultan, a renowned Isfahani beauty, aristocrat, poet and lover of her cousin Valeh Daghestani, another aristocrat and distinguished poet. Anyone would have predicted a life of love, poetry and luxury for them, a long spring that would fade naturally into the orange-pink and red of the sky as the sun inclined towards the west for them. But everything went wrong for them.

Ashraf Ghilzai, a tyrannical Afghan warlord, deposed Shah Tahmasp, King of Iran, and put the citizens of Isfahan to the sword; his military marauded and savaged and ravaged the city, the Ghilzai not the least bloodthirsty and ravenous among them. He took Khadijah as his woman, a much-desired war booty. Then, when Nadir Quli Khan (later known as Nadir Shah Abdali, then Durrani) defeated and routed the Ghilzai warlord and restored Shah Tahmasp, Khadijah Sultan, along with everything in the Ghilzai's palace, fell into Tahmasp's possession. Only a few years later, Nadir Quli Khan (named Tahmasp Quli Khan by the Shah) deposed Tahmasp and placed his infant son on the throne. A royal court and pavilion were established at Chihil Satun, and the baby was crowned as Shah Abbas the Third, honoured and salaamed by all, whether military chief or mullah or aristocrat. Those who dared even whisper in opposition were either strangled, or dragged before Tahmasp Quli with halters around their necks, and were made to swear in public the oath of allegiance to Shah Abbas and Tahmasp Quli Khan.

Poor Khadijah now fell into the hands of Tahmasp Quli. Valeh Daghestani and his family had fled to Hindustan immediately after

Nadir's first advent into Isfahan. Khadijah, friendless and now without honour, was, it was rumoured, assigned a small cell near the stairs that led to the cellar. She had been suffering from the disease of the lungs for some time, and though she was, technically, Nadir's woman, he was rarely, if ever, reminded of her to summon her to the harem. Valeh and his family were doing well under Muhammad Shah, the Mughal Emperor, but lacked the means and the courage to return to Iran, not to speak of Isfahan from where Tahmasp Quli ruled in the name of Shah Abbas the Third. Mounting a rescue for the God-and-man-forsaken Khadijah was out of the question.

In such a world, and in such times, could a powerless, patronless girl like Nurus Saadat hope for an unmolested life, or any kind of life at all? It is certain that Labiba must have thought on these matters, just as Nurus Saadat did, lying sleepless in her room, night after night. Yet, in spite of her proven strength of character, Labiba found herself unable to broach the subject with her daughter. The time to map out her daughter's future was staring her in face, now that Nurus Saadat was about to enter her fourteenth year.

One day, suddenly, the abscess that was hurting both of them quietly in their hearts burst open. That afternoon, when Nurus Saadat returned from the schoolroom after reading with her tutor her lesson on Nizam-ul Mulk Tusi's *Siyasat Nama,* a famous treatise for kings and statesmen written in the eleventh century, she went straight to her mother. Her face was flushed. She sat down next to her mother on the divan, practically touching thigh to thigh, something which she never did. She said after a moment of quiet, perhaps after collecting herself: 'Amma, Akhund Agha was telling me today that I have read *Siyasat Nama* with him better than any young man whom he taught.'

'As Allah Wills,' her mother said with a smile. 'And why not, my little lady is one among thousands. None would have a son even remotely bright like my dear daughter.'

Saying this, Labiba Khanam raised her daughter's chin, intending to kiss her forehead. 'But what is this? You are crying?' she said in surprise. 'Why, what happened? Are you out of sorts? Or do you want something to eat?'

Nurus Saadat choked back her tears with some difficulty and said: 'Akhund Agha believes me to be superior to boys. Amma says the same. But am I really so?'

'I for one have no doubt. And not because you are my child.'

'So then . . . so then . . .' She tried her best to keep a check on her rage, and finally failing, her temper flared up and her words, like a basin full of live coals, scattered over her mother.

'Then which King's Vizier am I to become? Which madrasa will I head? And if not these, which house is the one whose courtyard would be brightened by my feet? I am no boy. And I may be your darling baby, but the world knows me by a different description!'

It was a long time, and certainly for the first time since she settled in Baghat, that Labiba found herself at a loss for words. After a moment's stunned silence, she was about to open her mouth to reply when Nurus Saadat hurled away her bag of books, and smashed her lapis lazuli inkstand so hard against the wall that it broke. A spray of ink shot against the wall and the ceiling.

'I am not a boy!' She was weeping in impotent rage, her hands gathered up into fists, as if looking for something to hit or break. 'All my faults would have been hidden had I been a boy. And why should a girl be compared to a boy, after all, why not the other way round? Tell me, had I been a boy, would there not have been dozens of offers of marriage for me? Had I been . . .'

She gulped down her tears, but was unable to go on.

'Even then I'd have worried for you, darling,' Labiba managed to get in a word edgeways, 'though not in the way as I worry for you now. Please understand, my child, you and I cannot change the way of the world, its customs and laws, its prejudices—'

Nurus Saadat cut her short, perhaps for the first time in her life. She cried: 'I hate the world, I hate it, do you hear?'

'Yet, we women have to find ways to subsist and thrive within those very customs and rules of the world,' Labiba spoke as if she had not been interrupted.

'I defy the world and its customs! I spit on them!' Her tears began to flow again, and Nurus Saadat was now sobbing and talking at the same time, like a little girl, helpless. 'Having read so much, what did I learn, what did I gain? If I was designed to live my life as a dancing and singing woman, why all this play-acting? If it's written that my place is in hell, why was I allowed a glimpse of Paradise?'

Labiba Khanam now found it hard to control her own fury. 'So I am your enemy, am I?'

'Yes, you are!' Nurus Saadat howled. 'And always were my foe.' She ripped apart the pillow on the divan, strewing soft white feathers like snowflakes. 'Were you not my enemy, you'd have tried to make me something on your model. You wouldn't have deceived—'

'I deceived no one!' Labiba raised her voice to her daughter for the first time—it was a time like that, the time for unpleasant firsts—'You are not a dancing woman's daughter. I was born in a respectable family, but Fate—'

'Fate? Fate, or the Will of Allah, or the Edicts of the Elohim of Our Prophet Moses, aren't these deceptions too? Why did you not kill yourself if a dancing girl's life wasn't acceptable to you?'

Nurus Saadat now realized that she'd transgressed far beyond the line, far above her station. She, of all people, had no right to put Labiba Khanam to the question. She now saw the reality of what she had learnt from books in hypothetical narratives: children can be cruel to their parent without meaning to, without realizing it at all. She mopped her eyes with her tiny handkerchief; made a vain attempt to smooth the cover on the divan, to gather the feathers and stuff them back in the pillow as an act of inadequate atonement. She had unconsciously moved away from her mother in her rage, now she came closer, close as could be, put both her arms around her mother's neck, nuzzled and tried to tickle her. Then she said in a small voice muffled by Labiba's fragrant neck and bosom: 'Amma. I have done a great wrong. Please

212

forgive me; I was carried away by my foolish temper. I swear I won't
do it again. But what can I do, Amma? Night after night I lie sleepless.
What will happen to me? What will happen to us?' She wailed. 'Who
else is there before whom I can let go, but I shouldn't have done it. Say
you forgive me. Please.'

Her tears were wetting Labiba's neck and flowing down her breast,
moistening the bodice, but Nurus Saadat didn't try to do anything about
it. She wept, as she had never wept. Her large, enchanting, greenish-
blue eyes had never shed so much water. Labiba took her daughter's
feverish hands in her cold hands. Tears flowed down from her face to
Nurus Saadat's hands, but to no cooling effect.

This was the first and the last conversation, if conversation it was,
between mother and daughter on the subject. Perhaps both knew and
understood that the die was cast, the decision taken, and both knew
that their decisions were one and the same.

But the Scribe of Destinies had apparently something more, if not
something else, written on their Parchment of Fate. Events happened
which were apparently of no import, but could have potential for
change, to another direction, if not towards amelioration.

One evening, shortly after what we narrated above, the steward
in charge of giving appointments and setting up meetings, called on
the *hajib* and reported to the chief of woman guards that an envoy
had arrived, dispatched by Etmad-ud Daulah Navab Qamaruddin
Ahmad Khan Bahadur Nusrat Jang, Minister in Chief to the Emperor
of Hindustan. He desired to be presented before the Khanam. If she
so pleases, he can be invited to visit the next evening to make his
salaams and present the Missive of the Chief Minister of Hindustan
to Khanam sahib.

Labiba Khanam was a little surprised, and somewhat perplexed.
What business could the Minister in Chief to Muhammad Shah
Padishah Bahadur Ghazi have with me, she wondered. But the puzzle
could be solved only after granting him admittance. It didn't seem
expedient to send him back without meeting him face-to-face.

The next day, Labiba Khanam entered the divan khana at the appointed time and commanded the envoy to be escorted to her presence. The room where she sat was large, with a Kashani carpet spread from wall to wall. The carpet was light aquamarine in colour with no design or another colour breaking its expanse. Carpets—much smaller, but quite profusely coloured with floral designs—from Nayin, Bokhara and Kirman had been spread throughout the chamber, in an apparently casual manner, as if someone had thrown them there with no thought to create an effect. But actually, each of them had been placed after considerable thought, and with the view of giving the effect of casual elegance. In all the four corners, pressing down the main carpet, were solid heavy brass weights, designed like small, high-necked domes, and shining as the result of some few hours of daily rubbing. Inlaid attar boxes in oakwood from Kashmir and containers for cardamoms and other exotic condiments, again made of brass, and again shining like mirrors, were placed on small tables in several places on the floor. There was a large, low, circular table in the middle, breaking the profusion of colours created by the carpets. On the table was a large vase, displaying the flowers of the season, especially the roses of Shiraz and the tulips of Tabriz.

The walls were sparsely decorated with framed calligraphy, in the *vasli* style made popular by Hindustani calligraphers. The ceiling was covered in brocade, twisted in the middle to give the effect of a flower, and the wrinkles thus created in the ceiling cloth looked like large flower petals. Four candelabra with thirty-six candles each hung in four corners of the room. The candle shades in a candelabrum were all in different, very light colours: pale blue, sea green, burnt orange, and so forth.

In front of the main entrance door, at the far end of the room, Labiba Khanam sat on a low wooden platform, covered in dark-blue Kashmiri carpet, in the centre of which was spread a heavy silk coverlet from Yemen. The legs of the ebony platform, inlaid with ivory, were visible below the overhang of the carpet.

Labiba had on a loose, longish pair of trousers, partly Turkish and partly Hindustani in style. Made of peacock-green Hindustani silk, its other Hindustani element was in its borders, heavily embroidered in gold at the bottom. The bottoms were very narrow, almost like jodhpurs, just above the ankles, then the pants rose like a storm, in great width and breadth, almost like bellows. What saved them from seeming bulky and billowy was the pleats which divided the trousers from above the lower calves into soft, watermelon-like slices which gathered to become one at her waist. Around her waist, she wore a narrow golden zone, woven out of pure gold thread. The zone could be clicked open or closed with a solid gold catch, encrusted with a single golden topaz. She wore a narrow tunic in turquoise blue; its long sleeves were somewhat flared, to echo the pants, and again, to echo the pants, they were very tight at the wrists. Its neck and collar were decorated with small, natural pearls from the Persian Gulf and Sarandip. The bigger ones came from the Gulf. She wore a sleeveless vest above the tunic in back velvet whose dark colour was offset by a profusion of white sapphires and pink rubies woven along the neckline. Her nose and earlobes were devoid of ornaments, but she wore a necklace of medium-sized smoky topazes, each stone surrounded by glittering crystals.

To one side of her throne-like platform could be seen her dainty shoes, made of white buckskin. The shoes were shorn of jewellery, but were hand-painted, with floral sprigs. The painting deceived the viewer into imagining that the sandals were made of paper. She sat in the formal fashion, with her feet tucked under her thighs. Someone who viewed her from the side could occasionally glimpse a delicately painted toenail; or sometimes the whole pink toe or a part of the heel or sole could be seen, tantalizing, inviting kisses or adoration. She always sat in that same posture throughout the sessions when she sang. Never changing her side or stance, her face never revealed the strain that she must be undergoing, sitting that way, hour by hour.

She wore no weapon, but two Kurdish lady's maids stood behind her all the time, a dagger hung by their waist in a chased steel scabbard. The silver hilt of the dagger, inlaid with brass worked over in gold, could be seen prominently against the waist. Many more armed guards, all women, were never far from her and could even be occasionally glimpsed standing behind the arras, the light glinting on their weapons.

In order to gain the divan khana, one had to pass through a veranda, an enclosed courtyard, and then again a pair of double verandas. Entering from beyond the main door, hidden from view, and stopping under the central arch of the inner veranda, a lady's maid salaamed and spoke: 'It is to submit before Grand Khanam sahib: Rai Kishan Chand Ikhlas, envoy to the Exalted Presence, Navab Qamaruddin Khan Bahadur Nusrat Jang, Chief of the Ministers to the Emperor of Hindustan, desires to be presented.'

Labiba Khanam made some small, almost imperceptible sign, or gave permission with a very softly spoken 'yes'. The maid went out, walking backwards, and presently returned, came to the door of the divan khana, and announced: 'Rai Kishan Chand Ikhlas sahib has come from Delhi.'

His age nearer forty than fifty, his complexion very dark brown, Rai Kishan Chand Ikhlas was a little above six feet tall. His eyes were black and their eyelids wrinkled in two like a piece of silk—a sure sign of large eyes and large lids, marks of beauty in both male and female in Hindustan. Such eyes were called *ghilafi* (covered). His face was beardless, but the moustaches were of above-average thickness, their corners bent towards the mouth. The drooping moustaches emphasized the strength of the well-formed chin. His white, even teeth were slightly reddened with betel juice, and his face was the picture of good humour—it seemed he was just about to smile at some small joke. His cap, somewhat boat-like, was of heavily embroidered white cotton with a couple of inches worth of even more heavily embroidered border which had a hint of gold in the design. The cap was slightly rounded at the front, its edges raised a bit. The cap was worn slightly askew, revealing a little of very black, very dense hair worn in long locks according to the fashion then current in Delhi. He wore a five-stranded pearl necklace around his neck, and a silver ornament shaped like an amulet, adorned with very small beryls, light blue and with a dull sheen. He wore a long cotton tunic, onion coloured, with natural stripes in the same colour. Over the tunic, he had a short, velvet blue jacket, called nima. It had no formal buttons, but two round silken balls on both sides, hung upon the main tunic by golden loops. One side of the nima was drawn to the left and wrapped so that a part of the chest was uncovered, and the fabric of the long cotton tunic was so fine that the chest muscles could be seen clearly, creating the illusion that there was nothing under the nima. Similarly, in spite of the long sleeves, the broad and strong wrists were visible under it because of the fineness of the fabric.

He wore wide-bottomed trousers, in the best Delhi style, of the flowery silk called *phoolam*. To round off the ensemble, he wore a heavy Kashmiri woollen jamah of an even wider girth. Heavily pleated, it cascaded around his lower body from the waist. Over the jamah on his waist, he wore a silk sash, embroidered again in silk, Kashmiri style. The bejewelled handle of his dagger could be seen clearly, the dagger in its chased silver scabbard hanging by his left side. He wore light leather shoes which had, in the approved Mughal style, no walls above the heels, and the shoes would have resembled casual slippers but for the blue, red and green leather that had been used in their making. There was no ornament on the shoes, except that their ends were elongated and curled like a peacock's head. Behind him were a couple of bearers with covered trays on their head.

Rai Kishan Chand Ikhlas removed his shoes at the entrance to the chamber, took one step inside, and stopped there. He salaamed three times, bending low, and then he folded his hands on his chest and spoke in a clear, polite and firm voice: 'May your prosperity and fortune increase. I, the envoy of the Exalted Grand Vizier to the Emperor of India, present myself before Your Honour with the Grand Vizier's generosity-scented letter.'

The maid beckoned to him gently to advance. He raised his head, entered upon the Khanam's presence and sat down on a small Bokharai carpet, his feet tucked under his thighs in the approved fashion. He chose a carpet that wasn't too close to her, but not so distant either that normal voice couldn't carry to the interlocutor. Now he raised his eyes upon Grand Khanam, and that one glance was sufficient to slay him with the sword of desire.

There was a faint, but warm and welcoming smile on Labiba Khanam's face. She was, at that time, two years shy of fifty, but not by any means did she seem to be above thirty-five or thirty-six. And on that day, because of the foreign visitor sent by a Minister of the Realm, she had made her toilette with some care. Kishan Chand Ikhlas felt perspiration break out on his face. He lowered his eyes, intending to feel for his kerchief from under his collar, and his eyes fell on Labiba Khanam's shoes. His first impression was that they were made of paper, a child's playthings. But the next moment he realized with some surprise that they were the manufacture of his own land: shoes so thin and light and delicate that they barely lasted a day or two of wearing. He had the insane desire to advance and clasp the shoes to his bosom. Fortunately, that moment passed immediately when he saw a maid put before him a small, light occasional table on which were a small Chinese plate, piled with dry fruits, a Turkish cup of coffee, and an engraved and gem-encrusted box of attars.

Before he could address those items, it seemed to him that Grand Khanam's eyes were on him, and she was saying something: *'Ahlan wa sahlan,'* she said, using the Arabic words of greeting universally used in the medieval Muslim word. The words meant: 'You are of us, please feel at home.' She continued, using a famous line of a Persian verse:

Oh you, your coming here is the cause of our heart's happiness.

It seemed to Kishan Chand Ikhlas that a water-harmonica was being played somewhere behind the curtains. The speed was slow, evocatively slow; each note was clear as crystal. There was invitation in the notes, to come closer, to hear with your ear close to the source of the sound. Kishan Chand Ikhlas was willing to sacrifice himself a hundred times for the notes to go on tinkling, for the pure cuckoo-like voice to go on forever, even if it wasn't he who was being addressed. But Labiba Khanam was saying: 'Etmad-ud Daulah Bahadur has sent you as a sample of the shadow of his comfort and kindness in order to greet and elevate us who lie so far away from him.' She quoted a line from Hafiz:

It should cause no wonder, should the king favour the beggar.

Then she went on: 'I am grateful to him, body and soul. It would be my fortune's elevation to give up my life in sacrifice for his sacred existence. Please command how I may be of service to the Exalted Slaves.'

Kishan Chand was still in the land of enchantment, lost in the thrill of her voice. He now came back to the present world, and in some confusion, tried to remember what he was supposed to do next. Thankfully, he recalled immediately that he was there to deliver Etmad-ud Daulah's missive to the Khanam. He removed the purse that reposed under his sash, undid the strings and took out the gold-calligraphed message from the Vizier, placed it on his two hands with a *nazr*, or formal offering, of five gold coins. He then rose, made a salaam, and extended his hands towards the Khanam. Before his action was complete, another maid appeared, a small silver tray in hand, and accepted the missive and the nazr, and placed the tray with its contents on her head on behalf of her mistress. She then stepped up to her and placed it before her. Labiba Khanam unrolled the letter, which was rolled up like a cylinder and tied with a golden thread, and read it carefully. She smiled with some pleasure or approval. Before looking up, she read it over again. This is what the letter, written in the florid Persian of the time, said:

Possessor of the Sign of Advancement of Fortune, whose
foundation is fortunate and auspicious, Colour and Fragrance of
all roses and rose gardens, Venus of the firmament of music, vocal
or instrumental, Ruler of the kingdom of coquetry and style of
beauteousness, Labiba Khanam, Etmad-ud Daulah Muhammad
Qamaruddin Khan Nusrat Jang makes the submission as follows:
that the wedding of my only child, a daughter, is fixed to take
place with my sister's son, Riayat Khan, son of Zahir-ud Daulah
Navab Azimullah Khan, on a date in December 1743. On this
auspicious occasion, I wish to organize an assembly the like of
which the eye of the Ancient Heaven even would not have seen.
And it is obvious that such an assembly wouldn't be worthy of
such description if that Dear Lady were not there to enhance
its elegance and lustre. Details of the journey, expenses of the
passage and all such will be laid out before that Dear Lady by my
envoy, Rai Kishan Chand Ikhlas. I hope I will not be turned down.

It seemed to Rai Kishan Chand's anxiety-filled mind that her second
thoughts were not quite receptive to the proposal, for a small line of
worry wrinkled her brow, though it disappeared within a millisecond.
Kishan Chand Ikhlas was quite sensitive to it, but he daren't speak until
spoken to. Labiba raised her eyes to Ikhlas and spoke in a soft but grave
voice: 'His servant is grateful with her heart and soul to Etmad-ud
Daulah for remembering her and increasing her value, but . . .'

She stopped and Kishan Chand Ikhlas felt as if it was not she who
had fallen silent; it was his breath, which had stopped its to-and-fro
movement in his breast. What did the 'but' mean? What was to follow?
He feared unsuccess for his embassy; he naturally feared the loss of
face back in Delhi. Worse still, he feared lifelong disunion should she
refuse to go back with him. He concentrated his entire strength of
mind, the whole power of his spirit, in willing her not to refuse the
invitation. He couldn't ask, he couldn't question. He just looked at
Labiba Khanam with hopeful eyes.

After a long interval, or so it seemed to Ikhlas, because it wasn't actually more than twenty or thirty breaths, Grand Khanam resumed.

'But, my fear is that I will be a total stranger in Delhi. I don't know the language, nor am I familiar with the rules and conventions of the society there. I have no knowledge about the arts of that place, except that since the time of the Exalted Presence, Amir Khusrau, may God have Mercy upon him, it has been five centuries now and there have been numerous masters of the art since then, his disciples and the followers of his disciples. Delhi is even now home to musicians of excellence. I will be no more than a tongue-tied sparrow among them.'

Ikhlas now openly produced his handkerchief and dried his face and forehead. Then he spoke slowly, with clarity and deliberation: 'I do not dare disagree with what Grand Khanam's commands. I can only quote the proverb, "Each flower has its own colour, its own scent." You have your station; the masters of Hind have theirs. As regards the problem of language, in the Exalted Court of Shahjahanabad, the Presence will encounter numerous prattlers in the Persian language, like your servant. And there is no lack of Armenian speakers there, either. You will have your appurtenant instruments and your *saz* accompany you from here. Ghazals, or *soz*, will be entirely in Persian.'

He paused, swallowed, continued: 'And the common speech of Delhi is called Hindi, or Rekhtah, and it is so close to Persian that if you . . . if you were to accord to me the honour of accompanying and escorting you, the time spent on the journey will be sufficient for you to acquire that tongue.'

Kishan Chand Ikhlas had his eyes on Labiba Khanam as he spoke. He could not help himself against what was almost impoliteness on his part: his eyes should have been looking down, or in front. He should not have had them on Grand Khanam's face. But with every word that he spoke, he felt that he was becoming spellbound, more and more ensnared by her compellingly desirable person, the delicacy of her graceful bearing, her alabaster-like complexion which seemed to be internally luminous, her eyes, bright with some inner beauty, their blue-green colour iridescent, as if consciously casting their spell on him. Eyes, which not only reflected the expressions of her face, but also perhaps her real thoughts, with no attempt at concealment. The eyes seemed to have a marvellous vitality of their own. As the flames of the colourful candles became bolder, or sometime tremulous with the effect of the breeze, Labiba Khanam's eyes almost reflected each change of light with a light of their own, as if answering the movement of the flames.

'Very well,' said Labiba, 'or rather, extremely suitable and correct. But the journey is very long and often arduous if not clearly hazardous. There is also the problem of acclimatization, if not of acculturation. The climate of Delhi, I hear, is very hot. I will, in any case, be a stranger there,' she concluded with a half smile.

'The Presence will travel in maximum comfort. She would feel as if she were riding the Flying Throne of the Prophet, the Presence, Sulaiman. And as this servant submitted a moment ago, the Presence shall not be a stranger in Delhi.' He paused, tried to look her in the eye, and resumed: 'Prime Ministers and Princes don't invite strangers to their assemblies. You are not a stranger for them. If you'd permit me, I will personally provide security and stand guard upon you at all times.'

This last sentence he uttered with wistfulness, a half-open entreaty that held a colour of desire, which couldn't have remained obscure to Labiba Khanam. He continued, desperate not to let Labiba Khanam raise any new objection: 'It is true that the weather in Delhi ranges from very hot to very cold. But it's a leafy city, madam, there are more gardens than bazaars there, I daresay. Then we have cool, airy homes, stepwells with sleeping space. There are basements in most houses, plenty of ice and the lightest possible clothing to keep us cool.' He paused in some confusion, fearful that he was sounding like a professional guide. But he saw that Khanam-e Buzurg was listening, and his own tone was grave and respectful, not that of a professional caravan manager or guide.

He continued: 'Presence, there is no question of you feeling that you are among strangers. You'll be the personal guest of the Presence, the Minister of all the King's territories. You will have a house of your own, everything will be as you desire and command. And believe me, madam, everyone there will consider it an honour to carry out your slightest wishes and to make themselves familiar with your auspicious temperament, your preferred way of spending your time.'

Saying this, Kishan Chand Ikhlas beckoned to the men standing behind him, outside the door. They advanced, placed the two trays at the feet of Labiba Khanam, and removed their covers. Kishan Chand said, 'The thousand gold mohurs are a present, a nazr, for Your Honour from the Exalted Etmad-ud Daulah Bahadur. There are also a few dresses, full outfits, for your Exalted Servants. These small offerings are not conditional. You may or may not honour my land with your feet, which are always auspicious wherever they go.'

Labiba half rose from her set, made a low salaam, and said: 'May Allah grant more victories to Nusrat Jang Bahadur. His generosity has made my dark house replete with gems whose lustre illumines the dark. I will remain grateful to him.'

Kishan Chand could barely suppress his smile of delight. 'So, what are the orders about having the luggage made ready and loaded on the pack animals?' His body, and not just his tone of voice, seemed to radiate joy.

For the first time in the meeting, Labiba Khanam smiled an unconstrained smile. 'Not so quickly, please. I need some time to make my decision. I'll let you know about it the day after tomorrow.'

Kishan Chand's face fell, quite palpably. He was about to beg permission to rise and leave, when Labiba Khanam, conscious of the effect her words had on him, spoke again: 'You didn't take a look at the coffee, or even sample the attars. Please detain your noble self here some more. You are not staying somewhere far, or are you?'

'It is the nurture and nourishment given by the servants of the Presence, I am quite all right and comfortable in my lodgings.' Kishan

Chand spoke with unintended fervour. 'I am servant to your command. I can't go anywhere.'

The fervidness, not quite so hidden in these words, must certainly have been apparent to Grand Khanam; how much devotion, desire, how many unopened blossoms of longing peeped from behind the formal words, which are normally devoid of serious intent and meaning. But Labiba deftly avoided taking that direction. On a small gesture from her, the maid brought a new cup of coffee, removing the old one. Ikhlas was just about to pick up the new one when Labiba Khanam spoke: 'Rai Kishan Chand Ikhlas, is the word "Ikhlas" a part of your name, or is it a takhallus? Does your Elevated Temperament incline somewhat towards poetry?'

Hearing his name from the lips of Labiba Khanam transported Ikhlas; he felt such freshness, such an affectionate, homey flavour in the experience, as if Labiba hadn't spoken his name, rather, she had placed her hand on his shoulder. He felt a little tremor in his whole body and didn't dare lift the coffee cup lest he betray his thrill. Again, he swallowed before he could articulate his response: 'This insignificant particle of dust has the takhallus "Ikhlas". I am a pupil of the Presence, Mirza Qubul Beg Kashmiri, may his generous inspiration continue to spread far.'

'Pupil? Sorry, I don't understand. Music is a discipline that is certainly acquired from an ustad, but an ustad in poetry? That is something new. Are not poets supposed to be the disciples of God himself?'

'You are quite right, madam, quite correct. But it so happens that for the last four or five decades, the composing of poetry in Rekhtah, or Hindi, has been popular in the Exalted City of the Sultan. Poetry in this tongue was not much known or practised there before. Thus the newly fledged birds in the rose garden of poetry felt that they stood in need of some wise and experienced person to teach them to fly in the firmament of Rekhtah. The idea, of having ustads, became very well liked, and it was only a few years before high-ranking ustads found themselves educating many pupils in the art and craft of Rekhtah poetry. Young poets who wrote in Persian thought: so why not we also find a master ustad for us from whom we may derive inspiration and beneficence in the field of poetry?'

'Well, that may be so. But how do they derive benefit and inspiration from the ustad?'

'Oftentimes, the ustad substitutes a superior, more meaningful or idiomatic word or phrase for what the pupil had written. He teaches by precept and practice. Sometimes, he even goes to the trouble of substituting a whole line for an existing one. Or he may find the pupil's word organization in a line or verse to be dull or what we call "slow". If that be the situation, he may improve the line, or have the pupil try again.'

'Pardon me, but I couldn't grasp the meaning of the phrase "dull, or slow word organization". Would you, by "word organization", mean metricality?'

Rai Kishan Chand Ikhlas found himself with a problem to which he didn't seem to have a solution. How to define 'slow' or 'dull' organization? The definition of 'word organization' was easy enough. He answered after some thought: 'Your Honour must have heard of Imam Abdul Qahir Jurjani and his theories of metaphor and suitability.'

Labiba interrupted, 'Indeed, I do. *My* ustad taught me those things.'

'Well, then, let Your Honour call to her brilliant mind the formulation of the Imam that true eloquence consists in the order in which the words are arranged in an utterance. It is possible to have many arrangements; the best one has the most lustre, and the most sharpness.'

'Yes. I know. He has cited the Quran in this connection.'

'Perfectly correct, Your Honour. So if the arrangement of words in a line is not the best possible, if the line has more words than it needs, or if all its words are not fully effectual—these defects, or lack of qualities, render a line dull or slow, even if it doesn't have any obvious shortcoming.'

Labiba smiled her world-conquering smile. 'Well, I must say that's a good way of looking at verses. Have the ustads derived this method from Arabic, or from Sanskrit, which I understand is your most ancient tongue?'

'Madam, I have mentioned Jurjani. The rest of the idea naturally flows from Jurjani, though the formulation "dullness" or "slowness" is indigenous to us, I believe.'

My God, this discussion, almost like a viva voce test, must end here, Ikhlas said to himself. While he loved hearing her speak, he was fearful of sounding like a pedant. But he had, it seemed, aroused Labiba's interest. She now asked: 'Are there rules for these things, or does it all depend upon the ustad's knowledge and intuition?'

'There are rules, and there aren't,' said Ikhlas. 'What is most important here is not pedagogics, but the ustad's intuition of the language, and his experience as both reader and mentor.'

'That's very good indeed. But tell me, will you now permit me to partake of the pleasure of your poetry, which is joined with maximum expressiveness, I am sure?'

Again a tremor overtook Rai Kishan Chand's whole body. Should he recite some verses from a narrative poem about love? No, that would be presuming too much, he told himself. Even so, wasn't there a whole world of possible intimacies, of present appreciation and enjoyment somewhere in those plain words? 'You, permit, me, partake, pleasure . . .'

Truly, it was like the entry of the morning sun's rays into an underground dungeon! But he couldn't recall a single verse from his own poetry. And even if he somehow dredged out a few, it was most likely that they wouldn't impress this exceedingly intelligent lady, and he would lose this unique opportunity of speaking directly to her without betraying himself. God forbid, he might lose even the little credit that he'd gained in her estimate so far.

'My verses are unworthy of being presented before Your Honour. In this refined chamber it would indeed sound like the screech of a kite,' he replied, fearful that his refusal to say his own verses may sound pompous. He went on, somewhat tentatively: 'Should the Presence permit, I would like to obtain the honour of presenting before Her a ghazal from Mirza Bedil sahib, our greatest poet.'

'That's not a bad idea at all. Please to say his verses before me.' Labiba Khanam seemed quite willing to hear an Hindustani master, for many of them had reputations extending beyond Hindustan to Iran and even beyond Iran, in both East and West.

Now which ghazal of Bedil sahib should be suitable? Ikhlas suddenly was unsure, and worried. He called upon Bedil's spirit in his heart and said, 'Ya Abul Maani, Master of Poetic Themes and Subjects, please make easy this predicament for me. I'll visit your Radiant Tomb to pray and have a quantity of sweets distributed to the poor.' As he uttered these words in his heart, he thought he saw a page from the *Complete Poetical Works* of the master, dead these many years. The page was like an illuminated and scented manuscript, and he could read every word. By Allah, how suited to the occasion that ghazal was! He loosened his stance, resumed his posture, making himself more comfortable, and began to recite in his tuneful voice:

> *It would be cruelty, if desire drags you to excurse in a garden—*
> *You are no less than a freshly blossomed rose: open the doors*
> > *of the heart and go into that garden.*

Labiba was thrilled, and moved to some kind of pain, as if the tip of a very fine needle had touched her heart. She hadn't changed her stance during the entire conversation, but now she sat up with renewed interest. Rai Kishan Chand's eyes were half closed; he was swaying to the music of the words and fully lost in their mysterious message:

> *Do not choose the labour of pursuit after the musk deer whose scent*
> > *wanders away*
> *Create a problem for you with the thoughts of those curly tresses, and*
> > *enter Khotan, where all the musk deer are.*

227

If Divine Emanation doesn't cast a spell on you in desiring the physical existence
Who pulled at the hem of your shirt to bring you into this ancient caravanserai?
Your desire became your good, and your evil; your breath of life, your beast and your insect:
Who, with this madness, became your guide that you came into the world of I, and You?
I bore the anguish of waiting for you; in the path of thoughts of you, I am become dead—
Extend one foot towards asking about me; come for a brief moment, like the life in the body.
I thought but a little, and ran away from the ambiguity of existence, like the breeze
Cut open the knot of the dewdrop's reality and come into my heart.
You don't have the desire for height, nor do you have lowliness; you have neither the clamour of the drunk, nor do you have sense, or intelligence—
What's the use of your existence, fruitless like the morning? Be a breath of sound and come into song.
Why do you borrow the strength to struggle, just to suffer the pain of martyrdom without blood money?
Tear down the door of questing; enter the paradise of the state of safety and wellness.
What is the mirror upon which you bend so intently that you are oblivious to so much leisure?
You are no more than the power of sight of a slaughtered one. Raise your eyelashes and come into the shroud.
Ever comes the cry from the angel of the divine assembly:
Enter the seclusion of the school of fidelity through the door of not going out.

Come out from this cage, Oh Bedil, if desire tugs at you for the other side:
You are not all that happy in the stranger's state, so I say, 'Come back into your home.'

Kishan Chand Ikhlas could never forget the mood and emotional affect of that evening. Outside in the park, the dark green of the poplar and the elm and the lighter green of the chinar had become almost black with the deep red of the dusk behind them. Light no longer filtered into the divan khana through the lattices, and the candles, each in its candelabrum, seemed to have become brighter, more colourful. One by one, the high, glazed casements caught the fading, darkening light, their flimsy curtains fluttering a little as if moved by the power of poetry.

The two maids-in-waiting were spellbound as Ikhlas recited. Now, they broke out in spontaneous applause in unison, carried away by the occasion. Labiba was almost in a trance, striking her thigh with her hand, as if keeping time, muttering, '*Marhaba! Subhanallah!* Absolutely enchanting!' Now when the poem was over, she cried: 'How unusual the metre, how unfamiliar the words! But by Allah, what force, what invention of theme, what flow, what rhymes! Simply unmatchable!'

Kishan Chand Ikhlas noted Labiba's astuteness in knowing the metre and describing it as unusual. The metre, though not unknown to the experts, had been but very rarely used in Iranian Persian, as its structure was considered unsuitable for Persian. It was one of Bedil's achievements that he wrote much in this metre, and with great distinction and felicity. Ikhlas bent in salaam and now said a rubai, adapting his tone to the rubai's rhythms:

Mirza Bedil, who shows the way in poetry,
Is the true Messenger, the Protector, the Head, in the land of poetry—
He is unique in creation of styles of utterance
By Allah, for poetry, he is the God of poetry.

'Well and truly said,' said Labiba, and asked, 'who wrote that rubai?'
Rai Kishan Chand Ikhlas was almost intoxicated with so much attention, so much direct interlocution. He spoke, in a voice that was slightly choked, trying to keep a hold on himself: 'The poet is the

Presence, Bindraban Khushgo. One of the ablest and best drilled pupils of Mirza sahib, whom God has placed among the best.'

'So, do I understand that Mirza Bedil is no longer among the living?'

'He was joined with Allah's Truth a little above a score of years ago, madam. My dear and revered father, may Allah keep his shade on us for a long time, has also the honour of being one of the Exalted Mirza sahib's pupils.'

Labiba fell silent, as if in thought. Then she said, in a tentative tone of voice: 'May I ask something, if it won't be unpleasant on your temperament?'

'Your word, and unpleasant, dear madam! Please ask whatever you desire to know.'

'Well, actually, I was wondering . . . Mirza Bedil was perhaps Muslim. And you . . . ?'

'I am Hindu, Allah be praised. The worshipful Bindraban sahib is also Hindu. We in Hindustan, especially those who are in the profession of authorship, speak Persian, and all Hindustani communities, whatever their creed, have friendly and brotherly relations with each other.'

'And the Jews, and the Nazarenes?'

'They all keep to their ways and paths, without let. The Jews have been there for a long time now, certainly many centuries. The Nazarenes are comparatively newer, and all of them are in trade. In the glorious time of Emperor Shahjahan, Lord of the Auspicious Conjunction, some of their tradesmen in the eastern territories began to convert people, almost forcibly, to their faith. Condign punishment was visited upon them. They remained quiet for quite some time, but of late their activities have been on the increase. We don't mix with them much. Anyway, as the poet said:

Paradise is where there is no sickness or discomfort,
None have to do anything with the other.

He smiled, 'Perhaps that's why my land is called *Jannat nishan*—Paradise-like.' He had been somewhat more comfortable during the exchange, thinking that some rapport had begun to exist between them. So, he plucked up his courage, half rose, and submitted: 'I may now be granted leave to depart. I will present myself the day after tomorrow on your summons.'

'No, you don't need prior appointment. Please trouble your feet and extend your benevolence at this time the day after. You'll find this servant waiting.'

Perhaps those last few words had some extra meaning? Or am I reading more than she intended? Ikhlas quickly played the words back in his mind, but said nothing. Labiba rose to bid farewell to Ikhlas and was just about to put her feet into her shoes when Kishan Chand Ikhlas moved up quickly; in fact, almost ran up to Labiba and helped her put the shoes on. In this process, his hands touched, almost caressed her rosy toes and heels. A frisson, almost erotic in character and also somehow shocking, ran through his body, as if he'd run his index finger upon the sharp edge of a knife. He retired at once, made three quick salaams and stepped out, walking backwards, uncertain on his legs.

*

That night, and the following day, mother and daughter sought each other's views no less than three times about Etmad-ud Daulah's invitation. Nurus Saadat observed: 'Amma, I don't see any problem with going to Delhi. But to undertake such a long journey, stay there just a few weeks and then come back, facing again the hazards of the journey without sufficient rest and recruitment, seems not a proceeding in accord with prudence, or good policy. The times are turbulent in the extreme, and the route is not of the safest in many places. Luck may favour us and keep us safe on the outward journey, but to trust to your luck for a second time so soon, seems to me somewhat unwise.'

'So, you are in favour of my turning down the invitation?'

'Nooo, no. I don't say that,' she said, trying in her heart to understand what exactly she wanted to say, and resumed a few seconds later: 'There is another question, though. Do we, in terms of money, stand in need of Etmad-ud Daulah's benevolences?'

'No, there's no need at present. But you say that the times are unfavourable, and in fact not favourable at all for women like us who have no male guardian. So there's nothing wrong in having, and saving as much as we can for the bad times that are sure to come.'

'Nothing wrong, except . . .' She hesitated to go on. 'Except that in the forest, a tree which has a beehive will always attract the bear.'

'But there is no protection in living without the wherewithal of life.'

'That is my real difficulty, Amma.' She drew a deep sigh. 'Neither does seclusion and withdrawal suit us, nor being in the public view.'

'But if you take account of all things, you'll see that plenty is better than scarcity.' Suddenly her tone became sharp, instead of conciliatory. 'Had Zohra the Egyptian not earned such immense wealth because of me, and had I not come away from there with a fraction of what was really mine, I and your father would have died like dogs and cattle in a drought.'

Nurus Saadat, intimidated, fell on the defensive. 'I am not saying anything against you, Amma.'

'No, but experience tells us that those who linger in the maze of "yes/no" too often and too long rarely get to find their way out. You must bear that in mind.'

The conversation hung there. Neither was inclined to pursue her thoughts to the logical end. The next morning, Nurus Saadat reopened the subject. 'Amma, what kind of country is Hind, and what kind of life can we expect to find in Delhi?'

'What's the point of asking if we aren't going there?' Labiba replied curtly.

Nurus Saadat was stung to the quick, and her native sharpness of temper asserted itself. 'Amma, you are not prepared to hear me out, nor do you open your mind to me!'

'So, you speak your mind freely. At present you are perhaps not minded to understand what I have to say.'

'I, and not understand your words? That's not possible, dearest Amma. But . . . I . . . I have a thought.'

'Yes? Come, tell me what is your thought, darling daughter.'

'Well, is it . . . is it really necessary to return from Delhi after a short sojourn there?'

Labiba was taken aback. Yes, that was a possibility. Why hadn't she thought of it? Nurus Saadat went on, a little more boldly now: 'Our future, as we see it from here, could be no worse in Delhi. Delhi, I understand, is a very big city, bigger than Isfahan, and perhaps even Istanbul. And our co-religionists who also speak our Armenian language are not rare. In fact, there is a city in Hind, though far to the east of Delhi, where our people abide in large numbers. The city, I am told, has the funny name of Kal-ka-ta. It is the seat of a Chief Rabbi.' She smiled wanly. 'Perhaps a longer stay in Delhi may open up new possibilities.'

'Where did you get to know all this, Nur?' There was a slight needle of sarcasm nesting in the apparently innocuous query.

'Amma, there are books and travelogues, and reports brought back by travellers and pilgrims. Hindustan is truly a very large country, and very rich, very prosperous. Our King Nadir Shah Durrani, whose Glory is that of Jamshed, God preserve him, brought back so much booty from there that he issued a general amnesty from payment of the state dues for three years in the whole of Iran; and I am told that it didn't make much of a gap in the coffers of the King and the nobles in Delhi.'

Labiba, somewhat nettled at the lecture from her 'little' daughter, retorted: 'Since when did you develop so much interest in wealth and money?

'Weren't you teaching me a similar lesson about money yesterday?' She smiled a sly, but loving and mischievous smile. 'But the question is not so much of money or means . . .' Her tone became somewhat tart, suddenly. 'The question is of possibilities.' She softened a bit, looked into her mother's face with obvious tenderness. 'You are worrying about me all the time, Amma. My future must be settled soon, one way or another. Delhi is full of all kinds of people, a veritable melting pot of creeds, races and communities. Isfahan can't hold a candle to Delhi, really.'

'So our beautiful daughter is weary, or bored, with Isfahan, nisf-e jahan?' Labiba spoke with a hint of levity, perhaps to indicate that she was not unhappy with the trend of the conversation.

'It's not a matter to joke about, Amma jan!' Nurus Saadat was still hurting somewhere by her mother's sharp tones. She always signalled her unhappiness with her mother by addressing her as 'Amma jan'.

'We have to give our reply to Agha Ikhlas tomorrow. We should give our answer on a full evaluation of our circumstances,' continued Nurus Saadat. 'Who knows, God has given us this opportunity so that we may eliminate, or reduce the element of chance from our lives.'

She smiled and spoke in her most winning voice: 'And truly, Amma, why should Isfahan, or any other city for that matter, claim a place in my heart? We are not native here, and Tabriz I don't remember at all. Our true native land, as you say, is somewhere much farther away in the West. You saw it last when you were no more than five or six. We are nomads of a sort, if one looks at our history. Perhaps Delhi will give us a home.' Her wistful voice was almost brimful of longing and not a little fear.

'Yes,' Labiba stressed the vowel in 'yes', as if she were wailing. 'Anything can happen, everything is possible.' Her eyes welled up. Perhaps she was reliving, even if for a moment, the forlorn scene when she faced the earthquake's devastation alone as a child of six years.

Nurus Saadat was puzzled. Perhaps Amma is unwilling to leave Isfahan, and feels coerced under what she sees as my importunacy? She broke into sobs and said urgently, 'Please. Amma don't be unhappy. You send your refusal just this minute, if you so desire.'

'No. Not at all. That's not the point, my little one,' said she through her tears, but didn't elaborate. Nurus Saadat was speechless, not daring to ask more, or make further conversation. Still, the matter came up again in the evening.

Labiba was unexpectedly in a sunny, friendly mood and it was she who opened the discussion. 'It's quite possible, isn't it, that we go there, make a long stay, look at the cultural and social environment there, gain some idea of further possibilities . . .' She fell silent, leaving her words to hang in the air. Perhaps she didn't need to elaborate what she meant by 'possibilities'.

Nurus Saadat was elated to see her mother in a better mood than ever before since the Hindustan question was under consideration between them. She said, 'Quite. You are quite right, Amma. Let's make an extended stay and see which way the wind of fortune blows. We should, of course, make it a precondition that should we decide to return, Etmad-ud Daulah will take full responsibility for our safe conduct.'

'Yes, yes . . . I too am more or less of the same mind. But . . .' Clouds of pain and dejection again appeared on her face and she fell silent.

'Why, you are again passing into dolour! What's happened now? Are you still vexed with me, Amma?'

Something suddenly caused a flood of sorrow and misery to wash over Labiba's face, leaving Nurus Saadat puzzled, concerned and apprehensive. This time, Labiba didn't just weep with tears. She began to sob, covering her face with her hands. Nurus Saadat almost cried out in shock and dread. What was happening to my mother? She looked at her in bewilderment and rose in a flurry to call a maid. But in her hurry, she stumbled, fell and crashed head first against the heavy bed frame. The skin broke and blood began to ooze out. Labiba, forgetting her distress, rose quickly, picked up the daughter, embraced and kissed her, cooing endearments to her all the time. She immediately found a fragrant balsam and tied a light bandage around her head.

After making sure that Nurus Saadat was in no real pain now, she spoke to her soothingly: 'Don't you be unhappy, darling daughter mine. Actually, I remembered my vow, which I made at your father's grave when we were going away from Tabriz. I'd promised to him that I would certainly visit his grave again at least once before I died. How could that promise be kept should we go to Delhi and settle or stay there for any considerable length of time? I might die in Delhi . . . This thought stabs me like a poisoned dagger at my throat. Dying is no matter, but how will I face your father if I do not carry out my promise to him?' She began to sob and weep uncontrollably.

Nurus Saadat put her arms around Labiba's neck, hugged her close and began to kiss and soothe her as if she were the mother and Labiba the daughter.

'There, there, my Amma jani,' she addressed Labiba with the appellative of maximum endearment that she kept for very special occasions. 'I almost didn't know him, but somehow my heart tells me that he would support and approve of anything which had the least potential for our good. And who says that—God forbid—your time in this world . . .' She choked back her tears and went on: ' . . . is soon going to end? You are so young, and as Allah Wills, quite healthy. And travellers do travel between Delhi and Tabriz all the time. It's not as if the road between the two cities is closed by war or such other conflict.'

She paused to mop her eyes surreptitiously with her sleeve. 'Allah Willing, I too will go to Tabriz with you . . .' Now she couldn't control her tears and was wailing and crying loudly, ' . . . and hug his tomb and weep for him.'

*

The next evening, when Rai Kishan Chand presented himself to continue and perhaps conclude his discussion, his heart sank to know that this time there'd be no meeting with Grand Khanam sahib. The shock of not being able to see her, and the dread of the reply being in the negative sent a feverish tremor down his spine. Anyway, he was escorted into the divan khana with the usual protocol and politeness, and was surprised to find Labiba Khanam seated on her usual seat, in the same manner and style as before. An ejaculation of surprise was about to escape from his lips when he realized his error: Something was different there.

Before he could fall into further error, Nurus Saadat rose to her full height in welcome. Rai Kishan Chand Ikhlas noted that the young lady was somewhat taller than Grand Khanam, and much younger. Another difference was her heavy tresses: extremely long and dense, they fell in two black, braided cascades, almost caressing her thighs.

'I submit my greetings. My name is Nurus Saadat. Amma has charged me with the responsibility of acting as your host. Please seat your noble self.'

The timbre of the girl's voice was exactly that of Grand Khanam, except she spoke with the lilt and soft, caressing modulations of a teenager, making her voice even more heart capturing. If Rai Kishan Chand hadn't first set his eyes on Labiba, he would say that he never saw anyone as beautiful as Nurus Saadat. If asked now, he'd say that he saw no woman more beautiful than Labiba Khanam and no young girl prettier than Nurus Saadat, nor did he ever expect to do so.

Rai Kishan Chand made a valiant effort to suppress his surprise and disappointment, again bent low in salaam to the girl, and saying, 'Very well. I present myself,' he took off his shoes and occupied the same seat which he had on his first visit. The self-confidence and near-haughtiness that seemed to flow out from Nurus Saadat's personality made it difficult for him to decide if he should open the conversation, or speak only when spoken to. His difficulty was solved by Nurus Saadat.

She inquired: 'Will you please let me know the number of stages from here to Delhi?'

Rai Kishan Chand's heart lurched high in his ribcage, as if a gun had been fired next to his ears. He paused, apparently to consider, but actually to collect himself: 'It is thirty stages . . .' He stopped, not certain

237

how he should address this stunning young beauty.

'You can call me Nur Khanam,' she informed him in grave tones. 'I will travel to Delhi along with you.'

Rai Kishan Chand Ikhlas felt his body almost float in the air, like a rose petal. But his heart was heavier than a stone. Such exceeding joy and such a weighty commission, would he be able to negotiate between them successfully? Such an occasion had never risen before for him in the past.

The details were worked out meticulously. Rai Kishan Chand found in Nurus Saadat a knowledgeable, expert negotiator and keen inquirer. On behalf of Etmad-ud Daulah, and in his own right as Plenipotentiary, Ikhlas accepted all the conditions and demands. He made no demands of his own, nor did he insult the girl and her mother by talking money and rewards and prizes. He just indicated, in veiled but sufficiently clear language that it might exceed their best expectations. With due design, but apparently casually and obiter, he mentioned that Etmad-ul Daulah once awarded a female singer called Bahina the Elephant Rider, the princely amount of seventy thousand rupees in jewellery, costly fabrics and a gold dinner service for one performance. This information was also intended to suggest that the leading dancing and singing women there were permitted to ride an elephant, a mount normally reserved for the royalty and the nobility.

The final point, clinched after a little more exchange of possibilities and proposals, was that the departure would take place late in the morning on the fifth day from that day. Ikhlas was reminded of the lines of the great seventeenth-century Persian poet Saib, of Tabriz:

> *As long as the flowers' fragrance causes the breeze to blow*
> *It is not possible to bar my access into the garden.*
> *Saib, open your wings and feathers, it is the season for Hindustan*
> *The heart can no longer be tied to the sights and sounds of Isfahan!*

It was agreed that those among the household establishment who desired to go to Hindustan would be taken on. The rest would have the choice to stay back, or get an honourable discharge.

*

Thus had it come to pass that that day was the commencement of the fifth week for Labiba Khanam and her party to have left home, having been travelling all this time. The popular and better-travelled route went through Tehran, then Mashhad, and then negotiating the difficult mountain ranges of Hindu Kush, arrived in Herat. From thence to Kabul, where they joined the Babari Highway to Peshawar, Lahore and Delhi. But the problem was the climate and the weather in Tehran and Mashhad. Both being situated in very cold territory, they could not safely stay there for fear of adverse effect on Nurus Saadat's fragile chest and throat. Above that, as the road entered the Hindu Kush at heights exceeding four thousand yards, it was freezing cold and subject to blizzards and rockfalls at the time of the year when they would enter the ranges. So, after full consultation with the caravaneer and other guides and the keepers of the various pack animals and mounts, they decided to strike due south. Passing through towns as far in the south as Yazad, Bafaq and Kirman, they turned south-east into Zahidan. From there, travelling just at the edge of the southern boundary of the desert called Dasht-e Lūt, to Zahidan, they crossed the river Helmund a few days later and travelled in comparative ease along the right bank of the Helmund, reaching Qandahar in four days.

They rested and recuperated in Qandahar for a week, replenishing provisions, resting the animals, and preparing them for the most difficult part of the journey. The human travellers were also on the verge of exhaustion and dehydration because of the weather, the terrain and the narrow, mountainous roads, all of which had been very hard on them.

They travelled up the rising road that climbed to Ghaznin through some of the harshest mountainscapes in the world. The knife-like edges of the rocks on both sides of the narrow, winding road seemed to bend threateningly towards them. The road from Ghaznin to Kabul was equally unwelcoming, but the rock on the sides of the road did not seem to crowd them like minatory shadows in a dense jungle. They travelled down into the pleasant valley of the river Kabul. From Kabul they descended in comparative comfort to Jalalabad and Peshawar, though the road now looked more like a waterless ravine presided over by dry, grey and somewhat decomposed rocks and caves—caves which could easily conceal an army of bandits.

Their normal route now was the Royal Shershahi Road, which ran from Peshawar to Lakhnauti in Bangalah. But as they left Peshawar and entered the arid valley of the river Sindh, they thought of travelling upriver by boat up to somewhere near Rawalpindi, the nearest point to Lahore. They were informed that the wide river was fast, but quite shallow and was not navigable by the heavy boats that they would need for travelling upriver. Anyway, the scene changed fast enough, the aridity of the river valley giving way to populated hamlets along the road. The country was green, and seemed good-natured in its generosity, permitting many kinds of cultivations and fruits to grow in profusion. They travelled almost due south from Lahore to Sirhind, and four days later, travelling via Panipat, they were in Delhi.

Rai Kishan Chand Ikhlas was with them through the journey. Like a shadow, or a protecting spirit, he was always there when they needed him. His considerable entourage and the squad of twelve fighting men, professional bodyguards that he had hired on behalf of Etmad-ud Daulah, provided sufficient security and discouragement to highwaymen and petty thieves. He always spoke to the two valued and adored fellow-travellers in Hindi, and encouraged Labiba and Nurus Saadat to speak only Hindi among them as far as possible. Very soon, they'd picked up enough of the language to understand conversational Hindi, unless delivered very fast. By the time they left Sirhind, they'd become proficient in Hindi speaking, except that they made errors in gender and couldn't use idioms and colloquialities with success.

One day, Rai Kishan Chand Ikhlas said a Hindi verse before them:

I had no desire at all to go keep company with the garden dwellers
A thousand roses opened their lips invitingly, but I kept to myself.

'Oh, only God is free from all blemish!' Labiba and Nurus Saadat cried almost at the same time. 'Who wrote those excellent lines?' Labiba asked. 'Indeed, it sounds like our Mirza Vali or Baba Fughani.'

'Well, my lady, this verse is from a man who, though young, has almost a preternatural quality of age and experience. He is unusually independent of mind, has a lover's temperament, self-respecting and also self-regarding to a degree. His name is Muhammad Taqi, his pen name Mir, but all of us speak of him and even address him as Mir ji, or Mir sahib. Although younger by far than me, he regards even the most senior ustads inferior to him.'

'Do you know him?' Nurus Saadat asked.

'Yes, Nur Khanam. Every man and child in Delhi knows him. And in Delhi every poet knows every other poet anyway. There would be scarcely a dwelling there which couldn't boast of being home to a poet or two.'

'Strange, isn't it?' Nurus Saadat said to herself.

'Not so strange really, Nur Khanam. In Delhi, the business of poetry, whether as vocation, or as an avocation, is highly regarded: it is one of the nobler things to occupy oneself with.'

It was the first time that Rai Kishan Chand Ikhlas had seen Nurus Saadat taking such active interest in anything from Hind. He sensed that Mir's verse had in some mysterious way found its mark in her heart.

'Would you like me to say to you a few more verses from Mir?'

'If it's no trouble,' Nurus Saadat began to say, but Labiba completed the sentence for her. 'That one verse has indeed lit a fire of interest,' she said.

'Actually, I know a ghazal of Mir's which is a kind of introduction to him. Would you like me to say that ghazal to you, honourable ladies?'

'That would be even better,' said Nurus Saadat, 'to know the poet before you know him in person.'

Ikhlas began:

Who am I, friends and comrades?—My spirit is sore,
A fire resides in my heart: I scatter flames.
My own passion brought me out from behind the curtain;
For, I am really that same one, Who dwells in mystery, in secret seclusion.
It is my radiance alone on the shores of the ocean of poetry
My thought swells in waves of myriad forms. I am the poet's freely
flowing creative intellect.
Every morning, I finger-wrestle with the sun
Nightly, like a comb, I travel in the shade of beauty's hair.
Whoever even saw me once, he became mad for me
It's I who disquiet and agitate the whole world's temperament
Do not, please, do not try to make me open my lips
I have a hundred utterances, all drenched in blood, buried under my
tongue.
Pale, and drawn, I grieve for the young verdure of this garden
Blasted and withered, I am one of its yellowed leaves.
The crush of passions in my heart confuses me always, without rest
Don't go after me now. None but God knows where I am at this moment.
My being is a mere suspicion, more imagined than real
Even so, I lie like a burden on your fragile temper.
I dwelled in comfort, unpolluted, and chaste
Certain things happened, I have been here for some days now.

In spite of her wonted self-assurance, Nurus Saadat was open-mouthed. Was this poetry? Clearly, there was much in it that she didn't get to, but what she did get was the fathomless force, force of such immense proportions, so overpowering intellectually and emotionally that she was left at a loss for even trite words of praise. Labiba Khanam was in better control of herself, though she was affected in a way that she hadn't experienced before. She said, 'Only God is free from all blemish! It seems the spirits of Rumi, Baba Fughani and Mirza Saib have been dissolved in this young man's blood.'

'He certainly seems a person to meet and to know!' Nurus Saadat spoke up, involuntarily.

'This young man will present himself where perfections like you are to be found,' said Ikhlas, happy that another opportunity had opened for him to visit them. 'If he doesn't come soon enough, I will happily escort him to your noble presence in order to kiss your feet.'

*

The first thing that Labiba Khanam noticed about the city of Delhi was its immensity. Well before they entered the actual city at Kashmiri Gate, they had travelled for more than an hour through bazaars, clusters of homes, shops, mosques, temples, gardens, coffee houses, a caravanserai—everything that one associates with a large city. At the Gate, which was at the end of a wide bend in the road, the numbers of people going about the city's business were so strong that the very wide and very tall walls of the city and the massive gate were all but hidden from view.

Arrived at the Gatehouse, they were subjected to routine questioning. The laissez-passer signed by Etmad-ud Daulah was more than sufficient to gain them quick entrance into the city, about which the Urdu poet Dagh said more than a hundred years later:

Evening here was like morning, full of radiance
Every particle here shone bright like a sun.
Rubies of Rumman turned dark at the sight of its stones
The mirror turned to water, confronted with its dust.
It was a city whose shade even was radiant like the light,
The tapers there put to shame the divine fire of Sinai.

They proceeded into the city, admiring the tall and beautiful caravanserai built by Shahjahan's daughter, Princess Jahan Ara Begam, and entered Phatak Habash Khan where a fully furnished haveli had been made ready for them. It took Labiba Khanam a few days to comprehend the extent and the historicity of Delhi and its various cities, for Delhi wasn't just one city. Its heart and its most prestigious and most popular city was Shahjahanabad, between which and the outermost city of Tughlaqabad lay many miles and many cities. Shahjahanabad alone was home to more than half a million people, and a hundred thousand more entered or left the city in a single day.

Rai Kishan Chand Ikhlas took leave after entrusting them to the care and management of the housekeeper appointed for them by Etmad-ud Daulah who owned the haveli where they were accommodated. Ikhlas reported at the haveli every day to make sure the guests didn't need for anything.

No meeting took place between Grand Khanam sahib and Etmad-ud Daulah over the next few days, so the nature of the relationship that might begin to exist between them was yet uncertain. Without being sure of his position in the possible imbroglio, Kishan Chand Ikhlas couldn't dare even to imagine what threads of intimacy might be possible, to weave and tie, between him and Grand Khanam sahib. He passionately hoped and desired that Etmad-ud Daulah not choose her for his own so that he could get a clear field. There was always the possibility that Grand Khanam may reject Etmad-ud Daulah's hints, but even then it would be impolitic and foolish for him to try and take a shy at winning the affections of Labiba Khanam. Desiring a woman whom Etmad-ud Daulah had desired, albeit unsuccessfully, would be suicide for Kishan Chand Ikhlas, or for anyone else, for that matter.

Thus he both hoped for and dreaded the day when the meeting did take place. The flames of longing and the light of desire shone strong enough in his eyes anyway for all the entourage of Grand Khanam sahib to see and know who was the light of whose eyes. The Grand Khanam's feelings were inscrutable. Though she maintained all the formal courtesies, she saw him only when she must, and left her own maid-in-waiting or Nurus Saadat to deal with him on most matters.

Etmad-ud Daulah and Grand Khanam sahib met, eventually, and both quickly won each other's respect. Etmad-ud Daulah was of a short stature. His frame was stocky, but not plump. It was clear that he was a physically active person, with no flab on his body. His humility and hospitability of temperament were proverbial. His remote ancestor was the Presence, Shaikh Shihab-ud Din Suhrwardy, founder of the Suhrwardiya chain of Sufis, a chain of great renown and strong presence in Hindustan. His own had been a family of worldly success and celebrity for the last many generations. Chin Qalich Khan Asif Jah Nizam-ul Mulk and he were brothers. Mir Baha-ud Din, his immediate ancestor, arrived in Hindustan during Aurangzeb's reign and was awarded the title of Ghazi-ud Din Khan Bahadur and appointed to many high offices. From that time to this, the family had been the very emblem of nobility, generosity and worldly prominence.

Having got rid of the notorious 'kingmaker' brothers Syed Abdullah and Syed Husain Ali within a short time of ascending the throne of Hindustan, the King whose Court Pavilion is the Sky, Muhammad Shah Padishah Ghazi, awarded to Muhammad Amin Khan the title and duties of Etmad-ud Daulah, and after his premature death the King Emperor appointed Qamaruddin Khan the Etmad-ud Daulah of the Empire with the additional titles of Navab and Nusrat Jang. This had happened about a score of years ago. Since then, Qamaruddin Khan had retained and discharged his duties for his Emperor with full merit and distinction. Contrary to other nobles of that age, Qamaruddin wasn't given to conspicuous luxury. He faithfully observed the tenets of the religion.

Whatever the future may have held for the Empire, when Grand Khanam sahib arrived in Delhi, the throne of Hindustan was firm under the august person of Raushan Akhtar Muhammad Shah Padishah Ghazi, whom some uninformed historians of modern India have given the gratuitous title of *Rangila* (pejoratively: 'Lecherous, or Given to wine, women and song'; neutrally: 'Colourful'). No one knows who exactly awarded that 'title', and when. It is possible that since in his time an entirely new style of music called 'khiyal' emerged against the dhrupad of antiquity, and Muhammad Shah not only promoted the new style but also perhaps composed a few songs (called *bandish*) in that style, he may have adopted Rangila as his pen name, just as Bahadur Shah II, the last King of Delhi, adopted Zafar as his pen name in Hindi and Shauq Rang (The Colour of Desire) for his Braj Bhasha and Panjabi poems, most of which were meant to be sung, like bandishes, to ragas.

Anyway, at that time, Delhi's writ ran almost throughout Hind and the Deccan. The power and the glory of Asif Jah Nizam-ul Mulk and Qamaruddin Etmad-ud Daulah were at their zenith. Nadir Shah came, looted, massacred, rampaged and ravaged, and when he left, it seemed that he was carrying away the wealth of not just Delhi, but of the whole world. Though it had been just a few years to that enormous and direful visitation, it was business as usual now in Delhi, with no visible signs of 1739, the annus horribilis of Mughal history.

Etmad-ud Daulah placed no conditions before Labiba Khanam. He merely stipulated that she sing at the more important of the assemblies organized during the marriage ceremonies. 'Barring that,' said he, 'you are free in every way. This haveli, its servants, male or female, stewards, managers, guards—are all in and for your service; their salaries will be paid from my personal treasury. Rai Kishan Chand Ikhlas will be your Secretary and Guide, and will be at your service without regard to any specified duty hours.'

He continued after a pause, and spoke most neutrally and in the plainest intonation, so as to obviate any notion that his meaning was that he might then need Labiba Khanam for some personal service. 'Once I am free from the business of the marriage, I will trouble you again for a further conversation.'

Etmad-ud Daulah watched Labiba from the corner of his eye to register her reaction, if any. Finding her as neutral as he was, he continued: 'I have just one more request. It is not quite personal, but I hope that you will grant it, because weightier matters might hang by it.'

Now Labiba was a little anxious at heart, but she revealed nothing in her mien or bearing. 'Please command,' she said. 'This servant attends your words with the uttermost deference.'

'According to the customs and manners of Armenistan, it's quite proper for that Portal to be known as Grand Khanam sahib; for that Lady's daughter the auspicious name Nurus Saadat is quite proper. But the problem is, in the land of Hindustan such names are considered appropriate only for the purdah-observing ladies of the families of nobles and princes. Thus it would seem expedient that these names are for the time being not put in use with regard to the Porte. It would be most excellent, therefore, should you assume for yourself the designation Bari Bai sahib, and for the young lady, the appellation Nur Bai sahib.'

Labiba Khanam didn't answer for a few seconds, but expressions of distaste and displeasure were clearly visible upon her face. Etmad-ud Daulah was good sense personified and his diplomatic skills were also well known. Before Labiba's face could register anything, he intuited that she was about to give a sharp and unfavourable reply. But he had his problems and answerabilities: the proud ladies of Hindustan would never countenance the use of 'Khanam' and 'Begam' by professional women for their names, however skilled or exotic they might be. It was not so much a question of vanity as protocol. Etmad-ud Daulah came with the plan that if Labiba didn't fall in line, she wouldn't be asked to perform anywhere at all, though there would be no diminution in her pay and her honours.

Bitter pill as it was, Labiba Khanam well knew that Etmad-ud Daulah wasn't presenting it to her on a whim. There must be imperatives driving him to place the condition that he did. Still, in order to test him further, she said: 'Etmad-ud Daulah Bahadur, I came here in search of enhancement of honour, not to lose what I already have.'

'I am sure madam understands my point of view well enough,' said Etmad-ud Daulah, rising. 'Please give your best thought to this matter,

Honoured Madam. I now beg permission to leave.'

'Etmad-ud Daulah Bahadur, I am your guest in Delhi, bound by your protocols. But in my house I shall remain Grand Khanam sahib.'

Etmad-ud Daulah rose, made one salaam, and said, 'My eyes are bright, my heart glad.' Then he bent his head in the Mughal fashion and placed his hand on the left side of his breast. Before he could put on his shoes, one of Labiba's maids sprang to do the needful. Labiba Khanam walked up to the very end of the carpet, made seven low salaams, and before Etmad-ud Daulah could turn towards the door, she spoke in her most dulcet tones: 'Your authority, your estate, may grow daily; your life, your wealth, your fortune may enhance. Please to honour this servant again. I will remain grateful as long as there's life in me.'

As she spoke, she accompanied Etmad-ud Daulah up to and then outside the door, thus deftly avoiding Etmad-ud Daulah's back to her and not obliging him to walk backwards from her presence.

Thus, with no clear agreement, nor any oral assurances, both the parties had agreed that Labiba Khanam, in her house, would be Grand Khanam sahib and her daughter would be Nur Khanam. It was left to the people and the ruling class of Delhi to name them whichever way they chose outside her haveli.

*

The dawn was a little way away yet. The muezzins' calls for the predawn prayer reverberating in lane and alley, street and avenue, and of course in the Pearl Mosque inside the August and Exalted Fort, had now fallen quiet. In Hauz Qazi, namazi people were quitting their homes and walking with hurried or quick steps to the little neighbourhood mosque for the namaz. The tiny neighbourhood was otherwise asleep. There was no one else on the street except the sweepers getting ready for duty. Their mouths and noses protected against the cold and the dust by thick kerchiefs, their upper bodies wrapped in coarse chadors, they bent a little into the wind to defend their eyes against the cold breeze which had freshened up a short while ago. Though the winter was unusually cold that year, the culprit at that moment was the brisk breeze, which was caused by the tunnel effect, because the road to the Qazi's mosque came straight from Khanam ka Bazaar, passing through tall buildings on both sides. There was thus, effectually, a tunnel from Khanam ka Bazaar to the mosque and the morning air often took advantage of it to almost whoosh through.

The water in the small tank, also called Hauz Qazi (the Qazi's tank), was at that time rival to ice in temperature; a film of frost on the surface made it look waterless. A young man appeared from the lower side of the mosque, his gait somewhat swaying, as if not quite controlled; he would walk quickly forward for a few paces, then he would take the next few steps with slow deliberateness. This was perhaps because his eyes were laden with the red haze of sleep, and he was balancing a large bundle of papers under an armpit. He balanced the packet on the wide edge of the tank, a rather precarious proceeding, in view of the breeze. He then bent over the tank, scooped water from it, perhaps to drink, perhaps to wash his face. Both were unlikely activities, because he could not have been so thirsty in that weather as to drink from the near-freezing tank, and the water was cold enough for any but the most determined to persuade him to wash his face in it. Perhaps he was extremely hungry and was trying to kill his hunger with cold water; or perhaps his temperament was so fiery that it needed to be cooled at all times.

He'd just scooped up the water when someone called out: 'Hey, dear young gentleman, arey Mian sahib, are you, by any chance, Muhammad Taqi Mir?'

The person who'd asked the question was a man of somewhat advanced years—at least that's how it appeared to the man's young eyes—genteel, reasonably dressed. He'd just come out from Navab Qamaruddin Khan Etmad-ud Daulah's haveli in order to do the predawn namaz in the mosque. The mosque was just about fifty steps away from the haveli. Lights were burning at the haveli's gate and inside the gatehouse; it was otherwise sleepily silent.

'I certainly am Muhammad Taqi, but what's that to you?' His tone was almost churlish, certainly sharp, as if he didn't care about anyone, anything, and wanted the world to know it.

He was twenty-two, twenty-three years of age, tall but slim. His wrists were strong and broad, his eyes, red with sleeplessness—or was it drink?—were still commanding, full of character, though it could be seen that they could twinkle with humour when the occasion demanded. His beard was not long or dense. In fact, it was quite thin at the chin, suggesting a strong and cleft chin. He wore his moustaches full, and heavy on the cheeks, giving the impression of Rajput side locks. The cheeks, which would otherwise look somewhat sunken, looked full on account of the moustaches. His head was without cap or turban, or even the light, small, fashionable turban called *thakhfifa,* which was tied loose and with apparent casualness. His hair was long, dense and bright black, worn almost up to the shoulder, something not quite in vogue at that time. Perhaps he made a braid of them but hadn't cared to do so at that time. The hair was straight, without any curls, and seemed in fact to have been combed and pulled back hard to lie heavy and unruffled on and below the neck.

He had a short, light, full-sleeved tunic on his upper body. It was called nima, or *angarkha,* depending on the style. The nima was worn waistcoat fashion. The fabric was woollen, russet coloured. It was called *banat,* but it was not of the best quality and its russet was now fading somewhat. Under the nima he wore a long woollen tunic. His trousers were of Aurangabadi *mashru,* with a faint design of sprigs and flowers, pretty, but not the heaviest of fabrics. His shoes were strong, but more suited for casual than outdoor wear. A dark brown-red sash around his waist, with which hung a dagger in such style as to suggest, for no apparent reason at all, that its wearer would not be averse to using it if occasion demanded. Overall, his demeanour had faint suggestions of a soldierly, rather than literary, temperament.

His face was tired, in fact somewhat drawn, and worn, perhaps because of lack of sleep, or exhaustion, or both. Having been called out suddenly by a stranger hadn't certainly brought brightness to his face or improved his state of mind. When one looked closely, one could, however, see small crow's feet at the corners of his eyes, and in similar fashion, small wrinkles of laughter around the corners of his lips.

On the whole, his personality had a strange power, or what the modern people would call charisma: a magnetism, a subdued brilliance which promised to make itself apparent at any time that he liked. His voice was somewhat harsh, or hoarse, in the appropriate Delhi fashion, but to the careful listener the slight lilt of Braj Bhasha could be audible and be a source of delight.

The stranger, having come close now, answered: 'It's nothing to me, Mian sahib. You don't know me, but your temperament is well known for its love of loneliness and avoidance of socialities. And your poetry is even better known.' A tiny smile appeared on Muhammad Taqi's face. 'I have often seen you in the mushairas. Above all else, Navab Riayat Khan sahib, son of Zahir-ud Daulah Navab Azimullah Khan sahib, is extremely keen to make your acquaintance.'

'If that is so,' Mir, true to his character, was suddenly a little choleric, 'he should have sent me a written invitation. What is the point and meaning of having me accosted at midnight by strangers?'

'Young man, you hardly let one talk to you for a moment without flaring up! All right, look, I am getting late for my prayers, just you sit awhile in my rooms. It's right there,' he said, pointing to the sky-kissing haveli. 'On the upper floor of the Minister in Chief's Gatehouse. My servant doesn't know you. Tell him my name and say that I have sent you. My name is Alimullah. I'll be back in a jiffy.'

Saying this, that person hurried on to the mosque and soon disappeared into it. Muhammad Taqi stood there, mute, lost in his thoughts, his bundle of papers forgotten on the edge of the tank. God knows who this fellow is, he said to himself. He is a regular goer to the mosque for prayers; that suggests he must be a good man. Perhaps he has some sense and ear for good poetry too. Otherwise, who cares

251

for poets and poetry these days? I never heard of this Riayat Khan Bahadur. Must be some blockhead of an ass, just as other nobles are these days. But I already have kicked away the so-called patronage and support of my uncle, more hangman than uncle. For how long could I tolerate and swallow his vitriolic observations offered under the garb of correction to my verses? For how long could I stand hearing him say in my presence, 'Muhammad Taqi filches my poetic themes but is unable to make creative use of them'? Huh, as if I am starved of poetic themes! And if I were to rob someone's verses, would it be from my noble patron, my uncle, who struggles to produce a finished verse? If one of his lines comes out right, the other will be invariably dull and slow . . . And how malicious, how vengeful he is! Was there anything deleterious that he didn't do to me when I was somewhat brainsick recently and believed that there was a beautiful woman in the moon who loved me . . .

'Arey Mian, you're still here, freezing away in the hellish cold!' Alimullah Khan cried from the doorway of the mosque. 'Oh, I understand. You were perhaps diffident to go into a stranger's home? All right, let's both go now. Really, isn't that something! I am back, having finished my prayer and you haven't moved! Come with me now.'

'Sir, I'll come, but I have a request.'

'Yes, yes, do tell me.'

'Don't ask me to say my verses to you.'

Alimullah Khan let out a guffaw. 'So, you don't trust me to understand your poetry, is that so? Young sir, there'll be many others requesting you for a recitation of your poems. I just wanted to know why you were going to drink from the ice-cold tank in this drear-nighted, coldest time of the year.'

A brazier full of hot red charcoals was cheerfully heating away the environment in Alimullah Khan's little bedroom. One could almost taste its friendly warmth on one's tongue. Muhammad Taqi, overcome by the combined effect of warmth and fatigue, felt sleepy and in order to ward the sleep off, rubbed his eyes hard as he said, 'Excuse me. There seems to be a tiny bit of a straw or grit in my eye.'

'It's no straw, nor grit, dear young fellow. It's the lack of sleep that hurts your eyes. My home is the home of a fakir; my heart is devoid of deceit and perfidy. Here, take this quilt and lie down in a corner there. Was this not one of your verses?' He recited:

Last night, when beating his head against the wall had no effect
Mir haplessly curled his body up like a foetus and slept.

Mir was astonished. 'Where did you get to hear that verse? I wrote it just a couple of days ago, and it's just that one verse that I did so far, the concluding verse of a ghazal to be. Now Allah knows best when I'll finish it.'

'Why, do you find it difficult to compose poetry?'

'Well, it is, and it is not either,' Mir yawned a huge yawn. 'In fact, if I get to compose a good opening or concluding verse, and it turns out to be really excellent, then composing the full ghazal . . .'

Mir collapsed in mid-sentence and fell asleep in a heap, not caring where he fell and possibly hurt himself in the fall. It must have been many nights since he'd slept, or maybe the environment in his uncle Khan-e Arzu's house was so incompatible that he was exhausted in spirit rather than body. Body and spirit responded almost involuntarily to the homey warmth in Alimullah Khan's humble quarters. Alimullah smiled to himself and carefully draped the sleeping young man's form in the quilt already offered to him, and busied himself in his diurnal, telling the beads and post-morning optional prayers which he performed assiduously.

Muhammad Taqi Mir slept till very late. He woke up only when he dreamt that he was extremely hungry and was feeding his face with shameless haste at some dinner party. As he woke up, he realized that he was indeed terribly hungry. He woke up and rose in a confused hurry from the floor where he'd laid himself down. Alimullah Khan must have left for work, he told himself. What next? That was the question. Before he could cogitate on this further, the door leading upstairs from the ground floor opened and a serving man appeared.

'I present my submissions,' said he politely but with no hint of sycophancy. 'Bathroom and the necessary are both prepared for you downstairs. By the time you have finished your ablutions, I'll serve breakfast. Khan sahib will return in about an hour and a half from now. He has left the message for you to kindly await his return after breakfast.'

Mir was impressed by the effortless way in which Alimullah Khan had organized things for him. By the time he was finished with breakfast, Alimullah returned, looking cheerful.

'Young sir, you slept deeply and well, as Allah Wills. I hope you are quite refreshed now.'

Mir muttered a few words of thanks, but Alimullah Khan came to his point quickly enough. 'You must be wondering why I brought you here as my guest though we're strangers. The fact is, I am employed at the court of Navab Riayat Khan Bahadur as assistant, and general companion. As I told you last night, his Exalted Presence views your poetry with favour and occasionally inquires about you. I thought, the young gentleman's temper is rather on the flammable side . . .'

'Not flammable, haughty and self-willed,' Mir interrupted smilingly.

'Well, be that as it may, but I still believed that it would be good for both of you remarkable persons to be introduced to each other. Some good might come out for you and I might earn some kudos from the navab.'

In reply, Mir recited from one of his longer poems. He spoke without passion, or rancour, as if making a mere statement:

I am that lips-parched and heart-burnt one
Whose lips even the ocean wouldn't like to kiss
I am the hurt and damaged one
Whose presence might enhance the desolation of mountains and
wildernesses.

'So young, and so bitter!' cried Alimullah Khan. 'Pray, why are you so?'

'Dear and respected Khan sahib,' said Mir quite seriously, 'it is more a matter of my obstinacy than my embittered spirit. I once said, "There're hardly any here, oh Mir, who understand you." I hate taking; taking from anyone at all, even if it's my legitimate right as a friendly or patronly present. But my problem is, my soul is not so uncaring either, that I could stay silent in scarcity, and not reveal my condition to anyone. The great Abu Talib Kalim described my dilemma a century ago with great force.'

Then he spoke Kalim's verse with a strange, but bitter power in his tone:

Acquire a temperament that may make you friends with the world
Or the courage to renounce, and leave the whole world.

'But even Kalim couldn't live up to it,' he laughed, though the laughter had a whole gamut of self-mockery buried in it. 'So how could I do what Kalim couldn't?' he concluded somewhat abashedly.

'So what is the story of last night?' Alimullah Khan tried to change the subject and also assuage his curiosity. 'Had you been in a controversy, or a contestation somewhere and tempers became fiery? Was that why you were drinking from that frigid pool?'

Mir laughed again. 'My dear sir, if I were to answer in the language of poetry, I would say that I drank cold water in that coldest of mornings because

Some kind of fire smoulders in my heart. If it ever blazed up, oh Mir—
It'll burn up my heap of bones like kindling.

'By Allah!' Alimullah Khan ejaculated the oath involuntarily. 'Mian, what an absolutely marvellous verse it is!'

'Yes, but if I were to reply in everyday language,' Mir smiled, 'I'd reveal to you that I had a few cloves in my pocket. I chewed them the whole night and my tongue was quite dry and hard as a result.'

Both of them laughed. Alimullah Khan noticed that Mir's face changed quite remarkably when he laughed. His somewhat bitter or sour visage changed into something that was delightful to watch: The crinkle-cornered eyes sent messages of bright enjoyment, a wave of lightness ran through his body, and it became clear that this young man knew how to enjoy life and knew the value of laughter.

'All right, but why did you at all have to walk homeless through the night? Please let me into the mystery, if you don't mind.'

'Well, there's no mystery really, dear sir. But a bit of a sad tale, if you know what I mean.'

'Sorry, but I really am unable to understand.'

'There are two tales, actually. But I am not sure I should reveal those matters to anyone, but the things that rankled with me most, are known to most poets of Delhi. So I can tell you briefly that I had been staying so far with my uncle whom you must know by reputation, at least.'

'Yes, the celebrated scholar and poet, the Exalted Sirajuddin Ali Khan, whose pen name is Arzu, but who is universally known as Khan-e Arzu.'

'Yes, quite,' said Mir dryly. 'Then you must also be aware that he is not quite my uncle. He is brother to my stepmother. I am sorry to say that he is jealous of my prowess and reputation as poet.'

'You don't say!' exclaimed Alimullah Khan.

A cloud of irritation appeared on Muhammad Taqi's face. 'That is my main problem,' said he, testily. 'Everyone believes my putative uncle Khan-e Arzu to be a saintly, selfless person. None is inclined in the least to hear my side of the story.'

'I beg your pardon. I'll keep an open mind. I have no reason to disbelieve you.'

'So. I told you he is jealous of my talents and not only privately, but also publicly scoffs at me, and alleges that I borrow ideas and themes from contemporary poets, even from him. Do you hear, sir? I, borrow themes from him!'

'Well, it certainly seems unlikely,' Alimullah spoke in a guarded and diplomatic manner. 'You are a major poet in your own right.'

'Indeed, not yet major, sir. But I am a poet who doesn't need to steal or borrow. There could be occasions, very rare occasions, when an idea of mine may, sort of, collide with Khan-e Arzu sahib. You know, "collide" in our parlance means "similarity", especially accidental similarity. The latest incident was the last straw on the camel's back for me.'

'It must have been rather harrowing, I can imagine. You are a proud young man, and extremely well thought of as a poet.'

'Apparently my revered "uncle" doesn't know it. Last night, in his divan khana, he insulted me twice at dinner in the presence of several important guests, including Anand Ram Mukhlis, Mirza Sauda and others. He alleged that for one of my recent verses I lifted the idea from a verse of his. A rather feeble one at that.'

'He must have been joking.'

'That's what you will say, I knew. But he does wear the garb of humour on such occasions, the more to make his barb sharply pointed. In the second example, he alleged that I plagiarized from that ball of lard, Rai Anand Ram Mukhlis. I could bear it no more and left the dinner on some excuse. And immediately left his cursed house, where I had even suffered madness . . .'

'I think the best construction in such matters is that one poet writes an "answer" to another's verse. You know, that's a well-known poetic device.'

'Yes, I know,' Mir said bitterly. 'Who would know the device of *javab* better than me, who am supposed to be plagiarizing away?'

'My dear young sir. You shouldn't take such things to heart. You are known everywhere as a poet of surpassing invention. What harm could possibly touch you from irresponsible, obstreperous noises?'

'That depends, dear sir, that depends.'

Depends on what? Alimullah Khan wondered, but kept quiet.

'So I just rose from the dinner,' said Mir with a stubborn smile, as if he wasn't sorry for his clearly hasty action. 'And wandered the city . . . in fact, I lost my way.' This time his smile was wry, a little abashed as well. But he wasn't sorry, that was clear enough.

'There is no doubt that Khan-e Arzu was very unjust to you,' said Alimullah placatingly, as if pleading on behalf of Khan-e Arzu. 'But he is your relative, a man of influence. You should have held on a little more and left him when you obtained a good job. Such a farewell would have been in accord with the demands of good sense.'

'Look, dear Alimullah Khan sahib, you don't need to coach me in the ways of the world. If I cannot carry on with Khan-e Arzu sahib, I don't need to put my feelings about him under a lid. And there is another matter—'

Mir stopped in mid-sentence. Apparently he had talked a little too freely.

'Sorry, I don't understand.'

Mir remained silent for a while and Alimullah didn't consider it expedient to speak. Let him take his time and decide, he told himself.

Finally, Mir resumed, in a somewhat subdued manner, 'I have written a poem about that matter and I don't think I should reveal much about it just now . . . All right, I want to tell you that some days, or rather weeks, have been very hard, very stressful for me. It happened some time ago. I was moonstruck, truly. At one time I imagined that I saw a beautiful woman in the moon, beckoning to me. I sort of fell in love with her . . .'

He stopped, feeling clearly diffident, and perhaps even sorry to have revealed so much to a stranger.

'So do I understand that Khan-e Arzu didn't get you properly treated by competent physicians?'

'Physicians? Huh. A hangman he would have preferred, not physician. A woman disciple of my father's saved me, may Allah give him of His Mercy. She had me treated and cured.'

'Allah, Allah! What times do we live in!' Alimullah Khan drew a deep sigh. He knew a different story, a rumour concerning Mir's love for a young girl in Khan-e Arzu's family, a small titbit of the kind much savoured by the bazaar gossipmongers, but this was no occasion to bring it up. Instead, he said, 'Tonight, when I attend Navab Riayat Khan Sahib Bahadur's Court, I will mention you. Perhaps God would suggest something to him.'

'God, the Lord of all Honour, will certainly vouchsafe you the highest of His Kindnesses. But please, don't say anything that may put your service in jeopardy, or which may even have a remote potential of loss of honour for me.'

Alimullah was slightly miffed at these innuendos. 'Such a thing will never happen, my dear young sir,' he replied tersely. 'I haven't been lighting the oven in the service of these noblemen. I know how to deal with them.'

Mir was properly contrite, but Alimullah still felt a little hurt. He went on, a little curtly, 'Right, let this matter pend here for the present. You be here until late tonight. Perhaps the navab may summon you.'

*

That night, in the assembly of Navab Riayat Khan, Alimullah Khan narrated the events of the previous night. The navab's comment was: 'Well, that young fellow does have a nice turn of phrase in poetry. Etmad-ud Daulah Uncle was mentioning him a few days ago. But what is it about Khan-e Arzu? The Khan is a friend of the Presence Etmad-ud Daulah Uncle. I hope the Khan won't take it ill? I mean, Mir's employment with me.'

'No, not at all, Your Honour,' Alimullah spoke with force. 'His Honour the navab's Ascendant Fortune and the authority and awe of the Exalted Presence, Minister of all the Territories, Etmad-ud Daulah Nusrat Jang, shall never let that happen. I am quite clear on it, Your Honour.'

'But how much truth is there in Muhammad Taqi Mir's narrative? I, for one, didn't expect Navab Sirajuddin Ali Khan to mistreat the fellow.'

'I have heard something . . . but, sir, let this be not allowed to go beyond here,' said Alimullah Khan softly, almost in a whisper, and looked at those present. The navab turned his head towards Alimullah and bent close, the better to hear what Alimullah would say, and everyone present pretended to be busy in some conversation or business of their own, to signal their total lack of interest. Now Alimullah proceeded to say, 'According to the investigation made by this slave, Mir had fallen in love with a beauty in Khan-e Arzu's family . . .'

'So what? Mir Taqi is a Sayyid; he's good-looking, reasonably educated. So why not marry them?'

'Doubtless. His Honour's Command is entirely correct. But Muhammad Taqi Mir, though born Sunni, is inclined now towards rejecting his faith in favour of Shi'ism.' He paused, bent closer, lowered his voice further, and then went on. 'It is said that he utters abusive words about the Prophet's first three successors, as the extremist Shias do . . . Khan-e Arzu, as Your Honour must be aware, is a staunch Sunni. He traces his descent from Shaikh Ghaus Muhammad of Goaliar, whose ancestor was Baba Fariduddin Ganj Shakar. As is well known, Baba Farid sahib was an authenticated descendant of the Presence Umar-e Khattab, the second Caliph. So how could he countenance such a proposal? He refused, and refused most sternly.'

'That is a rather sordid tale,' said the navab.

'There is more, Your Honour. Mir didn't take kindly the refusal or the manner of refusing. He now began to speak ill of the Khan among his peers, and even sometimes in the presence of the Khan's acquaintances.'

'That was very foolish, and contrary to good manners, however justified Mir's ire against Khan-e Arzu sahib may have been. Anyway, then?'

'Well, sir, it was then or maybe before that event, Mir suffered a mild to severe attack of melancholia. Khan-e Arzu sahib perhaps represented it as madness, even violent madness, among his friends. No heed was taken to procure treatment for him. Mir's story is that but for a female disciple of his father's, he might have been incarcerated in an asylum for the insane.'

'All this is too lurid to be true,' mused the navab, 'and doesn't concern us really.'

'There is another aspect of the matter, Your Honour.'

'You mean to say there's more! All right, let's have it.'

'Mir's story is that Khan-e Arzu sahib routinely and falsely accused him of plagiarism. From some of the examples cited by Mir himself, I could see that there was coincidence of themes, but Mir is a powerful poet. Possibly, he did what poets often do: he "replied" to whoever was the original author, and Khan-e Arzu sahib construed it as plagiarism.'

'Well, that is plausible. There is a whole device called *javab* for this kind of thing.'

'His Honour's command is perfectly just. Mir is proud of his perfection in poetry, and his pride is quite justified. He couldn't stand the innuendos, and the hostile environment, and so he quit.'

'So in your view there is nothing objectionable in his being presented before the Presence, my Uncle?'

'No, My Nourisher, sir. Mir is an honourable man, even if he is given to an occasional attack of the choler. In fact, I am sure the Exalted Presence, the Minister of all Dominions, would be pleased at such a prominent poet being among those who are attached to your Court.'

'But what about Khan-e Arzu sahib?'

'May the fortunes of your governance increase; Khan-e Arzu sahib is a great man in the field of learning. He is no pettifogger. And he is not a man of malice. Let Muhammad Taqi be out of his hair; for the rest, he may live somewhere, die somewhere, these will be matters of the least concern for the Khan. And after all, Mir is his pupil, and also related to him, even if distantly.'

'All right. Let him be presented to me tomorrow after the late morning prayer. I'll appoint him if I find him congenial to my temperament. A room opposite yours on the other side in the upper storey of the guardhouse is vacant. That room will be allotted to him. He will eat at our kitchen. He'll have no duties. Let him roam around, write poetry, whatever, but he must attend the evening assembly here, every day.'

*

Late at night, when Alimullah returned home, he found that Mir was there, and awake.

'Hey, Mian sahib, your job is done!' He affectionately slapped Mir on the back. 'His Honour of High Value has commanded your presence tomorrow, late in the morning. Beyond that, it's your luck. All details of your duties are decided. But, dear young man, you are not reputed to observe caution at all times. But tomorrow, please, if you find something there that is not congenial, just swallow it without a word.'

'That, dear sir, would be a severe test. But I will do nothing that may redound to your discredit. You'll see, everything will go right, as Allah Wills.'

'If you do get the appointment, your board and lodging will be here, at His Honour's expense. Sleep here tonight in my room. I'll have a cot and bedding made ready for you.'

'Alimullah Khan sahib, this servant is much bounden to you. As Allah Wills, you will always find me grateful, and conscious of the good deed you did for me.'

'Please. I have done nothing. All thanks are due to Allah. It was just the merit earned by me from early rising and doing the morning prayer without break that I caught a glimpse of you. Go to bed now. Start tomorrow with the prayer for success on your lips.'

Navab Riayat Khan's palatial residence was heavily decorated in anticipation of the wedding, which was quite close now. Preparations

were under way for the wedding party and the obligatory customs—
dresses, gifts of jewellery and expensive perfumes for the prospective
bride. Every man or woman involved in the preparations regarded
themselves as the most important person in the world. Inside the haveli,
there was a throng—makers of simple ornaments, makers of jewelled
ornaments, embroiderers, crimpers of silk and cotton fabrics, women
representing the above professions, Turkestani women bodyguards,
maids of numerous descriptions, everyone bustling away, or off.

Shahnai was being played at the main door of the zenana. In the
interior courtyard of the male court, a canal was flowing away in
quiet delight, shady trees thronging, clustering around the banks
and the length of the canal, wooden platforms with carpets spread
on them under the shades of the trees, all platforms occupied by
professionals—singers, sitar and shahnai players, poets, seated
according to their experience and status. The Chief Steward, called the
Ishak Aqasi, was escorting all comers to their seats in accord with their
importance and station, entertaining them with attar, scented betel
cone wrapped in silver or gold foil, and sweets of various descriptions.
He knew Alimullah Khan, and also knew that a new employee was to
be presented to the navab, so he let Alimullah and Mir go on ahead,
towards the inner of the three sequential verandas where the nightly
assembly was in session.

The staff bearer announced the arrival of Alimullah Khan,
accompanied by Mir Muhammad Taqi Mir sahib. The navab accorded
permission with a flicker of the eye, and as Mir advanced to kiss the
navab's hands, he said, with a degree of casual freedom and expression
of welcome reserved for favoured employees: 'Ama Mir Taqi, it's good
that you could come, I wished to know you.' In the meantime, Mir
had bent low in seven salaams. The navab continued, 'Come, sit here
just below my chair on my left side.'

Mir didn't sit at once. He folded his hands on his chest, as in prayer,
and submitted: 'Mentor and Guide, the Presence, Master of New
Themes, Mirza Bedil sahib commanded long ago:

From my handful of ashes, my heart's fire arose again
Messiah of Love, who is it who fans me with the garment's hem?

'For me, you are the messiah of love. Your summons was the fan of the garment's hem that reawakened and lit again my cold ashes. The slave praises you from the depth of his heart for your kindly unrolling of the carpet of generosity.'

'Right. If you will be fidelious with me, you will find me your supporter always.'

'Presence, this servant can only reply with this line of a rubai that I composed sometime ago:

It is absolutely not possible for my heart to lose connection with you.

The navab smiled and said, 'Correct, and full of rectitude.'

He was then about to turn his attention towards some other matter when he checked himself, turned to Mir and spoke half in jest, half in earnest, even anxiety; Riayat Khan Bahadur would lose face if Mir went back to his original lair. 'Ama Mir Taqi, will your heart not hanker after Khan-e Arzu and his learned assemblies, or will it?'

'Mentor and Guide,' Mir folded his hands upon his breast and submitted in a firm but polite voice, 'I am obliged for your concern about this humble servant, but this slave adheres to what Vahshi Yazadi commanded a century ago:

The heart is not a pigeon, that it should come back after taking off
If once I took off from a terrace, I took off.

'Well said by Vahshi,' said the navab. 'Oh yes, there's another matter. Alimullah Khan will spell out your duties to you; now tell me, what salary would you be expecting from us?'

'My Exalted and Honoured sir, what need could be there for a salary when there is so much already by virtue of your nurture of the destitute. A solitary corner, and the loving nurture of the Heavenly Orb of your Fortune, these are enough for me.'

Alimullah Khan was pleased in his heart at Mir's sophisticated speech and his refusal to accept nothing but the navab's patronage, but he also fumed inwardly at the clodhopper Mir's simplicity. These navab types often take things literally. Should that happen here, Mir would be left high and dry.

The navab was in his more practical mood apparently. He said quite seriously, 'No, no. That won't do. You should have some cash to defray your routine expenses. So come, accept twenty-five rupees per month.'

Mir bent very low, made three salaams, and before he could articulate his gratefulness, Alimullah Khan, noting a gesture of the navab's eye, submitted: 'Eight days from today, that is Friday week, the marriage party of His Honour, on whom prosperity rests, will commence its progress to the bride's mansion at 4 o'clock in the afternoon. It might be suitable for Mir Muhammad Taqi to accompany . . .'

'Quite,' said the navab and turned to look at a dealer in gemstones who awaited his attention. His chief wares consisted of pink rubies, almost onion coloured, and very bright. They were found only in the hilly valleys beyond Kamrup and were famous all over the world for their brilliance.

*

On Alimullah's recommendation and guarantee, the navab's chief accountant advanced the sum of seven rupees to Mir for purchasing his minimum necessities. The navab's tailor made for him a couple of reasonably fancy clothes for the wedding party. Thus Mir became a respectable member of the society, his attachment to Navab Riayat Khan adding some more weight to his respectability. Mir's days and nights passed in comfort and, more importantly, in peace, and the day soon arrived for the wedding party to proceed to the bride's haveli.

By this time, the fame and reputation of the party from Isfahan had ceased to be the talk of the town. Now it was taken as the established truth: The two Jewish women—mother and daughter, by all accounts—were famed beauties from Armenistan. They were so beautiful that the mother seemed more like the elder sister of the daughter. Speculation and rumour manufacture took off from these 'facts'. They were Jews from Firangistan, really, not Armenistan; they have converted to Islam at the hands of Etmad-ud Daulah; Etmad-ud Daulah has proposed marriage with the daughter; he will marry the girl with extraordinary pomp and splendour once he is free from the marriage of his daughter with Navab Riayat Khan; the mother is in fact already married, but is separated from her husband, she has come to India in the hope also of getting the marriage annulled somehow, then she will marry some Hindu grandee; half a million rupees is the amount paid to them in advance by Etmad-ud Daulah; this is over and above travel expenses, living expenses here, and the promise of rewards and presents from the elites of the city who will be soon inviting them to sing; some grand lady of the House of Nizam-ul Mulk in the Deccan has sent a message and costly gifts to the elder woman, proposing that they enter the bond of sisterhood with each other . . .

In spite of his promise, Rai Kishan Chand Ikhlas had been unable to organize a meeting between Mir and Nurus Saadat. This was principally because he didn't want to do anything that might be construed as his playing a game of his own behind Etmad-ud Daulah's back. Whatever was to happen should happen only after the marriage ceremony commitments of the mother and daughter had been concluded.

*

The actual number of the persons in the wedding party was two thousand, while there were five thousand attendants. Ahead of all were about three hundred persons on sumptuous howdahs on elephants; the elephants were even more sumptuously caparisoned than the howdahs. These were followed by another hundred and fifty to two hundred persons in hugely decorated raths: the theme of the raths' decoration was flowers, as against the gold of the elephants'. After them came about four hundred men on horses. Behind them, no one knew who was who, and where he was to be found. The servants, attendants, spear wielders, staff bearers, and camels ridden by armoured military personnel were to be seen all over, though it wasn't clear which of them were from the groom's side and which deputed from the bride's to protect the marriage party members, including the groom, who rode on one of the first five elephants.

Throughout the length of the road and the lanes through which the marriage party passed, the groom's officers had been scattering and throwing into the watching crowd copper coins, tessellated flowers in brocade, heavy garlands made of gold lace, one-rupee coins, and smaller coins, like *dam, chhidam, ganda*, even cowries. There was a fairly large component of gold or silver rings, very thin, but occasionally with a semi-precious stone inlaid in them. The soldiers and the policemen had their task cut out to ensure that the 'looters' didn't go out of hand. Even so, some few did suffer injuries, a broken leg or arm even. But many also became prosperous for life.

The technical name for the items that were being scattered, or 'thrown to the loot' was *araish*, rather deceptive, because it just meant 'decorative item, decoration'. Another word was *phulvari*, which was even more deceptive, for it just meant 'a small flower garden'. The items of the araish or phulvari were always scattered upon and thrown freely into the crowd of watchers who were entitled to grab or 'loot' as much as they could.

Etmad-ud Daulah, following his religious proclivity, had requested the groom's family that they not bring any drums, pipes and shahnais with the party, but not stint on the fireworks. The entire route, from Hauz Qazi, the groom's residence, to Khanam ka Bazaar, the bride's residence, was lighted with handheld single-candleholder chandeliers, called *kanwal*, two- or three-candleholding globes, called *mridang,* and lamps lighted upon poles. Shopfronts and available doors and walls on the route had also been lit with oil lamps. Even so, the smoke emitted by the lighting or produced by the fireworks seemed to create the effect of a fog in some of the more densely populated lanes and alleys. Large cherry bombs, of the size of small pumpkins, preceded every mounted segment of the party. Fiery arrows, called *baan,* and fiery wheels, called *charkh,* were everywhere.

Etmad-ud Daulah's younger son Mir Intizam-ud Din Bahadur stood at the end of the lane that led from Hauz Qazi towards Chowk Sadullah Khan, beyond which was Khanam ka Bazaar. Except for the groom, and his chief relatives, the rest of the party dismounted there and walked their leisurely way. The animals in the party were accommodated in the big maidaun of Bulbuli Khana.

Just before the arrival of the marriage party, Bari Bai sahib and Nur Bai sahib rode from their haveli on an elephant, organizing their timing such that they arrived at the wedding pavilion just a few minutes before the actual marriage party. Except for a small umbrella above it, their howdah was open, so its occupants were open to view. Delhi's idlers and lovers of the good things of life had a field day, standing on the road wherever they politely could, to warm their eyes upon the unique display of beauty on the elephant. They had no out-runners, but four torchbearers fore and after, and two lady's maids in a palanquin behind their elephant.

Nurus Saadat's beauty and person at that time were in the same springtime of perfection which had passed upon Labiba Khanam long ago—or perhaps not so long ago, because the mother still hadn't lost anything of her youth, apparently. It is said that there were some among the watchers and onlookers who lost their consciousness not because of the din and the smoke and the crush of the people, but because of the mother and daughter's surpassing, charismatic beauty.

It is obvious that their name and renown had reached Mir quite some time ago, just as it had numerous others. And it is obvious that like half the city of Delhi, he was also among the sight unseen admirers of their world-illuminating beauty and was keen to find an opportunity to visit them or meet them in person somewhere. He couldn't ask Alimullah Khan about them for that would be rank bad manners, and he didn't know Alimullah well enough anyway to ask him such questions. Ikhlas he could certainly ask, but he was aware of the delicacies involved and had therefore desisted.

Since Mir was among the almost last category of the members of the marriage party, he could scarcely hope to find a seat from where he could observe the Khanam sahibs well, if not from truly close. But his luck was on the ascendant those days. Samsam-ud Daulah Ashuri Khan, Commander of the Royal Arsenal, spotted him among the host. Mir had once been presented to Ashuri Khan's father, Samsam-ud Daulah Amir-ul Umara Shah Navaz Khan, by Khvajah Muhammad Asim, nephew to Shah Navaz Khan. That nobleman of blessed memory ordained for Mir a fixed stipend of a rupee a day, which Mir had been paid regularly during the life of the Amir-ul Umara. Now when the present Samsam-ud Daulah Navab Ashuri Khan observed Mir being pushed about in the crush, he dispatched a staff bearer to bring him up to a place close to him, and more important, close to the stage on which the mother and daughter had taken their seats.

Mir almost lost himself as his eye fell on Labiba Khanam; and Nurus Saadat quite devastated him. It was almost like Rai Kishan Chand Ikhlas at his first sight of Labiba Khanam. Worse, or better still, he imagined that Nur Bai sahib also cast a glance—no better than a passing glance, it must be admitted, but a glance nonetheless—at him. And maybe she did it again? Later, he wrote in one of his poems:

Was that a glance, or a calamity
for my heart?
Just that glance was enough for me
to bid goodbye to my fortitude.

269

My eye went towards her, my sense
also went away.
I drew a sigh, quietly
And my power of endurance went away.
The restlessness of my heart
behaved cruelly with me,
My strength, my forbearance
All played false with me.
Oh, how could I describe the way
She looked at me?
Her glance pierced and went through
my liver, my heart.
I just gazed at her, silent;
But what wasn't that I didn't say to her
In my heart?

Mir's heart was full of fear: should someone notice him in that state, there would be no end to the mischief that could arise: he might even be actively punished, or made to leave the city for casting lustful eyes on Etmad-ud Daulah's cherished guests. He suddenly espied Rai Kishan Chand Ikhlas, who sat on a chair just behind Nurus Saadat and her mother, in his capacity of Secretary and Steward to Labiba Khanam. Kishan Chand Ikhlas smiled when their eyes met. Both intuitively plumbed the depths of each other's heart. The way in which Kishan Chand Ikhlas's eyes caressed Labiba's face and breasts were enough to tell Mir of where the matter stood for him: there was no rivalry between them.

Mir doesn't quite recall the ghazals that Bari Bai sahib sang, and how, in what style, she sang them. All he remembers is that had he not fallen into the silver river of Nurus Saadat's face, he would have been prepared to die for Bari Bai sahib's voice, or kill Rai Kishan Chand Ikhlas should he have stood in his way to her. Those who were there, and who were careful enough to make note of things, state that Bari Bai sahib first presented the Hafiz ghazal:

Bright, because of the reflection of your face,
There's no eye that is not.
Favour and grace, from the dust of your doorstep
There's no power of sight on which it is not.

Subhanallah! Only God is free from all blemish! But that ghazal, so suited to the occasion; that poem, sovereign of all poems, that voice drenched in the soft, earth-like essence of the Iranian note call *ushshaq*, the voice travelling unobtrusively far, like the call of the cuckoo, the white neck and throat, itself like a book of poems, and above all of that, the face, working its magic without the aid of powder, rouge or beautification, like a princess from a magic land. It seemed as if there was no one, no one at all in that assembly, there was just a face, a voice. None among the audience dared move from wherever they may have been. A magical rope seemed to have bound them into immobility. For those who understood the finer points of the music, it was as if they'd been thirsty all their lives for just that draught of life-giving water.

And when she sang the following verse:

I have no strength to move one step from your street
Although in the heart of this heart-lost one
There's no desire for a journey that is not.

She inserted the following, even more appropriate verse from Mirza Saib:

Like the intent to travel to Hind,
which is in every heart,
The dance of a mad love for you,
there is no heart in which it is not.

271

The entire young audience now stood up, not in applause, but to sing along with her, trying to match note for note. The older people, slapping their thighs, began to keep time with her. She was so carried away by her own virtuosity and the hypnotic power of the response of the audience that she sang just these two verses for more than half an hour, and in spite of the cold weather, she felt the perspiration running down from her face to her neck. The audience must have been beside themselves, furiously calling out for encores whenever she paused to dry her face or draw a breath of rest.

Once or twice she forced herself to break etiquette, stop, and drink a little from the cup near her. She did, however, finish the ghazal; otherwise they wouldn't have let her rise:

But for this little thing that Hafiz is unhappy with you
In your whole body, there's no excellence that is not.

*

Mir returned to his rooms quite late. Alimullah Khan was, of course, with the groom and might not come back until even later. Mir lay himself down on the bed, closed his eyes and tried to sleep. But all that came to him was the visual images of Labiba Khanam and her stunningly beautiful maiden daughter, and auditory images of Labiba Khanam's singing. Try as he might, he couldn't summon sleep to his eyes.

Finally, as the false dawn was about to spread its blanch powder on the night's face, he rose, rubbed his face hard to improve the flow of blood to his eyes, and sat down to compose a *sarapa* of Nurus Saadat. A sarapa needed to describe a woman's beauty from the toe to the head. Why did he sit down to write the sarapa was a question that he couldn't have answered with any conviction. Perhaps he wanted to record Nurus Saadat's beauty for himself and for posterity; perhaps he wanted to make sure that he recorded his first impressions, impressions which could only be described with full honesty immediately after the event; perhaps he believed that they would never meet again and he wanted the freshest possible memory of Nurus Saadat's person as he saw it that night.

How can I say anything about her tall stature?
It seemed to have been patterned in the mould of desire.
Each place better than the other,
All of her delicate frame was worthy of love.
Her head of hair: fit to surrender the life for their sake
Curly, and proud the whole lifelong.
More heart-attracting than her forehead?
No, the false dawn's claim is fully false.
Should I tell you about her brow as she glanced at you?
A Doomsday's tumult on top of another such!
And oh, how wondrous it glimmers, the colour of universal popularity
On her face, as if it's a blossom of the rose!
Her tongue, softer and more delicate than a rose petal,
Flowers rain down as she speaks.
What can I say, except that there're none so sweet-spoken,
How I long for that tongue to have been in my mouth!
The morning beckons at her earlobes all the time
The pearl in her earlobe, like the morning star.
The corners of her lips, the desire of the heart and soul,
The eye finds it hard to pass them over.
Were someone to have something to do with those lips,
Why then shouldn't he call the Egyptian candy 'dull'?
Should you fall to talking of their sweetness
Your lips would stick to one another.
It didn't seem possible, the lips so crimson—
As if colour might fall from them, drop by drop.
And when I looked at the breasts, prominent, jutting
It seemed as if they'd snatch my heart.
From the plane of the chest to the nave

Is the silence zone—modesty prevents plain speech.
And below the nave, an unopened blossom,
It's the occasion to demur, not to talk.

Mir deliberately avoided the more erotic mode, because he felt awkward talking about Nurus Saadat who seemed to him angelical, unpollutable by the sordid business of touching and taking to bed.

It was high morning by the time he finished composing the poem. His eyes red, his heart prickling with desire and anxious hope: Should I start right this minute for Phatak Habash Khan, and present myself . . . Present yourself as what? A suitor? Will you not be kicked out in less than the time it'll take to say your name? There'll be dozens of guards, female and male, bodyguards, gatekeepers, all bent upon putting their hands on your neck and giving a kick in your pants. You are Sayyid by descent, were you made for such ignominy? He smiled a wry smile in his heart; perhaps his verse, composed long ago, was prophetic:

Mir wanders in dishonour, none bother about his state:
The business of loving lost him even the honour due to a Sayyid.

I think I should now go to Rai Kishan Chand, he decided on impulse, and immediately made ready to go . . . Go where? Well, there are only two places possible. And who knows, he might be right there in Phatak Habash Khan! And these verses? Should I say them to her when I get to meet her? Indeed, could there be a worse breach of manners, you stupid lout? Take the name of God, Mir sahib. You seem to have sunk both intellect and respect in a morass of infatuation. I shouldn't delay further. If Alimullah Khan chooses to return at this moment and if he sees me going out, head bowed and gait submissive like a hangdog, his suspicions will be aroused . . . Dress? No need to change it. No doubt it's rather crushed, this outfit, but I have to get out now, before Alimullah sahib returns. And I don't have many changes of clothes either. Let me behave like the indigent poet that I am.

He first went to Katra Neel where Rai Kishan Chand lived in his ancestral haveli, and was lucky to find his friend home.

'Mian jan,' began Ikhlas without preamble, 'I well know what brings you here on this sudden visit when it's not visiting time even! Boy, you are very lucky, but also unlucky.'

Mir's impatience redoubled at these words. He also began without a word of thanks or greetings, 'Why, why should I be unlucky, dear sir? But no, first let's have the good news about my being lucky.'

'You're lucky because Nur Bai sahib is acquainted with you.'

Mir felt as if the whole world was swaying before him. He, Ikhlas, the huge divan khana, all were lurching, as if he were in a small boat and the wind was freshening fast.

'She . . . she knows me? Knows *me*? How is that possible? Has she heard my ghazals somewhere? Does she understand Rekhtah? But how? Didn't I hear that they are from Iran and Armenistan?'

'There, there, dear fellow. Have some patience,' said Ikhlas. 'If you ask only questions, talking away like one demented, how can I tell you anything?' He smiled indulgently.

'Your slave craves forgiveness, Rai sahib, but please narrate everything quickly, in one breath.'

'If I talked that fast, what'll you understand?' Rai Kishan Chand chuckled. He was obviously enjoying himself. He then narrated the tale of Labiba and Nurus Saadat briefly. He told of their intention to sojourn in India for a long enough time, their interest in Mir's poetry, how they came to learn Hindi on the way. Mir's heart was flying high, far away among the stars, wondering and marvelling. He didn't pause to consider all possible aspects and consequences—there could be, in fact there was, bone-cracking hot sun just beyond the cool, amorous shade of that day. He just kept repeating, almost to himself, 'What grace! What glory! Maula is so kind!' It didn't escape Kishan Chand Ikhlas that Mir was invoking Allah, but using the word Maula, which loosely meant the same, but persons of Shia persuasion often use it for the Presence, Ali, the Prophet's son-in-law. He knew that Mir's Shi'ism was a cause of the rift between him and Khan-e Arzu sahib, but hoped that it might be a point in favour of Nurus Saadat, who was to all intents Iranian, though not Shia.

'Maula's kindness on this pitiful slave! Oh, I have not words . . .' Mir then realized that Rai Kishan Chand Ikhlas didn't apparently share his raptures. Something was wrong, he realized with a shock.

'Dear Mir ji, now descend from the seventh heaven please. Listen to me, these are matters of this world, not a lesson in the love poems of Nizami.'

It was as if Mir were struck by a flying rock. 'Matters? Matters of this world? Rai sahib, what else could there be now?'

'You know I am an employee of Etmad-ud Daulah, and these women . . .' Mir hated for his angelic beings to be called 'these women', but it was more important to listen to Kishan Chand Ikhlas than argue with him. So he kept his patience. '. . . are his guests, or rather, his servants. He even has changed their names from Grand Khanam sahib, or Labiba Khanam, and Nurus Saadat, or Nur Khanam, to Bari Bai sahib and Nur Bai sahib, just like superior nautch girls.'

Mir hated all this narration, especially the change of names, which, although apparently acceptable to the ladies in question, was worse than gall and wormwood to him. He broke in sharply: 'Well, how are we concerned with all this? How does it affect me?'

'Ama, won't you try to understand'? Ikhlas said testily. 'Those people are servants to the Minister of all Territories; I too am servant to the same Grand Vizier. To introduce you to them, or have anything to do with your establishing a connection with them would be a serious mistake. Not just a mistake. I could easily lose my job on this.'

'But I hear that Khush Hali the courtesan is employed already with the Minister of all Territories.'

'Ama, don't be more dense than you can help. These noblemen have dozens like them around. They hang out at their portal, hoping to be noticed.'

The phrases 'hang out at their portal', 'hoping to be noticed', were as bitter cups forced to Mir's lips. He had to swallow the insult, but he was stung, as if it was he who was insulted.

'So?' Mir's choleric temperament came quickly to the fore. 'What have I to do with it? *You* are not in play.' He paused, realized that he was being stupid to speak thus to Ikhlas, and said: 'All right, dear and kind sir, I understand well enough now. But you are an employee of Etmad-ud Daulah, I am not. Am I not free to act as I please?'

'Looked at from one angle, dear young fellow,' Ikhlas smiled, but a little sarcastically, 'you too are in his employ. Not directly with Etmad-ud Daulah, but with his nephew and son-in-law. I do my duty to warn you about the good and bad of it. The rest be with you, but do please bear in mind that an ember from the fire of your desire shouldn't strike the hem of my humble garments.'

Mir was properly contrite; all things have diplomatic and bureaucratic dimensions, he now realized.

'I can swear by all that is holy, dear and respected brother, I will cease and quit well before any possibility of harm to you arises, however remotely, on the horizon.'

'Well, actually, you might do well to listen to me, young man. Etmad-ud Daulah Bahadur has the promise for seven singing sessions from them. Let's see which way the wind blows afterwards.' He quoted Khvajah Hafiz:

Who knows, it might indeed be the wind of hope
It may blow and join us with the friend whom we love.

Mir didn't fail to notice the 'we' used by Ikhlas and knew that it wasn't just rhetorical. So, he promised a sincere promise to abide by Kishan Chand's advice at all times.

*

It was as the great Sadi said, 'Like patience in the lover's heart and water in the sieve.' Mir wasn't going to abide by anything but his desire, hotter than any lust. He described in a small measure his state of mind in a long poem:

> *The dark dust of anxiety found its way out from his heart*
> *It was then like a storm in the city.*
> *A heavy stone, upon his head, all the time*
> *The time and space of living seemed to constrict him, all the time.*
> *His collar he ripped to shreds, his garment's hem disliked the new burden*
> *The hem and the collar became neighbours.*
> *Love trampled him, like a narrow, well-trod path*
> *Left on the wayside, like a footprint.*
> *The crazed lover, on his lips, always had*
> *This verse from some wise man:*
> *My heart cracked, and shattered into bits*
> *By God! By the Truth of God! By the Truth of God, by God!*

The thought often occurred to Mir that Nurus Saadat was herself inclined to look at him with favour, at least minimal favour. And obviously this was because of his poetry. Now if he didn't move fast enough at this stage of the affair, it was likely, in fact almost quite certain, that he would lose his chance. There was nothing stable in these matters, and as for the loved ones, their attention always wandered sooner rather than later. I am sure she'll never lack for lovers and suitors.

I am sure anyone with money or power could seduce her easily. These beautiful ones, especially the nautch girl types, hankered after power, which meant the holder of a powerful chair or office; or they ran after money, which anybody could have nowadays. Delhi was teeming with persons with money, and power, who were extremely experienced in these matters—matters of seduction, of coercion even. The loved ones have always been fickle, to one thing constant never. It was not difficult at all to make them change their mind with suitable enticements. Her possible suitors, or seducers, or lovers, had everything to aid and abet them in the conduct of love. And what was he? What did he have to show in opposition to his potential rivals who would pounce upon the opportunity almost before they even saw it?

I am but a poet, a young poet. My merchandise counts for nothing in today's world. No ships will be launched for it, no cannon fired for its sake, no armies march forth for it. My wealth is my lineage, my line that goes back to the Prophet. But love conquers and brings down all. He wryly recalled a verse of his own:

Sayyid or cobbler, what's needed here is fidelity—
In the business of love, do they ever ask about caste or creed?

He knew that in real life, fidelity, even from a Sayyid, wasn't enough. The business of poetry and the business of love didn't accept the same coin.

Granted that she knows me by name, but I have no means to convert that introduction in absence to a real face-to-face introduction. And I must have full regard for Ikhlas sahib's welfare too. Should some harm come to him by my indiscretion or impetuosity, I'll have no choice but to leave the city, go back to Akbarabad, and live in poverty and ignominy.

A strange thing was that although Mir had seen her for only a short while, and from some distance, yet his mind would drown into pleasurable imaginings the moment he thought of being alone with her. Erotic conversation would soon graduate to kissing, and touching, embracing and disrobing, reaching up to even those places towards which he'd made the coyest and briefest reference in his poem from which we quoted above. Later, much later, he would relive those storied moments and write about them:

The mouth waters looking at them
How delicious would those lips be which no one's ever sucked!
*

279

Could her body's pleasures at all be hidden
When her body seems to spring out from her tight dress?
*

It's many days, oh Mir, since she changed her clothes
But her body is all marked due to her old dress, it was so tight.
*

Were that silvery-bodied one to bare her body before me—
Not to speak of gold, or my plain existence
I would sacrifice my heart a hundred times over her.
*

Last night was the night of union; at just one of her coquettish moods,
I could surely die, last night:
My sleeping fortune was wide awake,
She and I came together at my home, last night;
She made one of her amorous plays:
For, she started, and suddenly woke up last night—
Were she to open her full face, it would be dawn,
Though we'd still to go one watch of the night;
She hid her face behind her tresses, and asked:
'Say, oh Mir, how much is now left of the night?'
*

I never could fully
Fathom the pleasures of her body
My eye always
Fell upon her soul.

How much, after all, did Mir see of her body? Her face and neck, her wrists and palms and fingers, maybe a fleeting glimpse of her heel, or sole of foot? But he imagined his kisses imprinted everywhere on her body. How many, and where exactly, and when, the count went on changing, if there could be a count. He wrote:

Wherever you look, on every spot

From head to toe, the heart commands:
Stay here! And stay for evermore.

The body's unfulfilled rapture, the rising graph of desire, like the pressure of blood inexorably rising in a super-heated body, the ever-erupting volcano of imagination, could poor reason or rationality even get a word in edgeways? Fortunately, it was the mundane physical barriers that withstood the storm of desire. He did nothing but write poetry, imagine himself in her company, and most unwillingly carry out the duty of nightly attendance in Navab Riayat Khan's assembly, fortunately shortened, or often not held because of his recent marriage.

He thought, and thought some more. Finally, he found what he thought was a clever though innocuous way to communicate with her. He wrote out, on a tastefully decorated sheet of orange-saffron paper the ghazal, 'Who am I, friends and comrades?' which Rai Kishan Chand had recited to her and Labiba during their historic journey to Hind. Below it, he quoted a famous line from a ghazal by Hafiz:

The view from the high canopy of my eyes is the
place where you are.

Below the line, he wrote, in smaller size of letters:

Writing made in submission, by Mir Muhammad Taqi,
known by his takhallus, Mir

He was about to seal it when he realized that there was no addressee mentioned anywhere. How will it reach her? Granted that I shall clearly instruct the messenger that the missive is meant for Nur Khanam sahib, but these brainless boobies, there can be nothing certain about what they do and what they don't. Who knows, they may deliver it to Labiba Khanam, and not even make clear to anyone the nature of their embassy. He gave the matter a great deal of thought and finally decided

281

that the letter contained nothing vulgar or objectionable; in any case, Khanam-e Buzurg was sure to get to know of the letter, regardless of whoever was its first recipient.

Once again, he went over the letter carefully, rolled it in the form of a key, sealed it and entrusted it to one of the cleverer boys of the neighbourhood. He gave him one dam in advance, with promise of another on his return and confirmation that it was indeed delivered at the haveli of Bari Bai sahib in Phatak Habash Khan.

He began to wait for the reply from the moment the young fellow disappeared from sight, his letter in hand. For many days, silence. Not to speak of a reply, not even an acknowledgement, not a hint that the letter had arrived where it was directed. Mir found excuses to go to Phatak Habash Khan, and go past the haveli like a casual passer-by. Sometimes he would tarry at a betel shop, or a coffee house, hoping that he might be noticed and invited in. Or some other possibility might emerge for sending another message. And . . . and . . . by God, it would be the True God's Benign Glory to bestow upon him the eminence of Alexander, so that Bari Bai sahib, or even Nur Bai sahib would be sighted somewhere at the gate, going in or coming out. Sometimes he would pray to be hit by a furious elephant, or a fast four-horsed carriage right at the gate of the haveli. Someone would, most surely, come out from the haveli to see to his wounds, and should he lose consciousness, perhaps take him inside the haveli and summon a hakim? She might, under the circumstances, even come out of her chamber to see the injured, hapless pedestrian.

It was Mir's sense of humour that saved him from another onrush of melancholia, or even mental derangement. He was no longer that very young and inexperienced man who believed that a girl of surpassing beauty beckoned him from the moon on moonlit nights. He could smile at his own Akbarabadi accent and intonation, just as he smiled a minute ago at the harsh *karkhandari* intonations— freely dropping the somewhat vague *ha* sound, and substituting the emphatic *ya* in its place, enunciating all the hard sounds even harder— of the boy messenger whom he had been upbraiding, blaming him for not delivering his letter. He could laugh at his own impatience, his own eagerness, juvenile at best, and futile and pointless at worst. Just as he could laugh at these idle things, he could also laugh at his love (or lust, or perhaps nothing but lust). He could see that his love-lust could also be a form of self-love, the expression of the desire to be admired by a beautiful woman of great refinement.

He had no illusions about his love, or about his own self. Neither one was from a world outside this world, not from another planetary land, not from an ultra distant star. What he was doing was play, *lila*, of the gods, or of men. I am not the first lover, nor Nurus Saadat the first beloved. Everyone believes their world to be very big, though in fact all worlds are very small, puny and insignificant. Of what weight are the loves loved here, the lives burnt and the souls reduced and diminished here? These are smaller than chess games played on the tiniest of boards. What is Lailah here and who the mountain-cleaver Farhad? What are their madnesses, their failures and successes?

I am a poet, perhaps a great poet, but a lover? I am just like any other lover. Not above him, not below him. All of us feel the same heat of lust when it boils over; all of us have the same self-regard, and perhaps the same contradictory desire to lose oneself in the ocean of love, to let oneself go, to destroy one's own self and be reborn in someone else's self. I am not alone in this. There have been others, there will be others.

No, I can't fly above the great poets, the great lovers. I love the body more than the soul. But, oh Mir, what body would that body be whose fragrance seems to be running away with me not only in my thoughts but also in my body!

Well, I can at least laugh at myself. Was it not I who wrote:

We've heard of sad people
But none could ever be like Mir
Who, when he heard the word 'Joy'
Said: It must be someone's name!

283

They say all the world is a stage, a dream stage at that. The madness of love, the convoluted tricks of reason, all are moving shadows. They say, this whole huge world, this universe, is a dream, being dreamt by another, even more Infinite Being. We are not our own dreams even. The immense *atman* has everything, is everything. So if I love someone, or someone loves me, it all comes to nix. They say, a Universal Consciousness is present everywhere, allwhere and we are somewhere in it, or not in it. It matters not at all. Others say, nothing exists but God. So there is nothing, or there is everything. We regard ourselves as sentient, but our sense owns nothing, it owes everything to Someone Else.

Do humans have a natural propensity for love? Am I acting under the impulse of something beyond me? But then, why should the desire to be a prey, to be preyed upon, to roil and roll in our own blood, ripping away the artificial dress of reason, wandering off without shame—why should these acts be meaningful for us in their own right? There must be some meaning there. Or is it all a throwback to the primordial times when Adam and Eve were at the mercy of the elements, and life could only ensured by being together, huddling together, sticking together? Had that not been the case, there would be no tribes, no communities, no peoples.

Remember, it was I who once said:

Love has churned out light from the darkness
If there were no love, there would be no manifestation.
Love is the causer, love the cause,
Love is the one which performs wonders.

But no, I am well aware that the realm of poetry is not the same as the world of men. They're not equal, not even parallel. Men want bodies. I want the heart of Nurus Saadat, but only for the duration that she makes her body my body. I should take off her clothes; keep awake the whole night, looking at her bare body. Stupid, am I not?

That's not what love is; that's not what love demands.

All right, then don't be vainglorious. Don't fly so high that your wings may be burnt off, making you fall to the ground with a big thump! Laugh, and be laughed at. Weep if you must, but then also weep at your grandiloquence.

Mir was not the same Mir now, but what he'd lost were his angularities. Nurus Saadat's love taught him humility, at least in the presence of love. He joked and played the games still, especially chess, of which he was something of a master. But he also knew that he was small. He could write any kind of poetry, but he could not command his kind of woman.

*

It had been many months now. Still, he waited for his reply. Not with the crazed intensity of the early days, but with a mournful, hopeful tristesse, as one looks at a disfiguring scar a hundred times a day, hoping for it to go away but not really believing that the hope would be fulfilled.

Bari Bai sahib made all her seven appearances contracted with Etmad-ud Daulah. Rumours were that they were now bound back for Iran. Others reported that they weren't going to return to Iran, but would be enhancing the life and soul of the city of Delhi. If one rumour caused a wave of hope to arise in Mir's heart, another would be like the insensible rock on which ten such hopes would crash, to disintegrate forever. It was like a hot, boiling bath followed by a cool, life-rejuvenating bath. He somehow forced himself to pick up the courage to go and ask Rai Kishan Chand about how matters stood in the haveli at Phatak Habash Khan.

He recalled, with a dolorous smile, a verse from his contemporary, Qaim Chandpuri:

Oh my heart, I don't say: give up your longings,
I just say: Desire just as much as you can afford to!

He also recalled that he was rather displeased with what he thought was the patronizing tone of the verse. But now it seemed so eminently appropriate. Yet, what exactly was the limit of affordance? Could he, could anyone, ever decide? No, Qaim sahib, or the protagonist of that verse, whoever he was, was being patronizing, after all. Come what may, tomorrow morning I will to Phatak Habash Khan and knock at their door.

He didn't sleep a wink that night. And perhaps it was the lack of the kindly moonrays of sleep, which suddenly caused the sun of his good fortune to rise to the apogee. He'd just risen from his bed that a messenger arrived from Kishan Chand Ikhlas asking him to come soonest.

Muhammad Taqi Mir traversed the distance with hands and feet aquiver, the heart aflutter, and the eyes bedimmed with fear. But the happy tidings there opened the floodgates of sunshine on his head and heart once again. Ikhlas was making ready to go somewhere, but he welcomed Mir most cordially and cried: 'Come, dear boy, let's embrace. Today is the day of Id.' He laughed in glee and continued: 'I am to report immediately at the Court of the Chief Minister of all the Territories, so I can't stay. But just hear this. It's something to your advantage. Congratulations!'

'What are you congratulating me for, Rai sahib? Let me at least know the nature of the situation, please,' Mir entreated.

'Mian jan, Etmad-ud Daulah Bahadur has commanded to Bari Bai sahib that the purpose for which she had been troubled to bring her noble presence from the city of Isfahan to the Sign of Paradise has now, by His Grace, been achieved and fulfilled. Now she is free to depart, or stay. Delhi is the heart of the whole of Hindustan; it is a heavenly stopping place. If she desires to continue her noble presence here, then the haveli is hers, all the staff there is hers to command. But she should now no longer feel bound to Etmad-ud Daulah Bahadur. All that is expected of her is to accept occasional invitations to trouble her noble self and enhance the splendour of the Ministerial Palace. Her unrolling thus the carpet of generosity would be much appreciated.'

Mir's mouth fell open, and refused to close. 'When . . .' he stammered, 'when did all this happen, and how? I hope it's not going to lead to some bad blood between them?'

'Ama, no. Not at all. One cannot even imagine the angelic and most sophisticated Chief of all Ministers Navab Qamaruddin Khan Bahadur to behave with any kind of meanness towards anyone.' Now he came closer to Mir on the divan and whispered, 'There are two matters, but one of them is rather in the nature of a secret.'

'Be assured. You know my nature. Whatever you reveal to me will remain between us always.'

'That's why I am making you privy to both things, Mian jan.' Ikhlas gently thumped Mir on the back. 'So the first thing is that Umdat-ul Mulk has petitioned Etmad-ud Daulah to permit him, Umdat-ul Mulk, to trouble the mother and daughter to visit him occasionally and perform.'

'Umdat-ul Mulk? Do you mean Navab Muhammad Amir Khan Anjam?'

'Who else? Are there many Umdat-ul Mulks around? The same, the Governor of Allahabad, the Commander of the garrison at Kara Manakpur, and inside the Fort, the favourite nobleman of the Khidev-e Hindustan, Muhammad Shah Padishah Ghazi, may God Perpetuate his dominions.'

'Really, are you not joking with me, Ikhlas sahib? Only God is free from all blemish!' Mir said. 'So Etmad-ud Daulah Bahadur agreed to withdraw? Well, he must be a person of a great and most generous heart!'

'Ama, many such as these Bai sahib types linger neglected in his pockets all the time!' Mir was again unhappy at the apparent disrespect to Labiba Khanam and Nur Khan Khanam, but he knew that he mustn't argue. Instead, he asked in a whisper: 'And what's that other matter?'

Ikhlas looked right and left, making sure that there were no eavesdroppers, and no one within earshot. Then he bent towards Mir and whispered: 'You know Intizam-ud Din Bahadur, don't you?'

'Yes, sure. He's the Grand Minister's son. On the wedding day, I saw him in the forefront, overseeing the marriage party's welcome and all.'

'Yes. Now it seemed that Intizam-ud Din Bahadur was taking a little more than normal interest in the affairs at Phatak Habash Khan, and he was rather more than particular about Nur Bai sahib. The Minister of all the Domains didn't obviously approve of this, especially in one so young. So long as they had some connection with the Minister, Intizam-ud Din Bahadur's interest could not be faulted. So, Etmad-ud Daulah Bahadur cut down the very root of the matter.'

His confidences over, Kishan Chand Ikhlas guffawed and Mir joined him. Mir's heart was a veritable house of fireworks, sparkling and heating the spirit. Since Ikhlas was to report for duty soon, they parted, each enjoying in his heart the future that was almost now on the horizon.

Reaching home, Mir wasn't yet changed into ordinary clothes, for he was too busy in thoughts of how again to approach Nurus Saadat, when a mace bearer appeared at his door, presented him with a rolled and sealed message, and went back, saying that no reply was needed or expected. Mir saw that it was his own paper. His heart sank, fearing that his message had been returned unanswered. As if he didn't deserve an answer, being unworthy of attention. He unrolled the paper and found that it was indeed his own paper, but with an addition. Just where he'd signed his name, he found inscribed in beautiful and minute calligraphy, so that the message would not run to the next page, the second line of the Hafiz verse of which Mir had made the first line his message. The line read:

Be kind; come down, for this house is your home.

The page fell from Mir's hands and he almost fainted. He didn't know what aroused him, but when he came to, he found himself thinking on the practicalities: When should I go? Should I send prior notice? Or should I send a message, asking for an appointment? Should I take some present with me? If so, should I present something only to Nurus Saadat, or should I have two separate presents? And what should the presents be? And if only one present is better policy, then should it be for the mother, or the daughter? Does the plain invitation contained in the master poet's line mean that it is a plain invitation indeed, with no frills attached, or required? But no one knows me there. If I go now, without appointment, what should I tell the guardsman, or to the maid if one comes from inside to inquire about me? Should I say that I am the poet Mir Taqi Mir, presenting myself on invitation by Nur Khanam? But if they ask for the invitation document? Should I produce this paper? But won't it constitute breach of confidence of some sort? She might not like it . . .

He was lost in these thoughts when he suddenly heard a shout: 'Hey, Mian sahib, Mian sahib, hey! Just be careful, sir! Move away, move over, please!'

In utter confusion, he sprang away from the voice and raised his head to know what was going on. He found that he was passing through the bustling bazaar area of Lal Kunwan. Not too far from Phatak Habash Khan. And oh, I can see the Khanam sahib's majestic haveli right there! By Allah, it's something like *Alif Lailah*! I was transported from my rooms to this place, leaving everything there as it was. But how? Then he looked down and saw the paper in his hand. So he'd set out, moving mechanically like a Chinese doll. While his brain was examining his thoughts, his feet were taking him where he wanted to go. It must be some sort of an occult confirmation for me to just go there. So let me go, then. Whatever is to happen, let it.

*

The tall, wide main gate of the Bai sahib's haveli was the scene of more activity than usual. The men mostly seemed to be from the craftsmen's professions. Perhaps some celebration was on the cards. He worried, if the guardsmen took me to be of the professional types, they might consign me to some side room, to await instructions? No, he must reveal himself boldly.

Now he was right in front of the gatehouse. A tall, powerful-looking person came out and spoke to Mir in Persian, stating rather than asking: 'Perhaps Mir Muhammad Taqi Mir is the honoured name of the respected portal?'

'Yes, sir. I am he. I am Mir the poet.' Mir was so flustered that he spoke in Arabic, and then realizing his folly, he repeated himself in Persian.

'Then, please bring your noble self inside. You are expected.'

Ya Maula! What is it that I hear and see! But Mir wasn't given time to wonder; the powerfully built, tall steward was walking purposefully, quicker than Mir, and soon led him to the door of a hall inside. He knocked, spoke something, perhaps in Turkish, to a maid who appeared, and withdrew.

The maid escorted him through a corridor, which opened upon the hall through a narrow side door, covered with a heavy curtain. The corridor was wide enough for two people to walk side by side, but the maid went ahead, coming to the end of the corridor from which two doors led into the interior. The maid opened one of the doors, which took them into a medium-sized, intimate-looking boudoir. The maid did a low salaam, told him in Persian to wait a while and withdrew silently.

Mir was surprised to have been introduced into a private chamber, instead of the divan khana. He noticed the quiet comfort and the warm ambience of the room. Wall-to-wall carpet, very light blue, or aquamarine, the unusual but very welcome fragrance of the attar of cloves, warm but not heavy; the room was not dimly, but somehow intimately lit, perhaps because of the very light turquoise-blue and jade-green shades on the candles. At the far end of the room, a door, again hidden by heavy Iranian or Uzbek tapestry; a little away from that door, a Turkish-style divan, with two heavy velveteen bolsters; in front of the divan, two stylish, padded, but rather uncomfortable chairs, obviously of Turkish or Firangi origin. An occasional table between the chairs and the divan; the table covered with cat's eye grey, embroidered tablecloth on which was a medium-sized, blue, yellow and green Chinese vase in the cloisonné style, heavy with flowers. Two small, niche-like alcoves, with two vases full of flowers, in a corner a small, very low table on which was laid out an unfinished game of chess. The chessmen and the board both were of ivory. A few books at one end of the divan; the volumes beautifully bound but clearly read, not just decoratively placed there.

Mir thought, where should I sit? On one of the chairs, maybe? Then his eye fell on his shoes, dusty, clumsy, utterly out of place there, in fact just the opposite of everything in that room. Mir was cursing himself for his thoughtlessness in not putting on better shoes. I should at least have left them at the . . .

'I present my submissions,' someone said in Persian. Mir raised his eyes, flustered, almost panicking. Nurus Saadat had entered the room from behind the heavily draped door so softly that he hadn't noticed the door opening. Nurus Saadat looked briefly at Mir, smiled, and went on: 'I am sorry I took some time. But won't you sit down?'

Mir's confusion was not quite abated, for he feared that Nurus Saadat must have been quietly noting his doltish behaviour and dirty shoes for some time. He, the poet who could compose poems at the snap of two fingers, found himself at a loss for words.

'I am . . . I am sorry,' he gulped, 'I was somehow lost. This . . . this chamber . . .' He stopped lamely.

'It's mine, my boudoir. Only some maids are allowed here.'

'I am privileged. Truly privileged . . .' He wanted to say an appropriate verse but nothing came to mind.

Nurus Saadat walked into the room. Did she walk, or float, Mir wondered. She came and occupied the chair next to Mir's. Why has she come so near? Mir was perspiring outwardly somewhat and profusely in his heart. What should I do now? Then, quite unknowing what he was doing, he left his chair, sat on the carpet, kissed her shoes, her feet, the soles of her feet, the toes, the ankles. He kissed each foot again and again, and all the time his tears flowed and wetted his collar, her feet, her shoes. Nurus Saadat did nothing to stop him, or move away from him. She just removed Mir's cap from his head and combed his dense, bright hair with her fingers. She played with his locks, tweaked them, gently pulled at them, then combed them again, and again.

Later, Mir was unable to say how much time they spent in that fashion. He says that he may have fallen into a light doze. What he did remember was the moment he tried to extend his hand above her feet, or attempted to kiss her on the face or lips, he was repelled most resolutely. All that he could do was to touch and kiss the occasional tress of her hair as their movements stirred it.

Whatever Mir remembered of their conversation that morning on that occasion did not perhaps take place then. It is possible that the two may have expressed their love for each other in some dreamy, or dreaming way. It's possible they did more, but there's no way to confirm this. What can be confirmed is that fifty or more years on, Mir composed some verses on separate occasions, perhaps commemorating that event:

She would put her feet on my chest
As she walked.
There was a time when she was here,
And she would do that.
*

Today
She permitted me
To put my head on her feet.
Now don't ask what great good it was
On me, and how much I am beholden to her.

'I thought of you often, and quite much. And you?' She spoke in Hindi, using the familiar *tum*. Her voice had a strong glimmer of Labiba Khanam's tones, but due to her youth it didn't have the strength and clarity of brass bells, the main characteristic of her mother's tones. At present there was an apparent artlessness there, but very clear modulation, like silver bells; delicate of form, her voice was oddly reminiscent of marble or alabaster artefacts, each line carved and chiselled with supremely careful artistry. Her Hindi was fluent, but Iranian-Persian intonations could be heard in it. She did occasionally falter in the matter of the gender of Hindi words—something that trips almost everyone who comes to the language somewhat late. She was yet unable to pronounce the retroflexes and the mixed consonants, but her enunciation gave her words a childlike rhythm, which was extremely pleasing to the ear and to the heart. Every time she softened a hard retroflex, Mir impulsively felt like rising and kissing her on the mouth.

'I didn't just think of you, or miss you,' said Mir.

'So? What did you do? Nothing?'

'I prayed for your long and happy life because you gave away to me the greatest possible wealth. *That*, I said to my heart, is generosity. And I prayed to my faith in your love, and faith in my God, that they never wane.'

'How does faith in your God come in here? I fear you are trying to travel in two boats at the same time.' She was a little serious, a little teasing.

'No. No. Not at all. We in Hind equate love with God and if I lose faith in God, I lose faith in love. And the other way round too. And I thanked my faith in my God that it vacated its place in my heart for you.'

'They said you are a fine poet,' she teased him again. 'Indeed, you know all sorts of specious arguments, and false prayers.'

'So long as love is, arguments and prayers don't matter. So my last prayer was to love itself, that it may not take away my life—of which your cruelty made a distinct possibility—so that I go on loving you.'

'Cruelty? What cruelty?' She smiled.

'Madam, don't you know that you are always cruel? Your smile kills me. Your voice takes away my voice. Your body drowns me in desire . . .'

She cut him short playfully and said, 'All right, all right. I confirm that you are a poet. You talk so well.' She delivered a playful slap on his cheek.

Mir didn't know if he should thank her for enjoying his conversation, but before he could decide, Nurus Saadat spoke gravely: 'Yes, you are a good poet. But what use would your poetry be if you didn't prove to be a good lover?'

'Good lover . . . ? That is . . . one who would die for you?' Mir was a little uncertain what he was expected to say.

'I'll tell you at some other time.'

Mir thought that Nurus Saadat was having some fun, but when he looked up, he was consternated to find that her face was extremely sombre, almost drawn, and perhaps there were unshed tears in her eyes?

'Dearest my heart, tell me what I should do, or not do,' he entreated, touching her slim fingers, so well made, but somehow feeling cold at that moment.

She didn't speak. Perhaps she wanted Mir to say something, and Mir wasn't able to fathom her purpose. In order to divert her, he spoke two verses declaring his love. It was as if he wrote them specifically for the occasion:

Does the morning sun rise with a radiance
Or do you?
Does the dew of the night possess a weeping eye
Or do I?
Look, that's your sword, here the basin to receive my head. Here am I—
Does anyone so play with one's own life
Or do I?

Mir imagined that Nurus Saadat would respond to the poetry with a smile of appreciation and enjoyment. But there were tears in her eyes now, quite openly. She was weeping! He was shaken to the core, and was also full of fear. Have I offended her, somehow? He didn't dare say a word, far less say something light-hearted. He tried to hold her hand, and ask what he should do to please her. But she pushed his hand away.

There was silence for many long moments. Finally, Nurus Saadat spoke: 'There are some fears in my heart.' Mir started, and wanted to respond immediately, but she raised her hand and said, 'That's all you need to do now. Just listen, or I'll fall silent, and won't then speak at all.'

Mir hung his head contritely and waited for her to go on. When she didn't speak for some time, Mir raised his hands, folded them in front of him, to beg her to go on, or to beg pardon. Nurus Saadat smiled in spite of herself.

'That's a good gesture you Hindis have designed! No need to say a word. Just fold your hands together and look dumb!' She laughed; her change of mood was surprising. And very welcome. The whole ambience changed from hostile to welcoming. 'And why do you people touch your ears and in fact pull them all the time?'

Mir tried a feeble joke: 'Yes, we pull at our ears. We don't eat them.' The point was that *kan khana* (to eat someone ears off) meant 'to be extremely and inanely talkative'. He was rewarded with a smile.

She said, 'All right, you, now listen.' She suddenly became pensive, almost brooding. 'I have been dreaming some bad dreams ever since I was small. I dream of mountainous, windy places. I am lonely there.'

She choked back a sob. 'The dreams are sometimes vague, nothing defined. Sometimes they are sharp, like the needle of the sun. Nowadays I have another dream. I dream that my dreams have become real.'

She was trembling a little. She pulled her feet up and bent the knees under her. Her delicate, pink feet were now hidden under her thighs. The tall neck, as it was raised a little, revealed a hint of small but pointed breasts, the narrow waist became still narrower. All these stances she had inherited from her mother, and her resemblance to Labiba Khanam was even more pronounced now.

Mir clasped her shoes firmly to his bosom, as if he could prevent her going away when he possessed her shoes. The corners of her huge eyes were bright with tears again. But she gazed at Mir's face as she said: 'I have to die alone. I have to suffer ignominy. And my mother . . . my mother will be . . . will be unhappy with me.'

'Darling, my princess, what is all this that you are telling me? Ignominy, lonely death—God forbid. This is not the time for you to die! You have just begun your life. And why should Khanam-e Buzurg be angry with you? Sorry, but these are dreams that happen when one has an upset stomach!' Mir tried to laugh, but the sound stuck in his throat.

Paying no heed to him, Nurus Saadat continued: 'I want such a one to be my lover who can save me from dying a lonely death, who can save me from my mother's disapproval.'

Mir was still unable to articulate; trying to find words, trying to clear his choked throat where the dead snatch of laughter was blocking it still. If it was the writ of fate, one could try to change the writ by prayers, charms, talismans. If it was a disease, one could consult Delhi's hakims, the best physicians in the world. If there was some jinn or evil spirit hounding her, one could go consult one of the many leading spiritualists in the city. But this was something else again. Was it superstition? Superstitions could also be got rid of by the arcane art of prayer, combined with talismans. Or was it premonition? Then there was no cure, he despaired.

Perhaps it is superstition, superstition about me. She doesn't want a Hindi for a lover. Perhaps some fakir made some prediction about foreign lovers when she was small, and though the words were forgotten, the effect had stuck in her memory. He began to speak in slow, deliberate words: 'Nur Khanam, I will go away from your life the moment the smallest shred of cloud appears on your life's horizon. Ignominy is unthinkable. I will go away even if I heard one whisper, one word spoken in sleep even. And Nur Khanam, you can never, never be alone. For, you are complete, self-sufficient in yourself. You don't need a host of lovers, or even a single lover to know that you are loved.'

He looked at Nurus Saadat. She seemed to be listening to his words, but her look was blank. Mir suddenly recalled some verses of the fifteenth-century Persian poet Jami. He began to say:

Absolute Beauty, free from the fetters of manifestation
By its own Light apparent to Itself.
A heart-comforting Beloved, in the secret chamber of the unapparent
A Beauty the hem of whose Dress is untainted even by false accusations
                                                              of blemish.
The morning breeze never plucked even one hair from that Beauty's
                                                              Tresses
The Eyes that never saw the grit of the kohl.
Making the Music of Love and being loved, alone
Gaming the Game of Love by Itself, all alone.

Mir could see that Nurus Saadat was listening, not dully and vacantly as before, but listening mesmerized by the powerful rhythms of overflowing sound, caught in the magic of words, words heated by the imagination, imagination such as is rarely vouchsafed to man. Mir cried, with almost the same passion as the passionate flow of the poem: 'Nur Khanam, you are none but a reflection of that Beauty, none but a beam of that Light. No loneliness can touch you, nor ignominy. No decline, no decay can come near you!'

Nurus Saadat's face brightened. 'How true! How absolutely true! Who is the poet? Let me hear more of him.'

Mir, exuberant in his heart that he could pull Nurus Saadat out of the pit where she was mired in despond, said more verses to her from the same section in Jami's poem. Nurus Saadat's heartbeat may have gone up, but her face reflected the light of heart-content. She pulled her shoes out of Mir's grasp, touched him on his face, and said: 'Do you know why I asked you to come today?'

'To raise my station, to heal the wound of my heart, what else?'

She shushed him, as if Mir were a child and she was chiding him.

'You men, you see nothing but your own selfish interests, you believe that everything is just so green and glowing with the power of the spring . . . You little fool!'

Mir was in raptures, being addressed thus. 'Your command is quite true, my Life, my World. I would love to be your fool!'

'All right, no more fooling! To business. Now listen. Umdat-ul Mulk has discussed with Amma. It has been determined that I'll visit nobody, sing nowhere, but at the invitation of Umdat-ul Mulk, and only where he wants me to go. He will give advance notice if he wants to visit, and give even longer notice if he wants me to come. I will do no duty but sing. You can see me and talk to me as a casual visitor at such occasions, but you will have to wait for my word to come here.'

'So, we can't meet every day?' Mir was upset, and worried.

'Very good, Mir sahib!' she laughed. 'So, you want to visit every day? Did you see your reflection in a mirror lately?'

Before Mir could retort, she said gravely, 'And look, please. Let no one ever get a whiff of when and why you come here.'

'I cannot dare disobey, my Life, my World. It would be a fool who would advertise his treasures. I won't deviate one little hair from your command, ma'am.'

'All right, go now. No more chatter. I know well. You men are ever shallow, ever deceivers. But remember, if you make my secrets open, you'll rue forever.'

She rose as she spoke these words, which were not delivered in a minatory tone, but playfully. Yet the careful listener could discern the undertow of serious concerns.

Then she said: 'Oh, there's another thing! I quite forgot to tell you. The day after tomorrow, I'll make my first public appearance in Delhi; in fact, it'll be the very first of my life. I will sing at the haveli of Umdat-ul Mulk. You must come.'

She turned to go. Mir stood, rooted to the spot. He bent his head in salaam, raised his right hand to the left side of his bosom, and was about to say, I will come, even if it costs my life, when Nurus Saadat raised her hand to do the salaam. Somehow, she stepped up as she turned, and found herself in Mir's embrace. Mir began to plant kisses on her face, lips, neck, nose, forehead, eyes, and did so with the vigour of youth and the passion and appetite of a starving young man. At first, Nurus Saadat resisted a little, but soon she gave herself to the pleasures and ecstasies that she had also perhaps been desiring in her heart. But she didn't let him go too far, and repulsed him when Mir tried to insert his tongue in her mouth. She kissed him gently instead and let her head rest on Mir's chest. When Mir tried other tactics and other places, she pushed him away, and said, 'No more, you! I'll slap you good and resoundingly strong if you persist!'

Mir tried again, half-heartedly, but knew that the time and the place were not right. Also, Nurus Saadat seemed to be tiring a bit. Recalling that moment later, Mir wrote a verse:

You start to wilt, as I smell you
How delicate, oh how fragile you are!
I touch you, and you seem to become grubby
How utterly light, oh how subtle and how soft you are!

Mir didn't remember much more of that morning: when did it progress to the noon, when and how he came out of the boudoir, and the haveli. But he remained proud of those moments all his long life. He could never relive them in his imagination, or fantasize about them, or even write a truly erotic poem about them. He was quite capable of doing so, and even openly erotic poems were not unknown in Persian or Hindi. Much later, he wrote an autobiographical poem, describing certain episodes in his life. In one of them, he said:

She was actually inclined towards me,
Though she was formally attached to another.
She was extremely careful, outwardly
But she met me often, secretly.

Gradually, our dealings became intimate:
She permitted me to touch her feet.
On occasion, she would stretch her legs
And let me touch my eyes to the soles of her feet.
Or she would smile, and put her feet on my bosom
Thus also she took my heart in her hand.
Sometimes she permitted an embrace
And sometimes, lying together, or side by side, breasts to bosom.

*

The next afternoon, Rai Kishan Chand Ikhlas appeared at Labiba Khanam's haveli, dressed even more smartly and opulently than usual. He had a servant by his side, carrying a big wicker basket; behind him, two others, carrying two large, covered trays on their heads. The covers on the basket and trays were red and blue brocade. The Rai sahib was immediately conducted into the divan khana as the servants waited in the outer veranda. Rai Kishan Chand remembered their first meeting in Isfahan—how far had he travelled since then, and Labiba Khanam? He wondered. He prayed that the outcome of today's meeting would be as auspicious and desirable as the one in Isfahan.

Labiba Khanam entered just a few minutes later. Rai Kishan Chand Ikhlas rose to his full height, made three low salaams, and said with a smile: 'Grand Khanam sahib, congratulations on the freedom of the morning breeze!'

Labiba Khanam got his intent, but wasn't quite certain, so she answered innocently: 'Freedom? Yes, congratulations to you, Ikhlas sahib. But why the word of congratulations to me specially?'

Perhaps she wanted Ikhlas to take full initiative, and ambiguity in such matters wasn't her style anyway.

'Exalted Portal, there was a stricture on the hearts. Now it's gone. You are free to choose, and I was not ever bound with any chains. I never owed, and do not now owe fealty of the heart to anyone.'

She laughed her special laughter, intimate, yet distant. 'Limbs tied up for long become paralysed. But limbs unfettered are liable to trip and break, especially if they are impudent.'

'The impudent are not faithful.'

'Correct, Honourable Ikhlas sahib. The playing field is here, so are the ball and the mallet.' It was clear that she was pleased with the conversation, and she was inviting for the next steps to be taken.

Ikhlas beckoned the bearers, who now came in, placed their loads on a low table, and salaamed the Khanam sahib three times. Then they took one step back, did three salaams, and went out.

'Rai sahib, what did you bring today? And for whom?' She was, it seemed, determined to be playful with him today.

'For one who has everything, and for whom there is everything from the assembly of all the horizons. But she lacks for one thing.'

'So, what's that thing? And is that what you brought today?' She was now openly playful, almost flirtatious.

'Actually, I bring it every day, but you don't ever notice it.'

'I see. But what is that thing? Rai Kishan Chand Ikhlas, you were quite a competent poet, but when did you enrol yourself among the people of Mir Haidar, the Master of Riddles?'

Rai Kishan Chand's heart leapt up, but he pulled himself back. Perhaps this wasn't the time to say what he needed so ardently to say. Let the conversation unroll itself further. But his heart said, what other occasion could there be? And if you don't have the pluck to say it, why did you come with such preparation? He recalled a line from Mir:

All this is mere talk; one can't really say a thing.

'Where did you go away, Ikhlas sahib? Should you not finish what you began? Or do the people of Delhi have a different protocol in these matters?'

These matters? What matters? His heart said to him, yes, there is invitation here. Accept it. This is no mere dalliance.

Finally, he blurted, 'The thing that your haveli lacks are Rai Kishan Chand's footprints, because at present they are not permitted to cross your portal.'

Grand Khanam certainly expected some such response from Ikhlas. But now that he actually said the words, she was shocked inside, and fearful. The thrill of the expected reply—the desired reply, in fact—was, in its own place, valid and suited to her estate. Her face was unable to express so many contradictory, complex feelings. It was far easier to weep, and that's what she did. Rai Kishan Chand found himself shaken inside, shocked beyond speech. Should he, somehow, take his words back? Should he rise and go close to her—as close as possible, under the circumstances—take her hand in his, and try to soothe her, console her, ask for forgiveness? He was about to rise when, by his good fortune, Labiba spoke: 'Rai Kishan Chand, you put me in a terrible predicament . . . I don't deserve the honour that you want to bestow on me . . .'

Ikhlas, fearful that she might now clearly say 'no' to him, interrupted impatiently: 'What is it that you say, madam? The honour is mine . . .'

He wanted to go on, but Labiba raised her hand in a strange, almost imperial fashion, to stop him, and spoke in a near whisper: 'After Bayazid Shauqi, and in fact even before him, I found no man who would even merit a glance from me.'

Tears welled into her eyes and flowed down from under her long eyelashes. But there was now a singular warmth in her voice and she switched from Persian to Hindi, using the familiar pronoun *tum*: 'I was extremely fearful when my heart began to long for your sight, to desire your company. I am married to Bayazid forever, I said to myself. I wasn't married to him just once, I was married and remarried to him with every breath in my life. Though I could see that you fancied me, in fact, you desired me with an ardent desiring, yet I didn't fear it at all. I feared for myself, and that fear is still present in me . . .'

She mopped her eyes and her face, now pale and somehow lovelier than ever before, and went on, '. . . I am a pauper, empty of hand and pocket in the business of love and desire. But I don't know from where

302

your talk always brings in treasure after treasure for me and overloads the hem of my dress with pearls of yearning and hope, even covetous hope. I didn't want the curtain to be removed, for the play of love to go to the next stage.'

She raised her eyes, her big eyes, smouldering with the heat of pain. Kishan Chand impulsively rose and moved up to her, touching her hand gently. She went on, looking at him with some affection and boundless pity: 'Ikhlas, the best part of my heart, the best part of my soul is now naught but shifting sand. Nothing can grow there. No love can green there. But I do hear you calling to me from what does survive, a very small part of my inner self.'

She fell silent. Perhaps she expected some assurance, some declaration from Ikhlas. She could give him only partially what she expected from him wholly. Or perhaps she was exhausted, both mentally and physically. Kishan Chand Ikhlas sat outwardly unmoving like a picture, inwardly listening to his heartbeat, beating for none else, only Labiba Khanam, however conditional would her love be for him. But he found himself unable to express these thoughts. Perhaps he thought it was derogatory to say, or imply that Khanam sahib could give him just a part of her love; it seemed to suggest a disability, a defect in one whom he only wanted to see replete with merit, and excellence, and goodness.

She now spoke in a tone of some finality: 'I don't know how much this apology of a life, where there is more ashes and dust than greenery, will suit you. It may be that you get tired, or bored with the desolation that is in me.'

'Don't say that! Please don't say that,' Ikhlas implored her. 'That will never happen. I will take what you can give; I will give all that I have.'

Labiba continued, unhearing, 'I am quite willing, happy in fact, to invite you to cross the threshold. But there is very little there to divert a young man like you and there is much barrenness. The winds of winter have made a wrack of my heart.'

'To me it is better to die in that wrack and barren ruin than to rule from the throne of Delhi,' Ikhlas spoke with great passion and determination. 'Both of us have, in our own ways, travelled far from ennui and boredom. And the colours of youthful loves and frolics of passion have long flown from our hearts. Lust you never had, and I have wandered through the lanes and by-lanes of lust and carnal desire for a whole lifetime. There's nothing there to attract, far less detain me.'

Labiba was silent, and still. Kishan Chand Ikhlas didn't know what she was waiting for, what more was it that she desired. He rose to his full height, to make one more attempt, to throw the dice one more time.

'What do you fear, Labiba?' he cried. 'You are the sun, I, a mere particle. However grubby and muddied the particle may be, it still shines when it reaches the sun's precincts. However much the sun darkens under an eclipse, it still can give a scar bright enough to enhance the incandescence of the heart, the brilliance of the shroud of love. Come, let's not tarry further, our lives are already more than half gone.'

He took another step towards her. She flinched a little, but then smiled and stood her ground. Ikhlas raised her chin and looked into her eyes, now brightening. He drew her towards his bosom. She made no resistance.

*

Umdat-ul Mulk Navab Muhammad Amir Khan Anjam's father was originally called Mir Khan. Aurangzeb, out of kindness and affection, added an 'a' to the name, making it 'Amir Khan'. His remote ancestor was Shah Nematullah Vali, a famous Sufi and poet of the sixteenth century. Navab Amir Khan was one of the favoured and prominent nobles at Aurangzeb's Court. His son inherited the father's name, and eventually, by virtue of his excellent qualifications and achievements, the title Umdat-ul Mulk, and the favours at the Exalted Porte of the Presence, Muhammad Shah Padishah Ghazi. He was Governor of Allahabad and Military Commander of the garrison at Kara Manikpur when he was awarded the title and summoned to Delhi.

Muhammad Amir Khan Anjam was slight, slim and of just about medium height. He was extremely agile, mentally and physically: each and every bone and sinew of his slight body seeming to be dancing with the brightness of wit and the luminance of multi-faceted accomplishment. In spite of his slight and, at first sight, insignificant body, he quickly became the dominant figure at any assembly because of his ready wit, his face radiant with kindness and his heart-warming smile. At the time that we are talking about, he had no equal in statesmanship, diplomacy, and administrative and financial acumen. On top of it all, there was his patronage of the arts and his legendary generosity. Numerous poets, singers, musicians and painters benefited from his Court through regular or irregular employment. He was a Persian poet of distinction and was even better known for his discriminating eye in matters relating to the appreciation of poetry in both Persian and Rekhtah. An acknowledged master in music, his name was taken with respect by ustads far and wide, who sang or performed at his assemblies with due deference.

Amir Khan Anjam would often crack jokes or indulge in witticisms or repartee. But he always kept his eyes low and his face straight: the sharper the repartee, the cleverer the witticism, the straighter his face. Because of his delicate features and small physique, he could be mistaken for a woman if he put on women's dress which he sometimes did in private and closed assemblies; such assemblies were devoted mostly to cracking or telling jokes, inventing wordplays, and the practice of the *zila*, sometimes called *zila-jugat*. Zila means 'side', and jugat means 'wisdom'. The idea was to construct sentences in which words from the same domain, or words having some similarity of connotation, whether directly or associatively, were used. The idea was not to use words with similar meanings; that is to say, punning was to be avoided. The intent was to mine the language from unlikely angles and use free play of association as a weapon of wit.

With the decline of the culture, the art of zila fell into disrepute, then desuetude. It was, in fact, not just frivolity, but could be used in poetry with much effect by the ingenious poet. Mir used it often and with such subtlety that all but the most discerning listeners failed to get the zila angle. The effect of zila is impossible to reproduce in translation, but here are a few examples from the poetry of Mir, with the necessary commentary:

> *How I wish I was one of this garden: like the scent of flowers*
> *I'd float with the morning breeze, enjoy myself, and then dissipate, like air.*

In the original, he doesn't say 'dissipate, like air'. He says, 'I would be air'. Apart from other resonances, there's an interesting zila here: 'to be air' actually means 'to disappear'. This meaning is not strictly relevant, but its associations with the whole theme would be obvious to an attentive listener.

> *My body acquired a heart, and fieriness shot through my whole body;*
> *It was such a spark that my clothing burnt.*

In addition to other metaphorical meanings, one must note that 'body' and 'clothing' have the connection of zila.

> *Well, only a fool or a simpleton wouldn't feel anxious after sending off*
> *a letter to her;*
> *I would be mistrustful, even if my courier were God's own messenger.*

There are two words, *qasid* and *rasul*, in the second line, which have the same meaning, 'messenger'; but rasul is almost exclusively used to mean 'messenger of God'. The zila should be obvious.

Going back to Umdat-ul Mulk Amir Khan Anjam's patronage of the poets, it is proper to recount here the case of the Iranian poet Shaikh Ali Hazin who arrived in India in 1746, a fugitive from the persecution of the King and in fear of his life. The first Portal where Hazin submitted his prostrations was that of the Umdat-ul Mulk. Umdat-ul

Mulk extended patronage to him far in excess of that irascible poet-nobleman's expectations. Over and above what he himself gave, the Umdat-ul Mulk introduced him to the Exalted Pavilion of the Emperor, Muhammad Shah Padishah Ghazi where he was immediately accorded protection and a cash grant of two million rupees. Ali Hazin stayed in Delhi for many years before travelling to the east and settling in Banaras where he died after a long sojourn, and was buried with full honours.

In spite of these generosities, Ali Hazin always remained critical of India, describing it, in his autobiography as 'a bedchamber with a dark day'. He looked down upon the Indian Persian poets, calling them 'inferior in theme', and deriding their language as not in conformity with the Iranian idiom which he regarded as normative. Umdat-ul Mulk, however, didn't withdraw his patronage from Ali Hazin, nor did he make any submission to the Shadow of God against him.

Two instances, one of Umdat-ul Mulk's happy understanding of the felicities of poetry, and the other of his ready wit, had been famous in history since decades.

Prince Ahmad Shah's foster brother Navab Ashraf Ali Khan Fughan, a poet of commanding reputation, presented the following verse before the Shadow of God:

Candle-faced beauty, don't let the moth have room in your assembly
My life for you, am I not enough for burning away?

Everyone praised the sweetness and spontaneity of the lines. Umdat-ul Mulk's comment was as follows: 'Honourable Navab sahib, the verses are luminous and the words most appropriate to the theme. But I have a suggestion: you say *ay tere qurban* to mean "my life for you". Now, if you said, *ay tere bal jain*, you'd be saying the same thing, but with the additional dimension of zila in bal jain because it means both "to give one's life for" and "to burn".'

The entire Court was unanimous in praise of the emendation. Even the Shadow of God uttered the following command with his

Miraculous Tongue: 'You spoke correctly, Umdat-ul Mulk. Your emendation inspired life into the verse.'

Khan-e Dauran Samsam-ud Daulah Abdus Samad Khan Bahadur Jang was known for his valour in battle, as also for his practical wisdom, but was sometimes found somehow to be vying with Umdat-ul Mulk Amir Khan in readiness of wit and framing apophthegms. Once he submitted to the King Emperor: 'Shadow of God, experience shows that those communities and groups of people who have the suffix *ban* in their names are evil natured, or disloyal, or both. Per example,' he continued gravely, 'this servant submits the following: *shuturban* (camel driver); *gariban* (cart driver); *sarban* (caravan guide or leader).'

His Exalted Presence looked towards Umdat-ul Mulk Amir Khan, who placed his right hand on the left side of his breast, bent his head, and submitted with maximum humility and graveness: 'Quite true, *mehrban* (one who dispenses kindness).'

The Shadow of God, unwilling to break protocol, didn't smile. But the corners of his auspicious lips quivered a little. As for those present at court, laughter, or even a grin, was out of the question. Everyone looked straight in front, with faces as wooden as if truly carved in wood.

Navab Muhammad Amir Khan Anjam's generous hand didn't fall short of reaching up to the young but promising poets like Mir. Thus both of them knew each other, and now, because of the connection with Navab Riayat Khan, Mir had no difficulty in being admitted into Umdat-ul Mulk's huge haveli.

At that time, Nur Bai's reputation—her beauty, youth and her proficiency in singing—was the talk of the town; even children were acquainted with her name. It was her first public appearance in the city that day, so a number of noblemen and rich merchants and officials arrived at Umdat-ul Mulk's haveli, some of them without even being invited. A crowd of spectators, hoping to get a glimpse of her, and perhaps even be lucky enough to hear a few of her words and notes of music, had poured into the street, thronging the gatehouse and its surrounds. Mir was luckier than most. He was allotted a seat among the poets and distant relatives attached to Etmad-ud Daulah, so he could clearly see and hear everything though there was no chance or question of looking her full in the face. Even so, he looked in that direction when he thought no one was looking, and once or twice could even look at her when her glance was on him, quite by chance. The Grand Khanam sahib was present, but she didn't notice Mir, and not to speak of Mir, she noticed none except Etmad-ud Daulah and Umdat-ul Mulk, rising to her full height to submit her respects to them. Others merited only a salaam, as she half rose to acknowledge their presence.

When the assembly was all set, suitable arrangements for the purdah ladies having been supervised by Umdat-ul Mulk's Chief Steward personally, and containers of betels, cardamoms, finely chopped dry coconut and betel nut placed at all strategic places, the hookahs removed from among the audience, Bari Bai sahib rose to address the audience. Speaking in Persian, she said: 'Worshipful Navab Umdat-ul Mulk Bahadur, Honoured Patrons and Dispensers of kindness and bounty, you are all connoisseurs, if not actually masters of the arts of music and of poetry. This little girl is a novice, a schoolgoing child in every sense of the term. It is for the first time that she is present before an open assembly—a galaxy actually, not just an assembly. Whatever she presents, please to look at her presentation with the eye of correction, and forgive her shortcomings. The convention is that the younger person is first afforded the opportunity to present her piece and give you a sample of her ghazal selection and her artistry of song. But this is a special time and special occasion, so I will open this assembly that rivals the Milky Way with a rubai from Maulavi-e Rumi. The little lady will also present a ghazal by Rumi, in her turn.'

Umdat-ul Mulk must have made some gesture, some beckoning movement of his hand, but no one could see it. The Chief Steward came forward, followed by two staff bearers, each holding a metal tray in his right hand. Umdat-ul Mulk removed a Kashmiri jamahvar double shawl from one of the trays and draped it around Nur Khanam's shoulders. From the other tray, he removed a bolt of Dacca muslin, so thin that the entire bolt had been passed through a silver ring and both its ends closed with two gold rings. This he presented to Bari Khanam sahib. Both rose to their full height and bent low in salaam before accepting the gift.

A hush now fell everywhere; even the buzz at the gatehouse became muted on all sides. Bari Khanam sahib looked at Umdat-ul Mulk, as if seeking appreciation from him, or even addressing the Rumi rubai to him. She sang in raga Bhairavi:

> *He, whom God has given a beloved friend like you*
> *Him has God also given a restless heart and a restless soul*
> *Now please don't have any expectations of service from him*
> *For, God has assigned him a wondrous duty!*

A spontaneous tumult of applause, appreciation and demands of encores arose from the audience. Khvajah Mir Dard, the prominent poet and musicologist, and his younger brother Mir Muhammad Asar were seated among those in the front. Khvajah Mir Dard sahib had not adopted the life of a Sufi yet, and occasionally attended such musical soirées as took his fancy. Both the brothers were beside themselves, repeating and humming snatches from the lines. Their throats dry, but their tongues untired, they were ecstatic in admiration.

In the meantime, the Chief Stewardess appeared from behind the screens and whispered something to Umdat-ul Mulk. He rose from his place and spoke softly to Bari Bai sahib. It appeared that the seating arrangements for the chief purdah-observing ladies were somewhat defective: some of the most eminent among the ladies, especially Mughlani Begam, the daughter-in-law of Etmad-ud Daulah, and wife of Mir Muin-ud Din Khan Bahadur, affectionately known as Mir Munnu, were unable to hear or even see the singers. Information was given that the seating was being rearranged, and so long as this was in progress, the Bai sahibs shouldn't be troubled to present their offerings.

By the time these whisperings were over, news came that everything was now to the satisfaction of the Exalted Ladies, and the singing may recommence. Nur Khanam rose to her full height, salaamed the assembly, and submitted that she may be forgiven for any faults that may be found in her performance. She first presented another rubai by Rumi, but the raga was Yaman Kalyan, a raga invented by Amir Khusrau. After a short *alap*, she came straight to the *asthai*. The words were:

When should be, and when should be, and when should be, and when?
Wine should be, and wine should be, and wine should be, and wine.
I should be, and I should be, and I should be, and I.
She should be, and she should be, and she should be, and she.

Oh, who can describe the effect of those incantatory, magical words, the nearly heavenly musical conjuration! The two most august brothers, masters of poetry, music and Sufism, Syed Khvajah Mir Dard and Mir Asar came almost into dance, reminding the audience of the whirling dervishes of the Mevlevia Sufis. Mir's face was wetter than his eyes, if that could be. He didn't bother to wipe his face, or dry his eyes. He just repeated, 'She should be, and she should be, and she should be, and she . . .' and swayed, and wept. He had no sense of what was happening around him, but others reported that quite a number of the senior members in the audience fainted and had to be attended to by the physicians. Many of the Exalted Begams had to be removed from the assembly because they fainted and had begun to wail, and also cry out applauding phrases directly as they were revived.

There was no way that one could compare the mature, true and flawless voice of Bari Bai sahib with the somewhat young-girlish voice of Nur Bai sahib. Bari Bai sahib's voice had a carrying power, a metallic resonance like that of large, ancient bells that had been ringing away since decades. It had a hypnotizing grace that needed a few minutes to create its full effect. Nur Bai sahib's voice had the clear effect of virginity, of the tinkle of silver bells. What it didn't have in depth and resonance, it compensated by fidelity to the raga, a fidelity that made her remain away from dramatic effects. Her words were clear, entirely undistorted by the pull of the raga; her voice had an even flow; her notes didn't break into passionate speed, but remained poised between slow and medium. She talked, rather than sang; yet there were some who said that she sang, rather than talked.

After the tumult died down, the instrumentalists retuned their strings, and the drone, which had been subdued through all this, became louder, insistent. Now Nurus Saadat began the initial, abstract rendering of the raga called Jogia, a raga suited to the midnight hour and to Sufi themes. After three or four minutes, she entered upon the text—a ghazal by Rumi:

My life and my love, joy in the two worlds, without you
I did not see
I saw numerous rare and wonderful things,
A wondrous thing, such as you
I did not see
They say: the scorching, burning power of your fire
Is lotted only for the denier, the unbeliever
Anyone deprived of your fire, except the arch unbeliever Abu Lahab
I did not see
On my heart's peephole, I placed the ears of my soul, intently
I heard a great number of words, but the speaker's lips
I did not see
Oh cup bearer, chosen of all, I swear by my two eyes
The like of you never came in Iran; the like of you in Araby
I did not see
Pour, pour the wine! So much, that I come down from the pedestal of
                                                          my being
Because in the realm of being and existing, anything other than hardship
I did not see
Oh you, who are milk, and sugar, and the sun, and the moon

Oh you, my father and my mother, ancestor other than you
I did not see
I am filings of iron, your love is the magnet
You are the essence, the root of all desire,
But in you, the least vestige of desire
I did not see.

*

After this assembly, the high reputation of mother and daughter soared even higher. They came closer to Umdat-ul Mulk and became more like client and patron. They had free access to him, and even exchanged jokes and said poetry to each other.

Umdat-ul Mulk's propensity for colourful clothing, and on occasion for women's clothing, grew as he grew older. Thus it so happened one day that he entered upon his assembly chamber wearing clothes that were more arresting than usual: he wore narrow-bottomed silk trousers, the fabric was bright orange and had very fine stripes in peacock blue. He looked like the embodiment of the rainy season; his dress immediately called to mind the call of the peacock, and the sound of rain upon the leaves.

After the salaams and greetings, Bari Bai sahib smiled, and said, 'Umdat-ul Mulk, today you have put on a really killing pair of trousers. Indeed, they kill like a beloved, a kafir.'

The basis of the witticism was the Hindi poetic idiom and also common usage, according to which the beloved was a kafir, because those who were in love were prepared to quit all: religion, faith, relatives and the life of this world. So a person who induced another to renounce his religion would indeed be a kafir. Thus kafir and a heart-stealing beloved were the same in most literary contexts.

She'd spoken softly, but not in such a low voice as to be inaudible to the necessarily select gathering. The older among those present cracked just a smile, the women giggled behind their wraps, the younger ones pretended to suppress a cough, by pushing their handkerchiefs in their mouths.

Umdat-ul Mulk observed all this, kept a grave visage, his eyes bent as usual. He answered, almost meekly: 'Yes, madam. But there is also a little *Mussalmani* in it.'

The assembly became the proverbial field of saffron at this cutting but extremely polished reply. Everyone laughed out as loud was as permitted by the limit of good manners. There were cries of:

'Wah, wah!'

'Only God is free from all blemish!'

'His Honour the Umdat-ul Mulk has performed the feat of answering a brick with a stone slab, and that too without transgressing the line of decorum!'

'Perfection, indeed, it is perfection!'

The basis of the extremely witty riposte was on the word 'Mussalmani' that means Mussalman-ness, or Muslimness, but it was more commonly used, colloquially, to mean 'the male member'.

Even Bari Bai sahib had applauded the navab's reply; but she wasn't going to admit defeat so easily. Once the sound of applause slowed down, she shot back: 'Sure, it's because of just that kind of double dealing the Navab is unable to look us in the eye and has his eyes always on the ground!'

The word 'double dealing' was absolutely unanswerable, given Umdat-ul Mulk's habit of never raising his eyes upon anyone. Still, he could have come up with something suitable, but it was getting late, so he removed an emerald necklace from his neck, its large, main stone cut like a square and suggesting a talisman, and presented it to Bari Bai sahib as reward.

*

Sometimes, Umdat-ul Mulk organized mushairas in his haveli. Better described as private assemblies of prominent poets, these gatherings were invariably attended by those who were lucky were to be invited; those who weren't, longed for an invitation to the next such occasion. Umdat-ul Mulk always invited the Bai sahibs to those meetings. Occasionally, he requested one or the other to sing some verses from the masters, and they readily obliged.

There was a mushaira of the above description on 6 January 1746 where almost all the leading poets were present. The exception was Mirza Mahzar sahib Jan-e Janan, who never went to any poetic literary gathering. Shaikh Ali Hazin, the Iranian visitor, was present. He was about to leave for the eastern territories with the view perhaps of settling there. Prominent among the Persian poets of Delhi who were present were Rai Anand Ram Mukhlis, his ustad and mentor Sirajuddin Ali Khan-e Arzu, Shah Nur-ul Ain Vaqif, Tek Chand Bahar, Mir Shamsuddin Faqir, Sukhraj Sabqat, who was one of the outstanding pupils of Mirza Bedil, and Mir Azal Sabit Ilahabadi. Those who preferred Rekhtah-Hindi, they recited poems in that tongue; many were more into Persian than Rekhtah, so they presented their Persian ghazals.

The meeting must have begun at an inauspicious moment: none of the ghazals recited scored a success. One of the main reasons may have been Ali Hazin who passed snide and sneering comments on all poets, whether Persian or Hindi, and clearly didn't care who heard him. The poets themselves, and the select audience (among whom was Mir as well) remained quiescent, for Ali Hazin was leaving Delhi anyway and also because he was a guest, of sorts.

Finally, the reciting candle was placed in front of Nur-ul Ain Vaqif, not the most senior of the poets, but because he was almost a Sufi now and rarely went out to such assemblies. Another reason was the passion, the almost mystical submission of the self to some Higher Being, the utter absorption in love, that were now the special characteristics of his poetic voice.

Mir remembered some of the verses that Vaqif sahib presented. He half sang, half recited, recalling the rhythms and power of a shepherd's song from his native Batalah, in Panjab. Swaying with the rhythm, and the passion of the ghazal, he recited:

It squeezes hard some times, some times it leaves it be.
My God, oh my God, what is it that the pain of love wants to do with
my heart?

You have no pity for a poor Mussulman?
You infidel, you fireworshipper
My heart, oh my heart!
You ask: who keeps you in such abject misery?
My master, my heart, my Mirza, my heart!

The words, the out-of-the-world recitation charged with music, the poet's utter absorption in the poem—it was as if, for the first time, the mushaira woke up to the truth and reality of poetry. Shaikh Ali Hazin had remained silent during the universal applause, his face expressing disapproval. Now he said, loudly enough for almost everyone to hear, though ostensibly only addressing Nur-ul Ain Vaqif: 'Shah sahib, your ghazal was nice, but by Allah, it wasn't Persian.'

A silence descended on the assembly. Those who, lamp in hand, were looking for their shoes, stopped where they were. The servants who were moving in to assist their departure, stood rooted to the spot. Suddenly, the noted Hindi and Persian poet Mirza Rafi Sauda spoke, with an edge to his voice: 'Shaikh sahib, ghazals are to be found in Hindustan too.'

Shaikh Ali Hazin was still oblivious of the audience's mood, and the provocative way in which he had addressed Vaqif sahib. He returned sharply: 'Well, maybe, but the poets here have no idea of the Iranian idiom, far less the sense of what constitutes poetic language.'

Khan-e Arzu now felt obliged to intervene, protocol or no protocol: 'Surely the Iranian ustads made creative appropriations in the languages of Arabic and Persian, even Hindi? Cannot the ustads in this land do the same?'

Ali Hazin, refusing to back down, spoke with his hated, almost racist pride: 'Are there any ustads of such calibre in Hind? Truth to tell, I have been looking for them.'

Khan-e Arzu refused to be baited; speaking calmly, he said: 'If Iranians can commit errors of idiom and usage in Persian, there can be masters of the Iranian idiom in Hind. One just needs the eye of justice to see this.'

Ali Hazin drew himself up, almost throwing his chest out. 'Only a native speaker can have the right and ability to use a language.'

Khan-e Arzu was still conversational. 'Shaikh sahib, it's not the question of the daily, almost unregulated colloquial language of the marketplace. The issue is of literary language. One can only learn it by reading the great masters.'

Now Mir stood up suddenly, and spoke almost as if he were giving a declaratory speech: 'Native speaker? Idiomatic language? The correct speech of the Iranians? All this is that much garbage!'

The audience was shocked, and also thrilled. Mir continued: 'Language is his who can play with it, as the child plays with its mother's body. Please excuse me, Shaikh sahib, but language is not a sacred widow casting a glance on whom may be considered sacrilege, or whose chastity should fall into jeopardy just because someone's eye slipped and fell on her veiled form. The poetry of the Iranians is becoming more and more routine, frozen in ideas of the old. You have begun to turn your eyes back upon the invention and the freshness of the Indian poets. Wasn't there a time in Iran when there were poets like Mirza Jalal-e Asir, Mir Tahir Vahid, Shaukat Bukhari and numerous others who never came to India but who loved to write the way we Indians do?'

Shaikh Ali Hazin was nothing if not adamant. 'There is a whole new movement in my country now, away from the artificial, convoluted dictions of the Indians, and back to the pristine manner of the ancients. We call it "The Literary Return". We don't need to learn anything from you.' He sniffed.

Mir folded his hands upon his chest, and spoke with a confidence born of an ingrained sense of superiority: 'Honoured Shaikh sahib, I present before you a rubai from Mirza Bedil sahib, may God enhance his station in Paradise. I expect Mirza sahib's words will prove to be the last word in this discussion.'

He looked around to see that he had everyone's attention, and then said the following rubai from Bedil:

An intelligence that understood the difference between black and white
Don't be sure that it understood the Secret of Truth as it really is.
I have uttered just a word, but after achieving the height of perfection:
You will understand only when you do not understand.

A clamour of applause arose, and people looked towards Ali Hazin to come back with an answer. Khan-e Arzu spoke softly to his neighbour, but clearly enough to be heard by all those who were near him: 'Muhammad Taqi is rebellious, and arrogant. But the truth is that justice is by his side in this.' He, and perhaps others among the audience, knew that Mir was in fact echoing Khan-e Arzu's theories in this matter.

'You spoke truly, Mentor and Guide,' said Anand Ram Mukhlis. His voice was high, and thin, though he was extremely fat, such that it was very difficult for him to rise quickly once he sat down somewhere.

Before there could be another comment from the audience, Shaikh Ali Hazin spoke with acerbity, in fact disdainfully: 'We have the likes of Sadi and Hafiz for our guides and exemplars. We never saw phrases like "Mirza, my heart, Master, my heart" in their poetry. And what does it mean to say that "You will understand only when you do not understand"? Such expressions are un-Iranian, of Hindi origin, they are examples of the convoluted way the Hindi brain works.'

This was as much of a racial slur as a literary statement. Tek Chand Bahar anticipated all non-Iranians and spoke sharply: 'Pardon my temerity, dear and respected Ustad. But the fact seems to slip your noble mind that poetry didn't cease to be after Sadi and Hafiz, and the loom of language didn't stop spinning after Baba Fughani, whom you have extolled in many assemblies. Please remember,' he paused almost with a dramatic gesture, 'if we treat you and them as normative, we give equal regard to Faizi, Bedil and Nasir Ali and Sarkhush and Waqif, though the nearest to Iran that they approached was a sight of the high road to Kabul.'

There was subdued, but quite audible laughter from the elders and barely concealed smirk from the younger audience at this cutting reply. Let Shaikh sahib answer that!

Someone ventured to speak, somewhat timidly, 'But didn't Abul Barakat Munir Lahori hold that the flights of fancy that abound in the poetry of the "newer style" poets are not in conformity with the practice of Sadi and Hafiz?'

Khan-e Arzu's followers glared at him, as someone inferior daring to speak in the company of acknowledged ustads. Khan-e Arzu said coldly, and not directly to the interlocutor: 'That dear gentleman has perhaps not seen my treatises entitled *Dad-e Sukhan*, or even *Siraj-e Munir*, which expose the weaknesses of Munir's positions.'

'And when my ustad and mentor the honourable Khan-e Arzu sahib publishes his totally unanswerable treatise entitled *Tanbih-ul ghafilin,* the entire shaikhdom of Shaikh sahib will be in jeopardy!' This was Anand Ram Mukhlis, again.

The discussion, or confrontation might have prolonged still, even though some among the audience were restless to leave, some even looking for their shoes, or staffs, and Mir was getting ready to deliver even more cutting arguments, when Umdat-ul Mulk's Chief Steward entered and submitted that the Presence, Navab sahib, was remembered by the Shadow of God. The gathering then more or less dismissed itself as Umdat-ul Mulk rose to say his excuses and thanks and goodbye to all the guests.

Shaikh Ali Hazin's brow was as knotted and his visage as thundery as ever. Shah Nur-ul Ain Vaqif was the happiest, for he hadn't needed to speak a word in his defence, or in reply to Ali Hazin's remarks, which were clearly in bad taste and far transgressed the protocols of guest and host.

*

The false dawn was just above the horizon when Umdat-ul Mulk came out, after a hurried toilet, to ride to the Emperor's Presence. It was darkening again, before the true dawn, and the predawn prayer goers were hurrying to the mosques. The day was Friday, the 6th of January 1746. It was not unusual for Mahabali to remember his chief advisers at all hours of the day or night, but such summons were never so entirely unexpected as the present one. Because of the unexpected summons, Umdat-ul Mulk didn't take the time to assemble his full navabi entourage and had left for the Exalted Fort on his elephant with just the front-sitter on the elephant, and the mahout. Of the out-runners, or outriders, he had none. He had just four armed horsemen riding in front.

Umdat-ul Mulk was one of very few nobles who were permitted to ride their elephant right up to the Auspicious Entrance to the Divan-e Khas, so he didn't dismount at the Lahori Gate, while his front riders proceeded to dismount from their horses. There was, in any case, no possibility of any danger inside the Auspicious Fort.

At the main entrance of the Divan-e Khas, Umdat-ul Mulk's mahout halted the elephant, gave an almost invisible and inaudible command to the elephant to stop side-on with the front platform so that the animal need not bend his massive legs, and Umdat-ul Mulk did not have to come down with the help of a ladder. The elephant was just a foot less in height than the platform, so the navab had no difficulty getting down. He dismounted hurriedly, not letting his front-sitter precede him. His front riders by then were on foot, and were some distance away yet. The drum was sounded, announcing Umdat-ul Mulk's arrival.

By the time the navab's feet touched the Auspicious Ground of the Exalted Haveli, two persons appeared from the two sides of the

320

gate, their faces effectively masked with wide handkerchiefs all over the face, except for the eyes, which barely showed behind the masks. One of the assailants struck a dagger into the navab's side, cleaving his liver almost in two. The second murderer struck him just under the sternum, finding the heart in spite of the navab's heavy cloak. He was dead before his body touched the ground.

The horsemen left their horses unbridled and sprang to the navab's rescue. Two of them tried to raise him up and provide some sort of resuscitation. But there was nothing there to revive, or even to help him breathe. The heart's main artery was gashed, the body's blood had flooded the chamber of the lungs, and even that was a matter of only a moment before death supervened. As they tried to lift the navab back into the howdah, the other two rushed off towards the Divan-e Am to stop the assassins or at least see which way they ran. But a massive and immense pile like the Red Fort, riddled with lanes, by-lanes, culs de sac, secret passages and concealed windows was an ideal place to hide, or escape. They found no one and nothing. The guards at both the inner and outer gatehouses swore ignorance of the entire matter.

*

Numerous houses, homes and hovels of Delhi resounded for many days with the sounds of mourning for Umdat-ul Mulk Muhammad Amir Khan Anjam. Numerous widows found themselves widowed a second time. Many orphans lost their parents again. Since the crime had been committed right inside the Exalted Fort and almost within the Emperor's line of sight, a number of rumour manufacturers openly blamed the Shadow of God for not only complicity, but also for actual planning and execution of the act. The motives stated were the dead navab's extreme closeness with Mahabali, and the navab's proclivity for cracking jokes sometimes even at the expense of the Shadow of God.

It was feared, they claimed, by the Emperor that the navab's closeness might bring him somewhat to the position of the notorious 'kingmaker' brothers who had actually ruled the Empire for at least a decade, killing or deposing or blinding the Sacred Presence as they willed, beginning with Emperor Farrukh Siyar of sacred memory, who was deposed, blinded and killed by the devilish brothers in 1713. The very first act of State and Policy executed by the present Mahabali, on attaining the Crown in 1729, may Allah Prolong his rule, was to have one brother killed and then defeat and kill the other in battle.

Another version of the story said that His Noble Presence the King Emperor had come to dislike Umdat-ul Mulk because one of his jokes had cut him to the quick. The position of Umdat-ul Mulk was a complex one at the Court, for he was a close advisor and administrative functionary on the King Emperor's behalf, but he could be also a sort of Glorified Joker, when the occasion so demanded. The tradition among the Mughals had been to give extremely wide latitude to the Joker. Even Dara Shikoh, who was known for his haughtiness, had once forgiven a Court Jester for a joke, which was vulgar and extremely offensive to the Prince in person. So, it is most unlikely that Umdat-ul Mulk's sense of humour was the culprit in the case.

The subtler spinners of stories averred that the killers were hired by Roz Afzun Khan, an eunuch close to the Queen of the Age, formerly known as Udham Bai sahib, and payment to the two murderers came from the private treasury of the Queen of the Age. The reason for her Exalted Presence's animus against Umdat-ul Mulk was her suspicions that the latter might not support the case of her firstborn, Prince Mujahid-ud Din Abu Nasr Ahmad (who became king as Ahmad Shah after Mahabali's death in 1748) for the throne. There were those who confirmed the hirer's and murderers' names, but said that the reason for the killing was Mahabali being upset by some of Umdat ul-Mulk's jokes.

Yet another tasty concoction was that some of the leading nobles did not approve of Umdat-ul Mulk's closeness to the Shadow of God. Some even imagined that Umdat-ul Mulk was secretly conniving at their being brought down in the Guide and Mentor's eye. They decided that Umdat-ul Mulk should be removed from the scene before some direness occurred to their careers at the Court. The principal conspirator here was either Imad-ul Mulk Ghaziuddin Khan or Safdar Jang. The future actions of the two could be seen as proofs—the former had Ahmad Shah, the successor to the present King Emperor, blinded and deposed in 1754, whereas the latter had caused his successor, Akbar Shah Secondus, to be assassinated in 1759. But while one could say anything with hindsight, at the time of narration, the two nobles were entirely innocent of any wrongdoing against any nobleman of the Court.

The last and perhaps the least plausible theory was that the murderers were no other than two disgruntled employees whom Umdat-ul Mulk had dismissed and banished from his sight.

Whatever the truth—and it has remained hidden to this day—everyone, including His Majesty himself, knew that it would be impossible to replace Umdat-ul Mulk Navab Muhammad Amir Khan Anjam, for he was like a large valley basin in which numerous rivers and streams converged to create a lake, placid but of fathomless depths. Some poet created a most appropriate chronogram: *gham-e umdah* (umdah's grief), seeing as how umdah means, among other things, a strong pillar that supports a structure; an excellent thing or object; a leading nobleman; and was of course the title of the dead man.

Be that as it may, Umdat-ul Mulk's murderers were never caught. And Delhi, the great forgetter, the great consigner of empires and people to the graveyard of oblivion, came back to its wild, wicked ways very soon. The Khanams, indeed, wore black for him for full eleven days.

After Umdat-ul Mulk, Grand Khanam sahib was in a quandary: to go back to Isfahan, or to stay on in Delhi? The comfort, the honour, the riches, that were her portion in Delhi could not be duplicated elsewhere, even Isfahan. And in any case, Grand Khanam sahib was also hopeful that the comparatively dry and hot climate of Delhi would keep Nurus Saadat's chronic pulmonary ailments at bay. So she stayed, but not attached to any nobleman or prince. On the contrary, she tightened and elaborated her protocol even more. She would occasionally appear at assemblies in the great houses, or at some rare moment invite a grandee to her haveli. She was, and yet was not, a professional woman. An eyewitness account, written in Persian by Dargah Quli Khan, the distinguished Hyderabadi nobleman, was something as follows:

Nur Bai is among the courtesans of Delhi. She lives with such splendour and is so inaccessible that even the richest noblemen seek a glance of her, and some even visit her at her haveli. Her house and establishment have the same pomp and ceremonious splendour as befits the highest people of Quality. The glitter of her divan khana, and when she goes out, the host of criers and outriders and attendants in the most splendid livery in her train, are as brilliant as that of any prince or nobleman.

Often, she rides out on an elephant, and the nobleman or navab whom she visits, presents to her at least one most valuable gemstone. And when she is invited somewhere, a big amount of money is invariably sent to her house in advance. The value of the purse that she would be presented after her actual visit can be imagined. There are many who have lost all their wealth upon her.

Nur Bai is absolutely unique in her understanding and appreciation of poetry and she has no equal in subtle and delightful speech. The way she talks, even in everyday conversation, the power of hearing drowns in the stream of the springtime. She uses idioms and idiomatic speech with such excellence that it seems her tongue fashions flower petals.

She is so well versed in the art of social intercourse, and the rules and protocols of conduct in her establishment are so refined that even the best masters in these arts should sit at her feet and learn from her. And she maintains such regard and practises such consideration on those who attend her assemblies that the most adept in these matters should become her pupils.

She organizes, or adorns the assemblies along with her troupe,
and each among that troupe is addressed as Begam, or Khanam.

Muhammad Taqi Mir and Rai Kishan Chand remained regular
visitors at Khanam sahib's haveli. There weren't so careful or secretive
as before, but weren't so blatant as to become obvious regulars. Mir's
visits and his devotion to Nurus Saadat were rather better known,
because he first came there a total outsider, whereas Kishan Chand
Ikhlas was the appointee of Etmad-ud Daulah to function as her
Secretary or as the Chief Steward of the Khanam's household.

Mir and Nurus Saadat hadn't yet progressed farther than hugging
and kissing, and occasionally touching the breasts, tentatively. They
enjoyed talking, and being intimate without words, almost like a
long married couple. Sometimes it seemed to Mir that Nurus Saadat
expected him to take some greater initiative; at least that's what her
eyes seemed to say to him, but he could never be sure, and determined
that an attempt not made was better than an advance repulsed.

It cannot be said that Mir was perfectly happy with his situation with
Nurus Saadat. He wanted more, but also he didn't want more. Nurus
Saadat seemed to him something fragile, something sacred, if not holy.
And he couldn't fail to notice the growing pallor on her face, in spite
of her obvious pleasure in his company. There was no apprehension
of Grand Khanam sahib disturbing their privacy, or showing any
kind of disapproval. Apparently, she was happy with whatever Nurus
Saadat desired, and knew that she didn't need to intervene, one way
or another. Mir fantasized about Nurus Saadat incessantly, but mainly
his imaginings were of regret that a lonely bed, and not he, was in
her embrace. Many years later, he recalled his feelings and his state of
mind in some verses:

Her face was always in my thoughts
And in my dreams, if I ever slept.
I, sad and broken-hearted on my bed

And her moon-radiant face on a pillow.
I, out of my mind, unsleeping, on my bed
With nothing but a peri-like form beside me.
My night spent with that illusory form,
And my day, in a state of woundedness.
All my friends became strangers:
They said, Mir has lost his mind.
So I, and they, stopped getting together
Everybody stopped visiting me
Love's intensity transformed me into something piteous:
The heart shattered, the liver turned to blood.
My whole being longed to sleep with her
My heart in disarray, wanting to be with her.

Yet Nurus Saadat stuck to her ways. Is it that she's testing me? Mir sometimes wondered. Or perhaps she is afraid? Or does she really want me to take the initiative? His mind was full of confusion, fuming with impatience. He was almost beside himself with his vanity on one side, compounded by his pride at being loved by one like Nurus Saadat, and Nurus Saadat's almost deliberate and palpable refusal to go beyond a certain limit, on the other. He didn't know anything about her medical history, or about her father's disease. Did he know those things, he might then have attributed a different reason to her caution, which Mir at present couldn't but see as unjustifiable pride.

All this, and Mir's own somewhat exaggerated sense of self-worth, led to an unwelcome and untimely rupture with Riayat Khan. Or rather, Mir dissociated himself from Riayat Khan and lost his livelihood as also the navab's protection and patronage.

*

It was an otherwise delightful assembly in the moonlit garden of Riayat Khan's haveli. Poems were being said and enjoyed, the hookah, and wine, flowed freely. Mir's ghazal on that occasion had been even more successful than usual. The navab deigned to hum a few of the verses to himself. As ill luck would have it, a young professional singer was also present and was hoping for his turn to come for presenting a ghazal, or even a khiyal, the fashionable musical mode whose popularity was greater than before since Mahabali favoured it above others. Two maestros, Sada Rang and his nephew Ada Rang, now attached to the Court whose Pavilion touches the sky, were credited to be its inventors.

Riayat Khan, in a mood of exuberance, commanded, 'Ama Mir Taqi, why not let Sultana, this young lad, learn a few of your ghazals by heart? By Allah, he's a fine singer, up-and-coming in the realm of music. His voice will adorn your ghazals!'

Mir was stung to the quick, or even more than quick. He said to himself: This brat of unknown parentage and base background, and a petty singer at that, he should have the privilege to sing my ghazals! And adorn them? Indeed, my need for daily bread has brought me to a pretty pass! My utterances, and to be vulgarized in the marketplace! He swallowed his pride, or rather swallowed a draught of blood, and said: 'The Presence of Great Value indeed enhances mine, but it occurs to this servant that Sultana is rather young and might be happier with some khiyals, rather than ghazals where it becomes an ordeal to observe the correctness of the raga and also enunciate the words clearly.'

'Ama Mir Taqi, what kind of talk is this? Arey, it won't do you any harm for the boy to sing your compositions! A ghazal is something, and a khiyal is something else again. I swear by your own head, please let him learn a few verses!'

Now Mir had no choice; further argument would be graceless and boorish. He quietly made the young fellow repeat five of his verses after him, to the clear gratification of the navab and others present. But once Mir left, after doing the usual three salaams and begging permission to go, he didn't return.

After a few days, he vacated his quarters in Etmad-ud Daulah's haveli

327

and moved into a garret in the massive haveli of Umdat-ul Mulk Amir Khan Anjam. He gave some vague reason to Umdat-ul Mulk's Chief Steward for needing to live there for a short while.

Some good things still happened to Mir. By way of indirect compensation, Riayat Khan took into employment a younger brother of Mir's, who was looking for a suitable station. Many weeks later, when Mir and Navab Riayat Khan met in an assembly of poets, the young navab was gracious enough to try to placate Mir by saying that perhaps he shouldn't have imposed Sultana on him. Mir was humble in his reply and submitted: 'Sir, Chieftain of Great Value, your slave is happy now. And he has recently obtained suitable employment, through a friend Asad Yar Khan sahib, at the Court of Chief Eunuch Navab Bahadur Khan sahib.'

A few weeks passed. Mir had apparently nothing against life except the continued cruelty of Nurus Saadat upon him. Then something happened which washed away all his complaints, all his disaffection, whether against the earth or the sky, as if he had been reborn, full of an unmatchable joy and assurance, or as if a shower of God's Grace had drenched his spirits to the full. His 'entanglement with the earth, his conflict with the sky' as he'd found himself writing sometime ago, disappeared, as if forever.

*

Mir had never heard of a place called Tisang, nor could he ever expect to visit such an obscure point on the earth. But a day came when both he and Rai Kishan Chand Ikhlas found themselves travelling, not without jerks and jolts, on the apology for a road that would eventually lead them to Tisang. This place, they learnt, was some distance from the big city of Merath (Meerut). A rather less forlorn place called Lavar was the nearest largish habitation.

It so happened that Navab Bahadur Khan possessed some property there, which had fallen into the adverse possession of a nearby petty rajah, more brigand than rajah. He ran away when Navab Bahadur Khan dispatched some troops to eject him from there. Now the Navab Chief Eunuch decided to visit there in person so as to establish fully the magnificence and manifestation of governance, and ordained that a troupe of high-class performers accompany him and a celebration be arranged for the dazzlement of the eyes of all and sundry. The principal performers were Bari Bai sahib, Nur Bai sahib, a young and beautiful boy singer called Mian Hinga, and some from the family of Ustad Sada Rang.

The caravan consisted of nearly two hundred persons. Mir was in it because he was an employee-poet at the court of Navab Bahadur Khan sahib, and Kishan Chand Ikhlas because Grand Khanam sahib never went anywhere without Ikhlas sahib in attendance.

The date was sometime in February 1748. Unseasonable rain, and more like a waterspout or cloudburst than rain, overtook them just after the caravan went past Sahibabad and turned left on the narrow and potholed road that led to Merath, only to find that the tiny Hindon River, which they had to cross, was in full flood. It was like the flush of a full moon on a dark, undulating plain. There was no suitable spot to pitch their tents on, nor a reasonably large village nearby where they could find roofs for so many heads. There was no option but to cross, and the crossing had to begin in makeshift rafts, which would take them to deeper water where the larger boats could be boarded.

For a city boy like Mir, and for some of the women, it was devastation unbound. In his long poem *Tisang Nama* that Mir wrote years later, he said:

> It was night when our road led us to the river
> And our eyes fell on the river's surface.
> It wasn't a riverbank; it was the skirt of a cloud
> Tied and twisted, made to look like a vast bellows
> The water was deep, and very dark

Every wave that rose, was headstrong, and malevolent
Even a typhoon would sweat in shame at the noise
Looking at the river, our spirits sank
The ebb, the flow, it took away our senses
Even Khizir, the Evergreen Guide, was green around the gills.

It's not necessary to recount further details of the journey. Suffice it to say that their route took them to Ghaziabad, and then bypassing Merath, they reached Tisang on the evening of the second day. The entire train was easily accommodated in the vast fortress-like house of the local grandee. Navab Bahadur Khan, disdaining to be the guest of a country dweller of inferior status, had his immense tentage pitched on the open land in the wide park around the house. Bari Bai sahib was also accommodated in a tent close by.

The wind suddenly freshened and blew somewhat menacingly through the park as evening began to fall. Darkness was not slow to follow. Nurus Saadat, who was no longer used to open, windy spaces, desired to be shifted inside into a room of her own. She feared, she said, that her tent might fly away into the night while she slept inside. She was accordingly moved into a small room, which looked out into the park.

The assembly that night was quite short, because everyone was fatigued out, and not many were even hungry. Immediately as the sun went down, the whole little town of Tisang sank into smoky silence; the sweet, nostalgia-arousing tinkle of the bells of the cows as they returned home died down well before it became dark. The occasional smoke arose from here and there: food being prepared for some latecoming worker from the fields, or milk being heated for a baby. Soon after the first watch of the night, the air grew still. Mir had been allotted a lowly room, almost a cell, beside the building. The only favourable aspect of the spare room was that its door opened on to a veranda, which gave on to a wide inner courtyard. So his cramped accommodation wasn't suffocating.

There was a small niche just above his cot; a candle was burning in it, giving out a feeble, but steady light once he'd closed the door. Bolting it from inside was not customary in rural Hindustan, so he just left the door ajar. He wrapped himself in the rather thin mattress provided by the host, turned his face to the far side from the door, and slept.

He felt that some person or thing seemed to have come between him and the candle. A thief was out of the question, and Mir didn't believe in ghosts or evil spirits. He opened half an eye, looked from behind a corner of the coverlet. He saw nothing. The candle? He noted that the candle was out. The door was closed, and the room was very delicately redolent with a fragrance about which he had never been able to decide if it was the scent of attar, or the natural fragrance of Nurus Saadat's body.

Fear struck him, all of a sudden, but not forcibly, and Mir was strong of body, actively interested in the art of armed combat, and didn't scare easily. Who is this, then? Is it a *being*? What does it want from me? Or am I dreaming? Could it be some sort of magic? But why me?

He heard, or felt, a very slight rustle just behind his head and ripped the coverlet off his body and left the cot in one strong, flowing motion. Now he stood before the door. There must have been a lamp or two burning outside in the veranda. Faint needles of light had crept into the room, through the cracks in the door, but the light wasn't enough to see anything except his body in the dimmest outline. Nurus Saadat put out her hand and touched him on the face . . . Nurus Saadat? His heart jumped so high under his ribs as if it would come flying out through his mouth, through his eyes . . . and should then stop forever, cutting off the blood to his brain. A very light laughter, almost like a simmer of laughter, a faint tinkle of silver on glass bangles. She came up and sat on the cot. The ancient, though tight legs and frame of the cot made a faint noise . . . of pleasure? Of acknowledgement that some new occupant of the bed had arrived? So, I can hear these sounds even while I sleep? Or dream? His throat was bone dry, raspy dry like parched sand. He wanted to say, 'Nurus Saadat, is it you? How . . . how are you here?' But he could utter only a croak, almost a dying croak, as if his larynx were under infinite pressure from all sides. His legs gave way under him; he slumped to the ground, against the bed frame on its longer side. Have I flopped down, or have I collapsed? Unexpectedly, he smiled inwardly. Isn't that a joke to beat all jokes? I am dreaming, and I know that I dream. But my hand . . . whose slippers, those slippers dearer than sweet life, whose slippers do my hand touch and feel? And whose feet are those, feet dearer even than those shoes? He tried to touch his eyes to a slipper, but it slid into his hands. Nurus Saadat's feet were cold, ice . . . Nurus Saadat's feet? Is she . . . is it she? He tried gently to rub the feet, to warm them, but his hand slipped up, by itself, as if it had a life of its own. Touching her . . . that Dream Being's ankle and above it. It was for the first time that Mir's hand had travelled that far upon Nurus Saadat's body. She wore Kashani double-sided velvet trousers, somewhat narrow bottomed, but loose, and quite comfortable. Fearfully, and overcome by desire, utterly lost in the heat of his blood, he wanted to explore further, farther. He touched what seemed to be a knee cap, then the smooth flow upwards of a thigh . . . But was it not that Nurus Saadat never wore velvet trousers? He raised his head to ponder, a fine length of gleam from one of the cracks in the door fell upon his eye, and then Nurus Saadat raised her head, and took one of his hands in both her hands and the same glimmer seemed to float on Nurus Saadat's eye, like a faint fire around an ember distantly descried. Mir's breath was now shallow, he seemed to be gasping for breath, and Nurus Saadat's breath . . . no, the breath of that Unreal Being was also short, and shallow. More than two centuries later, when their two beings were really the dust of forgotten dreams, someone wrote about such a moment: 'The darkness is soft because of her breath and her eyes glow like a green jewel.' That was what he, Mir, saw, but he had no sense, no realization yet of what was actually happening. His words had dried out on his tongue; the energy of desire had burnt them away like the mist of a cool morning. Later, much later, he transferred the episode to himself and wrote, 'Do look into the mirror, but look this way too, the wonderstruck eye of the lover gleams like a diamond.' But at that time, one of his hands was somewhere in her thighs and the other was still in his guest's cotton-soft hand. The gleam that had crept in like a probing needle for a small second, was gone, gone out, maybe? Or perhaps the breeze now blew in a different direction and so the luminant needle was looking at something else. He felt that his hand was being pulled, gently. He loosened his grip, letting himself be drawn towards the bed . . . or on the bed? He pulled himself together, trying to understand. He clasped the bed frame as fast as he could, as if . . . it was not the bed frame, it was Nurus . . . the Unknown Guest, and he wanted to take her in his arms. What should I do now? He asked himself. Perhaps she (that girl—Dream Being—Nurus Saadat herself?) desired him to teach her the ways of hugging and embracing and then lead her though the next, and then the next stages? Perhaps that was what Mir desired also from her? Or perhaps he was not more an adept of those paths than that . . . that Dream Being? Both were strangers to the arts of converting bodily desire to intimacy; nearness wasn't enough. Perhaps Mir, though not inexperienced, wished that she guide him, she take the initiative, or at least signal her heart's command to him, somehow. If she needed engagement, he needed permission, instruction. 'Pull and drag me to yourself boldly and impudently, I am sorry, I have never been exposed to all this. I don't know the way to embrace and board you,' as the Persian poet said. Suddenly Mir felt, or imagined his hands to be near the source of the honeyed stream of life. He knew nothing about Nurus Saadat's hidden features; had he seen or guessed something before, he might determine if the Dream Guest was Nurus Saadat at all. Wherever his hand reached, or slipped to, or fell, it felt softer, more tempting, and warmer with life than the last place. In the solitude of his little room he'd often fantasized about her body. Naked, how would she look? And the Mount of Venus where everything began, the lock which stopped the breath of being, or let it free, would it be plain, smooth, like an attar-seller's glass counter? Or would it be like the softest of the soft golden greensward that blows on the bank of a gentle stream? Mir's mind was now like a wheel of fire, gyrating in the vast expanse of his memory like a perpetual motion machine. Khusrau? Yes, Khusrau was somewhere around, to guide him. Guide him or put an either-or conundrum in front of him? He recalled, or did he visualize, faster than images moving in the Firangi box, faster than the play of light and shadows when the moonbeams touch the earth through a swaying tree? *The beauty spot upon the modestyplace of her whose lips are honey is what is left of the night on the sunstream; a place where a fly would lose its footing were it to alight there, and wonder of wonders, the beauty spot, though like a fly, doesn't lose its footing at all! The beauty spot on your modestyplace, oh moon, were it in the eye, nothing else would then be seen but the spot; God, oh my God, what an unsolvable riddle that is; there's a small sheet of ivory, and it has a spot and some very fine writing on it!* Is it double-sided velvet where my hand lies now, or . . . ? She, Nurus Saadat had her head on the pillow. Nurus Saadat? Yes, who else could it be? Her left wrist and palm of hand were on her brow, as if she was sleepy, or somewhat tired. Her eyes were shut, but she faced Mir, at least that part of her face which wasn't hidden by her wrist and palm. But her face didn't betray any expectation, or hope of future pleasures. Instead, it had gravity, a tension, as if she didn't know what was going to happen there. Or perhaps she knew, but was unable to ask. That Dream Being had no voice in her throat, so how could she ask? So did she desire a demonstration? Mir smiled in his heart, or thought he smiled, because he didn't really know who reminded him of Khusrau again. *Why, by your coquettish cruelty every day, do you decide to take my life? Why do you make me crazy, and give me an ill reputation? Of a night—inebriated—if I find you alone, I know what I should do, but if I don't, what will you do?* There was light again on her face from somewhere. The light revealed her dense, long tresses spread on the pillow, on the bed frame, even on the floor. Mir took his hand away from hers, placed it on her shoulder, then on her breast. There was a faint tremor there, but the rise of her bosom felt soft to pressure, and hard to the touch. He whispered, though the whisper came out like a dying breath, 'Nurus Saadat, do you feel cold?' She didn't speak. If it is a dream, he said to himself, did anyone ever have a dream so coherent, so much like real life? Perhaps his wandering fingers were about to find some way into the depth, where there was wetland, and a forest of silk, and the route ahead was narrow like a miser's eye, which can't see anyone giving or taking anything. Straight, but resistant, or non-resistant. That girl had her eyes still shut, though there seemed to be some faint movement of the eyelids and the lips. Slowly, ever so slowly, Mir raised Nurus Saadat . . . that girl's head, pulling it gently close to his face. He then used the rise of the neck to put his arm around it, so much that their mouths almost met. He was now sure that the lips of the Dream Being had opened a little; the faint light from outside the door enabled him to see pearl-white teeth, their pearly shimmer spread like a benediction over him and over her own face. Mir put his mouth on the mouth and experienced the thrill of a response, and a fragrance composed of apples and saffron. His tongue tasted the fragrance, and probed. *Putting her lips on mine, she said: Quiet, your life is now drawn upon your lips.* Her whole body was a delicate, almost non-existent tremor, warm and welcoming. Perhaps the tongueless body was striving to express itself and her clothes were the restraint on the body's self-expression. Mir bent forward a little and let his hand go down some, and yet more. She was so fragile, almost flimsy, that the hand could move over her almost by its own volition. (She's nothing but my imagination, that's why everything is so easy.) His hand was now on her waist, her hips. Those supports to the wall of Paradise, that pair of orbs, daystars that could arouse the Doom in the world, those soft and perfectly proportioned domes the colour of pomegranate flowers. Oh my God! How I wish this velvet wall didn't separate me from the velvet below! Mir's torso was now on the cot. Not much space was left on it now, but perhaps that other body had shrunk somehow, to make more room for him. Now the contours of that other body seemed more prominent. It seemed inevitable for Mir's hand to move upwards from the stomach and hips to the sensuously maddening, scented valley of the armpit and the breasts. *A pair of white orbs bright, rising from a bed of camphor-whiteness.* How I wish there was some more light, real light, for me to see. But there was some light radiating out from under her collar, as if morning was about to bloom there. *Her breasts nothing but light, and her bosom ever so soft and delicate; did anyone hear of one morning and two sunrises?* How I wish I could say this verse aloud. But people might hear, though this Dream Begam cannot, for *she* is not real. Nurus Saadat . . . the Dream Lady was now somehow sentient, for when he tried to direct his hand to the Mount of Venus, she held him by the hand and . . . that unreal hand of light . . . became real enough to direct Mir's hand between their two bodies, where breasts were meeting bosom, where stomach was joined to stomach, where pelvis was joined to pelvis. Then slowly, silently, stealthily, the little hand travelled down a little more. It seemed to Mir that the velvet under the velvet wall was learning to express its self; it was now on its way to abandon its silence. The knot that tied the body's tongue, undid itself.

*

Mir opened his eyes to find the sun streaming in through the cracks in the door, which was ajar, as he'd left it before he went to bed. The rosy pink fingers of the morning were like a draught of morning wine, exhilarating and life-giving. The candle in the niche was out. Or had it been put out? There were about three fingers of wax still left; so it was unlikely that it went out by itself. There was no sign of the nocturnal guest. (Nurus Saadat?) Not a single sliver of a bangle, a telltale hair or two, a thread of velvet, a twisted length of golden thread . . . there was nothing. There was, no doubt, the dampness of perspiration on the bed in many places. Mir sometimes perspired profusely in sleep, even at wintertime. The physicians said that this meant the slowing down of his blood during sleep.

Mir swore to himself all his life that he didn't wake up at all during that night. The first time he woke up was in the morning as described above. He had no special feeling of satisfaction, or achievement, because what happened couldn't but have been a dream. His desire for Nurus Saadat was ardent, and hot, as before. Nothing had changed, he insisted to himself. But was it true? Did nothing at all happen that night? He didn't know if he should exult at his great conquest, or be sorry that it happened only on the most unreal of planes.

Could Nurus Saadat dare to leave her room at the dead of night in a strange place, and visit him? Would Grand Khanam sahib not know? Or was she a conniver here? I beg refuge in God, Mir exclaimed to himself. I repent, I swear to do penance for this base insinuation. No, but did not Grand Khanam sahib sleep in her tent, in the park? Did not Nurus Saadat insist that she be given a room inside the haveli because she was fearful of the wild wind? So, Bari Khanam sahib couldn't have known . . . But could she not have changed her own sleeping arrangement and followed her daughter inside? No. Why should she? She would, in fact, have preferred to be alone, because of . . . of . . . Ikhlas sahib. Did Nurus Saadat take advantage of a situation that opened for her, or did she . . . did she connive at it?

Everything must have happened then as he dreamt it? I have nothing to go by, except images. Except imagined themes. That's what poets always do, he thought ruefully.

But it was reported later in the morning that Nurus Saadat was unwell. She was laid up with fever. Was it because of the physical, and maybe even mental, stress of the previous ast night? By God, can I ever forgive myself if that was the case?

*

They returned to Delhi. Nurus Saadat, as was the wont, entered her palanquin in strict privacy, screened by makeshift curtains held by her maids. Mir could get no glimpse of her then, nor immediately later in Delhi, for Nurus Saadat really had fallen into a fever which took many days to go away. When at last they met, in her usual boudoir, she was pale and wan, but made no mention of her illness, or its possible cause. Everything was as it used to be. Mir could never cross the lines which Nurus Saadat had drawn between them over the past many months.

Two months passed, and with them, the cold weather. The temperate weather helped Nurus Saadat to apparently recover her full health and energy. Unfortunately, the recovery was only a nine days' wonder, because she began to be often feverish, with loss of appetite. The physicians diagnosed 'heat in the liver', and treated her accordingly. Mir's meetings continued as usual, but they were often curtailed, because Nurus Saadat would tire quickly, and rarely permit even the wonted intimacies between them.

*

It can be said that much of the history of Hindustan in the eighteenth century is the history of treason and treachery and betrayal. One such betrayal occurred in late 1747 when Etmad-ud Daulah's nephew Shah Navaz Khan invited Ahmad Shah Abdali-Durrani to attack India and defeat what he believed to be the weak armies of the Shadow of God, Muhammad Shah Padishah. His reward? Etmad-ud Daulah would be removed from his post and Shah Navaz Khan made Minister of all the Territories, with an Emperor of his choosing.

Durrani believed that it was an appropriate case of the Chief Tusker nearing his death in the forest. Hyenas, jackals, vultures, other carrion eaters, see their opportunity and begin to gather around him, but at a safe distance. Muhammad Shah, his spies reported to him, was dying, and a deadly, bloody struggle for power was to ensue very soon. Shah Navaz Khan was one of the numerous carrion eaters, a lame hyena at best, and could be dealt with appropriately at the appropriate time. Right now, the moment was the moment of attack, and conquest.

Shah Navaz Khan gave the right of passage to Abdali-Durrani's forces, which ran through most of Panjab in a few weeks. What he and his forces did not know was that Muhammad Shah hadn't lost his grit and determination and cunning. He was on his sickbed, but had no intention of dying before repelling the Afghan invader.

An army of more than two hundred thousand mustered soon enough and reached Sirhind, under the overall command of Etmad-ud Daulah; his son Mir Muin-ud Din Khan Bahadur, affectionately known as Mir Munnu, was his Deputy, and effectively the leader of the royal forces. Rai Kishan Chand Ikhlas was Bodyguard Commander to Etmad-ud Daulah.

The battle was joined quickly enough, and remained inconclusive on the opening day. The next day was a Friday. Etmad-ud Daulah rose very early, as usual, and was at his predawn prayers when a shell from the Afghan's gunnery scored a direct hit on Etmad-ud Daulah's tent. He died immediately. Having the range now, the Afghan released a volley of shells, caused more damage, including to Etmad-ud Daulah's elite guardsmen and the adjacent tents. Kishan Chand Ikhlas, who was on duty at that time, suffered grievous injuries on his right leg and left shoulder. There was no choice but to immediately amputate the injured limbs, leaving Kishan Chand Ikhlas minus a leg below the knee and minus a hand and arm just below the shoulder.

The need of the hour was to prevent leakage of the bad news among both defenders and invaders, and to defend, if not immediately repulse the current artillery barrage. Mir Muin-ud Din Khan Bahadur, showing great presence of mind and fortitude of spirit, rode Etmad-ud Daulah's elephant into battle, dressing himself closely like his father. The ruse worked. The defenders didn't break ranks or even attempt a withdrawal.

Quite by accident, a couple of the Hindi artillery's explosive shells made a direct hit upon the Afghan's gunpowder magazine and the dumps close by. The explosions rocked the earth up to the city of Sirhind, killing many hundreds of the invading army within a few seconds. Many were vapourized, their bodies were never found, except a pitiful, twisted musket or a piece of chain mail for a missing soldier;

many more suffered grievous injuries. It was total rout for the Afghan army. The day was Friday, 22 March 1748.

The Imperial Army pursued the enemy up to Lahore, and beyond. It took a dozen and more years for Abdali-Durrani to recoup his losses. The Exalted Presence, Protector of the World and everyone's Refuge on Earth, Muhammad Shah Padishah, though on the sickbed still, dismissed Shah Navaz Khan from the Governerate of Panjab, appointing Mir Muin-ud Din Khan Bahadur in his place. It was an appointment which he held with distinction until his death in 1753.

*

Rai Kishan Chand, almost crazed with pain when not under heavy stupor induced by opium, was brought to Delhi in a specially designed bed and rath. Mir was among those who accompanied his old friend all the way. They arrived in Delhi late in April 1748, with the hot weather already knocking at Delhi's doors. In spite of the best care, Ikhlas's wounds did not see the way to healing. Sepsis supervened quickly, and because the wounds didn't admit effective bandaging, clean and open environment, and cool air were necessary to keep the flies away and avoid further deterioration by septicaemia, known as *zahrbad* in the medical parlance of the times.

In May, Ikhlas was shifted to Grand Khanam sahib's haveli with his father's permission. The *soleil* of Muhammad Raushan Akhtar Muhammad Shah Padishah was also westering by then. His sickbed soon converted into his deathbed. On 16 April 1748, he closed his eyes forever, having ruled and mostly governed effectively for twenty-nine years. Forty-six years old at death, his victory over Durrani-Abdali was to go down in the annals of literature and history as *fath-e Khuda saz*, a 'God-fashioned victory', which was the chronogram for the event.

The month of May 1748 was in its last days when that poet of surpassing excellence, that intrepid soldier and steadfast lover, Rai

340

Kishan Chand Ikhlas breathed his last. During his last days, Labiba Khanam had been almost continually by his bedside. His wounds had become gangrenous and foetid, so much that even his medical attendants hesitated to approach him, and never without a handkerchief to the nose. Labiba Khanam never used a handkerchief, even while cleaning and applying salves to her lover's wounds.

Kishan Chand had no sons. Achal Das, his father, and himself a noted Persian poet, lighted his funeral pyre. Poets, mathematicians, soldiers and noblemen attended the last rites at Nigambodh Ghat on the holy river Jamna. The old man mourned his son for the thirteen prescribed days, and then he tied the stone of forbearance to his bosom, never weeping, never complaining. The Grand Khanam mourned him for twenty-one days. Allah knows best the states of people's hearts and none knew how much and how long Labiba Khanam actually suffered. Mir was in constant attendance, and his greatest fear now was that the shock of Kishan Chand's death and anxiety over the continued ill health of Nurus Saadat might force Labiba Khanam to take to bed.

*

It was the middle of June in 1748 when Nurus Saadat said to Mir on one of the occasions when they were together: 'Today is our last time together. There'll be no further meetings for us.'

Mir couldn't believe his ears. 'What is it that you say? I'm sorry I don't understand.'

'Just this: Amma has decided to return to Iran. She wishes to go to Tabriz and spend her days caring for and meditating on Abba's grave,' she spoke in a listless voice, with a hint of weariness in it.

'And what about this whole household, the furnishings and furniture, the paraphernalia, and above all, you?'

'This haveli and all the furniture and goods that belong to the late Etmad ud-Daulah will be returned to his descendants. We'll sell the rest for whatever we can get for it and then head for home.'

She pronounced the word 'home' in a strangely bitter and ironical tone.

'But why? Just tell me what this place lacks that is to be had in Tabriz?' said Mir, wringing his hands, his brow wet with the sweat of fear and anxiety. 'And the climate there is also unsuitable for you.' He was looking for all possible reasons to dissuade Nurus Saadat from leaving Delhi.

'I am not a child now. I am fully grown up. My health is not all that feeble now. And if Tabriz didn't suit me still, I would go away to Isfahan.'

Talking just this much had made her out of breath. Mir protested: 'You are out of breath, you look feverish and warm to me. Clearly, your chest is weak. How can you say that there's no hazard to your health?'

'Will you just hand me the bottle of chest syrup and a clean cup in the cabinet there in the corner,' she said. 'The concoction, though unpleasant to taste, gives immediate relief.'

She spoke as if Mir hadn't interrupted. With a sluggish hand, Mir brought to her the medicine and offered to pour it in her mouth from the cup. She pushed him away. 'Hush! I am perfectly capable.'

'But you're terribly ill. You are *not* capable! Don't you see, you tire after even a brief conversation. How will you face such a long journey?'

'I'm not that sick!' she retorted. 'The patient always knows her condition best.'

Mir was about to shout, half in fear, half in resistance to her unwillingness, No! The physician, not the patient, knows best! But she put her hand firmly on his mouth, and went on: 'In any case, we'll undertake the journey only when I'm back to proper health. And a physician will accompany us.'

'But why? Why?' he almost cried out, beating his hand against his thigh.

'Sshh . . . Speak softly or else keep quiet.' She cupped Mir's face in both her hands as she said this, kissing him gently, robbing her words

342

of their apparent harshness, and in fact investing them with sweetness, and love.

'But why? Why, my love, my life, why? You gave me no real reason so far and yet you seem to have worked everything out, without even telling me!'

She ignored his outburst. 'Amma says that Etmad ud-Daulah invited us, gave us a home and honoured us. Umdat ul-Mulk treated us most generously. Rai Kishan Chand lived and died like the moth around the flame. Now that these three are no longer in this world, what's there to keep us in Delhi? Who will give us succour in times of adversity?'

'And you? Do you also agree with her? Will you be able to live without me, or you don't have any say in these matters?' The bitterness in his voice sounded a little like sarcasm.

Nurus Saadat's face reddened like a flare. She rose to her full height. She swayed slightly but managed to balance herself without support.

'Mir Muhammad Taqi, you presume—' She was going to say, 'you presume too much' but checked herself in time. 'You presume that a lover is all that a woman needs? I can live without a man but I can't live without my mother. You filled my being with new colours, but I owe that being to her.'

She was silent for a moment. Mir hung his head with shame. He seemed ready to burst into tears.

'I know I will never regain my former health. Tabriz or Delhi, what difference does that make for me now? The way Amma tended the festering wounds of Rai Kishan Chand over the past few weeks, the way she cleaned and dressed them, it was something beyond the tolerance of his brother and father even. The professional surgeon too stuffed his nostrils with perfumed cotton while dressing Rai Kishan Chand's wounds. Besides, he visited just once during the twenty-four hours of the day. You know the delicate refinement of my mother's temperament. Now if I were to become bedridden, would you be ready to nurse me in the same way?"

'Y . . . yes . . . of course.'

'Really? . . . Go on with you!' She smiled, looking at him affectionately. 'I know you men very well. Come, my life and love, you did say yes, just this much suffices for me.'

This was the first time that she had addressed Mir as her life and love. He felt a thrill of joy run through every particle of his being. But this was not the time for contemplation of the amorous paths. 'You could have tested me at least once,' he said, somewhat plaintively.

She laughed a little, but there was no sarcasm in her laugh. 'Forgive me, but you're not fit to be tested even. All right, tell me, where would you house me, and under whose treatment would you place me?'

Mir couldn't find his voice. She spoke: 'Look, I had told you long ago that I am troubled by dreams of dying a lonely death. I don't want to die alone. Nor do I want to offend my mother. Even her least displeasure will be equal to a lonely death for me. She won't be happy if I were to stay back here like a homeless waif at the mercy of whoever had the money and patience for me. I won't make her unhappy, at any cost at all.'

She was out of breath. She drank a little from the bowl of medicine, and went on, before Mir could find his tongue: 'Amma is wiser than us both. She knows Delhi is not for us now. Right now, there is no prop, no support for us. Soon enough, there won't be a roof over us.'

Mir, desperate for a convincing reply, could only end feebly: 'So, did I not fulfil your conditions? I protected you from the slanders of the world.'

'You're right. But if I hadn't kept your reins tightly in my hands, your love would have dragged me into the harsh glaring sun of the marketplace. It would have been fun for the world to see that Nur Khanam is tied to someone else but is another's beloved. You have nothing by way of restraint or patience.'

She smiled; this time her smile had a bit of playfulness too.

'No!' Mir cried, almost in tears. 'Don't slander me, please, my dearest dearest. I would never, never, let you down!'

'Have you forgotten your poems?' Again she smiled her almost miracle of a smile, as if the sun were rising in that little, half-lit room. 'Was it not you who wrote:

Hiddenness and beauty don't go together:
Was there anyone ever
Whose act of beauty failed to gain open expression?

'Okay, let that be, all this was just by way of jest. The truth is that I am beholden to you . . . and honestly, you are a fine poet. You say that the poet's world is something and the world of poetry is something else again. That which applies to the world of poetry need not necessarily be true for the world of the poet. Maybe, but the world of poetry is the truer one, is it not?'

'Nur Khanam, don't embarrass me any further. Please. I would give my skin to make your shoes if I could.'

'Look at my mother, ill fate dogged her all her life. Now it's I who am all that she has. How could I forsake her? Especially now, when whatever is left of my life and her own, depend on her.'

'I will not let you go!' he cried, almost shouting. 'Let me see the senior Khanam sahib just once. I will win her over.'

'No one's stopping you from seeing Khanam sahib. But you haven't answered my questions. Where will you keep me? What treatment will you arrange for me? Will you clean my soiled body if I were to become bedridden? Would you wash my soiled clothes?'

'These questions are hypothetical. Adam's children go through whatever they have to go through. Everything passes. I will endure and accept all that comes my way.'

Nurus Saadat said, 'Easier said than done . . . and if it were just for once, even a frail ant would bear the load . . . but to go through the same ordeal day and night and endless times? You are a human being too, and a male at that. And then, however devotedly you may tend me, but if by accident, or in a moment of thoughtlessness, you betrayed the slightest sign of irritation or weariness or disagreeableness on your face, I would . . . I don't know how I would react . . . swallow poison, or poison you even. It was, after all, one of your own great spiritual men, Mansur, who felt not at all the pain of uncounted stones that were thrown at him by the multitude. The hurt by the single flower that your other saint Shibli threw at him was ever so much greater.'

Mir spoke impatiently, 'You are judging me incapable without testing me even. This is grossly cruel.'

Nurus Saadat smiled a weak smile. 'Give up the thought of standing trial, you may end up losing face.' She quoted a line of verse, but she said the words with great tenderness and loving regret, as if a mother were forbidding her small child from undertaking some difficult task beyond the child's capacity. 'I'm not pronouncing you incapable, my love. But I'm fully conscious of our human limitations as well as I am aware of the oppressiveness of destiny. You are not aware of my mother's or her ancestors' history. If our people are fated to homelessness, then there's hardly anything anyone can do about it. Our homes will be destroyed before they are built.'

'But Nurus Saadat, is a short life full of happiness not better than living for ever like Khizir but full of pain?'

'How do you define happiness? And whose happiness is it anyway? Have you forgotten that we weren't brought here to seek happiness but to be slaughtered to death and to be burnt like flares of fires?'

Mir had no real answer now, except, 'Who says so? Life is not a straight line.' He paused, 'A single drop of joy in body and soul is sufficient to cool a whole sea saturated with poison.' He paused once more, 'but . . .'

'Yes, is it not this "but" which is most crucial? How long should one live and for whose sake? My mother's happiness resides in my life and you know that I may live longer if I'm in her care and have her approval. If I lived with you, my life would perhaps be shorter and my mother will be displeased with me too. However much you may be my friend and succour, if death visited me, and I was alone, I wouldn't be able to curse you even . . .'

She dried her own eyes, then Mir's eyes. 'Look, my life and my only love, don't come again to see me from now even if Amma sends for you.'

She wept profusely, copiously. 'I have somehow managed my feelings this time. If I were to see you again I just wouldn't have control over anything.'

She wept, her face buried in her pillow. She didn't even notice when Mir rose and left quietly.

*

The very next day after this conversation, Nurus Saadat took to bed. After many days of investigation and deliberation, the physicians diagnosed her with the same 'subtle and wasting disease' which had taken her father away. But while the disease had affected her father's bones, Nur us-Sa'adat's stomach and abdomen were affected. It appeared now that she had no more than six months, or even less, to live.

She became feverish every evening as the sun paled above. Even during the time when there was no rise in her temperature she would feel low, and hot, and listless. Her appetite was quite gone. And the irony was that medicines seemed to do her more harm than good. She would throw up the moment she took any medication. It was barely a month before she had been reduced to a bag of bones. Her diet comprised just boiled fresh figs and her medicine a chest syrup prepared according to the pharmacopoeia given in Avicenna's books. These were the only two things she managed to gulp down and keep down. She wouldn't even look at anything else.

Labiba Khanam pleaded with her, weeping, to permit her to send for Mir Muhammad Taqi. But Nur Khanam was staunch in her refusal. Finally, Labiba Khanam offered to postpone their decision to go to Tabriz.

'And, my darling, my sweet little baby, we can even cancel our departure if you so wish,' she said.

'Amma, you have made the right decision. Delhi is not the place for us now. And you have to fulfil the promise you made to Abba,' she spoke through tears and gasps for breath. 'And I want to die in your arms. I too have a right to the solace and strength you gave Abba when he was dying.'

'Your right is absolute, my life. I would give up my life in exchange for your cure; for that matter, if someone were to take my life and just extend yours by a few comfortable years, or months, even that would be the most absolutely right thing to do.'

'I don't want to live any more, my dearest Amma jani. What would life be worth after leaving Delhi? What right do I have to restrain you from leaving Delhi and imposing a third death on you? And if you were to leave me behind, I would be left alone. We are all bound to each other in such a manner that neither can we become free nor free each other.'

After a long pause, she spoke again, 'It would be advisable to hasten our departure from here. I would lose all if I were to die here. Bury me beside my father if possible, Amma.'

*

It was another month before all the preparations for departure were complete. First of all, they had to find a caravan, which would convey them to Isfahan or Tehran if not Tabriz. Appropriate arrangements for this kind of journey, complete with guards and escorts, were finally in place. An experienced physician was also engaged to travel with them. Muhammad Taqi Mir had kept himself abreast of all developments, and the day before the travellers left Delhi he had found a nook, ever so uncomfortable, in a window corner at the turning of Phatak Habash Khan Gate, and settled there, from midnight onwards.

The travellers set out in the morning. But Nurus Saadat's palanquin was covered from all sides. He wasn't even able to hear a faint clink of her bangles, let alone catch a glimpse of her. As he wrote sometime later:

Oh what's that thing for which
You went away, giving up desire and hope for everything else?
I would have at least looked at you in despair
But you even hid your face from me and went away

There were a few people from Etmad ud-Daulah and Umdat ul-Mulk's households come to bid farewell. All the people connected with the haveli were also there. Everyone from the haveli was in tears. Some even wailed aloud. Some others from the neighbourhood had foregathered too. Kishan Chand Ikhlas's aged and visually impaired father came, though in a palanquin. The air was rent with sobs far into the distance.

On the twentieth day of the journey, they were at a distance of three days from Herat. Nurus Saadat was almost in a coma. The physician told Grand Khanam sahib that they could reach Herat in one day and night if they travelled non-stop.

'The patient is in urgent need of a stopover and long rest,' he said. 'Besides, there are some renowned physicians in Herat. Who knows, they may think of something for her? Else, our young lady has slim chances of surviving the third morning.'

The Grand Khanam sahib ordered the chief members of her entourage, about thirty in number, to proceed at the speed of a forced march. They continued to travel all day. By the time it was evening, their climb into the mountains had begun to end and the descent to Herat was just to commence. But they had hardly reached the descending road when it began to rain. Nothing could be more fraught with danger than travelling down a sharp slope at night. Had the road been dry it would have been possible to perhaps hazard the journey downward even at night; but the rains had now prevented all possibility of travel.

Stopping was risky too, but at least the night could be passed in some safe place, hoping for God to do the best by them.

Stopping the caravan, Grand Khanam sahib sent two experienced scouts ahead to locate some safe spot like a cave or an overhanging ledge which could protect them from the rain and the fierce wind. The two returned in about an hour and a half with the good news that such a safe spot had been found. Moving as swiftly as possible in the indicated direction, all said prayers of thanks when they reached the safe haven, even if safe just for a few hours. The rain seemed to have thinned a bit. They would resume the journey very early the next morning before the false dawn if their luck held.

Nurus Saadat was still semi-conscious, but perhaps the windy, cold night and the rain had added a rattle to her breathing. The physician rubbed his large medicinal stone in water on a plate and said a small prayer under his breath and blew on it. He then placed a bit of the paste on her tongue. She seemed to improve slightly, and the noise in her breathing seemed to subside.

Labiba Khanam sat gazing at her daughter's face all night. When the noise in her breathing seemed to abate she felt relieved, believing that the medicine had proved fully efficacious. Suddenly, Nurus Saadat put out a weak, tentative hand, as if groping for something. The mother took her hand in hers, and began to recite prayers from the Midrash silently. She continued this till morning. Her mother didn't know when the breath finally left her daughter's body.

Nurus Saadat's grave was built in Herat. The tombstone had merely this inscribed on it in Persian:

Nurus Saadat
Left her mother's side at age 17 years and 7 months
Gone away from your mother, how fare you, my darling?

*

Labiba Khanam built a small but well-lighted, airy tomb over her daughter's grave. She would be there, day and night, in a tiny apartment she had built alongside. She sent back the members of the caravan and the physician to Delhi with generous rewards. As if in anticipation, Nurus Saadat had saved a lock of her hair in a heart-shaped silver filigree box. Along with it, she had written a page of Bedil's poetry in her unmatched calligraphic hand, with the instruction that the box and the page be sent to Muhammad Taqi Mir after her death:

> *Whatever the commodity of defeat and despair produces*
> *Finds its real worth and value at this Door;*
> *Your brokenness here is in reality a manifestation of wholeness*
> *Because the Ocean of Generosity is nothing but panacea through and*
> >> *through.*
> *The ocean that established the colour of the pearl*
> *Desires nothing but that the colour may fade, and the waves may break*
> >> *against the rocky shore,*
> *For the nature of the wave does not agree with security and wholeness*
> *The end and the beginning of the wave is to be broken;*
> *The spring cloud weeps for the rose*
> *That did not acquire the colours of fading.*

The physician from Delhi received this last memorial of the story of flower and stone with tears in his eyes, and delivered it with care to Muhammad Taqi Mir in Delhi.

*

Mir resolved many times to end his life. But whenever he set about actually doing anything in that direction, Nurus Saadat would appear before him and each time she would seem to be handing him what looked like a piece of paper or a letter. Initially, Mir took it to be a mere hallucination and an excuse or rationalization for the natural urge to stay alive. But soon after, he also began to see her in his dreams. In the beginning, the dreams too would be about her handing him a piece of paper. Then he seemed to notice that it was not a mere note or a piece of paper but an entire volume. Gradually, towards the end of this time of suicidal thoughts, he began to see her with pen and paper in her hands, writing something. In every dream he would also see himself endeavouring to see what Nurus Saadat was writing by going behind her and peering over her shoulder. Is she writing a letter to me? Does she want to send me a message? But just as he would go closer to her, she would vanish into thin air.

Mir had stopped writing poetry after Nurus Saadat's departure. He felt as if the doors of creativity and the magic world of words were closed for him now. And it was true that he was convinced there was nothing left for him to say to anyone, least of all to himself. You need a lion's heart, not a man's, to transport your thoughts successfully on paper. Still, there was a feeling of lack, a sense of unfufilment. Now, when he seemed to lack even the most primary words, how could he put anything to paper, or convey it to himself?

Gradually, his suicidal resolutions began to fade. Accordingly, his dreams too became dimmer. It was at that time, about one and a half years after having heard of Nurus Saadat's death that he wrote poetry again. He wrote this verse:

The stains of the tears of blood are now fading
The springtime of my collar now turns to autumn.

After writing this verse, Mir shed bitter tears, bitterer than any he'd shed when Nurus Saadat had gone away and when the news came of her being gone from the world. He knew now that the world had once again established its presence in his life. Now he realized that despite the best intentions, he would not have been able to provide the kind of service and tender care to Nurus Saadat that she had the right to expect from him.

After some time, Labiba Khanam disappeared from the side of her daughter's grave. Perhaps she went away to Tabriz. Or perhaps she went there only for some little time, and after performing the ritual prayers and service at her husband's grave, she moved to some other place. Or perhaps she started on her journey, but perished on the way. Anyway, no one ever saw her again in Isfahan or Herat.

The Sun That Rose from the Earth

I am the sun that rose from the earth
But the sky of poetry is bright because of me.

From the Ninth Divan of Shaikh Ghulam Hamadani Mushafi,
collected and printed 185 years after his death

1

Hayat-un Nisa Bibi, better known as Bhoora Begam, was the name of the chaste, purdah-observing lady whose house I sought. And her address . . . Well, that was the hard part.

It was now the third watch of the day and we had been seeking her home, wandering since the morning. But that house . . . it seemed absolutely unfindable, as if we weren't supposed or expected to find it. Actually, it was quite easy as far as the description was concerned: Go to Jhawai Tola, find the compound of Hakim Munnan sahib. There'll be a narrow lane commencing at the back of the said compound. According to my informants, it was a cul de sac, actually. The reason was that at the end of the lane, there was the haveli of some unfortunate individual who for some reason was regarded as an enemy by Mutamad-ud Daulah Bahadur Hakim Agha Mir, Prime Minister to the Kingdom of Oudh. A time came when that unlucky person also earned the displeasure of the Royal Court. That was enough for Agha Mir to swing into action. After all, an Officer of the Court who had never before hesitated to demolish the hovels of the poor, and dwellings of the rich, and even brought down a mosque or two, wouldn't ever demur in razing to the earth the haveli of an unfortunate individual who was no longer among the recipients of the King's favours.

Anyway, I was informed that just before the ruins of the demolished haveli, there was a rather dark and narrow alley. You enter the alley, wander along with its twists and turns until it brings you before the gate of a neighbourhood called Gandah Nalah, which means 'Filthy Drain'.

Once there, you should inquire about the homes of the descendants of Raja Jhau Lal, steward. Some live right on the side of the drain as you stand on its brink; some live on the far side of it. When you find those little homes, you should inquire again. Your destination will be very near from that place.

'The lady lived in one of those homes.' I was informed. 'I don't say "wife" because the Paradise-dwelling ustad did have a lady in the house, maybe his wife. But she was turned out of here when Shaikh sahib died. And Shaikh sahib, God may Bless him, you know about his relationships and friendships . . . don't you, dear sir? So, I don't know if we're talking about the same lady. Both possibility and reasoning indicate that it's the same lady. But you should go and inquire further. I have told you her name, so that should help.'

But the problem was that no dark and narrow alley, or any kind of alley, could be seen to start just before the demolished haveli. I had already made three fruitless circuits of Hakim Munnan sahib's compound. I asked many pedestrians—some seemed probable residents there—but to no result. The season of rains, the weather extremely muggy, and to top it all, the mud, and the smelly rotting garbage everywhere. I was quite tired out, but the unlucky fellow who followed me bearing two heavy metal trays, loaded with gifts for the lady, was ripping with sweat and falling with fatigue. He seemed disaffected enough now to quit at once, without waiting to be paid.

Certainly, I came from no other city but Lucknow and should have been reasonably familiar with most of the city's numerous neighbourhoods, but actually I belonged to Lucknow only in name. I was born in this city with Paradise-like surrounds and approaches in September 1793. Ill fortune followed hot in my pursuit almost immediately after that event. Kanji Mal Saba, Persian poet and my father of Exalted Memory, popularly known as the Silver Merchant, suddenly became a morsel to the Eagle of Death. He was called the Silver Merchant because buying and selling silver, silverware, all kinds of silver ornaments and bullion was his ancestral business. My grandfather, may God Show kindness to him, was the younger brother of the famed Lalah Chhunna Mal Dihlavi. The late Lalah sahib was almost an icon among the silver merchants of the Exalted City of Shahjahanabad.

My grandfather and his elder brother quarrelled on some trivial matter, but neither of the proud, strong-minded brothers was willing to take the first step towards making amends. After a few weeks of uneasy seesaw between filial love and filial duty, my grandfather took the high road to Lucknow, to strike out on his own in the traditional business. It was the beginning of the cradled-in-generosity rule of Navab Vazir-ul Mamalik Asif-ud Daulah Yahya Khan Bahadur Hizabr Jang. My grandfather grew the business so well and so quickly that he almost outshone his older brother in everything—wealth, honour and respect—and found renown within a few years of arriving in Lucknow with nothing but a hundred rods of pure silver, each struck with the seal of Emperor Alamgir Secondus Padishah Bahadur who'd ascended the Throne after his father's death a few years ago in 1754.

Change of water—or as they say in Persian, *ab gardish* (revolution of the water)—the stress and sorrow of having to leave his beloved Delhi, about which his friend, the great Mir Taqi Mir sahib once uttered the poignant, and perfectly true, verse—

It wasn't the lanes and streets of Delhi:
It was the pages of an album.
Each and every face that one saw
Was a painting.

—must have affected my grandfather, for his life was substantially shortened. He was called to the Presence of God in 1790, aged fifty. After him, the business, the wealth, the property, everything came into the hands of his only offspring, my Paradise-dwelling father, of angelic quality and nature. But he wasn't fated to stay too long in this ephemeral house. He wasn't certainly of such days where one could expect, or even apprehend the possibility of death. But there are thousands of excuses for death to visit one whom the Angel of Death decides to take for his own. He'd been running a low fever for some months. Occasionally, he'd also complain of an aching lower back. The hakims, diagnosing a general debility, prescribed strengtheners and conditioners for the heart and the liver. Their physic had little obvious effect, but he carried on with his business and management of his properties as usual, trying his best to live like normal people.

It was the third evening of the festival of Holi. My father took his bath, put on a festive dress, and went out to visit with friends. He chose his favourite, the white Arabian, for his ride. He was accompanied by his syce, and a number of other servants and lamp bearers. They'd travelled only a couple of hundred paces when they encountered a procession, celebrating some rich man's birthday. Someone's birthday became my father's death day. The Persian saying, 'One goes and is replaced by another,' seemed to be appropriate for such days.

The procession, as usual, consisted of spectators and actual participants in almost equal numbers. Fiery wheels and arrows, fiery and flying fortresses, many-coloured cherry bombs which rose up to great heights everywhere. The convention was never to use military fireworks on such occasions. Some devilish person somehow chose to explode an extremely loud cracker, appropriately called *hathi chinghar* (the elephant's trumpet), just in front of my father's speeding mount between its forelegs. The poor beast, delicate of temper and unused to anything frightening, was taken completely by surprise and stricken by terror. It reared to almost its full height and went wild, circling around the now-exhausted cracker like one demented. My father, enfeebled already by his long fever and backache, endeavoured as best he could to keeps his thighs tight and his reins loose, speaking words of endearment to his favourite horse. The high rear and the wild circling, however much he tried to control the two unnatural postures, were beyond his power. He lost his reins, letting the horse do its wild dance. My father's legs were torn away from the horse's back and he was thrown about twenty paces away, sustaining a severe head injury and instantly losing consciousness.

He was brought back home in a rath. Hakims and vaids and bonesetters and bone massagers were summoned. Their efforts brought him round within a few hours, but he was almost delirious with fever. All he could say about his condition was that he had a severe headache, and pains all over the body, especially his ribs and lower back. All this was predictable, and generally curable. It was the fever that was unpredictable, and no aetiology could be determined in spite of prolonged discussions and examination among his medical attendants.

My father never left his bed after that incident. Numerous inspections of his urine and phlegm finally led the physicians to the conclusion that he had consumption, not of the lungs but of the spine. The best known cure then was lying immobile on the bed and hoping for the best. No treatment for the phthisis of the bone was known then, or indeed for a very long time. He remained alive, or half dead and half living, on the bed for three months. I don't have the words or the knowledge to describe his suffering as the disease progressed at galloping speed. In fact, all that I have been narrating here is based on the stories told to me much after the event. I was an infant then, unaware of what was happening around me. I didn't know that I had even a father whom I had lost.

My mother almost lost her mind. With me suckling in her arms, she ran towards the stepwell inside our house, wailing and crying that she would jump into the well and give up her soul to Yamraj. And if she was stopped, she would perform the suttee over her dead husband, she declared. A number of servants, aided by some close relatives, pulled her back from the edge of the stepwell and took me away from her. The hakims and the vaids gave her the strongest sedatives that they knew. She would doze off and suddenly wake up, crying, 'Take me to the stepwell! What am I doing here?'

Fortunately, my mother's brother and some other relatives from both my mother's and father's sides arrived quickly; embers still smouldered on my father's pyre when they arrived. They collected the ashes that were to be scattered in the holy river Jamna at Delhi and at Brindaban. A third urn of ashes was to be scattered in the holy Ganga at Haridwar. Yet another was to be submitted to the care of Mother Ganga at Prayag. A fifth one was to be given over to the Mother at Kashi. The last urn was for the holy Ganga at Azimabad (now Patna) where my mother came from. A set of relatives on my father's side took the urns for Brindaban, Delhi and Haridwar, for they were almost in the same direction from Lucknow. They would travel almost due north, go to Brindaban first, near Mathura, then go on to Delhi, finally ending up at Haridwar to the north-west of Delhi. Azimabad was the easternmost city from Lucknow; Prayag and Kashi were on their direct route to Azimabad.

So that's how it transpired. My mother's brother persuaded his sister to come with him on the holy journey, taking me with her. He told her somewhat sternly: 'You can always do the suttee at Azimabad on the banks of Mother Ganga, or give yourself up to the Mother if you choose to. What is the point of doing the suttee in Lucknow, far away from all the holy places and the sacred rivers?' My mother pretended to be persuaded by the wisdom of these words, perhaps more out of terror than reason. But she acquiesced in the general scheme of going to Azimabad.

Among the relatives from Delhi was Lalah Ajay Chand, a cousin of my father's. They had been close since birth, almost like full brothers. In fact, he grew up with my father in Lucknow and was called to the family business at Delhi after he attained the age of decision. Now, the elders on my mother's side agreed that Lalah Ajay Chand would be the effective head of my father's business until I came of age. It wasn't clear, in the confusion and the pressure of grief, if my uncle Ajay Chand would assume full power of ownership over my father's business and properties, or would function more like a regent.

We arrived in Azimabad thoroughly exhausted by the journey and the long ceremonies on the way. Once the rites at Azimabad were over, my mother was transferred, almost by force, to a rural bungalow of my grandfather's, away from the noisy and moisture-laden air of Azimabad.

*

Once arrived at that small, extremely pleasant and airy bungalow just on the edge of the dark green and dense forest at Hazaribagh far to the south of Azimabad, my mother became permanently domiciled there. Caring for me fortunately overcame her desire to take her own life. A merry little waterfall hummed its music constantly just a little away from the bungalow, its salubrious surrounds alive with birds, and with the calls of smaller beasts like the wolf, the jackal, the hyena. Their voices were occasionally punctured by the growl of a tiger, the roar of a lion or the trumpet of an elephant. Wild buffalo, or gaur in local parlance, were often observed in large herds, their immense bodies shining red-brown when the light was favourable. Pheasants of all types, peafowl, pigeons were uncountable. Three kinds of mynah, two kinds of bulbul, two or three kinds of sunbird, beautiful slender waxbills tweeting and whistling for much of the day, especially when the rains came, woodpeckers and some migratory birds. And of course, the shrike, the falcon, the occasional eagle, even a fish eagle on rarer occasions. Kites, light grey, or off-white, or dark brown, policing the sky for any possible opportunity for food. The vultures, majestic in their ugliness, could be seen everywhere. Snakes were friendly visitors or residents, though the smaller ones sometimes fell to the notoriously bold mynah or a quick acting peacock. Typically, a mynah would blind the snake in two lightning punches into the eyes and would fly away triumphant with the hapless snake dangling from its yellow beak. We never molested the snakes; though we Vaishnavites didn't worship them, we venerated them. And the snakes seemed to know it. There was no case of snakebite that I could remember in the later years when I grew up and could understand such things. I saw or heard of no scorpions. Perhaps the air was too damp for them and the ground too moist to encourage them to go out in search of prey. There was no dearth of specialist individuals: some claimed to cure a person or animal of the often fatal effects of snakebite; some claimed to do the same for a scorpion's victim, or a swarm of bees. There were others who treated toothaches, jaundice or the effect of the evil eye. All such treatments were collectively named *jharna,* which means 'to sweep away, or to beat down dirty leaves from a tree'.

My mother never talked of Lucknow. She did not visit Azimabad even once after she arrived at the bungalow. It was some date in February 1825 when she closed her eyes for the last time. I was twenty-eight years old when she died. By then I knew something of life: wine, women, song, pretty boy-singers and dancers. I had been taught by tutors at home. There had been no talk yet of marriage, nor of going back to Lucknow. Perhaps my mother's people knew how it went with Lalah Ajay Chand, but my mother never inquired, never showed any interest at all. Lucknow, to all intents and purposes, was deadwood for her, burned with my father's funeral pyre.

We were prosperous enough, being fully looked after by my mother's people who were businessmen, but too proud to even show any curiosity about my father's business and estate. And I had no reason to think about it, so long as my mother was alive. I was happy with my friends, my studies were long since over, but my interest in Persian and Hindi poetry was as passionate as that of my Paradise-dwelling father. He was a great admirer of the Presence, Shaikh Ghulam Hamadani Mushafi, master poet in Persian and Hindi. Shaikh sahib had no home of his own when he initially arrived from Delhi to Lucknow. My father had him stay as house guest as long as he liked. My father became a prominent pupil of Shaikh Mushafi sahib who trained and instructed him in the finer points of Persian poetry ever since he became his house guest. Later, due to the connection of mutual respect and kindness on the part of Shaikh sahib, my father's continuing education was never broken until his much-mourned death.

A few weeks after my mother left us, burning the scar of separation on our hearts, the news of the departure from this ephemeral world of the Presence, Shaikh Mushafi reached us. His death had actually occurred in the year 1824, a little before my mother died, but the news came with much delay to our remote village. I was quite familiar with his name, and some of his poetry. It wasn't possible for Amma ji to talk about the past, or about my father, without the name of Shaikh sahib cropping up in some context. She didn't say so, but I could infer from the way she spoke about him that she didn't observe the purdah with him and he equated her with a favourite daughter-in-law, had he ever had one. Yet, in fact, my mother seemed to have assumed the role of a daughter, more than a daughter-in-law. Shaikh sahib had no wife or children when he arrived in Lucknow, and his personality tugged so at people's hearts; his conversation was so delightful but never commonplace that he sometimes seemed more enchanter than poet. Amma ji naturally felt somehow impelled to behave as his own flesh and blood. God knows Shaikh sahib had little by way of material benefit to give her, and she didn't need anything anyway, but Shaikh sahib seemed to be always bubbling with generosity, with love, with the desire to be good. I am sure he too looked upon her as daughter first, daughter-in-law second, and the wife of a pupil third.

My mother's place had little to keep me there after my mother was joined with my father in Paradise. My mother's enthusiastic accounts of Shaikh sahib as guest and substitute father, or at least father figure, and as poet and scholar, had created in me the feeling that he deserved from me the same regard and respect that my parents had for him. The news of his death came to me as a shock—it was as if I had lost yet another of my elders who were close to me. Sahib Ram Khamosh, courtier, Persian poet and nobleman with the Mughal Emperor and the King of Lucknow, and an admirer of my Shaikh sahib's, wrote a beautiful chronogram:

Sahib Ram composed the chronogram for his death:
The Book of Meaning and Reality disappeared from the world.

Since Shaikh sahib's pen name Mushafi means 'the holder of the Book', therefore the Holy Quran, Sahib Ram Khamosh was especially delightful in describing Shaikh sahib as 'the *Mushaf* of Meaning and Reality'. When this chronogram reached me from Banaras where Sahib Ram Khamosh had his own seat, my desire to have known Shaikh sahib, and now to know him as well as possible after his departure from this world of illusions, doubled and tripled in my heart. I decided to go to Lucknow.

Thanks to my tutors, I was pretty well versed in Arabic, Persian, Mathematics, Medicine, Arithmetic and Accounting. The love for Rekhtah I must have acquired from my environment, because my father wrote exclusively in Persian and was known as one of Shaikh sahib's best pupils in Persian poetry. I was reasonably acquainted with the works of the Great Masters of Akbar's times like Shaikh Faizi, Naziri and Urfi. Among the poets of the later times, I worshipped, like everyone else, the Presence, Mirza Abdul Qadir Bedil of Azimabad, followed by Anand Ram Mukhlis, and Rai Sarb Sukh Divanah, that redoubtable master of both Persian and Rekhtah. Among the Hindi or Rekhtah masters, I was familiar with Mir Muhammad Taqi Mir sahib, Mirza Sauda, Mir Dard sahib, and a host of others. The previous century was the century of the fullest flowering flush of Persian and the rise of the Golden Orb of Hindi from the earth which had lately been worshipful of only Persian.

I wrote a bit of poetry in Persian and, imitating my Paradise-dwelling father who was known invariably as Kanji Mal Saba, I found the pen name Vafa for me and loved to imagine my name Darbari Mal Vafa being taken alongside Kanji Mal Saba by the historian of the future.

I was bound for Lucknow, at least in my mind and heart. But the mind and heart are not space and time. And it was not just the distance. I had been out of touch with my relative in Lucknow, where he had functioned as my father's successor for nearly a score and ten years. Or he had been out of touch with me. So how to reconnect the threads which now felt nearly impossible to imagine as threads? My greatest fear was of rejection, and a pretence on his part of lack of knowledge of my existence. I could certainly ask my mother's people for support, and behave in Lucknow as if Lalah Ajay Chand didn't exist there, or anywhere else. But was it possible, I asked myself. The Vaishnavite Khattri-Bania families prided themselves on family continuities and standing by each other in all climes and at all times. So if I went to Lucknow and neglected to join with my father's people, the boot could very well be seen to be on the other leg: I was the defaulter, not they.

So I wrote to my uncle in Lucknow. I hinted that I wasn't interested in money or business. I wished to pursue the study of poetry with a prominent pupil of Shaikh sahib's, say Mir Muzaffar Ali Asir, and just needed a couple of comfortable rooms in our haveli to avoid having to look for a suitable dwelling.

The answer came, and it came quickly. My uncle wrote with obvious pleasure. There was nothing adverse in his tone and tenor, except for a very mild reproach for my having forgotten him. He concluded: 'All here are agog with excitement on your practical rebirth. Come at once. If you dine in Hazaribagh, drink the water here in Lucknow. Our eyes are avid for you here.'

*

So I started for Lucknow. I stopped at Azimabad to tell my maternal uncle and others of my intent to return. I assured them that I'd always be in touch, unlike Lalah Ajay Chand, whom everyone cited as the example of coldness and neglect towards the real successor to Kanji Mal Saba. I agreed, but 'I am not of Delhi entirely,' I said with a smile. 'Half of me is from Azimabad and Hazaribagh. It's the people of Delhi who're reported to be cold-hearted!'

They let me go, not without open misgivings about my future, far less my early return from the western territories.

I wasn't married, nor did I have much to do with women as young men of my age mostly did. I wasn't chaste, by any means. But matters of manhood and womanhood were not the axis of my life. Also, because of the almost total seclusion of the forest and the waterfall, and the innocent, beautiful creatures of God around me, I had become a sort of recluse, a contemplator, unversed and uninterested in the life and business of the world. True, my mother's devoted care and her family's wealth, generously given, had made all this possible. But there was no shame in it. I didn't invite myself to imagine what I and my life would be without them.

I used my knowledge of geomancy to divine the best day and time for departure from Azimabad, and accordingly, I departed from Mahendru Ghat near Bankipore in the old city of Patna. That part of the city was still known as Patna or Patliputra against the newer Azimabad, the new capital of Bihar constructed in 1703 by Azim-uz Shan, a son of the Paradise-residing Aurangzeb Alamgir, Emperor of Hind and the Deccan.

This was the second time in my life that I had occasion to cross the river at Mahendru Ghat, but it was virtually my first crossing because I have no memory of the infant more than a quarter century ago, or the crossing which he made with his distraught mother.

The magnificence and glory and glamour of the river amazed me. The very wide, smooth expanse of water, the innumerable lights twinkling from the rays of the sun as they met the endless, gentle waves that undulated like a vast chain mail whose wearer was the mighty Mother herself. The broad bosom of the river was like a field of play, if not a field of battle, because of the innumerable boats, budgerows and *morpankhis*. The morpankhi is a small luxury boat whose bow is fashioned like the front of a peacock, blue-gold-green with the peacock's pure blue head and its green-blue crest looking more like taffeta than feathers fashioned by the Great Fashioner. Its port and starboard resembled a peacock's wings. The budgerows were like floating luxury chambers: they had everything from a private bathroom and bedroom, to a dining room and an open deck for observation. They were lit up more like a festive home at Diwali. Then there were the smaller, less elegant and more agile boats for common transport, cargo and pack animals. Some of the larger passenger boats proudly unfurled two or even three tall sails made of tarpaulin. They had upper deck, lower deck and private bedrooms. They routinely travelled up to Fatehgarh far in the west. Some of them transferred to the deeper, faster Jamna and travelled right up to Delhi, though the riverine route was dotted with stony atolls and half-submerged islands.

I suddenly had the urge to make the entire journey by boat and enjoy the unusual life on and around a boat—I could clearly see freshwater dolphins, gharials, crocodiles and large turtles mostly near the far bank, except the dolphins who always gambolled in mid-water, leaping up or revolving like huge black balls. I was sure there would be more wonders on the way. But I was dissuaded from taking a boat through the journey because, they said, the journey after Ilahabad would have to be by road anyway, so keeping to the land route was preferable.

2

It was the auspicious day of Friday, and the date 7 July 1825, when we entered upon the city that rivals Khallukh and Naushad. Lucknow, or correctly speaking, Lakhnau, the city of colours and fragrances, almost like a second Shahjahanabad, the city which is the Capital of the Mughal Emperor, the city which is the place of all prosperity and the source of all government.

We entered the city from Alam Bagh. Our route, through Kara Manikpur, Salone and Rae Bareli, joined with the Navabi Road that connects Lucknow to Cawnpore. Skirting the graveyard at Aishbagh, we emerged before Akbari Darwaza, and came upon Chowk a little later.

Azimabad and Banaras were both great cities; even Ramnagar, the seat of the much-reduced Raja of Banaras, was prosperous, busy, bustling, full of trade and religion. But my God, my God! Lucknow was something else again. I wondered if Delhi could be more magnificent. And I saw both the good and bad sides of Lucknow right at my entrance into that auspicious city. I saw people unimaginably poor and even more filthy, all of them nearly naked—men, young and old, women, children, their faces and bodies caked with dirt, their hair dirty brown or pale brown because of constant exposure to the sun, matted and knotted like snakes, their faces and eyes almost feral. All of them were busy collecting, gathering, even looting small coins of copper, silver and gold, thick tassels woven with pure gold thread, thin rings of gold and silver, handfuls of rice and basketfuls of green vegetables. They were around a marriage party like wild dogs around a weakened elephant, trying to bring it down to its knees. The only difference was that the moment some unruliness was exhibited by any of the 'looters', he or she was set upon brutally by the soldiers, staff bearers and stave wielders attendant upon the marriage party.

These people, I was later given to understand, were called *shuhdah*—a word whose origin I couldn't ascertain—but they were of the inferior kind: a little above beggars, but not criminally inclined. A more depressing band of human beings I never saw. It was in shocking contrast to the resplendence of the marriage party. The groom was Nabi-ud Din Khan, nephew and adoptive son of Navab Khalil-ud Din Khan, Agent of the Presence, Rifat-ud Daulah, Rafi-ul Mulk, King of the times, Ghaziuddin Haidar Khan Bahadur to the Court of the Auspicious Navab Governor General Bahadur at Calcutta.

The contrast was even greater when one observed the riches, the sumptuosity, the rolling-in-wealth air of the city of Lucknow, the richest and the most refined city between Istanbul and Shahjahanabad. The city streets were sometimes unnegotiable due to the jam and crush of people, mounts, carriages and hawkers who seemed to have everything for a customer, from aphrodisiacs to building materials. Our haveli was in Khiyali Ganj, just a little beyond Akbari Darwaza, through a narrow lane. But it took me somewhat more than an hour to reach there.

The evening was fully blossomed in the sky when I reached my destination, to find both my uncle and aunt waiting for me. I was welcomed with genuine enthusiasm and pleasure, and was given a set of rooms in the older part of the haveli, closed since my poor father's demise. The rooms had been cleaned and aired and furnished in anticipation of my visit.

There was no talk of the purpose of my visit, nor of the duration of my stay in Lucknow. My uncle had me sleep the night in his room, and we spent the night talking of the past, the circumstances of my father's going, the changes in the family in Delhi and also the change in the political life of the city since Oudh became a kingdom in 1819. My uncle was clearly disapproving of the Navab of Oudh, Minister of all the Royal Dominions, having proclaimed himself King, as if there was no King in the Exalted Fort. But he acknowledged that the King, though he stood practically in moral and political fealty to the Firangi, was in better touch with his country and his people than the Royal Presence in faraway Delhi.

Morning came, and the first thing that my uncle did after he had washed and eaten was to present me a box full of papers and a key ring, actually a key chain—the keys were so many and so heavy—with which were secured the keys of our shop, our safe and everything else. He said: 'Mian, here are your papers of property and business, and the keys of everything that you own. One of the registers contains a full and verified account, down to the pettiest pie and cowrie, of the profits earned by your Heaven-dwelling father's business and properties after he became Dear to God. All this is yours from now.'

If there was any trace of sorrow, or unwillingness on his face, or demeanour, I couldn't discern it. I didn't know what to say, and how to thank him. It would be impertinent to thank him, and even more impertinent to show any kind of reluctance. But my uncle went on, after a moment or two: 'It's true that we spent most of the profit on our own selves, here and in Delhi. Some of it we invested in Delhi, in our own name. The remainder, which still was substantial, we reinvested.'

I wished now to intervene and say: 'Chacha, that's perfectly all right.'

But I bit my tongue back at the last moment. My words would have been insufferably patronizing, even though I wouldn't at all intend them that way. My aunt implored me with her eyes not to spurn her husband's words as untrue. But I had no intention of doing so. I tried to think of something to say, lest they misinterpret my silence as displeasure. My uncle now looked me full in the face and said: 'You may treat it as a loan, or as my fees for services rendered, or . . .'

Now I had no choice but to interrupt, without seeming rude: 'Chacha ji,' I said with my eyes downcast and voice the meekest that I could make, 'there is no question of loan or fees. It was your property so long as it was in your possession. Now you are giving it back to me somewhat greater in value than what my father of sacred memory left behind. I could want or hope for nothing better. And you must stay here in the haveli and help me run the business. You can be here for good, if you so desire.'

3

It took me many days to get over my tiredness and many more to become fully au fait in all aspects of my business. My chacha remained in Lucknow as I requested. He helped clarify any subtleties and solve any difficulties. Also, it was equally important for me to become acquainted with the leading nobles of the kingdom, and with other businessmen. My chacha cheerfully performed these duties for me. Now, having become comfortable in my new environment, I directed my energies towards my chief objective. My staff and my uncle certainly knew about Shaikh sahib's status as poet, and that he was no longer among us, but more than that they knew nothing, particularly because the Presence had left no offspring or even blood relation. No one seemed to ever have heard of his having a family. Fortunately, one of my assistant *moonshies*, Salar Bakhsh, popularly known as Mian Salaru, had some faint notion of his last-known address. He told me

that the Shaikh sahib of Sacred Memory had his last residence in a
house owned by him in Kalita Ganj, near Mansur Nagar. He was
buried in Mansur Nagar, in a graveyard near the Shrine consecrated
to the Presence, Abbas-e Alamdar. He didn't know who lived in that
house now.

Armed with this information, and with Mian Salaru as guide, I had
no difficulty in reaching Kalita Ganj and finding the house in question.
A pretty ordinary sort of residence, with no real personality, though it
was built of bricks and burnt lime, with a reasonably high plinth. The
main door opened right on the street, with no wall or garden around
it. There was nothing like a front veranda, or an enclosed hall for
the visitors. It had been painted with the usual white lime and water
solution, but the environment on the whole seemed rather desolate,
characterized by what could be described as soullessness. I later realized
that there was nothing wrong with the house, it was the occupant's
aura which made the house look uninhabited and lacking in welcome.
I knocked on the door, then rattled the door chain. I supposed that
the blessed ustad's wife, and maybe a maid, some attendant at least,
must be on hand to answer the door, but no one appeared for quite
some time. I was about to ask Mian Salaru to inquire next door, when
a hoarse, phlegm-laden voice answered peevishly: 'All right, all right.
Coming, I am coming. No need to raise a tumult.'

The door opened with a protesting, laconic sound, as if it opened
but rarely. One leaf was pulled inside, and a thin, emaciated person
appeared, filling the half-open door, not at all encouraging us to enter.
His beard, somewhat unkempt but quite white, covered a somewhat
receding chin. His eyes seemed to be in a permanent scrunch, as if the
light hurt them. He wore a long tunic of coarse fabric but indeterminate
colour, his pants were of the same cloth, short but wide. He wore no
waistcoat, nor jamah. His voice irritated and had the same ugly crackle
as his half-opened door: 'So? Who are you?'

'Is this the prosperous house of Ustad Mushafi?'

'Yes, indeed. That was at one time.' He revealed all his teeth in a leer. 'But now it is my prosperous house! The ustad's days are long over. His days were numbered anyway.'

'And you, sir . . . ?' I inquired, rather haltingly. His contemptuous leer was despicable but also threatening, somehow.

'Well, I am his younger brother Ghulam Samadani's brother-in-law's nephew. I have been in Lucknow since I was this high. And I am the sole heir to the ustad. Do you understand?'

'Indeed. But the ustad's honourable wife, the ustani begam? What about her?'

'What about her!' he flared up. 'She was his honourable wife? So you are among those who hovered around her!' Now he shouted, believing that his innuendo would have no effect on us. 'Who are you and where have you crept out from? She, that cheap harlot, and his wife! Was she ever married to him? Did she come here in a palanquin? Does anyone know who were her parents?'

He began to pant, like a dog in the sun, but this didn't tamp down his rage. He went on: 'I kicked her out. Do you hear, young man? And may I know who you are, asking about her? Another of her paramours, no doubt.'

He used the word *dhigra,* an extremely derogatory and offensive word. I didn't want to raise a shout, nor did I want to go away without knowing more, but I seemed to have no option but to cow him with threats, or assertion of my worldly position. It was clear that he was in adverse possession. But where did the poor soul go? Did she really have no parents or family?

I decided to persist with the soft approach for a little while more. 'But where did you send her to?' I asked, almost meekly.

'Send her?' he roared. 'She must have ended up in one of those prostitutes' hovels in Chowk. We of good birth don't interest ourselves in such matters.' He shut the door with a bang. I almost felt like rattling the door so hard as to break it down, get hold of the scoundrel by the scruff of his neck, deliver a kick in his pants, and send him tumbling into the drain.

But the day was saved for both of us by a gentle onlooker who approached and inquired: 'Sir, are you looking for the Presence, Shaikh sahib's bibi?'

'Yes, but this *Eblis*-begotten fellow is not willing to even give a civil word.' I fumed, but didn't fail to note that our good friend didn't say 'wife', or 'begam'. The word he used was the slightly pejorative 'bibi'.

'That scum, what should he tell you? His caste is unknown, his parentage obscure. He claims to be Shaikh sahib's relative by marriage. This was nothing but chicanery and the objective was to grab Shaikh sahib's little house here. He gave a few pieces of silver to the touts of the Kotwal and took what he wanted. The poor woman dragged herself out of here, weeping and wailing.'

'So, where can I find her now?' I asked with a heavy heart, convinced that I'd failed in my search. In reply, that kind person gave me the details of Filthy Drain and the homes there of Raja Jhau Lal's descendants, looking for which I had been wandering about for many smelly, sweaty and tiring hours. Salaru Mian wasn't with me today. Some sort of eye ailment had become endemic of late in the city, and Salaru Mian had fallen victim to it. His eyes closely shut, he lay quietly in his small home, alone, because he had no wife or children. I'd sent some palliatives through one of my servants and instructed him to stay at home until full recovery. Now it was I and my day labourer with his load. I was hoping that he would be helpful in finding the house, or the way to the house, but he turned out to an ignorant dunce.

Finally, we got there, and quite by chance. For, the individual had been a little inaccurate and we had been a little foolish. We found out that the narrow lane that we should have arrived at wasn't behind, but rather between the haveli of Hakim Munnan sahib and another haveli. They were so close together that we'd been constantly missing it, intent as we were in finding the lane behind the outer wall of the hakim's haveli. Once we found the correct lane, everything became easy. The lane was narrow, so much so that the sun could rarely penetrate there. There was another haveli at the far end of the lane; that lane narrower still, turned to the left, letting us out at the garbage-stricken rim of Filthy Drain. Actually, the point where the lane turned left had been partially blocked by a cart; the lane thus became darker, if that was possible, and the cart obscured the turn. Once the cart moved off, we could see almost everything, as in a mirror.

It was a small home, more like an inferior tenement, made partially of brick and masonry, partly of mud. There was a rather fragile arch-shaped bridge to cross the drain, then immediately the front door. The other rim of the drain was a little greater in elevation, so the puny little house seemed to be teetering on its edge. The drain was foul-smelling, the smell compounded by piles and piles of garbage, extremely popular with pigs and pariah dogs. The bricks that made up the arch of the bridge, and the plinth of the house in front of us, were starting to decay with the efflorescence of salt. The plinth looked in even worse state, but that must have been my jaundiced eye, because it was lichened with moss in many places. I was fearful in my heart to traverse the little bridge lest it might collapse beneath my feet. But I admonished my self: What folly is this? The bridge is only one short span and is in constant use. It should have fallen down long ago if it was so minded. And in fact, most houses in that neighbourhood were connected to the other side by only that poor little bridge.

Trying to walk gingerly and also swiftly, I crossed in less time than it has taken to write these words. I was in front of the 'front' door; there was no hall apparently, and the door was behind a thick and reasonably strong sackcloth curtain. I remembered a verse of the Presence, Shaikh sahib, and admired the immense range of his themes:

The light of your face is not reflected through it,
Moon-faced beauty, don't hang a sackcloth on your door.

There was no chain or ring that I could see, so I tentatively knocked on the door frame. Within a minute or two a young fellow, about ten or twelve years old, and barefooted, came out. He had on a short pair of trousers, somewhat narrow and reaching just below the knee. He wore no tunic, but a longish jacket like an oversized waistcoat. Both were of the coarse cotton cloth known in Lucknow as *guzzie*, much used by the poorer people. But there was no stain of oil, or black on his clothes.

'Sir, please command.' His voice had a sweetness and musicality that clearly belonged to our part of Hind. Also, rather surprisingly it was a somewhat educated voice. Having been here for just about a fortnight, I hadn't yet fully grasped the fact that I was in Lucknow where everyone spoke and talked with an air of refinement.

I was in doubt now. Was I at the wrong door? I stammered out my purpose, that I wished to pay my respects to ustani ji.

'Sir, do you mean from-inside-the-house of Shaikh sahib? You brought your noble presence here to call upon her?'

The readiness of his answer indicated to me that I wasn't the only visitor, or the first visitor there. There must have been other people, most possibly old friends of Shaikh sahib, or their sons, visiting, at least occasionally.

'Yes, if it's not too much trouble. I just want to make my salaam and pay my respect. I have no other business.'

'How should I introduce you? From where has the Noble Portal troubled himself to visit here?'

'Son, just say Darbari Mal Vafa, the son of Lalah Kanji Mal Saba of blessed memory, has come to pay his respects from the territory of Bihar.'

'Very well.' And the boy went and came back, lightning quick. This time he had a frayed mat and an equally frayed reed chair in his hands. He placed the mat in front of the chair, dusted the chair by blowing upon it, and invited me to sit in the chair. He went in again and returned with the same swiftness, this time with a small occasional table, more teapoy than table, in his hand. He put it on the mat and went back again, emerging a short time later with water in a large, polished white cup for me and in an earthen pot for my load bearer. Each and every movement that he made was fluid and unstrained, reminding me of the little rivulet and its fall near my faraway home at the edge of the forest in Hazaribagh.

'Very nice, young fellow,' I said, genial for the first time in many hours. 'You're truly an adept at your job! What is your name and where do you belong?'

'Portal, sir, my name is Muhammad Raja,' said he. 'And I come from a village called Kantit, in Mirzapore.'

I recalled that Kantit was historically known as a village where lived, or had settled, numerous good families of Muslims. Some Sufi shrines at Kantit were also well known. Muhammad Ibrahim, of Banaras, a learned man of great reputation who rose to be Grand Mufti to Jalal-ud Din Abul Mansur Shuja-ud Daulah Bahadur, hailed originally from Kantit. But I had yet to discharge my main purpose here, so I beckoned to the labourer to come up and make over his load to Muhammad Raja. The tray was loaded with a bolt of Bhagalpuri silk cloth, a hundred rupees in coin of the Royal Mint, and some sweets from the shop of Shaikh Koli, famous confectioner of Lucknow. The Bhagalpuri silk I'd brought all the way for presenting at Shaikh sahib's house.

There were indications of a hookah being made ready for me; I could smell the enticing fragrance of the charcoal of acacia-and-apple-fermented tobacco stealing out of the house. Muhammad Raja balanced the tray on his hands with some difficulty, went in and returned presently with the hookah. He placed it on the matting before me. I then heard a delicate footfall behind the door. I had my eyes staunchly down so as to obviate any suggestion at all that I was trying to look behind the heavy curtain. A small throat-clearing cough from behind the curtain, then a soft voice: 'Young gentleman, sir, it was more than enough for you to take the trouble and bring your noble presence here. Why such elaborateness of gifts, I pray you? I am entirely incapable of doing anything to give you adequate welcome. You shamed me for no reason, really.'

The voice was very soft, almost husky, or even somewhat choked.

I knew some ladies of extremely refined temperament who spoke in very low tones, as if they hadn't the strength to speak up because of sickness. Or perhaps my visit brought back active memories of the Presence, Shaikh sahib, and she was trying to choke her tears back. There was juiciness, almost sexiness, in the voice that one associates with the eastern climes, precluding one from gauging the speaker's age. Certainly, it wasn't the voice of a lady of advanced years.

'Worshipful Ustani sahib,' I submitted, 'it is I who am ashamed. You suffered a huge calamity and I wasn't here so that I could be of some small service to you. I just came from Bihar.'

'I am sorry your father was not during my time. I never saw him, but Shaikh sahib used to mention him occasionally. He particularly stressed the fact that he'd been your father's house guest for quite a while.' She quietly skirted her own story of woe; perhaps she didn't like to talk about her humiliation in front of a stranger. I liked her dignity and restraint, and answered in kind, talking about my father and me.

'Actually, I was just an infant when my father died. My mother took me away to her people in Azimabad and then Hazaribagh in Bihar. She brought me up there. She became a traveller to Paradise a few months ago.'

'I am very sorry, young sir,' she answered in the same husky voice. 'Only Allah's Name remains.' She then pronounced the traditional Quranic verse used almost universally to express sorrow when some loss or other painful things happen. 'Truly we belong to Allah and to Him we return.' She went on, 'How sad that you are now alone in this world.'

'Not so alone, ma'am,' said I, 'I came back here to resume my ancestral business and intend to stay here. I will try to be accepted as pupil by Khvajah Atash sahib or Munshi Aseer sahib. And,' I added somewhat diffidently, 'subject to your permitting me, I'll occasionally present myself at this door to submit my salaams.'

'Young sir, you are very kind. May you live for ages and ages. Do trouble your feet when you can. This servant will be deeply obliged.'

'Shaikh sahib regarded my Amma ji of blessed memory as his daughter-in-law. I believe that she didn't observe the purdah with him. And I am greatly desirous of learning more about Shaikh sahib's life and circumstances, if you make your kindness available to me.'

'Lal Mian, you are like a son to me, really. Please come whenever you want to. Talking about Shaikh sahib will divert me.'

'Very well, now I beg leave,' I said, rising. 'I will present myself soon to kiss your doorstep.'

'Lal Mian sahib, please abide for a minute . . .' Her voice was hesitant, bashful. 'I have a petition.'

I was rather worried, anxious not at her words but her tone of voice. She, who had been so self-possessed so far, why was she so shaky now? I had risen, so I stopped, and said, 'Please command.'

'You brought such a valuable bolt of silk for me. I mean to say, well, the matter is, I am an aged widow. It's of no use to me. And where should I wear the dresses, even if I had some made . . .'

I interrupted her, somewhat hurriedly. 'Well, I am not minded to take it back. Why not keep it for some future use?'

'No, no. That's not what I wished to say, Lal Mian. I . . . actually meant to ask if . . . if I could sell it off . . . ?

My anxiety left me. 'Exalted Portal, it's your property. Do what you like with it.'

4

The season of marriages started a few days later. The Hindu, the Muslim, the Iranian, the Afghan, the Abyssinian, the rich, the poor, all needed things in silver: the poor needed to have silver jewellery, an occasional talisman case, a glass, a key ring. The rich needed a full dinner service in addition to all of the above. I became so engrossed in procurement and sales that it was about five weeks before I could go to Shaikh sahib's. In order to overcome some of the shame of such prolonged absence, I brought some new presents with me.

The first thing I noticed was a coat or two of fresh lime and water paint on the house. The front had been tidied up; the curtain looked washed, or even new. Muhammad Raja appeared promptly, made three low salaams, took in my presents and brought back the message: 'Sir, Bibi ji desires you to enter.'

I was confused, if not alarmed. Enter where? Surely I didn't merit this kind of free and friendly, almost relative-like treatment? But I couldn't very well refuse, or start a question-and-answer session. So, most reluctantly, I pushed the curtain aside and followed Muhammad Raja into the house.

A very small inner courtyard, unpaved with brick or stone. One side of it, a narrow door behind a bamboo curtain: beyond it, most certainly the water room and the necessary. The other side had a small kitchen, and a somewhat raised but small veranda immediately in front. A couple of birds in cages—one of them a parakeet—hung on pegs pierced into the middle of the arches that supported the veranda's front wall and roof. A reed cot on the veranda, behind which was a wooden platform for doing prayers. The platform had a thin prayer carpet and a wooden stand for holy books, called a *rehl*. The cot was fully covered with a cheap but attractive bedsheet, of Farrukhabadi print, most probably. Beyond the veranda, a room, not much larger than the veranda in length, and also, apparently, in breadth.

The veranda was empty and the door of the room wasn't open. I didn't know where to sit, for to stand in front of the door or to sit on the bed seemed impertinent, or bad manners, at least. I sat myself gingerly at one edge of the wooden platform, not facing the door.

Muhammad Raja was engaged in preparing the hookah. I felt, rather than heard, the door open. I had my eyes strictly fixed on my shoes but I jerked out of my precarious seat and turned. Bhoora begam stood there, just inside the door. I bent low in salaam.

'May Allah Grant you a long life, Lal Mian. I hope you have been well. You remembered us after a long time.' Her voice the same as I heard on my last visit: musical, with the hint of the east—husky, soft.

I didn't know what to do: to keep standing and look strictly down at the ground (almost like a guilty man), or to look away and talk (most inappropriate, as if I didn't want to look at her). Perhaps she sensed my dilemma. She came up to the bed, seated herself on it, tucked her feet beneath her thighs, and gestured for me to sit on the wooden platform.

'Make yourself comfortable in your rather frugal seat, Lal Mian . . .' She looked up at me, indulgently, it seemed to me.

'Vafa sahib, after you left that day, I fell to thinking of those days in Shaikh sahib's life when I wasn't with him. You did say that your blessed Amma ji didn't observe the purdah with him. And you did so much kindness to me. My son, if I had one, could do no more, really.'

Her eyes were misting. I too could get to her real text somewhat: she was unutterably lonely. Choking back her tears, she spoke, her voice softer and huskier, if that could be possible.

'I am a woman of advanced years, and a widow. Your father was a special person for my Inheritor. So you're like one of my own. I didn't think it proper to be in purdah before you.'

She mopped her brow, or perhaps her tears. I now gathered up courage to raise my head and look at her.

She must have been forty-five, forty-six, just about average height, her body a little on the plump side. Very fair of complexion, heart-shaped face, but more inclined to youthful roundness, delicate bones, the face smooth, except for laugh lines around the eyes which looked somewhat faded as if the owner of the face hadn't been laughing much lately. Thin lips on which there was no redness but a thin crust of cakey, dark red caused by much betel chewing. The nose somewhat depressed, just as in many young girls with plump faces, by a residue of baby fat. Her upper wrap, or the dupatta, wasn't on her head, so the neck and the long hair could be seen. Dense, carelessly combed head of hair, as if the wearer of the hair didn't take much care of it. Still, the hair easily fell in a heavy braid down her back. The hair wasn't black, though it must have been golden brown many years ago. Her eyes very large and grey-green. There was no clear expression of interest on her face, but the eyes seemed to be bright and somehow more articulate than the face. Now I understood why they called her Bhoora begam. When I raised my eyes a second time, I noticed that the pupil of the left eye was very slightly out of true, almost unnoticeable, unless one was looking for the defect. But the eyes were still so eloquent, almost like a poet's, that even that little blemish seemed to enhance their attraction. I recalled the Presence, Shaikh sahib's verses. Written with her in mind, perhaps?

> *Your eyes practise the magic of Samiri,*
> *So it's proper for them to behave like the infidels.*
> *Oh! The people are prepared to swallow poison*
> *How green those eyes, like baby mangoes.*
> *How well they go with each other, oh Mushafi:*
> *The eyes so dark and green, the complexion so fair!*

I looked, and my gaze just refused to waver, my eyes refused to blink. Her dupatta was long enough, two and a half yards at least, but the muslin was far from fine, though perfectly white. A pair of narrow pants, made of the printed cotton fabric *mahmudi*, its colour a sort of greenish brown, the shade much like that of the little passerine songbird called *malagir*. Her long, loose tunic of the same fabric; she wore no necklace, nothing in her ears or nose; her entire jewellery consisted of a couple of thin gold bangles on each wrist, and a silver ring inlaid with a light-blue turquoise on her index finger. She could easily be taken for a serving maid at some grandee's house, but the softness of face, the refinement of deportment, the educated look, belied that impression.

A thousand questions rolled around in my heart: Was this begam a married or contracted wife to my grandfather ustad? Wasn't the Presence, Shaikh sahib a Sunni? And was this lady a Shia? I knew that the Sunnis don't recognize contracted wives. Perhaps that's why the poor lady was dispossessed so easily? But then how did she acquire this little apartment? Or is it on rent? If so, who pays the rent? For how many years was she with the Presence, Shaikh sahib? Where was she from originally? Her voice and intonation betrayed an origin in the east, apparently. But she certainly didn't look or behave like a prostitute, or a domestic call girl. What exactly is the truth about her? Perhaps God knew all, and none else.

She perhaps read something from the array of expressions passing over my face because her own face seemed to open a little, the reticent look replaced by something of a resolve to talk. She called Muhammad Raja to prepare the hookah anew and bring a fresh set of betel cones, then she said: 'I never saw your father, but I have read his account in the Biographical Dictionary of the poets, prepared by the Presence, Shaikh sahib in Persian. Actually, I didn't know about Shaikh sahib when your father died.'

Since she'd mentioned her lack of personal acquaintance with my father, her talking about this again and saying that she'd read about him in Shaikh sahib's book was perhaps a signal to me to begin my conversation, or questions, from there. So I said, choosing every word with care and deliberation: 'You and the Presence, grandfather ustad must have been together for quite some time?'

'Yes,' she said, and didn't go on. Perhaps she wanted me to put the questions.

'So you were married to him, or . . . or . . . was it a contracted . . . ?'

I felt diffident about using the word *muta*, the Shia term for a contracted marriage; a wife by contract was never really looked upon as equal to a properly married one, both were equal in theory so long as the contractual marriage lasted. Was she Shia or Sunni? I had no notion at all. If she was Sunni, she could take offence at the mention of marriage by contract.

A pale smile appeared on her face. 'Lal Mian, you have been to the house in Kalita Ganj, haven't you?'

Perhaps she meant that if I had been there, I would have found out for myself. Then, why this hesitancy?

'Yes, madam. I did go . . .'

'Then listen,' she spoke with some heat, 'I was with Shaikh sahib for twenty-six, twenty-seven years. Shaikh sahib was Sunni by birth, but in real life he was Sunni only in name. Among the Shia, he was Shia, even godless among the godless.'

She fell silent. I was unable to decide on my next question, so as to make the conversation proceed like a proper narrative. But she made some decision in her heart, and spoke:

'All right, I'll tell you about Shaikh sahib's beliefs at some other time. I know nothing about myself, if I am Shia or Sunni. I don't know if I am Muslim, even.'

My mouth fell open. I tried to say something, but my jaws wouldn't obey my brain's commands. Bhoora begam didn't even realize that she'd fired a gun right close to my ears. She went on: 'I was fifteen, or at most eighteen months old when my mother sold me at the haveli of Mirza Mangali of blessed memory. I don't remember the year or the month, but at that time he was in Banaras, and it was some time before he became the Navab and Minister of all Dominions, Mirza Saadat Ali Khan of Oudh.'

I wanted to interrupt and ask of the circumstances of the transaction, if transaction it was. But she didn't even pause for breath and continued in a monotone. 'Later, someone told me that my people were from Ghazipur, where the indigo and opium people are. But the Sahibs of Great Glory, as they put more and more land under indigo and then opium, cultivable land became scarce. Prices of grain went up, ultimately causing a famine. Mothers ran dry of milk in their breasts. Many of the poorest sold their babies to provide food for the growing ones and to ensure at least milk and water for the one whom they sold.'

'Oh my God! How appalling!' I ejaculated. But Bhoora begam was not now with me. She smiled a bitter smile. 'The begam of him who now rests in Paradise named me Hayat-un Nisa. So I became "the life of all women". I, whose own life was very nearly forfeit.' She tried to smile a second time, but couldn't manage more than a tiny sound of pity, or anger, maybe. 'Such are the games that Fate, or whoever it is, plays with us. A starving mother, a suckling baby. And she was named Hayat-un Nisa.'

She was now looking at nothing in particular. Suddenly the parakeet in the cage whistled, almost a human whistle. A smile came to my lips in spite of myself. I was going to ask something about the bird when she resumed her narrative: 'My mother must have gone away contented. Mirza Mangali sahib's was a very great house, after all. Firangis visited there all the time. Quickly enough, my hair grew out thick, and golden brown. My eyes brightened into their present colour of green-grey. Navab begam named me Bhoora begam because of these things. And the name stuck.'

'So, you were brought up in the haveli of the Navab, the Minister of all Dominions, according to the Shia faith?'

'Yes, this is true in a certain way. For actually, when I was five years old, Mirza Mangali sahib gave me away to his Captain of the Guards, Kaptan Fateh Ali Khan sahib, because they were childless, and his begam was extremely fond of me because of my looks. Kaptan sahib and his begam taught me the rules of the Twelver Shia faith. They had me educated. I was taught the art of reciting poems about Imam Husain and his Companions. I even learnt the more difficult style of soz, which is based on the khiyal style, but is entirely without any kind of accompaniment, not even the drone and the rhythm.'

'Yes, I know. I had occasion to attend assemblies of soz recitation in Azimabad.'

'I was particularly good at the *nauha*, which, as you know, is sung in groups actually, but I often sang solo. I was even taught Persian, a bit of Arithmetic, the finer points of ladylike deportment, and the culinary arts and sewing, certainly. I lived there as the personal maid to Kaptan sahib's begam, but I enjoyed all comforts.'

'So you were taken by the Presence, Shaikh sahib in marriage when Mirza Mangali sahib arrived in Lucknow as Saadat Ali Khan, Minister of all Dominions?'

She pulled a face, almost sour, a rather unexpected gesture, given her refined manners and speech so far. She fell into some thought, perhaps unpleasant to her. I was thinking of ways to bring her back on even track, when she drew a sigh, and resumed. 'So, Kaptan Fateh Ali Khan sahib rose in power and prestige when Mirza Mangali became the navab. He remained Captain of the Guards, but was also appointed chief of the armed forces with the title of Zafar-ud Daulah. I too grew into a healthy and active young woman. Shaikh sahib was often a visitor at Zafar-ud Daulah's, but I hadn't ever seen him.'

'So, did he send you a marriage proposal for you?'

Her face again clouded, with some pain, some unwillingness to recall something which was perhaps unpleasant. After a moment's silence, she spoke: 'I was grown up, but I knew nothing about the matters that transpire between the men and the women. All I knew was that people got married and then they had babies. There was a nephew of Zafar-ud Daulah's begam, a wastrel, a ne'er-do-well, but in spite of his being not employed or studying anywhere, he took great pains over his appearance. Always foppishly dressed, always trying to behave like a man about town with amorous and business interests everywhere. Whenever he came into the women's quarters, it was all I could do to avoid his flirtations. He would try to pull my dupatta away, or savagely pinch me behind, or put his obnoxious arms around my neck. I took care not to appear before him, or left a room when he entered, even though I occasionally earned a reprimand from Begam Zafar-ud Daulah for this stand-offish conduct. There would be occasions for him to dine late at the haveli and then stay over. Such nights were nights in hell for me, or like the tenth day of Muharram. I would somehow manage to stay close to Begam Zafar-ud Daulah, even sleeping the night under her bed. Once he spoke to me some words that sounded indecent to me. I took to my feet, regardless of whatever I had been doing at that time.'

'You didn't consider complaining to the begam?'

She laughed a short, hollow laughter. 'Lal Mian, even the begam's or Zafar-ud Daulah's blood relations didn't dare complain if some such thing happened to them. Inevitably, and invariably, it would be the woman who would be blamed. And I was a mere servant, however well treated by Zafar-ud Daulah and his begam.'

'So there was no question of your being . . . I mean, inclined towards him?'

'Incline towards him? That fellow who was more like a decked-up boy of the street? Never!'

'Then how did Shaikh sahib . . . ?'

'Well, that's what I am telling you about,' she spoke somewhat casually, as if the matter was of no real import, but it was clear that she was finding it difficult to express herself without recalling her emotions of that moment.

'One day, the begam said to me, "Hey, Bhoora, I don't know where the servants of the men's haveli have disappeared, let death take them. Now look, this betel box here, take it to Ustad Mushafi in the divan khana. And see, don't you at all stay there, even to draw breath!"

'I remember well. It was the winter of 1799. The noble month of Ramazan was to commence soon. A few days ago, the begam and the entire haveli had celebrated Zafar-ud Daulah bahadur's birthday with great gusto and merriment. On that occasion, I had been given a new jamah of *himru* . . . You must know himru?'

I truly wasn't sure. Few women among us Khattris wore a jamah. Seeing me hesitate, she said, 'It is silk from Aurangabad in the Deccan. Very bright, beautifully woven and embroidered, and very soft and light of weight. It was the envy of all my colleagues. When I moved about, I looked at the beauty, and the lowness, and the wide flare of it with true wonder and enjoyment. Hearing the command, I picked up the betel box with one hand, gathered the wide flare of the jamah in another, and practically ran out from the zenana haveli into the men's, separated from the zenana by a small corridor and a hall. I had been looking more at my jamah as usual, and not where I was going. I somehow parted the curtain at the door of the divan khana, and was across it in the wink of an eye.'

I marvelled at the dramatic narration. She should have been a dastan narrator, I said to myself.

She continued: 'I saw Shaikh sahib sitting on the divan. Though his eye wasn't on me, I was consternated to see him and burst out aloud, "Ouhi Allah, there's someone here!"'

'Lal Mian, how can I describe to you his personal appearance and his personality! If there's someone whom one could describe as enchanting and charismatic, it was he. There were numerous kinds of people visiting Zafar-ud Daulah all the time: Rajputs from Mandraja and Biswarah, tall, powerful Kanykubja Brahmins from Farrukhabad, Khans from Kabul, Iranians visiting as scholars or sightseers or businessmen. Furtively, somehow, we always managed to take a peek at all such visitors. But I never saw a more proportionately built man on whom every kind of dress seemed suitable. His complexion was fair, he was quite tall and big-boned. I could see his wide, powerful wrists and could visualize his well-made, full arms. His shoulder was straight, the neck high. He must have been no less than fifty then, and should have seemed unimaginably old to a young girl. But his soot-black eyes and beard, cut in the round, his long, bright black hair falling below the neck, and cut fashionably in one braid, all of it made him seem not old at all. He had a round, cotton chikan cap on his head, which sat slightly askew on his skull. The cap was a little taller than was usual in Lucknow. Perhaps he was observing the sartorial conventions of Delhi in this matter. A lock or two of the hair seemed to have liberated itself from under the cap and fell in artful disarray on his ear and forehead.

'He had the mouthpiece of the hookah—long gone out—in his left hand, apparently unaware that it had no embers, no tobacco left. In his other hand, he had a pen and he was apparently writing something in a fat book on his knee.'

'So you knew who he was, but not whether he was married, or otherwise involved?'

A cloud darkened his brow. 'No. And why should I have had any curiosity about his status?'

'I am sorry, I meant something quite different. But please go on. I won't interrupt you again.'

'He looked up when he heard my cry. I covered my mouth with my hand and took a horrified step back. My foot caught a wrinkle in the carpet, or maybe it was caught in the thick pile. I saved myself from going down in a huddle, somehow. He was looking at me still. Humorous mouth, long, straight nose, the eyes darkening with a smile. And what eyes were those—deep, dark and powerful. But his gaze had no lust in it, no contumely either, hidden under long lashes. Even the begams would envy those eyelashes. Quickly, I did a salaam and came back.'

I was afflicted by the ailment of undue curiosity, because in spite of my promise to listen without interruption, I blurted a question: 'At that time, Shaikh sahib's wife—I mean wedded wife—was already dead, wasn't she?'

She seemed to ignore my stupid question, and my breach of promise, and deigned to answer in conversational tones: 'No, the matter wasn't so simple, really. But I couldn't have known, or have had any interest anyway.' She attempted a wan smile; perhaps the memory of those days was more than usually murky in her heart, or joy and grief were mixed so in her past at that time that she couldn't decide if she should weep or laugh at it.

'A few days later I heard that Shaikh sahib had spoken to Zafar-ud Daulah about taking me into his home as a contracted wife. I wasn't clear about the difference between a *mutahi*, or contracted, and *nikahi*, or duly married woman. Nor did anyone ever ask me my preference. Many of the maids in the house had played about or were still playing in the field of love, all kinds of love, but I never encouraged, in fact spurned, their efforts physically or at least mentally to educate me in the body's pleasurable intricacies.

'And as regards marriage or muta, many of us didn't know either luxury, if luxury it was, and spent their lives in someone's big or small home, pleasuring them illicitly so long as our bodies remained young.'

Her story, or her narration of it, was at a stage when the role of the parents becomes inevitable. I was thus nearly forced to ask, when she paused for a moment, 'Your parents didn't come back ever to reclaim you, or at least inquire about you?'

'Parents, indeed.' She drew a deep sigh. 'I had no parents.' She paused.

I was rather taken aback, but let her take her time to elaborate her cryptic remark.

'A servant of Kaptan sahib's told me later that my father left my mother after some time and made a common-law wife of a forest-living woman from somewhere deep in the jungles in the south of Mirzapore. No one ever saw him again. My mother became someone else's kept woman.'

'So, they just dropped out and away?'

Her voice was very low now, almost inaudible, and strangled by tears. 'I don't know what befell her then. I even forgot her face, and then her motherly presence, after some years.'

'You never knew about your parents' religion. Or even if they were originally Shia or Sunni?'

'I don't know what is original and what its copy,' she answered somewhat sharply. 'Man's real religion is the religion that he gets from those who brought him up. Shaikh sahib used to say that religion, creed, caste, all these are fables invented by man to enable him to identify with each other and subsist in a society.'

'I beg your pardon again,' I said. 'I didn't mean to probe into matters of religion. I am not a religious man myself.'

'No. It's nothing, really.' She spoke with apparent equanimity, but I could feel, or imagine, maybe, a tremor in her voice. 'The truth is,' said she finally, 'my religion and caste were never disclosed to me. Perhaps because my parents were of some inferior caste, maybe not even Muslims.'

She suddenly rose, then sat down and asked Muhammad Raja for a cup of water, which she drank slowly. Her throat seemed not to let the water go down freely, and her breath was uneven. I was discomposed at my folly, worrying that she might even faint, due to the stress. I wanted to go summon a hakim, or an apothecary, when she spoke, with unusual firmness, 'You go now, Lal Mian sahib. I feel as if I am falling sick. I'll tell my tale, in full, if I live.'

She went into the room and closed the door. I too rose, hating myself, and hating myself even more when Muhammad Raja looked at me with reproachful eyes.

5

I wished to return soonest, feeling guilty and desiring to make amends. I also wanted to help her, quietly, if possible. Her little house—more like a doll's house—leaked and oozed penury and unfulfilled longing for a better life. Above all, I continued to be fascinated with my grandfather ustad's life and circumstances, and now I had the same avidity, almost bewitchment in fact, for his woman's life history.

I'd never yet known, or even clapped my eyes on an ustad poet. But I was certain that there could be no ustad like Shaikh sahib. I had read much of his poetry, and was struck by its plenitude. There was more splendour there, more activity of the daily life, more humanity, more wisdom, more *language* in fact, than almost anywhere else in Hindi poetry. The great Mir Taqi sahib was there, certainly, just a few years before Shaikh sahib, and he was everywhere regarded as the Lord of Poetry. But I think it was a matter of affinity, almost spiritual in character, similar to what some great Sufis had for another master, though that other master may have been less great than the one towards whom the novice or the tyro's heart inclined.

I remembered the words spoken by the Exalted and Honoured Presence, Shaikh Nizam-ud Din Auliya of Delhi when the Exalted Presence, Shaikh Sharaf-ud Din Yahya Maneri came to submit himself in his presence in search of Knowledge and Spiritual Perfection. Shaikh

Nizam-ud Din sahib's heart was attracted to Shaikh Sharaf-ud Din sahib, but the latter remained unimpressed. After the Presence, Shaikh Sharaf-ud Din sahib had gone, the Presence, Nizam-ud Din Auliya commanded: 'He's a rare and powerful being, like a griffin, but he's not destined to be captured by me.'

And that is exactly what happened. The Presence, Shaikh Sharaf-ud Din sahib found his destiny with Shaikh Najib-ud Din Firdausi, a major Sufi by all accounts, but regarded as lower in status than the Presence, Nizam-ud Din sahib. That was the case with me and Shaikh sahib. Mir Taqi was, by all accounts, greater than the rest, but my heart seemed to find its home in the poetry of Shaikh Mushafi sahib. Also, Shaikh sahib was my father's friend, and my father was not just his friend, he was also his pupil, and host, and Shaikh sahib had benefited from his largesse. So he seemed to me closest than all other ustads.

*

Bhoora begam fell ill, in right earnest. The city was suffering in the backwash of the season of rains. It was warm, muggy, airless, an invitation to the fevers, especially the fever that was preceded by the shivers, almost the shakes, and then the fever would rise quickly, faster than the Gomti in flood. Bhoora begam was afflicted by a pernicious variety of the shivers: it came every third day after the day of the fever. The foetid humours that rose from Filthy Drain obviously aggravated the shivers and also the fever.

There was no hospital, royal or private, in the city. There were a few Firangi practitioners whom the native populace, especially the poor, never consulted for fear of losing their dharma, or being prescribed medications with alcohol or pork as their ingredients. Hakims there were aplenty, and fewer vaids, but still quite a few. The medical practitioner never visited patients in their homes unless they knew them very well. Now, when every other house had a patient, it was inexpedient to go out on a house visit, leaving scores of patients or their attendants waiting. Bhoora begam didn't have the means or money to go to a hakim or vaid, so all she had was the medication Muhammad Raja could bring back after reporting the patient's condition to Hakim Munnan sahib, and getting the prescription filled by a cheap apothecary.

It was her day of fever when I visited. Her fair complexion, darkened and browned, her eyes shut, she was semi-conscious, but asked for water again and again. Muhammad Raja reported that Hakim sahib didn't want her to take too much water. She was extremely weak, hardly able to rise. A urine pot in china stood beneath her feet, under the bed. The whole house was simmering with the alkaline acidity of its smell. I placed some money under her pillow for her treatment, explained to Muhammad Raja some little homey methods of keeping the fever down. I put one rupee on the palm of a young fellow in the neighbourhood and instructed him about my addresses, and that he should not delay at all if Bhoora begam asked for me. He must come to me at the double.

Gradually, very slowly, she got better. Our conversations began again. In the beginning, as she convalesced, our talks were not long, and her voice was very weak. She got over her ailment and its aftermath in about four weeks, during which period I went to see her every week. I noticed that it wasn't just her illness that she needed to overcome; it was also her reticence, or shyness. Another new thing I noted was that she avoided telling a continuous story. She would often go off at a tangent and begin another narrative. We had left off when she was about to enter Shaikh sahib's home as a mutahi. But she didn't resume from there. She started quite somewhere else, came back to the muta, wandered away into another direction.

I could glean her story over those four and numerous subsequent visits. I think it's better policy now that I reweave her narrative in one connected account, though I'll retain her words, and the effect of her voice, as much as I can.

6

I entered Shaikh sahib's home as his contracted wife in the beginning of the fasting month of Ramazan. The year must have been 1799 or 1800. I entered that very house from which I was later ejected with force, and such ignominy. The begam of Kaptan Fateh Ali Khan sahib gave me away with four new pairs of clothes, all neither formal wear nor street wear, or whatever you might think they could be by way of wedding clothes: they were just four pairs of respectable clothes. The few silver trinkets that I had hoarded over the years, and the four or five pairs of my usual clothes, one pair of shoes, these constituted my dower. No one wept at my going, nor did anyone hug and kiss me before putting me in the palanquin. I didn't weep, as girls do when they leave home for the first time after marriage. I was sad at what I considered to be my expulsion from the haveli of Zafar-ud Daulah. But I did look forward to some independence, some real ownership of a house and its effects.

I knew nothing of physical love, or the method of going to bed with a man. Kaptan begam had explained to me, in as gentle terms as she could muster, the truth of the muta: it was marriage, albeit temporary; it entailed my 'serving' Shaikh sahib as all wives 'served' their husbands. The meaning of 'serve' was left to my good sense and understanding. Thus I was prepared for sex, a word that no one knew in my past life. Everyone called it *hambistari*, or 'sharing the same bed'.

The formal utterances of the muta were pronounced by Shaikh sahib in the haveli, so there was now no purdah between us. He wrapped me in a chador, picked me up like so much merchandise and had me ride a plain palanquin, covered from all sides. He rode his pony with me, as close as could be. Keen to talk to me, he told me a couple of funny, harmless jokes as conversational gambit, but I was too shy to answer. And worried, about my long-term future, and about the God-cursed hambistari in the short term. I couldn't imagine how it began, and what it meant to my body.

I was keeping the fasts of Ramazan, as everyone did in the haveli, and it was the third or the fourth day of Ramazan. Normally, the Shia weren't particular about keeping the fasts, or offering the five daily prayers. Their life centred on mourning for the Imam of High Station, may God send His salutations upon him; his martyrdom and his suffering—these were the driving force of their religious observances. Of late, things had changed somewhat, due to the influence of the Presence, Maulavi Dildar Ali sahib of Nasirabad, may Allah Raise his station; the five prayers, fasting in Ramazan and such other observances had resumed their importance and value among the Shia.

When Shaikh sahib came to know that I was fasting, his face showed a displeasure, and a disappointment, which he checked with some difficulty from converting into a howl of rage. He cooled almost immediately and began to kiss me. I sustained his kisses a few times, then pushed him away impatiently. He knew that hambistari while one was fasting was a major act of impiety, and one who broke the fast illegally was liable to do sixty continuous days of fasting by way of penance. Indeed, breaking a fast illegally without a valid medical reason was looked upon with as much horror as drinking wine. Shaikh sahib also knew that hugging and kissing one's legal spouse while fasting didn't constitute hambistari. So, while he contained himself, he was keen to do all the permissible things, and do them to the utterance.

I repeatedly repulsed his attempts at hugging and kissing and touching, and he repeatedly wooed me, almost assailed me, trying to take me in his arms and hugging me. Doubtless, it was fruitless as it was frustrating. Finally, he exclaimed: 'Hey, Bhoora begam, kissing and petting won't break the fast!'

I didn't know what to do. I clearly liked him, and in fact wanted to let him have his way with me, but I was shy, and also, I wasn't prepared to deliberately break my fast—that too for hambistari—and then have to do sixty continuous fasts after Ramazan. No, dear me, I wouldn't.

Suddenly, Shaikh sahib grinned in merriment, and said: 'Hey, Bhoora begam, did you hear? I actually composed a line of poetry.' He then recited:

Kissing and petting won't spoil the fast, I say!

Not giving me time to respond, he gave me a sort of reprieve.

'All right, give me a little time. I'll present to you some pearls of great price in a moment.'

His drive to go to bed with me apparently slackened for the moment; he picked up pen and paper, sat aside from me and began composing, often humming as he went. I ran my eyes around, without appearing to be curious, but there was no prayer mat that I could see, far less the Thirty Discourses. There was a water room next to the lavatory. Quietly, I rose, did my ablutions, and began to do the afternoon prayer, though I couldn't quite determine the direction of the Kabah.

I hadn't risen from the prayer mat when Shaikh sahib came from behind, pinched my cheek, forcibly turned my face towards him, and implanted a resounding kiss on my mouth.

'*Tobah!*' I exclaimed. (Later I found out that this way of saying tobah, 'I repent', commonly used to express displeasure rather than repentance, though informal, was used by Shaikh sahib in his poetry. He was so free and informal in poetry.) 'You spoiled my namaz, and also my fast!'

But Shaikh sahib never heard me, far less heeded me. I was rubbing my mouth and face with my wrap, my back half turned from him. He said, 'Please observe, and listen.'

Well, I do agree that the month of the fasts is right here
And has spread through the world the word of chastity
Let's see, what would be the ultimate result of my pining for you.
All right, this slave makes his slavish submission and states—
The prisoner of ancient pain will be liberated from sorrowing, and
Kissing and petting won't spoil your fast!

How much longer should I go on, to give words to my desire?
All that Mushafi wants is that you do as he wishes

You're still in control, do try to understand, don't act as if you don't know!
Come, put your arms around my neck, let some of my longings be satisfied
The prisoner of ancient pain will be liberated from sorrowing, and
Kissing and petting won't spoil your fast!

I had no sense, far less knowledge, of poetry, or how and why poems are made. But even I could see that Shaikh sahib had the capability to compose poetry, and poetry that was free from defect, at the drop of a hat, as they say. That afternoon, he composed dozens of six-line stanzas of the poem, from which I remember these two. But he didn't say to me all of them. I thought I wasn't missing much, because the rest of the stanzas would be similar. Much later, I found out that the poem contained references to some other woman too. But by that time I was quite used to Shaikh sahib's nature. Generous to a fault, he never forgot his old lovers, regardless of who took the initiative in severing the connection. And a drove of beauties was always around him, willing him to love them. My first few years with him were torturous upon me because of his open and unashamed love for other women. I think he was quite unable to help it. Eventually, I taught myself to reconcile with it as a fact of life. I tied the stone of endurance on my breast and carried on as if nothing had happened.

Oh, I went a little ahead of myself with my narrative. Coming back to that first day, I spent that whole day listening to Shaikh sahib's verses, enjoying his jokes and witticisms, feeling my own blood heat up in the proximity of his words and his person. I let him have his way with me that night and made him truly happy.

It was the very zenith of winter at that time. I forced myself to leave his side very early before dawn to ritually cleanse myself in the icy water in his water room. I was fossicking through the house and the kitchen for something to eat as the customary breakfast before starting the fast. Shaikh sahib suddenly appeared, kissed my forehead, and recited some stanzas. His style of recitation was extremely resonant, and was somewhat close this time to singing, or loudly humming:

Your kindly, generous eyes fell on his state,
Otherwise, he, with his wounded liver, could never have had such luck
But when fearless, he became bold in touching you
Your face reflected the effect of bashfulness:
Last night, Mushafi blessed you from the depth of his heart
And touched and kissed you and prayed to take away all possible
misfortune from you.

Darling, when his hands fondled and caressed your body
It thrilled, and quivered, like the river's wave
Oh, what could I tell you about his great good luck!
Pulling and struggling, we came to the middle of the night:
Last night, Mushafi blessed you from the depth of his heart
And touched and kissed you and prayed to take away all possible
misfortune from you.

Could I ever give words to those scenes and that moment! The night so cold, my body cold with the bath and hot with his kiss, his poem. I began to shiver out of shame. 'Please. Stop please.' I whispered and tried to scrunch my body so as to reduce my shivers. Shaikh sahib brought out his double shawl and draped me with it. (Later, I came to know that the actual addressee of the poem was someone else. The original line was: 'Oh, what could I tell you about his great misfortune!' and he changed 'great misfortune' to 'great good luck' to suit the occasion.

From then on, it became my routine through the month of Ramazan: I did service for Shaikh sahib for almost the whole night; I would leave him for my ritual cleansing, and prepare my frugal breakfast well before the close of time for breakfast; I'd then spend my day fasting and doing prayers. But I wasn't at that time sure if I should thank Maula Ali for having made me a contracted wife to Shaikh sahib, and making me the centre of his carnal attentions. Was it good luck, or bad? I couldn't determine, and felt unhappy. In the haveli of Zafar-ud

401

Daulah, there was admittedly more physical comfort, and of course nothing of the strenuous nightly duty that Shaikh sahib extracted from me. But I was not free there, I had no security. I had no protector, no true claimant or inheritor of my remains. And this Shaikh sahib, he clearly seemed to be a human butterfly, alighting where his fancy, or even whimsy took him, and flying away when sated. He might not let me go so long as I was young, or youthful, and he pretends to be heads over ears in love with me. But who could ever depend on youth? How long could youth last?

I had known girls or women of symmetrical, well-formed and elegant bodies lose their all in no time to a wasting disease, or to a tumour in the stomach. If disease didn't ravage, there was childbearing, suffering the overpowering pain which slacked and loosened the best of bodies. And then there was the harrowing, endless service in the bed. The list of the ills to which the flesh was heir to was endless, really. You became dry like a broken branch, shorn of leaf and blossom, more a necklace of bones fit to be worn by some evil spirit. And then, it took no time for the woman to lose her place in her man's heart, to fall from his attentive gaze just as her body fell from its peak of beauty.

And that was the case of married women. The fate of us, in contracted marriage, and having no home to run away to, can best be left unasked.

Shaikh sahib pleased me, no doubt. Pleased me no end, in fact. He had an indefinable magnetism, a power to please women. (Even boys, I later found out.) I could only long for, and never attain the stage in our relations when he would love me as much as I loved him. I could serve him, in every possible way, with all my ability, devote my heart and soul to loving him, but what did all that count for, if he didn't love me back? As they say, the blind man will believe only when he can see with his two eyes.

There was another thing to consider: Shaikh sahib was not destitute, but he couldn't be called prosperous, or even a man of means. His employment with Sahib-e Alam Prince Mirza Sulaiman Shikoh Bahadur was over. True, his differences—some would even call it feud—with Sayyid Inshaallah Khan sahib were long over. Insha sahib was now re-employed at the Navab Vizier's court from where (and from Lucknow as well) Navab Asif-ud Daulah Bahadur, the Navab Vizier, had banished him. He was reported to be the favourite of Navab Saadat Ali Khan Bahadur, the new Minister for all Dominions. But Insha sahib was busy all the time striving for and trying to retain the pleasure and affection of the new navab. He couldn't have the time or inclination to let the navab look at a potential rival.

Unhappy with the unfair and partisan treatment at the hands of Prince Mirza Sulaiman Shikoh Bahadur, there was a time when Shaikh sahib had practically shut himself up in his home. He didn't go to any mushairas, never went calling on his other patrons, living the life of a recluse. Later, at the persuasion of some of his closest pupils like Muhammad Isa Tanha, Nur-ul Islam Muntazir, Pandit Bidya Dhar and Haidar Ali Karam, he began attending the monthly mushaira in Rausha Ara Bagh, outside the city's limits. Zafar-ud Daulah occasionally sent some cash or goods, some came in from his pupils. Occasionally, a prominent nobleman or an admirer of ample means would send something, though not in the form of a monthly stipend. All this was sufficient to live an austere, if not comfortable, existence. We didn't lack for the necessities of life and ate reasonably good quality food twice a day. That was enough for passing the days, and I certainly was not born on a feather bed with a silver spoon to feed me with. In fact, I couldn't have expected better from life anywhere else.

Occasionally, it had seemed to me that Shaikh sahib didn't do a proper marriage with me because he was hard up, and was not prepared to assume the responsibilities of marriage, followed by the inevitable children, then their education, marriage and all the attendant burdens. But that was in the future yet. At that time, it seemed that Shaikh sahib had nothing to do but bed me and admire me and heap praises upon me. He would follow me around that small house as I did the prayers, or cooked food for him, or did the laundry, or took my bath. He would stand at the door of the water room, not to peep, but to hear. The tinkle of my bangles, the soft clash of the dipper on the brass bucket, the sound of water splashing upon my body as I poured it over me, the rustle of the thin towel as I vigorously rubbed my body, my soft humming as I dried my body, my rising from the wooden bath mat, pushing it away with my feet. He seemed to know every sound, and he seemed to love every sound.

In those days, a person who didn't know him intimately would believe that he was infatuated with me, or that he was a sex-starved adolescent, not an old man of fifty. Every gesture, every word apparently affirmed that he would not now look at anybody at all, woman or boy. He liked my body which he stated was superbly proportionate; he liked my stature which he declared was the most *mauzun*—suitable, or measured, neither too tall nor too short. He praised my dress sense—as if I had a whole wardrobe of dresses—and claimed to admire me in whatever meagre clothes I wore. I always looked angelic to him.

The month of Ramazan was over, and I for one wasn't unhappy to see its back—I would now be spared the punishing experience of having to bath in near-freezing water at least three hours before dawn every day to make myself ritually clean to observe the fast. It was my first Id after leaving the haveli of Kaptan begam, so she sent me a new outfit for the occasion. I put it on, and was getting ready to go to the haveli when Shaikh sahib composed a verse quite offhand, as if he knew it by heart:

I would never ask you to put off your clothes
If you took to always wearing clothes like this.

I reddened, and made to hide behind the door of our room. Undeterred, he said another verse in a somewhat louder voice:

Mushafi, you must somehow manage to get a peep at her today
For your beloved has put on a new dress.

Yes, all that was there. But I had some other problems too. For one thing, I could never divine his religion, or at least his beliefs. Nor did he ever open the subject himself. It seemed that he would rather avoid talking about it. Throughout the month of Ramazan, he behaved as if that month didn't exist: he didn't fast on a single day, didn't do any of the things that people did during that month; he gave no importance to the breaking of the fast just after sunset, which was something of a ritual which even non-fast keepers observed. Many people who don't fast for any reason at least do the five prayers regularly during the month, and take care not to eat anything openly. Shaikh sahib couldn't have cared less for such niceties. The Prophet's hadiths, his biography, books of mourning in the Shia style, poems commemorating the martyrdom of Imam Husain, lives or hadiths of any of the Shia Imams—his house was totally innocent of things of that description. He didn't even have a copy of the Thirty Discourses.

He never uttered a word which suggested that he was a Shia or a Sunni. I never heard him speak of any of the universally admired Sufi saints like the Presence, Shah Mina sahib of Lucknow, or the Presence, the Sultan of all Sufi saints, Nizam-ud Din sahib of Delhi.

He did do one observance: he went to offer the Id prayer, though I didn't know if he went to a Shia mosque or a Sunni one. Early in Ramazan, his pupil Pandit Bidya Dhar had made him a present of a Kathiawari pony, very sturdy, very spirited and playful, and extremely good-looking. That pony and Shaikh sahib were inseparable whenever Shaikh sahib went out. So he rode that pony to the Id prayer, and I suspect for showing off his pony rather than for putative piety.

Kaptan begam had sent a small, everyday kind of palanquin for me; obviously, I deserved nothing fancy. I felt a pang of bitterness for a moment, and then instantly scolded myself in my heart. Clearly, this plain palanquin was a favour to me. I didn't have the right to be called back to celebrate Id at the haveli, though it was all that I had by way of a parental home.

It was decided that Shaikh sahib would pick me up from Kaptan sahib's place after he was done with the prayer and with meeting his friends. But in the event, he didn't show up until late in the night. I mourned my fate as the day wore on, knowing full well that Shaikh sahib wouldn't have dared do this to me if I were his wedded wife. I felt myself welling up inside, and finally began to weep. My friends and former colleagues tried to console me, but I went on, spoiling their Id along with mine.

At last he did appear. He seemed somewhat abashed. Perhaps he'd heard about my lachrymose day. But I didn't say a word in reproach, nor did he attempt any extenuation. The moment we reached home, I said, without looking at him: 'You must have eaten. I am feeling rather sleepy, so I am off to bed.'

Saying this, I shut the door of our room with a bang and fell on the bed, dry-eyed, but seething inwardly. There was another, smaller room which could be used as a spare bedroom. Shaikh sahib may sleep in it, or spend the night walking about, or do what he wished. I wasn't going to speak to him.

Shaikh sahib cried out, in apparently genuine remorse, 'Arey, arey, Bibi. Just listen. Please listen to me!'

But I was having none of it. He knocked on the door a few times, and knocked again, and again, after a few minutes. But I barely heard the knocks. It was all I could do to prevent myself from breaking into a loud wail, like an angry child who is helpless to get rid of something that he hates. For the first time in my life, I wished that I had my parents so that I could run away to them and never have to bear the company of such as Shaikh sahib.

I wept myself to sleep. Shaikh sahib might have renewed his knocking, but I didn't hear it.

I was still in the Ramazan mode, mentally, so I woke up much before the dawn, then realized that the Ramazan was over. And Shaikh sahib was not by my side on the bed. I couldn't immediately understand, and was shocked. Then I recalled the episode that happened late last night. Worried and ashamed, and almost in tears again for quite a different reason, I tried to push the door open, praying to Maula Ali, Solver of all difficulties, that Shaikh sahib may have found comfortable sleep in the other room. And if he went away, leaving me alone, and perhaps locked in? In spite of the cold weather, I began to perspire as I fought a biting wave of cold fear piercing my spine; my throat felt dry and my lips cracked as if in a fever.

I tried to push harder, but the door wouldn't open. As if something obstructed its opening, something heavy . . . Ya Ali! What could it be? I would have cried out, had my throat muscles not been dry and stuck together. Hai Maula, Solver of all difficulties, what if it is some evil spirit! Some ghost or *churail*, envious of my comfort in Shaikh sahib's love, might have come to take him. No, Shaikh sahib is gone, surely he's gone, leaving me locked to die beating my head against the door.

Unfortunate that I am, I shouldn't have succumbed to my fury. Men have been like that, didn't I know? They spend their time loitering, roistering, ogling the women. Id or Muharram, all are the same for them. I tried to recall the prayer to Maula Ali which begins, 'I call upon Ali . . .' and tried to peep through a crack in the door. But there *was* an obstruction, and it was very dark still. I saw nothing but darkness, or maybe a dark form . . . ? I now almost thought to ram the door, using my slight body, but the door . . . it opened because that obstructive thing moved of its own accord! I could descry Shaikh sahib rising, his eyes sleepy, a slight smile on his face. Ya Allah! He was wrapped in the very shawl with which he'd covered my skimpily covered body on that memorable first night. He'd slept the night, hugging the doorsill.

I was perspiring still. But Shaikh sahib now rose to his full height, dressed in white, his well-proportioned body like a sleek marble column. Before he could speak, I rushed out almost blindly, and hugged him for all that I was worth, and cried, my voice choking with tears and shame: 'What is it that you've done? Why, you could've caught your chill of death!'

'So, I should have broken down the door?' He let out a good-humoured guffaw. 'I would have broken my property, you would lose nothing! Is that what you wished?'

He was such an irritating dear. A man, and he shouldn't lose his temper at being locked out, or anything else at all. Suddenly my fear converted into fury. I cried angrily, hugging him still: 'Look here, he is laughing and I am half dead!' I spoke through a rage of tears. 'I waited, waited for you all the livelong day and you spent your Id among those whom you call your own, as if I am nothing! I am nobody to you!'

I began to wail aloud. He spoke no word, just smiled and listened. I don't remember if he was smiling bashfully, or sarcastically.

'Tell me, tell me now! Are you Shia or Sunni? Why didn't you marry me?' I hit him on his massive chest with my small fists in impotent rage. 'Tell me, I say! Why didn't you marry me? Am I your kept woman?'

Shaikh sahib took both my hands in one of his, massaged them affectionately for a moment, and finally opened his mouth. I remember his hands were warm against mine.

'Yes, I am Sunni by birth, but actually . . .'

'I know nothing of your actuallies, they're always equivocal. I want to know this minute,' I raged. 'I know that contracted marriages are a major sin in your creed.'

'But they are permissible in yours. Is that not so?' He spoke indulgently, with no hint of argufying.

'But *your* religion doesn't recognize contracted marriages. So, I am no more than a plaything for you, a petty kept-miss to use and discard? If that is what I am, I will quit this house this minute and go hire a garret for me in Chowk.'

'Shush! One doesn't say such words!' he said, as I tried to disentangle myself from him. But he held me tight.

'Don't you dare speak to me thus! I am no baby.'

'All right, all right. I'll make a proper marriage with you, I swear. If you want I'll swear by the Exalted Portal, Imam Husain's brother Abbas. Or I'll swear by that even more Exalted Presence, Bibi Khadija, the Prophet's first and dearest wife!'

In spite of myself, I smiled at his childlike assurances, even giving details of the personalities by whom he was willing to swear. But my resentfulness supervened. 'Swearing by the holy persons is sinful. And I wouldn't believe the likes of you even if you took an oath with the Big Bread in your hands!'

I could see, or perhaps I imagined, a darkish wave of shame run across his face. Perhaps he understood my aggravation. Perhaps his talk of marriage was merely to assuage me at the moment and he didn't ever intend to keep his promise. And I believe he realized that I had seen through all his oaths and promises. He raised my face with his index finger under my chin, and spoke in a wonderfully gentle, reassuring voice: 'Have some patience. All in good time. I'll certainly marry you. There's no blame on you for being a contracted wife, and I am not going to run away.'

Was there a genuine fragrance of truthfulness in those words? Or was it my imagination? I am sure I was, as always, willing to believe. But Allah, those words, that promise, that voice, fluty-sweet, delicate juice, like the best Kashmiri apples, that smile, heart-winning, disarming. I'd heard of a mantra called *mohini*. Once you pronounced it with some person in mind, that person became amenable to what you desired from them, your slave to all intents and purposes. So did he pronounce the mohini for me and make me like wax in his hands? I didn't know, and I didn't care. Swaying in those waves of sweetness and delight, my head against his shoulder, my eyes closed, I intoned: 'I will never ever release you from your promise. Sir, do you hear me? Remember that I will grab the hem of your garment on Doomsday and supplicate justice from Almighty Allah.'

As if I believed him. I was letting myself flow away on the wave of his voice. And he wouldn't be Shaikh Ghulam Hamadani Mushafi who couldn't placate the hardest woman, break down the resolve of the most unwilling woman, seduce the most elusive butterfly to land on the palm of his hand. He enclosed my waist in his arm, held my head close to his chest, and walked slowly into the room at whose

409

doorsill he'd spent a whole cold night, alone.

He held me and lay with me throughout the day, unheeding to the calls and knocks of visitors, even the water carrier's, the sweeper's, the next-door neighbour's. Perhaps he'd organized food for his dear pony when he returned last night. But I didn't inquire. Perhaps one of the persons who knocked was the stable keeper, come to report about the pony.

Late at night, he went out. How late will he be in coming back now, I wondered. But in the event, he just went out the Akbari Gate, walked up to the iron bridge where perfumers' and bakers' establishments crowded out everything else. He bought a couple of fat, fragrant and soft saffron-breads and crisp kebabs, went on to the Katra of Sayyid Husain Khan to buy a small leathern bottle of the oil of henna, and came home in just a few minutes, with a ghazal on his lips:

One who is brimful of humanity
Woe is to me, if such a human being were ever to be separated from me!
In a whole lifetime, I saw numerous beauties
But never did I see one like you.
My friend, love's street is such a street
Where a man loses all reputation as he speaks a word or two.
He would, if he so desired, make flowers and springs from my ashes
He, who makes a human being from a handful of dust.

7

Marry me he did, but after many years. It was almost the end of the year 1813. The winter came early that year and ruled us poor earthlings with unusual severity ever since it made its advent upon Lucknow. Shaikh sahib went out early, telling me quite casually that he would come back with some friends for dinner a little past midday. Who and how many, these details he didn't impart, nor was this his wont to tell me. Where he went, at what time, or after how many hours I should expect him back, such details he deigned never to tell me.

I cooked with some care, took my usual freezing bath, put on fresh clothes and was drying my hair in the inner courtyard's welcome sun when the door chain rattled with the peculiar rhythm that Shaikh sahib had adopted, perhaps unconsciously. I knew it was him, and ran, taking care to put my upper wrap properly over my head. I opened the door to Shaikh sahib and two others. I immediately recognized them: Khvajah Haidar Ali Atash, Shaikh sahib's most prominent pupil, and Shaikh Imam Bakhsh Nasikh, whom I knew as Lucknow's leading poet. I'd seen them before, but never in such homey circumstances. Khvajah sahib came once in a way to share our frugal board, which was just above sustenance level. They'd never come together, and they surprised me, actually. I worried if there was enough food to go round. Had Shaikh sahib warned me before, I'd have put up the best dinner that was possible for me.

Most cordially, I invited them in, spread a couple of dhurries, the best that we had, and requested them to be seated while I prepared betel for them. I didn't observe purdah with these two, the nearest to true friends that Shaikh sahib had in Lucknow. Indeed, Khvajah sahib, for all his dervish-like ways, was almost a son to Shaikh sahib. And Nasikh sahib was his protector and friend. Khvajah sahib was tall, very spare, with piercing eyes. He wore his hair long and braided in a single braid that always came down his left shoulder. He wore Delhi-style loose and wide trousers, a simple, short tunic in wool with a nima of the same fabric. A tallish, four-cornered velvet cap, lightly embroidered in gold and worn askew, adorned his head. His beard was ample, but not too long, and was still black, for he was, at that time, less than forty years of age. He always had a dagger stuck in his simple cummerbund. His whole demeanour suggested that he didn't care who liked him, and who didn't.

Nasikh sahib was of a truly commanding presence, but no one would have believed, at first acquaintance, that he was a poet, and that too of surpassing brilliance. Very dark of complexion, almost black, tall and hefty. His head was shaven clean and bright. I think it was lightly oiled. His strong chin looked even stronger in the absence of a beard. Under his compelling eyebrows and wide forehead was a pair of the most magnificent moustaches. In spite of the cold weather, he wore just a long, loose tunic in muslin, and instead of trousers, he wore what was known as a lungi, or *tahmad*—just a wide and long piece of heavy cotton cloth wrapped around the lower body. That style and outfit were, I was told, specially favoured by wrestlers and professional body developers. Around his neck hung a long and heavy necklace of a stone that I couldn't identify. He always carried a long and heavy silver-headed and iron-ferruled staff in his hand.

Shaikh sahib's instruction to me had been to always regard these two as my own brothers and make them my confidants in every matter that I wanted, even those, he made clear, that I couldn't confide to him. Though both Khvajah sahib and Nasikh sahib were around forty years old, long past the time when one marries and raises a family, both were unmarried. Khvajah sahib because of his unworldly, fakir-like temperament—and also I think because of his never having money. Nasikh sahib was very rich, even by the lights of rich men like Zafar-ud Daulah. But he didn't marry because . . . well, because he . . . because he didn't love women at all. You know what I mean.

I sat on my tiny wooden platform, making up betel cones, my head bent, and demurely covered with the wrap. I did notice that each of them went into the water room, made the ablution necessary before doing a prayer, and returned quietly to take his seat. Ya Allah, is there going to be a religious ceremony—perhaps a Shia ceremony, for the two guests were Shia—but why, and why just these three? My heart was beating fast. Is Shaikh sahib going to give me away to someone else? But to whom? Surely not to one of *these* gentlemen? I trembled with anxiety, calling upon Maula Ali with as much ardour as I could muster.

Suddenly, Shaikh sahib called out loudly, in a more than usually

412

resonant voice: 'Hayat-un Nisa bibi, come and sit here with us.'

I nearly fainted. He had never called me Hayat-un Nisa, far less Hayat-un Nisa bibi. Surely, some catastrophe was to overtake me! I left the betel box where it was and trembled up to Shaikh sahib.

'No, not there. Sit in front of me.'

Unable to understand what was going on, I rose and sat on the edge of the durrie, so that Nasikh sahib and Mian Haidar Ali were to one side; I was before Shaikh sahib in my precarious stance. Nasikh sahib rose and wrapped around my shoulders, and over my existing one, an extremely fine, red muslin dupatta, heavily dotted with gold work. He wrapped it so that a part of it hung over my forehead like a bride's veil. Shaikh sahib then spoke the marriage oration, Sunni style, in Arabic. He then said, in the gravest and gentlest of voices: 'Hayat-un Nisa bibi, popularly known as Bhoora begam, you are a free woman, not at present married to anyone. I, Shaikh Ghulam Hamadani Mushafi, take you in marriage in lieu of three hundred royal rupees, payable at once, and with Shaikh Imam Bakhsh Nasikh and Khvajah Haidar Ali Atash bearing witness to this act. Do you accept me in marriage?'

My quiet sobs converted to loud wails. Shaikh Nasikh, unfamiliar with women, Khvajah sahib unmarried, what could those poor singletons know why I wept? They looked at Shaikh sahib and then me, back and forth, like a pair of puzzled, helpless marionettes. Even Shaikh sahib was uncertain for a moment. He said, 'There's nothing to fear, nothing to worry about. Just say the words—I accept—that's all.'

But I wasn't going to stop tearing. Or try opening my mouth. I seemed to have lost the control over my muscles. I had no strength but to howl, or shed big, silent tears.

Shaikh sahib put out an encouraging hand to touch me on the head, but I shied in fear and shrank back. Shaikh sahib spoke as if he were a divinely inspired guide to a child separated from his mother: 'Say I don't accept, if you want it that way.'

'N–no. No, I accept.' I was barely audible.

'Did you hear?' Shaikh sahib asked the witnesses.

'Sir, we did.'

'Then let's raise our hands in prayer to God.'

The three of them prayed, Nasikh sahib and Khvajah sahib silently, Shaikh sahib in whispered but audible tones. When my tears slackened, I rose, touched Shaikh sahib on the knee and shoulder, and let myself slump against the shoulder. Shaikh sahib held me up, and said: 'Today it's our day to serve the food. Brides of a few minutes don't do domestic work.' He then looked at Nasikh sahib who rose and presented to me a heavy red *dosuti* bag. He put it at my feet. Later, when all was quiet, I opened the bag; it was full of bright new coins: full three hundred rupees. I later found out that it was a non-reclaimable loan from Shaikh Nasikh sahib.

I shook the bag and peered into it. There was no document. I then didn't even think why not.

8

By that time, I'd become fully acquainted with important points about the appreciation of poetry, about the different ways that poets expressed themselves and what was special about each ustad. I was also blessed with a good memory from the very beginning, so I could now recite from memory, verses not only from Shaikh sahib, but also from others whose poetry was recited or discussed in my immediate vicinity. I think I also came to understand, I mean understand as much as anyone could after long and intimate exposure without being truly learned.

There were four components to Shaikh sahib's temperament: self-regard and self-respect; love of poetry and understanding of poetry; love of beauty; and humour and wittiness. I believe that but for his sense of humour, life would have become intolerable for him; it was so full of setbacks, slights and failures, especially in his agonistic contestations against his peers that an ordinary poet would have long conceded defeat and quit the field of poetry in favour of something less demanding.

Mir Taqi sahib in Hindi, and Mirza Qateel in Persian: he recognized just these two among the contemporaries. He doubted if Mian Jurat and Sayyid Insha were truly solid in their learning. He believed that poetry and erudition went together. About these two, he said that singing, playing on the veena, mimicking those around you, these could make you a musician, or a professional mimic, or *bahrupiya* as they say. But these aren't what go in the making of an ustad. He disliked needless display of Arabic and Persian in Hindi and disliked pedantry even more. Once he wrote a chronogram for someone whose name was Mufti. Somebody said, 'Sir, you have, in the interest of the metre, depressed the name so that the last *i* isn't fully enunciated.' Shaikh sahib commanded indifferently, 'In my own poetry, I have depressed the "i" of my name Mushafi a hundred times in the interest of the metre. I don't have time for your inane niceties.'

His view was that when a word became native to a certain language, it should be used according to the norms and conventions of that language, and not those of the original language. There was no need to valorize words of Arabic and Persian origin as if they were the deer in the sanctuary of the Kabah—unmolestable, to be left exactly as they were. In fact, in one of his rubais he equated Arabic and Persian words with the crow, clever but having a harsh, unmusical voice. He said:

Oh Mushafi, it can never have the value of a bulbul in the rose garden,
Even though the crow is clever, and sharp.
If you use grave, and heavy words
You will, unjustly, make an ogre of the Rekhtah!

An example of his sense of the self, and his hatred for sycophancy was his reaction to the unjust, in fact cruel and derogatory treatment, to which Mirza Sulaiman Shikoh Bahadur subjected him. Shaikh sahib didn't succeed in his effort to wash the dust of malice and displeasure in the Sahib-e Alam's heart because in the long 'apologetic' poem that he wrote for the purpose, he practically insulted the Prince by clearly insinuating that the Prince was fickle of temperament, and was like wax in the hands of his advisers. He wrote:

> *Your temperament is so plain and clear,*
> *That you give credence to whatever someone reports to you about*
> > *someone else.*
> *Your advisers are such, that if someone made a small error in the*
> *execution of his duties*
> *They can't even think of finding ways to meliorate and improve it.*
> *But your sacred temperament, unheeding*
> *Gives no thought to what this insignificant one submits.*

No doubt he wrote panegyrics, praising his patron to the skies. But that was the convention, and that was what everyone, including the great Mir Taqi Mir sahib, did in his panegyrics. In fact, the more extravagant the praise, the better the poem. Everyone knew that a panegyric was, by its nature, a poem full of flights of imagination and hyperbole. The poet even praised himself in such poems. Shaikh sahib, once in his panegyric addressed to the Presence, Imam Ali, may Allah's Salutations be on him, began with a resounding boast:

> *The time of Mir, and Mirza Sauda, is over:*
> *It is my age, I rule everywhere.*

In another panegyric, addressed to the Son of the Mentor and Guide of the Universe, Mirza Sulaiman Shikoh Bahadur, he practically rebuked him for being incapable of discriminating the false from the true:

> *Don't look at me; look at my pages of poetry,*
> *The Presence, Ali's word was not just a casual thing (he said: don't pay*
> *heed to the utterer, pay heed to the utterance).*
> *For an eulogist like me, it was but inevitable that there be an eulogized*
> > *one like you.*

If you are among the followers of Ali, the Leader, I follow Qambar, his slave.
Master of the land, don't let justice slip your hands
Even if you, the nurturer of the people, can't do any nurturing.

There was a gentle hint, or reproof in the lines about Imam Ali and Qambar. Mirza Sulaiman Shikoh Bahadur was Sunni, like all his House. He became Shia in Lucknow when he settled there as a royal guest of the Minister of all Dominions whose House was Shia. Shaikh sahib most appropriately hinted at the Prince's departure from his ancestral faith, and by bringing in Qambar, he hinted that both he and the Prince were 'from the same place' as Mir Taqi sahib wrote in one of his ghazals.

Shaikh sahib's life was spent in looking for a patron, and in writing encomia and eulogia for his daily bread providers. He once wrote, and this is quite true for him:

All the means of earning money ceased to be
So, having no choice, I became a poet.

And there's no doubt that he hated being where he was. He didn't love money: he loved knowledge, and thought. Once he wrote, and again, it was quite true for him, though he used Aristotle's name, and truthfully, because he admired knowledge and those who produced it:

A thousand pities, that a man like Aristotle
Should have been ensnared in honour and glory, leaving the land of
learning.

This ghazal he wrote while I was with him, listening to him talk, and hum, and also crack jokes when he didn't get a line, or an idea right. Fearfully, I asked him, 'Who is Aristotle?' He replied, and there was gusto and warmth in his voice: 'Bibi, he was the teacher and the guide of us all. Whatever we know and understand of the world, we owe it all to him, and Ibn Sina, whom we call the Presiding Master. Then Ibn Rushd, Abdul Halim Sialkoti, Mulla Mahmud Jaunpuri, these are our teachers and leaders. Aristotle became tutor to Alexander, and became a courtier to all intents and purposes. He had to leave his beloved school and stop teaching.'

I listened, open-mouthed. Shaikh sahib knew so much, he wasn't just a versifier, I told myself in my heart.

'Look at Khan-e Allama, a man to rival even Ibn Sina in learning. He worked so hard to place his patron Navab Saadat Ali Khan on the Navabi seat, dispossessing Vazir Ali Khan. And what did he get as reward? Practical exile to the English Lord's court as the Navab's representative. He didn't even die in his native land, but in Bengal, in faraway Murshidabad. Would he not have been infinitely better off, though infinitely poorer, but happier, had he not been a courtier?'

I understood some of his discourse, didn't understand much of it, but a question arose in my heart which I couldn't resist. Somewhat fearfully, I asked: 'So the commands of the Prophet and the utterances of the Innocent Imams aren't sufficient to know the world?'

He smiled: 'Bhoora begam, not just the world, but the whole creation. And it's essential to have both, reason and religious tradition, to understand it. Allah himself commands in the Quran repeatedly: "So why don't you apply your reason?" Why did Allah grant the power of perception? Listen to me:

The Tablet, the Pen, the Chair, the Throne, the Skies
All are all on High, but are under the power of Perception.

I didn't understand properly, but I was frightened, terrified even. Who is this Perception, Death take him, this thing of Disgrace? I beg protection from Allah—is Perception superior even to the Glorious Imams, the Hadith and the Quran? I feared for Shaikh sahib in the Afterworld. How will Allah and Maula regard him for such blasphemies? But I already said, I never could get to the truth of his beliefs. He wrote panegyrics in praise of the Imams of High Station; he wrote panegyrics also in praise of Sunni Sufis and saints. Today he declares the Shia to be illiterate and erring. Tomorrow he fulminates against the Sunni. And as far as doing the prayer, fasting, or reading the Quran is concerned, I never saw any such act occurring from him. He was extremely well versed in Arabic, but I never saw a religious paper in his hands. During the last years of his life, he did occasionally read from the Quran, or say the last prayer of the day. But I anticipate.

He now spoke with not a little passion, continuing his discourse: 'Do you hear? The world is stuffed full to overflowing with evil, cruelty and injustice. Honesty and Truth make their appearance here but rarely. I am sure Allah has delegated the management of this world to Satan.'

Then he said a verse which shocked me into a daze. I was half dead with terror. This was the verse:

Wasn't it He who raised this infinitude of mischief
By pronouncing 'Be!' and the universe of possibilities came into being?

'Allah! Please repent. You say such things in front of me and make me party to your sinfulness!' I slapped both sides of my face lightly in token of repentance and renunciation. 'What is it that happens to you now and again? Don't you have to appear before God on Doomsday?'

'Bhoora begam, had there been justice, there would be no Firangi here, no martyrdom for Tipoo Sultan, nor would a man like me, peerless in his times, wander here and there, making one of the night and the day, just for a piece of coarse barley bread and an earthen cup of cool water.'

I had no answer. He recited his verse with such bitter vehemence, with such a world of regret that I wished I had everything and I could give it him:

Mushafi, my hands remained empty when I lived
So what use if they coat my book with gold when I am not?

'For Allah's sake. Please be quiet now. Allah Sees and Hears everything. He is the Greatest Doer and Fashioner of all solutions! Should He be so Minded, He would have your doors and walls coated with gold!'

'Does your precious Allah have so much time, Bhoora begam? Bu Ali said that God cannot know the specifics of things.'

'Who is this Godless shameless Bu Ali whom you think is your friend? Firangi fetters are preferable to such company,' I cried heatedly.

He guffawed. 'Yes, his friendship seduces you in going astray!'

His brow knotted suddenly, as if he were trying to arrive at the solution of something abstruse. 'But please do think. He Exists by Himself in the State of Total Purity. How is it possible for Him to decline, and come down, and organize a court of justice like the kings and the chiefs of police? The matters of the world are bound up with the devices and management of God's slaves. Now what happens is that the management and devices of those who are honest and pure, are trumped by the cheat, the unscrupulous, with their chicanery.'

I put my fingers in my ears. 'Please to stop. I will hear no more! Please go into the water room and rinse your mouth well to clean it. Repent so that the rust and blackness of denial may be washed away from your heart.'

He laughed at my words, unheeding and free from fear of divine retribution. He may have been . . . well, how can I call him kafir, or one who is not in Islam? I can swear that he had more honesty, more scrupulousness in keeping his promise, or holding others' goods and money in trust, than any Maulavi or nobleman that I knew. In giving due regard and respect to people consonant with their position, he was most careful, most thoughtful. Maybe, during his quarrels with Sayyid Insha sahib, he may have polluted his tongue once or a few times in saying bad things about Sayyid sahib and his army of louts. Those events happened before my time. I was with him for close on thirty years, and I can say with full responsibility that I never ever heard him use bad language, or impertinent words, against anyone at all.

I think that he would have managed well enough with the noblemen, the rich and the elite, but for his self-regard, pride even. In the haveli of Kaptan Fateh Ali Khan, I had, on numerous occasions, seen the poets demeaning themselves, saying bad things, shameful things about their rivals, doing anything they could to ingratiate themselves with Kaptan sahib. Shaikh sahib never stooped low. His head was always high. Once in a weak moment—because I was pregnant then—I said that if we were rich, I would have a gold amulet made for my firstborn. Shaikh sahib's brow clouded for a moment, but he spoke nothing, and changed the subject. Then, apparently apropos of nothing, he said, 'Here, Bhoora begam, I just composed this. Tell me how you like it.'

He said, to my chagrin:

I am rich, oh Mushafi, by the wealth of poetry
What value has gold or silver before me?

From that day, I never brought up such foolish things before him. The baby was lost, and I have always believed that it was God's punishment for my folly and avarice.

He was indifferent towards money, but was never indifferent, far less overbearing, with young talent. He encouraged all the tyro poets who came to him, offering correction if they so requested, though he knew they were too poor to enrol as pupils. He even wrote ghazals, qitas, rubais and celebratory poems for those who came asking for these. They rarely paid him and he never demanded.

He knew that talents differed. He was prolific, and extremely comfortable at composing poetry. But he was a realist too. He knew that he, or in fact no one, could maintain the highest standard all the time. With admirable self-knowledge, he once said:

Oh Mushafi, it's difficult to consistently compose excellent ghazals
Well, actually, it's in the proportion of one verse in ten, quite by chance!

421

Sometimes I inquired the specific meaning of one or two of his verses. He would lightly say, 'Don't ask me what I meant. I am lost in poetry and poetry is lost in me!' Once he said this verse to me, by way of his fullest explanation:

I give my life as sacrifice to poetry, oh Mushafi
And poetry gives its life as sacrifice to me.

I thought, and thought. What exactly was he saying when he said 'poetry gives its life as sacrifice to me'? Did he mean that poetry would come to him always, as a lover comes to his beloved, at the risk of life even? Or did he mean that there could be no poetry after him because he'd brought it to its highest station? I never could ask him, nor solve the question myself.

9

His love of beauty? You must have judged already. I can't do more than say to you a verse of his:

From the Noble Master of Mecca, to the wise intellectual
There's none who doesn't in his heart harbour the desire for a beautiful
person.

I think that he coveted loving more than being loved. In his home, I always had love, and a courtly lover's attention. What were his interests and entanglements outside, I can't say. Before me, he certainly had many beloveds, maybe a score or more, including a boy or two. I suspect that sometimes he'd have more than one affair going at the same time. His poetry certainly suggests this to an attentive reader. He often spoke and talked in the rhythms and the idiom of a lover of the bazaar, the gathering or dwelling place of beautiful people, but always like a honey bee, travelling and flitting from place to place.

I think I told you some time ago that very few women could resist him; I could say the same about effeminate boys, all bedecked, turned out like the beloveds of yore. Here is a verse of his, perhaps it dates back to his Delhi days, but it seems authentic enough as a mirror to his loverly activities:

Mian Mushafi, you didn't let go a single boy
You're really something like a master at your job!

You can see the pun, don't you? It seems to be a tongue-in-cheek confession of a boy lover. But I really can't say. Poetry is an unstable site to dig for the poet's personal life. You know that these ustads revelled in new themes, outré subjects, always on the lookout for that which surprised the audience with a fine excess.

You don't think so? Well, I lived with him for nearly three decades. I got to understand at least his bent of mind. Not for nothing he admired Nasikh sahib and Atash sahib, who wrote a poetry quite different from his own, and in fact once he said to me that he would write like them from then on. Can you imagine another ustad like him? Willing, and able, to write in the 'new' manner being made popular by his pupil, and a friend very much younger? That's why it's not important for me to know how many women and men he loved, and the duration of each affair. Poetry and love of beauty—these were two inseparable aspects of his life, like the two sides of the same coin. He used to be irked by Sayyid Insha precisely for that reason. He used to say: 'This man, so talented, so brilliant, learned to boot, looks to nothing but his audience. He doesn't look to the heart, the hands and feet, and finally, not even at his own self. He concentrates only on making an effect. Now, that's not how the best poetry can be made. A poet should strive for newness, but newness in the world, not in an artificial, shallow courtly audience.'

This was really far above my comprehension, but I knew that what he said was genuinely profound, something which Mir Taqi Mir sahib would perhaps understand and maybe even approve.

Shaikh sahib then recited some verses from a ghazal by Sayyid Insha sahib, and continued: 'Such brilliance, such power, but nothing inside. The man doesn't want to look at the body, at the most beautiful thing God made.'

He then recited a couple of verses of his own:

It won't surprise anyone, if
your rosy-white beauty turned rosy
The spectators' retina.
*

Doubtless, her body was worth seeing
But I couldn't see a thing
When she removed her clothes.
*

How to write about the way
Her waist connects with her buttocks?
It's like drawing the picture of two hillocks
With a brush that has just one hair!

I redden and blush, whenever I think (and the truth is, I try *not* to think) of this verse. He told me that the ancient Hindus described a beautiful woman's gait as *gaj gamini*, which I think means one who walks like an elephant, swaying as if to music. And it was the heavy buttocks which made her walk so. He said: 'Do you see, Bhoora begam? It's easy to say gaj gamini, for it's an established theme: the beloved walks with a swaying gait, why? Because her buttocks and breasts are so heavy, and her waist so slim, that she can't balance herself. Now I describe the waist to be hair-thin, a well-known theme, but give a totally new metaphor for the buttocks. The rest you can see.'

As if I could see anything, reddening, furiously blushing, my eyes on my toes, and trying not to giggle. But Shaikh sahib was lost in his poem, and the sensuality of it.

You ask: There must be someone who hurt him, at least one who didn't succumb to his charms, somebody on whom his enchanting personality didn't work.

Actually, that's of no interest to me at all. Pardon me, but it's you men who compare conquests, tell tales, count the number of beloved-lovers they had. There was no reason for me, really, to be inquisitive. I did see someone called Makhfi mentioned in one or two of his rubais. But since *makhfi* means 'hidden', perhaps Shaikh sahib was being discreet. Anyway, Shaikh sahib has described her as a 'she-butcher's daughter'. Whether this was metaphor or reality, I don't know.

You may have read in Saadat Yar Khan Rangin sahib's account of some events in his life that Rangin sahib was in love with a 'butcher's daughter'. I don't know if the two are the same lady. Perhaps both were burning themselves into kebabs for that same woman. There were rumours that the woman's father was sworn to make mincemeat of Rangin sahib, who was almost an aristocrat. Was Shaikh sahib also stewing in his own juice at Rangin sahib's success? Only men know about such manly things. I wasn't even born when those matters transpired.

There was one, I know for sure. She lived with Shaikh sahib without marriage for a year, a year and a half. But she wasn't happy with the lack of comfort, not for Shaikh sahib, but for her own self. Finally, she—may her beauty be singed in hell—left him, falling for the blandishments of a woman whose profession was to connect and separate people. Some say that Shaikh sahib had her abort their baby because he feared for his good name. Fear? Shaikh sahib never feared anyone, man or God.

Go on with you, Vafa sahib, you are again pining to know about Ismat! They say Ismat behaved extremely badly and even cruelly with him. Shaikh sahib never spoke of such things. I really don't know much, but a very curious incident made him open up about her. For all I know, he may have regretted making me his confidante about this part of her life. Here's how it came to pass: He was laid up with high fever and was often delirious. Hakim sahib assured me that he would respond to treatment, but this was just the fourth day; the kind of fever that Shaikh sahib had would take at least five days to come down. I should not worry, but apply frequently a cold compress to his forehead whenever he became delirious. It seemed that he also hallucinated, and took the bygone days for real days. I was putting a cold compress on his forehead when he haltingly, but clearly enunciated a line from a rubai:

I'll die, always calling out Ismat, Ismat!

I didn't immediately realize that it was a line of verse. How could I know who this Ismat—may her face be slapped blue—was? Impulsively, and most solicitously, I inquired, with all the innocence of a very young and inexperienced girl: 'Should I send word to her? Where does she live?'

Suddenly, he opened his eyes, ever so expressive, but red with the fire of fever. Also, bright, so bright as if they never saw a day's illness. He beckoned for a cup of water. I quickly brought it to him and made him sip it slowly, but he drank the whole cup, actually quaffed it, in no time. The surprising thing was that he fell asleep almost at once after he'd drunk the water. I began to worry, and fretted that such a quick intake of water might have harmed his liver, like a sudden insertion of a thorn. But what could I do? I must wait. Still, I shook him gently once or twice. He half opened his eyes, spoke nothing.

As the day crept to its close, I could see that the crisis of the fever was past. I was sitting near him, on a small stool, supporting my elbow on the bed frame, my chin on my palm. He put out his hand and I took it into mine eagerly. Then he moved his fingers on the palm of my hands in a marvellous, loverly way, as if he were writing something on it, maybe a message?

I held my hand there, but he half sat up and whispered, 'Bhoora, I'll tell you a story.'

10

Those were the days, oh Mushafi, when eager to steal a glance
I wandered the lanes and streets of Delhi for years, looking for Ismat's
house.

I'd just arrived in Delhi a few months ago. It was my misfortune that love for beautiful people, and my memories of people and things that were past, had added themselves to my desperate search for livelihood. Instead of being a thing of joy, love became another affliction for me. Unhappy and angry at someone, I'd left Amroha for Aonla. A thousand regrets that the lamps that lit the assemblies there were put out well before it was morning.

Thanks to the depredations and militarist adventurism of Zulfaqar-ud Daulah and the Marathas, in the wink of an eye the rose garden that the Rohillas had nurtured for over five decades—trimming the old and planting the new—was devastated and laid waste. That paradisal assembly was turned within no time to a zone colder than the coldest hell, more desolate than a burning ghat. I rose and, stumbling, falling and raising myself up on the potholed highway, arrived in Lucknow. I presented myself at the Court Pavilion of Mirza Sauda sahib, but I found that he had more time for carding and combing the coats of his silken-haired dogs than for a literary tyro like me. I was, after all, nearly forty years younger than him, and he was the acknowledged master from Hind to Karnatak, the favoured poet at the Court of the Minister of all Dominions, expert at panegyric as much as at satire; his age as a poet was almost twice as much as my biological age.

Finding little to interest me in Lucknow, I was soon on the high road to Shahjahanabad. There was a doe-eyed beauty in Amroha; one blink of her eye was like a stab of a lancet into my heart. Her memory hurt me in Lucknow. In Delhi, nearer from Amroha than from Lucknow, her memories redoubled their cruel awls on my heart. I hated myself for quitting her. After all, what she said about my being without employment was no taunt, but because my own heart was on the defensive in this matter, her words hurt me more than a dagger.

I didn't have much education at that time. All my boyhood, all my youth, I squandered on flying kites, playing marbles and looking covetously at the young girls of our neighbourhood. But that eloquent ruby which had dazzled my heart and whose tresses, curl upon curl, had entangled my soul, was something else again. She played on my heart like a sitar under the hands of a master, or a flute at the lips of one who could make the flute talk almost like a human being. I wrote:

I gave away my heart, oh Mushafi, as a present to someone
Now the rest is luck: happen what may.

My heart craved to look at her always, with she close to me, so that I could hear her and look at her and marvel over both her voice and her beauty, all at once. But she was constrained by her people to observe extreme discretion. Clandestine meetings are not conducive to giving the reins to one's desire. Once, just to test the waters with her, I asked quite casually, 'Hey, what do you think of us getting married?' She laughed her full laughter, flowing with good humour, and also derision: 'So? What will you eat? And what would you feed me with? You think these pranks will last long on an empty stomach?'

I felt as if one of the big, tiger-striped bees had stung me. 'Do you not desire going to bed . . . ?' I said lamely.

'Yes, I do. Truly.' She spoke deliberately, emphasizing every word. 'But I haven't given thought to all this. If you were of some substantive capacity . . .'

'I am a poet!' I said hotly. 'There'll come a day when I will be an acknowledged ustad. Chieftains and rich nobles will be my pupils. You'll see!'

Again, she laughed. 'All right, come to me then. Then I'll see about your proposal.'

I rose abruptly and made for the door. She called out, and kept calling, 'Hey, hey! I was just joking. Just listen! I give you the oath of my own life!'

But it was the first time I'd experienced blind, burning anger, at my shame and the most cutting slight to my vision of my destiny as a master poet.

There was none at that time to stop me from going where my fancy took me. Two of my brothers were dead; a third had left the mundane world to become a fakir. I said goodbye to Amroha, and came out alone to settle my account with the world. And the laughable part—it didn't seem laughable to me then—was that let alone the wherewithal to fight, I didn't even have baggage, except the illusion, or delusion, of becoming the master poet of my time. How I wish I could see into the dark abysm of time, and could see these verses inscribed there, verses that I composed nearly half a century later:

> Now the poets' life and means of livelihood is
> That they hawk poetry's merchandise from door to door.
> None accept it even for free
> Humiliated, they come back home. Woe is to poetry!

But at that time my ambitions were high, and despair was down on the ground. The failure even to win a good position in Lucknow couldn't disconnect the thread of hope. If nothing, my fluent temperament and my constantly active creativity was instilling the colour of brilliance in my poetry: I was becoming known as an up-and-coming poet, invited to mushairas and private assemblies where sessions of poetry were held invariably after dinner and before the nautch girls took the stage.

One day, at an assembly in the public hall at Khvajah Mir Dard sahib's, I saw her. And was entirely unable to move my gaze away. It wasn't that she was outstandingly beautiful. But it was her total presence, her commanding confidence, her dress neither loud nor subdued, just as it should have been, her stance firm and comfortable, and not thrusting or loud. I didn't know what to do, where else to look. Each and every particle of her body, every bone and every sinew, seemed to dance with desirability, charged with the honey of womanliness. Oh, the way she arranged her dupatta back around her shoulders and upon her head after an excruciatingly brief glimpse of the rise of her breasts, the movement of her fingers as she flicked back a heavy, rebellious braided tress, which seemed to cling to her neck caressingly like the blackest of ebony snakes around a branch of the sandal tree. Everything of her seemed to cry out: I am made for desire; I am made to be lusted after; I am made to pierce the hearts and livers of men.

I was trying to pluck up courage to ask her name from the person who sat next to me when he half exclaimed to himself, somewhat satirically: 'Ah! So, Ismat Jahan has brought her noble presence here today!'

Ismat Jahan, what a lovely, lovable name. I wanted to say that name over and over again, to myself, or aloud, or to no one else. I wanted to start composing for her a sarapa then and there, but erotic thoughts blocked my imagination. I saw nothing but her body beneath those magnificently simple clothes, so appropriate to her personality. As Urfi said:

I opened my eyes on the beloved's face
Ashamed, my sight ran away.

It was just thought, and speculation, and hope, hope rolling rapidly like a river. I knew somewhere in a corner of my brain that it wasn't hope, but it was the deceptive face of ebullient youth which beguiled me. But at that time, I didn't even know who recited what, and what I recited. I don't know if she somehow felt the hot breath of my desire reaching her. But I was sure that she would have eyes for none but me, once she knew who I was. Who . . . I . . . was? Did I even understand what I was saying?

Back home, I asked some friends of my confidence about her. All of them were united in discouraging me. One of them, much aware of women like her, said: 'Mian Ghulam Hamadani, your dice is stuck in a bad, bad place. Foolish young man, this is not Amroha. If you want access there, you must have to be made of gold. Your handful of dust will avail you nothing at that portal!'

My friends' admonitions called to my mind a rubai of Shaikh Abu Said Ab-ul Khair sahib, may Allah Increase his station in Paradise. How I wish today that I'd paid heed to what he commanded seven centuries ago:

Someone asked me: Who is your beloved?
I said, it's she, so why do you ask?
He flopped down and wept over me aloud:
How will you live at the hands of such a one?

But I was on fire. I heard nothing, heeded no one. After many weeks of inquiry, I did get to know her address. But knowing the address and visiting the address were two different matters. By now I'd got to know more about her: she was patronized by the elite of the land, not just of the city. She was immensely rich. And equally disdainful of petty poets and penniless admirers like me. Sometimes, I purposely made my way to her street, hoping at least to get a glimpse of her. I saw nothing but richly caparisoned elephants bearing golden howdahs, carriages bedecked like brides lining both sides of the street, and Ismat Jahan's lackeys—tall, imposing Abyssinians, short, stocky Telangas—forcibly removing, summarily ejecting any loiterers, however genteel-looking.

I wrote a ghazal during those days of despair:

My heart impels me to wail, and to weep
I should gladden my heart at least with tears, and weep.
I have been kept alive in your disunion, so
That I remember how you look, and weep.

Finally, one day, I did get to cast my eye on her: not really looking in its proper sense, but something, something very like it. One of her Abyssinians, cruel as hangmen, was absent from the door, perhaps gone inside to report something. The other one was flirting with a betel-seller woman next door.

Suddenly, a tumult. Subdued, but a noise certainly, presaging some important arrival. It transpired that Afrasiab Khan Bahadur had sent his personal rath to fetch her. Ismat Jahan begam had refused to go a number of times in the past, but today she had indicated her consent. Hence the rath. I crossed the street in almost one step and practically pasted myself to the wall at the other end, near the betel-seller from where I could clearly observe her doorway, without appearing to loiter. By that time another doorkeeper was right at my head with his staff, bidding me wordlessly to go off. But, oh my great good fortune! She appeared in the gateway. And I could observe her in motion. As the great Nizami said many centuries ago:

> *So fresh and fluid, her body seemed to ooze out from her dress,*
> *Her tresses, playful, seemed to fly away from her hands.*

A very mild whiff of living good fortune, the highness of her star of destiny, reached me wafting upon the air, like the air itself. I bent low in salaam. A casual glance, at me, or perhaps at some other at beauty's door. I made to say something, but words stuck to my palate, or my tongue seemed to stick to my palate. Oh, I was happy being permitted to do my humble salaam. As the Persian poet said:

> *He who practises love, brings submission*
> *Because love has nothing to do with those who don't know how to submit.*
> *An erect neck doesn't go with loving*
> *For, the practice of love doesn't tolerate those who are frivolous.*

I am sure she remained unaware of my existence, but I am sure the heat of the desire blazing in me, and the flames of my conflagrant love must have been felt by her, even if transiently. But how could I say a word to her when I didn't have the strength to even take a look at her?

It happened a few times after that momentous moment: I would be lucky enough to find her coming out or going into her gated haveli. It gladdened my heart to find more and yet more occasions to fantasize about her; those little glimpses were a yet stronger spur to my charging love. Sometimes, I'd find out that an assembly of poets was being organized there and I'd irrigate my crop of desire with the water of hope that I too would be invited there. I would build castles of hopes and amatory dreams, but it was as the Persian poet said:

None in that assembly spoke ill of me even,
Though I kept my ears close to the wall.

I knew at least this much from my cautious inquiries: she was 'attached' to no one, but she didn't have a loving corner in her heart either, for anyone. All had the same word for me: Mian, rid your heart of all thoughts of her. If she were to place you on her head, it wouldn't be out of love; it would be just because it made it all the easier for her to throw you down her balcony.

And on my side, my absorption in her was so great that I always persuaded myself as I went out, perhaps this time, surely this time, she is going to look at me with some interest, no, not regard, but with curiosity at least. As Amir Khusrau said:

I am intoxicated with joy: She saw me last night in
her street and asked,
Who's this fellow? They said, he's a pauper, he begs for alms around here.

Some day will dawn soon, I told myself when my heart became a target for her barbs of indifference yet another time; some day when she will look at me she'll know that I'm not a stone or rock on her street. I am a human being. How well the Persian poet said:

433

She's inconsiderate towards me each day
And I deceive my heart, she won't do it tomorrow.

The day did come, after all, against all possibility. It was the Fair of the Sticks. The sticks, profusely decorated with colourful flowers and fragrant grasses and golden festoons, were taken out to celebrate the Janam Ashtami, and also, on different dates, in honour of certain Sufi saints, like Shah Madar whose shrine is not in Delhi, but whose 'sticks' are celebrated everywhere around here with great gusto.

So I too, mood scattered and heart screaming with unhappiness, decided to visit the fair, hoping that she might be out there and I might get to look at her in a comparatively open environment. And that's what did happen. I was browsing among some florists' shops when I noticed her buying some posies and flower garlands at the next shop. I stood, rooted on the spot, hoping to find some way to approach her.

It seemed to me that I had just grown up, it was my first day of puberty. I was so thrilled, so overawed with fear and hope. A wave, a thrill, ran down from my heart into my loins. God, I could faint right here. Please, please, let me keep my head. I was a moist log of wood smouldering for ages, it seemed to me. Now it would flagrate or explode, as I knew such wood sometimes did. I felt in the pocket of my coat, hoping against hope to find some money there. It must have been Shah Madar sahib's spiritual beneficence that I did find a few petty coins, not enough for a bouquet, but for a nosegay. I threw the money, picked up my petty merchandise, and almost ran to the rath where the drapes were just about to be drawn. I presented the nosegay, bent as low in salaam as was appropriate. I was rewarded with a very faint knit on the brow, a slight movement upward of a bejewelled hand towards the forehead. Then a brief beckon to the maid who sat opposite. This was both a gesture of acceptance of offering and command to the rath driver to move. Hai! What should I do now? Where should I go? Run after the rath?

I took my courage in both hands and spoke the verse of an old

Persian poet Jamali with all the mellifluousness that my throat and lungs could command:

My dress is made of the dust of your street
And that too is rent in a thousand places by my flowing tears.

My arrow hit the target plumb centre. A subtle, fleeting smile on her lips, though it didn't reach the eye. She whispered something to her maid who raised her eyes to me, darting and black as the bumble bee, and said, 'Bibi ji says she has seen you around somewhere. But she cannot stay here at present. She commands that you trouble your feet to the haveli sometime.'

The rath was already almost in motion as she spoke; it turned a bend and disappeared from my view. But the whole world was in my view now. I could see everything with a clarity that I didn't believe was possible. My feet were with the clouds moving lazily across the half-blue sky. I could see everything from there and the wonder of it all was that I could espy the colours of the children's clothes, hear their chatter and the whistles that they blew. I could talk to them, tweak the ear of one or another, tell them a joke, sing them a brief song. And the whole plain, the whole village of Khvajah sahib, and then the villages and monuments beyond, I could see them all from on high. They were at my feet.

Morning dawned, intoxication gave way to hangover, bringing practical matters to torment me. What should I wear? I was used to wearing everyday clothes at all places and I didn't have too many of them anyway. I needed fancy clothes, or at least new clothes. What should I take with me as an offering? A rubai or a ghazal?

Then it occurred to me to consult Hakim Qudrat-ullah Qasim sahib. Poet and biographer of poets, he was a man of affluence and influence. He would know all about such things. I was comparatively free with him in spite of the difference in age and rank. Another connection common between us was that both of us were disciples of Our Mentor and Our Authority the Presence, Maulana Fakhruddin sahib. Yet another connection was our friendship with Hakim Sanaullah Firaq, poet and physician, and Maulavi Nur Ahmad sahib, a lover of poetry.

The decision once made, there was no difficulty in putting it into effect. I went out to call on Hakim sahib; his house was in Kucha Chelan, not far from where I lived. Hakim sahib's words were heart-warming to me, but also discouraging, in fact, heart-lacerating. He said: 'Mian Mushafi, going there is no problem. If you wish, I can accompany you there and introduce you properly. But you aren't going to make any impression on Ismat Jahan. In fact, you'll be on ice there, all the time, liable to slip and be expunged as a fool.'

'Hakim sahib, I am sorry, but I would still like to try. I have an invitation of sorts, after all.'

Hakim sahib smiled—a piteous smile? I should hope not—and said: 'Dear boy, she is faithful to none but to gold, yellow or white. You have nothing, not even a piece of unstamped copper. Even the extremely rich dance to her tune . . . Well, she is a woman of the bazaar, after all. One shouldn't expect anything different from her. But she seems to be exceptionally faithless, and unfaithful and uncaring.'

'Why is that so? Why is she exceptional?'

'Well, there is a story about her,' Hakim sahib spoke somewhat hesitantly, as if in doubt.

A story? I was thrilled in my heart. Was there something special there? But I waited for Hakim sahib to go on.

'I heard that there was a young Maulavi called Khairuddin who taught at the madrasa of Ghazi-ud Din Firoz Jang. Very young, very talented, they say. For some mysterious reason his heart tugged at Ismat Jahan's heart. She too was reputed to be interested. But some mysterious complications arose and the plant of their hopes failed to green and grow. So she changed, and changed so that she became almost like a city-killer. Everyone loves her, she loves no one. She plays with them, drains them of all, and she kicks them without remorse.'

'Allah, Allah. And that poor Maulavi?'

'He became a poet, he writes with the pen name "Ismat". He has given up the world to all purposes.'

Hakim sahib had an enigmatic expression on his face. Perhaps, God forbid, he saw me as another such?

My heart sank and became cold as dead. What did I have, except a flood of desire and rising youth? This wouldn't be enough to entice Ismat Jahan. And even if it did happen, what about the aftermath? True, I was good-looking in those days, strong limbed; I often practised physical exercises at a convenient akhara, or wrestling arena, even in Amroha. But Delhi in those days was teeming with handsome youths, examples of male youth and beauty and physical prowess, from as far as Armenistan to as near as Kabul. Then there were those master womanizers, the Kyrghiz, who came a few years ago with Abdali and never returned. Faces rosy pink like freshly ripened apples, tall in stature, strong white teeth, penetrating almond-shaped eyes, chests strong and wide like steel chests, and strong legs and arms like the smooth and thick branches of elm or birch. They had everything, and they were always available for hire as soldiers or bodyguards, and relentlessly pursued the women of the neighbourhood. They never seemed short of money. So where did I stand in their competition?

Seeing me lost in thought, Hakim sahib spoke kindly, 'Mian, where are you lost? Have hope, and faith. I'll take you there tomorrow. What will be, will be.'

Hakim sahib then loaned me two half gold coins. Called *nim ashrafi*, the value of two was equal to one gold coin. I knew I could perhaps not return them soon, if at all. I think Hakim sahib was of the same thought, but he was quite willing, and able to do generosity with me.

I immediately bought an expensive cloak and a muslin tunic and a nima to go with it. Shoes were another purchase that I made in I don't remember how many years. These left me with half a gold coin and some change, so I regarded myself opulent, and well able to buy Ismat Jahan's favours, if need be. We rode in Hakim sahib's open palanquin.

437

Throughout the journey, passers-by, shopkeepers, shoppers, recognized Hakim sahib and greeted him. There was the usual crush of mounts and carriages in front of Ismat Jahan's haveli. My mortal enemies, the Abyssinians and the Telangas, sprang to salute Hakim sahib, but apparently they weren't of more weight than dry blades of grass for him. Their hands were still in the air when we passed inside through the spacious gate.

I was surprised to see that we went up the stairs only to face another guardhouse. This one was commanded by Abyssinian and Turkmenistani women, every inch warriors and every inch intimidating. They looked at us but indifferently and said, 'Please to go down the other side through the stairs.'

We descended into an enclosed garden. Very green but not dense. Orange, lemon, litchi, berries of many types, and a few mango trees, very small, as if they were maintained to be that way. Flowering shrubs of many varieties, but none growing wild or too tall. Prominent were the champak, the *gul-e chandni* (moonlight flower), magnolia grandiflora and the hibiscus. A square masonry-built platform right in the middle, with a water channel running around it; the channel was fed by a larger and longer channel that came from somewhere at the far end of the garden and disappeared under an ornamental bridge at the other end. Colourful fountains, their shallow basins carved from pink marble. Some of the thorny and greener trees like lemon and the *falsa* berry had very fine wire gauze erected around them, so fine that it could be discerned only after some effort. These trees were indeed evergreen, ever-fresh cages, full of twitter and song from all kinds of tiny birds. Then I noticed the pigeons: fantails and hooded jacobs, and tall majestic shirazis, followed dutifully by tiny *chua chandans*, more turtle dove than pigeon in appearance; plump, small *khurd nokhas*, distinct from the rest by their very short beaks, cooing and pecking food from the grass, a couple of maids following them to make sure that their droppings or any seeds or blades of grass scattered by those untidy birds were picked instantly.

At the far end of the private garden in front of us was a dazzling white pavilion in two storeys. On the terrace roof, strutting birds, watched over by another attentive maid. Peacocks I could identify, but not the others, slimmer, smaller, with golden bodies and long, golden tails—some Chinese fowl, apparently. Then one of our Indian hill pheasants, magnificent in red and blue with blue-green crests—was there a birdhouse here, or a menagerie for display?

A gold-brocaded curtain on a door at the end of the terrace attracted my attention. Two female guards stood there, erect and unmoving. Hakim sahib gestured to me to follow him without tarrying to gape at the birds.

We entered. I gaped some more. It was almost the Hall of Public Audience in the Fort, except that no one was standing; people sat on carpets, supported by bolsters, with the wall at their backs. Hookah and betel were much in evidence. Musicians, male and female, busy with their instruments, tuning and tightening them very softly. The front seat with a golden-brocaded fat bolster was empty. A maid stood behind it, a heavy peacock fan at the ready. Very delicately scented air, the attar of henna pervaded gently, though I could see no sprinklers. Then I realized that there were four ornamental chandeliers hung at four corners of the roof: they were not chandeliers, there was some pressure mechanism at the top through which the very fine spray was disseminated throughout the chamber.

It was Abul Hasan in the Arabian Nights. It was not me. How could I reach that pedestal, far less stay there? I was going to wake up soon and be kicked or dragged down the stairs into the street.

She entered. She recognized Hakim sahib before everyone else and took a graceful step or two towards him.

'I submit my greetings. Allah, Hakim sahib, you quite erased my name from the tablet of your heart!'

'No, there's nothing like that, Ismat begam. But you know, it's the world. Always one thing after the other, otherwise who wouldn't love to come here to your assemblies?'

439

She smiled, but there was no invitation there. Everything was from a distance.

'And this is my friend Shaikh Ghulam Hamadani, just arrived from Amroha. He's a fine poet, his pen name is Mushafi. He was keen to touch the frame of your Prosperous Door.'

'Very well.' Now there wasn't the faintest grace of warmth in her voice. She didn't look at my face, nor did she let on by gesture or phrase that we'd met just yesterday and I'd been asked to come here.

I bent low in salaam. She said: 'I submit my respects. Please seat your noble self.' Then she turned to other guests. In the meantime, a maid had brought in a silver tray with betel cones and small nosegays. I was going to put out my hand when Hakim sahib nudged me with his elbow. My God, I was supposed to put something in the tray before picking up the cone or nosegay! God, oh my God, Hakim sahib's money was meant for this purpose. And if I'd spent the whole two half mohurs! I was drenched in sweat, as if someone had poured a whole pitcher of water on me.

With some difficulty, I pushed my hand into my pocket, brought up the measly half mohur, put it in the tray, and picked up a cone with almost trembling fingers, fearing all the time that I might commit the unpardonable sin of dropping the cone on the carpet.

Hakim sahib too presented some offering, but very discreetly. I couldn't guess what it could have been. Salaaming everyone and accepting the greetings of all, Ismat Jahan began to sing. It was a ghazal from Amir Khusrau:

Praise be to the Maker, how expertly and deftly He painted
Such a form from mere earth and water!
It would never be bright enough like your beauty
If the sun were a guest at your assembly.

Can you imagine my folly, my naivety? I actually assumed that the ghazal was sung in praise of *my* good looks, or to express joy at *my* arrival there! I smiled to myself, and worse still, smiled at her, in token of my appreciation. She made a half smile occasionally, as some singers do. But I was quite certain that she was reciprocating my smiles.

There followed another ghazal, and then the assembly came to its end. Everyone stood, made formal salutations to Ismat Jahan and to their acquaintances, and made for the door. Hakim sahib rose, so did I. But I stood, rooted there. Surely she'd have something to say to me. Another invitation, at least. Or perhaps she was in a flirtatious mood and wanted to enjoy that mood in my company? Hakim sahib was clearly uncomfortable at my loutish delay, and made to leave a number of times. He even looked at me from the corner of his eye. Ismat Jahan salaamed him for a second time. There couldn't be a clearer dismissal. But I stood, until Hakim sahib caught me hard by the elbow and practically shoved me along.

Ismat Jahan turned to go in. And a young merchant, practically coated over with gold and loaded with pearl and diamond, followed her inside with an almost proprietary air. He obviously intended to stay the night.

I burnt with rage and felt sweaty all over with shame. It seemed to me that my clothes would catch fire instantly and my sweat would steam away into the air. I beg forgiveness from God. Such strumpetly conduct, and such cold lack of care for me! How I wished the earth would open and I would disappear down that hole.

We returned. Neither of us spoke. I was fighting my burning pain and hurt. Hakim sahib was quietly aware of my state of mind:

How could Mushafi recover from his burning madness?
His brain boils and sputters like a pot over the fire.

Hakim sahib broke the silence after he reached me home in his palanquin. As I alighted from the palanquin, he said: 'Mian Mushafi, enjoy this verse from Raja Chandar Bhan Brahman, and eject and reject everything else:

The merchandise of your beauty sells in a strange bazaar
None can get it and a whole world is the buyer!

'Right, goodbye. You'll come for the mushaira at my house the day after, won't you?'

Hakim sahib clearly meant that even that filthy rich merchant prince wouldn't enjoy her for any length of time. I should be among the buyers, but not actually aspire to get her.

'Yes, surely,' I could articulate with some difficulty, my voice like a lamp that had just gone out, leaving a little wick which would glow weakly for just another moment.

11

God bless him and forgive his sins, what an excellent word of advice Hakim Qasim sahib gave me. How I wish I had listened to him. But, hai, what station of love it was from where Mirza Jalal Asir, the Iranian poet and nobleman, wrote:

How could one tell the heart not to be in love?
Granted that the heart would listen, but what should one say?

I tried to put my pain into words in a ghazal:

If there was a peri before me, I would not look at her
Please close my eyes, so that I may see no one else.
The love-blood that fires the heart, has been poured in my body
I should at least look at the red rose, if I don't see the little buds.
She in whom my heart inheres, she who has taken my life
How can my life go on, if I don't see her?
My life is because of you, you're my liver, my heart
Looking at whom should I live then, if I don't see you?

I made it a practice to visit there. Very often, I couldn't get admittance, and when I did, it was always in public assembly. And the same episode would prick my eyes like a needle at the end of every assembly: some young merchant, some nobleman's son, some Maratha chieftain, would follow her into the inner chamber. As much as I could manage, I brought small presents, but she never looked at me, far less at my baubles. If I was lucky someday, she would command me to recite a ghazal, or compose something extempore to suit a particular occasion, like the sighting of a new moon. Those things weren't any problem for me. My verses, though, weren't always ennobled with her praise.

If not every day, I'd visit every third or fourth day, witness the play of harlotry and come away firmly convinced that I won't visit again. But I beg God's pardon that I didn't stick to my proud resolve for more than three or four days. The longest gaps were when she was out of town.

Two years, two and a half years, passed in this fashion. During this time, which wasn't too bad for me as poet, but barren in the sense of getting gainful employment, there was just one occasion when I was granted something more than a marginal hanger-on's status. Once, and just once, was I permitted to come close enough and get a small sip from the ocean of pleasure, that river of honey and song which I was still deluded enough to believe was my ultima Thule.

I'd purposely delayed making my departure—as I did as often as I could. She was to go out somewhere, and quite by chance she followed me down on the silent stairs. Her entourage was still to make an appearance. She paused, looked at me with some interest, as if waiting to see if I approached near. I trembled up the two stairs that separated us and hugged her as if clinging to her for dear life. I felt her breast crushed against me, I kissed her lips, I touched her back and tried to caress her hips as I made an attempt to insert my tongue in her mouth. But I was repulsed, almost pushed aside and down the stairs. I looked at her face, trying to espy a tremor of desire, a ray of encouragement. But there was no expression there.

I stumbled my way down in a blind haze, quite forgetting the absence of any sign of approval or invitation on that imperial, imperious face. I knew now that I was the chosen one. I knew I had the road open to me, right up to her bedroom.

Oh, the magic thrill of that embrace, the hot sherbet of enjoyment that flowed from her lips! I lived, and relived, those moments over and over again a thousand times, without satiety, without boredom. I'd break those few moments into a hundred parts and enjoy each part separately. Now I was imagining her look as I was two steps down from her; now I recreated my trembling steps which ended extremely quickly in a whirlwind of hugging and crushing and holding and touching. I relived each part separately. Then, sometimes I thought I'd missed one step, one stage in re-enacting the scene, and would begin all over again.

I even remembered with pleasure my caressing her back, my trying to travel down her long braid like a rope, rappelling down to her hips and buttocks, and how rudely was my hand shaken off. I knew even then that she desired those things, but in privacy. I remembered the glow on her face, the white flash of her neck, the brow crowded with impudent tresses, the moon from behind the cloud. I thought on all this for so long and so much that the journey of a couple of steps became as long as the longest night of separation.

I went away for three, four days. I had hopes of employment with a noble in the employ of Mahada ji Sindhia and he'd ordered me to accompany him to Kol, ninety miles away, where Mahada ji had his headquarters. Returning late at night, I lost no time in presenting myself a little before the appointed hour of her music session.

I was informed that she was gone away somewhere. Kunwar Mahindar Kishor, the son of Raja Jugal Kishor, was her escort.

'Where did she go? And why?'

'How are you concerned with the why and wherefore of it, Shaikh ji?' the Abyssinian sneered. 'And as far as where is concerned, it is some place called Sultanpur, beyond Qutub Sahib. There's a lake there. The idea is to enjoy boating and a little bit of shooting for the water game there.'

'When will they return?'

'Well, something like five, seven days. The great ones do what they like. And who are you to be showing curiosity about these matters? Now get a move on. Get.'

Seething with anger is not the phrase I wanted. No words could come near to describing how I felt. And greater perhaps than the damage to my pride, or indignation at what I saw as her unfaithfulness, my worst tormenter was ethical and religious indignation. Imagine, I who never had observed any of the rituals and practices of my religion, and who certainly had broken many of its commandments, was angry at her for being immoral! I'd forgiven her all her immoralities, all her shameless harlotry, her giving herself to people for money—I'd rationalized everything, was prepared to countenance all her past flaws. But to behave with the same sacrilegious contumely as before was something I coud never forgive. I'd expected her to behave, more or less like sharif Muslim women now that she'd become mine.

She, in the arms of that uncouth young man, sharing her bed with him, I couldn't take that from her, from anyone.

I returned to my hovel, making many different vows, each direr than the other. Worse still, I composed a rubai, assailing Ismat with abuse and reviling her. Making a wordplay on the word *ismat*, which means 'chastity', I wrote:

Is it not a matter of sadness that with a beauty of a houri
Ismat should indulge in sinful transgressions?
Mushafi, it's quite like the saying:
The Abyssinian is called Mr Camphor!

I was unlocking the chain on my door when I saw Hakim Sanaullah Firaq; he'd come calling on me. My love for Ismat Jahan—or infatuation, if you would have it that way—wasn't much of a secret. I welcomed him in, and before even offering a betel cone, I recited my rubai, placing the poor man in a dire quandary. Praising the rubai was as bad as dispraising it. Still, he had no choice but to admire the witticism in the last line which is a Persian line from a rubai, but is used as a dictum or apophthegm; the other three lines nobody remembers, actually.

I committed folly upon folly. I didn't desist saying the scurrilous rubai to anyone whom I met over the next few days. It was Delhi, you know. Scandals, rumours, poems, especially cruel and abusive poems, were enjoyed more than the choicest foods and tobaccos. Above all, there were quite many in Delhi who had been spurned by Ismat Jahan, or who had lost their all for her sake, but had still been kicked with disdain from her company. They took vicarious revenge on her by publishing the poem far and wide. And it wasn't just revenge: it was my fate being sealed with Ismat Jahan every time the rubai was recited.

So, I waited and fumed for many days before I had news of her return. I shouldn't have gone there. It was impossible that she didn't hear about me in Sultanpur—it wasn't all that far, but I, stupid young fool from Amroha that I was, I presented myself at her haveli at the usual time of public assembly.

There seemed to be rather more than the usual rush there, all affluent and far better known than I. Ismat Jahan, perhaps paying heed to the larger crowd that day, promptly made her appearance. She, who barely looked at me, if at all, recognized me instantly, and said: 'Please to come, the High Portal Shaikh Ghulam Hamadani Mushafi, from Amroha!'

There was something very wrong, but I could say nothing. I had my eyes firmly on my feet. How ill formed and dirt crusted they seemed! She went on: 'Please command, your poetry is brightening day by day, we hear.'

We hear! Could there be anything more ominous? I croaked like a starving toad: 'Yes, madam. You are very kind.'

'And this rubai is an instance of the Portal's miraculously composed poetry?'

I looked up. She had a paper in her hand, and I could see my cursed rubai clearly inscribed on it. How I hated to be a poet. I would have preferred to be a street sweeper.

'Madam? I don't understand.'

'Well, is this rubai which ends "The Abyssinian is called Mr Camphor" your composition of excellence?'

By that time, everyone, even her black cat, had eyes and ears for me alone. I was wordless.

Suddenly, with a savage movement of fingers and hands, she tore up the paper, and then crushed the poor scraps under her foot. And then she rubbed her foot upon the carpet. Was it further to derogate and censure those puny pieces, or to cleanse the sole of her shoe, I couldn't say then, or now. But she was speaking to me: 'Now go back to the hole from which you came out head first. I shouldn't see you around here from now.'

The world was dark in my eyes anyway, worse still was the hurt of humiliation and loss of honour. And the matter wasn't remediable either, by any means at all. I stood, silent, unmoving, as if I'd been turned to stone. Suddenly, someone coughed behind me. I didn't have the power to turn and look, but it seemed to me that someone had coughed to suppress or disguise a snicker.

I turned, like a blind man who'd lost his stick. Thank God I reached the door without walking into someone or stumbling. As I reached the door, that cursed door, I wished I never saw it. I was about to push aside the curtain when someone pulled my sleeve from behind. I started and turned to see. It was that very maid whose eyes were black as bumble bees: 'Bibi ji says that there'll be Abyssinians and Telangas at both ends of the street watching for you.'

I didn't know if she spoke with pity or contumely, but the message was clear enough. I said to my heart bitterly: not just that little alley, the whole surface of the earth is closed for me.

I lived in Delhi for many years after my exile from paradise, but never again could I set eyes on Ismat Jahan. I sent numerous messages,

447

letters, poems of apology through different intermediaries, but no reply came. It was as if I were a stain on her wall, which she had had scraped off by an iron implement.

The days would pass one way or another, but my nights were always a torment; her memory shook me nightly like a fever that never abated. I slept fitfully, but upon awakening, the name Ismat was on my lips. The days were slightly better, but there was no lack of occasions to remind me of her and of my few moments with her, and the features of her body and face, which were like a die stamped upon my heart which didn't let the impression fade. I was a proud man once, proud of my manness: I used to say that there could be no sorrow in love which a man would be unable to get over, to resist the flow of time from becoming a river of regret. Now I knew better. Now I knew how well Mirza Sauda sahib had commanded:

Oh heart, didn't I tell you not to let love inscribe its scar on you?
Did not that one scar ultimately bloom into a red rose-garden?

But I was right, in a way. Once we get used to weeping, then weeping and singing lose their separate sense. Much later, I composed the following verse, trying to tell the world the true end of the story of love:

Love squeezed my heart, so much
That, not to speak of blood, even the colour of desire didn't remain in it.

12

'You made no mention of the differences between the Presence Shaikh sahib and Sayyid Insha,' I once observed during one of our conversations.

'What could I tell you about those things? I wasn't with Shaikh sahib in those days. Whatever happened was quite repugnant to Shaikh sahib's temperament. But I believe Sayyid Insha too didn't feel that he should be congratulated for what happened between them.'

'But they never made up formally.'

'No, but the old enmity disappeared. You'll recall that the Presence, Minister of all Territories, Asif-ud Daulah, whose station now is in the Paradise of Eden, responded to Shaikh sahib's plaints and dealt justice to both. He banished Sayyid Insha sahib from Lucknow. There didn't pass much time on this when Maula recalled the Presence, Minister of all Territories. Then Sayyid sahib returned happily and resumed his home here.'

'They must have been meeting frequently, or going to the same mushairas and assemblies?'

'I don't remember any such occasion, but I didn't necessarily know where Shaikh sahib went or with whom he spent his time. Yet I do remember a verse of Shaikh sahib's deploring the deaths of Insha sahib and Qateel sahib:

Mushafi, how could I be happy with my continued life?
Don't I remember the deaths of Qateel and Insha?'

'What was the reason, or the foundation for differences developing between the Presence, Shaikh sahib and Sayyid sahib? Didn't you tell me once that Shaikh sahib had the knack of winning over anyone, as if he knew the mohini mantra?'

She reddened. 'I don't say this of everyone,' she smiled, blushing still. 'But he was able to cast his spell quickly on those he desired to . . . love.'

'Who was closer to Shaikh sahib's heart? Sayyid Insha or Mirza Qateel?'

'I think he was a little irked with Insha sahib's desire for everyone to praise him and like him. I remember someone talking at Zafar-ud Daulah's about Insha sahib. He said, Insha sahib desires everybody to have nothing but admiration for him. Then he quoted a verse of Insha sahib's which went:

If you felt a little offended that I said you are beautiful, and elegant
Then please don't mind, look at me. So let me be beautiful and elegant!'

She concluded, 'I believe it was quite true that Insha sahib was a great admirer of his own talents, and maybe even his good, manly looks.'

'Was this because Sayyid sahib had some problem with himself?' I ventured.

'I don't know these things,' she said with a hint of pique.

I was abashed. I had no reason to go into matters which could be of no real meaning to me, or to her. I was concerned with facts. Still, I made another foray into the unknown. 'I sometimes feel that Shaikh sahib was much more open-minded in regard to the non-Muslims. He looked for merit, not parentage.'

'You don't understand, Lal Mian,' there was a hint of admonishment in her tone, 'in those days and among those people, there was no special feeling about being Muslim or non-Muslim. They were people first, scholarly people, poets, artists. It didn't matter if Mirza Qateel was a convert from Hindu to Muslim. It didn't matter that Tika Ram Tasalli or your own father were Hindu.'

'I beg your forgiveness, but I wasn't talking in terms of religion.'

'Then what was your context? Why bring up things that couldn't be there?'

'No, madam, I shouldn't have spoken thus.'

'Shaikh sahib wrote a panegyric in praise of Tika Ram Tasalli, who was his pupil, not his patron,' she went on, as if I hadn't spoken.

'Yes, madam.' I was still penitent.

'And he treated your father as his own son.'

'Actually, I expressed myself wrongly, ma'am. I meant that Shaikh sahib was extremely open-minded, and in fact believed in the unity of all religions.'

'Yes, you may be right there. Also, he practised no religion in a formal, ritualistic sense; he did believe quite firmly that all human beings and their beliefs came from one source. You may call it a Sufistic idea if you wish. But he was no Sufi either. He wrote a beautiful verse once, stating clearly what he believed.'

She then recited, almost sang in an undertone, the following verse:

Differences of faith and religion robbed it of all the purity,
Otherwise, in fact, there were a hundred pitchers, but the water was
drawn from the same river, upon the same bank.

'As Allah Wills!' I exclaimed. 'Only God is above all blemish! What a wise and extraordinary thing to say, and what a beautiful way of saying it!'

'Yes, it is from his seventh divan.'

'Praise be to God, you loved him and his poetry too!'

She reddened. At that time she looked inexpressibly sweet, in fact, desirable. I changed tack hastily: 'I think I am right in saying that he bore no malice towards anyone.'

'Yes, quite. He once wrote a panegyric in praise of the Presence Ali, Peace and Salutations be upon him. He wrote two verses in it which give an indication of his true nature. He said:

I am not sorry if I praise myself
But my poetic temperament should never oblige me to satirize anyone.
The reason why the elders viewed personal satire with disfavour
Is that even words can cause hurt.

I made bold to say: 'But he must have, at some time or other, been displeased with you?'

'The truth is that it did happen, once or twice, but only for a tiny moment or two.' She smiled a shy, somewhat abashed smile. 'Once, though, he was angry with me for almost a whole day.'

'Arey wallah!' I exclaimed. 'Really? But why, and when?' In my eagerness to probe I forgot to observe the first rule: do not show any undue curiosity.

Apparently, she didn't notice my transgression, but she didn't let me go on. 'Some other time, maybe,' she said, without any suggestion of evasion. 'Right now, I will tell you about certain of God's creatures whom he wholeheartedly disliked, with no let-up ever.'

I almost held my breath and spoke after a beat or two. 'Oh, and you haven't mentioned him yet!'

She laughed, a genuine, open laugh, not a guffaw, but a friendly, slightly coquettish laugh as a girl would with another. 'Not him, them,' said she, trying to check her laughter.

'I'm sorry, I don't understand.'

She took a small sip of water, organized herself, and spoke in a normal voice. 'The Firangis. The Firangis were his pet aversion.'

'How did that happen?' I exclaimed. 'Was there something special about the Firangis? There weren't many Firangis around in those days, were they?'

'What do you mean by something special?' she replied stiffly. 'If you mean that he gave away his heart to one of those blue-eyed red-faced ones—death take them—who are free with all men and, yet, Shaikh sahib didn't succeed with her, you are very wrong.'

I'd done it again. I should keep a sensible tongue in my mouth, I rebuked myself in my heart.

'No, not at all, ma'am. I am sorry I didn't choose the best words. All I meant was if some Firangi pupil had displeased him somehow.'

'Why should he then despise the entire nation of the Firangi, Lal Mian?'

She was still miffed with me, but continued in a more even tone. 'No, please understand me. He disliked the Firangis as interlopers in our land. He didn't like their military tactics which he saw as based on fraud more than anything else like military superiority. He wrote a verse towards the very end of his life.'

She recited:

How well these Christians know perfidy and machination,
Before the start of fighting, they always bribe their opponents'
commander to desert their master and come over to their side.

'This, it seems to me,' she continued, 'was what he must have observed over a lifetime. He didn't like their looks, and in fact he wasn't alone in this. Shaikh Nasikh sahib also has verses derogating the skin colour of the Firangi women. Shaikh sahib regarded their colour as unattractive, insipid. He said it forcefully in a verse which goes like this:

I just cannot like a beauty so insipid
What can I say, how devoid of taste is the colour of the Nazarene people!

'Wah, wah,' I said, 'how apt, but how courageous to speak so disparagingly of the race which was hot in pursuit of power all over Hind and Deccan. But I recall something else in that context: what is a "biskut"?'

Then I recited the following verse from Shaikh sahib:

The mean sky, like a Firangi, devoid of colour
Has just two biskuts, called 'sun', and 'moon'.

She laughed with pleasure. 'What a delightful verse! It took a person like Shaikh sahib to compose such a theme, and so well. Actually, a "biskut" is something which the Firangi calls "biskote", or more commonly, "biskit". Our "biskut" derives from the former. These are round, thick tablets, fairly large, and lightly scented. Sweet or salt, they are eaten at breakfast or teatime.'

'Indeed. So Shaikh sahib liked them?'

'No, he was just using a new theme. The sun and the moon are insipid things, he says, practically useless, like the Firangi biskut, because one can't fill one's belly with them. The sky is the traditional enemy in Hindi poetry: unsympathetic, even cruel.'

'An excellent verse, and you explain it so well. It is by your ascendant good fortune that these things are made easy for me!'

'I think what Shaikh sahib resented most was the Firangi's looting the wealth of Hind, his dispossessing or draining away the power of our kings and rulers, and the pride and the hauteur of the Firangi, bordering on insolence. They believe that they are superior to us in every way, even in religion.'

I quite agreed. In fact, I could myself think of many verses from Shaikh sahib on those themes. I said to her one or two of them:

Whatever wealth, whatever splendour there was in Hindustan
Was drawn out by the infidel Firangi through his schemes.
*

I'll be persuaded that they can challenge Muhammad's Way
Only when I see their faces rosy pink on Judgement Day.

She smiled with pleasure, and also maybe with approval of my choice, because she'd just described the Firangi women as red-faced. We Hindis didn't really like the florid faces of the Firangi, but in Rekhta 'to have one's face red' means 'to be successful, to be honoured'. So, Shaikh sahib had made a marvellous wordplay there.

'Now please narrate to me the matter when Shaikh sahib was angry . . .'

She interrupted me. It was a rare occasion for her to do so. She said: 'Some other time, please. I don't feel too well today. I'll tell you the whole story, I assure you.'

13

As I made my way to her puny home for my next visit, I scolded myself in my heart for being so importunate to know the story of grandfather ustad sahib's displeasure with her. Perhaps it was something too personal to be revealed to me? I shouldn't have been so childishly reckless. I decided that this time I won't raise that question at all.

I found her actually unwell. Muhammad Raja said that she 'had pains' in her body. I didn't quite understand. Was it a fever? Or the onset of lumbago? Living as she did in an extremely damp place, lumbago wasn't out of the question. She lay in bed, her head wrapped in some cloth, like a bandage. Her face was drawn, with the shadow of the lack of sleep in her eyes.

I asked, 'What is the problem, ma'am? Did you consult some hakim?'

'No. I am sorry, but it's not a matter for the hakim. I have these pains regularly. Not to worry, I'll get well soon. Tell me your news, Lal Mian sahib, how's the business these days?'

'Oh, the business is perfectly well. But I don't want to see you unwell. Let me send Muhammad Raja to the hakim.'

'It's nothing at all. I have . . . I have them regularly. Come, let me order some tea for you.'

Stupid dolt that I was, it dawned upon me only now that she must be having the time of the month. No wonder she was so reticent about it. Thank God I didn't press her more, though such follies were not unknown from me where she was concerned.

I looked at her face somewhat intently. She was clearly in pain, but somehow she didn't look her age now. She looked younger. Or I must have judged her age wrongly when we came face-to-face for the first time. Or she was one of those women who remained fertile longer than usual. I rose in some confusion. 'I'm sorry. I'll go away now and trouble you later. I didn't know . . .'

'Please stay, Lal Mian sahib. I'll order tea from Rakab Ganj for you. Muhammad Raja will bring it in a jiffy. They make good tea there. Let him prepare the hookah in a minute. I'll share the hookah and the tea with you.'

'Since when did you develop a taste for tea, may I know?' I spoke hesitantly, for fear of offending her again, but the fact was that very few women drank tea those days, so it was proper to ask her a question or two about it.

'Actually, Shaikh sahib learnt to drink it when he was in Delhi. He preferred coffee for himself actually, but said that tea was good for the headache and the . . . cramps, you know.'

Muhammad Raja brought tea in a glass flask, or wide-mouthed bottle, wrapped thickly in a towel to keep it warm. I didn't think much of it, for it was what they called Kashmiri Tea in Lucknow. Very thin of texture, milky-sweet, and flavoured with saffron. We in Bihar drank stronger tea. I believe the less affluent used some spice, like cinnamon, instead of the saffron.

'So the Presence, grandfather ustad was mindful of all your needs though his circumstances were sometimes rather straitened.'

'He wasn't indigent, but not affluent either. Occasionally, he would be rather hard up, but it didn't prevent him from being generous. He always said, "Give, so that you may be given." I sometimes quarrelled a little with this doctrine, but yes, essentially he took good enough care of me, and he never turned anyone down, far less me.'

'So it's not true, what some say, that he was sometimes obliged to sell his poems for money?'

I could see her face tighten, and realized that I had let my tongue run away with me yet again. In no time she flared up; throwing off her chador and shawl, uncaring even to cover her upper body, she sat up straight, the pains forgotten. She cried: 'I say let the two-mouthed rope sting them in their graves, those who say such scurrilities. Maula shall certainly direct his ire at them. Let them confront me, those misfortunate ones who say his poems of the last years were sold for money!'

I rose and folded my hands in submission. 'I am truly sorry. Ustani sahib, please believe me I meant no ill. I just mentioned something I heard from the vulgar tongues.'

She wiped her tears with the back of her hand. 'Let them burn in a furnace, those idle gossipers in the bazaar! Please listen to me attentively, sir. He certainly stopped going out after the bitter episode with Sayyid Insha, but he never stopped writing. How could he not? Poetry was the breath of his life. And he never lacked for money, and he never ever asked for payment from those to whom he gave away his verses sometimes to encourage them.'

'I am sorry. Please. Let it go now. Please forgive me.'

But she didn't hear. She was speaking as if dictating an important statement to someone, loudly and clearly, so that there should be no mistake.

'He was a person of great kindness of heart and purity of mind. He didn't conceal or play down his preferences. There was none, there *can* be none to match him in giving regard and attention to his juniors and paying respect to his seniors. He could give away a whole ghazal to some pupil if he praised it somewhat more enthusiastically than usual. If someone gave him money, he didn't refuse it, but he didn't expect it, far less ask for it. He used to say that it was a true Sufi who didn't expect, but didn't refuse a gift.'

She stopped for breath, and then before I could insert a word in edgeways, she went on: 'I will have you know, sir, that everyone loves their children. He had no children, but always said that his poems were his true children in spirit. He would never let go casually or for money anything that he wrote. Does anyone let go of their children? And if some pupil put a rupee or two at his feet as a token of gratitude, was it selling his poetry for money?"

'No, certainly not, ma'am.'

'Then from whom did you buy that trash about Shaikh sahib selling his poems? And do you think his creativity could be blocked even if he was obliged to sell his poems? He wrote a whole divan in Persian in reply to Naziri's divan during his days of reclusiveness. He wrote a prose narrative in Persian. He finished yet another divan in Persian. And all this during those four or five years. So you think he sold off all that?'

'Please. Forget this mistake. It was just that. A foolish mistake. I'll always remain ashamed that I brought such words to my lips.'

Her temper was cooling now, a little bit. She drew a sigh. 'Look, Lal Mian sahib, you are as my child, according to the relation, if not according to my age. Shaikh sahib was such a generous man that he would give away the clothes on his body if someone approached him and if he was really needy. He wrote:

Mushafi is such a man, that if he were short of money, ever
He would pay his servant with his whole Divan.

'Wallah, what power of expression, and what generosity of nature!'
'Not just that, Lal Mian, you don't notice that he would *always* have a manservant, even if he was poor. He lived in style. He wasn't like those puny poetasters who look to their patron for the day's bread.'
'Madam, I quite understand. But I am new to these parts and don't really know the literary and social mores here. That's why I said that foolish word. I hope I am forgiven.'
She was now her usual, soft-spoken, low-voiced self. 'Shaikh sahib wrote a small account of his family and its traditions. He called it *Majma-ul Favaid* (Collection of Useful Points). It's in Persian. During the time he was composing that little book, he wrote a ghazal in which he put in subjects and themes that were . . . well, unorthodox, if not contrary to religion.'
She'd now brought up not one, but two new things which I felt I must know about if I really wanted to write about Shaikh sahib. But I wasn't sure how to phrase my questions. She had just been seriously offended by me; I should now put every foot forward with the greatest care. But inquire I must. So I said somewhat casually: 'I haven't seen the *Majma-ul Favaid*. In fact, I believe no one has.'
'I have his manuscript and could lend it to you.' She smiled an apologetic smile before proceeding, 'Though I'd prefer that you read it here. It's a small book, actually.'
'Very well, ma'am, I'm deeply obliged. I'll trouble you about it someday soon.'

'Thank you, Lal Mian sahib, I will be always bounden to you for your consideration.'

She fell into thought, or maybe she was weighing her next words in her brain. I didn't want to hurry her, avid though I was to hear more about her or Shaikh sahib.

'There isn't much about Sahib's beliefs in *Majma-ul Favaid*, in fact, it reads like a romance. But it reveals Shaikh sahib's pride in his ancestry. He seems to have developed his ideas about God, and religion, and the destiny of man much later in life.'

'One could say his experience of the world taught him many things?' I hazarded.

'Yes, but I also believe that he was a hakim, a man of thought in his own right. He didn't like to accept things blindly. I remember he often said to me, "Bhoora begam, the Ultimate Reality, the Greatest Reality, is Man." I would be worried sick at such obviously irreverent words. "What is it that you say?" I would cry in distress. "Allah, His Prophet, the Quran, the Imams, the Day of Judgement—all these are nothing? Is that what you say?" He would smile and reply, "Dear Begam sahib, I don't speak from the point of view of the Books and what's inscribed in them. I talk the language of Reason." I would cry, "Please, do please leave these matters to Imam Ali sahib and his followers, his interpreters. We aren't supposed to obey the voice of Reason. We must obey the voice of our Faith!"'

I wasn't a devout Hindu, or a devout anything, except a student trying to understand my hero, one of the greatest poets of Hind. I did follow the usual rites and customs, some of them clearly modelled on the practice of Muslims, many of the rest handed down from generation to generation over centuries. Having a competent and pious pandit to do the prayers and services was enough religion for me. As I heard Bhoora begam talk of Shaikh sahib's belief in Reason and not, presumably, scripture, I was unsure about what I should do. If I agreed with Shaikh sahib's ideas as recounted by his wife, I might end up offending her for she was a devout Shia Muslim herself, whatever her origins. And

I also didn't wish to start an argument with her. For once, I held my tongue. She went on: 'It was the peak of summer. The night hadn't cooled the air, and the walls and ceiling were still almost smoking. We lay in the courtyard, Shaikh sahib on his cot and I on mine. Neither of us could sleep. The air was alive with the mosquitoes and the bed was crawling with bedbugs. Shaikh sahib had a hand fan with which he was fanning me. I had on a very loose, short pair of trousers, made of the perspiration-absorbent coarse cotton cloth called *susi*. My tunic was actually a muslin choli, very short, though not loose. One of the pants legs was rucked up in my efforts to combat the bedbugs. Now with his vigorous fanning, the other one also blew up, revealing much of my legs and thighs. Before I could pull the trousers down, Shaikh sahib smiled and spoke a verse; he must have composed it at the spur of the moment:

> *Well, at least there was a whole bazaar of beauty open before me*
> *I am grateful to the bedbugs for keeping me awake.*

I couldn't help smiling with pleasure. Only a poet of Mushafi's calibre and creativity could bring bedbugs into a ghazal. But the subject, the lady herself, was before me, so I couldn't very well admire it openly.

'Indeed. Very interesting!' I said somewhat non-committally.

Bhoora begam continued: 'I said, "Go on with you, sir! You can make poetry from bedbugs, perhaps you can teach them poetry too! But do something for the heat of the night, worse than that of the day!" Quite late, I fell into a warm, uneasy slumber. I'd wake up from time to time and see Shaikh sahib writing something. This wasn't unusual. And it must be the ghazal whose one verse he'd said to me earlier in the night, I thought.'

'And was it the same ghazal?'

'No, to my misfortune. It was something quite different. Eighteen verses in all, of which seven were in the qita form, which is continuous, like a narrative or argument. And it was quite . . . quite shocking.'

Shocking? I was piqued. Hey, was it something obscene or pornographic? I'd heard say somewhere that all the ustads wrote some pornography on the sly, for the delectation of themselves and their friends. Occasional obscenity in humour or satire was of course nothing new. But Shaikh sahib never wrote a satire on any one, I knew.

She seemed to have some difficulty in going on. I made to rise and say, 'Let's postpone the account for some other day. I don't want you to tire any more. You've been talking for some while.'

'No. Please don't go away, Lal Mian. I might not have the strength next time. I'd extracted the paper from under his pillow as he slept. I read it and it seemed that if someone cut me, I would not bleed. All my blood seemed to congeal.'

She called Muhammad Raja to bring back a paper folded inside a small purse in her box. When Muhammad Raja brought it to her, I saw it was a half sheet of thin paper, yellowing and with faint black handwriting on it.

She began to read a poem from the paper:

One night, I travelled farther even than the caravan of human tears
Searching everywhere to find Nonspace.
Suddenly, an angel from the Unapparent called out,
Young man, what are you doing here, wandering from place to place?
I said: I looked for the House of the Maker of all creatures everywhere
     in the lower world.
Finally, I was given the clue to go to the Heights of His Throne,
But my heart asked me: Did you really reach your True goal at all?
Your bravery was your guide and brought you here,
But let someone tell you now: Where is His Dwelling, his Trace?
Displeased, the Angel said: You have no sense, no understanding;
Why look vainly for Nonspace? Where is Nonspace?
Go, excurse the realm of the physical bodies, in the world of the living:
There, you shall find the Dwelling and the Sign. There is no Sign, no
     Dwelling here.

461

She fell silent. The poem was obviously finished. Perhaps she expected me to comment? Or was she looking for words herself? Timidly, but with clear enunciation, I began: 'Ustani begam, it doesn't lie in my mouth to comment on the poem, or on the subject. But it seems to me a clear declaration of some sort . . .' My voice trailed off.

'Not some sort,' she said gravely. 'At that time at least, it struck me as a clear declaration of irreligion.'

'I wouldn't go that far, ma'am,' I said, equally grave. 'I should say that he places matter above the soul, or believes the service of man to be the true service of God. God lives here, in our hearts, not in some non-human space. That can be treated as a Sufistic doctrine, not irreligion. He uses the word *la makan*, which is often taken to mean "the place where God dwells". And he says *nishan*, which also means, "dwelling, abode".'

'These are rationalist constructions, Lal Mian sahib. The maulavis would never fall for such meanings. I feared for him. I feared that the strict maulavis, Sunni or Shia, would condemn him as Godless, as anti-Islam. Just look at the sheer power of his poetic utterance. The words speak for themselves.'

'Sure. But he is a powerful poet. And essentially, all such things are taken under the umbrella of "creation of theme". And that is a legitimate poetic practice.'

'I don't know. This is not just poetry, or creation of theme. He is denying . . . denying the existence of God. I was so fearful, and angry then.'

Again, I was about to rise and end this sorry account, at least for now. But she gestured for me to stay. She asked Muhammad Raja to bring her some water, which she drank slowly, deliberately. But her eyes began to flow.

'I don't know what devil of misfortune came to possess me that night. I was absolutely determined in my mind: I must save him from the opprobrium of the maulavis and the fires of hell.'

'I won't say it was some "devil". I would say you believed it to be

462

your duty. And Shaikh sahib's safety and welfare and always wishing him well, that was your first duty, I think.'

'Yes,' said she. 'Or maybe not. I should have trusted him to know better. I shouldn't have done what I did. It was quite disproportionate.'

She put her hand into a box which Muhammad Raja had just brought to her. When she took her hand out, I saw two separate scraps of paper, with extremely refined handwriting in the *shikasta* mode . . . Was it the original draft, and had she torn it into two?

I ventured. 'Is this the handwriting of the Presence, Shaikh sahib?'

'Yes.' Now she was unable to speak further. She nodded, and waved the paper's two halves.

God, my God! A poet, and so proud and intellectually profound a poet as Shaikh sahib, he sees his own paper disrespected thus? Would he permit anyone, but anyone, to do this?

'I had the paper in my hand when he woke. Not waiting even for a moment, I spoke loudly, almost as if I were admonishing him. "What is this that you have written here? Don't you fear God?" I upbraided him, I railed at him, reproaching him for endangering his and my own religion, pushing us towards eternal perdition. Shaikh sahib didn't show anger at me. He just said, "Bhoora begam, you had no right to do what you did. And it doesn't behove you to sit in judgement upon me, to be the censor over my poetry. I believe Man to be all and everything. Our Prophet, let my life be sacrificed for him, was he not human?"

'I interrupted him rudely: "I know not these niceties. For me, it is Allah's Prophet, and after him, the Imam. I don't want to know more." And . . . and I ripped his ghazal into two and threw the pieces, almost at him.'

'Oh, *inna li'llahi wa inna ilahi rajiun!*' I ejaculated. 'Truly we belong to Allah and to Him we return. That was very bad, really.'

She said sharply: 'For you it was very bad, what do you know of what happened with me then? He said, very gently, "Bhoora begam, you have lost your mind. It's not free from risk to talk to you now."

463

Saying this, he took his cloak from off the clothes' peg, and left, not even bothering to put it on.

'I realized what had happened only when I heard the quick rattle of the door chain. But I still wasn't back in my senses. I thought: Oh, he must have something urgent to do. He'll return presently.'

'So you waited.'

'What else? I couldn't very well follow him out, could I? I waited, and then began to weep loudly when the door chain didn't rattle again. My heart consoled me, convinced me, he'll come back, surely. He cannot have gone away. This is his home . . . But if he didn't return for many days? How will I stay here alone? Surely I don't deserve to be left alone, like this? To be deserted? I'd heard of men deserting their women, married or not. Should I be an exception? Why should I deserve exceptional treatment? Shaikh sahib was my husband, according to my lights. I should have followed him blindly, not challenged him.'

'So did you try to call out for a neighbour, or go out to seek help?'

'Where could I go? We were not prosperous enough to invite guests or go on social visits. In the eyes of the world, I was only a mutahi. Married women disdained to have anything to do with me.'

'But Zafar-ud Daulah Bahadur was there. You must have been going there sometime? And there was Khvajah Atash sahib . . . And there was the manservant, wasn't there one?'

'You don't understand. I needed to go out before I could reach Kaptan sahib. The manservant belonged to a realm outside my zone. Going to an unmarried man like Khvajah sahib without Shaikh sahib's authority would be the greatest folly. And I didn't know how, or where. I couldn't very well walk about the streets, asking for the way from absolute strangers.'

'Yes, I am sorry. I didn't see it clearly. You were practically a prisoner.'

'And at risks of all sorts if Shaikh sahib didn't return soon. I could still not envisage his going away forever. And actually, I'd never suffered harshness or anger from him. So I didn't know what exactly his absence meant.'

'Yes, also, you couldn't leave the house empty, and locked. Shaikh sahib could return while you were away.'

'A few hours passed,' she continued valiantly, though she did now seem to be tiring. 'I began to explain to my heart, look, Bhoora, you were nothing. You could have been killed or sold in prostitution or starved to death. Allah and Maula Ali took away your parents, but they nurtured you, gave you a safe home, food, and even marital stability of a sort. Do you think Maula will forget you now in your hour of distress?

'Then I bathed, put on clean and proper clothes, and began to pray. I thought up as many names as I could remember of saints who are friends to women, and prayed to them one by one to intercede with Allah and Maula Ali on my behalf. I promised to give alms in thanksgiving, vowed to light lamps for forty days in many holy places.'

She paused, perhaps she was reliving those intense moments of piety and prayer. I didn't dare interrupt her. She put her hand into the box again and produced another paper.

'Then I took out a nice blank page from his inkstand, washed off the encrustation of ink from the pen, and wrote this.'

She put out her hand. I took the paper. In a pretty, but rather unformed hand, was written the same ghazal, all eighteen verses of it, the margins justified, all lines straight. Below the last line was inscribed in red, bright even now:

I seek your pardon.

Your maid,
Bhoora

Below it, in a firm and beautiful hand, was the line of verse in black:

Actually, Mushafi was never angry at you.

'So when did he return? You presented this paper to him?'

'I was tired and sleepy, having wept and wailed so much. But I saw that there was some time yet for the prescribed hours of the afternoon prayer to be over. So I stood on this little wooden platform with a prayer mat on it and began to do the prayer.'

'And Shaikh sahib made a sudden entrance?'

'No. I'd bolted the door from inside. Suddenly, I heard the rattle of the door chain, in Shaikh sahib's wonted rhythm. I'd know it in thousands. I stopped my prayer, sprang down and ran. But in my hurry, or maybe due to some rush of blood to the brain, I swayed and fell, and my head struck a corner of the platform, just below the brow.

'I began to bleed. But I got up and ran, opened the door, and fell into his arms. Shaikh sahib saw the blood all over me and construed it another way . . .'

There was the light of a true smile on her face and it was the first time through all these days that I saw such a smile, lighting up her whole being like a lamp. She touched a corner of her brow where I could now see a scar. She passed her hand over the scar caressingly, as if it was her dearest possession in life and the prettiest thing on her face.

14

The years 1539 and 1540 were extremely hard and arduous for the Exalted Presence, Nasiruddin Muhammad Humayun, Padishah of Delhi. His armies suffered defeat after defeat in every important engagement. In the beginning of the year 1540, Sher Khan Suri delivered a crushing defeat to his army numbering more than a hundred thousand, not counting the elephants and horses and guns, at Chausa in Bihar. He not only put the Imperial Army to flight, he pushed it back vigorously up to the river Ganga, and continued his pursuit even across the flooding river.

Sher Khan immediately declared himself King of Hindustan, assuming the title of Sher Shah. He proceeded with his immense army towards Agra and Delhi. In fact, the Imperial forces were not in such disarray as appeared to Sher Khan's spies. Aware of the whereabouts of the Emperor himself, who, after breaking camp at Chausa, was camping at Qannauj many miles away, the Royal armies proceeded there at the double. Loyal chieftains and generals were busy preparing for a final confrontation, reinforcing themselves by conscripting the irregular armies of the navabs and rajas of Oudh, and enlisting the standing forces of similar noblemen in the vast area between Farrukhabad and Kol in the north-west, not too far from Delhi.

The high roads of power for Humayun and Sher Shah were going to be separated soon with Humayun leaving the arena in disgust and defeat. But at that time, Sher Shah was merely Sher Khan in Mughal eyes. Rumours of the decisive-to-be battle at Qannauj had thrown the ryots in confusion. They couldn't decide whether to pay homage and present the golden garland of fealty to the Taimuri Pennant which seemed to be losing its effulgence, or present the flowers of faith to the Suri Rose, which was brightening red with the blood of battle.

Sher Khan had, of late, adopted a new and rather liberal policy which was to have important consequences for governance in Hindustan. Non-Afghan tribes and groups of proven valour and loyalty, who also exhibited clear signs of the ability to lead, were inducted as Afghan. This was executed in an elaborate ceremony, something like the rite of passage, after which the newly accepted chieftain and his horde were accorded a new, Afghan name. These new inductions were not just from the non-Muslim Rajputs, but many Muslim non-Afghans, many Brahmins and Vaishyas were also subject to the rite of passage, subject to their having proven qualities of bravery, loyalty and leadership. Conversion to Islam was not a condition.

When it came to defending Sher Khan, the novitiate Afghans were loyal and strong like walls which had been strengthened by pouring liquid lead in their interstices. Among themselves, though, they hadn't given up their local, sub-tribal prejudices, rivalries and conflicts. The Lohanis, for example, were extremely hot-headed. They looked down upon all, even the Afghans, original or newly admitted. Jalal Khan

Lohani, son to the Sultan of South Bihar, regarded as inferior every other person who was not from his sub-tribe. Sher Khan was his tutor and mentor. He straightened him out in a very short time, and inducted him as a proper Afghan.

The Sarang Khani Afghans were originally of Turkish extraction. They were known as 'Children of the Turk', because many were born to the slaves or maids of the Turks, or were fruits of intermarriage between the slaves. By virtue of their martial qualities, they became de facto Pathans (not Afghans) over the years.

The Farmulis were originally children of the Shaikhs, that is, just one level below the Sayyid. Many were born out of wedlock, and came, over decades and centuries, to be identified with the Pathans.

The Qaim Khanis were originally Rajput. So they were in conflict with everyone, the Farmulis being their favourite aversion, because the Farmuli could trace his ancestry, putatively, to some Shaikh of high standing.

Gradually, Sher Khan knit these broken and disparate pearls of valour and loyalty in one brilliant chain, admitting them, subject to their proving their worth, as true Afghans.

We speak of the time when the Battle of Qannauj was some while away. The Farmulis and Qaim Khanis of Amroha, Sambhal, Hatim Sarai and other population centres were busy in warring out their own conflicts. They didn't want to support the Emperor, but were awaiting an outcome in favour of Sher Khan before throwing in their lot with him.

About thirty miles to the north-west of the ancient town of Amroha is a village called Shaikhpur. The Farmulis ruled the roost here. About six miles to the south-east of Shaikhpur is a smaller village called Manjhavali. Most of the population here was Rajput, and some lesser communities. A narrow dirt road joined the villages. Shaped like an arch, it ran from Shaikhpur to Manjhavali, its peak being the location of a hamlet called Dharaora Malkaoan; none but the Farmuli lived here. There was a yet smaller hamlet, called Akbarpur, a bit off the road, and almost inaccessible in the bad season of the rains. I say 'was' because Akbarpur no longer exists on the face of the earth. All that remains is alkaline land, or dark-grey and desolate scrub, occasionally broken by stunted copses of deep-green and brown palash trees. A somewhat forbidding red appears to explode here in some of the spinneys when the palash bursts into flower with the early rains.

Though we were almost all of us Shaikhs in Akbarpur, the long and violent hand of the Farmuli Afghans kept us in constant terror. There were quarrels day after day, involving the use of staves and swords; false or made-up allegations of wrongful possession of one party's land by the other (mostly us, from Akbarpur), accusations of the Akbarpuris cutting off a mango or rosewood tree, and so forth. Matters could become bloodier if a girl of one clan ran off, or was taken away, by a hot-headed lover from another. Even if the girl had chosen voluntarily, allegations of kidnapping and abduction were bandied about, leading to bloodshed, or the homes of one party set on fire by the other.

We, the children of Shaikhs from Akbarpur, were scholarly types or agriculturists. The Farmuli regarded themselves as masters of sword and cutlass. Well supplied with weapons and manpower, they almost always ended up winner if the dispute between Shaikh and Farmuli turned into organized battle. The state of the land was in turmoil ever since the battle between the Khidev-e Hind the Exalted Portal Nasiruddin Humayun and Sher Khan had been running wild and hot. Even in normal times, there were few who'd hear sympathetically a complaint from a Shaikh-born against a Farmuli.

Shaikh Qavvamuddin was the leader of our community in Akbarpur. Rumour began to circulate one day that the young son of the haughty and almost lawless Bilal Khan of Dharora Malkaoan was found murdered in mysterious circumstances. His headless body was found in a lonely place, but his head was discovered in an almost impassable clump of wild filbert and dark acacia, among dark brown-grey, thick and extremely thorny tall bushes and many smaller shrubs. Now, whether based on the truth (no inquiry had yet been made by any party) or trying to capitalize on the occasion to reduce the Akbarpuris even more, it was strongly bruited about that the murderer was a Shaikh's son from Akbarpur, and the reason was stated as a rivalry between the two for the favours of a young, rather promiscuous shepherdess who lived alone. It was further stated that action from Dharaora Malkaoan would start the next day, after the burial of the young dead was complete.

The pity of it was that Shaikh Qavvmuddin did nothing, even on hearing the reports of his own spies, about the next morning being a time of attack and danger. He did not evacuate any women or children, didn't alert the young men, except in a casual manner. Thus there was no real preparation for what the next day would bring. Worst of all, they didn't commandeer and collect all the grain in the village in anticipation of a siege. Women were busy in cooking and feeding, and the men gathered in a few half-hearted defensive positions.

As the night deepened around us, we saw lights from torches and open flames advancing toward us. Some of us believed they were ghouls or evil spirits, and began to recite whatever prayers they could remember. Some of the braver ones advanced to the limits of the village, only to find that the lights were ominously near and they could descry the glint of weapons in whatever light could reach them.

We decided to retreat, but by the time we even thought of it, our entire village was encircled by harshly burning lights and fully armed marauders. The younger raiders were in our midst in no time. They had naked swords in their hands, their faces hidden behind black masks except for small apertures for the nose and the eyes.

At first we believed it to be a strategy of disguise. But we were soon disabused. They hadn't come to plunder: they had come to burn. We were like field mice caught inside the maze of a cornfield after the corn has been harvested and the hard, dry stumps are set on fire so that the ashes could be used to strengthen the soil for the next crop. We had nowhere to go. Within a short time, everything was burning, and the smoke was so dense that the most intrepid of the young men, who wished to run to the rivulet that flowed a few hundred yards away to fetch water in their pitchers, couldn't see the way even a few feet ahead of them.

Shaikh Qavvam's wife ran into the barn adjacent to the house and hid her suckling infant under a load of hay, hoping that she might save the baby thus, not stopping to think that if not the fire, the smoke would extinguish the life in the elfin little body. But she could see nothing, think nothing. There was nothing to see, nothing to see by, except the red-black flames that swayed like serpents' tongues and the yellow-blue blur of the fire from the burning thatched roofs, the rafters that supported mud roofs, and the flimsy doors that were supposed to protect the sparse and paltry homes.

Half-burnt bodies of the dead smelled like burnt mutton, fat from the bodies fuelled the flames, and shadows mixed with the living dead as they tried to crawl away to a lonelier death. Shaikh Qavvamuddin had been among the first to be killed. The raiders now impaled his wife's body on a spear and decided to enkindle the barn. The fire was slow to ignite, perhaps because of the water pitchers stored there and the urine of animals having moistened some of the upper part of the hay. It wasn't clear to the raiders, nor the victims, how murderous the fire was, because the raiders were busy looting and the victims were trying to find a way to escape. The smoke prevented clear vision for both.

It had been an hour since the raid on Akbarpur began. Now there was another wave of outsiders. These were spectators, some even with their wives and children, to enjoy the free fireworks show. They ran through the invading horde on horseback, or rode their dromedaries and ponies into the melee. Among them was the wife of a leading zamindar, Shaikh Mammu by name, from Shaikhpur. They were childless. When Shaikh Mammu's wife noticed that a barn in front of her was on fire, she cried, 'Stop! Please stop! Perhaps there's some poor, dumb animal in there. I won't let the helpless thing burn to its death!'

She drenched her dupatta in water, wrapped it around her face, and ran into the smoke and the incipient fire, not fearful of a falling rafter or burning door. There was no animal there. But a baby. Cheerfully sucking at its thumb, half hidden from the eye by the hay and straw around it. It was as the Presence, Ibrahim, Prophet of God, Peace be upon him, saved from the raging fire by Allah's Command: *Oh Fire, become cool and safe for Ibrahim.* Shaikh Mammu's childless woman was awed by the sight, not unforgetful of the Quranic tale. The fire of motherhood overcame the fire ignited by the beastly human. She wrapped the baby in her dupatta, covered the bundle under her long tunic, and brought it out safe, still sucking at the thumb.

Just look, there was yet another miraculous event that occurred then. Just observe now the Doing of the Revealer of Subtle Points and the Maker of Wise and Delicate Occurrences! The woman who rescued the baby named it Nizam, quite ignorant of the fact that its own parents had named it Nizam.

Twelve years passed. The adoptive Nizam was given all, and more than all care, all comforts, all affection and love that he would have got in the loving arms of his biological mother. But Destiny's games are inscrutable, strange. Who can know the Secrets of God, the Possessor of all Strength and the Master of all Matters? One day, Shaikh Nizam's classmates taunted him about his being without a father, and of obscure parentage. Shaikh Nizam broke down and ran away to his mother in tears and cried that he must know his origins or he won't eat. Having no choice, the wife of Shaikh Mammu told the boy his real story.

Nizam, who until that moment had grown up in pride, even vanity, and believed himself to be the real child of Shaikh Mammu and his wife, had looked down upon everyone else as inferior and even low class as compared to him, found the world go dark in his eyes—he was without father, without mother, and worse, he grew up and was nurtured in the home of those who were the murderers of his real parents! That whole day and the following night, the poison of shame, and pride, and the sense of having been cheated, boiled in his heart like water constantly heated in a small pan over the hottest of fires, the fire of helpless rage. Before it was properly morning, he let himself out of his false home and ran away to parts unknown.

Travelling alone, or sometimes with a trustworthy companion, Nizam went all the way to the Deccan, undergoing the hardships and the delays and the disappointments that attend a homeless, penniless traveller. Each day over his long travel, he shook the dust of memory from the hem of his tattered garment, trying to push the past away from him so much that it should become incapable of being imagined even. He arrived in a small town, where a poor water carrier took pity on him and made him his house guest without inquiring too much into his antecedents. Thus, the guest became a member of the household, no longer a transient visitor, but a sharer in the hot and cold of his patron whose love soon assumed the character of parenthood. Nizam became the adoptive son of the water carrier and began to bring in water for a Sayyid family of note.

Days passed, became months, and then years. Nizam had by now become a true son to the water carrier, having shaken off the memories of his past, which was now not only far away in physical distance, but also from his mental landscape. In spite of all the changes and vicissitudes of life, and the insurmountable distance from his true parents' loving arms, the ray of good fortune and the light of good birth was still refulgent on his brow.

The lady of the Sayyid's house took notice of him and she at once saw that the boy couldn't be the progeny of a lowly water carrier. That rare pearl couldn't have been found in the stream of water bearers. Finally, one day, she asked him plainly: 'Who are you? And to which community do you belong?'

'I am the progeny of the Sayyids,' Nizam spoke without thought, without pondering the facts of his life.

The Sayyid lady was pleased no end. She cajoled and prayed and persuaded the water carrier to surrender Nizam to her, to be brought up like the Sayyid that he was. She declared him her own, clothed him in the richest clothes, gave him the richest food, and appointed the most learned men of the day to tutor him and train him to grow into a Sayyid gentleman. Soon, Nizam's heart and brain were well watered with the life-giving streams of learning and knowledge. The plant of wisdom grew deep into his psyche, and the cool breezes of rectitude, fanned upon him by the branches of that tree, made his face bright with content, the light of knowledge and wisdom, and the inner comfort of spirit, so much so that he became the envied of all.

Nizam, when he finished his education, was widely regarded as decorated with the gems of knowledge and grace, and the custodian of all sciences, all laws of good behaviour, and all the arts of civilization. The Sayyid, of Elevated Lineage, had a young daughter whose beauty put the effulgent moon to shame and who was well versed in all the domestic arts and sciences, home management and the niceties of self-beautification. The Sayyid married this daughter to Nizam.

Now, the world has never lacked for the jealous, the talebearer, the slanderer, the calumniator. In those parts there were many such who had been seeking the hand of the Sayyid's daughter in marriage. They inquired deeply into the origins and the family connections of Nizam, and it became quite clear to them that Nizam was no Sayyid. The rivals then went post-haste to the Sayyid and alleged to him: 'Your son-in-law is no Sayyid. He's not even a progeny of the Shaikhs. He's a new convert to Islam!'

By mischance, evidence of the truth of their accusations became available soon when some jobless youth of village Shaikhpur and places nearby arrived in Nizam's city in search of employment. When they saw Nizam in enjoyment of all luxury and respect, the fire of jealousy burnt high in the fire grate of their chests. Promptly, they propagated the news that Nizam was no Sayyid, nor even Shaikh, and was in fact a new convert, a foundling.

The sons of the Sayyid of Exalted Value held that they had been disrespected by Nizam and that the stain on their honour was unwashable except by the shedding of Nizam's blood. Fortunately, their mother, the Lady of Exalted Portal, didn't support them in their scheme. She said: 'What has happened, has happened. It cannot be written back. Nizam is after all our son-in-law. It is improper to take the life of any child of the Prophet Adam, and especially one who has become our relative, even if by deceit. Better it is that our daughter and her husband are both banished to Nizam's place of origin. Everyone is happier to be where they came from.'

So that is how it came to pass. Nizam and his bride were sent off on their way to Hind, with great pomp and splendour, with money, jewels and a horde of attendants.

Now it so happened that some events occurred on the way which made Nizam's splendour to rise even further. His wealth, the number of his retinue, his pelf, his awe among the people, equalled the sultans and rajas of the land. Nizam's prestige spread through the four corners of the world. Wherever their caravan passed, people foregathered to see the thrilling sight, believing that a heavy-drawing army of some great sultan was passing under the command of a world-conquering commander-in-chief.

Now Destiny so designed Nizam's fate that his caravan passed through the territory of Rangar Rajputs. One of the chieftains, being much struck with the glory and splendour of Nizam, offered his virgin daughter in marriage to him. He accepted, after obtaining the willing consent of the chaste and purdah-observing Sayyid lady, his first wife. Numerous offspring were born to them from that marriage.

As ill luck would have it, the Sayyid lady's arms remained empty of a baby which she could fondle, and suckle, and bring up. Shaikh Nizam sorrowed over this greatly, until the Sayyid lady herself commanded to him: 'Your seed will not sprout from my womb. You make another marriage, and that lady should be from your own community.'

In accordance with her desire, Shaikh Nizam tied the thread of marriage with a young daughter of a Shaikh, newly converted to Islam. Barely a year had passed that the daughter of the Shaikh gave birth to a baby boy. There was great rejoicing at this auspicious event. But the black smoke of vanity and egotism also began to rise, and coil, and twist in the new mother's brain. She became inordinately proud, presumptuous and overweening, regarding herself superior to all because she was the mother of a boy baby, which was not a boon granted to the Sayyid lady.

When the daughter of the Shaikh became too overbearing, so much that she began to openly disrespect the Sayyid lady, that noble lady was driven to pronounce a malediction upon the Shaikh's daughter. Within a few days, the boy died, and shortly thereafter, its mother also returned the gift of life to the One Who Gave it to her. All over the place, the fame of the miracle-working daughter of the Sayyid spread its awe and fear among the people, Hindu or Muslim. Now Shaikh Nizam and his servants acted according to nothing but the movements and beckons of the Sayyid lady's brow.

Some time passed. Now the Sayyid lady commanded her husband to marry yet again, within his community. So the marriage did take place, and the new wife became pregnant by the Wish of God, and was delivered of a boy baby at the end of the prescribed months of pregnancy. The mother brought her son to the Sayyid lady and, placing it at her feet, implored: 'You are both mother and father to the baby. I am just a servitor.'

The Sayyid lady passed her hand on the back of the mother and on the head of the newborn, and said: 'Yes, this is my baby. But you are its wet nurse. Take him, nurse him and nurture him.' And so it was done.

Now, there have been twelve generations after that boy of fortune and exaltation, and I am the last of that twelfth generation. I am childless. My brothers too are childless. So now the continuity of our ancestor's seed depends upon the spiritual offspring of this sinful one. Only Allah Remains. All else is to be effaced. And always Remains the Face of Your Lord, He Who has all the Majesty, Bounty and Honour.

I, Shaikh Ghulam Hamadani, of Amroha, then Delhi and then Lucknow, narrate the story and of what passed over my ancestors, in this text called *Majma-ul Favaid* so that the people of the coming times may learn and draw lesson from it. I record these facts also to affirm that I am from an honourable origin, and not like the common herd.

15

It seemed to me that the Presence, grandfather ustad's narrative was more like a dastan, an oral romance, or an extended tale of the kind grandmothers told their children to make them go to sleep. It was the material of folklore, at best. But I wasn't going to suggest any such thing to Bhoora begam. All I thought of obtaining from her was some details about the Presence's own life that were missing from the narrative. So on my next visit, I asked her, 'Do you know the date of composition of the *Majma-ul Favaid,* ma'am?'

'I don't know for certain, but it was before he solemnized the marriage with me. That year and month, I remember, were February 1821.'

'Shaikh sahib writes in the book that he had been living in Lucknow for three decades.'

'Yes, that should place the probable date of composition at 1819–1820.'

'I hope I won't offend you, but Shaikh sahib doesn't mention you by name, and just says that he and his contracted wife have been together for about twelve years, and that there are no children from this union. This should mean that your total number of years with him should have been nearly twenty-seven.'

'Yes, that should be the case, more or less.'

'Pity Shaikh sahib didn't make any additions to the book. Had he done so, he might also have recorded your name and the fact of your marriage with you.' I spoke somewhat cautiously.

'What difference would that have made?' She drew a sigh. 'The real proof was the marriage document, and it was never written. Khvajah sahib and Nasikh sahib, who were witnesses to the event, were around. But nothing could hold before a court of law without paper.'

'Those gentlemen didn't oppose and resist your ejection and dispossession?' I was still very tentative in my tone.

'There was no time, no opportunity. The burial, the next day's Quran-reading session of the Sunnis, the Shia assembly of the third day, all happened according to the schedule. Nasikh sahib, Pandit Bidya Dhar and others were in the forefront in organizing those events. It was quite late in the evening after the Shia assembly. Everyone went home to relax. In the dead of night, some persons, who were for me as cruel and heartless as the murderers of Imam Husain, may Peace be upon him, and let there be Maula's curses on them—arrived with a gang of supporters and forced me to evacuate the house at once.'

'I'm so sorry. How sad that you were compelled to leave that very night. Could nothing be done at all?'

'Tell me, what could be done, and by whom?' She spoke with a touch of asperity. She remained silent for a moment or two, then spoke in her normal, melancholy tone. 'During his last days Shaikh sahib employed a maid to help me in running the house because much of my time was spent in tending to him in his frequent sicknesses. She was a kind and gentle widow. She took me to her narrow quarters for the night. I was allowed to take nothing.'

'So, none of the neighbours came to your aid?'

'Who would risk insult and injury for my sake? Still, as a result of the neighbour's urging, they came the next morning to say I could take away my own clothes and Shaikh sahib's personal papers.'

'Zafar-ud Daulah Bahadur didn't come to your aid?'

'He had inquiries made and found out that if the matter was pushed further, some extremely reputed and respectable names would be in jeopardy, for they were behind the usurper.'

'Indeed.'

'No, please don't say a thing against them. They bought this house for me for five hundred rupees. I had only three hundred, my dower actually. Kaptan begam paid the rest. She found Muhammad Raja to help me live a somewhat normal existence. Initially, she even paid his salary.'

With my usual insensitiveness, I said: 'How I wish Shaikh sahib had left some papers to prove your status as wife. I think it was a serious omission not to leave a written marriage contract.'

She flared up immediately. 'Why, why was it a serious omission? Even if there was something written, it was just a paper. Worms could have eaten it, the damp could have destroyed it.'

'True, we are no one to censure the Presence Shaikh sahib for doing, or not doing something.'

'Yes, and I didn't insist, for fear of annoying him. Worse, I feared that it was somehow inauspicious to ask him for paper, as if, God forbid, he was going away shortly. It seemed selfish, if not avaricious.'

'But he could have executed a will, even without telling you.'

Her face darkened. Suddenly she seemed to have aged. Her cheeks looked sunken, her eyes hollow. I was about to rise in alarm when she whispered: 'It seems you know nothing about Shaikh sahib's last days.'

'I am sorry?'

'He had been unwell for some time. He fell ill, suddenly, with a new illness. One morning he woke at the usual time, but didn't rise. He pulled me by my dupatta and gestured that I sit beside him. There was agony on his face. The agony of concentration. It seemed he was unable to speak. "Ya Allah! Have pity on us! Has he been struck dumb?" I cried to myself and asked the old maid to come running and help me. But help me in what? I just pointed to him and tried to say, "Please. Is he stricken dumb?" But all I could say was, "Please." The old woman understood me as saying that Shaikh sahib needed help to rise. She made to put an arm under his back, wanting to push him up. Shaikh sahib shrieked an almost unhuman shriek: Eeeeeee! I stepped back from him. Allah, what is happening here?

'His face reflected no pain, but a spasm of concentration, his jaws were shut tight, his eyes were bulging out. A vein was prominently throbbing on his forehead. He had his fists tightly squeezed shut. He beckoned to me, perhaps he noticed my fear. A crooked smile appeared on his face. It slackened a little. But instead of articulating something,

479

he burbled and gurgled like an infant. I thought he might be asking for water, but when I brought the cup to him, he waved it away.

'I brought him a sheet of paper and a pen. For, it seemed to me that he was unable to speak for some reason, but must be capable of writing what he desired, or felt. He took paper and pen and tried to write, but nothing but meaningless squiggles resulted.

'I ran to the Quran stand and picked up the Holy Book, trying to fan him with a riffle of its pages. I'd heard that the air from the pages of the Quran could cure dumbness. He shook his head somewhat emphatically, and looked at me with pleading eyes, as if asking me to understand what he wanted. I was at my wits' end, and could do nothing but to ask him through the sobs I was trying to choke back: "'What is it that you desire? Please give some hint, some indication?"

'He uttered a meaningless squawk, but it seemed to me that he was trying to say something like "you". He almost croaked something like "Tu . . . tu . . . tu . . . Eu . . . u . . ."'

'I then realized that his power of speech wasn't impaired. But he seemed to have forgotten the shapes and sounds of the words. He could neither write, nor speak, except in some sort of symbolic, childish sounds. I asked him: "Do you want me? What should I do?"

'He uttered sounds like tu . . . tu . . . but I could discern a sound like pa . . . pu . . . pupee. Perhaps he was asking me to summon a pupil of his? I asked: "Should I summon Khvajah Atash sahib?"

'He smiled with some content, as if I had asked him the right question. I dispatched my old maid to go to Khvajah sahib, come back with him, but also ask him to have a hakim come here immediately.'

'Pardon me,' I interjected, the fool that I was, 'but it doesn't seem to me that Shaikh sahib had lost the memory of words . . .'

For the first time, she became angry with me. Her eyes blazed, her face reddened up to her earlobes with displeasure.

'Lal Mian sahib, I expected you to understand the Presence, Shaikh sahib and his mind better. At least by now you should have become familiar with the workings of his mind.'

'I am sorry,' I stuttered. 'But losing one's memory for words . . . ?'

'What else?' she almost cried at me. 'Don't you see? He was not stricken dumb. And he had his senses intact. His face, its tension and the signs of concentration, were clear to me as the symptoms of something else. I could understand that his cry of "Eeeeee" was actually his effort to say "here" or a similar word, like "I". He was trying to say "you", but could only articulate it partially. Similarly, he wished to say "pupil" but could merely say the consonant and its attendant vowel.'

'I think I understand now. Shaikh sahib was the greatest poet of the time. Even if he lost the sound and shape of words for some reason, he couldn't let himself be entirely silent. So you had to decipher, or decode, everything that he said?'

She sobbed and spoke through her tears. 'I think if there's anything of mine that will please Maula when I lie in my grave, it is how I tried to interpret, to decode, Shaikh sahib's words and never let him feel neglected or ignored. I just watched his lips all the time.'

'So Khvajah sahib and the hakim came, and tried to treat his condition?'

'Yes, both were entirely consternated at first. Khvajah sahib knew a little bit of medicine, and the hakim sahib was of course an experienced physician. Both confessed that they had never come across such a case, and in fact couldn't put a name to it. After considerable thought, hakim sahib diagnosed a partial paralysis of the brain, affecting the "speech centre". He did prescribe some nerve medicines and also some general medication designed to tone up his physical condition, and suggested that we consult a Firangi doctor.'

I pondered briefly, but didn't find anything to say. To express sympathy was all right, but I couldn't think of anything concrete. But my businessman's mind wouldn't let go of the fact that Shaikh sahib should have left a will, or some paper to protect Bhoora begam's interests. Perhaps he didn't love her enough? No, I think the main reason would be that like most unbusinesslike people, Shaikh sahib never gave thought to writing a will.

481

It seems she could read my thoughts. She said: 'Do you understand now? It was inappropriate to blame him for not preparing a will. He was given no time.' She began to weep. 'I spent all my time looking at him, trying to understand what he desired. I had no time for thinking about such worldly things.'

I wanted to say: There can be no world without worldly things. But I held my tongue. Instead, I asked, 'So did the Firangi doctor come, and was his prescription of some use to the patient?'

'Initially, I resisted the proposal, but came round finally when I realized that there was almost no hope and I mustn't deprive Shaikh sahib of the best that could be done for him.'

'The doctor must have charged some fee?'

'Yes, he did,' she answered with some distaste. 'But the fee was paid by Shaikh sahib's pupils, though Khvajah sahib was in extreme need himself. Perhaps some of the others paid.'

'Obviously, his visit didn't do much good.'

'Well, I resisted his medications too, initially. His diagnosis was the same as hakim sahib's. I feared his medications would have alcohol, or the extract of pig bones. But he assured me that that wasn't the case at all.'

'Yes, but his time had come. I hope . . . I hope . . . his ordeal didn't last too long. I mean, he didn't suffer much.'

'I am not sure, but I hope.'

'Well, you suffered much, and you served your illustrious husband well. He must have been pleased with you. The woman whose husband dies happy with her is assured of Allah's Pleasure.'

'May your words be auspicious for us.' She drew a sigh of hope. 'His illness didn't last long. He seemed to have caught the chill that night, which caused a fever to arise later in the day.'

'He was sick for just a few days?'

'No, but not long. I wasn't counting, but I think it was a couple of weeks.'

'We are of Allah and to Him we return.' I uttered the Quranic verse pronounced on occasions of loss or death. I rose, gave some money to Muhammad Raja, and went out, promising to return in a few days.

16

Merchants, they say, serve no one. But the fact is the merchant is slave to the meanest customer, the smallest buyer or seller. My promise to return in a few days remained only so much breath. Two months passed before I could get around to visiting her. I always obtained news of her through my clerk, and sent some money and victuals every fortnight or so. She didn't ask me to come, nor did she remind me of my promise to visit soon. She was a woman of immense self-respect and independence of mind. She knew that I must be busy, and knew better than to supplicate me for a visit or aid above what I sent to her.

The rains that year were extremely intense. And it rained even long after the season of the rains was putatively over. The city drains were unable to handle the immense outflow of water. On top of it was the stoppage of all riverine traffic of goods, and substantial reduction of road transport for other merchandise. The prices began to rise, bringing good cheer to us merchants, but causing hardship to almost everyone else.

Still worse was the strong and continued hot sun that followed the much-longed-for departure of the rains. Buildings, already enfeebled by continuous wetting and buffeting by the rains, now began to crack and crumble. Grain, stored in temporary sheds as always, began to rot. Vegetables became scarce. The drains and tributaries of the Gomti which helped much to remove and carry away the city's garbage, began to flow back, pressed by the rotting garbage and filth. The sun caused more rot to the storage, and generated countless insects and bugs and worms in the drains and other ponds where the water had been awaiting evacuation in the natural course.

Inevitably, cholera began to be reported from the narrower

and denser parts of the city. Chowk, Nakhas, Gandah Nala (where Bhoora begam lived) and Akhara Bhim were the worst affected. Soon, the disease assumed the proportions of an epidemic. Every neighbourhood was reporting two, four, even more deaths every day. Women and children were the chief victims. Women would be attacked by fits of vomiting and diarrhoea as they worked in the kitchen, or did household duties. The children were often left alone while their parents were at work. Neither children nor women were capable of explaining what was happening to them. Working children, or children big enough to be allowed out to play, died in the largest numbers. The little souls at play wouldn't even realize what struck them when they began vomiting copiously, and sooner rather than later, their bowels began to open in spite of themselves. They would be half dead by the time they reached home or found succour on the way.

Hakims, vaids, experts at shamanistic practices, ojhas, maulavis who claimed to know the antidote to cholera, none were spared by the disease, so much that their diminished numbers began to cause concern. The Exalted Presence, Protector of the Faith, King of the Times, Ghazi-ud Din Haidar Bahadur imported medications from Cawnpore, Sitapore, Ilahabad even. The medications were distributed free, and widely. But what was the cure for cholera? The fever had to take its own course, the vomiting and the diarrhoea could at best be combatted by rehydration and some strength-giving medicines. But the epidemic gave no leave for even these treatments to work. Even the Firangi doctors accepted defeat for they had no idea of the aetiology of the disease. And the Hindis were always diffident of going to Firangi doctors who were few and far between anyway, and had the reputation, perhaps wrongly, of being inordinately expensive.

The affluent began to leave the city. Merchants like me loved their business more than we feared death, so we stayed. And Khiyaliganj, where we had our haveli, was comparatively safe. On the third day of the real panic and the move among the rich to evacuate the city, I decided to go see Bhoora begam and make sure that she was all right.

I'd just started when I saw Muhammad Raja come towards me. Breathless from running hard, he could barely speak for a few seconds. I expected the worst and my worst fears were true. Bhoora begam had cholera, apparently. She had fever, she was vomiting, unable to hold down even plain water, and her bowels were not in her control. Muhammad Raja narrated through tears, saying that he had brought some medications from Hakim Munnan sahib, but Baji jan was unable to swallow it.

I obtained ten seers of ice, had a jar filled with the standard medicine, the Javarish-e Shahi, and packets of the Joshandah to combat the fever. I had all this loaded on to my carriage, put ten rupees in the palm of Muhammad Raja's hand, and instructed him: 'Go with absolute haste in this carriage. Have small packets of the ice made and instil the iced oozings into her mouth every fifteen minutes or so. If she can swallow, give her a spoonful of the Javarish-e Shahi every hour, and boil one packet of the Joshandah in clean water and drain the concoction in a clean cup, make her drink it when it cools a bit. If you feel that she is very hot, spread the cold pack on her face and neck, and press it gently. Do this until you can see her fever coming down somewhat. I'll follow in a few minutes with Hakim Munnan sahib.'

The poor, almost illiterate boy, just about twelve, thirteen years old, couldn't be expected to take decisions and actions with the fineness that was needed. But he was at the moment my only hope. By the time I'd finished instructing Muhammad Raja, a message arrived from the haveli that my chacha was perhaps yet another victim of the cholera. I decided to go the haveli first, organize treatment for him, and then go to Bhoora begam's and look after her.

Fortunately, my chacha had not been totally overcome by the disease. His fever was down, his vomiting was less, but he still had the runs. His two sons, fourteen or fifteen years old, found themselves utterly helpless. So I thought it expedient to sit by chacha's bedside

485

and be sure that he was on his way to recovery. I stayed with him for almost the rest of the day, leaving him only when I could see that he was getting clearly better.

I reached Filthy Drain about the evening. I had Hakim Munnan sahib with me. The moment her door opened, our nostrils and senses were assailed by the sharp, rancid smell of urine, and the denser, heavier smell of the runs. I thank God that I didn't commit the folly of putting my handkerchief to my mouth and nose. Hakim sahib, of course, knew better.

We entered. Muhammad Raja wept, and said, 'Baji bi hasn't opened her eyes for the last many hours now. There's no strength left in her. I tried to feed her the medicines that you sent with me. There was no benefit. Worse still,' he spoke through his tears, 'she's so . . . so dirty and smelly. How can I clean her and change her clothes? She is not even responding to my pleas.'

I consoled him the best I could. Hakim sahib felt her pulse. By the slight gesture of his head, I deduced that her pulse was very weak. Her face was pale, almost bloodless, and her eyes were shut. I called out to her by name. She half opened her eyes, but tried to pull her sheet over her body; perhaps she didn't want her to be viewed by males who were strangers too.

She drew a sob-like breath, tried to cover her face with her hands. I noticed that just a day and a half's illness had reduced her so much that the bangles on her wrists hung loose. Her fingernails were almost white. Hakim sahib raised her lower eyelid to examine her state of anaemia: The eyes were almost white; the pupils, once as green as green glass bangles, had lost their brightness and liveliness. Although her collar was quite wet with water and perspiration, yet whiffs of heat rose from her body and touched us like hot exhalations rising from the hot earth after a blast of rains.

Hakim sahib opened his mouth to say something, but a spray of vomit escaped her throat, wetting her collar again with its vomitous, foetid smell. Then, quite without any warning, the runs began again.

She almost doubled in pain, then flopped back on the bed, quite unaware of what her body was doing to her.

We came out of the room. Hakim quickly wrote the following prescription in Persian:

ruby-red rose flower leaves, cooked in sugar = six tolas
plain vinegar and honey = four tolas
extract of roses = eight tolas
extract of sweet fennel = quarter seer
These to be mixed thoroughly and drunk.

He said, 'Let this prescription be filled as quickly as possible. The dose is one large spoonful. I will administer the first dose myself, then the same dose is to be given here every half hour by the patient's attendant.'

I entrusted the paper to my syce, instructing him to have it filled as soon as possible. Hakim sahib spoke to me in a low voice: 'In certain cases of cholera, this prescription has proved efficacious, but the patient is in a bad way. I can't hold out any hope. It is in the Creator's Hands.'

'I know,' I replied in the same tone. 'But we must try.'

'Yes. I'll visit again tomorrow, but let me be kept informed of the developments at least twice in the night.'

My syce and carriage bore Hakim sahib to his dispensary, the syce to bring back the medicines at the earliest. I then had the neighbourhood water carrier and a sweeper, both women, summoned through Muhammad Raja. I put twenty-five rupees in the hands of each. I said, 'Bring in adequate quantity of water every day to wash and sweep the house, clean the lady, change her clothes as many times as needed. You'll be paid this sum every day as long as you are on duty here.'

Twenty-five rupees was a sum that they couldn't have earned in a whole year. They agreed willingly and began their job at once. The prescription came back shortly. I had one dose administered to her in my presence, and then I went out, to let the washing and cleaning be done thoroughly.

487

Perhaps the cleaning up, the full bath in cool water, fresh clothes, or the medicine—perhaps a combination of all these had their effect. The water woman came out with the message that Bibi ji wanted me inside. I took Muhammad Raja with me and went in.

Bhoora begam was barely able to speak, but her eyes were half open, her face was less pale. She raised a trembling hand to her brow, then she gestured towards the little box that sat next to her. Muhammad Raja brought the box nearer to her hands. She looked at me with imploring eyes, gesturing towards the box.

In a low, but distinct and deliberate voice, I said: 'Bhoora begam, I clearly understand your intent. I'll take in my custody all the papers of the Presence, Shaikh sahib that are contained in that box. I'll take proper care of them, and will also have provision made for Muhammad Raja. But there's no hurry at all.' My eyes misted over. 'You will get better, fully better, as Allah Wills.'

Her eyes began to flow. She didn't bother to wipe them, but looked at me as if she knew very well the truth of my assurance—it had the same value as one given to a child to pacify him.

'This . . . this . . . Right now, please.'

'I understand, madam. I'll take the papers away right now.'

I passed my hand on Muhammad Raja's head to console him, and give him moral strength. 'Raja mian, I'll leave my syce here. Inform me immediately of any change in her condition. Don't worry about the lateness of the hour. Just send him to me if you want to report something.'

I salaamed Bhoora begam, picked up the box, said goodbye to the women, and left. I drove the carriage myself because the syce was to stay there overnight. My heart warned me that I wouldn't see her alive now. And that's how it happened. I returned very late from my uncle's quarters and it was about two-thirty in the night when I prepared to sleep. I hadn't set foot on the bed when Muhammad Raja arrived, weeping. Bhoora begam was no more. To Allah we belong and to

Allah we return. I prayed in my heart that she may be raised with my grandfather ustad on Doomsday, that they may be together always:

Mushafi, the moment this curtain of the body was pulled aside
Understand that every impediment was removed.

Early in the morning, I sent the information of her passing to all his friends and also to Kaptan begam. I got myself ready and arrived back at Bhoora begam's with money for what was needed to be done: the shroud, the grave-digging, the many kinds of incense, the spices that needed to be mixed in the water for bathing the body. Among the first to arrive were Diwan Durga Parshad Muztarib and Pandit Bidya Dhar, Shaikh sahib's oldest friends. The ladies from the house of Munshi Muzaffar Ali Asir and Mir Mustahsan Khaleeq—dear pupils of Shaikh sahib—organized the bathing and all the other rites. She was buried in the graveyard close to the shrine of the Presence Abbas, where Shaikh sahib had his place of eternal rest.

After the male assembly of the third day, I intimated to those present that the dead lady—may Allah Bless her—had entrusted Muhammad Raja's care to me. If agreed to by those who were the closest to the family, I would sell her house and give the proceeds to Muhammad Raja and let him go back to his home in Mirzapore. Everybody praised my proposal.

After the epidemic receded, I sold the house and its appurtenances for three hundred and fifty rupees, the prices having fallen much due to the epidemic. I added a hundred and fifty of my own and sent off Muhammad Raja with a reliable caravan. He said goodbye to Lucknow with wet eyes and choked voice. I recalled the opening verse of a poem by Shaikh sahib. It was my last counsel to him:

So long as there's breath in body, we have to be restless, in distress
The bubble can separate from the wave only when its breath is gone.

17

That year, the endemic contagion of the cholera decided to revisit Lucknow. The return was only about a couple of weeks after it had waned, and it was more murderous than the first one.

Darbari Mal Vafa's chacha was fully better in about a week's time. The grief of Bhoora begam's passing was also becoming less hurtful by the day. Darbari Mal Vafa was now making his mind ready to expand in the form of a regular narrative the notes that he'd recorded privately after each meeting. He was thinking in terms of compiling a full biography of his grandfather ustad, a biography that also contained some information about his chief pupils, examples of their poetry, and the Shaikh's corrections upon them where such corrections were possible to be retrieved.

He had begun collecting examples of the pupils' poetry and brief accounts of their circumstances, and samples of the Shaikh's corrections on their poetry. A number of Shaikh sahib's most influential pupils, like Kunwar Sen Muztar, Durga Parshad Muztarib and Khvajah Haidar Ali Atash actively supported him in the project. While he thought the Life should be as detailed as possible, he wasn't of the view that accounts of his married life, or lives, and the important women in his life like Ismat Jahan, Bhoora begam and others, should find a place in the Life.

Shaikh Nasikh sahib took a different view. He felt that while too explicit and descriptive accounts of all important women need not be entered, exception should be made for Bhoora begam. He believed that that lady had much to do with Shaikh sahib's intellectual and artistic achievement, and that lady herself had had an unusual life, so she must be given adequate space in Shaikh sahib's biography.

After many days' indecision, Darbari Mal Vafa decided to abide by Shaikh Nasikh sahib's advice. In fact, now that it was decided to give space to Bhoora begam, it was necessary to give a full narrative of her expulsion and dispossession from her home, not omitting to mention any who had had something to do with her expulsion. He did not fear public censure or disapproval. Once he decided to tell the tale, he'd tell it clear and plain.

In Bhoora begam's box were the manuscript of the Presence Shaikh sahib's eighth divan, a manuscript of the *Majma-ul Favaid* in his neat calligraphic hand, and a ninth divan, containing the Panegyrics in draft form. The eighth divan and the *Majma-ul Favaid* were ready to be formally calligraphed and its authentic copies published. The collection of the Panegyrics needed much work before it could be readied for publication.

There was a separate bundle of papers in the box, aside from the draft divan of the Panegyrics. He opened it to find a long satire on Mirza Sauda, composed by Nur-ul Islam Muntazir, a brilliant pupil of Shaikh sahib. There were also some satires—scurrilous poems rather, composed by Shaikh sahib and his pupils during the unfortunate dispute with Sayyid Insha sahib. Without revealing this to anyone, Vafa decided to destroy all those papers. The actors in those distressful episodes were long dead and he was sure that Bhoora begam would be happy at the papers' destruction.

Darbari Mal Vafa had planned to start getting all the divans of Shaikh sahib calligraphed for publication by the finest calligraphers of the day: Hafiz Muhammad Ibrahim and his chief pupil Munshi Mansa Ram Kashmiri. The gilding and washing over with gold water, and the writing of the main headings, were all to be done by Hafiz sahib, the rest by Munshi sahib. But there's a Persian line, which has become proverbial:

I have some thoughts, but what thoughts do the Heavens have?

Or it could be altered to:

I have some thoughts, but what thoughts does the epidemic have?

The *cholera morbus* didn't take many days to return, as if it lay in wait for people to be deceived enough by its departure. Those who'd emptied their wonted domiciles, and had run away to nearby places like Mohan, Unnao, Cawnpore Sandilah and similar towns, came back, but weren't properly settled in their homes before the cholera overtook them again.

Twenty-two days after Bhoora begam's demise, Darbari Mal Vafa imbibed the cholera. By three o'clock in the morning, his vomiting became almost continuous. By about two o'clock in the afternoon the next day, Darbari Mal Vafa closed his eyes on this transient world. All his plans to protect, preserve and publish the works of his grandfather ustad, his own ambitions to become an ustad poet, were burnt into dust with his earthly body.

*

An oil portrait of Darbari Mal Vafa hung in his chacha's divan khana for many years. In the loot and pillage of 1858, it fell to the hands of an English soldier who sold it to a discriminating superior officer for fifteen rupees. Changing hands again once or twice, the painting found its resting place in the Victoria and Albert Museum in 1879, when the India Museum maintained by the British East India Company was merged with the V&A Museum.

An extract from the descriptive catalogue, placed beside the painting, is as follows:

A Hindoo Businessman of Lucknow, by Muhammad Azam. Circa 1825, 30" x 24", Oil on Canvas, British-Indian Style

The information given in the extract is accurate, except for the identification of the subject. Portrait painting in oil had become known in Lucknow by about 1780, but didn't immediately become popular. The Indian portraitists and landscapists began to use the oil on canvas technique by about 1815 and soon became as proficient as their foreign competitors, especially the German Johannes Zoffany, the uncle and nephew Thomas and William Daniel, and Robert Hume, to mention only the most prominent.

Mildred Archer, the most famous modern historian of western-style painting in nineteenth-century India has described these Lucknow painters as 'Company Painters', though they weren't employed by the British East India Company and show little influence of the 'Company School' which excels mainly in anecdotal paintings.

In any case, the portraits of Muhammad Azam were clearly influenced by Zoffany and Hume. They didn't much stress the sitter's inner life and character, but gave their best attention to the outer details, the sumptuous dress, the pomp and splendour. Azam was especially good in representing fabrics like silk, velvet, brocade. It seemed to the viewer that he was actually touching those fabrics, and the pearls; what is also evident is the full confidence of the sitter in his environment, in his excellence of status.

Muhammad Azam painted Darbari Mal Vafa's portrait to present his person as a prominent businessman of Delhi. He wears an orange velvet coat in the Delhi style, and wears a four-cornered black velvet cap, again in the Delhi style. The novelty here is that the ornamental plume or crest of the hat has been shown higher than normal and, instead of colourful feathers, its beauty is enhanced by a large yellow topaz. He has a silken cummerbund in sky-blue, by which is hung a dagger in a bejewelled sheath. Darbari Mal Vafa sits in the traditional style, his feet tucked under his thighs. This posture has made the lower hem of the coat open a bit. Under it, a glimpse of light purple-grey muslin tunic can be seen, as also a hint of a sky-blue velvet short coat whose cut-off sleeves are also seen.

The sitter's complexion is light brown. He is a slim, but obviously a tall and powerful man. He is beardless, revealing a strong chin, and moustaches in the Delhi Hindu fashionable style come down to the ends of the mouth. His dark eyes are not on the viewer, but bent in reflection, emphasizing the long eyelashes.

On the whole, the sitter is a person of substance, very good-looking, and clearly well educated.

There's a heavy brocade bolster behind him, but he doesn't lean against it and sits with shoulders squared. There's an open window behind him through which can be seen a part of an indoor garden. In the far background is a bamboo frame on which is a rich vine creeper, showing unripe grapes. In the foreground, a few rose plants can be seen.

There is a solid silver inkstand in front of the sitter, but slightly to his left. In his right hand he has a quill pen with which he writes something in a thick book. The spine of the book can be dimly read as something pertaining to the Life and Works of Shaikh Ghulam Hamadani Mushafi. There is nothing to suggest a merchant's profession for the sitter. He does have a heavy key on the right of him, and it might have led to the supposition that he is a businessman. Actually, the key is the symbol of the Treasury of Knowledge, not the treasury of a merchant. In the words of the immortal Omar-e Khayyam:

Although I am elegant of face and sweet of scent
My face is rosy like the poppy, my stature tall as a poplar;
I failed to discover why in this pleasure house of dust
Eternity's Painter Painted me such a beauty.

Timecompression

Shaikh Ibn-e Sukaina commanded:
God has the Power to expand time for any of His slaves
and lengthen the duration of time while it remains short
for the rest of His slaves. In the same way, God sometimes
compresses time, so that a long duration of time is experienced
    as short.

From Hamid Hasan Qadiri's Urdu translation of some tales of
miraculous events narrated by the Iranian Sufi and poet Abdur
Rahman Jami (d. 1492) in his *Nafakhat-ul Uns*

1

I lay upon the bed, turning from side to side. Not because something exercised my mind, or some anxiety's thorn pricked my heart. Sometimes it happens, at least with me, that almost as soon as it's evenfall, or when I retire for the night, I know that sleep won't come easily tonight, or perhaps not at all. I recalled some lines from Kaifi Azmi, though not from where I first heard or read them:

Sleep won't be possible on the pavement
tonight.
It's a very hot wind that blows
tonight.

Actually, for us Indians it's the cold weather that's much more direfully deleterious than the summer (so I think, at least). We, the dwellers of hot North Indian plains who walk barefoot on the rock-hard earth baked by the baleful blaze of May or June, experience the hot weather as something else again. The scorcher, the sun, my God, how hot the air is, as if fire rained from the sky. The earth is so violently, blisteringly hot that you could roast chickpeas or rice on it, as if on a griddle. And the sun so strong that the kites quit brooding their eggs . . .

Kites quitting their nests? Why kites alone, pray? I remember this idiom, if idiom it is, from when I was little. And it was always a puzzle for me: Why single out the kite as the one who quits her brooding? I stood in too much awe of my father and my tutors to make bold to ask them, why should the kite leave its eggs? Did it mean that the heat would incubate them without the kite's assistance? Or did it mean that if the kite continued trying to hatch them, the heat would addle the eggs? But this must be true of all birds, so why the kite alone? Was it because it's only the kite that drops its eggs in May or June? But that doesn't seem to be a likely explanation. There are thousands of kinds of birds, it mustn't be only the kite among them which breed in the summer's heat.

When I grew up and picked up some smattering of linguistics, I found that language is an arbitrary being. It's often illogical, even crazy. I recall a similar incident of a few years later, much before I studied linguistics. In one of the stories of the *Alf Lailah* (*The Arabian Nights*) that I read in Persian translation, I found the sentence: 'It was so hot that the chameleon's liver was on fire.' Why chameleon, and why his liver alone? The Persian for 'chameleon' is *hirba* and our Persian teacher informed us that in Urdu we called it the *girgit*. He also informed us that some people said *girgitan*; perhaps the creature sounded more menacing with the long *an* sound attached to its posterior.

But our teacher didn't (couldn't?) explain why it was the bad old chameleon (a creature always feared by us as extremely poisonous, whose long, thin tail seemed like a weapon, not an appendage) whose liver was burning, and why the liver alone. Both the questions remain unsolved for me to this day. Maybe I should have read Ornithology and Herpetology if I wanted to solve these language puzzles.

Well, here I was, in my ancestral village, and it was hot. Not the apogee but early May, and the temperature was nudging 105 F in the shade. Kaifi's poem (if his it is) led my thoughts away to faraway, forgotten readings, but the fact was that I was sleepless. I don't think it was the hot night and the somewhat inimical westerly wind that blew away my sleep. As I said above, it was just one of those things. I lay in a huge four-poster under the ancient neem tree that had given us shade and comfort for more years than I knew. There was a maidaun before our front door, a not very imposing one, but big and wide, and when you entered through the door you found yourself in a narrow hall leading into a long gallery, on both sides of which were doors which opened on to houses occupied by my grandparents and uncles. The bed belonged to my grandmother, and my hosts had brought it out specially for me. The bed, its *nivar* tape which was wound on the frame to provide a strong, resilient foundation on which to spread the bedding, the bedding itself, all these were in good shape, though it must have been more than sixty years since she died. In all my years when I was growing up and she was alive, I never saw or heard her leaving the village, or even the house which she ruled with benign despotism. I don't know if she loved me; I certainly had no feelings for her. In fact, I don't remember her ever losing her composure or showing her affection openly.

The only time I heard her being benevolent, or soft, or affectionate, whatever, was when I heard her speak of some delicacies that someone had brought as present: 'These I'll give to none else but my Bhoj.'

Bhoj was the nickname of my father who was the youngest of seven sons. She had no daughters. Ours was a fairly religious Muslim family and to give the nickname Bhoj to the youngest son was somewhat unusual, but I saw that everyone was quite comfortable with it. Bhoj is the name of a legendary Hindu king, after whom a part of the province of Bihar is named Bhojpur, and the language spoken in a large part of the valley of the holy river Ganga is called Bhojpuri.

My grandmother has been dead close to seven decades now. Many of her grandchildren and grand-nieces now work, or have even settled in foreign lands. For them, things of seventy years ago would seem like prehistory. For me, though, matters of seven decades or somewhat more seem like yesterday, and are certainly part of my own history.

During my grandmother's times, her big four-poster and in fact all other beds and cots were the cantonment, or even tactical headquarters of a whole army of bedbugs. They would bite all night long but we boys would sleep uncaring, and in fact even unaware of that formidable army. No mosquito, no bedbug could ever hope to vanquish or even breach our walled forts of sleep. My older cousins, though, used to often describe their nights with this verse of Mir Taqi Mir:

Finally, my sleep interrupted early
I spend the rest of the night awake and alert to hunt down
the bedbugs.

Only God would know how many of the forts, barracks and colonies still survived in those beds. In mine, it was silence and peace for the present. I lay, content to wait for sleep, unharried by bugs or mosquitoes. In the half-light of the stars, I could see across a fair bit of the maidaun in front, except where my view was blocked by a small mosque built for the convenience of my grandfather in his last couple of years when he'd grown frail and unsure on his legs and couldn't comfortably go to the main mosque of the village, a few hundred yards away.

What I remembered from childhood of the pre-mosque days were a few mango trees in the middle distance, some barren or fallow lands followed by green fields, and two or three narrow dirt paths which seemed to converge on our house and went their mysterious way beyond it. These paths ran through green fields where wheat was grown, and the light, soft-green of the wheat fields produced a soothing sense of life, growing effortlessly, almost without human aid.

Our house was large, but it had no formal main gate, far less an enclosing wall to keep out strangers. So sleeping outside, under the dark-green neem tree produced a sense of openness, of vastness, though not nearly as interesting as the life around the open well that was at some distance from the house. There was no bar of caste or religion there. The well was accessible to even the lowest of the low caste, and equally, to people comfortably off, *sharif* Muslim families. High-caste Hindus never came there because the well and its surrounds were polluted and the pollution there was an ongoing activity. The well, therefore, was the haunt of many kinds of people—women, boys, artisans, day labourers—and it never seemed to be less than throbbing with life until late evening.

So the expanse open before one who slept in the open in the space in front of our house seemed uninteresting, even uninterested in who was sleeping, who was sleepless, who was in pain, who was being bitten by the bugs. The world of the maidaun at night seemed unconcerned with who slept early, who slept late, who was a stranger, who a native of the vast house behind. No, stay awhile. In those days no one, but no one, could think of sleeping late. My grandfather and others woke up well before the false dawn to do their prayers, then they came out almost in a procession for the predawn prayers in the mosque. None, therefore, could even think of sleeping late in that place.

And not just the early prayer goers, there was much else to waken, or gradually waken the sleeper in the open: the changes in the rhythms of the colour and movement of the breeze, the flow of the night seeming to slacken once the heart of the night had been reached, the imperceptible—but audible to the unconscious mind—lowering of the whispers of the night, the slow, very slow retreat of the darkness, the feeling—again imperceptible to the outer sense, but clear to the unsleeping organism called the Mind—of the eastern horizon approaching near and the receding of the mysterious west where the sun had gone down to bed the night before, then on some extremely deep level of the senses, the awareness of the massive wall of darkness morphing first into the grubby half-light of the green and brown of the reed thickets, then their dense greenness separating itself from the surrounding dark and becoming half visible as long leaves swaying in the whispering wind, the swaying then changing into the outline of other leaves and plants from the lightest green to the darkest.

These, and many other things not describable in mere words, would never leave a sleeper in the open unawakened as the sun rode higher upon the eastern horizon.

Now the skies in our modern cities are generally invisible, hidden behind the noxious veil of dust and smoke. And in the land from where I'd come, it was a noteworthy event if a smatter of stars could ever be seen in the night sky. And here in this sleepy village? A half moon in the sky, the neem's higher branches making a dark green-brown cluster or moving curtain. With the slightest freshening of the breeze, the leaves parted a little, giving occasion for a tiny moon-ray to touch me, lessen the sense of dark, a silvering of the edges of some of the leaves giving a softened lustre to the shady tree. I am reminded of a verse by the nineteenth-century Urdu poet Shaikh Nasikh:

How can I go into the garden at night when my lover is not with me?
Moonlight converts every leaf into a dagger.

In the city where I have my home now, we went to work at a time when the morning hadn't spread over the land. Some travelled twenty miles to work, some even farther. Those who could afford a helicopter, and were lazier than most, would have a helicopter land on top of the building where they lorded it over the rest of the world. True, they did leave home much later than us, but they travelled up to the roof by a fast elevator and took a protected step or two into their ride. Before travelling up, they would be in the shower or the dining room, and would never have occasion to look at the sky, far less descry the stars, mostly invisible anyway, or even the paling moon of late morning. By the time we, and they, returned to our homes, the evening light would have bloomed fully on the horizon, inevitably pursued and overtaken by the darkness of the fuggy air and the night itself shrouding the sky. So, unless there had been a storm overhead, the helicopter riders always remained insensible of the world that fed them oxygen, and they returned uncaring into their secure cocoons.

I remembered Robert Louis Stevenson's phrase 'living slumber' which he used to describe the human sense of sleeping under the sky. It occurs in his travelogue, written in such exquisitely elegant prose that I know I couldn't write a paragraph like it in a hundred years.

But I wasn't sleepy yet, so I was deprived of the pleasure of Stevenson's living slumber. I recalled that at the end of the maidaun and to one side of it, my grandfather's cousin Subhan-Allah had his house,

504

unimpressive from outside, but fairly open and full of leaf and plant inside. It was a low house, single-storeyed as most dwellings were in our village. So it was possible for us to see behind and somewhat to the left of it, a large, unusually dense and dark green-brown tree, massive and somewhat frightening in its dark amplitude. I don't now remember the kind of tree that it was: peepul, mango, rosewood, jackfruit. It wasn't a banyan, that I remember. At night, the tree always seemed to me to have come somewhat closer, nearly overshadowing grandfather Subhan-Allah's house. It was well known among us boys that the tree was the abode of a malevolent *baram* (some sort of evil spirit in human shape, but somewhat amorphous). The baram eyed every passer-by, especially those in their early youth, with a greedy, glowing gaze. So what did he want? None could give a satisfactory answer but there were a number of theories, each more frightening than the last.

It was believed that the baram quested eternal youth, and the best way to achieve this was to get hold of a youngish human and absorb his spirit, just as we sucked and chewed the sugar cane, absorbing the juice and spitting out the rind.

It was also said that he was more bone than flesh or sinew, and he craved youthful boys so that he could strip the boy off his flesh and clothe himself in it.

It was also believed that the baram was, for some unknown reason, imprisoned in that tree, and he needed some fresh and strong human being so as to use him as transport and go to distant places and hunt for blood—human or animal.

It was reported that once the baram did carry off a young farmer and promised to give him very nearly boundless strength, the strength of a young stallion, provided he would let the baram ride him of a night. The farmer could then take on the strongest challenger or enemy, and beat him. It wasn't known how the farmer escaped the baram's clutches, but it was rumoured that he had to bribe the baram with a bit of his life juice and that's why the farmer was growing paler every day. His identity, of course, was as secret as the baram's itself.

505

Some of my older cousins were past masters at narrating the most hair-raising tale with a straight face. One of them told me that, actually, our grandfather wrote out a talisman for the farmer, to be enclosed in silver and worn at the midriff. That's how the hapless farmer—not so hapless really—escaped the baram, and the rumour that he grew pale and wan every day was just that.

Another cousin of mine was fond of repeating the following with newer and yet newer embellishments: One of our grandfather's farmworkers was given the duty of guarding the harvest at night. He reported before my father the next morning, shivering and feverish, and said: 'Maulavi sahib, I am not going to do any guard duty at night. Someone, a baram or a *betal*, appeared at the top of a neem tree after midnight. Baring his long teeth he jabbered all night, threatening to carry me off the next day.'

My grandfather then wrote a charm in the Bhojpuri language to this effect:

This man is my farm labourer
Don't let anyone threaten or obstruct him.

He folded the paper eight times, instructing the labourer never to unfold it and always wear it in his turban.

The baram, betal or whatever it was, never reappeared, as stated most forcibly on oath by my cousin, aforesaid. I don't believe in such things now, but I was quite sure at that time that the reason the massive shadow, that huge tree, appeared closer at night was because the resident-prisoner baram was trying to give himself some mobility by pushing that tree around. That forbidding tree was not visible tonight. The house of grandfather Subhan-Allah now consisted of three somewhat squat storeys, but enough to hide the tree, if it still existed. There was nothing now to discern beyond the house. If I survived till morning, I'll certainly go out in the blinding blue sunlight to investigate if the tree was still there.

Survive? Is there an issue of survival involved here? Why shouldn't I survive the night? I meant to say 'stay', and my senses, somewhat wetted by the sleepy shower of an unexpected snooze, enunciated 'survive'. No, that won't do. I am staying the night anyway. There was no if or when about it. All this damfool talk of ghosts and evil spirits has addled my brains.

In my boyhood I was an avid reader of ghost and horror stories, perhaps because my head had always been full of fear of the unknown, fear of solitude, empty houses as the abode of the jinn, the residence or visiting place of mysterious evil spirits. Empty spaces were the stamping ground of churails, women who were in themselves evil or were dwellers of caves, burning ghats or abandoned houses. They could assume any female form but had no control over the shape of their feet: the feet were made backwards, toes in the back and heel in front. This was one sure sign for anyone accosted by a churail in however alluring an attire or attractive female form she appeared in. In their own, original selves, they were of course coal-black, of short or somehow deformed body.

In the village of my childhood, fearful beings dominated our imagination: jinns and evil spirits (of huge variety, from ghost to betal, and the churail). Almost everyone of my peers claimed at least one encounter with one or more of those abominable characters. I don't say 'things', for they were real enough for us. The strange thing was that I never associated them with the notion of death, nor did I fear meeting my death at the hands of those beings. What I feared most was being captured or taken possession of by an alien being, or imprisonment in a lonely place; or things that I didn't know and couldn't understand who created them and why.

When I grew up, my taste for terror or horror or ghost stories also grew, to the dimensions of almost an irresistible habit. This weakness for thrilling books remains to this day. When I grew older and became a person of some means, I bought all kinds of such books almost compulsively. Soon, I had a veritable library of such literature. I recall with regret the large number of ghost story books, anthologies of ghost or horror stories, thrillers that I gave away for lack of space. Some of them I have now bought again at excessive price from specialized book dealers because they've become collectors' items, classics of their genre. In spite of having given away quite a good number of them, I went on buying and reading such books. Today, my library overflows, bursting at its limits, and those few hundreds of slim volumes would not really make a difference now, but my library would have been the richer for them. Names like M.R. James, Algernon Blackwood, Oliver Onions, H.P. Lovecraft, E.T.A. Hoffman, Sheridan Le Fanu, Robert Bloch, Oscar Cook and Dennis Wheatley are still active in my brain as the creators of doors to a world that is very real but inaccessible by normal means.

I don't know if I took to those writers because of my bent of mind—isolative, uncommunicative, suspicious of strangers, believing that there was more evil than good in the world—or if my reading of those tales made me believe that the world was full of uncommunicable, dreadful, inimical things. I still have a sneaking fear of the (in modern parlance) paranormal, or (in my vocabulary) supernatural. My reason doesn't believe but my heart somewhere, somehow, does.

How childish, how callow my temperament is! I can not only recall those unfamiliar, far-off things, but they still fill me with a vague fear, a sense of realness, not just as *stories* or *tales* recalled from the page of memory or the pages of past books, but something that I can almost sense close to me on this ancient bed in this insomniac night.

No, I think I am sleepy somewhat. But I also think I shouldn't sleep, I should be alert to something or someone coming. T.S. Eliot, in his *Gerontion*, said:

> *Signs are taken for wonders. 'We would see a sign!'*
> *The word within a word, unable to speak a word.*

But Jesus refused to show him a sign, when Matthew cried for one. So, signs mean nothing. But am I waiting for the past, my past, to embody itself before me? No, I don't want that, however potent the past may be in my imagination. There was a ghost in Thomas Lovell Beddoes's poem *The Phantom Wooer*. He loved for the future, wanting his lady to die so that she could join him in—where? Well, somewhere:

A ghost, that loved a lady fair
Ever in the starry air
Of midnight at her pillow stood;
And, with a sweetness skies above
The luring words of human love,
    Her soul the phantom wooed.
Sweet and sweet is their poisoned note,
The little snakes of silver throat,
In mossy skulls that nest and lie,
Ever singing, 'die, oh! die!'

Now this was really a frightening poem (or experience?). What surprised me as much as the terror that struck at my soul was the phantom's certainty that his (its?) lady would join him (it?) as a ghost once she died, and that he (it?) could take her with her song, that she'd be enchanted by the song, or was it the singer? In the shorter last stanza we are told that the poisoned notes emerging from the silver-throated snakes are dearer and dear as the night passes, or as the nights pass:

Dear and dear is their poisoned note
The little snakes of silver throat

To me, the most surprising thing about the poem—apart from its imagery which clutches one by the throat—is the ghost falling in love with the woman. In our culture, jinns, other spirits of the Unseen, do fall in love with a nubile girl, especially if she ever stood under the sky or a pomegranate tree at night with her hair undone. But an

Englishwoman of the nineteenth century? Ghausi Ali Shah sahib, a well-known Sufi of the early nineteenth century, would magnanimously write charms or amulets for the women, Muslim or Hindu, who were visited, or possessed by a jinn, a ghost, a spirit, whatever. He also used to say that such visitations or possessions don't happen with Englishwomen because the Firangi's fortunes are in the ascendant.

2

It's clear that it's not going to be morning any time soon. There used to be a largish pond right behind our house. It was called garhi, the feminine gender of *garha* and just means 'a ditch'; a garhi should have been much smaller than a casual ditch, instead of being a pretty large pond. Anyway, who can understand or explain the vagaries of language? Our garhi, or largish pond, may or may not have been deep, but it certainly seemed so to me. I never saw anyone fishing there, but it was my most favourite place. Full of a variety of life, subtle changes over the day, and occasional meeting place of friends, especially to pick the peepul's ripe berries—very small considering the mammoth size of the peepul, but delicious, at least to us who were always hoping to be regaled with sweets and delicacies.

The pond was alive with leeches, numerous kinds of small cockle shells, dark little gnats which ran around near the shore, searching for food, presumably. (What did they eat, small as a point they were, and where was their mouth?) Tadpoles and baby snails appeared and disappeared mysteriously. But the most interesting of all were the water ants, dark grey, thin, with tall feet and longer than their land-living counterparts. Today their mental picture puts me in mind of high-speed, high-mobility pinnaces, or the long and narrow but extraordinarily manoeuvrable boats of Kashmir called the shikara; for some unknown reason as usual, for I never heard of them being used as hunting boats, though shikar means 'prey', or ' to hunt'. To me those elegant creatures, the water ants, were incomparably faster, and more engaging than any other thing in the pond. Their legs were very long and slim, like the jokers in a circus wearing very tall crutches. They swam (or ran) extremely fast on water, like the hunting hounds about whom I'd read in my storybooks.

I don't now recall if the water ants traversed the whole pond (it seemed quite wide to me), or they returned from halfway. There wasn't enough light there, and I was short-sighted and couldn't anyway pursue their journey with my eyes. Maybe they did run the whole breadth, but to me they always seemed to have returned quickly enough to make me assume that they didn't go more than a yard or two. Their territory seemed to be rather confined, but within it they did run around with a degree of self-regard, or feeling of importance, as if the whole pond existed only for them. Often I saw them change course suddenly and expertly without breaking their rhythm. This happened surely when they were menaced by some bigger but invisible beast of the deep? Or were they just gamesome, frisking about like baby colts or other cattle babies in a meadow? I don't think I ever saw a real meadow during my childhood. But my imagination was full of vast, undulating curves covered with thick weeds and tall grasses waving to the visitor. It must have been in such a meadow, I imagined, that Rustam would rest after a long and hot day, and would dismount from his powerful, yellowish horse whose body was covered in orange-red rosettes, and let it graze. (I'd read many *Shahnama* stories in Urdu, hence my familiarity with Rustam and his steed Rakhsh.)

Or I'd sometimes imagine the water ants, so busy and active on the wide surface of the pond, as very light, nimble frigates (though I didn't know the word 'frigate', nor even 'pinnace' then) going out to do quick battle and returning after inflicting damage upon the enemy. Or perhaps they were light passenger ships, busy in transporting intrepid soldiers to the larger ocean. They would then transfer to the vaster, heavier, lumbering battleships. Thus they were actually—how thrilling!—in the business of seamanship and long, adventure-filled ocean voyages. Not like that rather hapless Sindbad the Sailor whose ship always suffered some shipwreck. These boats were truly stable and expert floaters, managed by skilled sailors.

Snails there were aplenty: some were roundish, like small domes. They were dull brown or grey; others were long and slim, about an inch or more, pinkish, spiralling up or down, depending on how you looked at them. Some were truly ill formed, like a hunchback sadhu who wore long, matted hair all over his head like some huge turban. They were no patch on my favourites, the highly mobile, energetic water ants. The snails were almost always lifeless, the organism inside them having perished in some prehistoric time. They were quite hopeless, really. They looked clammy and soiled, but were actually dry to the touch.

There wasn't much display of colour or form there. How I would have loved to be allowed to go to the riverbank and collect shells in all sorts of shapes and colours. But going anywhere near the river, or lingering on the bank was quite a no-no, even if I was with a chaperone to prevent me from falling into mischief.

I don't remember seeing real leeches there, but there were a number of live snails, going about their quiet business almost imperceptibly. But one could sometimes observe two thin, liver-coloured and clammy-looking tongues emerging from the sides of their dome-like bodies. My village friends always warned me against them. Don't ever touch those harmless-looking tongues. They are razor-sharp and the moment the tongue touches you, it'll leave a thin, red mark from which the blood would well up in no time. They are not snails really, they are leeches of a kind. I had often been slashed by the long, green-grey leaves of certain kinds of reeds. Their edges were sharp, really sharp, and you stood in severe danger if you let your finger or palm run against them. Now it occurs to me that it must have been some kind of a spoof: the thready 'tongues' were nothing more than the snail's frail legs, with no power to bite.

The peepul tree that stood almost at the edge of the nearer bank of the pond was my friend by day and foe by night. I could hear in the night its bright-by-day but black-by-night leaves making many kinds of noises, soughing loudly like the panting of a large beast. The wind seemed to be passing right through my room, above my bed, though at night I kept all windows and the solitary door tightly closed, especially as soon as I sensed, or imagined, the stars shining out of the darkling sky. Yet, those nights were the hardest ever, the most terrifying in my young life. Everybody in our large family ate early and so did I. My mother and other daughters-in-law stayed back in my grandmother's house, which was joined with ours by a longish, but enclosed and narrow lane. The women would stay talking adult, womanly things, I presumed. Childbirth, cookery, sewing, needlework, news of the family, I imagined. My grandmother didn't encourage discussion, or even mention of rumours or gossip. My father stayed back for my grandfather's nightly assembly of sons, nephews and cousins. The year was 1943 or 1944 as I remember. There was no radio, no newspaper arriving daily in the morning. Our best source of news was the odd traveller who came from the city, armed with the latest news or the previous day's newspaper. (I recall a small procession of young boys, including me, and sweets being distributed to them on the occasion of what was announced as 'the conquest of Tunisia'. The procession was led by one of my older cousins.) I sensed that some government directive and money would have come from the city. Since my grandfather's family were all extremely religious, they must have discussed matters of piety and religion as well.

For my father everything was as it should be: He taking his place in the assembly and using his superior knowledge of English and History on occasion, and I, safely ensconced in my father's bed in our little home. Nothing could harm me, or no calamity strike me while I slept in the secure zone created by their prayers for me and by our grandfather's huge house.

But the truth was entirely different, I regret to say. As I said, our little abode was connected to the back of grandfather's house by a long, narrow alley. In the small triangle created by the junction of the two dwellings, there was a small lavatory. No bathroom, just the necessary. It was never used as far as I knew. It had a small window opening on to the pond, and two narrow doors for the two sides of it, one opening into the alley and the other opening on to grandfather's house. It must have been assumed by my parents that anyone entering the alley from any side would easily be detected. And I, eight or nine years old, reading English and other modern subjects at school, could fear nothing.

But oh, my parents' ignorance, or the nescience of the reality of childhood. How could they know that that exceedingly neighbourly, friendly, leafy peepul transformed itself into an enemy, and not just any enemy: an enemy who bore some nasty grudge against me, or who was a vile being somehow convinced that I had been disrespecting him during the day and should now be punished for my intransigence. He made the winds run over my bed and my roof like charging steeds to threaten me out of my senses. And perhaps those eternal friends, the water ants, the cockle shells, the snails, and numerous other beings who lived a secret life in the depths of the water crawled out of their havens, crept up that monstrous peepul and transformed into all kinds of supernal but malevolent beings: the churail, the baram, the murderous *pishach,* the man-eating or man-threatening ghost, the jinn, the witch-like woman who always wore black and danced under the solitary peepul, rifle in hand. Sometimes I believed I could see her burning, ghoul-like eyes. No, perhaps it was that massive peepul himself who became an equally vastly proportioned jinn? Or was it that, taking advantage of the malefic wind, one of the blood shedders, the pishach or the baram, was about to slither down the tree and fly in with the winds and take me off?

Every night I did battle with the peepul, that massive, black-as-pitch inimical being who stood there—no, who kept creeping up to me to take me unawares. And then, there was the wind that roared above and over my body like a hundred railway engines. And every morning I would find the same peepul, smilingly beckoning, cool, shady, generous in dropping its berries for us. Countless were the times when under the noontide sun, fearful of being swept off by the hot western wind, I would sneak out with my friends to pick and enjoy the somewhat crunchy, lightly sweet peepul berries. Once, one of my friends put a brown, dry and hard dropping of a goat in his mouth mistaking it for a berry. (I can assure you it wasn't me.) This was an occasion of merriment for us, but also of re-establishing our solidarity. For, if the secret leaked out, each of us was sure to be treated to a sound thrashing.

I've come today to my village, back after more decades than I care to remember. I've come to open a school established by me and my peers on a part of the ground where our grandfather's house stood. The neem tree at the door, under whose shade ate all the males of our family and any stray traveller who happened to pass by, or stay for the night, is no longer there. The tree which now gives me shady breeze at night is barely thirty or forty years old. The peepul and the pond behind the house have disappeared. A visitor today would be convinced that it was never there. The modern Urdu poet John Eliah wrote about his dislocation and the tearing up of memories by the uprooting tempest of Partition:

As if we never belonged here
As if we were the dust, were never from the sky.

How right, but what did my poor friend know about us who always belonged here and never went away, but had their whole childhood, their boyhood, their growing up into men, their friendships and their rivalries taken away with the trees that were cut, sunk with those ponds and lakelets whose waters were drained away, removed from the lanes and pathways where there's no room now to frolic with a ball, or even walk carefree walks, for they have been converted into dwellings?

You who stand at the gate of the city
Profusely weeping, speak
What did you do with your youth?

515

I recalled Verlaine's lines, perhaps not very accurately, but good enough for my purpose. No. I am not one of them. I never was torn from my living roots. I have achieved something, I am a fairly important person now, invited here to open the new school building. I am no longer that little boy-child who would inwardly fume against my father because he'd never let me have my fill of mangoes or musk melons at dinner time. Did I not belong here, truly belong here? Or perhaps not? But if I didn't, who else would wander, letting the dirty yellow blood of memory still course in his veins, blood that entered my being with the churails, the jinns, the winds which frightened me with a speed faster than any bullet train, the outrageously alien beings who smiled at me nightly and beckoned me with their long-nailed fingers, dried up and claw like?

But that world was wonder-striking in every way, it ever called us to display our mettle, our courage, our lack of fear, while our hearts quaked with dread. I am reminded again of the privy which stood in the triangle at the end of the lane that joined my little home and grandfather's much bigger house. No one ever used that necessary but it always had a sort of mysterious, snaky smell. The story (or the truth) about it current among us boys was that were someone to go there at a fixed hour and say 'As-salam alaikum' for forty days without break, a jinn would appear on the forty-first day, willing to do whatever you wanted of him.

I was too lily-livered ('whey face', as Shakespeare said so powerfully) to try, but I understood that many years ago someone did. On the forty-first day he perceived a figure higher than any palm tree, but his head somehow was still under the low ceiling. The figure said, 'Wa-alaikum-as salam' in a sonorous, but very hard voice, as if many bulls were bellowing in time. What happened afterwards, no one knew or was willing to say.

3

But the ancient peepul tree was right in front of me now. Our little home had fallen to ruin a long time ago, my grandfather's front rooms had gone the same way. Now there was nothing to impede the eye from reaching the far end where the pond lay and where the peepul stood.

Just a minute. The peepul and the pond I knew disappeared ages ago. It couldn't be that they now came back at night to welcome (or menace) me. Oh yes, it does seem that someone is descending from a height, maybe down the neem under which I sleep, or am trying to. The figure is dim and grey, tall. No, not very tall, but dense somehow, as if wrapped in a heavy cloak. Cloak? In the summer? Actually, the peepul is now behind the man . . . the figure actually. Behind the figure there's something like a blue-black light, and it highlights the figure, no, the man, moving towards me. The light is very faint, but I can now clearly see that person and the peepul behind him.

It must be a man, a traveller, most probably. There's nothing to fear. He must be a very old man, though. His clothes are not worn out, but they look frequently used and washed, inclining to the thinness of texture which is characteristic of very old, very well-worn clothes washed many times over.

The stranger now stands at the foot of my bed. No, I'll never let him sleep on my bed. I want to rise and ask him his name and purpose. I also want to call out to the muezzin sleeping in the little mosque about fifty yards from me. But my body seems to be rigid somehow, and the muscles of my voice box seem twisted into a dry knot. I am rather aged, but well preserved and have felt nothing unusual about my body or throat ever.

It's not very hot, but somehow I feel perspiration flowing down my forehead, collar and armpits. I should rise, dry out the sweat drops, and if possible, organize something like a handheld reed fan to help circulate the rather tightly packed air around me.

The light is now not only behind the stranger, it also seems to surround him. Now I can discern his features clearly. But why the hell doesn't he speak, tell me what he wants? Not very tall, but stout and sturdy, a body clearly used hard and well. White-striped black cotton turban, heavy and tight, a short tunic, very short so that a part of the stomach could be seen; the tunic was almost like a *shaluka*, much favoured by working men and women. It was a two-piece dress, worn with straps or jointure on the shoulders, with or without sleeves. The sleeves are of proper length, but I can't determine the quality or actual colour of the fabric—must be coarse cotton, I think. A half-sleeved short coat over the tunic, it seems to be of some flowery fabric, white on black or blue. Short but heavy cotton trousers ending midway at the calves, somewhat loose below the waist. A sash or cummerbund tightly worn around his middle, a dagger hung from it. (Is he a dacoit or a fugitive criminal? But the dagger's in its scabbard.) The handle of the dagger protrudes prominently. It's shorn of any ornamentation, made of bone or some hard and seasoned wood. So also the scabbard. I can't see if he is wearing any kind of boots. He wears a short necklace, mostly of silver with a stone in the middle, perhaps a pale turquoise. His moustaches are a little longer than usual, but not of much thickness, but the ends are firmly twirled at both ends. His pepper-and-salt beard is cut short, but is dense and pointed. He cannot be a dacoit or robber. They travelled in a band, didn't they?

Again, I tried to rise, but it was useless. My throat too was dry and tight as before.

'I make my submissions to His Honour the Khan of the Age. How is His Honour feeling today?'

A strange voice, somewhat hollow, the tone and tenor quite different from the rustics of our part of the country. But it didn't seem to be that of someone from the western districts. He seemed to be a man who had been around Persian speakers for a long time. Iranians speak faster than us of the eastern climes. This man's enunciation was surely somewhat faster than normal for us. His body language certainly revealed a certain servile, menial temperament, but the voice was strong and forcible.

A cool blast of sleep touched me. My eyes began closing of themselves. The air had grown cool and sweet.

4

The Lord of the World, Sikandar Sultan Lodi, son of Sikandar Sultan Lodi, had been ruling with magnificence and glory the territories of Hind, Panjab, the eastern tract that lay between the two rivers, Bangal and Bundelkhand for more than twenty years now, with an unrivalled concentration on the business of strong governance, impartiality and justice for all his subjects, and with a power and pelf not seen for the last hundred years. Now this was to be the last year (1517) of his auspicious reign, but no one knew that the star of the ascendant fortune of that great Sultan now hung precariously just above the horizon.

Having decided to leave the Presence, Delhi, the city inalienably joined with power and delight, the capital of Islam after the great city of Istanbul in Rum, the Lord of the World chose a new place for his capital just north of Gwalior and due south of Delhi. He named it Agra after a village nearby on the bank of the holy river Jamna, and established it as his new capital in 1504. The Lord of the World spent most of his time and attention on creating new buildings, gardens and dwellings for himself and his subjects in Agra. This did not detract from his sovereign might and awesome majesty through the Sultanate. Peace, amity and security was the rule of the day. In his Sultanate, enriched by conquest and trade, and ruled with an iron hand under a velvet glove, through numerous police stations, superintendents and middle-level managers, even the smallest untoward occurrence anywhere was reported promptly to the capital and almost invariably came to the Sovereign's personal attention. It was commonly believed that the Lord of the World controlled a number of jinns who were in constant attendance on his august Presence. The jinns immediately informed him of whatever was worth being brought to his wise and benevolent intellect. This, it was said, was in the tradition of Sikandar Bicornous, Lord of everything that was between the two horns of the cow which held the whole world aloft upon her head.

I, Gul Muhammad, approximately fifty years old (my real age was known only to my mother, but she went to her heavenly abode a long time ago), came to Delhi with my father who left the ancestral village quite young to become one of the doorkeepers at the haveli of Khan-e Jahan Lodi, also or better known as Masnad Ali Khan. I was the only child, so I was indulged by all, allowed to play and eat to my fill. When I was four, five years old, my father submitted me to the educational charge of the permanent maulavi at the haveli where he'd been trying for a number of years to educate the children of the servants employed at the haveli. Then at the age of eleven, I was sent to the madrasa of the renowned Shaikh Bhikari sahib of Delhi, son of the world-teacher, the Shaikh of the times, Allah Diya sahib of Jaunpur.

For three, four years I was subjected to the rigorous teaching regime of the madrasa where the motto seemed to be 'spare the rod and spoil the child'. The Shaikh sahib was more of an orator and mentor, so the actual teaching was done by his pupils. I must say that I studied best as I could, going up to some of the advanced texts of Logic and Literary Theory. Other than those, I picked up a nodding acquaintance with Astronomy and Astrology, and that was all I could show by way of my education.

I had some interest in poetry, so I became a regular student-learner at the assemblies of Shaikh Jamali Kanboh. There I picked up some practical points of the art of poesy, but showed no real promise. Once I composed a ghazal on the pattern of a famous ghazal of Hafiz of Shiraz, the Voice of the Occult. Shaikh sahib scored a decisive line through my composition and commanded, in Persian: 'Mian sahib, you will never be a poet. I see that you have more aptitude for swimming and wrestling. You could make a good soldier.'

It was a bitter pill, but I swallowed it quietly. Shaikh Jamali sahib would see me more with bands of kite fliers on the bank of the Jamna, swimming in the stepwell at the shrine of the Presence Nizam-ud Din Auliya sahib, or bending in obeisance at the training arena of Ustad Bhupat Rai, the great wrestling master. Be it the flowering of the Basant, or the days of assemblies to celebrate the Prophet sahib's *meelad* (birthday), or the merrymakings during the festival of Holi, I'd be invariably found where there was opportunity of sport and singing and exchange of jokes. And there was nowhere in Delhi which was not enhanced by the Presence, Jamali sahib. From morning till afternoon he would move around in the city in his large, open palanquin, teaching or pronouncing blessings upon whoever happened to supplicate him. So the Shaikh was well acquainted with my antics and skylarkings.

I couldn't become a man of learning or a poet. All that I gained for my intellectual labours was that I became known among my friends as Maulavi Gul Muhammad. The small Persian and less Arabic and Arithmetic that I imbibed from the schools became my passport to popularity among both the learned and not-so-learned. My father's house to eat and sleep, the various assemblies of the Presence, Delhi for activities like swimming excursions, mushairas, taking the air in one of the numerous gardens created by Sultan Firoz Tughlaq of blessed memory, now Resident in Paradise; but I needed little more. True, my father tied me in the nuptial knot when I was seventeen. But my wife lived in the village, leaving my activities untrammelled. So I had as much interest in domestic activities and caring for my wife and child as any bon vivant in Delhi.

I lived carefree so long as my father lived. Barring an annual or biannual visit for the festivals for which I made special preparation, I rarely visited my family. Life couldn't be happier. But my father died at about the end of the third year of my marriage, taken off by an epidemic of the *taun*, or the plague, commonly known as 'the Firangi disease', for it was rumoured to have originated somewhere in the territories of Firang countless miles away. The potent contagion lost no time in travelling abroad, and since then it appeared every decade or so in the territories of Hind, leaving homes and even whole neighbourhoods bereft of the breath of life.

I sorrowed for my father most profusely and long, for now I must needs to look for employment, take care of our meagre agricultural holdings and, most urgent of all, provide for my family. The services of my blessed father stood me in very good stead, for when Khan-e Jahan Lodi heard of my bereavement and my dire financial distress, he introduced me to the Khan of the Age, Asad Khan, son of Mubarak Khan, who immediately appointed me 'single' foot soldier in the regiment maintained by him.

*

'Do you hear me, honoured sir? Are you paying due attention?'

'Yes,' I said, irritated and bored. I turned on my other side and went to sleep. Or perhaps I tried to fall asleep. The night was cooling; I tried to wrap the bed sheet around me and shut my ears.

We were called *ahadi*, meaning 'single', but we were regular combat soldiers—single in the sense that we fought on foot, unsupported by a horse. The Lord of the World, Sikandar Lodi, had a standing army, always willing and prepared to fight for him to its very last breath. We supplied our own weapons, uniform and horse, if the latter were needed. We were paid regularly a salary of twelve rupees a month. The Lord of the World provided living space in the form of tents, erected in cantonment fashion in wide maidauns, or large houses in which fifteen or more soldiers could live comfortably.

I was employed in the regiment of the Khan of the Age, Mubarak Khan, but that was only a formality. Like all soldiers of the standing army, I had the Lord of the World as my real master. The Khan of the Age just testified to my cleanness of character and my physical health, and requested the Paymaster General that my name may be entered among the soldiers of his regiment.

When my father died, it had been ten years for the Lord of the World, Sikandar Lodi, on the Sultan's throne. All the four directions of the world reverberated with his illustrious name as a just, strong-minded and generous ruler. The power of his rule, his coin, stretched from Hind to Sind, from Panjab to Bangal and from Delhi to Dhaur Samudra. One incident was often cited of his sense of justice and generosity. It was as follows: A poor farmer of Sambhal, which is situated at some considerable distance south-east of Delhi, while ploughing his meagre field, was astonished to hear the point of his plough hit something hard. Further digging at that place turned up a bronze jar which was found to be full of ancient gold and silver coins. The local chief, when informed of the finding of the treasure trove, promptly confiscated it and didn't even specify if the confiscation was in favour of the Sultan, or his own self. The Sultan demanded a full report when he was informed of the matter by his own spies and news bearers. The local chief reported back to the effect that the finder of the bronze jar was a no-good, illiterate farmer who didn't deserve the bounty.

The Lord of the World issued the following edict: 'Be it known to that fool, the Chief of Sambhal, that the Power Who ordained the finding of the treasure by the farmer Knows more about the worth and value of the finder. The treasure must be returned to the farmer with recompense paid by the Chief of Sambhal promptly on sight of this Command, on pain of the blaze of the Sultan's displeasure destroying him and in no time bringing him down from his cushioned bed to hot cinders and ash.'

The chief was so shaken by the Sultan's peremptory command that he immediately rode out to the farmer, returned the bronze jar with its contents intact, paid him a hundred rupees from his pocket, and obtained a satisfaction certificate from the farmer.

It was reported once from Thanesar, in the territory of Panjab, that the local Hindus have rebuilt an ancient pond there and hold a monthly fair at the site. They also offer obeisance and worship to the water god there. Bells and conch shells are also employed. The local chief prayed for guidance and orders from the Lord of the World. The Sultan considered the matter in religious assembly and ordained that since the pond was a historic artefact and no disturbance of the peace was apprehended by its reconstruction, the pond may be officially declared property of the Hindus, and religious rites and ceremonies allowed to be performed there without the least let.

There was a standing army, eighty thousand strong, in Delhi and its environs in battle-ready status. Tughlaqabad, Ghiaspur, Kelukheri, Begampuri and Siri, ancient cities of Delhi and many of them former capitals of the Sultanate, were surveyed to locate slightly elevated, large, green and water-fed maidauns for erecting barracks and for housing some elements of the standing army. My regiment lived in tents near Ghiaspur, just a little away from the holy river Jamna. Only those who have observed the mighty river can imagine its width and depth and fast flow. When it came into real flood, showing its displeasure to the people there, the entire area from Ghaziabad on the bank of Hindon down to Okhla in the south-east would overflow with water for days and days. That's why the people there had satirically named that whole area Patparganj (that is, land whose alluvium is renewed every year by river waters). Actually, there was nothing there but weeds and wild berries and mosquitoes, sundry biting gnats and creepy, stinging insects and creatures.

Allah, Allah, those were the days! My pay had become seventeen from twelve rupees a month in my ten years of service. The rupee was called *tanka* those days. It was divisible into one hundred copper coins called *bahloli,* for it had first been issued by Sultan Bahlol Lodi who now resides in the highest level of Paradise. The bahloli was so strong that it sufficed for a trip to Kol (modern-day Aligarh) eighty and more miles away if the traveller rode his own horse. I'd made some good friends too. In their company I occasionally visited the nautch girls, did a bit of drinking just as all soldiers did, and still saved four or five tankas for sending home. Maulavi Gul Muhammad had fallen by the wayside, replaced by Gul Muhammad, the armoured infantryman.

It was now the twenty-first year of our Sultan's benignant rule. My daughter was shortly to enter her thirteenth year, an age quite suitable for marriage, which might become overdue in a couple of years. Word came from my home that it would be very desirable for her betrothal and then marriage to take place before the next season of rains. I was summoned to settle all the issues.

Although the Lord of the World, Sikandar Lodi, son of Sikandar Lodi, placed much stress on the Muslims to observe the law of the Shariah strictly in all matters, and especially in the ceremonies relating to marriage, yet we Muslims of Mewat and its surrounding areas still had more than a smack of Hinduism in our life. Except on Fridays, we normally wore Hindu-style dhotis, one end tucked at the back, dividing the two legs clearly into two. Our women didn't observe purdah, but when they went outdoors the upper edge of their saris was worn on the head in a long veil, like an overhang which made it difficult for anyone to look them in the face. Every home had a box in which money was religiously deposited every month to defray expenses at Holi, Diwali, Id or Shab-e Barat. We gave or accepted no dowry but the girls' people always came in strength for the betrothal ceremony which itself cost very nearly as much as the wedding. The bride's farewell ceremony, called the *rukhsati* among other Muslims, and *gaun* or *gauna* by us and the Hindus, was almost always much later than the wedding itself. We didn't marry off our children when they were very young, but we did behave like the Hindus in observing the long gap between betrothal and marriage.

The month of Jaishth was ending, the cooler, rainier month of Asarh was about to begin in a few days when I started for my village. I had managed to assemble a capital of three hundred, three hundred and fifty tankas for I knew that the marriage ceremonies—in spite of what my wife may have collected over the years by way of the bride's jewellery and the groom's clothes—would certainly cost almost all that I was taking with me. I decided to start before the early evening prayer. The day would have cooled by that time and after I'd travelled a stage from the border of Delhi, I could spend the night at an inn and make a very early start the next day, reaching Nangal Khurd, my village, by the evening on the third day. I didn't have much by way of effects and baggage because all the essentials, and more, could be organized from in and around the village, and it was a job best done by the women anyway.

I rode alone with just my horse for company. I was a soldier, after all, and didn't have anything to fear from stray highwaymen. The chief road was mainly clear of the villainous and the miscreant. My route took me to Wazirpur just outside the city, running parallel to the Firoze Shahi Canal up to and much beyond Wazirpur. It then made a sharp turn, to go to Hissar. Darkish, dense trees lined the road all the way. The gloaming on the western horizon and something like mist on both sides of the canal created something of a tunnel effect for me.

After a few miles from Wazirpur, the canal and the road made a sharp turn, making it impossible to see what lay next. Once you entered the bend, you were more or less isolated from the rest of the road, back or front. But that was nothing to worry about. Under the strong rule of our Glorious Sultan, the roads were safe everywhere, and I was only about fifteen miles from the main city anyway. The place where the road suffered the bend was not too far from where I proposed to spend the night. So fear-free, humming a ghazal of Hafiz Shirazi, I let the horse trot at a comfortable pace.

I noticed a small culvert on a dry waterbed which would soon overflow when the skies opened up. On the farther side of the culvert was seated an old woman, truly decrepit, her head practically devoid of hair barring a few white strands, her threadbare wrap barely covering her head, not to talk of her upper body. A truly poor specimen of the begging humanity, I said to myself. Before I'd crossed the culvert, she spoke in a loud, but prayerful voice: 'God saves the singleton and the doubleton!'

By this time I'd crossed the culvert. The old woman, again speaking up, but in a most humbly pleading voice, said: 'Give something in the name of Allah. Have pity on the poor helpless widow!'

I thought, I should not be uncharitable at this time. I was on my way to perform a noble deed, so let me make an auspicious beginning here. So thinking, I thrust my hand in the pocket of my shaluka to bring out a small coin or two, bending a little to the left so as to drop the coin in her lap.

Someone pushed me violently from behind. I was almost unseated, but my left hand was still in my pocket. Furiously, I half turned towards my assailant to deliver a choice word or two of abuse. But someone shot a strong hand around my neck and shoved me towards the first assailant. I was still trying to take out my hand from the pocket when my horse lost its footing and reared up. This was enough to uproot me from my seat and make me lose my grip on the reins. I didn't see what happened to my poor mount because a coarse, black cloth smelling of vomit, sweat and blood was thrown upon my head, totally blinding me. I found myself fainting, my last thought was for my poor little girl, how would she get married if I was robbed and killed here? The cloth was tied around my neck and head, and a handful of it was stuffed into my mouth, but still I tried to draw my dagger, hoping to account for or least one of the villains. They don't realize who I am. They'll know soon enough.

I was almost suffocated now, further wasting my breath in trying to draw the dagger and disentangle my other hand from the pocket which was now quite twisted. I tried to shout with all the lung power that I had, 'Motherfuckers, don't think you can get away from me!' But all I could utter was a nearly inaudible croak. By now they had tied me up like a trussed-up goat being taken to the slaughter, or a criminal being prepared to be strung up the gallows. I felt my strong leather purse, tied to my lower back under the shaluka, being snipped off with more dexterity than running a sharp, hot wire into a pat of butter.

To add more insult to injury, I heard my horse whinnying a bit, but then pacified with a few words of comfort and affection and a loving chirp or cheep, like a kiss, repeated three, four times. These fornicators' sons were past masters at horse enticing and stealing, I knew well. What I didn't know was that this patch of road became prone to highwaymen after sundown. I heard faint sounds of the horse moving away from me, disappearing soon enough. Of the highwaymen and that accursed woman I heard no footfall, no sound. In fact, but for that harridan's two utterances, the entire operation had been silent, like a female cobra. I hadn't heard them breathe, far less cough or clear the throat.

I determined that they didn't want to murder me. It would have been simple, with me tied up and helpless. So robbery was their motive, not murder. I was furious at myself, at the whole army of the Lord of the World, an army whose very name cast a deadly fear in the enemy's heart, an army that had subjugated a huge area on all four sides of Delhi. And here I was, trapped like a wretched mouse, helpless, bereft of everything, like a naked earthworm. Was this how a member of the world-beating army behaved? Fie upon a Sultan and his Sultanate that a member of his military force should be overpowered and robbed less than a stage away from his capital!

But what should I do now? I thought with almost a tearful despair. I'd nothing but a few bahlolis and a little food that I'd packed and hung with my saddle strap. It was likely that some other pettier thief or robber would make away with those, and also make away with my life before he left me. I couldn't call out, I couldn't move, I had no slack in my mouth to try to spit out the gag. In fact, I might even draw it deeper in my effort to get rid of it. I might choke to my death.

I must return to Delhi, to report the outrage and . . . and try to raise money. But how? That was the damnable question.

How much time has passed? It must be dead dark around me now. It must certainly be long past the *maghrib* namaz, which takes place just before sunset. But I could hear nothing, no sounds of the cows' bells, of songs sung by the farmer or the shepherd as he returned to his merry home after the day's labour. No birds seemed to sing as they returned after chattering over their food from all over, talking companionably among themselves—a chief characteristic of the parakeets as they returned in their hundreds to roost in their favourite peepul or neem. Maybe they weren't returning yet? Maybe the dusky red of the evening light wasn't yet quite painted upon the sky. So, it wasn't the time yet for the birds to return. Or perhaps my ears were stunned due to my futile attempts at raising a shout, so I couldn't hear anything at all.

Is it very late now? Is there none coming home or passing this way on their legitimate business? Why should they? Only cretins like me didn't know about the perils of this road. All sensible persons would naturally keep away after dark. Did I hear a tiger's roar a minute ago? No, there are no tigers around here. I shouldn't give way to my foolish, defeatist fancies. But weren't there panthers and cheetahs here aplenty? Well, the cheetah wouldn't hurt a human, even a helpless one. But the panther was something else again. He was fond of shedding blood for no reason. Panthers roamed around on the moist, leafy bank of the Jamna from Delhi to Karnal, like the bulls set free to wander the streets as an act of piety. The panthers were so audacious and unafraid of the smell of the human that they often occupied the solitary homes in the countryside vacated by people due to floods or departure to the city in hopes of getting employment. Also, there were wolves and hyenas to fear.

But wasn't I rather far from the Jamna and its immediate valley? I shouldn't mistake bushes for bears. Sultan Firoze Tughlaq, who now dwells in the Eternal Paradise, built this canal for the express purpose of bringing the water of the Jamna to places where its water couldn't reach due to topographical obstacles. But didn't the moisture around the canal and the dense trees here create an environment like the leafy bank of the Jamna? The Almighty must have Accorded a very high place to the Sultan of blessed memory because of his canals and the profusion of free inns and caravanserais that he erected on their banks. Also, there were caravanserais on the road to Kol, to the north-east. His provision for free food and shelter to all travellers could be my salvation today.

I tried to rub against some stone the ropes that restrained my wrists. But I couldn't see, and I couldn't find a stone however much I groped and felt on the gravel road. And my hands were tied at my back, making all such efforts futile anyway. My ankles were tied even harder and my efforts to rub the restraints against the gravel availed me nothing but scratches and scoriations which would have been bloody, but I couldn't know.

Have the dogs stopped barking? Or are they terrified of a wandering panther, or pack of wolves? But was it not a pack of jackals howling away their peculiar howl—whooaan whooaan whooaan—in some nearby field? I remembered the delegations or ambassadors who often arrived here from China. Many of them had unarmed combat experts in their entourage. One of them told me that some of the more consummate artists in unarmed combat were capable of artificially puffing up their bodies when they were bound and made helpless, so that they could wriggle out of their bonds when an appropriate opportunity came to exhale the extra air from out their tissues and sinews and thus loosen their shackles without having to wrestle with their fetters and fastenings. How I wished I had learnt that art from him! But even then, it would have been useless here, for I had been taken by surprise.

The night must be pretty far gone, without doubt. But is that some rustling, some scraping of a shoe on a bark, some dry twig cracking under someone's foot? Or is it a whisper . . . two whispers? Two persons? Are those sisterfucking pimps coming back? I strained and strained, there was nothing but an empty humming in my ears; perhaps the muscles of my tired throat were aching, or the small amount of air in my comprehensive gag was circulating aimlessly?

No. Wait. There are bells! Is it a temple somewhere nearby? No, I knew the road was pretty bare, tree lined and enclosed on one side by the canal. It was a measured, sedate, stately bell. Surely, there was the gap of a few breaths between rings, and surely there was some small difference in the tone of the bells? Two bells, and certainly an elephant! Robbers don't ride elephants. It must be someone of substance! My heart leapt up in my constricted ribcage. Deliverance must be near, for the sound of the bells was travelling towards me . . . it slowed, stopped. I heard someone say: 'Chait Singh, look, there is something or someone on the road. Man seems to be dead, or unconscious.'

The voice was that of a nobleman, not that of a military man. Its owner was someone sophisticated, used to an easy life of command, not the hard din of battle.

'No, don't get down. Just approach as near as you can, then observe carefully.'

I intensified my efforts to writhe about and roll away from my place to show that I wasn't dead.

'Exalted Honour, it seems to me the dacoits attacked someone and wounded him grievously, leaving him for dead.' A very meek and somewhat frightened voice reported.

'Oh, so it's some wounded man? Perhaps an enemy brought him here with the intent to throw him into the canal and ran away when he heard us approach. All right, advance just a little more.'

'Presence, this could be a trick.' The voice still reflected terror in no small degree. 'It could be that someone is after us for some reason . . . maybe there are thugs around, intent upon doing some mischief to Your Honour.'

I further intensified my rolling and writhing and trying to call out. This time I even succeeded in producing some strangled sounds.

'Trick? What trick could there be? Man, you seem to be a total loss! What could happen to us here? You expect some ambush? There'd have been dozens of arrows inside us by now if it was an ambush! All right, get down now and ascertain the state of the poor fellow!'

'Your Honour, sir . . .' The voice was still full of doubt and unwillingness while I tried to produce some real sounds from my constricted throat.

'Man, you are an utter coward, really. All right, do it like this. Let the elephant go even closer, and then command it to pick up that bundle-like thing. Don't you hear him groaning or trying to speak? Command the elephant to wrap his trunk round him and bring him up to us.'

Chait Singh must have moved the elephant ahead, for I could now hear his whispered commands to it. His words I couldn't determine, but he must have spoken decisively because soon I felt something like a very thick and massive python wrap itself around my body and pick me up with no apparent effort. I wasn't fearful, but certainly felt intimidated, and tried to make myself as small as possible. But I was no match for that cloudy, cloud-like power. In less time than it takes me to say it, I was lifted up and deposited gently somewhere between the mahout and the owner. At least I presumed so.

Chait Singh, and maybe his master too, helped me get rid of the foul gag, wet and sticky with spit and also the extra string that the bastards had tied over the cloth below my chin so as to prevent any light from penetrating inside. It took me sometime to regain my voice and I told them my story, swallowing and pausing for breath frequently. The Master of the elephant said gravely: 'So, Ahadi ji, you were doubly lucky. They didn't take your life and then we turned up soon enough.'

'Each hair in this servant's body will remain tied with the knot of your nobleness towards me. I was quite certain that some carnivore would eat me up before the night was out.'

'Well, you were certainly visited by a calamity but were let off cheaply enough. Forget what happened. It must be God's will. I am for Bahadurgarh and can take you there with no trouble. Afterwards, you may do what you think best. Arrangement can be made for you to stay the night there, if you wish.'

'It's the kindness and nurture of your gracious self to pay so much heed to a poor traveller. It would be well if I could reach Bahadurgarh under Your Honour's protection. I will leave for Delhi in the morning.' I spoke as calmly as I could, suppressing the pain and grief in my heart. I drew a sigh and bowed my head in acquiescence to my fate, or to my saviour, I wasn't sure.

'Very well, Chait Singh, let's go ahead. And yes, Ahadi Gul Muhammad, make sure that you're leaving nothing behind.'

'Sir, what's left now to leave here? The servants of the Presence rescued me from certain death. I am quite content. Please to order the elephant to proceed.'

We exchanged more information about us as we progressed. The good name of the Master was Sri Raghuraj Bahadur Singh. He was going to a relative's marriage some place beyond Bahadurgarh. He too had started late, but that had turned out to be the reason for my redemption from the direst of fates.

We reached Bahadurgarh soon enough and they said goodbye to me before a small caravanserai. The few bahlolis that I'd left were enough for a night's board and lodging, and a seat early in the next day's bullock cart to Delhi. I had four companions in the cart but they were too busy talking about the crop, the produce and the best price for it to be had in Delhi. We made it to Delhi well before afternoon prayer.

5

Was there anything changed in Delhi? Nothing, but nothing. It was I whose status, fate and state of mind were unrecognizable from the confident soldier of the Sultan of Hind and Sind who had set out for his home, making plans for his dear daughter's rosy future. How could I, if at all, organize a loan or contribution of three hundred, three hundred and fifty tankas? I had nothing to offer as security, even if I could find a benevolent—a contradiction in terms—moneylender. My friends were notorious for their thriftless ways. The Khan of the Age was most probably in Agra, in the service of the Lord of the World. His Honour Khan-e Jahan Lodi was away on some military campaign. I knew no other nobles, or rather no other nobles knew me. Any of those two could, if they so wished, relieve my distress in no time, but they couldn't be expected to come back in the next day or two, and spare time and energy to listen to the travail that I'd endured. My revered teacher Bhikari Shah sahib would certainly help, but I couldn't imagine greater shame than asking him for money when I'd done scarcely anything, any service, for him.

Also, how could I reveal to anyone other than my closest friend that I, a sturdy and experienced armed soldier of the Lord of the World, became such an easy prey to a gang of petty highwaymen?

Lost in these thoughts, cogitating over my shame and also all the possibilities to retrieve the situation, I arrived at my barracks quite late in the day. I was happy in a way, for everyone would be on duty somewhere and I could escape their pitiless barbs for a few more hours. But I was chagrined to find my close friend Muhammad Alam Bihari the moment I set foot in my tent whooping out to me: 'Hey! Are you Gul Muhammad, or his ghost? What are you doing here, and why? You should have been in Nangal Khurd long ago.'

Most reluctantly, and cursing him and seething inside, I directed my eye at him. He was half sitting, half stretching on his hard bed, a long rosary in his hand which he'd been obviously telling.

'So, our pious man,' I bit back a stronger word, 'is telling the rosary of a thousand beads! When and how this conversion, dear man?'

He guffawed. 'What are you trying to hide, old fellow? Did you lose all that money on some harlot?'

'Please, let's both be serious now. First you spit it out. Why these beads, and why aren't you on duty?'

'All right, I'd taken a vow to recite salutations to the Holy Prophet a thousand times when my mother got well. I got the good news late last night. And now, what's the matter with you?'

Extremely loath, and with downcast eyes, I narrated my sorry tale. But before I could come to the end, he hollered: 'Oh, oh, oh! By the doorstep of the Presence Nizam-ud Din Auliya sahib, you are a fool to have fallen victim to that she-devil of a hag and her satanic brood! I thought you knew about them!'

I almost fell into a red-hot ebullition of temper, but I held my patience. I swallowed, kept silent for a couple of beats, and then said: 'Right, wise man, you know all and I am a cretinous fool. But what's going on here? Don't pretend to be Amir Khusrau and don't talk in riddles.'

Alam realized that he'd almost been baiting me, sprinkling salt on my burns. He now spoke gravely: 'I am really sorry, yaar. I thought you knew, or I would certainly have warned you. That woman, just beyond Wazirpur at the end of a culvert, waits for the unwary traveller, and her three sons sit in ambush in a coign of vantage under the jutting edge of the culvert. When the harpy notices a lone traveller or two, she sings out, *God saves the singleton and the doubleton!* If there's a larger party that she espies, she sings out, *There's safety in numbers!* When the satanic clutch hear the first signal about the lonely traveller, they spring from their hide and overpower the unfortunate one in no time. They don't kill, but rob him of his last penny that they can find.'

'There's no power and no strength but in God.' I uttered the Quranic verse which we use also for expressing disgust and unhappiness. 'But what do I do now? Who will lend me so much money? And if someone does, how will I repay it?'

'Hey, man! There are numerous lenders. Go to any moneylender, there's wealth enough to borrow. But before they give you any of their wealth, they take away your mental health.'

'So what should I do? Commit suicide? Who will then provide for my poor daughter?' I retorted sharply.

Muhammad Alam was a little abashed and fell silent. I too fell silent, embarrassed at having lost my temper. He was only trying to help. After a few moments, Alam raised his head, but without looking at me, suggested: 'Shouldn't you . . . I mean, shouldn't we approach our friends?'

'No, not at all! What will my daughter feel at being married by subscription? She'll swallow poison and go to sleep for ever.'

'God forbid! I don't mean that we should go from friend to friend, begging pan in our hand. I thought that we could borrow from two or three of our more affluent friends . . . on soft rates . . .'

'Who will believe it?' I cut him short brusquely. 'Who in this world will believe that the girl's father borrowed from friends on soft terms? No. That's not workable. Muhammad Alam, please, don't flatter me to deceive.'

Muhammad Alam could perhaps see that I was on the verge of tears. It wasn't a theoretical problem that I was faced with. It was a life-threatening situation. But he had nothing to offer, really. He bent his head, idling picking at his beads. Seeing that he was as clueless about a solution as I was, I angrily removed my turban, hurled it against the wall opposite, and cried bitterly: 'All right. I'll leave for Nangal Khurd right now. I'll go and stretch my hands before my wife's people, begging them to give me money and make me their slave. I will draw the water and hew the wood for them for the rest of my wife. Bastard, why didn't you forewarn me?'

'Save your breath and save your temper, dear brother,' he said without raising his head. 'Tearing your hair and clawing at your body will avail you nothing.'

'So what do I do? Drink your foul blood?' I shouted.

He smiles a wan smile. 'I'll lance my pulse right now and let you drink your fill, if that could help.'

I struck my forehead with both hands and cried: 'All right, to Nangal Khurd I go. Happen what may, I must give away my poor daughter in marriage on the appointed date.'

Both of us were quiet for a full minute, each of us pondering solutions where perhaps there were none. Finally, and still avoiding my eye, Alam spoke in a low voice, somewhat tentatively: 'Listen, yaar. There could be a solution here. I'll explain if you promise not to take offence.'

I pulled a face. 'I'll try anything unpleasant, if it works out.'

'No, hear me out first. Please. Have you heard of Amir Jan?'

'Who? Amir Jan, that courtesan from Jaipur who lives with the pomp of queens?'

'Yes, the same. Gul Khan, have you heard that she helps out people in distress such as you?'

I was angry at the preposterous idea. 'Help? What help can she give? She lives on other people's riches. She drinks and eats money. Her job is to close her fist on your money, not open her fist for you!'

'Forbear, my friend, forbear,' Alam said coolly, presuming that I was willing to consider his proposal, whatever it was.

But I was still raging inside. 'So I am listening, aren't I? Or should I shove myself into your mouth?'

Alam ignored my rudeness. 'It's heard say that she is not a courtesan by birth. In fact, she was the loved daughter of a very good, but poor family in Jaipur. The parents had the sense of honour and integrity that one associates with people of good upbringing. They didn't want to marry her off to just any comer. They were looking for a groom of good birth, education, means also, if possible.'

'I can understand,' I said. 'Who would know the alarm, the anxiety of a poor parent better than I?'

'So they thought themselves lucky when a young man, matching precisely the description of a most suitable groom, appeared and was willing to marry her. It was like a blind man being offered the gift of sight. They didn't hesitate and married their daughter off without delay.'

I could now anticipate what was going to come. Such stories were, sad to say, not at all rare in any society today.

Alam went on: 'The blackguard took her to Delhi, used her to his heart's content, then he sold her to a whorehouse. The parents heard of the terrible tidings much later and were horrified. The father preferred to pretend that his daughter was dead, but the mother did everything possible to bring her back. She pronounced upon her the oath of her milk, entreated her most abjectly, finally even threatening not to own her before God. But the daughter wasn't to be appeased. She sent word to the mother that they would now be face-to-face on the Day of Judgement and she would demand justice and retribution from God. As of now, she was no more in this world.'

'I now remember hearing of her somewhere, but not her history. I know that the whole of this vast capital city is willing to do her bidding, to carry out her smallest wish. But . . .'

'I know,' said Muhammad Alam. 'She receives her admirers by appointment, doesn't go to anyone's mansion, be he prince or nobleman.'

'So, how can we expect her to rescue us, if she won't see anyone, unless she wants to?'

Alam said, 'Don't be impatient. Apparently, you know something about her, but not all.'

'You mean I should approach *her* for help?'

'Actually, many people in your situation do. It seems that she has quite a substantial amount of money put by, a sort of charitable fund, for precisely such unfortunate individuals and families. She gives interest-free loans for the marriage of poor girls and such.'

'But how should I approach her? Do you think someone will give me an introduction?'

'Brother, do you imagine that the destitute, the wretched, the desperate, wait for someone to volunteer to take them there? Such people go, try their luck, leave everything to fate, that's all.'

'Will *you* come with me?'

'Why not? Do you think I tell you all this just to divert your mood?'

'Still, how shall we get past her door? What could we say to her to carry conviction?'

'Your father was employed at the Khan of the World's haveli. I hear the Khan is an occasional visitor there. You are employed with Asad Khan, the Khan of the Age. We'll begin with their names. And remember, all are not cast in the same mould. Each bundle of straw gives a different flame when burnt.'

I was lost in thoughts of rejection, humiliation, the ignominy of having to ask money from one who was after all a dancing girl, a woman of no virtue. But if persons like the Khan of the Age were visitors there, what shame would attach to me?

I knew this was a specious argument, but the drowning man clutches at straws. And if we succeeded, it was all to the good. If we failed, we failed. We lost nothing. I drew a deep sigh, and said: 'When should we go?'

'Right now. As they say, one doesn't need to consult an almanac to do a good deed. Don't hesitate, I say. As for me, I'll finish my thousand salutations to the Prophet when I return. Indeed, I hereby vow to repeat them and pray that the merit that may accrue thereby should go to the Presence, the Holy Ghaus of Jilan who, I understand, always helps those who are in need.'

'Jazak Allah!' I uttered the most common Arabic prayer to express gratitude. 'May Allah Give you good recompense. I'll owe you forever.'

'There's nothing owed and nothing to repay. Come on, onward to Amir Jan!'

*

Was it a dancing girl's mansion, or a noble's haveli, or king's castle? I was utterly lost at the splendour, the opulence and the display of power. Two mountainous elephants at the massive gate, a spacious and fortified guardhouse on both sides; the upper floors of the gatehouses were high-ceilinged airy rooms, perhaps for the guards to live and/or sleep there when off duty. The guards were all women, or perhaps it's not quite right to describe them as mere women. Very tall, very strong muscled, standing erect. Clearly they were from faraway Caucasus or Uzbekistan. It was a posse of twelve, fully armed. Fair complexioned but the blood of youth and power so coursed in their veins as to make them look tawny; eyes slightly smaller in proportion to the face, but perfectly almond shaped, brown or green in hue. Their breasts rising up from under the tunic, hard but forbidding in their aloofness. They wore tight shalukas with long sleeves; the muscles of the forearms seemed to be straining against the rich fabric. Their trousers extremely tight and looking almost pasted to the body, giving the impression of the legs' utter preparedness to march ahead, or even kick someone. In spite of

such emphasis on tightness, there wasn't the least vestige of the intent
to reveal. Gold-embroidered caps on their heads, a brocade sash around
their narrow waists. That was all by way of physical adornment. The
entire assemblage was in dark blue silk, further accentuating the effect
of masculinity. They stood erect, looking with disdain at the world as
it passed before them.

The elephants compensated for what the girls lacked in decoration
and rich adornment. They were covered with heavy blue velvet
embroidered profusely in gold, with a number of small gemstones
thrown in, a spacious howdah in silver rode on their broad backs;
each of their long tusks wore eight large rings in gold; their forehead
painted with flowery designs in ochre, their bells heavy and brilliant
in burnished copper. They faced the river Jamna, which was just about
a mile from the mansion, and one could see large and small boats
floating or at anchor.

Following a flick of her commander's eye, or maybe of her own
accord, a guardswoman approached and, looking me straight in the
eye, said: 'Yes?'

Her tone was not hostile or rude, but entirely devoid of
encouragement or cordiality. I stammered my well-rehearsed statement
that I was a poor man, soldier by profession, and wished to pay
obeisance to the Honourable Lady for help. I didn't mention that I was
robbed, just that I was supremely needy.

She gestured towards Muhammad Alam. 'And this person is with
you? Why?'

I told her about Alam that he was a fellow soldier. I mentioned
our connection with the Khan of the World and the Khan of the Age.

One of the guardswomen, acting on some gesture from
somewhere, went inside. Somewhat shrunken with awe, we stood
in the sun quietly, trying not to sweat. There was no suggestion that
we could sit, or come nearer, in the shade. The alley, or in fact the
street on which Amir Jan's haveli stood, had just one or two houses,
fairly impressive neighbours. But there was nothing like a stream of

passers-by. Of shops, there wasn't anything much but an attar-seller and a florist on the opposite side of the haveli. I thought I should buy a garland of roses and another of large jasmines, to present if and when we gained admittance. But I couldn't pluck up courage. Who knows, my puny present may be construed as impertinence. We stood, trying not to betray any impatience, trying to dry our sweating faces by stealth, running our hands on our faces and swiping them on our sashes.

Suddenly, there was some command from the interior, because the commander of the guards beckoned with a supercilious finger for us to approach. As we approached, the huge gate was opened, and as we crossed the threshold it was promptly closed.

I'd expected to encounter a private garden when we entered from the inner gate of the guardhouse. There should have been double verandas on three sides of the garden, and a secure path leading us to some kind of sanctum. But there was a narrow and obviously high set of stairs to our right, and a covered alley, which was well lit with lamps placed in niches at suitable intervals and redolent with an extremely pleasant scent. We walked the length of the alley and came to a set of rooms. Thank God we were now asked to sit and wait. Even our soldiers' feet were tired and heavy with standing and also, I suspect, due to our inner tensions.

A half hour, maybe, or more, passed. We were then summoned by another martial-looking woman, slightly older than the women at the gate. We were ushered into a hall—no, not a hall but rather an enclosed polo field. Sorry, I am exaggerating, but the hall was of truly immense proportions. I can't describe any details because I, and I am sure Alam too, didn't have our eyes for anything at all. We just looked ahead, hoping not to stumble. The only thing I remember is the profusion of all kinds of lights creating another day, competing with the day outside.

'My submissions,' someone spoke in an indescribably sweet, musical voice. The voice was just above a whisper, but clear like the tinkle of silver spoons against china. 'You are employed with Khan-e Jahan Lodi Masnad Ali Khan?'

'No, Ma'am. We are foot soldiers in the regiment of the Khan-e Duran Asad Khan. My late father was an employee of His Honour Khan-e Jahan.'

'Please state your purpose again.'

I spoke in fits and starts, trying not to fumble too much. This time, I narrated the facts of the robbery, trying to be as succinct as I could. Between one utterance and the next, I had my eyes firmly to the floor, but I could occasionally sneak a glimpse of the unbelievable durbar. She sat on an ornate ebony chair, two maids fanned her with peacock-feather punkahs. To her right and left stood young Uzbek guardswomen, fully armed, two on each side. I didn't see any appurtenances of dancing or singing. There were, instead, a half-dozen or more large brass cages in which sang and strutted birds which I couldn't even begin to identify. I recalled that the Presence, Sultan Firoze Tughlaq who now rests in God, had an entire pavilion built in front of his palace, called the Kotla, in which he had assembled and put on show the bones, feathers and even full skeletons of all kinds of birds and mammals. Perhaps Amir Jan had taken a leaf out the blessed Sultan's book.

She heard me out without interrupting me. After I finished, she beckoned to one of the girls who stood before her. She went in and promptly returned with four guzzie bags clinking with coins. On another brief gesture from Amir Jan, the maid placed the bags in my somewhat quivering, somewhat unwilling hands. Amir Jan spoke in the same dulcet, but somehow commanding tones: 'These are four hundred tankas: three hundred and fifty for what you lost, and fifty from me as marriage gift to your daughter.'

'Ma'am . . . but it may take me some time before . . .'

'You should devote your energies now to the marriage preparations. Fifty tankas are not a loan, for the rest it's up to you. In your intent you should be honest that you will return it to me. There is no time limit.'

I wished to make some more submissions, but Amir Jan turned her face away, and her maids and bodyguards bent to us in salaam. That was all there was by way of farewell. No words were spoken.

*

My darling daughter was married, and married with more lavishness and ceremony than was usual for families of our status, thanks to the extra fifty tankas from Amir Jan. I sent a formal invitation to Sri Raghuraj Bahadur Singh. He couldn't come, but sent a brocade wrap, five tankas and a basket of fruits and sweets. In accordance with the commandment of the Sultan of Exalted Station, I took care to avoid explicitly non-Muslim ceremonies and displays. But there was one thing which was universal among the Muslims too, though strongly disapproved by the Sharia. The 'bride's farewell' took place not immediately, but after an appreciable lapse of time; in our case, I could get it reduced to two months after much arguing and cajoling.

The news came of the sad departure from this world of the Sultan of High Splendour, Lord of the World, Sikandar Lodi, on his way to Delhi from Agra. *To Allah alone we belong and to Him we return.* The eye of heaven will now never see a Sultan of such grandeur, such awesomeness, such firm control over his people. Perhaps it was not an auspicious step for him to transfer to Agra from Delhi. Agra didn't become all that our Sultan wished it to be. He needed to bring back his magnificent self to Delhi again and again. His health was failing, but none could imagine that his end was so near. Some even said that the move to Agra cost him his health and hence his life.

Changes were inevitable consequent upon the Sultan's departure for Paradise. Who knew which noble would now be elevated as Khan of the World and who would be vouchsafed the rank of Khan of the Age. How will it fare with Asad Ali Khan in the Exalted Court Pavilion of the new Sultan, no one could know. I had the good excuse of my daughter's farewell ceremony, which was to be some time later. So I remained at home. After the farewell, I told my wife that there wasn't any hurry even now. I should wait to see how things developed. The coin and the Sultan's august name in the Friday Orations were now changed. The regiment of the Khan of the Age might even be disbanded. It was thus better that I devote my energy for some time to my neglected cultivation and watch the turn of the events. And in fact, I did need to rest a while after my recent traumas.

One whole year passed. My fields gave a good yield, better than the previous years. I made some money there, and some more through coaching many young men of my and nearby villages in martial arts and the art of unarmed combat. By the end of the second year, I could foresee that in another year I would be able comfortably to pay back Amir Jan's loan. There were no significant developments yet, except that the new Sultan, the Lord of the World, Ibrahim Lodi, had brought back to Delhi the court, the armoury and the chancery from Agra, which retained its strategic position in the campaigns against Raja Man Singh of Gwalior, and other petty kings and rajas farther south. The stations of the Khan of the Age and Khan of the World were still vacant. Perhaps the new Sultan, may his rule and dominion live forever, was of the view that the Khanates didn't need to be filled. I'd heard nothing from Muhammad Alam for many months now. Perhaps our regiment was disbanded, after all.

Unto my daughter was given a beautiful son three years into the marriage. The usual celebrations and merrymakings ensued. I said in my heart that this was an auspicious augury for me to return to Delhi, repay Amir Jan, and seek my fortunes anew.

It was early winter. The days and nights were glorious, made even sweeter by the occasional drizzle. I started out for Delhi on a sunny day, the village astrologer confirming that all the stars were favourable for me to start immediately, or at best, within three days. I invoked Allah's Blessings, and had a coin dedicated to the Imam-e Zamin (the eighth Imam of the Shias) tied on my left upper arm. My wife made an offering to some Hindu devi and vowed to give all of it in alms when I reached my destination safely.

It was the October of 1521. A bright, heart-warming and beaming day; some clouds in the sky far above suggested that there might be some occasional rain during the course of the journey. Kites and a solitary hawk or eagle watching on the earth from the high heavens, the eternally hungry crows keeping themselves vigilant for carrion or live prey, sparrows in their hundreds fossicking through the fields as the early wheat crop was gathered. Every sort of game, animal or bird, apparent everywhere in a crush of hoofs, horns, claws and feathers. The orchards were alive with peafowl, the trees colourful with green pigeon, the road and the fields on both sides busy with the coming and going of blue bull, blackbuck, four-horned antelope, spotted deer of all sizes and hog deer; black or grey partridge, mountain and plain quails strutting around, as if it was they who had called up the nice weather. All were out to welcome the winter and to forget that there were such things as fiery, stormy days roasted alive by the westerly wind.

I rode no horse but travelled with a small caravan: I had a good amount of silver with me and there was safety in numbers anyway, and I'd already been purged of false pride in my prowess and status as a fighting man.

We reached Delhi late in the afternoon, just after the asr prayers, on the third day. The world was the same, even if the Sultan was new. Great cities did not change as people do. The open maidauns in front of the Paradise-abiding Sultan Firoze Tughlaq's Kotla were unpopulated as before. Matka Shah sahib's shrine, then the ancient Fort of Rai Pithaura, and between them somewhere, hidden by dense trees and foliage, the shrine of Bibi Fatima Sam; eunuchs and *zananas* (men who dressed and lived like women) singing the praises of the Exalted Presence Nizam-ud Din Auliya sahib and offering cool drinking water to all comers, Hindu or Muslim, were in place as before. The mausoleum of my Paradise-dwelling Sultan was nearing completion in the centre

of an extensive garden. Sultan Bahlol Lodi, now dwelling in the shade
of God's Throne, was buried quite a distance away in Khvajah Sahib,
but his coin was still the coin of the realm.

6

I had little hope of finding, far less rejoining my old regiment. Still, I
went to our old barracks merely in the hope of finding someone with
whom I could stay the night. My heavy purse, big with money, didn't
make it an attractive proposition to stay in some inn or caravanserai,
where most probably I'd have to deposit the money with the innkeeper,
thus attracting attention to myself.

Ghiaspur was there where it should have been, but there was no
trace of my regiment. All I could find out was that Khan-e Dauran
was in Bharaich, in the eastern territories, on some campaign. His
regiment may or may not be with him. I decided not to waste further
time, for it was early evening now, and decided to stay at one of the
caravanserais established by the Paradise-abiding Sultan Feroze Shah
Tughlaq. The nearest such establishment, as far as my memory went,
was in Badarpur, on the border of Tughlaqabad. Delhi was far enough
from there, and Ferozabad, the neighbourhood near the Feroze Shahi
Kotla where Amir Jan had her haveli, was still farther. Still, good sense
suggested that I stay at the caravanserai in Badarpur.

Morning dawned. I spent more than usual care over my personal
appearance, put on new clothes, slightly more expensive than I
normally wore. I hadn't surrendered my money belt to the mistress and
slept with it under my pillow. Thank God it was quite safe and intact. I
was so keen to revisit Amir Jan, or maybe to repay her loan, that I set
out without eating breakfast. Fortunately, the mistress could get me
a suitable horse on hire, and the distance didn't at all seem forbidding
in the hopeful pink of the morning. In point of fact, it took just over
an hour at an easy trot.

The bank of the river Jamna was active as usual, but what was going on there at the mansion? Did it not seem somewhat forlorn, or was it my imagination? The massive gatehouse was dismally devoid of guard or elephant. The exterior looked grim, disconsolate. The attar-seller and flower-seller too were missing. I looked at the river, practically in front of me, to make sure that I was at the right place. I was. There was no doubting the place. Had she left Delhi for some other city, Agra maybe? Or finally giving way to her mother's entreaties, had she gone back home to Jaipur to a quiet life? Had she married again and settled with her new husband?

I decided to go on up to the riverbank and inquire there. I had taken a few steps when I noticed someone in an open palanquin coming from the direction of the river. Perhaps he could tell me something. I moved a little into the road, not to block his way, but to make it clear that I wished to speak to him. That gentleman was perceptive enough to realize that I wanted to ask him something. He bade his bearer to stop near me and craned his neck to look at me closely.

'Sir, do you need something?' he asked.

'No, not exactly, Honoured sir, but I was hoping to pay a visit to Amir Jan sahib.'

'Amir Jan? Sir, she is no more in this world.'

Shocked, I took an involuntary step or two backwards, as if to distance myself from the news. I spurred my horse so clumsily back that I almost lost my seat.

'What is it that you say, dear sir? The last time I met her she was in exceedingly good health!'

'It was no disease, sir. It was a calamity, a bolt from the blue.'

'Sorry. I don't follow. What could have happened to her? Please forgive me, but I am not questioning you. It is just that I had some urgent business with her.'

'Well,' he said wryly, 'that business must now await the Day of Judgement. She died by drowning not a couple of hundred paces from here.'

Finally, what I could glean from my kind informant was that Amir Jan had acquired a small, very stylish boat, a *morpankhi*, which is designed and painted to look like a peacock. She was so enamoured of it when it was delivered at the jetty that she desired to go out in it that very minute. Her guardswomen and the boatmen all tried to make her desist, because the river was in a mighty flood and was flowing even faster than usual. Already a heaving host of tumultuous currents, now the river was perfectly unmanageable. But she insisted and they couldn't resist her. The boat was cast off with her and some favourite guardswomen on board, and was handled by the most experienced boatman. But it seemed to have been pulled in quickly by a tremendous heave and thrown right into the midst of a whirlpool. That was the end of the boat and its occupants. The boats of their lives were swallowed by the waters of death. Not a single body was found for some days, except the remains of the boat itself somewhere near Kosi Kalan, fifty miles down the river. By the Glory of Allah, Amir Jan's body was swept to the shore on the third day to enable a proper burial.

'"To Allah alone we belong and to Him we return." Sir, I am much obliged.' I was almost in tears.

'Sir, it was hubris,' he returned. 'None should try to challenge the Force of Allah's Waters. But she was an unusually charitable woman. Perhaps that's why the river returned her body.'

'"There is no Lord and Master but You and I am become one of the sinners."' I recited the prayer of the Prophet Jonah. 'I am sure you are right, sir. The Prophet Jonah was also pardoned. Where was she buried, have you any idea? In Jaipur, perhaps?'

'No, sir. She'd left a will desiring that when her time came she should be buried in the graveyard facing the mausoleum of the Presence Sidi Maula, the Abyssinian. And her wish was carried out.'

'I heard that those who die by drowning are raised among the martyrs.'

'It is in Allah's Hands,' said he, gesturing towards the river.

'All of us will have to render our accounts on The Day. One hopes that she will be dealt with gently.' I replied. 'I must thank you, sir, for giving me all this information, or I would have been wandering everywhere, looking for her.'

We parted. But I had an urgent problem to solve. There was no way now that I could return her loan, so what should I do with the money? Give it away in charity with the prayer that the merit of it may be entered in her good deeds? Perhaps. Perhaps I should go back to Delhi and consult some pious man. But more important, I needed to visit her grave and say the prescribed prayers and Quranic verses for the peace of her soul. I knew quite well the location of the Presence, Sidi Maula sahib's mausoleum, and the graveyard opposite. It was just a few hundred yards short of the shrine of the Presence, Nizam-ud Din Auliya, Sultan of all Friends of God. The village of Ghiaspur was a couple of miles beyond the shrine.

The graveyard produced the illusion of a garden or orchard because of the profusion of fruit trees. There was no dearth of birds, rabbits and painted partridges, the male striking in black, red and blue, the female just black and grey spotted. Their call was extremely distinctive. A shed with a number of large and small pitchers full of water for pilgrims and passers-by, and a shallow but largish trough for bird and beast had been established there in the name of the Presence, Nizam-ud Din Auliya. I don't know who endowed it and from where the payment to the attendant and other expenses were met, but the water station was always busy. I decided to finish the business of Amir Jan, offer my obeisance at the shrine of Sidi Maula sahib, then Nizam-ud Din sahib, and go back to my inn at Ghiaspur. All this to be done during the day of which a substantial portion remained. I could return in good time for an early dinner at the inn.

I was somewhat surprised to see the water station abandoned, though some water containers were still there. It wasn't difficult to locate Amir Jan's grave because of the gravestone which clearly showed her name and requested the passer-by to pray for her soul. The soot stain in the niche where a lamp should have been lighted every night was very faint, as if there had been no lamp lit there for quite some time. I was saddened by the end of a magnificent woman who was queen-like in her style of life, and who considered herself equal, if not superior to the noblemen and the exalted Khans.

But there was something even more shocking. There was a large opening on the side of the grave that faced me. Allah, Allah, what splendour and what pride, what amour propre and what haughtiness! But she was now helpless against the grave robber, the badger, perhaps the snake even. I looked around for some lumps of clay and rock so that I could mix some dry grass or small twigs as a binder, wet the whole thing with water and close the gaping hole. There was no difficulty in finding those things. I came close to the grave so that I could fill the gap with wet clay and pat it closely shut.

But there was some light emanating from the grave. I stepped back in confusion and no little misgiving. Were the grave robbers still inside? But whoever saw a grave robber, or any thief advertising his presence with a light? Then what was going on here? From a safe distance, I gazed as intently as I could. The light was not pale, like that of a candle. It was light green, an uncommonly cooling light for the eyes. I screwed my courage to the sticking point and went nearer. The light was still there. If anything, it was stronger. I ran anxious eyes all round, hoping to see some pious visitor, some passer-by. But there was no one there. And something else: the birds had all fallen silent. The peafowl with their sharp, long, penetrating call seemed to have run away. The partridges seemed to have gone back into their bush and shrubbery. It was just like a full solar eclipse at midday when it seems that evening has fallen. The trees didn't wave their branches, the birds had disappeared in the fastnesses of tree and foliage. A dingy light supervened everywhere. But where was the occasion for a solar eclipse, any kind of eclipse here? It was broad daylight when I came, how could everything be so murky, so soon?

I turned to run away. But the light seemed to be inviting me. It was as if someone lit a lamp with green shade exclusively for my . . . my what? Delectation? God save me from such delectations. Oh my God, what had I done to merit this heavenly . . . this infernal invitation?

I drew near. Whoever thought of an invitation from a grave? No, I needn't tarry any more. This is certainly some jinn, or mischievous genius haunting this place. I have already recited in my heart enough verses of the Quran to suffice for a prayer for the dead. Let me take to my heels, reciting the Verse of the Chair—sure protection from all non-human, evil threats. But first I should recite the very last chapter of the Quran, renowned all over the world as the Chapter of Refuge:

Say: I seek refuge
With the Lord
And Cherisher
Of Mankind,
The King
Of Mankind,
The Judge
Of Mankind—
From the mischief
Of the Whisperer
Of Evil, who withdraws—
The same who whispers
Into the hearts of Mankind—
Among Jinn
And among Men.

I drew back, and found myself closer. What a strange pulling power this light has! Perhaps it's not Amir Jan's grave. Perhaps it is some powerful saint like Sidi Maula sahib, capable of changing the appearance of things, of changing the human heart and soul, who lies buried here?

Ya Allah, if it is some jinn, or evil spirit, please, let Amir Jan's soul, and her grave, be rid of that malevolent being. If it is a sign of the punishment meted out in their graves to the sinners, please, please, Ya Allah, as a sign of favour to Your Prophet and Beloved, let it be mitigated. I vow that once I am assured that Amir Jan is not undergoing punishment, I will, on release from this graveyard . . . go immediately to Nizam-ud Din sahib's shrine and spend the entire three hundred and fifty tankas for food to be cooked and distributed free to whoever comes there.

I certainly want to run away . . . But let me bend a little closer and see what else is there . . . No, it's not a hole, it's more like a secret door, operating on some kind of spring. I must have pressed the spring inadvertently . . . it's like a set of shallow stairs, as there are for going down into the underground cellars of opulent homes. There are many lights here. It's some occasion for the affluent, some celebration, perhaps. But inside a Muslim grave? My feet proceed unbidden towards the stairs. Can I stop myself? But now I am already down a few steps. What if that secret door closes when I reach the bottom? Was this something like Alladin's spurious uncle and the cave down which he went, and then the uncle clamped the cave shut when Alladin refused to surrender the lamp? But I have nothing to surrender except my own life. Let me go back. There's still time. When I look back I can see the hole . . . the door and the muddy light beyond it. It must be about three o'clock in the afternoon. I can comfortably make it to the Presence, Nizam-ud Din sahib's shrine, away from it all. He was God's chosen slave, he was also a refuge for the fearful like us.

7

A garden, extending far, as far as my eye could see. Water channels, ornamental ponds with silver and crystal fountains merrily singing away, each drop of the water bright with the reflection of the sun. But there was no sun that I could see. The light was cool, uniform, not throwing any shadows. But how was that possible? I must be dreaming.

Yes, I must be. But the water is lightly scented with the cool fragrance of keora, reminding me more of the eastern climes where the keora plant grows in abundance, and not the arid air of Delhi where I went to sleep. Went to sleep where? I don't know and I don't care. I am going to enjoy the rare sights and even rarer sounds here than cogitate on my mental or physical estate. There are many birds here that I can't identify. Their twitter is all around me, like the light, welcome showers of early winter.

It's certainly a meadow, an artificially laid and managed meadow. How else do I see white buck drinking water from a pond in the middle distance, which seems to be the twittery, raucous haunt of numerous large and small birds? I can see the great saurus, the golden pheasant, a muster of peacocks, a pandemonium of large hilly parakeets. The deer are drinking from various ends and corners of the pond. One of them looks back, observing something with large eyes, black as if with kohl, and now wider in surprise. Its long, graceful neck and head with two delightful, short and rounded ears make it a painting more than real life. There are huge birds, eagles, and even larger birds, perhaps they are the simurg of legend and the poets' world? Occasionally, a fish eagle swoops down and its silhouette is reflected against the water. Perhaps that's what startled the deer.

I walked on, not wanting my dream to end. One thing surprised perhaps more than most: there were women gardeners everywhere. No males, and the women dressed much better than any females I saw in Delhi, and all of them young, and more surprisingly, quite conscious of their youth and beauty. As if they were acting a part. I now saw a large white building, apparently somewhat farther than the pond in the middle distance. Fired with curiosity, I walked towards it, though sedately, not liking the heart-enticing meadow scene to end. But I'd walked only a few steps when the building stood, stately and aloof, in front of me.

Amir Jan's mansion, or a replica of it. I'd left it only a couple of hours ago, so I remembered it, well enough. The only difference was that this pile was all marble white while the real one . . . I mean the one in Delhi, was in red sandstone and grey marble. The one here seemed to be like a carafe of cool, snow-white milk. It seemed to tempt me to somehow lick it and swallow it, as children do with the cold foam of milk and sugar called *namash*. I looked to the right: it was right there, the thunderous river Jamna. There were no bathers at the ghat, but cargo boats, budgerows, tiny pleasure boats, large sailboats, ships, everything was as before. Lascars were busy loading and unloading. It was business as usual. It was broad day when I visited there first, but now it seemed to be evening at the ghat. No elephants, no Uzbek guardswomen were to be seen.

I entered boldly. It was the same again: a tall, somewhat narrow set of stairs on the right, not quite winding like the stairs inside Qutb sahib's tower, but certainly dauntingly high. In front of me, the usual closed path like a secure corridor. The baffling, uncanny and evenly spread bluish-green light seemed to be inviting me, and also following me everywhere. I didn't care if it was something like the land of magic. I had to go up and see where exactly this bewildering scene was located.

I went up, trying to keep count of the stairs, but immediately lost the count. Was it proper to count the stairs, at all? What was this outlandish structure? Will the stairs ever end? Why did I keep forgetting their count? Will these devilish—I beg Allah's Pardon, not devilish but puzzling—adventure ever end? I felt my gorge rise. It's not a place meant for the living? But am *I* alive? How do I happen to be . . . But the stairs suddenly ended, on a wide terrace, quite open but with an ornate marble pavilion, at one end. Something like an observation platform. I went up to the dizzy edge and looked all around. I could distantly, but clearly, see Qutb sahib's Tower. So I was still in Delhi, or rather, still in the same graveyard? No, but there was a door beckoning to me in the pavilion, which didn't seem to be as bright as the sky under which I stood. I hadn't noticed any door when I came up here a minute ago. I must have missed it. But how? The door was quite distinct and the distance wasn't much. Perhaps I was meant to enter, just as I was meant to enter the grave?

I went in. The light suddenly changed to reveal the same interior of the mansion where Amir Jan gave audience to me. I swear by all that is holy, I swear by the Exalted Doorstep of Sultan ji's sacred mausoleum, there was nothing different here. Amir Jan sat on a large ornate chair like a queen, two maids behind her with peacock-feather fans, guardswomen, armed to the teeth and of the same kind as I saw before, stood on both sides of her and at all the corners of the chamber. Some music was playing very softly, but I couldn't identify the instrument, or the source. Something like an organ, maybe? No one was looking at me. They seemed statues, but for the movement of the fans. My footfall was deadened by the thick carpet on the floor. I must state my purpose here. Let them not misunderstand me as an interloper. I cleared my throat. Suddenly, everyone seemed to be aware of my presence. One of the guardswomen looked daggers at me.

'Ma'am, I . . . I came . . . to repay . . .'

I wasn't allowed to finish my sentence. Amir Jan looked at me with boundless disdain and asked: 'Who is this man? How did he come here?'

I tried again. 'Ma'am, please. I want to repay . . .'

Now Amir Jan spoke in cold anger. 'Throw this man out. How dare he enter here!'

'Ma'am, I am your servant, Gul Muhammad, the soldier. Perhaps you don't remem . . .'

Now her countenance bore disgust more than anger. She turned to one of the guardswomen, practically turning her splendidly clad back to me, and commanded: 'Why do you stand here, gaping like fools? Don't you know we don't permit strangers here? Kick him out now. I don't want him here for a minute more.'

Two of them advanced towards me, daggers bared. A few more appeared from behind the arras, their faces cold and pitiless. Before I could react, the first two were upon me like lightning in human form.

'Vacate this chamber now,' one of them spoke with cold arrogance. 'Or this dagger will be investigating your insides.' She gestured towards the door. I was mesmerized, unable to move my eyes away from that murderous, dagger-wielding beauty. What if she does stab me? But now, all the women who had appeared from behind the arras encircled me and moved towards the door. I had no choice but to move with them. But before I could take my first stumbling step, one of the encirclers, a tall, extremely handsome Abyssinian, shook me by the shoulder, as if waking me up, and pushed me.

She followed me across the pavilion, her grip still strong on my shoulder. The stairs no longer looked winding, or narrow. She practically walked me down, not letting me stop to catch my breath. The lights still pursued me. She reached the door, opened it on the inside, patted my shoulder, and beckoned to the door, but her eyes somehow seemed to say that if the time and place were favourable . . .

There was no garden now. In terror and confusion, I looked back. There was no door, no mansion, no view of the river. But was it a bazaar in front of me, or was I dreaming again? Young, handsome, well-dressed men, enjoying or trying to enjoy a glimpse or two of the beautiful, youthful girls and women and beardless boys rolling along in the bazaar; it's clear that they are not shoppers, they are enjoyers of life; the women also seemed to be enjoying the attention that they could clearly perceive from behind the curtains of their palanquins. And some were fearlessly, without the purdah, seated on sumptuous open palanquins or raths, surrounded by admirers and handmaidens ready to do their slightest bidding. I could clearly see some of them, behind the purdah or without it, huge black eyes like the ripe jamun fruit, or black and brown eyes like the sherbet of hibiscus flowers. If I imagined for the tiniest moment that one of them was looking at me, life seemed to course anew through my tired body.

Shops, bursting with merchandise. You can buy here an ostrich egg or a fan of ostrich feathers as easily as a real, live ostrich looking at the world with mournful eyes from behind a movable shuttering loaded on ox carts. Unbelievably large heaps of precious stones on display velvets in the front part of the jeweller's shop; gold and silver seem to be of no account here. A wide canal running through the length of the bazaar, with flowering shrubs on both sides. The water of the canal clearer than any mountain spring; passers-by freely dipped their hands into the water and drank from makeshift cups fashioned with two or even one palm of the hand. And the water was fully free from dust or garbage. I could see the stewards of the canal, long staff in hand, watchful and ready to swoop upon any passer-by foolish enough to try to drop some garbage in the water. Their assistants had fine nets fastened to the end of long poles. The moment a dead leaf or flower petal falls into the water, they extend their poles like large, long pelicans with a big crop hanging from the neck.

I was unable to count the birds and animals on display or for sale. The whole bazaar rang with their calls. Trainers of all kinds of animals—from elephant to partridge and quail—put up their myriad shows, from dancing to fighting. Open perches on large, hand-driven carts; numerous pigeons perching on them, or flying back to them after wheeling in the sky as high as they could. Another cart had open perches practically studded with small birds. Some of them fly around and return to their open home, undaunted by the spectators stretching their necks or hands the better to observe them or even touch them. They're obviously trained to fly free and come back, as inspectors doing their rounds.

I could see dancers and singers, but I could hear no sound. I could see their lips moving, their hips gyrating, their breasts jutting, mocking at the spectators. I could see the musicians playing on their instruments, almost in a frenzy, but no sound reached me. Was I dreaming? Or was it another act of magic wrought upon me by Amir Jan . . . or was it her ghost? But Muslims never become ghosts, we don't believe in ghosts. Supernatural control of time and space, then, but for what purpose? What objective could be fulfilled for Amir Jan by deceiving me thus?

I couldn't hear the music here, nor the sound of people walking and talking, carriages passing, their drivers calling to clear the way. But I'd heard everything spoken in Amir Jan's pavilion.

. . . I should go back, to Delhi, or is it some other city? Must be Delhi because I clearly saw Qutb sahib's Tower in the far distance. Maybe the river that I observed wasn't Jamna, but is there another city with a tower identical with Qutb sahib's? No, I can't truthfully say that the tower I saw was identical to Qutb sahib's. I saw it from a far distance, after all. So it could be a superficial resemblance. But nothing was beyond God's Power. Perhaps there is another city somewhere which is just like Delhi and its river just like the Jamna, and its tower just like Qutb sahib's? God could certainly create another Presence like the Exalted Qutbuddin Bakhtiar Kaki sahib in some other city, even in some other world. I have somehow travelled to another city and the rest must be daydreams. But was there another Amir Jan, dead or alive? I clearly remembered my informant telling me that Amir Jan died by drowning some time ago. But I did see her, or another like her, just recently . . . then a new thought occurred to me: The Amir Jan whom I saw didn't at all acknowledge me. She didn't seem to be aware that I was her debtor, or that she had a debtor at all. She didn't recognize my name, treating me as a stark stranger. So was it another Amir Jan, in another country? In fact that mystery woman never revealed her name to me. It was I who assumed her to be Amir Jan.

I suddenly felt dizzy, as if I were spiralling down from a height. I squeezed my eyes shut while I could hear the wind rushing past me at great speed.

*

I opened my eyes to find that the pressure on my ears and my brain was very nearly gone. I lay, foetus fashion, and suddenly realized that I hadn't actually fallen: I had rushed out of the opening in Amir Jan's grave as one pursued by unnatural beings. I didn't look behind once I dimly glimpsed the aperture in the grave. I sprinted up the stairs, not stairs, no. It was a gentle slope. Anyway, I sprinted, panting and exhausted, and fell down, scrunching my body like a foetus, and fainted.

It was evening now around me. I could see the lights in the shrine of Sayyid Bhoore Shah sahib, or maybe in the much larger shrine of Baba Nizam-ud Din sahib, Sultan of all friends of God. It was just a few hundred yards from Bhoore Shah sahib to Sultan ji sahib.

Stiff limbed, I rose and shook myself like a dog. I dusted the detritus of scrub and bush off my clothes as best I could, and prepared to leave. It was quite dark and I needed to put each step carefully.

. . . But where was Amir Jan's grave? If I came out through the opening in it and collapsed in front of it, then where was that grave? And why do I believe that it was evening? I entered that grave just after the time for the afternoon prayer, which was at about one in the afternoon, it being just the beginning of winter. At this time of the year sundown in Delhi was well past five o'clock, in fact nearer six than five. I was inside that . . . that . . . grave for the best part of three hours, at the most. So the time shouldn't be much past four in the afternoon. Frantic, I looked all around like one deranged. All I could see was scrub and skirl, shrubs or small trees of wild filbert, henna, clumps of reed growing from scree and stone. There was no sign of Amir Jan's grave. Granted that it wasn't very prominent to start with, but it had a headstone with her name on it. And where was the water station dedicated to the Presence Sultan ji sahib, and where the nearby well?

I lost my wits for the second time that afternoon and began to bound like a frightened hare. But there was no path marked, no indication of direction, except the distant lights. I might tumble into that well . . . I pulled myself short like a horse whose rein is pulled violently. Panting, I stopped to reconsider my state. I must decide upon my course of action with a cool head. The first thing was that for whatever bizarre or curious reason, it was no longer the time of daylight. Night was upon me and there could be no question of my spending the night here alone, exposed to the weather and creeping creatures, and worse still, to whatever ghost or *efreet* was after me—night was the best time for the subterranean being to hunt me. Plucking up courage, I raised my head and looked around again, my sight dim with terror. But it was the same view. I'd made no mistake. I wasn't imagining things. So, I must now put each foot forward carefully, lest I step on a snake or scorpion, or stumble into an open grave. But where were the well and the water station? Perhaps the well had dried up and someone had it closed to prevent the unwary from falling into it. And when the well dried, the water station closed too.

. . . But wasn't it just this afternoon that I went down into the well . . . no, no, into the grave, and both things were functional? Allah, what sin had I committed? I was not the first man to borrow money to get his daughter married. And was it a sin to try and pay back my debt?

I began to walk with extreme care, as if on eggs. I kept in my mind the location of the lights that I saw when I quit . . . came out of the grave. I dragged myself sometimes, sometimes I crawled, having wrapped my turban on my hands and arms, thus creeping like one fettered. I hoped that no scorpions lived there, but I could do nothing to fend against snakes or poisonous chameleons. In fact, I was prepared to be stung by a snake but not spend a night there, or anywhere within sight of the graveyard, even if some safe place could be found.

I managed to crawl out, or stumble out, whatever. The lights were now brighter and clearer. The mausoleum of Sidi Maula sahib was perhaps hidden somewhere behind the dense growth of trees . . . but there was no dense growth at the time . . . shut up, you stupid footman! Don't think of those things now. Try to escape unscathed from this place.

There used to be nothing but dense undergrowth between the Presence, Sidi Maula sahib, and the Presence, Bhoore Shah sahib, from where one could clearly observe the shrine of Nizam-ud Din sahib, the Beloved of Allah. But where there used to be a narrow footpath joining all those holy places, now there seemed to be a sort of road.

I faced the Exalted Threshold. A number of people were coming out after the prayers; some waited at the Presence Amir Khusrau sahib's grave, where qawwali was being presented. Some of the poems were in Persian and I could understand the language well, but some were in some sort of language like Hindi, which I could recognize and understand, but couldn't speak because it was quite different to the Hindi that I was used to. But this country must be Hind, and this city none other than Delhi? I noticed everybody was clad somewhat differently from what I used to wear. Their trousers were very wide, very long, such that their feet were quite covered by the trouser bottoms. They did have turbans of many varieties on their heads, but they wore another, much shorter dress above their long tunics. Oddly enough, the sleeves were long, but cut away from above, near the elbow, thus the lower part hung loose. I couldn't fathom the reason for this. Another thing that looked quite unusual to me was the fabric, of their tunics; it wasn't plain grey or white, but printed with flowers, or stripes. Their trousers too were of the same type of striped fabrics and in many colours. We always favoured dark grey, or very dark green, almost black, or heavy red, like the oil expressed from mustard, for our trousers.

I stood at the sacred threshold, looking at everyone blankly, like a cretin, not knowing where to go, or what question to ask to gain some enlightenment. One or two visitors stopped short for a moment, looked at me casually, and passed. Some just stared surreptitiously. Finally, I noticed someone who seemed kindly and sympathetic. As he passed by me, I spoke up in my best Hindi: 'Sir, please. I want to ask something.'

The stranger looked hard at me. I couldn't be a beggar. Possibly a traveller from some far country. He answered in gentle tones: 'Please command. What service can I do for you?'

His voice had a sophistication, a cordiality that I could never hope to match, especially in the Hindi that those people spoke. He spoke as if he was in no hurry, that he didn't at all mind being accosted by a stark stranger.

In confusion, I switched to Persian: 'Honoured master, is this city Delhi or not?'

He smiled briefly. 'My master asks something strange. But certainly, this is Delhi. What did your kind self imagine it to be?'

'No, no, sir, nothing of the sort,' I returned quickly. 'But this city is rather different from the Delhi that I knew.'

'My life for you, has my respected friend come to Delhi after a long time?'

I didn't know what to say to this. My head began to ache and my heart began to beat fast, as if I had been doing some rigorous duty. I felt giddy and fell down in a faint.

When I came to, I found myself lying in a bed in the outer veranda of my benefactor's house. A physician had been and gone, diagnosing shock, fatigue and an empty stomach, with gases rising from the pit of the empty stomach and pressing on the diaphragm. I had nothing like the grand mal or some such malady. He had some smelling salts and herbs placed under my nose, ordered light food and complete rest, and left, saying that the patient would be his usual self by the morning.

I was happy that no inquiry was made about my origins. My benefactor, whose name was revealed to be Hamiduddin, simply took me for a traveller from some distant land. A small town called Isa Khail in Sind was the farthest place from Delhi that I could imagine without having to dissemble much (where I could easily be found out). So I pretended that I had been in Isa Khail for a score of years and had been employed as armed guard at the gate of a local nobleman. I came to Delhi just the last evening, having left home in search of a better fortune. Being almost a stranger now in Delhi, I'd lost my way and couldn't regain my caravanserai, which was the reason for my further confusion of mind.

Hamiduddin believed my tale, imagining that my faint was merely a passing episode, caused by fatigue and anxiety. My somewhat incoherent conversation at the shrine he put down to the above reasons, and the difference in my Persian accent and my comparative discomfort in Hindi was because of my long sequestration from Delhi. But why was my stomach empty? That may have been a puzzle for him, and was certainly a puzzle for me because according to my calculation I'd eaten only a few hours ago.

My host must have believed that I was somehow short of money and hadn't been able to buy food for the many hours that I had been wandering. He was too well bred to tax me on this matter. But my biggest problem was to explain why Delhi was so unfamiliar to me. I thanked my stars that I was able to invent a nobleman in Isa Khail at whose gate I was employed as an armed guard. Hamiduddin smiled good naturedly, and said: 'That's very well, sir. For, we are in the same profession. I am employed as armed guard at the *deorhi* of the Khan of the Age, Abdus Samad Khan sahib.'

I wasn't familiar with the word 'deorhi'. It was clearly not Persian, but I imagined it to be something like the chief entrance to a grand building. But I was fully familiar with the title Khan of the Age.

'So Asad Khan sahib, son of Mubarak Khan sahib, no longer occupies the position of Khan of the Age?'

He knitted his brow in concentration. 'Sir, I don't know any Khan of the Age called Asad Khan, son of Mubarak Khan sahib. Abdus Samad Khan has been Khan of the Age since the auspicious times of Raushan Akhtar Muhammad Shah Padishah Ghazi, who now dwells in Paradise.'

My head reeled again. Who is this person with the long name? He is remembered with such awe even when he's dead. I tried to gain control of myself, leaning back against the bolster, pretending that I still was quite tired. I stammered out the question: 'So the Lord of the World Sultan Ibrahim Lodi is no longer Sultan?'

This time the knitted brow of my newly found friend indicated a little pique. He was quiet for a few moments, then spoke gently, but with a hint of suspicion: 'Sir, you seem to forget. There never was a King named Ibrahim Lodi on the throne of Delhi.' He paused, and thought some more. 'Oh, do you mean a Sultan Ibrahim Lodi of Delhi, who was many centuries ago defeated by our King Zahir-ud Din Babar in the battle of Panipat? Yes, that Sultan was killed in battle, and is buried in the very maidaun where he tasted defeat and then death.'

He looked at me intently. He seemed to be trying not to revise his opinion of me as an honest traveller. Darkness overtook my eyes and senses again. My Lord of the World, our Sultan Ibrahim Lodi of Exalted Station, son and successor of Sultan Sikandar Lodi, dead and buried in some unknown battle plain? And what's this about King and Padishah? Our rulers always referred to themselves as Sultan.

Seeing me so pale and perhaps sick, Hamiduddin hurried to say: 'Sir, your distemper seems to persist. May I venture to suggest that you eat something and retire to an early rest. Did you mention a Firoze Shahi caravanserai? We could go there in the morning. I am not familiar with a hostelry of this name, but there used to be a well-known hostelry called Arab Sarai near Khvajah Sahib. It's now full of little apartments, but perhaps we could find out more about the Firoze Shahi caravanserai there in the light of day.'

'I will remain bound to you always, my kind sir. But I think I could find a guide here who could take me there. I don't want to incommode you further.'

'Tut, I won't hear of that. I am at your service.'

But I could see some doubt, if not suspicion, lurking behind his cordiality. Perhaps he was thinking of disabling me when I slept and handing me over to the police? But I had no choice. If left here alone, I would wander the city, a *shahr-e ghaddar* if there was one, that is, a city where one could easily lose oneself, or fail to recover it if he lost something. *A betraying city*, that was the true meaning of the phrase. It would as easily betray me to hostile elements as lead me to my extinction. I must ask some more questions, the better to ready myself for eventualities.

'Kind sir, what is this place called, where you have your auspicious residence?'

'Sir, this is the village Khirki, not too far from Badarpur. You may have heard of its famous mosque?'

My heart leapt up and then came back with a thud. Khirki village and its mosque? The Heaven-abiding Sultan Feroze Tughlaq built it in mid-fourteenth century. But Khirki was well outside all the possible cities of Delhi that existed in my time! Thank God many things of the remote past are still there, and the Kotla of Firoze Shah was far, far from here. So my pretence of having somehow lost my way could pass muster. But how much time has passed since the martyrdom of the Lord of the World, Sultan Ibrahim Lodi? I clearly remembered it to be 1521 when I left home on this accursed trip. So what was the year now? Better keep full control on yourself, and don't at all say anything indiscreet. By and by, I'll get to know more.

'Indeed, sir. I know about Khirki village and its magnificent mosque built by one of the Tughlaq Sultans.'

'So perhaps you'll recall more in the day. Please eat something and rest.'

Putting aside my misgivings, I did what my host wanted. I made him agree to my proposal to hire a horse early next day and go to Delhi. Belatedly, I remembered my horse which I'd left at the graveyard. I hoped someone had rescued it.

8

Hire a horse I did, and set out for Delhi. But the thought of what would have passed over my other horse was eating into me like a canker worm. I hoped and prayed that the poor beast that I rode now may have a safer passage through life.

Quite on purpose, I passed close to the mausoleum of Sidi Maula sahib, may God Elevate his stations, and the fateful graveyard where Amir Jan was supposedly in eternal rest. There was no sign of urbanism in the little population that was around the mausoleum now. Apparently, some gypsies had occupied the area some years ago and now lived there in rural style. Their women, bereft of purdah, or of signs of female modesty, busy in doing all kinds of work from cooking to fetching water; the men lording it over, lying on reed cots, enjoying the mild sun and smoking something from out of a closed container to which was attached a short pipe. Whatever it was that

565

they smoked—it wasn't cannabis or marijuana—had a penetrating, acrid smell. I thought it extremely disrespectful for someone to smoke that stuff right beside the mausoleum of a Sufi of such eminence and state, and also in front of the graveyard where lie buried generations of eminent citizens of Delhi.

There was no attendant, no one offering a prayer for anyone. I didn't even see a grave with a gravestone; all the graves were denuded of their covering—dust or cloth or greenery—and were almost level to the ground. My heart trembled and my knees became dangerously shaky against the horse's side. Allah, what place is this now? Is Amir Jan really buried here? Was there anyone at all who went by that name? And I? Am I another spirit, resurrected much before Doomsday? Or am I what the Hindus call a pishach, a demoniacal being, delivered to the earth for wreaking mischief? Mischief upon whom? Wasn't it I who was having all kinds of mischief done to me? Enough. Let's pass as quickly as we can.

A little ahead of the shrine of Nizam-ud Din sahib, close to Bhoore Shah sahib's grave, but set back quite a bit from the road, I noticed a tall and extremely pleasing edifice in white marble and red sandstone. The dome, in white marble, was designed somewhat like a huge turnip, but had an extraordinarily cooling and refreshing effect. One never saw domes of such delicateness and superb proportion in my age. The Lodi mausoleums were built like fortresses, the total effect forbidding, as they were perhaps intended to be. But this building seemed positively to invite you to enter: cool, soft, peaceful, almost like a preview of paradise. It couldn't be a palace and must be a mausoleum, but I hadn't seen mausoleums with gardens laid around them. Fortunate was the person whose progeny possessed such good taste and spirits so informed with such filial love that they built surpassingly beautiful homes for their dead forbears.

I turned my mount to the right from the mausoleum of Bibi Fatima Sam, friend, and some say even equal of Baba Farid sahib, Mentor to Nizam-ud Din Auliya sahib, may their souls be blessed by Allah and

His Prophet forever. Just a little ahead, and still to my right, I could still see, or imagined I saw, traces and remnants of the Indraprastha Fort, built, as the Hindus say, five thousand years ago. It was just a huge, flattish mound now, overrun with grasses and Delhi's hardiest jungle dwellers, the henna shrub and the stunted wild filbert, which must have been around from even before the Indraprastha Fort. I was now passing the shrine of Matka Shah sahib, with its ancient water station manned as usual by eunuchs and zananas singing the praises of the Presence, Nizam-ud Din sahib. But there weren't enough people around, certainly not as many as in the times past. The jungle had been creeping upon them, stealthily or even openly claiming its property back.

There was nothing left between Matka Shah sahib's shrine with numerous water pitchers, or *matkas*, arranged around it in profusion, and the historic Kotla of Feroze Shah, may Allah Bless him. I thought of the few Arabic poems that Bhikari Shah sahib taught me, laden with grief for the bygones who had left nothing but a few half-burnt pieces of kindling, traces of camels tethered to comfortable date palms, which themselves were forlornly dry now, a few lengths of rope which helped to erect the beloved's tent. Was it not the same here? Those poems were not mine, but it seemed to me at that profound moment that I wrote them, and I wrote with my Delhi in mind.

I was now convinced that the Delhi that I knew was long gone. My patrons, my masters, my sultans no longer ruled the territory of Hind. I knew not where they lay, or if their enemy, or Time, the greatest enemy, had deprived them of their resting places too. I recalled that my Lord of the World, Ibrahim Lodi, Sultan son of Sultan, had issued his commands for construction of his illustrious father's tomb, suited to his achievements and his awesome presence as Ruler. God knows if my Sultan, poor Ibrahim Lodi, was allowed leave to finish the mausoleum or not.

People, and dwellings, even small bazaars began to be seen once I was past the Kotla and the magnificent obelisk which the Paradise-abiding Sultan had brought here from hundreds of miles away and installed in the Kotla. What a feat of logistical planning and engineering it was. It had stood here, proud and inviolate, for countless centuries now. I recalled with a shudder that I still didn't know what year it was and who the ruling prince was now.

I turned to the right again, that is, in the direction where the village of Ferozabad was to be found. But there was nothing there. Just the immense riverbank, a few wretched-looking huts of fishermen and out-of-work lascars. There was no haveli, not even that sky-touching gatehouse through which two elephants could comfortably pass. With some difficulty, in the middle distance I could discern a few grassy knolls, almost invisible under the thick foliage. So that was all the relict that Amir Jan—if Amir Jan's mansion it was—left for her future mourners. I suddenly called to mind my money belt and felt for it somewhat apprehensively at my waist, under my clothes. God be praised, it was all there. I could hear, or feel the hard clink of the metal when I shook the belt vigorously. Surreptitiously, I put my hand under my cloak and tunic, untied the mouth of the belt, and extracted a coin. It was a sultani, a gold coin first issued by the Tughlaqs and continued by subsequent regimes.

So there was a measure of satisfaction, or consolation, here. I was present in the time when those coins were current. Or at least I knew someone who was from those times and who could give me so much money. But there was more discomfort here than satisfaction, I realized after some thought. There was—or is?—a real world in which Amir Jan and her mansion existed; in which I was robbed by highwaymen and in which I returned to my cantonment; in which Muhammad Alam accompanied me to Amir Jan's and in which she gave me enough money to solemnize my daughter's marriage with appropriate ceremony; in which I earned money enough by honest labour to enable me to repay Amir Jan's loan.

Ya Allah! Then the world in which I returned to Amir Jan's palace to return her money, and I found nothing of Amir Jan but news of her death by drowning, was also the same world in which I was now! So what happened to me at Amir Jan's grave a couple of days ago was also of this world? But . . . but her grave, even almost the whole graveyard, had vanished when I came out from it after just a few hours! So in which world did my encounter with the 'dead' Amir Jan take place and where was I now?

I didn't know whether I should howl in rage and terror, or go jump into the welcoming waters of the Jamna, regarded as holy by so many of my countrymen. Will the holy river give me peace?

I'd advanced a couple of steps towards the river when I heard a muezzin's call to prayers. Which prayer, I didn't know or care. But it seemed to me that I came awake from a horrid dream. There was Allah, the Owner of that mosque, there were His slaves, being called to serve Him. Whatever my circumstances, but my Allah existed, existed somewhere, and in the here and now, we were His slaves, ready to do His Bidding, to answer His summons. *Alastu bi Rabbikum?* Am I not your Lord and Provider? He had spoken to all human spirits on the day of creation. And the spirits had answered, *Bala!* Yes! Allah, my Rabb, was still there. But why did He then Make me submit to such travail? No, it doesn't lie in my mouth to question Him. He must Know His Purposes better than us, His foolish and ignorant creatures, as He Himself Pronounced in the holy Quran.

True Lord or not, so many men and women served Him and had faith in Him. At this moment in my life, this call from His House cannot but be meaningful.

I turned north-east, towards the direction from which the sound of the muezzin came. That direction also indicated more people activity, shoppers and promenaders. It was a very busy market, buzzing with wheeled vehicles and palanquin bearers. There was an odd kind of vehicle, almost open, pulled by a powerful horse, driven by a man who sat on a rather elevated seat in front. Two or even three people seemed to be travelling in it pretty comfortably, because one of them reclined against a bolster, his legs stretched. Somebody called out from the sidewalk, not much of a sidewalk really, but a path sort of separated from the main carriageway. So I heard the shout: 'Hey! Hey, Mian tangawallah, here, here!'

The driver then turned, stopped the vehicle, and spoke politely, 'Sir?'

I thus knew that the odd-looking but comfortable vehicle was called a tanga. But there were more palanquins, open and shut, than other vehicles. Most of them extremely sumptuous, the bearers in some sort of livery which seemed different for every vehicle. Another, even more outlandish than the tanga, was something like a small, balconied chamber pulled by bearers. It was very ornate, closed from all sides, except a small door on both sides for entry or egress, and a balcony in front, a sort of protection against the rain and sun. I assumed that those who rode in such vehicles must be women of quality, and maybe men as well, but the vehicle seemed eminently suitable for privacy and purdah.

It suddenly occurred to me that the bazaar in which I was, was somewhat like the one that I observed inside the grave of Amir Jan— or whoever that being was. I didn't go deeper into the busy street, but walked more or less parallel to the river, in a generally northerly direction. But I did notice one thing: everyone on the road, shopper, visitor, worshipper, idle saunterer, was armed. Some were doubly armed, with dagger and sword. Was it because these people were fond of fighting and showing their prowess, or because they felt insecure, I couldn't say. But they all seemed content with whatever they had, and inclined to laugh and joke more often than those in my time. I was wary of walking anywhere near the edge of the pavement for fear of being dragged under the wheels of the tanga and getting into a fracas which I could never win, and also would run the deadly risk of exposing me as one from another age.

Walking gingerly, trying to enjoy the unfamiliar but attractive sights, I found myself in front of a—pretty was the word that came to mind—mosque. I'd already noticed a superabundance of mosques and mausoleums in this city. It wasn't the case in my time. The two minarets were very tall and slim, almost like reed pens pointed upward in the sky.

The domes were in marble, with stripes in black. The whole pile oozed delicate subtlety. There was a large caravanserai right adjacent to it, its main approach chock-full of all kinds of vehicles. So this hostelry is still in use, and busy enough for me to take almost anonymous shelter here, I said in my heart. But that beautiful, sweet-looking place of worship kept dragging me towards it.

According to the inscription on the tall main gate, the mosque was called Zeenat-ul Masjid and was built by Princess Zeenat-ul Nisa Begam, daughter of Mohyiuddin Alamgir Padishah Ghazi, in 1707. Was it 1707 really? I rubbed my eyes hard, trying to improve my vision, if at all possible. Yes, the date was 1707, without doubt. By God, I don't deserve such punishment, fraught with so much mystery. I clearly remember the year when I left Nangal Khurd. It was 1521 and the Lord of the World, my Sultan Ibrahim Lodi had been the ruler of Hindustan for just four years. So was this mosque built very nearly two hundred years later? Was it not just Ibrahim Lodi, but much more, that had come and gone since then? With tottering, faltering steps I went into the mosque whose loveliness was now like a draught of poison to me. In the mosque's extensive courtyard was a grave. Fearfully, I approached it and found that Princess Zeenat-ul Nisa Begam, the builder of the mosque and daughter of Emperor Alamgir, was buried in it. The year of her death was inscribed as 1711. The mosque looked old enough. Doubtless, many years had passed since the Princess was joined with God. So what would be the year now? It must be 1735 or even later. Perhaps the Ahmad Shah Padishah whom Hamiduddin had described as the King today is King in the eighteenth, and not the sixteenth century?

I had been deluding myself so far, unwilling to face the palpable, tangible reality that had been teeming, surging around me. If the Seven Sleepers of Ephesus could sleep for three hundred years, if the Hindu King Muchkund could have slept on and on for thousands of years, could I not have fallen asleep somewhere for a few years or even maybe a couple of decades? Perhaps I never did visit Amir Jan's mansion to repay my debt to her. Perhaps I fell asleep somewhere on my way and slept for . . . well, many years, let's say. I slept and dreamt. Dreamt of all that had happened to me. I was, after all, serious in my intent to repay my debt. So it was natural for me to have dreamt what I did.

As for the changes around me, I rationalized by imagining that in this world of being and non-being, of creation and destruction, what took centuries to make could be unmade in weeks, if not days. Now the mosque and its founder had destroyed all my illusions. I'd lost not just a few years or even decades. My loss must be counted in centuries.

I removed my shoes, went into the mosque, performed the ritual ablutions at the ornamental pond, and prostrated myself. Imagining myself in his Immediate Presence in the mosque, I let myself go. I wept and begged and entreated Allah to save me from disaster. You are the Wise, the All-seer, You are Lord of all the Worlds, the Most Kind and the Most Benevolent. You know I am not a sinful man. I don't deserve what befell me. Please. Please, for the sake of Your Prophet Muhammad and his beloved daughter Fatima, free me from this calamity. Allah, what would have befallen my wife and children? How would have my unnatural absence gone for my poor mother? If You do not Wish me to join them, please take me off from this world.

Overcome by fear and anxiety, and exhausted by my tearful prayers, I felt decrepit and debilitated. A number of people came into the mosque to pray, but they left without inquiring from me why I was so distraught. Perhaps the spectacle of an old man weeping and grovelling made them uneasy: I may have aroused the King's displeasure, or even God's wrath, for some bad thing that I did. It was better not to put their hand where it didn't belong. So everyone stole away quietly.

As I wept my heart out I felt lighter in spirit. I don't know after how many years—centuries—I wept like this, perhaps not even on the death of my father.

I went out to the ablution pond and did my ablutions again. I did a brief namaz and prayed to Allah to guide me to the right path, diminishing my fear and sorrow, and that I may get news of my people.

But what news could I expect now? If the dates before me were correct, there was a distance of more than two hundred years between me and my people. Was there anyone left there at all, my distant progeny through my daughter? Or maybe not even that. God knows I did nothing to deserve this punishment, this continual punishment. Should I quit the world of the common people and go live in a mountain cave or remote forest, like many holy men of yore? Should I remarry and establish a new home, new family? I had money enough to start me on this sort of familial venture. But was it worth it? What assurance was there that a similar calamity won't overtake me again?

In the past I had just that much interest in religious observances as any foot soldier in a powerful ruler's standing army. I would occasionally pay obeisance at the shrines of our great Sufi saints, and that was all. I wasn't even particular about doing the Friday prayer, or keeping the fasts of Ramadan. But now my tears and my humility-laden questions and my prayer did some good to me. Perhaps it was a blessing from that pious and charitable lady in whose mosque I was. Whatever be the cause for determining my course of action, I immediately decided to convert the intention into action.

I went to the mistress of the hostelry and explained to her that I was a traveller from the land of Sind, arrived here in search of opportunities for a better life and would like to stay as a guest in the caravanserai so long as I didn't find some settled employment. She asked my name, which I truthfully told her. Oddly enough, she wasn't curious about my luggage, nor about the place in Sind from where I hailed. I, as a pre-emptive measure, volunteered the information that I'd been robbed of all my belongings somewhere near the canal at Wazirpur and I spent the previous night with a friend in his house near Khirki. The mistress was now joined by her husband, and both were quite satisfied with my account, which was coherent and plausible enough.

I inquired about the rent: it was one and a half paise per day for the room. Food would be prepared according to my wishes, the price of which would be charged separately. For the toilette, there were many excellent bathhouses in Daryaganj nearby, where I'd be charged nominal fees.

I now presented the smallest coins that I had, called chhidam, and as the name indicated, each was worth six dams, the dam being the lowest coin in my Delhi. I was in difficulties immediately. The mistress exclaimed: 'Hey, Mian sahib, where did you acquire these foreign coins? I never saw them before. To me they seem to be the currency of the country of jinns! I am afraid to even touch them. Please get me the coin of the realm, or I am afraid I won't be able to offer you a room.'

I tried to explain to her that the coins were the currency of Sind, from where I came. But the more I stressed the genuineness of my chhidams, the more obdurate she became in her adverse view of the money. She began to become suspicious, as if I'd acquired the money by robbery or looting some foreign travellers. She said: 'Mian sahib, if you are agreeable to my advice, you must at once go the Kotwali police station, and show these to the Kotwal. They should know what exactly these things are, and how much value they have. I am not going to accept them.'

As she raised her voice, her husband turned towards us to pay more attention to what was going on. A couple of the guests who were staying there immediately became curious. In the Delhi of my days, people were exceedingly fond of all kinds of show of high spirits, carry-ons, quarrels, spectacles, whatever. They would assemble at the spot in no time and would even attempt to take part in whatever fuss or commotion, or noisy activity was going on. Obviously, their tendency to enjoy any kind of ruckus had strengthened over the years. I could see that I would be inviting trouble all round if I persisted in my efforts to convince mine hostess, especially now that her husband was inclined to join the scene. I removed the bead necklace that I wore round my neck. One bead was fine gold, a few silver, and the rest were coloured glass. Even one of the silver beads would suffice for my room for many days. I offered the necklace to my host and hostess, and said: 'Here, keep this for now as an advance. Kind gentleman and lady, let me go out to the money changer and get this cleared up. In the meantime, hold the room for me.'

The mistress cooled down a bit and wordlessly accepted the necklace. I prayed for my grandmother in my heart because it was her wedding present to me. Leaving the inn, and placing my horse in the care of the syce there, I walked towards the bazaar which, as I'd noticed on my way to the mosque, was alive with activity.

I entered through a massive gate in red sandstone. The gateway's inner width was sufficient to let two carriages pass comfortably. Even so, the multitude of people visiting the bazaar had created a narrow footpath around it. I later found out that the bazaar was called Daryaganj, perhaps because of the river close by; *darya*, as we all know, means river or ocean. The name seemed suitable from another angle too: there was a virtual flood of people rolling in and out of the place. I soon noticed the plenitude of commodities and merchandise, and also specialized wares in the shops. What was equally interesting, though somewhat jarring, was the fact that most of the shops had criers, or canvassers, who tried to attract the shoppers, or even the passer-by, to the merchandise.

I could hear many languages spoken and could see that the throng of visitors consisted of people from different climes: Arab, Iranian, Abyssinian, Firangi, Uzbek and many more. I felt a degree of comfort, for I wouldn't stand out in this host. More interesting from my point of view was a whole wealth of money changers. Many casually displayed their wares even in front of their businesses, with coins of all types heaped on carpets, and a crier exclusively to watch the hoard against the petty pilferer. Trying to behave like a nonchalant stroller rather than buyer or seller, I cast casual glances into quite a few money-changing shops and at the items. Concentrating my fortitude on the business in hand, I gingerly approached a shop where the crowd was relatively sparse. I haltingly said, 'As-salam alaikum.'

'Wa-alaikum-as salam, Mian,' he answered cordially. 'Please

command. What service can I do for you?'

He must have taken me for a foreigner, because he spoke in Hindi, but enunciated every word clearly, as if speaking to a child. I took out one tanka, which I'd already removed from my money belt into my pocket, and switched to Persian, showing the coin to him: 'Sir, what price would you like to give for this?'

He peered closely at the coin, then spoke with a hint of doubt in his voice: 'Sir, may I touch it and take it into my hand?'

I thought for a moment, then said, 'It's all right.'

He rubbed the coin between two fingers, looked at its obverse and reverse carefully, clinked it against another silver coin, and said: 'Sir, may I ask the origin and provenance of this coin?'

I narrated my story of Sind, which by now I had rehearsed often orally and in my heart. For further effect, I added the entirely apocryphal story that in my country, each such coin was equivalent to one Egyptian silver *darham*. After consultation with some neighbouring money changers, he offered to buy the coin for two and a half Delhi rupees and said that a lot of ten or more would fetch a better price.

I decided to change five tankas for the present. Then I thought of bringing out my bahlolis and chhidams to have them valued. But my heart suddenly began to ache, as if some constriction was preventing easy flow of blood. Oh, those were the days when everything was familiar, the earth and all its sights were my childhood friends. And now? Was now real, or then real? I felt for the coins in my belt. The coins at least were real and worked both then and now. I had enough to last me for a couple of years at least. But if I became known as one who seemed to have an apparently unending supply of ancient tankas which he changed to Delhi rupees often, suspicion was bound to arise. Had I found a treasure trove? If so, this should have been reported to the King, not changed and spent recklessly.

All right, all right, I was caught in enough straits of my own to need to imagine more. But try as much as I could, my heart remained sluggish. I must find some means of living like the common man that

I was. I couldn't let myself dangle in uncertainty and doubt. I had some facts by now, from casual inquiries and by listening to people's conversations without appearing to eavesdrop. The King in Delhi was indeed Ahmad Shah, and it was the second year of his reign. I found that these people counted the years in three different ways: the hijri, which I was quite familiar with, the Hindu calendar, called the *saka samvat,* which I knew about but was not familiar with, and the *san-e julus,* that is, the year of ascension of the ruling Prince. Thus, it was 1162 hijri, 1676 saka, and 2 julus. By Firangi reckoning, not that anyone ever used it, it was 1748. These emperors were Turk-Mughal and the founder of the dynasty was Zahiruddin Muhammad Babar whose army defeated and slew my Sultan Ibrahim Lodi.

Questions and doubts again assailed me. What was the truth about me? Did I die centuries ago, but the Angel of Death somehow mislaid my soul? No, such things never happen. I am being the more fool in giving way to superstitions. So, was I dreaming? But dreaming when? Is *this* a dream—the beautiful mosque, my hostess, the money changers, my coin? If so, what was the nature of my experience inside Amir Jan's grave? I wanted to say filthy words about her, but somehow my tongue couldn't utter them. Poor woman, she seemed caught in the same web as I. I recalled a Brahmin's discourse that I barely heard and paid attention to long ago—how long ago? Let's not get into that for the present. His teaching was something like treating everything as unreal. Then how did we exist? Well, he said (somewhat smugly, I thought), there is a Universal Consciousness somewhere, and that Cosmic Consciousness brings us into existence in Its Imagination. At that time I disdainfully dismissed it as garbage, garbage of an overheated imagination. But suppose that pandit was true? Suppose it was nothing real that was happening to me, to anyone. It was all in the imagination of that Being (not necessarily divine, because the divine didn't enter that scheme of things). This didn't explain what happened to me. It only described it, but description doesn't fill the belly of the inquiring mind. I couldn't even be sure that the world which I encountered in Amir Jan's grave was not the same in which I now was.

I was left where I was. But where was I? My knees felt tottery and I had a strong urge to pass water. So strong was the urge that I knew if I didn't relieve my bladder now I would wet my pants.

I looked around for a bathhouse and, luckily for me, I was almost in front of a mosque which was on the upper floor, but whose entrance and the stairs that led to it weren't difficult to make out from where I was. Like an impatient young boy in a hurry, I bounded up the stairs, entered the mosque's urinal, and closed the door. I relieved myself, but stood rooted to the spot, uncaring of the acrid alkaline smell and the narrow space. I didn't want to go out and face the fearful and almost threatening world outside. I'd never imagined, far less experienced, the state of being totally alone. Even an orphan would have a home, and if not home, a village or neighbourhood where people knew him, at least by face. But I couldn't count on finding one familiar place in this sprawling metropolis, more like a necropolis for me.

Was someone knocking at the door? I opened the door with a bang and came hurrying out, my eyes unable to see much because I had just quitted the dark urinal and here there were lights galore. Or maybe my senses were still mixed up. I stumbled against the doorsill and collided with someone who was just climbing up to the mosque. An extremely friendly, but somewhat mocking voice, reached my confused ears: 'Hey, young fellow,' said he as I collided with him again in my shame-ridden effort to rise. 'Are you drunk on the seed pod? Then you should have stayed at home and enjoyed your roaring drunken, sloshing in it on your bed!'

He used the word *doda,* which I wasn't familiar with, but my confused brain told me that it must be something inducing intoxication.

So shaken and embarrassed was I by my faux pas that I found my knees buckling under me. I dropped down to the floor with a dull, foolish-sounding thud. The stranger gently put his hand on my shoulder, almost as if he were my older brother: 'Please. Do rise now.

I hope you didn't hurt yourself?'

He held me with a very strong arm as I tried to rise and steady myself.

'No. No. Not at all,' I raised my eyes to him and stammered out an apology in Persian. 'I am quite all right, sir. Please to forgive me, sir. Actually . . . actually I felt rather giddy all of a sudden.'

'Oh, I am sorry, you poor gentleman. You seem to be a stranger in these parts. Do you need a physician? Or should I help you reach wherever you happen to be staying?' His Persian was a hundred times more fluent, refined and idiomatic than mine.

Now I looked at my kind stranger, and was stunned. By Allah, how soft and sophisticated, how delicate his general appearance was! His bones light but strong, the structure of his face extremely proportionate, like a beautiful ghazal; but still, it was not lacking in masculine authority. He was tall, slim, very fair. Smiling eyes, deep and dark as if full of wisdom and penetration. More remarkable than the exceptionally large eyes were his eyelashes. I'd heard but never actually saw that some women (and the occasional man) had their eyelashes so long that they seemed to hang above their eyes like a curtain. Yes, I did see such eyes now. When this gentleman raised his eyelashes to look at something, it seemed as if two little lamps had lit up. Very neatly cut and styled beard, not too long, but pointed and short. His beard was jet-black, his moustaches well formed, of medium density, but twirled upwards at both ends. His thin but expressive lips had a light coat of redness, perhaps because he was fond of chewing betel, or perhaps they were naturally of that hue. He wore his hair long, well combed and hanging down to his shoulders, hiding the slim, fair neck, which still gave the hint of being there because the hair was gathered up behind the ears.

He wore, or rather carried on his head, a light turban in sky-blue silk, expertly twisted and sitting easy on the head, revealing the fair forehead and permitting some locks of hair to hang as side locks. His tunic was muslin, of the same colour as his turban, somewhat tightly stretched on the wide, leonine chest, and so fine that one could glimpse the muscularity under it. Over the tunic he had a fashionable short coat with cutaway sleeves, revealing the wide, proportionate wrists under the tunic. The short jacket was of blue velvet from Kashan, with small, white gemstones around the collar. Nothing was overstated.

I eyed him unashamedly, then ran my eyes to the lower body—frankly, to enjoy the show of the same phenomenally suitable clothes that the man must have worn on his lower body, and I was not disappointed. He wore very wide-bottomed trousers in dark blue, striped silk. His shoes were brilliantly black with some silver ornamentation. But I didn't want to stay too long on the shoes because I was told by my father that gazing at someone's shoes was rude. I went back to his upper body and saw what I'd missed the first time around: He wore a wide sash in leather, the kind of Yemeni leather which is coloured delicately in yellow, blue and red, and tradition has it that it feels slightly scented because of the dye. I never could test this supposition because the leather was frightfully expensive in my Delhi, and I imagined it should be the same even now. The belt had gold buckles and was worn tight to emphasize the narrow waist and to let a dagger, whose handle I could see was jewel encrusted, hang by the waist in its gold-worked scabbard. He wore on his neck a necklace the pearls of which must have come from Serendip. They went so well with the neck that it was impossible to imagine them without it.

He must have been of my age, that is, about fifty, but I looked entirely uncouth and steeped in rusticity before him. His face looked so fresh, so soft that it seemed he was a mere student and had just come out of his madrasa. His whole personality and person seemed to radiate a youthful light.

For a moment I shrank in shame: how rude and how intrusive to be gazing at a total stranger as if he were a painting on display. I realized that I hadn't even answered his question. But it occurred to me that he was quite used to being gazed at by strangers, or even friends. He seemed absolutely unselfconscious and looked at me with mildly interested eyes, waiting for me to come back to the world of ordinary men and women. He must have observed that he had stunned me into speechlessness. He didn't at all look directly into my eyes, just stood quietly observing my fascination. Neither shy nor irritated, he looked entirely natural.

It occurred to me all of a sudden that it wasn't only I who was looking at that, to me, unfamiliar King of Beauties. There were some who were observing me and smiling to themselves. And some others were looking at that marvel of comeliness as if they knew that he liked being admired. I started, as if coming awake suddenly, and took a step towards him, intending to touch him or hold the end of his long tunic. Then, realizing the folly and inappropriateness of the gesture, I stopped short and said meekly: 'Sir, indeed I am a stranger here. I beg your forgiveness . . .'

Before I could conclude, an older gentleman practically rushed out of the mosque and, freely taking the beautiful stranger's hand into his and then putting his lips to it, exclaimed: 'By Allah, Mir sahib, how lucky I am that you lingered here a while,' and gesturing towards me, he continued, 'or I was intending to come visit your auspicious house.'

'As-salam alaikum, Mian Sharafuddin Payam sahib, how nice to see you here. I was getting introduced to our new friend here . . . Brother, your verse about the young fellows of Delhi wearing their caps askew was really something! But just wait awhile.' He turned towards me and resumed: 'Mian sahib, have you come from far? I was submitting a small inquiry about where your noble self stays at present.'

By God, how mellifluous that voice was, how strong and manly. He spoke so clearly and with such quiet emphasis, as if reciting a poem in an assembly.

'Sir, I don't have a proper address yet. For the present, I have a room in the hostelry near Zinat-un Nisa's mosque. As for my origins, I come from the country of Sind and go by the name of Gul Muhammad.'

I noticed some people smiling, not only at my accent, but also on my saying 'Zinat-un Nisa's mosque'. I should have said Zinat-ul Masjid, or at least Princess Zinat-un Nisa. All right, I said in my heart with some disdain and disgust. Do they not know that I am newly arrived here? What a fate it was for me. I was not a newcomer, but still I was a stranger.

'Mian sahib, then you wouldn't have seen much of the city. Let's go stroll in Chandni Chowk, enjoy a bit of coffee and conversation in a congenial coffee house.' He looked at Sharafuddin Payam, as if inquiring if he would like to accompany us. Payam sahib must have been waiting for the kind gesture, and said eagerly: 'Very well, sir. Your servant intended to go towards Madrasa Rahimiya anyway, and hoped that he could be given the opportunity to accompany Mir sahib and his guest.'

'Then, sir, Bismillah.'

*

We came out. I was the last, gingerly descending the steep stairs. Mir sahib must have been some sort of a public hero. Every second or third passer-by greeted him with a smile, and it was the effort of everyone to stop him and exchange a few words. Mir sahib always managed to avoid wasting time, but said a brief, good-natured word of inquiry about him or someone in his family. I watched him almost avidly—he spoke politely and diplomatically, but his words were never devoid of substance. I found myself enjoying his company, and felt the cloud lifting somewhat from my heart.

I would sometimes manage to fall behind, to observe him from a few yards behind and watch his gait and bearing. I found that his gait was as attractive and as full of music, colour and rhythm as his person. He walked at medium pace, but his tall, spare body created the impression that he walked fast. His hands moved back and forth in gentle time with his legs. It was as if he were rowing a boat, so rhythmic was his progress through the crowded bazaar.

I noticed that everybody said 'Dilli' instead of 'Dihli' as we used

to say. It jarred upon my ears. 'Dihli' was so musical, so appropriate
somehow. We had a proverb: 'Dihli, the *dihliz* (threshold) of Paradise.'
Some others, especially those from the eastern parts of Hind, said it
also as 'Dihli, the *dihri* (doorsill) of Paradise.'

Time and the distance passed quickly. I enjoyed Mir sahib's
sparkling conversation as much as his popularity and the sights of
the long, arrow-straight Daryaganj. I was almost at ease now when,
quite precipitately, I suffered yet another shock. My legs refused to
move, as if millstones were tied to the soles of my feet, and my heart
had stopped beating, caught in a monstrous vice, and all the blood
in my body had been drained into my brain. I felt my head bursting
like an over-soft watermelon. I tottered, and tried to take the support
of the jutting board of a shop closest to me. But my body refused to
cooperate. Mir sahib immediately understood my condition, and shot
out his hand to grab my shoulder in a strong grip, immobilizing me. A
part of my brain was grateful to him, while another part marvelled at
the phenomenal force exerted by him. So much power in such a slim,
apparently delicate, if not frail frame! I found out later that Mir sahib
was one of Delhi's leading masters in unarmed combat, especially
in wielding the short stick, and was a regular visitor at the wrestlers'
arena near his house. There he practised fist wresting and similar arts.

But at that time I had in front and to the right of me an immense
maidaun full of people, acrobats, shops of all kinds, curio dealers and
practitioners of numerous arts. In the immediate front background
was that red sandstone fort, towering, colossal, threateningly gigantic.
It was the bazaar and the fort that I saw in my dream—no, not dream,
but in the subterranean world under Amir Jan's grave. I looked to my
left, hoping that the apparition would go away, but there it was, the
prodigious, prosperous bazaar with the canal bisecting its length. So,
was Amir Jan also transported from our age to this?

Mir sahib's kind and solicitous words brought me back from my
shock and fear: 'What is the matter, Mian Gul Muhammad? Are you
taken ill?'

'No, no, sir. It was just giddiness, again. Perhaps due to the change of air . . .' I finished lamely.

'We are quite close to the best coffee house in town. Just you get a hold on yourself for a very little while. Then we'll rest and talk. Are you sure there is nothing seriously wrong with you?'

'No, sir. I am perfectly all right now.'

*

The atmosphere in the coffee house was redolent with many kinds of agreeable, though modern, aromata. The chewing of betel was quite common in my age, but the additive of tobaccos, each of a different kind and flavour, was new for me. More surprising still, a variety of the tobacco was put in a small bowl to which were attached a longish tube and another bowl which, I found out, was half filled with scented water. In the smaller bowl, tobacco pellets were placed at the bottom and covered with live coals. As the tobacco began to heat up and burn, it would produce an extremely delicate, enjoyable and penetrating exhalation. This indicated that the instrument was now ready for use. The aficionado put his mouth to the mouthpiece attached to the user's end. As he drew at the pipe, a brief gurgling sound emerged and the smoke of the most delectable flavour exuded from his lips.

There was a space reserved for eaters for whom choice, saffron-scented naans and spicily fragrant meat dishes were ordered from the nearby eatery. The scent of these mingled with the other scents to create a wonderfully refreshing air.

We talked and exchanged repartees, the repartees mostly limited to laughter and enjoyment on my side, and the actual words or phrases produced by Mir sahib and Payam sahib. By now I got to know more details about Mir sahib. His full name was Sayyid Muhammad Ali; he wrote poetry, mostly in Persian, with the pen name Hashmat. Their origin was from Kashmir from where a remote ancestor had arrived to find employment with the then Mughal Emperor. Some of the family later became attached to prominent noblemen at Court. Sayyid Muhammad had two other brothers, named Abid Yar Khan and Murad Ali Khan. They were gemologists and also dealt in gemstones. Expert swordsmen and horse riders as well, the two were employed in the jewellery treasury of Muhammad Shah Padishah whom God summoned to His Presence in Paradise a year ago. The family was so rich that it was often said in Delhi that the goddess Lakshmi had permanent residence there.

Mir Muhammad Ali was not in anyone's employ, though he was nominally attached to the regiment of Navab Qutbuddin Khan. He was rarely, if ever, summoned to active duty. He had plenty of money of his own and then to spare. His nominal employment with Navab Qutbuddin Khan was because of his proclivity for the martial arts and the prestige that redounded to the court of the navab for such a distinguished person being in his employ. He was unmarried, and spent much of his time in reading or writing poetry and enjoying the company of beautiful young men. As I said just now, he wrote mostly in Persian. He was the pupil of the famous Persian poet Mirza Abdul Ghani Qubul Beg, of Kashmir. He wrote occasionally in Hindi or Rekhtah (the latter name was becoming more common, I understood, though it was the same language). He occasionally mentored young Rekhtah poets, and his most renowned pupil was Mir Abdul Hayy who wrote with the pen name of Taban. I later learnt that Taban sahib's most popular verse went like this:

Whoever doesn't acknowledge Hashmat's mastery, oh Taban
Is the enemy of Muhammad, and of Ali too.

Since Mir sahib's name was Muhammad Ali, and Taban sahib was also a Sayyid (a descendant of Ali), the verse became quite delectable, and justly popular.

9

Gradually, and very slowly, I began to feel at home among the poets and the mirzas of Delhi. I could never be a mirza myself, but in the company of poets and some more or less free-livers, I became used to their ways. It had been an uphill task, and no less dismal and tough than it would be if I were in a foreign country. The main reason for Delhi becoming somewhat agreeable to me and the small modicum of stability that accrued to me was because Mir Hashmat got me employment as foot soldier in the regiment of Navab Qutbuddin Khan sahib. Mir Hashmat then helped get me a suitable house in Kucha Chelan at a monthly rental of two and a half rupees. He also helped me find a nice old lady to cook and keep house for me at half a rupee per month. She was to board with me, which was no problem.

My footman's job didn't entail living in Moradabad, which was the headquarters of Navab Qutbuddin Khan sahib. I was required to go out only when there was field activity. You shouldn't be surprised at the disinterested help and easement provided to me by Mir Hashmat. The whole of Delhi acknowledged his lionheartedness, his munificence, his generosity. Everybody knew that if there was anyone among the renowned men of Delhi who exceeded everyone else in modesty, selflessness, capability and humaneness, it was Mir Muhammad Ali Hashmat.

His company rekindled my interest in Persian poetry and literature. Maulana Jamali sahib's admonition notwithstanding, delivered oh, so many centuries ago, I reapplied myself to the business of poeticizing. In those remote times, there was none but Maulana Jamali whose prowess as poet was respected by all. Now, in this Delhi, I found that not only poets—who practically overflowed from every neighbourhood—there were Sufis, engineers, architects, astronomers, philosophers, scholars of religion, astrologers, experts in mechanics, not to mention sports and martial arts. Wherever you raised your eyes to look, you would find an outstanding person in one or more of those disciplines.

Persian, and then Hindi poetry was the paramount activity—
practically a craze—in non-religious and non-scholarly areas. Especially
since Hindi poetry became popular, poets emerged from all walks of
life, from artisan to soldier to nobleman. Hindu, Muslim, even the
occasional Firangi, was like the moth on the taper of poetry, or crazy
after the universal beloved called poetry. And the strangest thing in
contemporary Persian literary culture was that the poets of Delhi
openly regarded their mastery of the language as superior, or at least
equal to the Iranians. Gone were the days (as in my earlier life) when
the Indian generally deferred to the Iranian in matters of language and
literary practice. It was only my ustad Maulana Jamali who was rated
generally as a near equal of the Iranian.

An important thing that I noticed was the presence of many Hindu
masters of Persian. This I could perhaps directly attribute to my
Lord of the World, Sultan son of Sultan, Sikandar Lodi, who threw
open the doors of official employment to the non-Muslims, thus
inaugurating a long and illustrious line of great non-Muslim Persian
poets, lexicographers and grammarians.

An interesting incident happened just a few years before my arrival
in the city. The Iranian nobleman and distinguished poet Shaikh Ali
Hazin arrived in Delhi and was patronized by the Emperor Muhammad
Shah and Umat-ul Mulk Amir Khan Anjam. But the Shaikh was a
conceited person, and had nothing but contempt for the Indian Persian
poets. He refused to mix with them, far less fraternize with them.

A very interesting and piquant situation came to pass one day. Mirza
Abdul Ghani Beg Qubul Kashmiri, the ustad of Mir Muhammad Ali
Hashmat and many others, arrived at the Shaikh's door, wishing to pay
him respects and courtesies. But the Shaikh sent word that he was not
home. It was clear that the Shaikh considered it beneath him to open
his doors to a mere Indian poet.

The next day, Mirza Qubul sahib revisited the Shaikh, accompanied
by a host of his pupils, including Mir Hashmat sahib. Ali Hazin, churlish
as ever, sent word that he was not home. Qubul sahib commanded: 'All

right, we'll wait here until Hazin sahib returns.' So he and his pupils spread mats at Hazin's door and made themselves as comfortable as possible. Finally brought down to the Indian earth from his Iranian sky, Ali Hazin was obliged to receive them. Now Qubul sahib and everyone else recited their poems. In the end, Hazin sahib offered to say some of his own ghazals to his unwelcome and uninvited audience. But they refused, saying that his poetry was so popular and well known that they didn't want to trouble him. The Shaikh got as good as he gave, or even better, because within a few hours, the incident was on every gabby tongue in Delhi.

But I was telling you about Mir Abdul Hayy Taban. All of Delhi knew and talked about his utter devotion to his ustad. It was absolutely unquestioning, bordering on prayerful obeisance. Yet over and above that, his physical beauty was the stuff of legends. It was said that his beauty and grace would eclipse even the begams of the royal palace. I even heard once that the Exalted Presence Ahmad Shah Padishah, Emperor of Hind and the Deccan, had a secret desire to observe him. This was possible only when Mir Abdul Hayy had occasion to attend the Court, but he was not interested in the pomp and splendour of kings and emperors. The Exalted Presence then devised a stratagem. He had been informed that on certain days and at a specific time Taban would appear at the balcony of his house. Something like the royal practice of granting the people an opportunity to gaze at their Lord and Master early in the morning. Even Emperor Jahangir, I was told, who kept late hours in the night, would make it a point to appear at the balcony of the Royal Residence at four o'clock in the morning. He would then go back into his bedchamber to sleep some more. This practice, or actually an important rite connected to the Royal Presence, was called *jharoka darshan* and continued to this day. So the Emperor ordered that he be kept informed of Mir Abdul Hayy's appearance at the balcony. If free from onerous business at that time, he would like to visit at least once. So once it happened that he had the time when the news came, and he rode out. There was the usual host below the balcony, enjoying the radiant beauty and charismatic personality of the young man. The Emperor and his suite duly arrived, but there was hardly any possibility for the Royal Presence and his cortège to remain for any length of time in such an open place. The Emperor then asked for a glass of water—the emperors drank only the holy Ganga water, which was always kept handy—and an ornate glass with a matching tray was presented to him. He, on the pretext of imbibing the water, stayed as long as he could. The gaze was made easy by the eleven-foot elephant, with the howdah on it being just a few feet below the balcony.

I am sure the story is apocryphal. Yet there can be no doubt that Mir Abdul Hayy's looks were perhaps the most admired thing of beauty in Delhi at that time. I was extremely keen to make his acquaintance, but was in such awe of his reputation that I thought I should make his acquaintance when others were present, and not in his dwelling, so that I may not be seen as particularly seeking introduction to him. I noted that most people referred to him by his full name and rarely by his mere pen name. This was surely a mark of deference.

And the other thing about him, perhaps equally celebrated, was his drinking. Whenever he was the subject of conversation, which was often, the first thing people would ask if he was sober at that time. He talked wisely and well when he was not in his cups, but when he wasn't sober, he was easily aroused to high dudgeon, but never, I was told, in front of his ustad, far less with the ustad himself. What went on between them, apart from mutual admiration and love—as between two human beings—nobody could tell. Shah Mubarak Abru, a well-known Hindi poet of the last generation, wrote a long poem which he titled 'Sermon', to a boy who had the potential to set up as a 'beloved'. Among some most elaborate points of instruction on make-up, cosmetics and general deportment, there also occur the following lines, clearly condemning sexual relations between the boy-beloved and his admirer:

But beware of the wanton
The lustful, the unchaste, the obscene at heart,
The base in spirit, the profligate.
There are some others in these times, base and low-born
They have acquired the practices of the Indian-born nobles,
They gaze at the pretty ones
And have evil in their hearts.
The ones whom you know to have no love in their heart
You don't need to look towards them.

But who knows what goes on behind the doors? Yet, as the ancient saying goes, the censor has no business inside the house. But who can stop the tongues from wagging? Mir Jafar Zatalli, another famous Persian and Hindi poet and satirist of a couple of generations ago, wrote a whole ghazal and numerous verses satirizing and castigating pederasty. But Jafar Zatalli was generally ignored as a pornographer himself, and a clown; Mirza Abdul Qadir Bedil, an extremely respected and renowned Persian poet, a little older than Mir Zatalli, wrote a fully pornographic ghazal making mercilessly savage fun of the pederasts.

Anyway, these matters were of no interest to me. I was curious to find out if there could be any human being more beautiful than Mir Muhammad Ali Hashmat. He was not young, though he couldn't be described to be in his decline. To me, and I am sure to others, he looked much younger than his age, and some of his manners and gestures seemed quite like those of an inexperienced or unworldly young man. Yet, his voice was not high or piping as is a common characteristic among pederasts or effeminate persons. His tones of voice were always full of authority and confidence, never unctuous. I have told you about his physical prowess and his love of martial arts. There were many stories of his personal bravery, but I omit them because I have more important things to narrate.

Umdat-ul Mulk Navab Amir Khan Anjam was a person remembered by many. He died by assassination just a few years ago. People said that he who didn't see the Umdat-ul Mulk should look at Mir Hashmat. The only difference was that Umdat-ul Mulk was small, almost petite, and Mir sahib was tall. Umdat-ul Mulk always dressed flamboyantly and would sometimes even wear female clothes. It suited him uncommonly well. Putting on female apparel had no appeal for Mir Hashmat. Like Mir sahib, Umdat-ul Mulk was also known for his military prowess and his learning. He was a diplomat of distinction. Mir Hashmat was a long-time employee of Umdat-ul Mulk, and after the latter's assassination, went into Navab Qutbuddin Khan's service. It was at Qutbubuddin Khan's that Mir Hashmat made the acquaintance of Mir Abdul Hayy, who was at that time a pupil of Shah Hatim's, the famous Hindi and Persian poet. Mir Abdul Hayy was so taken with Mir Muhammad Ali that he immediately said goodbye to the senior ustad and became a pupil of Mir Muhammad Ali.

Mir Abdul Hayy had been, for many years now, a sort of informal employee, or companion, to Qizilbash Khan Ummid, a poet and a nobleman. It was said that every evening, Mir Abdul Hayy's was a sort of meeting place of good-looking and 'beloved-like' young people. Some said that Mir Abdul Hayy used to introduce some of them to Qizilbash Khan's haveli for song and dance sessions, while some of the youth, it was rumoured, stayed the night at the haveli. God knows best. In my very short acquaintance with him, I never saw or suspected any such thing. Of Qizilbash Khan, I have no opinion, for I never knew, or even saw him. Mir Abdul Hayy, no doubt, had a boy companion, Sulaiman by name, very sweet-looking, nothing brash. Down was beginning to sprout on his face, yet he looked comely enough. Mir sahib took him everywhere, except to Mir Hashmat's assemblies, as I heard.

Another house where Mir Abdul Hayy Taban was a regular visitor was the monastery of the Presence Mirza Mazhar Jan-e Janan, a leading Sufi and a prominent Persian poet. He occasionally composed Rekhtah, and Mir Taban was better known there as a poet and raconteur. These special sessions were held once in three or four days, and were restricted to some chosen friends. Here, jokes were cracked or exchanged; some said some of the jokes could even be risqué, but never vulgar. Another favourite activity was punning: they loved conversing in puns, most of which were, naturally, created on the spur of the moment, and preferably in verse. Sulaiman never accompanied Mir Abdul Hayy Taban to those sessions either. Mir Taban too didn't drink even one drop the day he was to go there.

I cannot accept—unless it be by direct personal knowledge—that a Sayyid of commanding reputation and ample means, a frequenter at the special assemblies of one of the leading lights of Sufi Delhi, whose followers came from many foreign parts too, could ever fall so low as to act as—let me say it—a pimp for an aristocrat, or anyone for that matter. Jokes and repartees were an important part of Delhi's social and literary culture. I can understand Mir Taban regaling a select company with jokes and puns, but I can't imagine him behaving or conducting himself like a procurer.

In fact, the first extended speech that he made when I first met him was a slightly wicked joke. Mir Muhammad Ali Hashmat invited me to his home one day, saying that Taban would be coming later, and I could have a nice meeting with him in other jocund company, with a bit of wine to ease and enhance the flow of words. He also mentioned that Taban wanted to present a ghazal that he'd written about Mir Muhammad Ali. Since I lived quite close to Mir Hashmat sahib, I arrived there shortly after the night prayer. Mir Abdul Hayy arrived a few minutes after me. He entered in a sort of rush, kissed the hand of the ustad, then kissed him on both cheeks. Joining his hands on his chest in the universal sign of meekness and submission, he said: 'Ustad knows where I spent the evening! I swear by the spirit of the Khvajah of Shiraz, my throat is parched and my breath of life is now about to expire through my dry lips. Sir, for the sake of the Saqi of the Day of Judgement (the Prophet's son-in-law, Ali), please to let me first embrace the fair and rosy pink Armenian. Later I'll submit to you a sizzling joke.'

I didn't know at that time that there was an allusion there to a verse from Mir Taqi Mir sahib:

How fair and rosy pink it came out!
The wine is surely the daughter of an Armenian.

Mir Muhammad Ali smiled, and beckoned the servant who stood behind, somewhat to the left. Well drilled as he was in the protocol, he went in behind the curtain and promptly returned bearing two metal trays, chased and lightly ornamented with designs. On one of the trays were two glass bottles with long, thin necks and a long silver glass. One of the bottles had a colourless drink, the colour of the other was red, presumably some kind of Armenian wine. On the other tray were smaller bowls of roasted and salted almonds, cashew nuts; another contained several kinds of condiment.

Mir Hashmat commanded his servant: 'Hey, Mian Bahadur, aren't you forgetting Maulavi Gul Muhammad sahib? Or you think he doesn't care for the better things of life?'

Bahadur hung his head in apology. 'Presence, it just slipped my mind. I will remedy the lack in a moment.' He went in and brought back a similar glass on a tray. In the meantime, Mir Abdul Hayy took his seat on the carpet, leaned against the bolster, and began to pull at the hookah with obvious enjoyment. Red lines had already begun to appear in his eyes in anticipation of embracing and kissing the mouth of the Armenian's daughter, or in commoner parlance, the daughter of the vine. I took the opportunity to take a good look at him.

If Mir Muhammad Ali's charm and elegance, and his appeal to the eye and the heart were contained in the stateliness of male handsomeness combined with a maximum degree of feminine grace and subtlety of proportion, the younger Mir sahib's charm consisted of a miraculous metamorphosis of feminine, silky gorgeousness into the exquisite masculine delicateness of a willowy young man. And it seemed, to me at least, that he would remain so all his life. He must have been no less than four or five and thirty, but looked boyish, and with a dignity and a sense of puissance which would, I was quite convinced, totally overawe a mob of depraved, low life and aggressive characters, that is, if ever occasion arose for such a mob to come anywhere near him. Yet, in spite of being possessed of such striking presence, he didn't seem vain, or conceited. He hadn't deigned to enhance his good looks with external aids.

It is true that excessive indulgence in wine had worked to drain his complexion of some of its pristine freshness and give it a dry, chalky effect. A second, and somewhat more intent look revealed lines of some tiredness around his lips, but there was no question of him not being mistaken to be anything above four or five and twenty. His complexion pink and fair like that of an Iranian youth, his face open and good-natured, he wore on his head a twisted short, black silk turban which had fine but prominent green and blue stripes, giving the impression of a peacock. His nose was slightly raised in the middle, giving a vague hawk-like effect. Large, greenish-blue eyes, very self-aware, his dark beard cut short and fine, with moustaches of the style but with a hint of twirls on both sides. His oval face had somewhat prominent cheekbones, but nothing like the Mughal emperors. The high cheekbones only helped enhance the fine proportions of the face.

He wore the usual tunic in fine muslin, very long. It was light pistachio in colour with a hint of yellow. He wore no short coat, but a long cloak, or the *qaba*, slightly cinched at the waist. The cloak was green silk, but somewhat shimmering, like taffeta. Maybe the effect came from the Aurangabadi silk-cotton fabric called himru. The cloak was open, hence his scarlet silk sash seemed somewhat loosely tied. His dove-grey trousers were wide and long, according to the current fashion. There was a necklace, not too long, around his slim neck; the stones, all cabochon, were ruby, carbuncle and amethyst. A short, unsheathed dagger hung upon his chest, held with strong, black silk thread, worked in gold and silver, and brought down from the neck by being first wound around the shoulder. What a pleasing effect, I said to myself, what a quaint mixture of the deep green of maturity and the rosy spring of youth! Bringing the weapon down from upon the shoulder was a practice recommended for very young practitioners, but only experienced experts wore it unsheathed upon the chest.

He had jewelled rings on the index finger of the right and the ring finger of the left hand, and a plain, wide ebony bangle on his left wrist, which played exceedingly well with his fair and slim wrist. The total impression of his person was so soothing that it seemed to radiate some sort of soft light through his clothes.

Like his ustad on our first meeting, Mir Abdul Hayy seemed also to be aware of my gaze on him. And like Mir Hashmat, Mir Taban was also entirely indifferent to it. In fact, he seemed to be waiting for me to finish my inspection of him and only then extended his hand towards me, and half rising from his seat, he said: 'By Allah, dear sir! So you are the famed Maulavi Gul Muhammad of whom my ustad, the Presence, spoke often. So much, that I was extremely eager to make your acquaintance, so thanked be Allah that my desire was fulfilled today!'

Although Mian Taban was much younger than I, his beauty so fully enraptured me that I rose to my height, shook his hands, and said with a feeble smile: 'I hope to God that I didn't disappoint you!'

'Disappoint me? No, not all, sir. In fact, I found you better even than what the Exalted Presence had commanded. Here, please enjoy the hookah, and this too.' He extended towards me the mouthpiece of the hookah, and prepared two full glasses. Placing one before me, he raised his and drained it in one gulp. By Allah, this surpasses everything! If there was ever a master drinker, it is he, I said in my heart.

Mir Abdul Hayy must have noted my consternation, and said to me: 'Yes, my worshipful sir. Please to attend to an opening verse by Sayyid Khvajah Mir Dard sahib, may his life be long. He is the son of my Exalted ustad's friend, the Presence Khvajah Nasir Andlib.'

Then he recited with rare passion:

People say that it drinks, but what does the bottle know of inebriety?
The poor thing has earned a bad name because of the daughter of the vine.

Before I could respond, he went on: 'Now, Maulavi sahib, did you ever encounter such perfection? Mir Dard sahib is still quite young. In fact, he is much younger than I. Tell me, is it not a miracle, this verse?'

Mir Muhammad Ali sahib murmured, 'Indeed. It is here that our Rekhtah exceeds anything ever composed by the Persian masters.'

I couldn't find words adequate for the praise of this verse. My heart was just ecstatic. More than the verse, I admired the ingenuity of Mir Abdul Hayy for so brilliantly exculpating himself from the blame of being inordinately fond of his cups, and presenting himself as the blameless bottle which willy-nilly imbibes the intoxicant and remains essentially unaffected. Thus, Mir sahib implied, he and wine went together, just like the bottle and the intoxicant. I wanted to express agreement with Mir Hashmat sahib, but I knew I wasn't apparently educated enough, and I could not, of course, declare my origins and claim a knowledge that was hundreds of years old. But this was my destiny, my burden. I must bear it as cheerfully as I could.

'Only God is above blemish,' I said. 'But I know not if I should admire the transparent conscience of Mir Abdul Hayy sahib, or extol that other, younger, Mir sahib. By Allah, I am already drunk with pleasure.'

Abdul Hayy Taban smiled with pleasure, but in the meantime he had filled another glass and drunk half of it. Now he quaffed the other half. Mir Hashmat looked at me encouragingly, as if hinting to me to let Taban sahib go his own way and I, my own. Mir Abdul Hayy's temperament is his own, his preferences are his own.

I was trying to make bold to ask why Mir Hashmat sahib had no glass in his hand. But luckily, Bahadur mian, as if on cue, came in with a small cup of opium dissolved in water, or maybe wine. On another tray, he had a small cup containing dark and thick coffee, and a bigger one of tea brimming with steam. Mir Hashmat sahib took a delicate sip of opium and chased it with a gulp of hot, sweet tea. He swayed with pleasure, his eyes closed. His face lit up and when he opened his eyes, they seemed brighter than ever. I knew the opium imbibers' eyes became duller and sunken as the poison hit the body. Many of them couldn't stand bright light. But he wouldn't be Muhammad Ali Hashmat if he were to behave like the common or garden opium addict.

Mir Abdul Hayy was filling his third glass when a servant announced the arrival of Lala Sukh Raj Sabqat.

'Ahlan wa sahlan, let him come in at once,' Mir Hashmat sahib said with eagerness. 'And Mian Bahadur, get a full flask for Sabqat sahib.'

'Very well, sir.' Bahadur went in to fetch his wares. Sabqat was ushered in by a servant. Mir Hashmat half rose from his place; Mir Abdul Hayy and I rose to our full height and paid our obeisances. Sabqat sahib bent in salaam to Mir Hashmat and embraced him. With us, he salaamed and shook hands, then placed his right hand on his left breast, indication that our place was in his heart.

Everyone in Delhi knew Lala Sukh Raj Sabqat, distinguished pupil of Mirza Bedil sahib who was joined with God a score or so years ago. Sabqat sahib was a surpassing master of Persian, and adept in the art of social manners and behaviour. He was attached to the court of Etmad-ud Daulah Mir Munnu sahib. After the martyrdom of Etmad-ud Daulah in the recent battle of Panipat, Sabqat sahib had resumed managing his family affairs. The following verse of Sabqat's had been on every lip in Delhi since he composed it many years ago:

He, absorbed in the task of taking care of me, and I, carefree
The business of being a slave is also in a sense the business of being God!

Mir Abdul Hayy and he were old friends, though Sabqat sahib was many years older. Similarly, Kishan Chand Ikhlas, another prominent Persian poet of Delhi, had been great friends with Mir Taban in spite of the age gap between the two. Taban sahib wrote a Hindi verse about Ikhlas sahib:

His conversation, his poetry, are redolent with love, oh Taban
And that's precisely why for Kishan Chand ji, I have ikhlas.

'Ikhlas', the pen name of Kishan Chand ji, means 'pure attachment, sincere friendship, purity'. So, its use here was appropriate and quite piquant. It hadn't been long since Ikhlas sahib left us for his heavenly abode, and everyone who was anything in poetry remembered him with kindness. Also, his account of the Persian poets, called *Hamesha Bahar* (Everlasting Spring), was quite popular.

Sukhraj sahib, after having made the courtesies, said: 'Hey, Mian Abdul Hayy, my heart had been fretting and pining for your company these many days. Today I was passing this way and I thought I should drop in. I know the hour is late, but I couldn't restrain myself from waiting on Mir sahib for a brief moment. And it would be like icing on the cake if you too were here. And so you are! *Alhamdu Li'allah.*'

He paused for breath. Taban sahib immediately spoke. 'Sir, I have always submitted that you must regard this Exalted Portico as your own court. By His Grace, you were granted the will to come here. Come, let's celebrate your coming with a glass.'

Mir Hashmat sahib, who had closed his eyes and was swaying gently, now opened his eyes. Profound and intense were the words that came to mind, looking at those unforgettable eyes. He said: 'Honourable sir, regale your noble self with this new wine in an old flask.' He waved lightly towards a flask which was brought in as commanded by Mir Hashmat sahib. 'It's not harsh like the Firangi ones that Mian Taban favours.'

As Bahadur poured a glass for Sabqat sahib, I concurred in my heart with Mir sahib about the harshness of Firangi wines. In my time Firangi wine, and why wine alone, the Firangi himself, was entirely unknown and obscure. Now their wines, and in many places their soldiery too, were in circulation, and no one was shocked.

Mention of the Firangi wine, and now its effect on Mir Taban, called to my mind an exquisite verse of Mirza Jalal Asir. The wine had brought a roseate hue to his face, mitigating to a large extent the chalky dryness which was rather noticeable when he entered. The warmth of the wine, and his pleasure in it, had run a very soft carmine on his fair countenance, very nearly transforming it. His face was flaming, and the fine red strands of intoxication that had now begun to run in his eyes reminded one of the fine streaks of fiery red that shoots through dark clouds at dusk. His delicately chiselled lips had a sanguinity which was much above the redness caused by the chewing of betel. But there was no fumble in his voice, far less a slur. He talked without the least stutter, and sat as upright as before.

In spite of the fact that I might be regarded presumptuous, Mirza Jalal Asir's line shot forth from my mouth:

Wine became the oil of the rose for the bright lamp that is your face.

Mir Hashmat sahib looked up, startled. He forcibly struck his hand on his thigh and exclaimed: 'Hey, you tyrant! What a line! You doubled, no, you tripled the pleasure of this delightfully tipsy assembly. May the Lord keep you happy always. Who wrote that line, pray?'

Without waiting for me to answer, he repeated the line once, and then again. There was an almost enchanting cadence in his voice. I knew that he never said his poems in assemblies, so very few people were familiar with his unique style of recitation. There was a slight rolling tremor in his voice, something like what the master singers called *gitkiri*. I never expected anyone other than a master singer to have command over it. As for Mir Taban, and Sabqat sahib, both were lost in the mood and the remarkable image. Taban seemed entirely unaffected by modesty or bashfulness. Obviously he was not one given to false modesty. He knew he richly merited that extraordinary line of verse.

'Sir, it is from Mirza Jalal Asir,' I submitted, and quite on impulse, recited the whole opening verse:

The wine glass struck a new hue on your Firangi face
Wine became the oil of the rose for the bright lamp that is your face.

'Oh, oh!' cried Mir Hashmat sahib, as if stricken. 'Mian Sabqat, did you hear? That lovely fellow was an Iranian, but he never came to Hind and always composed in our style.'

'Yes, Your Honour,' returned Sabqat sahib. 'The Iranians, what do *they* know of these subtleties? It is our invention, in fact.'

Mir Abdul Hayy looked at me with his big, bright eyes. 'Our Khan-e Arzu sahib is quite right. Nowadays it is us, the Indians, who have the competence of native speakers in Persian.'

I was apprehensive that my own incompetence would be betrayed once they began discussions about competence in language and the native speaker's prerogatives. Naturally, I knew nothing of the developments over the last two or more centuries. And in any case, in spite of my years with Bhikari Shah sahib and Mulla Jalali sahib—may Allah grant coolth and fragrance to their graves—I was never a capable scholar of Persian, or anything else. So I hurriedly changed the subject and interjected: 'Quite, my dear Sir, but what about that promised joke. You promised . . .'

'Yes, sahib,' added Mir Hashmat. 'Let's have that joke, Mir Abdul Hayy.'

'As you command, sir. I beg to submit that there is one person, well known, who was a petty dealer in fruits and vegetables.'

'Let's not have his name mentioned,' interrupted Mir Hashmat.

'As you command, Guide and Mentor. So fortune smiled on him and he became rich beyond his dreams because he somehow obtained a lucrative post at Court. As we all know, Umdat-ul Mulk Amir Khan sahib was a frequent visitor at Nur Bai's, the most famous courtesan of that time. They punned and joked and exchanged witticisms. Now our friend thought that Amir Khan and Nur Bai are no more, but this Khan is here, and also Shamshad Bai, our famous singer.'

'Heh!' Sabqat sahib snorted. 'Umdat-ul Mulk and this puny Khan of obscure origins!'

Mir Taban continued. 'So this person visited Shamshad Bai who received him upstairs, a rare honour. But this maximum fool, this horrid old man, at the time of departure, takes his leave with these words: "Bai sahib, it's very nice you received me in your upper storey. But I didn't see your lower storey."

'Bai sahib says, "Your Honour, didn't you come through that very storey a few minutes ago?"'

There was loud laughter all round. More visitors arrived as the time passed. I knew Sharafuddin Payam sahib, but many I didn't know even by face. They talked until late into the night. I observed that though they were apparently concerned with nothing else, but poets and poetry and affairs of the heart and good living, they were at a deeper level very conscious of the revolutions in the clock and the time, the hot and cold of politics as it changed in favour of one prince and then another. They were very aware of the inroads of the Firangi, his devious ways, the internecine rivalries of our nobles and aristocrats, the advent of Nadir Shah and his bloodthirsty, rapine and avaricious savagery in Delhi. Though it was now almost eleven years since that monstrous visitation, and Delhi had recovered much of its former sheen, they realized that the Emperor must be fully supported by his nobility, and unless the nobility themselves joined to form a leaden wall, affairs of the State would remain shaky and vulnerable; Delhi would soon cease to be the Centre of the World.

The guests began to rise and take leave, but Mir Taban reminded his ustad: 'Guide and Mentor, you have no interest in my ghazal?'

Mir Muhammad Ali smiled. 'I was hoping you'd have forgotten by now.' He turned to the guests. 'Honourable sirs, Mian Abdul Hayy has a ghazal about this worthless slave of Allah. Please to tarry a while and hear him.'

Everybody postponed their departure, most willingly. Mir Taban recited his famous ghazal whose opening verse was:

In the whole world, and through my life, I am
your friend, Hashmat,
Now what should I have to do with worldly wealth, Hashmat?

There were seven verses, and not one did have even a whiff of physical desire, carnality or unusual intimacy. Each verse was cordially applauded by all except Mir Hashmat, who sat quiet, with bowed head. Only at the end, he raised his eyes to Mir Taban and commanded: 'As Allah Wills. Very nice ghazal.' He added with a smile, 'But you could have chosen a better theme.'

There was general laughter and congratulations to Taban sahib. Sabqat sahib accompanied me up to my humble lodging in Kucha Chelan. He lived a little farther, in Hauz Qazi near Mir Munnu's haveli. Again and again, he would recite Mirza Asir's opening verse and almost dance with pleasure.

10

Months passed. Life became more or less serene for me. I enjoyed meeting with the Rekhtah and Persian poets of Delhi. I met Shah Hatim sahib once or twice; Mirza Rafi Sauda sahib, Nurul Ain Vaqif sahib, and many others. I saw Mir Muhammad Taqi Mir sahib but twice, but not so as to get to know him. Sauda's reputation was exceedingly high in both Rekhtah and Persian; Mir Muhammad Taqi sahib had made his place among the poets of Rekhtah, but he rarely went to any assemblies. I was given to understand that he had some sad things happen to him recently, so he didn't enjoy company as much as he did before.

I became a regular visitor at both Mir Hashmat sahib's and Sabqat sahib's. Sabqat sahib knew some of the leading pupils of his blessed ustad, Mirza Bedil sahib, so I got to know his circle almost as well as the circle of Hashmat sahib. I tried to spend my idle time in briefly visiting some of the more remote places of the older cities of Delhi. The present one, I knew, was almost always referred to as Shahjahanabad, and was founded by Emperor Shahjahan in 1648. I once went as far as Wazirpur too, but it was a very different place now and I was as much a stranger there as I was in Delhi. Only the canal remained, may Allah Increase His Favour upon Sultan Firoze Shah. Yes, and that accursed bend in the road where I was robbed and catapulted into that dreadful chain of events which put me here, the loneliest of cities. The road was not as well looked after as before, but it was the same road, without doubt.

I thought of my valiant benefactor and saviour, Sri Raghuraj Bahadur Singh. Could any of his people be found still? This thought redoubled in me the desire to make some serious effort to investigate Nangal Khurd and if there were any there who would remember my poor people.

Thus it was Wazirpur again which was my undoing. It was here that I resolved to send someone to Nangal Khurd. But what I discovered about its present state convinced me that there is no justice in the world. The universe is without compassion, if not actively hostile to the world of men. I was fated (if there is something like fate) to live homeless, trying to understand the true meaning of loneliness. Occasionally, I did think of marrying, but directly as the thought came to me, my heart would well up with blood and my eyes with tears. It seemed to me that I was thrusting another woman upon my poor blameless wife. Reason told me that there could be nothing, no remnant of my wife, two and more centuries later. But I might have progeny living still. What would they think of my new wife?

In my confused state of mind I didn't stop to consider how I would explain myself to my people, or progeny, if any were extant. Here in Delhi I could afford to cheat as much as I possibly could. But what should I tell the people of Nangal Khurd? After all, I was trying to find them precisely because Nangal Khurd was my ancestral home many centuries ago.

I nevertheless dispatched a professional sleuth and searcher to Nangal Khurd, and through his absence on this commission, I prayed for him to bring good and positive intelligence about my wife or daughter or her child. I didn't see the absurdity of my beseechings to God. If they were dead, they couldn't come back to life, and if they were not dead . . . what were they then?

Anyway, the sleuth returned. His report was that he couldn't find the village Nangal Khurd. Inquiries further afield revealed that there was a village of this name, but it was washed away in a flood many years ago, perhaps thousands of years ago. No one survived, nor buildings nor graves. The place where the village was has since been bare and uninhabited. Much of it is covered by living jungle now, while some of it has become too alkaline to permit any growth.

I didn't leave my quarters for many days and ate but little. I wouldn't let the lamp light my grieving home. After my maid left, I would extinguish all the lamps. Rising early the next day, before the arrival of the maid, I would give the food to dogs, cats, stray cows or bulls, whoever would take it. When she rattled my door chain later in the morning, I would open the door rubbing my eyes hard, pretending to rub away the sleep from them.

I knew all this was futile, insipid, of no use. But I knew this from the beginning of my second life. I have no home, no hope, no friend. Nor did I have the content, such as the poorest of beings could find at least once in their lifetime. I was certainly a jinn, thrust into some odd human body punitively because I had offended the king of jinns. But there still was a thread, thin such as a spider spins, by which hung the body of my more dead than alive hope. Perhaps . . .

This perhaps was the thread by which I dangled and swung, day and night, from mood to mood, from the breath of life to the sting of death. Granted that my family were all dead. But their children, great-great-grand-infinitely remote children, must be there somewhere. They must be cultivating their lands, planting their gardens and orchards. Those orchards must have mango trees, their faces aglow with the rain, their breasts heavy with fruit.

But everything was against the thread. Everyone wanted me to sever it. Why not sever my jugular and bleed away my life? But grandma used to say that he that kills himself becomes a ghost. Yet am I anything other than a ghost now?

My maid was convinced that I had lost my reason. Perhaps due to loneliness? She spread a quiet word about my state among the neighbours. Within a few days, some kind-hearted old ladies took upon themselves the charge of finding a wife for me. Thus, every two or three days, a lady, fully wrapped in her chador, would appear at my door, with another woman in tow. Sometimes that other woman would be bold enough to have her face not wrapped in her chador. The woman in tow was a *kutni*—or a professional finder and promoter of suitable marriage proposals. I would decline their offer or suggestion as politely as I could. Still, some of them returned, with a newer proposal and more details. I was hard put to find fault with the poor woman whom they suggested would make a suitable wife for me. Finally, my kindly ladies decided that there was no oil to be pressed from these sesame seeds, and desisted and left me alone.

*

I hadn't visited Mir Muhammad Ali sahib for many days now, sitting at home, moping and inwardly groaning, nursing my wound. I knew there was not a little of self-pity in it. But I didn't care. If God didn't take pity on me, at least I could. One day, early in the morning, a messenger arrived bearing Mir Muhammad Ali's summons. 'Come at once,' he wrote, 'and come prepared to remain out of town for a few days.' I was surprised, both at the contents of the message and at the fact that this was the first time that Mir sahib had sent for me. I was a little hopeful too. There was a change in the offing, it seemed to me, and even if the change results in nothing, it always brings some hope. I packed a few things, rolled my bedroll, and handing over the keys of my rooms to the local prayer leader, I sent word to my maid to visit once a day and take care of things for a few days. I'd be returning soon.

I had hopes, but not unmixed with apprehension. In my time there were no firearms; we fought with arrows, then hand to hand if it came to that. The army now practically lived on the fumes of gunpowder. On my first acquaintance with the terrifying objects and weapons of war, I was naturally filled with terror and uncertainty, and with difficulty managed to enlist for training before actually reporting for duty. But I had never fired a shot in anger and had never been in front of live fire.

'Mian sahib,' Mir Hashmat exclaimed when we he saw me, ready for instant departure. 'You are very welcome. We leave for Moradabad straightaway, I and the rest of the regiment.'

My heart missed a beat. This seemed like a military operation, not a hunt or excursion for entertainment. But I maintained my calm and said, 'Most certainly and with pleasure,' said I. 'Do we know the nature of the duty, sir?'

'Yes. Briefly, the Rohilla Navab, Muhammad Ali Khan, is dead. His two older sons are in exile at Kabul. The Rohilla tribesmen wish to install Sadullah Khan, the youngest son, in the deceased navab's place.' The story was somewhat murky and the details were missing about subsequent events. The Governor of Moradabad was mobilizing, presumably on orders from the Emperor. But no written commandment was at hand. It was certain that the navab wouldn't take such an initiative without orders from the Exalted Fort.

Anyway, the message was from Navab Qutbuddin Khan, Governor of Moradabad. He expected the entire regiment to arrive on the scene and confront the Rohillas, not to fight maybe, but to overawe them with the might of the Royal forces and prevent the recalcitrant tribesmen from installing Sadullah Khan without the Emperor's orders.

'So we go, Maulavi Gul Muhammad,' concluded Mir sahib, 'and we go fast. We should let them have a taste of the Emperor's displeasure and imminent retributive action which, they should be convinced, will be eminently condign.'

The whole regiment, nearly five hundred men, was assembled by early evening. We started at once, so as to do at least one stage by nightfall. The next stages we covered at the speed of a forced march, stopping only the minimum hours of the night. We thus reached Moradabad in three, instead of the usual five days. We were informed that Navab Qutbuddin Khan sahib was camping at a place called Dhampur, at a distance of about forty miles, and awaited our arrival. We rushed off to Dhampur, although many of us were now visibly tired and did not like the prospect of any possible engagement with the enemy without rest and recruitment.

The Governor was camping in a small, undefended fortress at a distance of two miles from Dhampur. According to the spies, the Rohillas were expecting to confront the Royal forces on the bank of the river Ram Ganga, reinforced by the arrival of fighting men from some other tribes who had been undecided so far.

Navab Qutbuddin Khan had had the area surrounding his fortress reconnoitred and chose a suitable field of battle, keeping to his back a heavily wooded patch of slightly high ground, rising a hundred feet or so, overrun with thick undergrowth, the trees mostly stunted wild filbert, dark acacia, palas and sal. The idea was if they were forced to retreat, they should withdraw into the woods which, being on high ground, would be practically impossible for the enemy to storm, or even advance upon stealthily. The navabi forces were almost entirely infantry. We didn't have any kind of cannon, drawn by bullocks or camels. We had no support from light cannon mounted on elephant or camel. The lightest of Mughal artillery were *shuturnal*s, a pair of heavy guns firing grapeshot, mounted on the two sides of a camel. We had some of these, but it was clear that they would be an impediment, rather than support, in the battlefield that the navab had chosen.

Deliberately, or in honest error, the spies' information was wrong on all counts. Instead of the assumed thousand or two partly armed and straggly forces, the Rohilla were ten thousand strong, and armed. The enemy had actually surrounded the woody knoll, hiding themselves behind the thick, apparently impenetrable bush. Most of our hundred vanguard were killed in the first encounter. Those who escaped, arrived with the dismal information that we were surrounded. The redoubtable Ram Ganga was behind the enemy. So neither help nor escape was possible that way. The hoped-for retreat strategy had been stillborn because of the Rohilla positions behind and inside it.

The Rohillas took the initiative and began shelling soon after the remainder of the vanguard finished their full report. Apparently, they were quite aware of the weaknesses of the Royal forces. Very soon, once they had their target, the shelling became intense and well placed. We couldn't retreat into our supposedly safe resort.

The navab took the only option available: charge the enemy lines. He took it most valiantly, leading us on his horse all the way. The fighting soon became hand to hand. Qutbuddin Khan and Mir Muhammad Ali seemed to have sealed a pact with Death not to approach them. I was just behind them. It was bitterly cold and windy, such that our blood seemed to freeze when we were cut. The party was over just after midday. The Rohilla butchered every man jack of us.

*

As if in an earthquake, my bed began to shake and jump up and down like a demented monkey. I woke up, barely escaping being hurled down from the tall bed.

'What did you say? All were killed? No one survived?'

'No, Your Honour. None.' He spoke in a low voice, laden with grief.

'So are you . . . Are you dead too?'

'Sir, that is something that I don't myself know. Your Honour can decide best.'

The low, laden voice was becoming lower every moment. No, it was fading.

'Hey, hey! Stop! Please stop!'

But the dark, bluish, blackish light was dissipating in the dawn. I could see nothing. Someone began to play the Bhairavi on the shahnai somewhere. Then even that sound faded away.

11

When Abdul Hayy Taban heard of Muhammad Ali Hashmat's death in the slaughter of Dhampur, he threw down his turban, ripped his collar, and said a Hindi verse from Mir Hashmat in a choked voice:

When autumn was upon the garden and became forcibly known to the rose
The bulbul wept, and cried: Woe, Woe! The Rose, the Rose!

From then on, he wore black and became a recluse, so that he stopped going even to the select assembly of the Presence, Mirza Mazhar sahib. Once, that Exalted Presence sent for him, something which he almost never did. But he said to the messenger: 'Go with folded hands and submit that Taban is no longer there.'

Soon after, he gave up drinking and fell ill. The physicians strongly admonished him and ordered him to resume drinking.

'Wine now is absorbed in your tissues, into your bones even, like blood. It is now a fifth element of your temperament. You will die very soon unless you return to your old ways.'

Mir Abdul Hayy, though suffering exquisite torture caused by the denial of wine from his system, wept and said, 'No. Forever no. What face will I show to Mir Hashmat sahib, to God, if I break my vow of abstemiousness?'

The day he gave up drinking, Taban wrote to all his friends, saying, 'My time is come. Come and see me and let me see you, before I go. Please forgive any wrong that I may have done you so that I may go as light as I came.' Friends came in their numbers. Some would look at him, weep and go away. Some would sit by his side, trying to divert him with pleasant talk and witticisms.

On the eighth day of sending the letters, Mir Abdul Hayy Taban turned his face upon the world.

On him be God's Mercy, oh Mir, Taban's grief scars my heart
May he have redemption, he was my friend too.

A Note on the Type

Dante was the result of collaboration between Giovanni Mardersteig, printer, book designer and typeface artist, and Charles Malin, one of the great punch-cutters of the twentieth century. The two worked closely to develop an elegant typeface that was distinctive, legible and attractive. Special care was taken with the design of the serifs and top curves of the lowercase to create a subtle horizontal stress, which helps the eye move smoothly across the page.